"An engrossing epic."
—*Entertainment Weekly*

"Extraordinary. . . . Kevin Baker is quickly altering the landscape of American historical fiction."
—*Christian Science Monitor*

"With *Paradise Alley*, Kevin Baker emerges as our finest historical novelist."
—Peter Nichols, author of *Evolution's Captain*

"Brilliant. . . . An exploration of love and loyalty and bonds among three women, and a complex look at their relationships."
—*Hartford Courant*

Paradise Alley

PRAISE FOR *Paradise Alley*

"[A] richly detailed, impeccably researched drama. . . . Baker's success as a historical novelist rests on his superb ability to bring contemporary understanding to consequential events of the past by creating fictional yet totally credible characters whose lives are deeply affected by these events."   —*Booklist*

"[A] huge success. . . . Fascinating, instructive, never pedantic."
                                                                    —*Houston Chronicle*

"Inspired. . . . Vividly entertaining, and its themes are as timely as any drawn from this morning's newspaper."   —*Baltimore Sun*

"A page-turning epic."   —*New York Post*

"Deftly plotted, fabulously detailed, and never less than absorbing. An authoritative blend of documentary realism and driving narrative that's just about irresistible."   —*Kirkus Reviews* (starred review)

PRAISE FOR KEVIN BAKER

"Extraordinary. . . . Kevin Baker is quickly altering the landscape of American historical fiction."   —*Christian Science Monitor*

"With *Paradise Alley*, Kevin Baker emerges as our finest historical novelist, illuminating a critical and unexplored moment of the Civil War with a compassion and vitality reminiscent of Tolstoy. Baker's novel of immigration, slavery, rage, and rebellion miraculously captures not just the essence of our nation's past but of where we stand today. *Paradise Alley* is a powerful and unforgettable book."
                                        —PETER NICHOLS, author of *Evolution's Captain*

"Kevin Baker is perhaps the most ambitious American novelist working today."
                        —DARIN STRAUSS, author of *Chang and Eng* and *The Real McCoy*

"Baker is a master. . . . *Paradise Alley* probes the primal mysteries of those opposite poles, love and war, with skill, drama, and deep humanity."
                                                                    —*Edmonton Journal*

"*Paradise Alley* is a first-class work of historical fiction by a master storyteller. Baker achieves an epic and accurate weave of truth and imagination, a seamless saga of cruelty, courage, and human struggle set during the bloodiest urban uprising in American history."
                                        —PETER QUINN, author of *Banished Children of Eve*

About the Author

The critically acclaimed novel *Dreamland* established KEVIN
BAKER as "one of America's best new writers" (*Boston Herald*). Now, with *Paradise Alley*, he emerges as one of the
most important voices of his generation. Baker is at work on
the third volume of his "City of Fire" trilogy. He is also the
author of the novel *Sometimes You See It Coming* and served
as chief historical researcher for the nonfiction bestseller *The
American Century*. He is married and lives in New York City.

PARADISE ALLEY

A Novel

KEVIN BAKER

Perennial

An Imprint of HarperCollins*Publishers*

Gift Book

Fic
BAKER
K

To Ann and Bruce Baker, who have
always been there for me,
and whose kindness and generosity
has been unstinting—and, as ever,
to Ellen, with love

A hardcover edition of this book was published in 2002 by HarperCollins Publishers.

PARADISE ALLEY. Copyright © 2002 by Kevin Baker. All rights reserved. Printed in the United States of America. No part of this book may be used or reproduced in any manner whatsoever without written permission except in the case of brief quotations embodied in critical articles and reviews. For information address HarperCollins Publishers Inc., 10 East 53rd Street, New York, NY 10022.

HarperCollins books may be purchased for educational, business, or sales promotional use. For information please write: Special Markets Department, HarperCollins Publishers Inc., 10 East 53rd Street, New York, NY 10022.

First Perennial edition published 2003.

Designed by Lindgren/Fuller Design

Map by Diego Maclean, copyright © 2003

Library of Congress Cataloging-in-Publication Data is available.

ISBN 0-06-095521-X

03 04 05 06 07 ❖/RRD 10 9 8 7 6 5 4 3 2

6/29/2009

DRAMATIS PERSONAE

Ruth Dove, a ragpicker, from Paradise Alley, in the Fourth Ward of
New York City

Billy Dove, her husband, a shipbuilder and escaped slave

Dangerous Johnny Dolan, Ruth's former lover, and a criminal

Deirdre Dolan O'Kane, Johnny's older sister, and a former domestic

Tom O'Kane, Deirdre's husband, and a private in the Fighting 69th

Maddy Boyle, a hot-corn girl and prostitute

Herbert Willis Robinson, her lover, and a writer for the New York
Tribune

Finn McCool, a Tammany ward heeler, and assistant foreman of the
Black Joke Volunteer Fire Company

George "Snatchem" Leese, a bloodsucker

Black Dan Conaway
Richard Feeley } soldiers of the Fighting 69th
John J. Sullivan

Horace Greeley, editor and publisher of the New York *Tribune*

Henry Raymond, editor and publisher of the *New York Times*

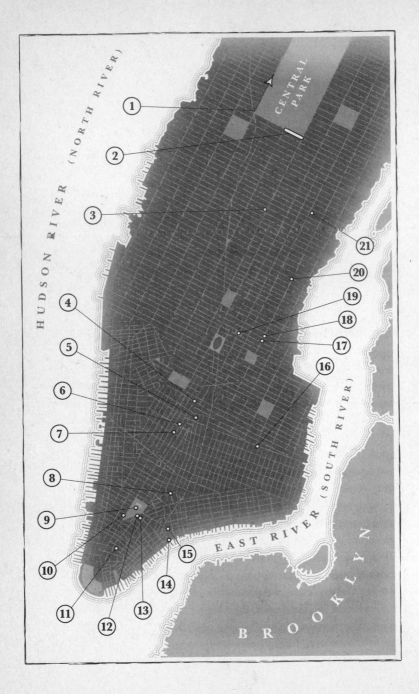

Key

1	To Seneca Village
2	Pigtown
3	Colored Orphans' Asylum
4	Police Clash With Mob
5	Police Headquarters
6	Metropolitan Hotel
7	Saint Nicholas Hotel
8	Five Points
9	City Hall and City Hall Park
10	Astor House Hotel
11	Sub-Treasury Building
12	New York Tribune
13	New York Times
14	The Sailor's Rest
15	Paradise Alley
16	Place of Blood
17	Armory
18	Union Steamworks
19	Gramercy Park
20	Murder of Col. O'Brien
21	Ninth District Provost Marshal's Office (Draft Office)

Monday
July 13, 1863

I am a rambling Irishman
Ulster I was born in
And many's the pleasant
day I spent
'Round the banks
of sweet Lough Erne
But to be poor I could
not endure
Like others of my station
To Amerikay
I sailed away
And left this Irish nation . . .

"THE RAMBLING IRISHMAN"
Traditional

❀ · 1 · ❀

RUTH

He is coming.

Ruth leaned out the door as far as she dared, peering down Paradise Alley to the west and the south. Past the other narrow brick and wood houses along Cherry Street, slouching against each other for support. The grey mounds of ashes and bones, oyster shells and cabbage leaves and dead cats growing higher every day since the street cleaners had gone out.

Fire bells were already ringing off in the Sixth Ward, somewhere near the Five Points. The air thick with dust and ash and dried horse droppings, the sulfurous emissions of the gasworks along the river, and the rendering plants and the hide-curing plants. It was not yet six in the morning but she could feel the thin linen of her dress sticking to the soft of her back.

"The good Lord, in all His mercy, must be readyin' us for Hell—"

She searched the horizon for any sign of relief. Their weather came from the west, the slate-grey, fecund clouds riding in over the Hudson. That was how she expected him to come, too, fierce and implacable as a summer storm. His rage breaking over them all.

He is coming—

But there was no storm just yet. The sky was still a dull, jaundiced color, the blue tattered and wearing away at the edges. She ventured a step out into the street, looking hard, all the way downtown, past the church steeples and the block-shaped warehouses, the dense thicket of masts around lower Manhattan.

There was nothing out of the ordinary. Just the usual shapeless forms lying motionless in the doorways. A ragged child with a stick, a few dogs. A fruit peddler with his bright yellow barrow. His wares, scavenged from the barges over on the West Side, already pungent and overripe.

Nothing coming. But then, it wasn't likely *he* would come from the west anyway—

With a muted cry she swung around, then ducked back into her house, bolting the door behind her while she fought for breath. *The idea that he could have been coming up behind her the whole time.* She remembered how quickly he could move. She could feel his hands on her, could see the yellow dog's bile rising in his eyes. That merciless anger, concentrated solely upon her—

She had not truly believed it before now—not even after Deirdre had come over to tell her yesterday afternoon. Standing there on her doorstone, one foot still in the street as if she were hanging on to the shore. Wearing her modest black church dress, her beautiful face even sterner than usual. She was a regular communicant, Sundays and Fridays—no doubt especially agitated to have to see Ruth on the Lord's day. She told her the news in a low voice, all but whispering to her. Deirdre herself, *whispering,* as if somehow *he* might overhear.

He is coming.

He had come—all the way back from California. It was a fearsome, unimaginable distance. *But then, what was that to a man who had gone as far as he had already?* A friend of Tom's, a stevedore, had seen him on the docks—as stunned as if he had seen Mose himself stepping off a clipper ship, back from his bar in the Sandwich Islands. Coming down the gangplank with that peculiar, scuttling, crablike walk of his, fierce and single-minded as ever. Moving fast, much faster than you thought at first, so that Tom's friend had quickly lost him in the crowd waiting by the foot of the gangplank. Already disappeared off into the vastness of the City—

Which meant—what? The mercy of a few days? While he found himself a room in the sailors' houses along Water Street, began to work his way relentlessly through the bars and blind pigs, sniffing out any news. Sniffing out *them.*

Or maybe not even that. Maybe he had hit it right off, had found, in the first public house he tried, a garrulous drunk who would tell him for the price of a camphor-soaked whiskey where he might find a certain mixed-race couple, living down in one of the nigger nests along Paradise Alley—

No. Ruth calmed herself by sheer force of will. Picking up a broom, she made her hands distract her. Sweeping her way scrupulously around the hearth, under the wobbly-legged table even though she knew there was no need, they would never live here again after this morning.

When she made herself think about it logically, it wasn't likely he could be that lucky. He had never had much luck, after all—not even with herself—and his own face would work against him. He couldn't go out too bold. They would remember him still, after what had happened with Old Man Noe. Men would remember him, would remember *that*, and keep their distance. Maybe even turn him in, for the reward—

They still had time. A little, anyway. She and Billy had talked it out, deep into the night. Time enough for Billy to go up to his job at the Colored Orphans' Asylum in the Fifth Avenue today, and collect his back wages. Then they would have something to start on, at least, to see them through up to Boston, or Canada.

Why aren't we in Canada already? We should be there—

She swept faster, in her anger and her frustration, kicking up the fine, black grit that crept inexorably through the windows and over the transom, covering the whole City over, every day. They had talked about leaving, all these years, but somehow they had never actually gone. She had put it down to Billy's moodiness and his obstinacy, the lethargy that seemed to hold him sometimes, particularly when he'd been drinking.

Yet it was more than that, and she knew it. They both felt safer here—on their block, miserable as it was, in the bosom of their friends and neighbors. They told themselves there would be risks if they ran, perhaps even worse risks. A white woman and a black man, with their five mixed-race children, moving through one small town after another, with no real money to sustain them. They would be leaving tracks for him like they were written in the sky—

So where were they to run now?

Ruth forced the question from her mind. *It didn't matter now, now they had no choice.* She had everything packed and ready to go. In a little while she would get the children up and give them their breakfast. They would leave as soon as Billy got back from the Colored Orphans', with the two weeks' wages he was owed.

She would stay home from her job with the German bonepickers, it would be safe enough here for the time being, on their street. At least that was what they had told themselves. It was too bad Tom was off with the army, but there was Deirdre. They could count on her to keep an eye out, at least. Ruth had seen her when she'd first looked out this morning—already sitting by a window, standing the watch.

Deirdre knew well enough what to expect from her own brother.

All it required was a few more hours of grace, then they would be gone. Over to Hoboken on the Desbrosses Street ferry, then a schooner up to Halifax, or Montreal. Or if they didn't have enough money for that, they could just set out at random, across the countryside, head west or north—

There was a low, rumbling sound. She risked poking her head out a window, wanting to see if it was storming after all. But no—the tattered yellow sky still hung balefully over the harbor, and the North River.

The sound went on and on—one continuous, unending roll of noise—and she realized it must be something man-made. Something both more and less than the daily going to work, the bawdy, boisterous awakening of the City that she liked to listen to every morning from her doorstep before joining it herself. This had more of a purpose, a direction. The sound of hundreds, even thousands of feet, and voices, moving relentlessly, indivisibly north, toward uptown.

Something had been brewing in the City all weekend, she knew, though she had barely set foot outside her home. There were little things she had picked up, when she poked her head out to throw the washing water in the gutter. Something in the snatches of talk from the men in their taverns, and the brayings of drunks on street corners. Something in the agitation of horses, the thinning of traffic, the urgency of a policeman's voice. In the unhappy silence of the other women on the block like her—listening and waiting.

The men were unhappy, and when men were unhappy, no one

could rest easy. Something about the draft, but whatever it was, she knew it would be bad for people like them. Maybe, at least, it would delay him—

A couple hours' grace, that's all we need. Surely that is possible.

She tried to think, to make sure there was nothing she had forgotten. Her memory had never been very good since her time with Johnny Dolan. She would leave the beans or the corn bread over the fire until they burned. She would forget to run an errand, to get something important, unless she carefully thought out everything on her way to work in the morning, or while trying to fall asleep in her bed at night. Sometimes she thought he had knocked it out of her, beaten it right out of her brains—

What needed to be done, then? She forced herself to concentrate. The children were still asleep in the back room but she had their things bundled up beside their beds. They could carry that much on their own. Everything else was already tied up and waiting by the back door—their bolt hole—where it could be easily tossed into the barrow just outside.

There was little enough. Her kitchen wares, two tin pots and an iron frying pan. Six long spoons, a few bent knives and forks. The two other dresses she owned, plus another small bag for her underclothes, and the ribbons she wore in her hair on special days. Billy's one suit, and his shirts and his overalls. His seaman's kit, and his tools, still as meticulously wrapped and oiled—and as untouched— as when he had first purchased them, over a dozen years before.

There was almost nothing of a more personal nature. Only their Bible, and a few books that belonged to Milton, their oldest boy. The framed daguerreotype she had finally persuaded Billy to have made of the whole family. All of them in their best clothes, standing solemnly around Billy where he sat in a broad, cushioned chair. The paterfamilias, a little stand in the picture parlor tucked carefully behind his close-cropped hair to make sure he held his head steady, the rest of them clustered all around him in various shimmering shades of light. Hers the only fully white face, looking bleak and blanched, nearly invisible next to the rest of them.

She had wanted to have one made of the little girl who had died, of Lillian, who had passed from the croup before she was two. A proper funeral picture, made up with the girl in her best dress, lying in the coffin, but Billy had stopped her. It was too dear, they needed to spend the money on the living, and she was glad he had persuaded her now. There was no need to haul the picture of that poor dead girl up and down the roads, as Ruth had once hauled herself. She would be left behind where she lay, out in the pleasant, shady cemetery in Brooklyn—

That was all. Everything they had to show for thirteen years in this cramped little house. They could be gone in a moment, out through the back privvy lots and down to the ferries. Gone before even he could catch them—

All that remained was that *thing*. His magic box. She paused over it with her broom in hand, as if considering whether to just sweep the whole thing out the door, out of their lives. The strange pile of gew-gaws and odds and ends which Johnny Dolan had put their immortal souls in danger in order to have. Somehow, she had never been able to get rid of it.

Because of what it had cost?

It lay in a far corner of the front room now, like some malevolent old dog. The black, funereal cloth that still covered it now coated with dust. The same cloth they had found it in, had brought it all the way here from that ruined abbey outside Cork. She folded the cloth back, staring at the cracked glass. Behind it lay the whole collection of shiny odds and ends that had fascinated him so, and that she had not been able to so much as look at since he had gone. The broken sword and the blackamoor's ear, the miniature engine and the giant's eye and the pictures of lovers, and a thousand other wonders. All of them once glued and arranged so perfectly within the box, now mostly jumbled together in a heap at the bottom.

Yet still it shone. Deep down, through the depths of all that junk, still glinted dozens of tiny mirrors. Glued to the back of the cabinet, meant to make it all seem larger, more splendid, to gleam like jewels. In the yellow morning light, she caught a dusty, broken reflection of her own face. Squinting, peering ignorantly back through all the wonders, impossibly old and distorted. Her cheeks beginning to hollow, the lines creasing her chin and brow, her brown hair starting to grey.

She threw the cover down over the box and went back to her sweeping. She wasn't sure why she had never gotten rid of it, sold it off long ago to the street sweepers for whatever pennies it would bring. Was it to remind herself of her sin—of all her sins?

Or was it the last hold Johnny Dolan still had on her? Some lingering hope that if she kept it, the box might appease him even after all they had done to him.

If he returned. When *he returned*—

She thought she would leave it. It might at least slow him down for a few more hours while he brooded, and wondered over it like he always used to. Maybe even make him forget about them altogether.

Or would it simply be another track for him to follow?

She had to stop then—crouching down, nearly doubled over in her own front room. To think of *him* again. The return of that presence she had dared to believe she had shaken out of their life forever—come to repay her now for all she had done. Worse yet, come to visit all his fury upon those she loved, on Billy and all the rest of her family, he would not care who he hurt. If he could catch them—

Of course he would come back. Of course he would, after the trick we played him—

He is coming.

❦ · 2 · ❧

HERBERT WILLIS ROBINSON

The boy grins up at me from the gutter, his face smeared with blood. He squints into the morning sun, and wipes a hand across his mouth. Spreading more gore from ear to ear, as if to make a threat, like running a finger across his throat.

But no—he is neither grinning nor threatening, only trying to see who I am against the yellow glare of the sun. My shadow spreading over his playground, the pool of blood on which he is sailing his paper boat. As he looks up at me, distracted, more thick fingers of blood creep slowly up his little boat. They collapse its sail, pull it slowly down into the gutter. He shrugs and produces another brown scrap of butcher's paper, folding it expertly into a set of three triangles. He christens it and launches it, on a fresh red stream eddying up through the sewer grate.

My streetcar arrives and I swing on up over the boy, on my way to the *Tribune*, where I am employed writing articles for Mr. Greeley's newspaper. The faded yellow signboards on the side of the car loom inches from my face:

TREMENDOUS EXCITEMENT: THE IRREPRESSIBLE CONFLICT! ONLY——
——R. H. MACY——
CAN PROVIDE BOTH THE ENORMOUS REDUCTIONS
AND THE SUPERB QUALITY THAT WILL SATISFY BOTH HIM
AND HER AND LEAVE YOUR HOUSE DIVIDED NO MORE!

I move back out of the inner car, clutching one of the outside poles by another adamant sign: *NO COLORED PEOPLE ALLOWED IN THIS CAR.*

Out here at least the air is not as close as it is inside, fouled with sweat and body odor. The car jammed already, mostly with workies and mechanics, sewing girls and maids making their way to their jobs. Not yet six o'clock in the morning but they are in a holiday mood. Singing and joking, even rocking the car on its rails, the sour smell of whiskey seeping through the windows.

> *From Eighth Street down*
> *The men are making it*
> *From Eighth Street up*
> *The women are spending it*
> *And that's the story of this great town*
> *From Eighth Street up and Eighth Street down—*

Today is Getting Out Day. Today is All Fools' Day, today is Carnevale and Christmas and the Fourth of July, all rolled up in one. And all that's needed is a match.

All weekend I went among them as a spy. That is my job, as a reporter. Listening to them in their taverns, on their street corners and in their parlors. Posing as the out-of-town drummer, the friendly, credulous stranger. There were the usual wild oaths and threats, the drunken boasts—but something else as well. Something real, some kind of dangerous undercurrent beneath all the loose talk. Like all the blood and offal the butchers shove down in the gutters until, when it rains, everything comes bubbling up, the streets swimming in entrails and pigs' ears, cloven hooves and horses' teeth, and puddles of blood.

Trouble in this town usually starts like a musket flash, sudden and unpredictable. A fight, a joke, a routine arrest. Some halfhearted protest that turns into a riot before anyone can quite understand what is happening.

But this is different. More deliberate—even, perhaps, intentional. I don't mean that there is some outside conspiracy, a little group of men sitting around a table in a cellar room. Those rumors have been flying for weeks now, at the Union Club, and the bar in the Astor

House, and in the lobby of the St. Nicholas Hotel. Confederate agents have slipped over the border from Canada. Hired assassins have been brought over from Ireland, the Knights of the Golden Circle are stashing muskets in a secret basement in the Five Points, ready on a signal from Richmond to fire the town—

The usual nonsense. The wild talk that precedes any real crisis in the City, like the seabirds swooping in off the North River ahead of a storm. No, what I mean is that *they* have been talking. The Other City, the Dark City, the City with Its Face Turned Away From Us. The City of Night, the City of Fire, murmuring in low, deliberate, angry voices that we can never quite make out. The workingmen in their party halls. The fire companies in their station houses, the gangsters in their subterranean hideouts. So much talk, so much plotting, bubbling slowly to the top.

It started when the new Draft Law was announced. All able-bodied men, ages twenty to forty-five, married or single, are now eligible to be drafted by lot into Mr. Lincoln's army, and shipped south to the war. There to be fed on wormy hardtack, and saltpork, and butchered by incompetent generals while their families try to subsist on begging and government relief. *Unless*—and, ah, there's the rub!—unless they have three hundred dollars to buy themselves a substitute. An easy enough thing, for any man of means—but two years' salary to an Irish hod-carrier from the Five Points—

The relief that swept the City after Gettysburg faded, when the casualty lists began to trickle in. Loyal Republicans who had illuminated their windows and put up bunting to celebrate found their stoops blackened with tar the next morning, ominous crosses chalked on their doors. Then, last week, the Provost Marshal's patrols started working their way through the Fourth Ward, demanding that men give up their names. There were fights, and arrests, brick chimneys toppling mysteriously off rooftops, just missing the Provost's guard.

The draft was scheduled to commence last Friday, up at the Ninth District office, on East Forty-sixth Street by the Third Avenue. Right to the end, no one thought they would really go through with it—not in this city full of Democrats and Copperheads. By the time I arrived, the mob was already filling the street, a boisterous crowd of workies and their wives. Plainly uncowed by the handful of police and the squad of invalided soldiers standing guard—shouting out their insults and scatological comments.

"Three hundred dollars! Oh, you can take that and shove it up my—"

"Oh, they will, Billy boy! Oh, they will!"

Nervous, rueful laughter floating up from the mob.

"Three hundred dollars! Tell Abe Lincoln to come an' collect it hisself!"

"Oh, he will!"

Nevertheless, they went ahead with it. The soldiers hauled a big, squared wooden drum up into the open window, and mounted it on the scaffolding there in full view of the crowd. A well-known blind man was led up by the arm, and the marshals gave the drum a heavy, lumberous crank, rolling it over and over until it resounded like thunder up and down the street, silencing even the mob.

Then they opened the hatch and plunged the hand of the blind man deep inside. Watery yellowed eyes staring straight ahead. His fingers rooting in the drum like so many thick pink pig snouts until he had dredged up the first handful of names, written down on simple scraps of paper. An impressively groomed and uniformed major plucked them one by one from the blind man's palm, unfolding them and reading out the names and addresses in a fearsome voice:

"O'Donnell! Thomas! Fifteen Great Jones Street!"

The crowd began to hiss and groan, and I saw the two pickets standing at either end of the drum exchange nervous looks. They held muskets with fixed bayonets, but it was clear to me that if anything had started, they would have bolted like rabbits.

"Condon! Jack! One-eight-four Avenue A!"

There were more groans, more hisses and boos—but nothing else. No well-placed brick or two that might have set off a whole barrage, provoked a volley. The spark wasn't there yet. The crowd was in too good a mood, the weather too moderate still. As the next few names were called out there were more catcalls, more rude noises, but even most of this was good-natured.

"Brady! Patrick!"

"Good for you, Brady!" someone in the crowd yelled out, and then everyone was laughing. Soon every name was greeted with a joke—

"O'Connell—"

"How are you, O'Connell?"

"O'Connor! Sean!"

"Good-bye, Sean!"

"A rest from the missus for you, Sean!"

"Old Abe's done for you now, Sean me boy!"

—the whole scene devolving into another extended street-corner entertainment. The kind *they* love—like a good dog fight or a family argument. At one point a particularly ignorant young *b'hoy* walked out of the crowd when his name was called and, with a resigned shrug, pulled himself up through the window. The major looked as if he were going to have a fit of apoplexy, his face reddening and his hand reaching for his holster, wondering what kind of prank this was.

"Who the hell're you?"

"I'm McMullen, sir. I'm here to give meself up," the lad said.

The crowd roared, the whole exchange like a scene out of some Paddy stage farce. The major cursing at his would-be recruit—"*Get the hell down from there, goddamn you, man!*"—the youth just grinning sheepishly back at him.

After that it was clear nothing was going to happen. The crowd was almost festive, so close to the end of the working week. Soon they began to drift away, to their homes or the local taverns, looking for new entertainment. The blind man still rooted for names, handing the little white pellets over to the bellowing major until the office finally closed its doors in the late afternoon. The marshals hauled the drum down from its platform then, and shuttered the big open front window, the guard of invalided soldiers hurrying away, grateful to be going back toward their barracks on Governor's Island.

Yet the whole time there was another draft going on as well. I could see it on the fringes of the crowd—the boys, runners for the volunteer fire companies, scurrying back and forth to tell their wards and their blocks who had been drafted. After a while another fringe of young men began to gather—butcher boys and apprentices, gang *b'hoys* and fire laddies. Their hands in their pockets, looking angry and sullen. Walking back and forth, smarting with the insult, repeating the same things over and over to each other.

"*Three hundred dollars! Sold for three hundred dollars, when a nigger goes for a thousand!*"

They lingered still, muttering on the edge of the crowd, as if waiting for something to happen. But it never did. The spark never came, and soon they drifted away with the rest of the crowd, looking back over their shoulders at the shuttered draft office.

The streetcar struggles futilely down the First Avenue, the horses slipping and falling on the slick granite paving stones. Our driver curses and whips at the other teamsters with their wagon loads of dry goods and potatoes, beef and beer. They curse back, cutting across our rails until we are slowed almost to a standstill. My stomach lurches and my poor heavy head feels as if it will topple like a twelve-pound shot from my shoulders and roll up and down the aisle of the car, at peace at last. I jump down at the next corner, deciding it will be quicker to make my way to the newspaper by foot.

The cars should operate on steam, of course, but after several spectacular crashes, the Common Council banned all locomotives south of Forty-second Street. Instead, they are unhitched from their engines at the Grand Central Station, hooked up to teams of horses, and pulled the rest of the way downtown. They make no better progress than the ambling stagecoaches or the omnibuses, or, for that matter, the dauntless pedestrians, picking their way past endless piles of steaming manure and teams of rearing horses.

This is the way we live *now*, in the City of Smash and Burn, Sulphur and Blood. Nearly one million souls, packed down into the tail end of Manhattan island. Some few thousand more scattered among the villages of Haarlem and Bloomingdale, the rambling shantytowns of niggers and Irish niggers around the central park they have finally laid out above Fifty-ninth Street. A city where herds of pigs still run loose in the streets. Where stagecoach drivers race and whip each other along the avenues, and steam ferries race and collide and explode in the harbor. The population double what it was twenty years ago, and double again what it was twenty years before that. And every year, the City getting denser, louder, filthier; more noisome, more impossible to traverse.

Presiding over it all is our upstanding Republican mayor, fuming regularly and ineffectually over each iniquity like some Italian volcano. Just beneath him sit our unspeakable aldermen and councilmen, better known as The Forty Thieves. Would that it were so. In fact, there are eighty-two. (Only New York City would take it upon itself to support a legislature of bicameral crooks.)

And beneath *them* a whole vast, imponderable hive of crooked street commissioners and demagogues, dead-horse contractors and confidence men, hoisters and divers, shoulder-hitters and fancy men, wardheelers and kirkbuzzers and harlots. And all of them with a profit motive, all of them with an angle and a game, and an eye on the main chance. So many with their hands out, so much corruption that even if you wanted to clean it all out you could never do it, you could never even get past the first, most inconsequential layers of dirt.

In short, it is a great town in which to be a newspaperman.

HERBERT WILLIS ROBINSON

I am a connoisseur of hangovers.

To the uninitiated they may seem merely unpleasant, but to the more experienced there are both fine and subtle gradations. Wine is the worst, even a good wine. The sediment clogs the mind like grit in the gears, and roils the stomach. A brandy hangover, on the other hand, is like a bell smashed with a hammer, ringing, but clear and hard. Sweet liqueurs fill one with a sense of sticky self-disgust the next day, like wriggling on some gigantic curl of flypaper.

No, the best hangover is just the right combination of beer and whiskey. Beer to fortify the stomach and give it something to chew on. Whiskey to soften the mind to a cloudy, cosmic mush, sparked by flashes of completely unjustifiable optimism. Done properly a good hangover can carry one through the next day like a thick cotton cloud, leaving everything a little unclear but at a sublime distance. A bad hangover can make one wish to die or—same thing—swear off drinking altogether.

This is not a good hangover.

There was no avoiding it, though. When you wish to know what men are thinking in New York, you must go to a saloon. Over the week-end, all last Saturday and Sunday, I worked my way down through them, and in this town you can find every gradation. There are high bars and low bars, blind pigs and blind tigers and respectable snugs. Free-and-easy halls and bohemian bars and groceries, elegant club rooms and hotel bars on the dollar side of Broadway, hose joints and clip joints and shock joints and dives.

I worked my way down to the very bottom layers of sediment and sentiment, determined to hear the Other City where it was murmuring. Disguised again as a drummer, a rube—even *one of them*. Until by Saturday night I had reached the very worst crimp bars along the waterfront—The Morgue and The Yellow Man; The Glass House and the Hole-in-the-Wall. Terrible places, with their paint thinner passed off as alcohol, and a side business in murdered and shanghaied sailors. Bars where you go only to prey or to be preyed upon, or if you are too weary anymore to tell the difference.

Near midnight on Saturday, I found myself outside Finn McCool's place, The Sailor's Rest, where a few years ago Slobbery Jim knifed Patsy the Barber over twelve cents they had stolen from a murdered German. It is no more than a sagging, ancient pile along South Street. The nasty, ironic name, carved on a wooden board that made an awful creaking and flapping sound above the entrance. The saloon itself like all such places, furnished with no more than a bar, a few tables, and some long benches pushed up against the walls. Shelves filled with dusty, opened bottles of brown and amber liquid. Crude prints depicting the usual gabble of Irish heroes in America: O'Connell and Mitchel, and poor old Corcoran, and Meagher of the Sword.

In the back hang the slitted red curtains of the Velvet Room, with its solitary bed and notorious trapdoor. Most of the crimp bars have something like it—a room where strangers too drunk to know any better are plied with a great, complimentary bowl of whiskey or rum and escorted through the thick red curtains to sleep it off. Only to awaken the next morning well on their way to China or Peru or Shanghai, not to be seen on the dockside again for years—if ever.

Something was up, I knew from the moment I walked in—something beyond the usual shenanigans. I had been here before on a Saturday, had even taken Maddy to such establishments. There was always a fiddler, and someone banging away like a pagan on a goatskin drum. The red bombazine curtains blowing in the window, the only light a couple of smoky-wicked whale-oil lamps. The men dancing wild reels and polkas across the sawdust floors, with young girls just over from Ireland, who showed their teeth when they grinned.

This night, though, there was no lunatic drummer, no dancing. There was, only, a palpable sense of menace. The saloon was packed, but the men sat nursing their porter and ale, speaking in low and bitter tones.

I stood at the bar, where I could pretend to drink while I looked them over. Many of them were the same men and boys I had seen at the draft, brooding at the edge of the mob. Fire laddies, especially from the Black Joke company, and butchers' assistants, and gang *b'hoys*. Daybreak Boys and Swamp Angels, Dead Rabbits and Plug Uglies and Roach Guards. All of them repeating the same muttered litany:

"Sold for three hundred dollars! When a nigger goes for a thousand—"

The very spine of our City, such men are—the ones who do all the low jobs and the hard ones, who keep the whole great machine running. Indispensable men, really, and doing it all for wages that will barely feed them.

How I loathed them! I know I should love the poor, but I don't, they are dirty and loud. Dressed up in their ludicrous gang paraphernalia—stovepipe hats and soaped temple locks, gaudy kerchiefs and baggy Oxford pants tucked into the tops of their boots. Brass knuckles and giant Bowie knives falling out of their pockets. They jeer and heckle in our theatres, shout obscenities at each other on the street, break up any political meetings their masters don't like. Always bellicose but helpless, cynical but self-pitying.

I want to love the poor, but I don't, perhaps not even Maddy—

"Drink up!"

McCool's bouncer trudged over to force a whiskey on me. She is a famous harridan of the ward, a six-foot-tall Irishwoman with red hair down to her knees. They call her Gallus Mag for the bright yellow suspenders she uses to keep her skirt up, though she wears a belt as well—a revolver and a slung shot tucked conspicuously into the front of it.

"C'mon now, don't make me get rough with ya!"

The Mag has brass claws on her fingertips, and when she smiles you can see that her teeth have been filed down to long, white points, as sharp as a rat's. It is said that she will bite the ears off any customer who doesn't go quietly, and that she stores her trophies in a tall jar of formaldehyde that is prominently displayed on the bar. It is the saloon's running joke. Greenhorns reaching into the jar for the usual pickled eggs jump in the air when they find themselves holding an ear. It never fails to get a good laugh.

I duly ordered up a drink, and Gallus Mag grinned and slung it across the bar to me. I took a sip, tried not to make too sour a face, and failed—the whiskey's flavor and body no worse than the finest acids. Gallus Mag, watching for my expression, burst into laughter, throwing her head and her long red hair back, and setting the whole bar laughing along with her. I grinned weakly, trying to hide how much I detested them all.

Usually Finn McCool himself was behind the bar. This night, though, he moved among his customers like a venomous bee, spreading his poison from one little cluster of men to another. Shoulders rounded, prematurely wizened head sunk nearly to his chest. Going about his duties as a Tammany ward captain, and assistant foreman of the Black Joke.

The Black Joke and the other fire companies are the breeding swamps of our wonderful new mass democracy. There are dozens of such companies, supposedly protecting our highly combustible City. In fact, they are little more than headquarters for our street gangs and political machines—you go tell the difference. They pull their machines recklessly through the streets, brawl with each other over the Croton hydrants while our homes and businesses burn.

Each company has dozens of members, necessary to tote the heavy wagons by hand through the narrow lanes of the City. All of them volunteers, nearly all of them Irish by now—rough, arrogant young men who love to paint gaudy scenes on their fire wagons, hold elaborate chowders and dances.

They are cultivated by aspiring Tammany Hall politicians such as McCool. Dispensing favors and gossip, perennially booming his brother, Peter, who is the captain of the company, for alderman. Usually, on a Saturday night, Finn's saloon would have been lousy with the leaders of the Democracy—but for some reason there was no sign of them now. In fact, they had vanished from every dive I visited, all week-end.

No Captain Rynders holding court in the back rooms, his omniscient gambler's eye flitting over everything. No Fernandy Wood, oozing his smug, perfumed way through the crowd. No sign of the enormous Tweed, with his oddly open, innocent boy's face—the monstrous mirror image of Greeley's own. All of them conspicuous in their absence. Their disappearance as unsettling as the flight of birds, or the howling of dogs and cats before an earthquake—

"Ye see how it is," I heard a low voice behind me. "Ye see how our Mag deals with them who like to overhear what they shouldn't."

I took a small sip of the varnish the Irish giantess had served me before I turned around. There was McCool, perched by my elbow, a smirk creasing his face, nodding significantly at the jar of ears. Seeing through any disguise I might want to adopt.

"She must be a regular Circe," I told him.

I had noticed long ago that the ears, bobbing there in the deep, red liquid behind the glass, looked suspiciously pointed and large and hairy, even for the sailors and bummers who liked to frequent The Sailor's Rest.

"Who?" McCool asked.

"Circe was a witch with a habit of turning men into swine."

"Ah, but the bitch was a liar, then. For it don't take a woman to turn a man into a pig."

"No?"

"No. All you have to do is treat men like swine an' they will live up to the rule every time."

"Is it swinish, then, to stand up on two legs and fight for our country?"

I was drunk enough to be that reckless with him, though I suspected I had nothing really to worry about. Finn could have already had me beaten to a pulp; thrown into the black and oily river outside, or shipped down to Port o' Spain, had he chosen to. No, there had to be some reason he *wanted* to speak to me, a reporter for Horace Greeley's *Tribune*. Something he wanted to find out—

"Strange how it becomes *our* country when there's fightin' to be done," he said, with a smile that went as deep as his teeth. "Anyway, I gets confused these days. Is it the country we're still fightin' for? Or is it the niggers."

"Do you not think slavery is evil, then?"

"There are many evil things in the world. But I don't remember Abe Lincoln come hallooin' about with half a million men when all of Connaught was starvin' to death in its cabins."

"Do you mean to stop the draft?" I asked him straight out.

He gave a short shrug, and stared at me more intently than ever, as if he didn't quite understand the question.

"But it don't matter what I want to do."

"Is that what you're telling those men?" I asked him, gesturing over at his clientele, the fire laddies sullenly nursing their drinks.

Finn only shrugged again. The grin gone, but a slight frown along his forehead now, as if he were trying to explain something to an exceptionally dull child.

"You go ahead an' see," he said. "You go an' draft the men who put out the fires in this town. Honest workingmen, what never wanted a thing from this life but to raise their families an' love their wives."

He was well into his campaign speech by now, I knew, but there was something in what he was saying that chilled me to the bone nonetheless.

"You go ahead an' ship good Irishmen south like so many niggers, while their wives an' families have to beg the relief agency for money to eat. You just start that drum rollin' again on Monday morning an' you see what happens."

He nodded curtly, then went back to his rounds, moving away as abruptly as he had appeared. I decided it was time to take my own leave, making sure to leave a healthy tip for the female behemoth behind the bar.

Once outside I walked immediately over to the dockside—even leaning out over the water. There, deep below the shifting currents, I could see the remains of an ancient ship. There was little enough of it left—a couple of broken spars, a few planks of its bulwark visible along the shallow, silted bottom. The name, in gold-painted letters— *"JERSEY"*—just barely illuminated by the lanterns from the ships riding at anchor beside it and the lights from the dockside bars. One of the ancient British prison ships from the Revolution, left to slowly fall apart and sink into the harbor.

Thousands of men died on such ships, chained in the holds for years, allowed up for exercise only at night. Never seeing the sun before they perished from starvation, or the fevers. A typical, diabolical British punishment. Taking men who claimed to fight for freedom—some great, glorious, abstract notion of freedom—and putting them to the test. Making sure they would never again have the simple freedom of standing outside on a brilliant day.

I had seen the *Jersey* many times before, though. My real attention was focused on the door of The Sailor's Rest. As I watched from the corner of my eye, a huge, hulking shape ambled slowly outside and pretended to light up a pipe. *Someone meant for me?*

Yet even as I watched him, I glimpsed another figure—one rising noiselessly from where he had hidden himself in a pile of old rope and crates. He came straight for me, making the blood freeze in my veins. Some desperate rummy or thief who had spotted my suit, or my watch fob, and my unsteady gait.

The hulking figure by the door was on him as quick as a dog upon a snake, slung shot in hand, moving with extraordinary speed and silence for such a big man. He seized my would-be assailant by the neck, giving him a single sharp blow. The man fell at his feet with a low moan—my protector lifting him up immediately, dumping him into the black river where he sank with a small splash, barely audible in the night. Then he moved back against the wall, watching me again, no longer bothering to fiddle with his pipe.

I knew then that Finn McCool wasn't trying to find out anything at all. Rather, that he was trying to deliver a message, had even provided protection to make sure I got safely off the docks with it.

"Like all cowardly criminals, they're trying to set up an alibi for themselves in advance."

Later that same Saturday night I stopped in at 300 Mulberry Street, the police headquarters, to see Superintendent John Kennedy, chief of the Metropolitan police. He only nodded, head down, making another notation at his desk when I told him all that I had seen and heard. Still working away vigorously although it was the early hours of Sunday morning by then. He dismissed the whole idea that the mob was beyond the control of Tammany, or Mozart Hall, or all of the endless layers of demagogues and scoundrels in this City.

"The big fish have swum away, so no one can blame them. McCool would have us believe the mob is beyond his control—but I'd wager good money he's only taking orders from afar. Maybe even Richmond!"

John Kennedy is one of those brisk, efficient Irishmen, a testament to what the race might do if they could only stay away from the drink. His uniform as neat and pressed as McClellan's itself, his white beard trimmed close to the chin.

"I understand the Black Joke lost thirty men to the draft. Including their captain," I told him.

"Yes, I've heard that." Kennedy nodded again, barely bothering to look up.

"They're all up in arms," I went on, ticking off all the murmurs of revolt I had heard among the fire companies. "Also the Shad Belly, and the Dry Bones. Even the Big Six is supposed to be ready to go on the warpath, though I can't imagine Tweed would allow them to get mixed up in anything."

"Yes, I know. The fire laddies all want to be exempted from having to serve in the militia again," Kennedy acknowledged drily, unsurprised. "They all want it back the way it *used* to be, before the war. But where would we be then, if we gave them the old exemption? Nearly every young man worth his salt is a volunteer fireman in this town. Who would do the fighting for us?"

There was another brisk shuffle of papers. The sheer masculinity and vigor of such men as Kennedy is overpowering. Skin as pink as a pig's, chin cut sharper than a clipper's bow. He seemed to me Father Christmas and an Old Testament prophet all rolled into one—ready, alert, faintly amused. The sort of captain one might have trusted with the defense of a city, in medieval times.

"Nothing to worry about!" he assured me. "They should have made their move on Friday, when the mob was already out."

In the amber glow of the gas lamps, men bustled impressively in and out of his office, bringing endless dispatches and telegrams. Kennedy perused them all, jotting his notes on each one before passing it over to another subordinate. His lieutenants were as neat and well-groomed as their chief, collars buttoned up to their throats despite the wilting heat.

"Now it's too late," he went on. "We're ready for them. I've canceled all leaves, called in every man I have. They know better than to try anything, now that we're prepared."

Together with Commissioner Acton, Kennedy has made the City's police as honest, as reliable and efficient a force as we have ever had in the City. His Metropolitans were created by the state legislature just

six years ago, a last desperate effort to do something about Mayor
Wood's corrupt old Municipals, who had reached a new nadir of
depravity. Fernandy Wood refused to yield, of course, standing on
high, constitutional principles—not to mention the bribes that were
the lifeblood of his administration.

A judge then sent the Metropolitans to arrest *him*—the mayor of
the City—and before the whole thing was resolved, our rival police
departments, Metropolitans and Municipals, actually got into a fight
on the steps of City Hall. Burly, uniformed policemen, wrestling and
punching and gouging at each other's eyes, right out in broad daylight. If the Seventh Regiment hadn't happened by and broken it up,
they might all have killed each other. Has any city, down to ancient
Rome with its gladiators, ever offered its citizens the spectacles that
New York does on a daily basis?

Since then, though, Kennedy has cleaned out the deadwood, whipped
his police into shape. His headquarters is more efficient than that of
any division staff I saw down in Virginia. Laid out on a table in his
office is a map of the entire City, with pins stuck in it indicating
the locations of the police precinct houses and the draft offices; City
Hall, the Sub-Treasury building down on Wall Street; the major banks
and stores, the homes of leading citizens, and all the other potential
targets.

"Any trouble will probably start at the provost's office. But we also
have to cover the shipyards, and the ironworks along the rivers. Then
there's the Union Steam Works *here*, and the State Armory *there*—"

He pressed a pink, clean-nailed thumb down upon the old steam
works, at Twenty-second Street and the Second Avenue—important
only because it was made into a munitions factory after Bull Run. Just
below it on the map, at Twenty-first Street, is pinned the State
Armory, where the army has ten thousand rifles stored.

"—but we've already got the Broadway Squad there. It will take
some mob to get past *them*. Even if they do, we have telegraph opera-
tors at every precinct house. We can rush men to any trouble spot,
anywhere in the City, within minutes!"

There was no reason to doubt his system. Yet I couldn't help noticing how many pins there were in his map. A whole City, the greatest
in the Americas, to be held by his twenty-three hundred Metropolitan
officers.

"How many men can General Wool let you have?" I asked him about the City's army commander.

Kennedy frowned a little at this, but stood up straighter than ever.

"Not many. Mead stripped the City of every man he could for Gettysburg. Maybe fifteen hundred, at most, and a lot of them Invalids."

He tried to reassure me again as he showed me out, squeezing my arm and balling his other hand into a confident fist.

"There is no cause for alarm. The important thing is to stay on top of them! Give it to them good and hard before they get started!"

We passed on out through the headquarters, back to the streets and the usual chaos of a Saturday night in our City. As we went through the station house, though, I noticed what any sentient New Yorker does every day—that all of the men policing his City are Irish. Great big bruisers, to be sure, even their long mustaches bristling aggressively. Polite and well-groomed, a trim-looking fighting force if there ever was one. They even have to pass a literacy test now.

Yet they are all Irish, all the same, right up through their captains and commanders, and Kennedy himself.

We cannot do without them. *But if there is real trouble, what will they do?* Can we rely on them—if it means putting down their friends and neighbors?

Or is the enemy already inside the gates?

⚜ · 4 · ⚜

RUTH

Seven o'clock.

The block was nearly silent. Usually by this time of the morning there would be a small riot outside her door. The street teeming with men and women joking and jostling each other on their way to work. The shopkeepers and vendors making their long, singsong pitches.

But today none of the little shops across the street was opening up. Their doors and windows were still shut, though Ruth could make out shadowy movements behind some of them. Their owners were still inside, she knew, watching and waiting. When anyone did move down the street, they walked with quick, jerky movements, heads pivoting as if to see what might be coming after them.

The back lot was just as quiet. She peeked out there—*Just to be sure, just to make certain he wasn't coming that way.* Usually, by this time, there would be a commotion there, too, as whole families made their way down and out to the stinking back privvies. But there was nothing now.

She peered past the privvy shacks, at the back of the tenements on the next block, where the Jews lived. They were a family named Mendelssohn, a glazier and his wife, and their three daughters. She knew them a little, mostly from fetching water at the pump or exchanging nods with the woman when they were both hanging their laundry on their roofs, above the reeking gulf of the back-lot outhouses. All of them murphys, they wouldn't take a drink between them. The eldest daughter dark and beautiful of face but lame, walking with a cautious, lurching tread. Sometimes Ruth would stand by the back door on Friday nights and listen to the strange songs and chants coming from their kitchen, spy the candlelight dancing through their windows.

"The Jews are a mark upon us," Deirdre liked to fret, but around the pump in the morning, the women were divided. Some said they were indeed a mark, and a bad element, but others felt they might be good luck, at least if one knew how to use it.

"Have ye touched the oldest one's leg?"

"No, it's the *hair* you got to touch, to get the luck. Otherwise it's no good."

"No, it's the leg, of course, that's where she was smote—"

They would argue on and on—and find ways to sidle up to her, to run a hand along the Mendelssohn daughter's head or her hip when she was in the pump line, thinking she wouldn't notice. Ruth thought that she did, that she could see her eyes go wide and her body stiffen whenever she felt their hands grasping at her. Yet she had never noticed that anyone along Paradise Alley had much luck, no matter where they contrived to touch the Jew girl.

She saw no one—but now she could hear the noise again, rising up from all around her. The same marching sound she had heard before. The low, ominous murmur of men's voices and the tramp of their feet, as if all the City were on the move.

The mob was out.

At least they weren't stopping yet. Still moving uptown, past them, God's mercy for that.

Billy was still uptown, at the Colored Orphans' Asylum at Forty-third Street and the Fifth Avenue. He would be trapped up there, she realized with a jolt, unless he was already swinging back down the Bowery. She tried to picture him—moving warily but fast, his pay in his pocket. They could be out of the City before anything even got started—

No. She forced herself to face the truth of the situation. It was no good to do otherwise, she had learned that if she had learned nothing else in this life. Better Billy go to ground, and be safe, if the mob was really out. Even if he got back in the next few minutes, it still wouldn't be a smart idea to head out on the streets now.

Ruth ran her eyes over their possessions, waiting by the door. All her thoughts of how free she would feel, how relieved once they got on the ferry, dissipating instantly. Instead, she forced herself to think about what they had, here and now, and what they would need.

There was enough food to last a few days, she had seen to that for their travels. *What else, what else?* Water. They were nearly out; she hadn't sent Milton to the pump last night, figuring they would be gone. There was no help for it now, she would have to go out. She took a deep breath, picked up the two buckets by the door.

She looked in on the children again in their room, thinking she would simply lock them in while she walked to the pump in the square. But Milton, her oldest, was already up. He smiled sheepishly at her from the bed where he lay, reading his book. Looking serious at once when he saw her face, listening with her to the growing noise outside.

"What is it?" he asked, and she had to smile despite her worry, just to look at him.

Her boy. Her firstborn. Always so quick to understand, to sympathize.

"Nothin' to fret yourself about," she told him, as easily as she could. "Just some men about—"

"Are we goin' still?"

"Well, I don't know now. Not right away, at least."

It had been impossible to keep their preparations from him, the boy was too alert for that. *They had not told him why, at least.* She had never told him much of anything about her life before his father. It was not so much to spare his feelings as she was ashamed to have him think of her like that, the way she had been, when she had lived with Johnny Dolan.

"Where's Da?" he asked.

"Up with his orphans—"

He looked a little relieved, she was sorry to see. Billy was always too hard on the boy. He never liked him reading so much, even though it was he who had insisted on sending Milton to the free schools for as long as he could go. He wanted him up fresh and well rested when he went out to help him on a job.

"You're no good to me like that," he would harry the boy, especially when he was in his more sour, hungover moods. "You get up from that bed, you come in to wash, get your breakfast, first thing you do."

But there was no stopping him. Milton reached for a book when he woke up in the morning, he read after supper until he fell asleep before the coal fire in the grate. He would rather read than sleep, or eat, and she tried to puzzle out what he was at now. Once it had been patriotic histories of the nation, books such as *The Life of Washington,* with the picture of the fine man on the white horse.

These days, though, it was a different kind—adventure stories of some sort. She read the title slowly out loud, sounding out the letters—*"The-Green-Aven-ger-of-the-Fields."* Knowing he would like that, and indeed he beamed at her, a great, delighted child's smile.

Sweet, sweet boy, as sweet as the berry—

She forgot sometimes how young he still was. Dark-eyed child, with his big book, sneaking a look back at its pages even now. It was he who had taught her what reading she knew. Nearly fourteen, still without so much as fuzz on his smooth, almond-shaped cheeks but so serious at times that he seemed much older. His body already as taut and muscled as a man's, from the full day's work he put in whenever his father could find it for him. Taller than she was now, and as black as his father—darker by far than her other four children, who were more the color of coffee cut with milk.

She feared for his color. She always feared for him when Billy took him out on jobs. Knowing how the dockworkers and the street cleaners would spit and curse at him for his darkness. Knowing that he could not walk for more than a block without some hard word. She couldn't stand that for her boy, her favorite, she knew, though she tried to deny to herself that she had any such thing.

"It's not so bad for him," Billy would tell her. "Better that he's black like that. It's the mixin' they don' like. It's the thought of how that happens, makes 'em crazy."

The boy would only smile again, proud to do a man's work. But she knew how it hurt him. She could see the fear and the bewilderment in his eyes, the way he shied when he saw any group of Irish toughs coming down the street. How he flinched from their curses. *Hey, nigger. Hey, contraband—*

His father cursed him when he saw that, telling him to walk like a man, but she considered that useless and foolhardy advice. Ruth only wished there was some way she could protect him. Instead, she ended up depending on *him* to keep the other children in line, help her with the chores and errands when he wasn't working. He was such a trustworthy child, had always been so, reliable beyond his years.

"I have to go out now. To get the water—"

"I'll go do that—"

He was already putting down his book, ready to go in a moment.

"No!" she told him, more quickly than she wanted to, trying to keep her fear off him. "No, I don't want you to bother yourself."

She smiled at him, tried to make light of her own anxiety. "It's just to the pump, anyhow, and I got to have a talk with Deirdre—"

"All right," he said evenly, from behind his book, its wild, melodramatic cover. Two men fighting with sabres over a prostrate woman— one of them, no doubt the avenger himself, swathed from head to toe in green.

"All right," he repeated, seemingly accepting everything she said on the face of it. "I'll get breakfast."

But he was too smart, Ruth knew. She could see from his eyes that he knew something more was going on.

"Go ahead an' read for a bit yet," she said, trying to distract him. "You can let these sleep, no sense gettin' 'em up yet."

She looked over at the others, the younger ones—Mana and Elijiah, Vie and Frederick. Still asleep in their beds and cots piled around the small room, drooling and whimpering fitfully in the heavy heat. She couldn't help leaving him with a final warning, even though he didn't need it, even though she knew it would only alert him the more.

"Whatever you do, though, don't let 'em go out. Y'hear me now?"

"All right."

The eyes solemn as a bishop's, watching and waiting. She made a decision. There was no hiding anything from the boy, she might as well make sure.

"Just be sure ta bolt the door behind me, an' don't open it. *Don't open it for no one but me,* d'ya hear? Not even if it's just one person, sayin' he needs to come in for some'tin'. *D'ya hear me?* I don't care how sweet he is to ya—not one person!"

"What person?"

"Never you mind."

She hadn't meant to sound as harsh as she did. It was impossible to explain it now, even if she could.

Oh, but that she could rip out her past, just for the sake of this boy—

"It don't matter who," she said, softening her voice. "All sorts of shanty trash are out there today, stirred up about the draft, or some such. Someone tries to come in anyway, you get t'others, go out the back door down to the O'Kanes. The *back* door now, d'ya hear?"

"Yes'm."

He nodded gravely and she smiled.

Best to make it a duty, another task for him to carry out, he was good at that.

"Good then. I won't be gone a quarter hour, don' worry."

She backed out of the room, to give him some privacy. He had already become painfully modest, sleeping in longjohns or his pants even in this heat, lest she see him naked in the morning. She let him put on his pants and shirt before he escorted her to the door. There she swung up the solid ash bolt, breathing a sigh of relief when she heard it swing back down after her, once she had stepped outside.

He was a good boy, he could be relied upon. As much as anyone could, if he *came by—*

The women of the block stood at the pump like a row of brightly colored flowers. All of them at least slightly different shades, even sisters and sisters, the mothers from their daughters. There were women and girls from the Islands, blue- and purple-black as plums. Runaway women from somewhere in the South, faces the color of fine chocolate or well-used leather, or brushed with just the faintest trace of red, or olive. Women from Hamburg and Bavaria, or from Leinster or Connaught, like herself. Faces originally whiter than white, freckled and pale as the hide of a pale horse—but browning now, weathering as they all were, under the hard summer sun of the City.

Each of them looked relieved to see someone else out on the otherwise deserted street. Waiting where they did every morning, to fill their buckets at the green wooden Croton hydrant that lay beneath the shadow of Sweeney's Shambles.

Paradise Alley was not really a street or even an alley at all. Rather it was a passageway, never more than nine feet wide, that led into the Shambles—the huge, connected double tenement on Cherry Street that loomed above them, its walls and even its windows perpetually blackened with coal soot. Ruth and her family rented rooms just outside the tenement, in one of the few remaining houses crammed into the tail end of the block, where it slanted down toward the south and west. Most of the houses less than thirty feet deep and twenty-five wide, two stories apiece and another half story, which served as workshops for the tailors and carpenters and shoemakers who had first rented them. Not that there was anyone left on Paradise Alley with such skills anymore—

The Croton spigot was the only one for three blocks, so women came from all over the Fourth Ward—the Jews from the next block, and the women from the tenement, and even Deirdre, swapping stories and telling tales. Most days they liked to extend this chore, chatting and watching idly as their children tried to murder one another in the street.

Today, though, they were more taciturn, almost tongue-tied. Scuffing at the ground with their shoes and fiddling with the wooden buckets. Tersely sharing what bits of news they had.

"I hear they're goin' out at Owen's, and the Novelty—"

"Henry says any shop what don't turn out, they'll burn."

"They burn the whole town, they can—"

Their voices low and jumpy. Filling the buckets quickly, anxious to be back inside, behind their own shuttered windows and bolted doors.

"Why would men *do* such things?"

"They won't do 'em," snorted Mrs. McGillicuddy, a towering Kerryonian from the Shambles. She wore her hair tied up in an even higher topknot, against the heat, and Ruth could see the exposed white skin along her neck already turning a bright shade of pink.

"They get in ten blocks of the telegraph office, they'll be shot down like dogs," Mrs. McGillicuddy insisted, her hands stuck on her hips, as if challenging any of the others to contradict her.

"The same goes for the armory, or City Hall, or any codfish Republican's home. You know it as well's I do."

"*Then* what'll they do?"

They all fell silent. Knowing only too well what the men were likely to do then, what they did whenever they were frustrated. If they could not get to the mighty and powerful, it was all the more likely they would come on the block. This street of tenements, of whores and niggers and half-castes, open to all—for all to do as they liked. Yet even as they realized their common danger, their talk became more fractious, echoing the arguments of the men.

"Can ya blame them, though? Three hundred dollars it is, and a man can buy his way out—"

"An' no exemptions for the fire laddies, or the police! No other exemptions at'all!"

The complaints tumbling out. Ruth, and the women of color, and the other white women who were married to Negro men lowering their eyes as if they were somehow responsible.

"I hear the abolitionists is puttin' all the good Irish men in the front lines."

"*I hear they're bringin' a hundred thousand freed slaves to the* City, to take their jobs—"

"Me sister's husband went for nothin', went off right away an' got his leg shot off in Virginie. What good is he now, I want t'know?"

"Beggin' for money from the City, like some street whore—"

"Can ye blame them? Three hundred dollars an' ye can buy yer way out, just like that! When for a thousand, you can buy yourself a whole—"

The woman trailed off in mid-sentence. The Irish conscious at last of the others in their midst. Ruth took it all in. Saying nothing, but thinking of how Billy would jump up from his chair with the newspaper, dancing about in his rage whenever he read anything about the money.

Three hundred dollars? Three hundred dollars! Goddamnit, but I'd go to the war for half that! For nothin' at all!

She had been hurt, because she was sure that he meant it, and made him stop his talk.

What would we live on, then? Have ya thought a that? What would we live on then?—though it didn't matter. The government was not taking any black soldiers, for all the wardheelers loved to harp on it in their street-corner orations:

Ya don't see a single black face among the ranks then, do ya? Ya see all the faces of Ireland, doin' their duty an' fightin' for the Union, but ye don' see a black face among 'em. They're just markin' their time, waitin' to take your job, your wife—

"Here's herself now. Up bright an' early for once."

Even the black women nodded in agreement, happy to change the subject.

"She'll bring the devil down on us today. Wait if you don't see—"

Ruth looked down the street to see Maddy Boyle walking toward them with her bucket. Moving with that free, open-legged gait that made them all stop to watch her, men and women alike. *Maddy the Whore.* She walked with her head down, the usual, slightly lopsided grin on her face, as if she was nurturing some secret joke.

"God bless all here," she said very loudly when she came up to them, looking them each directly in the face, the edges of her mouth twitching with mirth now.

The women nodded curt hellos, or stiffened and moved away, depending upon their morality. Yet there was something more to their reaction today than gossip and resentment, Ruth thought. They seemed almost spooked by Maddy, shying away from her when she came near like skittish horses.

Men came to Maddy's house—they all knew that. Day or night, brassily ringing the little bell out front, or giving some prearranged tap, as soft as a pigeon's wing upon her door. Butchers and longshoremen, and sailors striding bowlegged down the street as if they could scarcely keep it between their legs. Gentlemen, looking dismayed and furtive. Black men and white men, Irishmen and Yankees. They came two and three at a time, while Ruth wondered if she made them wait downstairs in the kitchen.

And sometimes there were disturbances in the night, drunken singing and fighting out in the street. Ruth always liked to look out from their bedroom window just to see, wondering at the thought of all those men fighting over Maddy. Other families on the street cursed at her from their windows, and threatened to run her out. Maddy held her own, cursing back at them like a sailor until they put out their lights and slammed their windows shut again. They had always been a little intimidated by her. She had some rich gentleman who kept her in the house, and her prices were beyond what anyone on the block could afford. Their sons and husbands acted stupefied when she walked by, the women muttering about her casting spells.

She took her place in the bucket line, still wearing her secret smile

and a fine, embroidered frock. It was yellow as a summer daisy and
indecently thin to wear outside. Nothing more than a dressing gown,
dearer than any dress any of the other women at the pump owned, but
stained with dirt and ash, maybe even a little blood. Maddy oblivious
to both how fine it was, and how it looked. When she caught the other
women staring at her, she only grinned back, making eyes at them and
sticking her tongue out like a madwoman.

"She's the one." Mrs. McGillicuddy nodded significantly, not bothering to keep her voice down. "She's the one we got to look out for."

The others all knew what she meant.

"Sure, she'll bring 'em right down upon us—"

Maddy seemed not to hear them, rocking slowly back and forth
where she was. Still grinning her little smile, the tongue lolling out of
her mouth. *Like a child*, Ruth thought. Then her head snapped up—
and she jerked an enormous, ancient pistol out from the folds of her
dress, laughing when the women closest to her fell back over themselves.

"What do I care if they do?" she exclaimed triumphantly, turning
around and around in the street, waving it at them all. "They'll get
more'n they wanted if they do!"

"Jaysus, put that away before y'do some real damage with it!"

Mrs. McGillicuddy tried to sound scornful, but even she could not
hide the fright in her face.

"Ya see? The girl don't have a half-wit a sense."

"She'll bring it all down on our heads!"

That was the fear they shared. Maddy brought men, and men
brought trouble. Even so, Ruth had an irresistible urge to go up to her,
to ask her about the gun.

"D'ya really know how to use it?"

Maddy turned her gaze on her, and Ruth smiled without thinking.
How pretty, how young she still looked, Ruth thought—as opposed
to her own self. She doubted if Maddy really knew who she was, for
all their years living on the block together, but she smiled radiantly
back at her nonetheless, as if they were the oldest of friends.

"Sure, what's there to know?"

Maddy shrugged grandly, brandishing the weapon before her.

"It's a gun, you pull the trigger."

"And you could kill a man with it? Just like that?"

"In a trice!" Maddy told her. "Just let 'em try a thing with me!"

She handed the pistol over to Ruth, who balanced the barrel gingerly in her palm as she thought about it.

Just one shot. Just one clear shot and that would take care of even Johnny Dolan—

❧ · 5 · ❧

DANGEROUS JOHNNY DOLAN

The soft, pink nose nuzzled his cheek, pushing him gently but insistently out of his sleep. He blinked up at a pair of moist blue eyes, hovering above him, sensitive and inquiring.

He swung himself up at once, fully conscious now. The eyes already dropping back, disappointed—but still he swatted at the inquisitive, rubbery nose. The creature skittering away down the alley, oinking querulously.

"Get on with ya!"

He had laid down with pigs before, but there were stories of them eating men who had gotten too drunk in the Water Street alleys. When the beast lingered optimistically, Dolan tossed an empty bottle after it, chasing it off into the street. Then he twisted around, leaning on the brick wall he had been lying against to hoist himself up, grabbing up his bedroll and the little sailor's bag of his belongings. Carefully checking to make sure they were all still there, along with the boots on his feet, the shiv and the razor hidden in their sides and soles, the slung shot in his pocket.

He stretched, and turned back toward the wall to urinate. Studying, as he did, the other still forms that lay in the piled muck and garbage of the alleyway, buried beneath old coats and scraps of newspaper. Wondering if they would be worthwhile. The chances were great they had already been picked clean by a bartender or lushroller, but who knew, maybe the stench had put them off—

He kicked the closest man over with his foot. His face lolled back, yellowed as varnish. An overcoat wrapped around his body, even in this heat. Dolan had rummaged through his pants and vest before he realized he was dead. He stood back up, crooking his head to one side as if to study the man, divine his secret.

How was it so easy to slip off this life?

He kicked at the bum's little feet, as shriveled as the rest of him. Not even a pair of good boots on him, the patent leather worn through with holes the size of silver dollars. He kicked at him once more before he left him.

Lucky for you, then.

He stood at the mouth of the alley. Completely still, the way he always was while he tried to decide what to do next. Giving away nothing, committing himself to nothing, only his eyes flickering all around him, taking everything in.

All of it so much the same, even after so many years. The rancid fish stink of the waterfront, human and animal waste bobbing openly in the water. The aroma of coffee and ginger and cinnamon, nutmeg and lemons and oranges piled up in their crates. The ships tied up to the wharf like so many racehorses, their black bowsprits craning out over the street, straining at their hawsers.

Fourteen years. Yet here he was again.

His joints and back ached from his night in the alley, and he rubbed the few coins he had in his pocket together, ruminating upon them. *Get a room today or go out looking?* Nice to have a place, a place of his own, even if it was only for a few hours. A hole to rest and figure in, and lay his sailor's bag.

But any place he could afford was bound to be a flea pit, somewhere he'd have to watch his back and his things night and day. Worse yet, it was one more chance for him to be recognized, the other boarders or the proprietor sticking their noses into his business. Trotting off to the police, perhaps, to see if the reward was still good over that business he had had with Old Man Noe, so many years ago.

No, better to keep walking. No sense coming all the way around, five thousand miles, just to end up hanging from a gibbet—

He had made sure to get off the gangplank in a hurry, keeping his eyes down. You never knew who might be watching. The endless, shifting crowds of pickpockets and day laborers and drunkards, killing

time along the docks. Watching, always watching. It was the one thing
they had to do that didn't cost money. It would be a mistake to waste
money on a bed, for all he knew *they* had already moved on, would
certainly have done so if they had any sense at all.

But then, if they'd any sense they never would have crossed him—

Fourteen years. First the voyage 'round the Horn, then all that time
in the prison the Vigilantes had sent him to, in the foothills of the Sierras. Sawing planks or breaking rock, chained to a line of other men.
The jail hadn't been that tough, just a stockade of logs, stuck out in
the wilderness. Once he had even gotten hold of a file from the saw-
house, concealing the thing up his sleeve. Working assiduously at his
irons every night, after the other men in his cell were asleep. Waiting
until he was out on a party felling trees before he cut the last strand of
metal and simply ran off blindly into the woods, certain that no man
could catch him then, no matter what he had to do.

But he had had no food and he couldn't trap any game, what with
having to stay ahead of the dogs every day. He had never encountered
trees—*forests*—like that before, and before long he had no idea where
he was. That was the point of the prison, stuck out in the wilderness
so far that no white man could ever find his way back. And every
morning there were the dogs again, and the men on horseback. Chasing him farther up into the mountains until finally—starving and
bruised, his boots in ribbons, flesh cut and welted by brambles and the
whiplike tree branches—he had been run out on a cleared white rock
ledge where he had wept, and howled like a wolf in his rage and his
frustration.

He had wanted to simply throw himself over the edge, then and
there, but he couldn't make himself. *Not so long as they were alive. Not
so long as they had what belonged to him.*

He couldn't let himself go, not so long as he could think about that.
Thinking, that was the damned shame of it. He'd always been cursed
with the ability to think, he'd known that since back in the poorhouse
in Cork city.

*Whereas other men were just insensate lumps of desire, no better than
hogs—*

Because he could think, he had let them chain him up again and
march him back to the prison. He had let them give him six months in
solitary, and his sentence doubled for trying to escape.

All that useless time. Thinking about nothing but what it would be like when he got back here, to the City. But what was time, time *or* distance, to the likes of him? Now he had come back, just as he had sworn he would. Now he could think to some purpose, more than just to keep himself alive.

Back to claim what was his—his wife, and his treasure. So where to look first?

He kept still for a little longer, in the shadows of the tavern. *Best to try that niggers' nest first.* The Nigger Village, up in the scrub woods and the swampy lowlands above Fifty-ninth Street, half a mile or so past Pigtown. If they were foolish enough to be there still, thinking they would be protected by *his* people.

Well, they would see about that. There wasn't a whole city of niggers that could keep them safe from him.

He rubbed the coins together again. Enough for a drink, anyway, though he had no real idea what the price might be anymore. *At least one drink, he should have that just to take the edge off the thinking—*

He went around a corner, to the saloon he'd noticed the night before. A name he remembered from the old days, though he wasn't quite sure why: The Yellow Man. He tried to walk over to the bar as inconspicuously as possible, with his head down. Even so, the barman gave a start when he looked up. The other men along the rail backing off ever so slowly, the way they would when they didn't want to give offense—but didn't want to be too close, either.

At first he was afraid he had been recognized, but when he looked into the yellowed, mottled mirror behind the bar, he saw what the truth was. He hadn't looked in a glass since Galveston, had no idea just what he was like now. His tar's clothes filthy from the ground out back. Rough patches of whiskers sprouting along his cheeks and chin, choppy stubs of hair sticking straight up and turning a steely, grey color. His face still lined and jaundiced from the case of the yellow jack he'd picked up in Panama. That had delayed him another three months, even the whites of his eyes turning a jaundiced, yellow shade.

He smiled back at himself in the mirror. *Barely human.* It was just what he wanted. All but unrecognizable, yet fierce and frightening. *This way no one will interfere with me.*

.   .   .

The bar was a rough, dilapidated place. There was an old stove, a few
tables and chairs with more men slumped over them. The usual yel-
lowing illustrations of George Washington, and Emmet on the gal-
lows, and Will the Pirate tacked along the walls. He put a coin down,
and pointed to one of the barrels stacked up behind the bar and labeled
simply "WHISKEY," hoping to hide his ignorance of just what he
should order, or how much it might cost.

The bartender picked up the coin, nodded, told him, "Thirty seconds."

Dolan had no idea what he meant. All he could do was grunt back
at him, making a barely human sound of assent. He was still off, he
knew, from all those years in the prison. It was fine that his looks
would frighten away the curious, but he was still sunk into himself,
still moving and talking almost like an idiot, or a dumb beast. He had
to rouse himself, had to match the pace of the bustling, treacherous
town all around him—

The barman grabbed a grey rubber hose that hung down from a
barrel behind him, just as one hung down from each of the other barrels on the wall, like so many rat tails. He pulled away at it, priming
the hose with a steady, masturbatory tug. Until at the precise moment
when he felt the whiskey begin to flow he pulled out his pocket watch
and handed the end of the hose over to Dolan.

"All right. Thirty seconds."

Dolan wrapped his lips obediently tight around the hose end—
tasting the thick, acrid residue of onions and sausage, all the tastes
from the hundreds of other men who had already sucked from the
same hose that day.

Then the whiskey hit—wiping out every other sensation in his
mouth and throughout his body. It was the harshest thing he had ever
tasted, like pure iodine burning out the back of the throat. More camphene than whiskey, over some little time it would strip off a man's
insides like paint thinner. Burn right through his gut, wipe his mind
blank as a slate. *That would do it, that would stop the thinking.*

He hung on, not even pausing for breath, determined to get every
last second of his time. *It would do for now.* He kept sucking it down,
letting it stir the last flakes of salt cod in his stomach to a boil, wanting

it to churn up his head as well. When at last the barman ripped it out of his mouth, he nearly reached for the knife in his boot, wishing nothing more than to be reconnected to that hose.

Instead, he stood there for another moment, with both hands on the bar while he collected himself, making sure that his legs would still carry him.

"Another?" the bartender offered a little warily, having caught the look in his eyes when he pulled the hose away. But Dolan shook his head.

It was time. *After fourteen years it is time. It is goddamned well past it.* He swung his sailor's bag over his shoulder, and stretched himself like an animal, flexing every part of his body. Then he strode deliberately out of the bar and into the great City, his head glowing beautifully as it swelled and opened before him.

❧ · 6 · ❧

HERBERT WILLIS ROBINSON

In New York the machines don't work and the men won't. The street-sweepers are on strike and the machines they brought in to replace them don't clean anything, they only wet down the trash and scatter it around. New piles of trash spring up around them—empty bottles, cabbage leaves, fish bones, scraps of clothing. (It is the iron law: Wherever there is a pile of trash, New Yorkers will throw more and more, pretending that is where it is supposed to go.)

Dead horses line the gutters where they fell. That's the surest sign of how hot it is. The worst heat of the summer yet, humidity already thick enough to make you feel as though you washed in molasses.

Two brawny Irish laborers wobble on ahead of me, arms around each other's shoulders, drunk as lords at seven in the morning. There is no doubt about it, something is in the air today. They thought it was a good idea, having the first day of the draft on a Friday. Get it started, get it over with, and let things cool down over the weekend. Instead it just gave them time to talk and plot, away from their jobs, just gave the heat time to settle itself upon us—

I am still headed down the island, toward my place of employment at the New York *Tribune*. After I stop in at the *Trib*, I must get back up to Paradise Alley and check on Maddy. She won't fare well if there's trouble. Maybe I can convince her to come up to my house in

Gramercy Park, take shelter in the servants' quarters—though I doubt it. She refuses me everything now, things for her as well as for me. She refuses even to play our little game anymore. Relying, instead, on that big horse pistol she has gotten hold of. Brandishing it in her little hand with a laugh— *If there's trouble, I can take care of meself*—

My Maddy. Still so willful, so beautiful, even though she rejects me. She's seen so much in her life. But she's never seen a mob.

The boy gazes up at me from the gutter. The pool of blood engulfing his paper boat, dragging it down into the whirlpool. He wipes his hand across his face, smiling, spreading the blood from ear to ear—

I don't know why his face stays with me so. Most days I would not look twice. You can see one like him on almost any street corner in town. Just another child of the City at his play—

At Eleventh Street I stop to watch an Irish construction crew, putting up a double tenement on the site of Abraham De Peyster's old mansion. I can never resist pausing to watch the City make itself over again, its constant risings and contractions like that of a giant anaconda, or a copperhead, shedding its skin.

I have been watching this same crew for weeks, toiling in its pit of yellowed mud. By now they are so familiar I can identify most of them by sight. The big, red-bearded fellow, a natural captain of men, who is the foreman. The short one, slightly hobbled, but built thick as a bull in the chest, able to lift whole beams by himself. Two others, both with dark complexions and thick, curly beards, who look enough alike to be brothers, perhaps even twins. All of them in their stiff canvas pants and work shirts, filthy bandannas tied around their necks, identical bent straw hats to shield them from the broiling sun.

Day after day they nibbled away at old De Peyster's stately Dutch brick home and garden, determined as ants, with only the most primitive of tools, shovels and picks and sledgehammers, even their bare hands.

Question: Why is the wheelbarrow the greatest invention of all time? Answer: Because it taught the Irish how to walk on two feet.

It is good to see someone—anyone—working again, after all the strikes in the last few months. The strike of the longshoremen, and the gasmen, and the streetsweepers. The strike of the tailors and the hat-blockers, the ship's joiners and the ship's caulkers, the coppersmiths and the carpenters and the machinists and the hod-carriers—

It is a pleasure to watch even such a thing as this go up, to reassure oneself by its steady progress, day in and day out. No hoosiers or lumpers here, my little team has been at it without pause. As soon as they finished leveling De Peyster's house and gardens, they began putting up the tenement houses on the same site, using the same sal-vaged bricks and timbers. Nothing is ever permanently discarded in the City, save human life.

There has been little enough construction for the duration of the war. Even Dagger John's enormous new cathedral lies dormant and moldering along the Fifth Avenue, due to the shortage of manpower. But the tenement has risen steadily through the spring, and early sum-mer—three stories high, rooms eighteen feet by twelve, with a single stinking row of privvies in between. More than likely the men who have built it will occupy it themselves, building their own homes here, the roofs above their own heads—

"Cave in! Cave in! Men in trouble!"

It happens slowly, yet all at once—like dropping a tea kettle and watching it fall, knowing the damage it will cause before it even hits the floor. There is a groan that seems to come from deep within the earth, then an awful tearing noise as the building collapses, and then the men disappear under all the old brick walls and timbers and earth.

The red-bearded foreman, with his usual apprehension, nimbly jumping clear at the last moment. The squat, hobbled little Vulcan and two of the others scrambling up immediately from the ruins. They jump back in before the great white-grey cloud of dust has even set-tled. Impervious to their own danger, sending up the cry even as they dig frantically into the rubble:

"A hand, a hand! Men in trouble!"

The whole neighborhood is there in an instant: passing grocery clerks and bank messengers, teamsters jumping down from their wag-ons, leaving their packages and carts where they stand in the street. Women running to the site still barefoot, tying black shawls around their heads, coming straight from their kitchens or the cellars and back tenements, the laundries and the factories. All of them leaping into the treacherous hole to help dig out, hauling out whole beams, scratching up bricks and stone with their hands.

Their urgency is so desperate, so terrible to behold that, before I know what I am doing, I run in myself. There I am, right down among them, slipping and sliding into the excavation, useless though I am. Turning this way and that, trying to find something, anything to carry out.

There is another harsh, inchoate cry, of triumph and of fear. They have found the buried men, and now they haul them up—the two black-bearded twins. Surprisingly short and thick-legged so close up. Eyes lolling back lifelessly in their heads and every inch of them, even their curly black beards, now covered in white mortar dust. They lay them out on the ground, try desperately to push life into their lungs, breathe it back into their mouths. I wait with them, looking just over their shoulders, enflamed to be so near to this scene—to *them*.

Yet it is all futile. The diggers have become the dust they are buried in. The men pumping at their chests and mouths back away, and the horde of women gathers in around them now. They are their wives and daughters, sisters and cousins and neighbors trying to exhort them back to life—caressing their brows, wiping the dust from their beards and cheeks with their aprons.

It is to no avail—now they see it is to no avail, and send up a long, wailing keen of despair. Clapping and grasping their hands together, raising their heads and their hands to the sky. Their faces looking hollowed and ancient, distorted beyond all human recognition. Their wailing is a weird, unearthly sound, straight from some ancient, heathen village, out on the bogs.

I clamber up from the pit as fast as I can, brushing what dust I can from my suit. In my haste I bump into one of the new foundation walls. I barely touch it—but the wall begins to come apart immediately, the bricks sliding off, one after another. Even though it was laid down weeks ago, the mortar has reliquefied in the humid, swampy heat.

I stare at it, mesmerized. The mortar is now nothing more than a slimy grey paste, oozing out from between the bricks it was supposed to hold in place. This is plainly the cause of the cave-in. The worthless mortar, provided by some contractor who was hoping—what? That it would not give way until the tenements were all finished, and filled up with families, and he was well away?

I scramble back up to the street, no longer so concerned about the condition of my suit. Just wanting to be gone from that place, the keening going on and on behind me and the grey mortar still leaking out, dropping bricks into the yellow mud.

HERBERT WILLIS ROBINSON

Seven-thirty, and I reach the *Tribune* building still trembling from the cave-in. My face and new suit covered in dust, in the dust from those men as well as the house they were building. *What was I doing, jumping right in like that? Trying to save them? They could not be saved—*

I try to shake the dust from my suit, from my head. I don't feel up to facing Horace just yet. Instead of going on into the *Tribune,* I linger across the street by the *Times,* where Henry Raymond, Greeley's old assistant and constant thorn, is passing out carbines to any of his men who want one. He guffaws when he sees me, nearly swallowing the cheroot that is dangling coolly from one side of his mouth.

"Good Lord, man, but what happened to you! Does Horace make you put in Sundays on his farm now?"

I try to look amused, and force my hands to stop trembling. *What a strange day this has been already! First that boy, running his finger along his throat. Then the cave-in—*

"If you were any kind of newspaperman at all, Henry," I tell him, doing my best impersonation of Horace, "you would know that the future of our nation depends upon sound, scientific advances in agriculture and animal husbandry."

Henry guffaws appreciatively, and keeps handing out guns. A small, dapper man, his face swaddled in a thick moustaches and sideburns; Raymond was never an abolitionist, always preached compromise for the Union. Now, though, he seems to be positively hoping for trouble.

"Jerome is going up to the Armory," he tells me, coolly smoking his cheroot while he waits for the flashy stock plunger who is his leading investor. "He is going to get some Gatling guns from the army. With those mounted in the windows, I may actually *invite* that lot to try us!"

He stubs out his cheroot and gestures contemptuously across Park Row, toward City Hall Park.

A huge crowd is gathered there now, behind the high, iron fence of the park—more of the workingmen and women I have seen on the move all morning. They mill about, trampling the neatly planted flower beds. Doing nothing else as yet but talking to each other, listening to a few soapbox orators.

"Just give them a few hours to get drunk," Raymond assures me. "The police should have moved them out from there already. But of course our noble mayor has been caught napping."

So has Superintendent Kennedy, apparently, for all his assurances. There are only one or two Metropolitans in sight, fewer even than there would be on a normal working day, treading fearfully about on the far edges of the crowd. So much for staying right on top of the mob and hitting them.

"What about the Common Council?" I ask.

"Those Copperheads!" Raymond snorts, his eyes shining with disgust. "It's a wonder they're not out here leading the mob."

"But what about their ordinance?"

There was talk that The Forty Thieves might pass a midnight act, offer to pay the three hundred dollars needed for substitutes on behalf of any man who wanted one. Such a bill would be extravagant and craven, a complete capitulation to the mob—and something that just might save the day.

"Yes, I heard that, too," Raymond says drily. "But where's the angle for them in *that?* Where's their share, eh? Better we should have provided our councilmen with thirty dollars for each *recruit*. The Sixth Ward alone would've taken Richmond two years ago!"

He offers me a revolver, and after a moment's hesitation I thank him, and shove it hastily into an inner breast pocket of my dusted suit. Raymond grunts with satisfaction, then leans in more seriously.

"At least you've got sense! I've been trying to get your employer to take some guns all morning. They will come, you know."

"Yes."

"The pigheaded old fool!" Raymond swears.

"Yes."

In the newspaper business everyone feuds with everyone else, but Greeley more than most. His fissure with Raymond dates back to the man's employment with Horace. (Something about Raymond lying close to death for two weeks in his boardinghouse, while Greeley neglected to so much as send a copyboy to check on him.) Then, of course, Raymond had to go and aggravate everything by building his bigger, grander new *Times* building, catty-corner from the *Tribune* across Nassau Street—

Bidding him good luck, I cross over at last to Horace—and walk into chaos. Editors and reporters and apprentices are running up and down the halls, making any preparation they can think of. They are filling buckets of water, shuttering and bolting the big glass windows on the lower floors and stuffing water-soaked bales of paper up against them. All repeating to each other whatever scraps of gossip and rumor they have heard, no matter how insane. (Once a newspaper has been shut up, what choice do we have but to tell our lies to each other?)

Greeley himself adamantly refuses to make any preparations for the mob, though it's well-known how much they despise him for his abolitionism, his Republicanism; his repeated jibes at the Irish and Catholics in general. He is, instead, in one of his martyr moods. He stands now behind his tall painted composing desk, tousled white hair and neck whiskers ringing his absurdly round, pink, affable face like that of some superannuated cherub. Wide blue eyes blinking innocently, hands clasped together with that air of perfect, childlike serenity that makes friends and enemies alike so wish to strangle him.

As I watch he rejects all pleas from his adjutants, Sydney Howard Gay and James Parton, that he arm the staff, insist on police guards, flee—do *something*.

"In a republic, we are always at the mercy of the people," he tells Mr. Gay, who is nearly in tears. "If, after all our efforts here, we still must live in danger that our establishment will be burned and our very persons assaulted—well then, so be it. We must acknowledge that everything we have tried to do over these last twenty-two years has been a failure."

The very fact that he is on the premises before noon, though, belies Greeley's tranquility. Either that or he simply wanted to get away from the woman up on his Chappaqua farm whom he calls Mother—and who is better known around the office as The Irrepressible Conflict. It is a brave man indeed who would rather go home to Mary Greeley than face down a mob.

"No, far be it from us to add more blood to a nation already awash in it—"

Beneath those pious blue eyes, I detect a deeper uncertainty. Like most men who have strong opinions on everything, Greeley does not fare well in a crisis. It was the same way when the war began. His first reaction was to write a pacifistic editorial opposing any attempt to keep the South in the Union by force—"Erring sisters, go in peace!" Within two months he was deluging Lincoln with telegrams on how to deploy his armies.

"Do you think there will be any *violence?*" he asks me now, as if "violence" were some kind of unthinkable consequence, here in this City, in the bloodiest war of our history.

"Nothing more than burning the town down," I tell him. "I suspect they will stop at Brooklyn, though. East River and all that."

"Are they determined to go through with the draft? It's madness! I told Lincoln—"

He cuts himself off, brooding. Running his fingers absently through the piles of foolscap and grass heaped on his desk, the pasteboard hatbox full of scribbled notes for his future editorials. Horace, with all of his hobbyhorses—his socialism and Fourierism, his enthusiasms for land reform and abolitionism, fantastic diets and free love. Some of it he even believes in.

"We must know things," he says, his newspaper instincts rising to the fore. Furiously scribbling down notes on his desk. "Have the police turned out? How many troops are there in the City? Can we count on any more from Meade? Where are the mobs gathering at present?"

He turns to me, wondering the same thing he asks himself when he turns his attention to any man. *What can I do for the Empire of Horace?*

"What are those spendthrifts on the Common Council doing? Where is our mayor?" he demands.

"Most likely in Long Branch, or Newport for the season."

"Find them, would you? It would be nice to know what they plan to do about the mob calling for our deaths."

"What about acknowledging our failure—" I try to ask, but Mr. Gay is already pushing me out the door.

Maddy. I should be with her already, up in the house I rent for her by Paradise Alley. She is my first charge, surely I should be trying to do what I can for her, trying something to get her to leave.

She won't go, though, I know that already. I stopped by to see her, too, during my peripatetic rounds this week-end. But she would not listen to my warnings, my worries. *She is so much like a child still, in mind if not in body.*

There is more to it than that, I know. She is still bitter—she has every right to be. I have betrayed her, though I never made any promises to her. I should get back to her now—but she will wait, I am sure of it. I still have time, to do Greeley's bidding, do my job, and get back to her. Just a little while more—

I go out the back door of the *Tribune* and pass into the City again. Going back out to the mob in City Hall Park. My pulse is racing, even to move among such people, but I am almost giddy to be there. Secure, as I am, in my disguises.

Instantly, I have become one of them, thanks to the treatment my clothes received in the construction pit. Not quite a workie, or an Irishman, of course, but one of that vast, *in-between* class that always mortars together the City. A printer's devil, or an itinerant craftsman, an egg dealer or a patent medicine salesman, down on his luck.

Just now we are being exhorted by a man on top of an orange crate. I recognize him, curiously enough; he is the barber from Christadoro's, at the Astor House. Normally a good-humored man, like all barbers, pleasant and amenable to whatever views on life or politics or women his customers like to spout as he guides a razor across their throats.

Now he dances atop his orange crate, still in his barber's apron and his gartered sleeves, leading the crowd in three wild cheers for

General McClellan, and for the *The Caucasian*, the banned Copperhead paper.

"And now three groans for the damned *Tribune*, and the damned
Times, and that goddamned Greeley! The old White Coat what thinks
a nigger's as good as a white man!" he sputters furiously, thrusting his
straight razor to the sky.

The men before him laugh, and cheer, and give three low, menacing groans on cue. Only in New York—a mob led by a revolutionary
barber.

Yet for all their bloodlust it is still a holiday for the crowd—a bit
of hookey from their jobs, with little real malice beneath their schoolboy cheers and moans. I take up a spot on the periphery of the mob
and stop to listen for a while, but soon this tonsorial rhetoric causes
my mind to wander. I become distracted, staring out through the iron
bars of the park at the rest of the City, at the passing scene of the City
that always fascinates me, as long as I can watch it from a distance.

Everything still appears to be normal there. Swaths of gold and
magenta shimmer along the dollar side of Broadway. The ladies trun-
dle between the milliner's and the department stores—as they have
for the last two years—shining in their plumed Imperial bonnets.
Moiré dresses ripple in emerald and amber waves. At the corners they
use the hidden strings of Madam Demorest's dress elevators to lift
their hoop skirts, and glide over the unspeakable filth and the pigs in
the gutters like so many balloons.

If, that is, one can really call them ladies. These days the shoddy
aristocracy and the old gentility are all but indistinguishable. We mint
millionaires faster than shinplaster money. Men make fortunes in a
month, selling the government saddles without stirrups, rifles without
barrels, uniforms that are no more than rags glued hastily together,
likely to fall to pieces in the first hard rain. They throng Delmonico's
latest restaurant to wolf down French partridges—though they still
balance peas along their knives and blow their noses in their fingers.

Their wives now swamp the jewelers, and string themselves up
in pearls. Styling their new-grown tresses into wavy wreaths, wrapped
around their plump, cheerful faces like a hangman's noose. They hold
grand balls, and powder their hair with gold and silver dust. On
Sundays they carriage about the central park with liveried footmen,
and camel-hair shawls. They summer in Saratoga, spend the winter

wrapped in sable and ermine, racing down the Fifth Avenue in their sleds, hurling snowballs at each other and giggling like schoolgirls.

All this golden lust. For all our complaints, the war has barely touched us—some of us. Across Broadway I watch the white-jacketed Negro waiters at the Astor House pull open the shades and, with immense dignity, begin to lay out the usual free food around the bar. There, inside its stoic Greek facade, the ancient Dutch-English aristocracy of the City still gather around its quiet courtyard gardens and fountain, supping on its twelve varieties of poultry, its forty brands of Madeira.

Whitman used to come in for lunch at the bar, before he went down to Washington to find his brother. Let someone stand him to a short beer, then spend the rest of the afternoon contentedly tucking into the steaming platters of roast beef and ham, and smoked turkey; the thick bread and pickles, sardines, and rounds of cheese; and the inevitable hard-boiled eggs (no ears, here). *A poet must provision himself like a camel or a wood tick*, he used to say, *get his meal when he may, and live off the remnants as long as he can.*

It was not so long ago that I was with him here, stuck in an omnibus when Lincoln passed through the City on the way to his inauguration. We watched the train of carriages that brought him and his wife to the Astor House, the mob crowding around for a glimpse of the great man. There was a sense of crisis in the air then, too—that light-headed, breathless feeling just before a thunderstorm breaks. The Confederacy was already forming, and a great throng had sprung up around the hotel, surrounding the new president-elect in his barouche.

Whitman didn't like the crowds. He leaned out the window, wrinkling his nose—sniffing the air as if he could detect the rot in men's souls.

"There's many an assassin's pistol or knife in a hip or a breast pocket, right here," he muttered dramatically, casting an eye over the mob. "Ready to strike, as soon as break and riot come—"

At least we will be here, then, at a safe distance, I thought, but I didn't say it. Just then Old Abe stepped out of the barouche with his usual lanky grace. I had seen him the year before, when he had come to electioneer at the Cooper Union, and he had been impressive enough then. Now, though, he seemed like some primal force—astonishingly tall and lean and muscular. His clothes black and simple, tanned Western face furrowed like the soil of a new-plowed field.

He ushered his short, dumpling wife into the hotel lobby—a gesture both gallant and prudent—before he turned back down the steps to face us again. Standing with his hands clasped behind his back, looking us all over with an expression of polite but detached curiosity.

There were calls for a speech, but he begged off, nodding and bowing slightly on the Astor House steps, bending his high frame like a bow pulled taut to the arrow. *The people, his master.* Telling them with his disarming honesty that everything was shifting too rapidly, that "before I should take ground, I might be disposed by the shifting of the scene afterwards again to shift."

That brought a laugh, and a hand from the crowd, and I thought then that I had been wrong, that with his long neck and stovepipe hat, his tousled hair and his apelike arms, Lincoln seemed like a very *modern* force. Some rude device, the engine of a Western riverboat, perhaps. A tinkerer's dream, with all his ungainly, misshapen, improvised parts, yet hammered nevertheless into a machine of formidable power.

Of course, after that we put him through all the usual inanities we inflict upon our politicians. Nothing would do but that he had to be presented with a wreath from the Astor House manager. Next a tall man insisted upon measuring himself against his height and, again with that casual tolerance, Lincoln agreed. Obligingly turning back to back with him—the crowd cheering again when the president measured two inches taller than the tall man.

At that he was finally allowed to continue inside, to his room and bed. As he went up the rest of the stairs, a spontaneous cheer rang out from the crowd—nothing else so rare, or so moving in this town full of professional agitators and pitchmen. He stayed his steps again for a moment, looking back, surprised for the first time, and more cries— real sentiments—poured from the crowd:

"God bless you, sir!"

"Stand firm! Stand firm for the Union!"

"It's a hard day's work you have!"

And finally, in a child's voice:

"I hope you will take care of us! We have prayed for you!"

He smiled, pausing once more at the top of the steps to address the crowd, that sly, gently ironic smile of his just touching his lips, though his eyes watered with emotion.

"But, you must take care of me," he said softly—and then was gone, into the shadows of the Astor House.

I saw him only once more before he left the City, before the war came. That was the following night, when he went to see Verdi's *Un Ballo in Maschera*, at the Academy of Music. Mrs. Lincoln had gone to a reception at Barnum's American Museum, with all its marvels—its white whale, and its Fiji mermaid, and a dwarf who could recite any passage of Blackstone's law by memory—and he was alone again.

I watched him up in the presidential box, his face its own mask. Sitting there high above the rest of us, listening to the divine music. Giving away nothing himself, nodding gravely to all who nodded to him. During the performance he sat slumped back in his chair, with only a single white-gloved hand visible from below. It seemed to glow in the darkness there, that white glove, swaying slightly with the music, hovering above us all.

I touch the pistol Raymond gave me, in my coat pocket. It breaks me from my reverie, returns me to the task at hand. There is nothing more to be learned from the crowd for now, so I sidle away—climbing quietly up the steps of City Hall, peering through the gracious glass Georgian doors. Looking for someone official.

Yet the building appears to be deserted. Its shutters and doors are locked up tight as a drum, its restful green awnings drawn in against the incendiaries. *Where could our government have gotten to?*

This is a fool's errand. There is no sound at all coming from inside—save for the ticking of a large clock in the portico, renowned for its accuracy. I pause to set my own watch by it, staring at the hands while they slowly, scrupulously tick away the minutes.

Maddy. I must get back to Maddy.

❦ · 8 · ❧

RUTH

When her turn finally came, Ruth drew her water and reluctantly left the other women where they stood. She hated to leave them—even Maddy, even as spooked as they all were, nervous as cats. At least they were something familiar, part of her regular morning chores on this unsettled day.

She was, as well, dreading what she needed to do next. She made herself walk the few yards down the block to the O'Kanes's house. Pulling on the bell there, balancing both the water buckets carefully in one hand while she waited for Deirdre to get to the door.

Of course Deirdre already had her water collected, Ruth knew before she was even inside. It sat distributed in buckets and pails in the front parlor, and the other rooms throughout the house—much more than her family could possibly drink, but handy for dousing any sparks.

She was always thinking, that one. Always thinking, the way Ruth herself could not, and looking ahead.

The children were already up and dressed, sitting around the front room as quiet and stern as little judges. The room itself was neat as a pin. Jammed with the oversized used furniture she and her husband, Tom, had salvaged from the old houses over in St. John's Park. This was Deirdre's greatest pride. It was furniture unlike anyone else had on Paradise Alley—an immense cherry and oak, fall-front secretary, a rosewood reclining couch, even a square piano they had crammed into a corner.

The O'Kanes's house was only a little wider than Ruth's own, but they owned theirs—the upstairs as well—and Ruth was sure that every inch of it was as immaculate as ever. The floor scrubbed nearly through. Handmade lace curtains hung over the windows, as neat as only the nuns could embroider. Pretty blue-white Canova porcelain plates sat on her shelves—and over the mantelpiece, in the place of honor, a proud brass crucifix and a colored illustration of Christ, holding open His Heart of Infinite Mercy.

Deirdre stood in the doorway, her face expressionless. Irked, Ruth knew, just to see her there. Her perfect light-brown eyes the same color as her hair, and cold and unblinking.

"Do ya think we ought ta go?" Ruth asked her haltingly, unsure as she always was around Deirdre.

She finally moved aside, letting Ruth into her house—but only after she had ushered her children out of the room, as if she were afraid they might catch something from her. They filed out at once, without a word of protest, and only then did Deirdre gesture for her to sit, in a French chair made out of chestnut and mahogany, with an upholstered seat. Ruth perched on one end, as uneasy as a sparrow on a weather vane.

"Do I think we should go?" Deirdre repeated her question back to her.

"Aye. Go, or do somethin', then—"

"Well, maybe it's you who should go, then," Deirdre said drily. "It's you who has a way of bringing him here, isn't it?"

"You know that's not true," Ruth said softly.

"Well, I don't know who it was, then. I don't know who it was who brought my brother all the way here from across the sea, if it wasn't you. I only wish to God you'd left him there."

Ruth said nothing, just watched Deirdre's face twist as she spat out her words, unleashing the whole tide of her frustration over Johnny, and the war, and where her husband had gone.

"It was Johnny Dolan what brung me," she said at last, quiet but insistent. Deirdre made a face but said nothing.

"It was him what brung me, you know that as well as I do, Deirdre Dolan," Ruth repeated, using her maiden name. "Like it or not, it was Johnny Dolan who brung me over. I'd've been dead without him.

❧ · 9 · ❧

THE YEAR OF SLAUGHTER—1846

I was born in the Burren, where it's said there's not enough water to drown a man, nor a tree to hang him, nor the dirt to bury him. We had a cabin on the land, not far from Ballyvaughan, and there the maidenhair and the roses and the orchids grew wild in the summer, and the white bones of the earth lay out in the sun.

In the winter, when no one went outside and there was no work to be had, they sat by the peat fire. Listening to their father tell his goblin stories, or about the time he saw Daniel O'Connell at the monster rally.

"The whole country turned out to hear Swaggerin' Dan. There was people everywhere. They filled the fields, an' the roads an' the fields beyond that. Made torches from barrels of tar, an' hogsheads of sugar. And Dan himself standin' there on the hillside with his chest puffed out like a strutting cock—"

Their eyes half-hooded, dreaming around the fire. Listening to the flow of their father's voice, while the banshee wailed around the cabin. Ruth, the oldest, sitting by herself in her emerging womanhood. Then the boys, Brian, who was her mother's favorite, and Sean and Liam, and the younger girls, Kate and Agnes, and Colleen, the baby. All of them half asleep, as groggy as bears in the smoky, dirt-floored cabin through the long winter months. No windows, or even a chimney, just the door left open enough to let the smoke out and the pig in.

How ignorant we was, and how helpless. It's a sin to be so helpless—

Their father telling his stories of the wider world slowly, solemnly, as if he were still working on each one. Mother quicker, but telling each one the same way, every time. The dance at the crossroads, or how they moved the cabin the day they were married.

They loved to hear them, nevertheless. The story of how the wedding party picked up the whole house: the thatch roof, and the sod blocks, and the foundation stones and everything inside. Carrying it half a mile, to where it still sat, out on the bony plains of the Burren, while the fiddler played, and the women cooked outside in the field, everyone breaking off from the work to drink or eat, and dance.

"Those days we still would dance at the crossroads of a summer night. The priest didn't like it, he thought it a pagan thing—"

Ruth could picture it. The whole village stepping softly, slowly through the fields so as not to wake the priggish priest. Whispers and muffled laughter in the grass. The young men in their gaudy waistcoats, carrying peat and sticks for the fire, jugs of poteen and fiddles under their arms. The swish of women's dresses moving through the high grass, the bright ribbons tied around their caps—

When the west wind eased, an' the winter ended, me Da would haul the seaweed up the cliffs, where the wide Atlantic throws itself up against the land an' the seabirds make their nests in the rock wall. An' me Ma would mix it up thick with the sandy dirt, an' the pig droppings, an' the lumpers would grow even in that. Until they did not.

They pulled them up in August—great, white horse potatoes. Stowed over the fire, on a plank just below the roof thatch. Cooked up with a little salt or, sometimes, for a special occasion, in a soup with a bit of herring and a piggin of warm buttermilk on the side. Not so fine as the red potatoes they grew down in Munster, but big enough to feed them all, and the pig as well until the following June. After that they would live on the American corn they got in the town, and most of the chickens, until it was August and time to pull the lumpers again.

The August Ruth turned sixteen they pulled the potatoes up and found the half of them black, and rotten to the core. The blight had

come before—never so bad, but there were still enough saved to get
them through the winter without eating the pig. And the next spring,
Mother tore up the old beds with her spade, and had the priest bless
them, and by August the horse potatoes grew big and white and coarse
again, and they said a prayer of thanks to the Virgin, and to St. Brigid.

But just two weeks after, Mother knocked a dozen lumpers down
for the supper, and cried out when she cut into the very first one. They
didn't have to ask what it was. The potato she had cut into was black
to the heart, though they had pulled it up from the ground whole and
white. She cut the rest open, one by one, her face set grim as a stone,
each one as rotten as the next.

*Da boosted us up on the plank o'er the fire, an' we threw down the potatoes
as fast as we could, tryin' to find any that was still good, and separate them
from the rest. But it was too late. They turned to black slime before our
eyes, even as he laid 'em out around the cabin.*

*We run out to the lazy beds then, to dig up the new crop an' see if we
could not find one or two that was still untouched. But even before we could
dig them out our nostrils was filled with the sweet stink of the blight. The
lumpers turned to shite where they lay. We skidded through them on our
backsides, laughin' and scramblin' in the potatoes, for what else was we
to do?*

*Have you ever had a nightmare come true? Have you ever had the worst
thing you can imagine happen to you? We always feared the potatoes
would fail, and we would starve. And then they did.*

After that there was nothing to do but eat the rest of the chickens. And
when they were gone, they ate the pig, since they did not have a thing
to feed it with anyway. Their mother spent all day over it, basting and
roasting it until the meat was ready to fall off the spit, and their father
carved it up deliberately, rationing out the great, greasy slices one at a
time.

They were ravenous just for the smell of it. None of them had ever
tasted real meat before, and they gobbled it down as soon as they held
it in their hands, letting it burn across their tongues and their cheeks.
While Da and Ma looked on, not eating, letting them have it all, every
bite, the tears streaming down their faces. For they knew what it
meant to eat the pig.

And that winter the wind blew all day and all night from the east, which was an unnatural thing, and it brought the snow an' the cold with it. Me Da walked his miles each day to the works, where he labored with t'other men building roads from no-place to no-place, for four and sixpence a week. He worked there in the road, with no coat and the shoes crumbling on his feet, until he died in the road, and was buried in the road, there under the rubbled stone.

In the third year of the blight, they came to tumble the cabin. Half a company of regulars, just turned out of bed and still half drunk. The nervous landlord's agent with his notice of ejectment hiding inside their bayonets. But that was enough. They called them from the cabin and out they came, the woman and her seven children. White as slugs, without a pair of shoes among them, pants flapping raggedly at their shins.

It was half an hour's work. The soldiers lifting the thatch off the roof with their bayonets, then pulling the foundation stones and the peat walls apart with crowbars. The agent reading his bill of ejectment in a loud, shaky voice—slowly tailing off to silence as the family made no objection. Standing out there along the white bands of limestone, blinking like moles at the sun glinting fiercely off the bayonets.

"All right," the mother said when they were through, and they trooped back into the wreckage of their home and began to set up their *scalpeen.*

They pulled out anything they could, the stools and straw bosses, the bedding and the blackened cooking pot. The soldiers ignoring them, their work done for the day, forming up to march back to town for their day's dram, the agent safe in their midst again. They heaped a few stone blocks and the tumbled roof up around their possessions as best they could. Then they crawled back under, out of the sun and with their bellies to the ground.

We ate the pig, an' when that was gone we ate all the turnips an' the black-berries an' the nettles we could find. We even tried to eat the flowers, for it was all that grew out there, the maidenhair an' the pretty roses, an' the blue an' yellow orchids. But we couldn't keep 'em down.

After that their mother went to the church, but two of the priests had died from the spotted fever, and the last one had no word from the

bishop, so he closed up the church, and went out to the works with the
rest of the men who could still walk there. Next she went to Ballyvaughan, to see if she might beg some flint corn there.

*An' that evenin', just before dark, I looked out from a hole in the thatch an'
I saw her there. A lone black figure on the road, holdin' her skirt out before
her, so that she looked like a sower upon the land. And not like a sower of
new corn but a sower of Death, so I knew from that moment on, sooner or
later I would have to leave.*

And after the flint corn ran out in the town, they gave them turnips,
which was actually an improvement. When they boiled them down, at
least the turnips weren't as hard and dense as the corn, which was like
trying to eat pebbles. But soon the turnips were gone, and they got by
on soup from the Quakers, until that ran out, too, and there wasn't
anything—there wasn't anything to eat at all in the town, or anywhere else they knew of, out in the desolate silence of the Burren.

*Have you ever had a nightmare come true? Have you ever had the worst
thing you can possibly imagine happen to you?*

Her mother lay on the hearth, her head against the four crude flagstones where they used to make their fire. Her voice no more than a
rasping whisper. Telling the old stories again, about how they used to
dance at the crossroads on a summer's night.
    "That was na twenty years ago—"
    Ruth tried to picture it, the way they always did. But in the end she
could only see the telling of the tales. All of them, her sisters and
brothers and her father still. Dreaming around the fire in the long winter months, when the banshee howled around the walls and there was
nothing to do but tell stories.
    But most of all she remembered the food. She tried to help it, but
that was all she could think about by then. The fat white lumpers,
boiled in the pot with a piece of salt herring, a piggin of buttermilk on
the side—

*The whole village, walking out to dance in the crossroads. Moving through
the fields at night, carrying their goatskin drums and flutes. The women,*

each one wearing a bright ribbon in her hair, skirts brushing through the tall grass—

She had never thought of her mother as old, but she reminded her now of a knackered horse she had seen in the town. Her cheeks caved in. Whole patches of her scalp bare, the brown, almost black hair she was so proud of almost gone now. The flesh hung like a loose blanket off her limbs, eyes spinning wildly in her head.

"*Bliadhain an air!*" she cried out. "*Bliadhain an air!* The year of slaughter!"

Ruth stared down at her, dizzy in her hunger, her mother's face spinning before her. There was no fire, and none of them had enough strength left to fetch more peat, to go out and find some, and cut it from the ground. The stones were still warm, though, and she laid her own head next to her mother's, staring into her decayed face, dropping into death.

I left them in the spring, when the red rock roses and the mountain aven grew, and the orchids turned the rock pink and yellow and blue in their abundance. I walked out an' left 'em there, in all that useless beauty.

There was a terrible stink, and Ruth could see something glistening, dark and wet along her mother's blanket. She raised her head, watching, wondering if she was seeing the very life drain out of her. But her mother's face seemed different, too, almost calm now, all but radiant with the fever. She gestured to Ruth, crooking one bony finger at her.

It was then that she saw the nail was broken, the finger bloodied and dirty. It was then that she saw the gaping hole beneath the hearthstone, that lay in the ground like an abscess.

"You must. Get him out," her mother commanded, pointing at something across the room, her voice barely audible, but triumphant.

"You must. Help him. Get away."

She turned her head slowly to look where her mother was pointing, thinking she must surely be mad now. But she was pointing to her brother Brian, the favorite. The boy sitting on the floor, staring dully ahead as he always did, but with something dribbling down his chin and chest.

Something he had *eaten*—eaten, when there was nothing to eat, nothing to eat in the world. And coughed it right back up, too. At least two turnips, and a potato as well, judging by the remnants on his shirt, and in a small pool in his lap. In his hand, Ruth saw, lay the old red handkerchief of her mother's. Covered in dirt now, from where she had wrapped the hidden turnips and the lumper in it, and buried them all away under the hearthstone. Until something had broken, something had ruptured in her and she had felt herself giving out, and realized there was nothing more she could do. That was when she had dug up the stone, dug out the last, few bits of food in the world—and handed them all over to Brian.

Ma made no secret of it now. Looking over at her, propped up on one elbow, Ruth could see her still gesturing—her face shining and victorious, even in her death agony.

"Help him. He must get out—" she was still whispering.

Ruth looked back at her brother where he stared, straight ahead through bleary, lifeless eyes. Her sacrifice too late, the food useless to him now. Still her mother gestured with her broken, bloodied finger for Ruth to do something, to help him, Brian.

Instead she crawled over to the others, huddled together under their blankets. Agnes and Liam with their eyes closed, dead or sleeping she wasn't sure. The rest staring glassily up into the thatch, their chests barely moving, if they were really still moving at all. She bent down close to see—

The old woman glared up from the hearthstones.

"Save him!"

Brian sitting, staring straight ahead, feet out before him. Bits of potato dribbled down his chest.

Don't die here.

"Get him out!" Her mother's dying words.

Don't die here, in this place.

Ruth heard the words in her own head supplanting them, and she began to crawl. Mad and shamed despite herself, despite the fact that it didn't matter, they were all going to die. She would not die there, with them.

She came out of the *scalpeen,* and the cool air outside braced her for the moment. She felt light-headed, but strong enough to struggle to her feet and walk. She knew she would not get far, but at least it was better to get out, and die like this, out in the raw, cool wind along the Burren than inside with them.

Her family—

I thought to go, so I went. I started to crawl, an' I did not stop until I was out of the scalpeen. *I thought just to go an' curl up in the lazy beds. But then I was out, an' I felt the air, and I said, All right, just keep goin' as far as you can.*

She kept going, lurching on out, away from the remnants of their cabin, out past the bare white rock and the bright riot of flowers.

10

THE YEAR OF SLAUGHTER

She walked out of the *scalp,* expecting to fall down at any moment. She walked on out across the Burren, past the lazy beds, and out of the last sight of their tumbled cabin. Walking just to see how far she could get, thinking, *Well, better to die out in the field, at least. Better to die out under the sky.*

She found herself at a road and she walked along it, though she did not remember where it was, or what way she was going. After many hours, though, she came to another cabin, one much like their own, and she went up to knock on the door. Not knowing what she could even ask for; after all, nobody in the whole county had any more to eat than what they did.

But when she went to knock on the door, she found it pushed open. What little there was inside turned upside down. The cabin plainly deserted, its people no doubt out on the road already.

The way we should've gone. Before it got too late.

She picked through the meager, leftover belongings of the deserted family—not surprised, in her near delirium, to find herself among someone else's things, someone else's home. She found a used shift she picked up—thin as an onionskin, but a shift nonetheless— then a shirt, and a pair of pants. They were too big for her, but she was able to roll them up and put them on.

She kept searching through the cabin after that, looking for food.

She could not find any, but she felt warmer in the found clothes, and the cabin itself, and after a time she lay down and fell asleep on the floor.

The next morning she woke up and walked back out on the road again, because she could not think of anything else to do. After a while she came to other cabins, and in nearly every one of them, she found *something* she could use. Most often scraps of clothes, or a few old things she might trade for food. Sometimes, if she looked hard enough, she could even find food itself—a few last bits of potato or turnip the departed had squirreled away under the thatch or the flag stones, forgetting even such scraps in their desperation to be away, off the starving land.

She had to be careful. Sometimes she came upon a cabin with bodies in it, already black and bloated from the famine dropsy, or the scurvy. It took her some time before she could steady her nerves enough to go in and search such cabins, trying to touch as little as possible, lest she come down with the *tamh* herself.

And sometimes there were still people living inside, or in the tumbled-down *scalpeens*. Skittish and wild, and fierce as wolves. Hovering under the thatch, liable to come at her with a knife or a stick if she surprised them. And sometimes she came across cabins that had already been picked clean, with bodies inside that didn't look as if they had died at all from the *tamh*, or the hunger.

She kept walking. She walked the whole length of the Burren, from Ballyvaughan to Kilshanny, from Lisdoonvarna to St. Mary's of the Fertile Rock. Through the little towns with their blue-slate squares, the markets empty and shut up against the country people. The empty pastures, and the fields lying fallow, and untended—

The town moved slowly through the field. All of them, men and women and children, bent over at the waist. Searching for any last turnip roots, the only sound the quiet sway of their clothing and the shuffle of their feet along the ground. She watched them, thinking about the town walking out by moonlight to dance at the crossroads, the ribbons tied in her mother's hair.

Her mother, walking along the road. The silent sower, holding her skirts out—

The roads were full of people now, walking out of the West.

Headed down to Cork, and east to Dublin, anywhere there might be food. The men and women moving slowly, steadily, as fast as the hunger would allow. Shawls thrown up over their heads, the loose, slouching plug hats pulled down over their heads. Unfired pipes shoved between their teeth in the rain, hands in their pockets. Walking out of the West—

In Limerick she saw the cartload of orphans, left in front of the poorhouse door. The house full, the door shut against them. People hurried past on the street, looking away. The orphans sitting up in their shirts, large-eyed and bald, like baby birds in their nest, too bewildered even to cry.

And near Tipperary she met a band of men carrying a black flag with the words "Flag of Distress" written on it. They looked as fierce and wild as wolves, armed with makeshift pikes and hoes, as if they were ready for anything. They asked if she wanted to join them, taking her for a boy. But then a man came down from the local works and gave them some bread and they melted away, as meek as lambs and glad to get it.

They huddled just inside the cave, waiting out the rain that fell in steady sheets. All of them, men and women alike, covered with makeshift shawls of one sort or another—blankets, tablecloths, skirts. Anything to cover them. Faces flushed with fever, talking together quietly as they waited, repeating the same hopes and rumors of the road.

"I heared there was flint corn at St. Brendan's Well."

"Ah, no, we just come from there," a grey-haired, stoop-shouldered man answered apologetically.

"Wait till the Liberator gets back from London, he'll see to us—"

"Did you hear what he told the Commons?"

The stoop-shouldered man recited as if it were a lesson he had learned by rote in the hedge schools.

" '*Ireland is in your hands, in your power. If you do not save her*—' "

"God bless him, Swaggerin' Dan!"

" '*I solemnly call on you to recollect*—' "

"Aye. They needs to recollect us soon."

"Takin' boats full a corn out of the country ever day, while they leave us Peel's brimstone—"

" '—*a quarter of her population*—' "

She leaned against the rock of the cave's mouth, listening dully to the others speak of the Liberator, Daniel O'Connell. Trying to look as inconspicuous as possible. Trying to look like a half-starved boy, in her scavenged pants and shirt, she figured that was safest on the road.

Not that she had seen one man in ten left with the strength or the inclination to interfere with her. Not that there was anything left to fear from these, jammed together in their cave. For all the angry words, they remained calm and placid, ready to accept whatever their fate might be. "It is the will of God," she had heard them say, then curl up and die on the spot.

The worst way to die ever discovered. Ruth feeling the same, feeling as if, in the end, life would just flow out of her like water draining out of the limestone after a storm.

And why, oh why, should anyone extend it so long?

"Look in here!"

Behind them, they hadn't quite noticed it, the opening into the rock stretched far back into the hillside. The walls straight and even, obviously the entrance to a dolmen—perhaps the tomb of some important, ancient king, like ones the farmers still found after a heavy rain.

"Back there?"

They peered down into the black passageway of the tomb.

"Are ye daft?"

"Why not? It's a king's barrow. Why else would they dig it so deep?"

"We were all kings in this land once, you know—"

"No sayin' what there might be."

"Sure, but it's a fool's errand. How would we even find our way?"

"I have matches!"

A mad-looking young woman, blue eyes spinning like cartwheels, held up a little wooden box. They simply stared at her, too polite or exhausted to ask why she hadn't traded something so valuable as a box of self-starting matches for a potato, or a lump of bread.

"Do you really got some in there? Do they work?"

"Sure!"

The mad young woman took one out, scraped it along the cave floor, and held the light up, grinning. Once-lustrous red hair matted down in loose clumps under her shawl, her stomach swollen—with hunger or a child, Ruth couldn't tell.

"Who knows? Who knows what gold they buried with their kings?"

"Our kings."

"All right, then. Anyt'ing we find, we split it all ways even."

"Agreed!"

She looked around at the twenty or so half-starved men and women and thought that if they found a gold crown and scepter, the first *gombeen* man they met could have it from them for a bucket of soup.

Dividing the spoils of their wishes—but that was all they had, after all.

She followed them down into the tomb, walking in a crouch under the vast stone slabs that stretched into the hill. The madwoman casually lighting one match from another. The air getting closer, damper, the sound of rushing water somewhere ahead in the darkness—

"Jesus God, what was that?"

An old man's voice pricked with hope as he stumbled over something in the pitch-black darkness, imagining it to be a king in his armor. Another match flared up, hovering over the ground.

"Jay-sus!"

They hovered around the rotting corpse, the cheeks collapsed, bones poking out through gnawed fingers that still grasped a blanket clutched up to the chin. No ancient, shriven king—just a woman dead some few days. They sidled slowly past her, moving still farther into the tomb. Tripping and bumping now into more bodies, some still breathing, laid down to die where they were along the cool, dark sides of the dolmen.

"Anything here's been plucked long ago—"

"Ya can't know," the stoop-shouldered man insisted mildly. "I heared there was a child found a gold collar, not two leagues from here—"

The match blew out, and they stopped where they were in the darkness, waiting while the mad girl fiddled around for another one. She was getting low now, they could hear her fingers scraping along the bottom of the wood box. They had moved past the bodies, too far down the winding passage for anyone more to drag themselves even for the privilege of dying alone. But still they were reluctant to go back without seeing the end of it.

The girl lit up another match, grinning triumphantly, and they shuffled slowly onward. The water sounded louder here, the air was a little clearer, and it gave them hope. There was a sudden curve in the passageway, one so well disguised they almost walked straight into the rock—and then they rounded the bend and came face-to-face with an immense skeleton, seated on a rock.

"Jay-sus, here it is!"

"Oh, we'll eat now!"

"Pig every night!"

The very sound of such words sent a pang through their shriveled stomachs, and Ruth considered again that they were mad. Undeniably, though, there was a skeleton. A formidable one at that, seated on its rock throne as serenely as if it had been expecting them. The bones indeed ancient, stripped of all flesh and colored a waxy yellow-brown—

"It must be Brian his own self. Eight feet tall, if he's a hand!"

"It's a king for certain. Who else could it be?"

But there was nothing else to the kingly skeleton—no royal raiments, or armor, or clothes at all. No gold crown or collar for them. And they understood, presently, that there was something else the matter, something altogether unnatural about the thing.

"Here, he ain't a king at all!"

"How d'ya know? How d'ya know?" the mad girl demanded, furious. Lighting up another match even though the first one already illuminated the small niche they were standing in, chasing away every possible shadow.

No one answered her, for they could see now the elongated jaw of the skeleton before them. The pointed teeth and long, extended claws of what was once a bear, or some other prehistoric monster, curled up to die in the tomb many ages ago. No king, no king at all—though nevertheless they stood staring at it for a few minutes more, compelled by its sheer size and mysteriousness. Before the stoop-shouldered man asked timidly:

"Well then, do ye suppose he et our king?"

.   .   .

The old women sat by the road, waiting for the burial cart to come out. She sat with them for want of anything better. They saw through her disguise, such as it was. Telling her she should get to a man while she still could, telling her she should get herself married, if that was what it took.

She barely understood, at first, that they were talking to her. The old women like so many crows, flapping their black-shawled arms and their gums, every tooth rotted from the lack of any food. Making soft, soothing, gummy noises, telling her what she should do—

"You bet' safe self—"

"You kin get ma'. Any ma' will do."

"Any ma' do."

—repeating that over and over, until the cart came, and they stirred themselves to walk after it. Rising up from the pile of sticks and black rags that they were. They started as soon as they saw it, fifty yards down the road, getting a good head start so they could keep up with it for a few paces, holding their arms and their mouths open in desolation, offering themselves up as mourners.

She did the same, with them. That was the custom, hoping the bereaved in their grief would throw a few pennies out on the road. But there were no bereaved here—just the cart man flicking the reins at his donkey. Looking straight ahead, the bare feet of the deceased bumping along in the back of the cart, sticking out of their crude linen shrouds. The old women following anyway, as long as they could. Holding out their arms still, their mouths too dry to keen, their tongues clacking dully against the roofs of their mouths.

One of them, the ablest, still managed to keep up with the driver, somehow. Holding on to the cart with one hand and trying to look up into his face. Ruth tried to move along with her, to hold her up. Listening to her rail at the driver though he looked straight ahead, as motionless and unseeing as his cargo:

"I am descended from perhaps as good a family as any I address, though now destitute of means!"

The old women walked on for a few feet more before they fell back, collapsed by the side of the road again, the cart rolling on to the cemetery.

. . .

The country around Limerick was mad with new roads. They ran straight and true as a leveling rod, and when she came to one she decided to take it even though she had no idea where it ran. But after a few hundred yards she noticed that she was the only one on it. The only sounds the crunch of her feet on the rubbled rock, the cries of the crows wheeling and diving ahead of her, leading her out along the treeless plain.

She walked along it for miles, nonetheless. The clouds streaming past her. Some dark shape seeming to pursue her, to run alongside her so that she thought it was a cloud at first, or maybe one of the wheeling crows, or the devil. But there was no crow that big, and after a time she realized it was her own shadow, slanting just off the road, wraith-thin and insubstantial, fading and evaporating with the clouds. She waited until it swung along in front of her, then trod it down under her feet, making it disappear.

The road seemed to run on forever, far out past the horizon, but that was an illusion. For after she had followed it all day, it only dipped down into a little dell and ended right there, in the middle of the plain. There was nothing more. No destination, no town. No direction signs to anyplace else, it just stopped. And there she stood, all alone with the crows careening around her at the road's end, and screamed into the silence.

She thought there was something wrong with the village when she was still half a mile away. The whole thing no more than a white smear on the green and lovely countryside. Twenty houses, crouched together on the edge of a bog. No smoke coming from the chimneys, no cows out in the pastures or pigs in the mud pens. No sign of anyone or anything moving in the whole village.

She supposed they might have taken to the road together. She had seen that, too: Villages that had subsisted in the same place for a thousand years, all picked up together and making for Dublin, or anywhere else they thought they might get fed. Thinking there might still be safety and sustenance in numbers, what had led them to huddle together in the first place. Only she knew, after months on the road, that there was no safety, there was no succor anywhere—

When she moved closer, though, she was sure she saw something. A few low shapes skulking between the houses.

She stopped where she was. There were always stories out on the road of men robbing cabins, murdering, even eating, the people inside. Thinking maybe she should try to walk around the village. Yet it was no more than the *suggestion* of movement, flickering off the whitewashed house sides. And anyway the shadows looked low to the ground, like those of children, or pigs.

She left the road when she reached the village, taking her added precaution, just in case. Creeping toward the back of the closest house, trying to keep as low to the ground as she could. Hearing her own soft footfalls on the grass. Smelling all the smells, and the absence of smells in the village. The odor of pig shit moldering in the sties, and the lack of anything cooking, of any fire on the hearth, and a general stink of putrefaction. *All the usual.*

She was just sidling around to the front of the first house when she spotted another fleck of movement, out of the corner of one eye. She swung about—in time to see the back legs of a dog, disappearing behind the side of the next house.

So that's what it was. She thought of trying to follow it, but she knew it was useless, that she didn't have the strength left to chase down and kill a dog. The village was still unnervingly silent, bereft even of the cawing and flapping of the crows that were everywhere else.

Best to see what there was and get out.

She went into the first house. It must have belonged to the richest people in the village, she guessed, a well-made home, of wood as well as stone, and blocks of peat. She knocked on the wooden door—what had once been a good door, swinging broken off its hinges now— then pushed it back and padded inside.

The house was a shambles. The plates and cups, the finest she had ever seen, and the solid wood furniture—all broken up, lying in a great heap by the fireplace. Even some of the hearthstones dug out and tossed around the room.

Slowly, the thought penetrated through the daze of her hunger: *They didn't just pack up and leave.*

She saw there was another, open doorway within the house and looked upon it with trepidation. The very idea of an inner room in a home seemed sinister to her, an obvious trap. But she needed to look, and in any case there was such a stench coming from it she couldn't believe anyone, man or beast, could be lying in wait for her there.

She stepped inside, and saw it was the bedroom, with a real bed, a fine embroidered quilt. Underneath it lay a man and a woman and two children—all of them dead, though not for very long. Their faces covered with large, red spots and sores. By the side of the bed stood a cradle, a dead infant inside that had been badly gnawed by something. *The dog*—

She crept back out without having bothered to make more than a cursory search for food, the stink becoming too much even for her. She stepped out the door, glad just to be back in the cool air—and as she did she saw the low, black shape pad quickly behind the next house.

Another dog—or the same? At that moment, though, she was startled by a sudden, *human* sound, coming from somewhere on the far side of the little village, a few hundred yards away.

It was the sound of a woman, she realized. Screaming something in a voice so high-pitched and desperate that Ruth could not even distinguish at first what she was saying. Instinctively, out of what dull concern she had left for another suffering creature, she took a step toward it, wondering what she should do.

Then she stopped, able to make it out now. The one word the woman was screaming, over and over again:

"Food! Food! FOOD!"

The same old cry. *But didn't she know there was no food?* And if there was, *she* would eat it—

The foolish boy, chin and chest covered with the vomit of his last meal. *She gave the last turnips, the last lumper to him, her eldest son, the half-dead boy. She had saved it while the rest of them starved*—

Ruth crept over to the next cabin—a poorer one, its walls made only of dried peat, and mud and straw. Yet inside was even worse than the first house. Here bodies lay all about the dirt floor, tossed and worried out of their death blankets—throats gnawed open, whole limbs pulled off and scattered about. She halted in the doorway at first, not sure at all about whether to go in. Then she made herself take a few steps, holding her nose against the stink. Picking up a poker from the fire while she tried not to look at the chewed-up bodies, jabbing under the stones, and the straw boss. Looking for a stray lumper, a turnip, a bit of Indian meal—

But there was nothing, and she backed out the cabin doorway. She was still trying not to look, her eyes cast to the ground—when she heard the growl just behind her.

She turned slowly, all the way around, and saw the dog head-on for the first time. Why it had growled at all, she didn't know. It could probably have been upon her without that inadvertent warning, could have torn her throat out before she even fully realized it was there.

The animal was large and mostly yellow, much bigger than it had seemed before, coming up nearly to her thigh. Its ribs showed through its patchy coat, and bits of blood and offal covered its snout. It growled again, and snapped its jaws, pointed yellow teeth flashing in its red mouth.

Something wrong with how thin it is—the thought floated through her head. Not that it mattered. There was nowhere to go, the cabin behind her had no door at all, just the rude opening in the peat. If she stepped back inside, she would only be trapped there—

She tried edging her way slowly around the side of the house, back pressed up against the crumbly peat wall. Yet as soon as she started to move, a large red dog trotted around the corner toward her, then two more mongrels after that. All of them, despite the chewed-up bodies in the cabin, looking as half-starved as the one already before her.

Something wrong with that—

Not that it mattered. She was stuck against the wall now, the lot of them growling and snapping at her. One of the dogs made a high, baying noise, as if it were a signal, and the rest of them began to move in on her. A dog circling to each side, cutting off any escape, as quickly and naturally as if they had done this many times before.

She hung back, too weak to do anything much else. She couldn't keep her eyes on them all, the way they were spread out, the best she could think to do was to hold up her arms and hope they wouldn't get through to the throat or the stomach right away. Give her a chance to run though she knew she wouldn't get very far, out along the open road, the open bog stretching out to the horizon—

The dogs hunched down. The baying over now, their voices back to low, throaty growls. *It was coming.* She braced herself against the wall, trying to watch for the moment they were ready to spring—when a man came around the other side of the cabin.

He was moving very fast, in a sort of crablike, sideways manner, a stout piece of wood in one hand. He was on the dogs almost before they knew he was there. Bringing the wood down on the head of the nearest one, sending it sprawling into the dirt with an awful crack.

"Ha!" he yelled out triumphantly, then pounded away furiously, pulverizing the downed dog's head, its ribs, its splayed and trembling limbs.

"Ha! Ha!"

The other dogs didn't run, even then. Instead they circled around and came back at him, one at a time as they got up their nerve. He dealt the first of them a solid blow across the chest but it came back up, still going for him until, with a lucky thrust, he stuck the stick as far down its gullet as it would go, sending the animal spinning and choking away.

But now the first dog, the huge, loose-skinned yellow mongrel, was on him, and he had lost his stick. Ruth forced herself off the wall, scrambling on her hands and knees to the choking dog, where it twisted around in circles on the ground. She grabbed at the end of the stick, pulling as hard as she could, trying to get it out without shoving her hand between its jaws.

But it was too late, the yellow dog had flung itself at the man's chest, its teeth snapping for his throat. He grabbed great clumps of its fur, actually pulling it closer to his face—then switched his hands suddenly to the dog's neck. Squeezing it down even as the dog cut through his shirt, raked his chest bloody with its nails, squirming and writhing to get its head clear. The man just squeezed harder. Compressing the dog's neck visibly, his face set in a terrible grimace only inches from its snout. His hands sinking deeper and deeper through its fur until, at last, it shuddered in death and he dropped it.

There were two dogs left, still skirting the fight, looking for their chance, but Ruth finally got the stick free and tossed it over to the man. He picked it up and shook it at the dogs—his hands bloody, his close-shaved head covered with red, glowing boils. They looked at him and trotted away, stopping only to snarl back over their haunches.

Why he didn't kill her then she never knew.

In fact, she understood it even less the more she got to know him. All she knew was that she had gotten to her knees, then stood up— staring at him there with the club in his hand, the dog corpses around him. Eyes filled with a yellow, murderous bile, as if he had the *tamh*, or something worse. She tried to prepare herself, tried to think of something she could say if he moved toward her. But instead he only dropped the gore-stained club, and knelt down over his kill.

"Good, good, good—"

Muttering to himself, kneeling in the dirt by the dead dogs. Prying open their jaws, staring one after the other down into their throats.

"Good, good, good," he went on singing to himself. "No spots on the tongue. Good!"

He pulled a knife out of his right boot and began to hack away at what was left of the pulverized dogs. It was a small blade, so small he hadn't even bothered to use it to defend himself against the dogs. But now, with much effort, he used it to saw their legs off, one after the other, then to tear their tongues out. She watched him, nearly mesmerized, there in the dirt of the road that ran through the village. While he barely acknowledged her, only glancing back up at her with a look that warned her not to make so much as a move toward his kill.

That was when the woman began to scream again.

"*Food! Food! Food!*"

He heard it, too. She could see he did, that it wasn't just her, the way he cocked his large, terrible head to one side. Listening as a dog might. Sizing up the sound with perfect, blank-faced equanimity, then scratching hard at one of the bright-red boils above his right ear.

"Food! FOOD!"

He tucked his butchering knife back into his boot, and looking back up at Ruth, gave her a command for the first time.

"C'mon!"

She hauled the pieces of dog along for him, able to keep from jamming the still-warm flesh and organs in her mouth only by thinking of what he was liable to do to her if she should. Instead she followed him down a row of cabins. Barely able to keep up with him, he moved so rapidly in that odd scuttle. He was obviously in much better health than she was, still strong and quick. Not even looking ill-fed, though where he could have found that much food she could scarcely imagine—

The screaming grew louder, the woman's voice sounding as if she were in mortal agony, and he began to walk even faster. At last they reached the house it was coming from, Ruth panting with the effort. The man looked at her curiously, waiting for her to catch up—then he pushed the door of the house open and stared hard into the gloomy inside. He walked in, motioning for Ruth to join him. She did as he wanted, though the stench inside was terrible, worse even than in the death cabins, and she swayed and tried to back out. But he only grabbed her by the arm, holding her where she was.

"Stay! I might need ye," he insisted, and pointed to the straw bed, in the corner of a dark room.

They lay there under the blanket, the woman and her husband, or at least that was who Ruth assumed they were. She thought it likely, for they were both very handsome, or at least they had been. The man still alive but too weak to do anything save move his eyes back and forth, his mouth stuck open. The woman lying flat on her back as well. Her eyes unseeing, staring up into the roof thatch. Still screaming out that single word to the heavens:

"Food! *Food!*"

And yet, Ruth could see, it was too late for food. All of their teeth were gone, her's and her husband's, their cheeks caved in like old grandparents. The skin already beginning to change. The man tall, with a broad chest. The woman with dark brown eyes, large in her head now, and her hair streaked with white. All but helpless now—

The man who had saved her from the dogs drew out his knife and picked at one edge of the blanket, turning it slowly off them. They made no objection, but lay where they were, the man still silent, his wife still screaming futilely. The two of them fully dressed, she saw— but their clothes burst through where their arms and legs had swelled up at the joints. She could not keep from looking at it, the dark patches of blood so thick under their skin it looked almost black.

The dog killer let the blanket fall and walked back out of the house, Ruth following him as fast as she could move. He squatted down in a little circle of white stones by the side of the cabin, a place where a vegetable garden had been before it was stripped bare, even the shriveled husks pulled out by their roots. There he picked up one of the white rocks, weighing it in his hand—then told Ruth to do the same.

"No," she said immediately, and regretted her bluntness as soon as the word had left her mouth. Yet he was almost gentle, this once, in his response.

"We'll need somethin' heavier than the stick. They're not dogs, you know—"

"I'll have nothin' to do with that," she told him.

"Won't ya now."

He reached over, grabbing hard along her arm.

"You will tell me what you'll do an' not do, will ya—"

She tried to shake herself loose from him, but he held on to her arm.

"Goddamnit, it's the black leg! Ye must've seen it before," he cursed at her. "There's not a thing to be done for it!"

"Still, I won't have it on my soul."

The dog killer snorted at this.

"Your soul! Worry about your belly first."

"FOOD!"

He scratched fiercely at his head again, listening to the woman inside.

"Besides," he muttered, "that screaming's got to stop."

He picked up the large white marker stone again and walked back in. She waited out in the ravaged garden while he did it. She could have run, down into the bog, or hidden herself in one of the cabins, and she didn't know that he would have come after her.

But instead she waited, standing in the garden. That was the decision she made then, knowing she could not last much longer without him. Standing in the garden, feeling the east wind blow through her hair. Waiting until she heard the woman stop—

After a few more minutes, the man came out of the house again, carrying the bloodied stone in his hand. He walked out and hurled it as far away as he could, out into the bog. Then he turned his eyes back upon her.

11

DANGEROUS JOHNNY DOLAN

He walked up past the jewelers' and watchmakers' shops along Maiden Lane, looking idly at all the shiny sparks and fawneys in their windows and thinking what an easy smash-and-hoist job they would make—

And what about my treasures? The whole collection of them he had hauled across the sea, miraculously safe behind their own glass case. His cabinet of wonders. *Where were they now?*

He didn't want to think too closely on that, just yet. *Most likely sold it off, or junked it.* Ruth had never appreciated what a thing like that was worth. No one had, once they'd reached Amerikay, which he had never understood. It had paid for their whole passage over, after all, and that was just peddling it through some Dublin popshop. Yet they had only laughed at him in that saloon Finn McCool had taken them to, cracked it and jumbled it all up, then handed it back to him.

Some plan to cheat him, no doubt—as she had done. Well, he would find out what it was worth now, one way or the other—

He turned north on Pearl Street, following it up through the Bowery. The sounds of dice and piano music already coming through the doors of the theatres and the free-and-easy halls along the street, even this early in the morning. The bars festooned with large window signs, advertising their attractions—

The Handsomest Young Lady Waiter Girls in the City!

We still live—beautiful danseuses, charming lady vocalists, attractive ballet troop!

Who Complains of Hard Times?? Free Lunch!

He stumbled, jostled by the crowd, though all of them seemed to be moving with him, toward the north. No doubt some new sensation of the City. *An opera singer or a stuffed ape, anything that would hold their interest for a few minutes.* He stared all about himself, a sense of panic rising in his stomach. Still not used to so many people after all those years in the prison—

That was when he saw the face. Looming above the crowds of sailors and shipwrights, teamsters and longshoremen moving slowly around the corner into Catherine Street. *His* face—Patrick's face. The one he had almost given over looking for, even in crowds.

Yet there it was. Taller than Dolan had thought he would be, but the right age. It might not be him. There were only so many faces in the world, and he thought he had glimpsed traces of it before, along Broadway, and on the Embarcadero, and all the way back in Dublin, for that matter.

Still, it *looked* like Patrick, the same distracted but friendly eyes, mouth slightly addled into a lopsided smile. It half-turned, to look back at something, and in profile it looked so much like Patrick that Dolan tried to fight his way up the crowd to him, forgetting everything else he had come to the City for.

But he was no longer so good at maneuvering his way along crowded sidewalks as he had been. He tried to shove his way past, only to run smack into more backs, and elbows. He followed the face—followed *Patrick*—on up the Bowery, unable to close the gap between them at all. Until just before Grand Street, when he was no more than ten yards behind, the face vanished, as abruptly as if it had dropped into the sea.

Dolan bulled his way through to the place where he had last seen it, but it was no use. He looked into every bar and store along the block, even knocking on the doors of homes, despite the risk. All useless. He tried to stammer out a description of the face he had seen, of Patrick, to the curious, wary faces that peered out at him. But it was as if he had forgotten how to speak their language. His words tumbled out in rough, useless fragments, which only further served to frighten them—

The face of me brother? Mine! Only younger. Like a boy, do ye have him?

The people he tried to speak to only shook their heads, and moved quickly back into the gloom of their houses and tenements. Dolan felt the old rage growing in him, but he kept it down. It just confirmed his decision not to board in some house. He was well past being able to talk civilly with people, to even seem fully human—

He backed out into the middle of the street, moving heedlessly around the horses and carts. Still wondering if there were some place he might have missed, some slit of an alley. They were common down here, he remembered, and most of them barely wide enough to fit a man. The young divers and hoisters used to light out for them when the police came down the waterfront—

Finally he spotted what he was searching for. A wide, dead-end cut, knee-deep in mud between two buildings on the east side of the street. Cat Alley, as he remembered. It was empty, but maybe there was another alley, a door at its end. He started down it, so engrossed in his search that he didn't see the man coming up behind him, the arm reaching out for him.

"Dolan! *Dangerous* Johnny Dolan!"

The voice boomed above his head. Arms as thick and long as a bear's grasping him around the shoulders.

"Dolan, it *is* you, ain't it? When the hellja get back?"

He let himself go limp, thinking he would have only one chance if it was the police, one opportunity to go for the long knife in his boot. But the great bear arms let him go, and turning he saw another familiar face, one he remembered by the huge protuberance that sprawled across it.

"Big Nose Bunker," he said in wonder, more to himself than the large man in front of him.

"That's right!" Bunker grinned, clapping him on the shoulder. "Ya knew me, too! Ah, there's the boy."

He remembered Bunker from when he had run with the Dead Rabbits. *A thief, but never much of one for mixing it up despite his size.* Now he looked nearly middle-aged—run to fat, his huge chest and belly crammed into a soiled black-and-yellow-checkered suit. He laughed unpleasantly and nudged Dolan with his elbow.

"I ain't seen you since Old Man Noe got his. Was it true what they said?"

"What's that?"

"You *know*."

"No. I don't know."

"*You know*—that you used to keep his eye in your pocket? The one you gouged out?"

Dolan stood for a moment in the entrance of the alley, shifting his weight from foot to foot while he thought. Bunker grinning obscenely at him through his thick, greasy whiskers—the whiskey and onion smell on his breath nearly sickening him, so like the hose he had sucked up to in The Yellow Man. Big Nose was always a free one with the velvet, as he remembered. It wouldn't take more than two or three drinks and he'd be telling everyone who'd listen that he had seen Dangerous Johnny Dolan himself on the Bowery, big as life.

"C'mon! I'll be dumb as an oyster!"

He grinned back at Bunker.

"C'mere," he said, reaching out to put a hand around his shoulders and drawing him deeper into the alleyway.

"C'mere. You wanna see somethin', I'll show ya—"

Big Nose walked right down the alley with him, still grinning lasciviously. Dolan smiling back at him, his arm firmly on his shoulder, until he was sure they were far enough down to be invisible from the street. Cat Alley hooked off to the right, and ended at the back of a derelict building. He remembered it. There were huge gaps in the brickwork of the abandoned building—enough for a man to pass through, clean out to Chrystie Street on the other side—

He stood before Bunker, still grinning, and pulled his thumb gouger out of his pocket—pretending to fumble it into one of the bright orange-and-yellow crates. Big Nose went for it at once, leaning over as far as his bulk would permit him, straining to see the disembodied eye of James Noe. Dolan shook his head in disgust, even as he reached for the knife in his boot.

As if an eye would last that long—

Big Nose saw the blade coming at the last moment, out of the corner of one eye, and stuck up his hand to block it. Normally that would have made no difference, but Dolan was still off, from the yellow jack and his night in the alley, and all those years in the prison. He half-staggered to one side, slashed wildly at Bunker's hand, and sliced off most of four fingers before Big Nose could stumble back, his eyes wide.

"Jay-sus, Johnny!" he protested, sounding affronted more than hurt as he stared down, uncomprehending, at his severed digits in the alley mud.

"Jay-sus, I ain't got any money, you know—"

"No. No, but you got a tongue now, don't ya!"

This time he pushed the knife, thick and sharp as a butcher's blade, right through Bunker's hand and into his gut. Big Nose wheezed out a scream, but they were too far down the alley and it went unheard amid all the hubbub of commerce, the roll of barrels and the horses and wagons and the shouts of men, marching along the street. He struck again and again, six times in all, aiming for the killing spot, the vital organs and arteries, before Bunker went down. Silent now but still looking a little baffled. A big, beefy slab of a man, falling slowly to his knees and then keeling over, face first in the mud. Johnny stood over him for a moment, wiped his blood on the tail of Bunker's coat, then leaned down and rifled quickly through his pockets, just in case.

"Ah, goddamn ya, Big Nose," he cursed under his breath, coming up empty-handed, without even some battered old copper watch he could pawn.

"Ya always was a fine one for the truth."

He ducked quickly through the crumbling building then, back out onto Chrystie Street. There he fell seamlessly into the crowd, marching with the rest of them to the north, forgetting about the face of his brother for the moment.

⋆· 12 ·⋆

HERBERT WILLIS ROBINSON

I abandon our abandoned City Hall, cutting around the crowd filling the park, and cross over a footbridge to the dollar side of Broadway. Here the sidewalks are nearly as full as they are on any Monday morning. Crammed with merchants and Wall Street traders, peddlers and messenger boys and visitors from out of town, all of them oblivious to the impending crisis. The flower girls are setting up their wares as usual, wherever they can find a corner or a fence.

I stop at the stand of an old Negro woman to buy a pear in syrup, served up in a clay dish, a good remedy for a bad head. The street throngs push past me, as impatient as ever. Yet standing there, slurping down my pear, I notice, crowds or no crowds, that more and more dry-goods stores are not opening up. Or they are closing down already, their tin-sheet shutters clanging on the pavement. Some of our merchants have gone so far as to hire toughs and paid them to swagger about outside their doors, pistols prominently displayed in their belts. I wonder how much use such men will be to them if the mob actually does come.

On Paradise Alley they know better. The only sound in the street is the buzzing of flies, hovering over the heaps of garbage and the horse carcasses. Every door is shut. You can almost *feel* them sitting inside, in the stifling heat. Watching every movement along the street—

I pull the bell outside Maddy's—outside the home I rent for her. It is a sturdy, old freestone house, dating back to the Dutch. One of a few remaining houses along the nub end of Cherry Street. Just down Paradise Alley, looming over them all, is the terrible double tenement they call the Shambles   an enormous, monolithic structure, its walls and even its windows perennially blanketed with coal soot.

I give a small shiver, as I do whenever I see that place, and turn away, ringing Maddy's bell again. There is still no answer, so I pound on the door with both my fists, instantly enraged by her insolence, then worried. Could she really be out on such a day? Foolish enough to be straggling back from some god-awful haunt of hers—

"All right, all right, if you're that desperate for it!"

The voice of a slattern, but I am relieved. At least she has had the sense to stay in today—

She opens the door, smirking up at me through her hair, and I realize it is all a joke. She knew who it was, must have seen me hurrying down along Catherine Street through her upstairs window.

"Oh, it's you," she says, coquettishly, sidling up against the doorjamb. "I'm sorry, I was expectin' a regular—"

Infuriated all over again, I seize her by the elbow and push her inside. She yanks her arm away angrily, reaches under her frock and pulls out the absurd horse pistol she's been carting about.

"Ya can't do that to me! Mind yourself, or I'll give ya a taste of this!" she screams, waving the enormous gun around in front of my nose.

I slap it out of her hand, the ball rolling harmlessly away as it hits the floor. I slap *her* then—once, twice across the face, as hard as I can make myself, assuming she is still drunk from the night before. I am immediately filled with regret, with anguish and self-loathing for my temper. Maddy bawls like a cat for a moment, then steadies herself, waiting to see what else I might have to say.

She is not someone who rattles easily.

"Amuse yourself with me some other time. Things are up today."

"Are they?" she asks, stabbing a hand at my crotch, expertly discovering the tumescence that has come over me since I pushed my way inside her home.

"Are they indeed?"

I shove her hand away, holding her arms by her sides. She stands there, a smirk on her face. Looking, God help me, nearly as young as she did when I first knew her. I feel a great tenderness toward her still. Looking at the way her thin, silken hair hangs down over her face. Wearing the fine yellow gown I bought her at Stewart's—though even in this light I can see she has already managed to stain it with food and ashes, maybe worse.

I don't know why she should hate me so, save for the fact that I have stolen her life.

"You have to leave this place," I tell her. "That pistol won't help with a mob any more than it did with me. You have to come with me."

"Why would anyone want to come *here?*" she brays at me. "It's your fine houses uptown they'll burn! Best you get back an' look after yourself!"

"I wouldn't rely on it," I say, as calmly as possible. "There will be police and soldiers to guard Gramercy Square. The mob will go where there is the least resistance."

"You think your soldiers will do any good? Those shot-up old men? I seen what *they're* good fer. Besides, they say there ain't a whole regiment in the City—"

She is trying to provoke me again, though I fear she is right.

"Look around you," I tell her, gripping her by both arms and making her listen. "Look at all the coloreds you have down here, many of them living freely with white people. Who do you think the mob *really* wants to burn? And when they come, they'll find you as well."

"And what'll you do with me?"

"I'll take you to the house—"

"You'll take me to the house. To *your* house, now."

"Yes, you can stay in the servants' rooms. If the mob does come, you can say you work for me—"

It is the wrong thing to say—and I know it only too late. She stiffens, that stubbornness falling over her again like a veil.

"I worked for you before. I do as I like now."

"When have you not?" I ask her, looking around me.

She has turned the home I rented for her into a bawdyhouse. There is an empty bottle of whiskey on the table, empty glasses lying on their sides, an open tin of sardines. The whole house smells rancid, almost as foul as it does outside. It doesn't look as if it's been washed or swept for weeks, though I give her money for a charwoman, as well.

I move back toward the door almost reflexively. Maddy only leers at me knowingly.

"Why'd ya really come? To offer me the chance to be your maid? Or were ya hopin' we could play your game again?"

She lifts the hem of her yellow gown up over her sex—up all the way to her small, round breasts—as wanton as a Water Street whore, and I am spellbound. *Even after all this time.*

"I can get outta *this* fast enough. All you have to do is fetch the chains—"

"All right, you've had your fun."

I want to walk out of the house, leave her to the mob. I want to throw her down on the day couch, have her right there. I want to save her from everything. And as always she senses my predicament, grins knowingly around her mat of hair. *These people*—

"If you insist on staying, at least take some real precautions."

I leave her the Colt revolver that Raymond pressed on me, showing her how to work the mechanism and turn the chamber. It won't be easy for her to fire, with her soft little hands, or to aim a weapon with such a kick. She can get off six shots with it, though, and the noise it makes will sound like a cannon. That might be enough to give her some running room, at least—

She stands there looking at it, caressing the smooth, white, ivory handle as if it's the best gift I've ever given her, better than all the dresses, and the toilet water, and the ribbons for her hair, over so many years. Better than this house, or all the tutors, or the piano. *A gun.* Admiring it, so childlike.

That cryptic note of triumph as she defies me:

"I do as I like."

My Maddy. My mistress, my love. A spewing whore—and I have done this.

Have I done this?

She used to be different, once—I think. *So was I.* We met so many years ago, when she was little more than a child, already a woman many times over, in this town.

I can remember the very moment. It was one of the few true spring nights the City ever experiences. I had stayed on at the *Tribune* offices well past dark, putting to bed the national weekly edition. Getting out the Word of Greeley for the nation. Knowing that it would be read by sheepherders out on the Ohio, homesteaders in Illinois, gold panners in the California foothills. The advance guard of empire, fending off flood and famine, bandits and savages. Hunched around their camp-fires upon the dark and illimitable prairie, reading whatever scraps of the *Tribune* they can lay their hands on. Asking each other in awe-filled voices: *Have you seen Horace?*

After my duties were discharged, I had stayed on, trying to work on my own book, a collection of sketches from life in the City, which I planned to call *Street Scenes*. This was my secret ambition, the book I had yet to tell even the other literati down at Pfaff's Cave about. Deep in my heart of hearts, I harbored dreams of becoming the American Dickens, of turning out a book of great social importance—and one that would also sell like hot mutton pies in the dollar stalls.

Yet somehow, the images I had gathered failed to coalesce. They stuck and shriveled on the page before me. I put it down to my fatigue, to my mistake in trying to plug away at what was my art only after I had done my necessary work. Frustrated beyond endurance, I fell asleep, drowsing in the warm room.

It was her voice that awakened me:

> *"Hot corn! Hot corn!*
> *Here's your nice hot corn!*
> *Smoking hot, smoking hot,*
> *Just from the pot!"*

The sound of a hot-corn girl, so close beneath my window that I could nearly hear the rustle of her shawl. How many times had I heard that same call! Usually at night, while I was trying to sleep—smoth-ered in my bedroom, shifting about under a single sheet. The cry of the girl, somewhere out in the vast City, coming through my window—

> *"Hot corn! Hot corn!*
> *Here's your lily-white corn!*
> *All you that's got money—*
> *Poor me that's got none—*
> *Come buy my lily-hot corn*
> *And let me go home!"*

Now, welling up around her cry, I could hear the omnibuses creaking their way up Broadway. The trill of the newsboys, hawking the late extras. A fire bell clanging, the eager young men in their red shirts rushing to the station house. The laughter of the rabbit sports on their way to a theatre, or a supper, or a whorehouse.

All the sounds of a great city turning into night . . .

It was that hour of the evening when the City is just picking up steam. That hour when the Wall Street merchants leave the exchange to wager in hotel bars and gambling dens. The workingmen speak earnestly in their lodges and political meetings. The gangs plot in their cellar redoubts, the smiling women walk brazenly through saloon doors. The theatres and the beer gardens fill.

The room around me was soaked in the agreeably pungent smells of my profession: ink and pencil shavings, blotter paper and Indian rubber and machine oil. Beneath my feet I could feel the throb of the first-floor presses, rolling out tomorrow's edition, to be sent out all over this City, the state, out to all the new lit outposts of our republic—and I could still believe then, with a glow of pride and satisfaction, that I was a part of it all.

> *"Hot corn! Hot corn!*
> *Here's your nice hot corn,*
> *This corn is good,*
> *And that I know*
> *For on Long Island,*
> *This corn did grow!"*

The girl's voice drifted up to me again. It was clearly the voice of a young woman, perhaps still a teenager. Brave and insistent, guileless and revealing despite itself, the way only a young girl's voice can be. I heard it tremble slightly. No doubt anxious she wouldn't sell all her corn before it grew cold and she had to take it back to the Little Water, or the Arch Block, to face another beating from her mother or her pimp (or both). Still, I could perceive, she tried to use her fear, to hit just the right note of girlish helplessness that draws men like flies.

They are our ideal of womanhood here in the City. When times are bad enough, you can find one on every corner: match girls or button girls, pear girls, and especially hot-corn girls. A small cedar barrel tucked up in the hollow of their arms, full of hot roasting ears of corn like some not-so-secret token of their real profession. These child-women, always half-naked, always barefoot. Always offering and plead-ing, alluring and bleeding.

"Hot corn! Hot corn!"

She was just below me—circled, I knew, by black-coated flocks of men. Men of business and young gang toughs, clerks and foreign skip-pers, aldermen and judges. Some of them buying, some of them leer-ing. Holding up the coins in their hands, just out of reach. The young rabbits and shoulder-hitters, with their string ties and top hats, push-ing their way through the crowds, picking their fingernails with their knives—

"Hot corn! Hot corn!"

There was a sudden, high-pitched scream, breaking the girl's litany. I was on my way at once, bounding out of my chair and office, down the stairs, toward the entrance, thrusting on my coat as I went. The *Tribune* has a watchman, and there were newsies, printers' demons, politicians, and editors everywhere, but who knows? One of our City's most charming attributes is that, while it is not nearly so dangerous as it might appear—*what place could ever be?*—the most evil things imaginable can happen anywhere, at any time.

I ran out the front door prepared, if not to rescue, at least to get the story. There was the hot-corn girl on the corner, still screaming bloody murder. Struggling to hold on to her cedar barrel, battling like the furies to protect her wares against—a herd of pigs.

They had already snatched most of her ears and scampered across to City Hall Park, snuffling and snorting, eating as they ran. Our politicians talk constantly of devising some way to rid our streets of the pigs, Greeley himself must have dedicated a dozen editorials to the subject. Yet somehow, nothing is ever done. They bust out of the pens where they are kept by the North River, run in packs on the streets. Smarter than dogs and twice as big, knocking over children and snatching food out of ladies' hands.

Even as I watched, three of them bullied the hot-corn girl about with an uncanny coordination and intelligence. Two of the porkers butting at the cedar bucket, trying to tip it over just enough so the third pig could stick its snout in and get at the remaining ears.

"Get away! Get away! Awful things!" the girl was screaming, flailing at them with her free hand.

The pigs slunk reluctantly off at my approach, sizing up my height and weight with their usual swinish sagacity. Back to scrounging in the gutter for their usual meal—old apple cores and sausage bits, turned oysters and butcher's offal and horse's remains, drowned rats and moldy pigeons. (Plenty to keep them fat and round until it is time for them to grace the best tables in Manhattan.)

On the street corner, the hot-corn girl was still screaming and crying, the young men grinning at her as they passed.

"There now, I've sent them off," I said bluffly, trying to comfort her, but she just kept screeching like a harpie:

"What'll I do? What'll I *do?*"—and without thinking I reached out, shaking her sharply just to get her to stop making such a horrid noise. She kept screaming—and before I knew quite what I had done, I had picked her right up off the ground.

There we stood, mutely looking each other over. Our faces inches away from each other. Her shoulders slender, even scrawny under her plaid shawl. I know I should have been captivated from the first, but in truth I thought she looked much like they all did: wearing the same shawl, the same spotted calico dress torn strategically along the shoulders and calves, showing off her legs up past her knees.

I could hardly guess her age—though whatever it was, she had not been a child for a long time. No one could be, out on the streets like that, in all weather, with all company. Her hair was lank and unkempt, her face dirty, her feet bare. Her hands, I remember, clinging to my arms. They were small, but rough and horned from shucking the corn each morning, roasting it dutifully in the street or in the corner of some tenement room.

How she clutched at me! *How savage she is,* I thought then, but at the same time, *How helpless. How unprotected.* Her wild green eyes alarmed but also calculating. Her face serious and wide and innocent while she tried to figure out who I was, and what the hell it was I wanted.

❧ · 13 · ❧

HERBERT WILLIS ROBINSON

Oh, my girl—

I picked her up, right there on the street. I picked her up, after the pigs had ravaged her wares.

It would have been easy enough to leave her, once she had stopped screaming about the pigs. It would have been easy enough just to go back to my warm room, and my useless book.

But I did not. Instead I pulled out some coins, dollars and half-dollars, thrusting them blindly into her hands, meaning to pay for the lost corn. Or at least so I told myself. I must have handed over to her at least ten times what her whole bucket of roasted ears cost. And when I did she looped her arm through mine, as passively as a child, and I realized I had bought more than just the damned corn.

What was I doing?

Yes, I am a bad man. I had been to brothels before. But she was still so young. Barely a woman at all. I had never been one for the child brides, for all the little Annabelle Lees who haunt our street corners and our bordellos in the City. Yet there was something that drew me to her . . .

I took a few, halting steps down Park Row, into City Hall Park, as if I were trying her out. Her hand so small, so light on my arm. She looked up at me with her eyes still questioning but docile, with that strange, childlike trust even the most jaded nightwalker must have to hand herself over to a strange man on a dark street.

"I know a place," I told her, and I began to walk more quickly now, my head down and my collar pulled up around my face, hoping no one would recognize me as I towed her through the blurred and crowded streets.

I could scarcely take her to my own respectable home in Gramercy Park. No doubt she lived in the Five Points, or in some Sixth Ward tenement—the Gates of Hell, or Brick-Bat Mansion, perhaps. That wouldn't do either. Who knew what ponce waited for her there, or if I wasn't being set up even then for some badger game—to be robbed of my purse, my watch, my life, once I had my pants off?

No, there was only one place for us. It would have to be one of the Seven Sisters, the row of seven whorehouses strung cheek by jowl along East Twenty-third Street. Each of them supposedly run by one of seven sisters from a distinguished New England family, who came each in their turn to the City, were debauched. As the story went, they then wholeheartedly embraced their sin and made a killing on it.

All rubbish, of course. The story was much too good on the face of it, the truth colder, as it usually is. The houses, like everything else in this town, owned by mysterious combinations of businessmen, managed by seven unrelated old crones who had never been anything *but* the merchandisers of young flesh.

I went to them more than I liked. They were the best brothels in the City, with velvet curtains and well-tuned pianos, good brandies and cigars in their parlors. The sheets were changed between customers, and the chamber pots were emptied. Every Christmas Eve there was a rollicking party, with games of blindman's buff, and leapfrog, all played in the buff, by the girls, at least. And every New Year's Day there was a formal open house, where gentlemen called to drink a cup of punch, and chat politely with the same young ladies, done up in their finest dresses and ribbons.

I took Maddy to my favorite house, the most respectable one of the seven, more discriminating than all but the best hotels, and a good deal cleaner. It was run by a particularly hideous old panderer, with the homespun nickname of Gramma Em. She bowed us in obsequiously, acting not in the least surprised to see me in the company of a bedraggled hot-corn girl, just picked up from the street.

Instead she took us immediately in hand from the doorman, leading us quickly and discreetly up the stairs. From behind the scrim that blocks the front parlor, I could make out the genteel silhouettes of well-dressed men and women in conversation, the sound of one of her girls playing a stately hymn on the piano—

Gramma Em tottered before us on the stairs, bent nearly double with age but surprisingly agile, holding a taper out ahead of her. She led us to one of the most private, removed back rooms on the second floor, around a corner at the far end of the hall.

"As you like it, sir," she murmured, pushing open the door and slipping me the key.

The room was anonymous but well-furnished. It was equipped with a functional, sturdy bureau, a vanity with its hair- and clothes-brushes. Writing paper and pen, an unopened bottle of brandy, a fistful of good cigars—in short, everything a gentleman could want in his club. Yet my taste in her house was all Gramma Em had ever presumed to know of me. She had never given the least indication that she was aware of my writings, or of where I lived, or who I might know, or even what my name was.

"Ring for the girl if there is anything more you require, sir."

Pulling the shawl closer over her shoulders, spectacles at the end of her nose, bestowing a benevolent, elderly smile on us both as she bowed herself out of the room. Yet I had seen her ruin a girl who had cheated her, a beautiful mulatto from the Islands she cornered in the downstairs kitchen, branding her on the face with a heated fork before anyone dared to stop her.

She closed the door—and I locked it immediately behind her and turned finally to my prize, the hot-corn girl. She stood on tiptoe on the edge of the rug, turning slowly as she took it in: the immense, canopied bed with its feather mattress, the lady's mirror across the room with its own brushes and pins, clasps and combs. Then, all at once, she skipped about the room. Moving so lightly and naturally she might have been flying. Her feet barely touching the floor, staring closely at everything. Running her hands over the smooth quilt, the polished furniture, running the brush through her hair.

I was sure she must be performing, playing the innocent for me just as she did for the men out on Broadway. I reclined indifferently on the bed and tried to ignore her, kicking off my shoes and lighting up a house cigar.

But she ignored *me*. She went right on flitting around the room, excited as the child she still was at heart. Only acknowledging me when she turned to share her excitement, dirty, innocent face flushed with pleasure over it all.

"Is this where you live?" she breathed.

I leaned forward on the bed—still not quite believing, watching her for a long moment before I stubbed out my cigar.

"Come here," I said, and patted my knee.

Like an obedient child, she skipped on over to me, up on my lap. She was so light, so small. Her boney, underfed hips and bottom cutting into the flesh of my thighs.

"So you like this place. How would you like to remain here for a time?"

I had a tried and true method of seduction—though, granted, I had only tried it out on whores. To steady her nerves and mine, I asked her questions about herself. About where she came from, about her family and what she liked and what she did with herself. All the time sliding my arms gently around her waist, holding her in some innocent, even familial way. Slowly, slowly beginning to stroke her breast, her neck. Rubbing her brow and cheek, getting her to relax back into my arms so that I could stop trembling myself.

Yet this girl was different. The moment my hand lit upon her thigh she lifted up her calico dress—pulled it all the way up over her head and let it fall on the floor, just like that. She was suddenly wearing only a rough, yellowed half petticoat. Still seated on my knee, her modest, smooth, rounded breasts fully exposed, the ribs showing underneath.

It was the body of a girl, but one already exposed to the hardness of the world, and suddenly I didn't know what to do with it. I wanted to weep, I wanted to worship her. I wanted to make it so she would never have to face anything hard or terrible again, and at the same time I wanted to fuck her.

"What do you like?" she asked me, innocently, parroting back my questions.

"What's *your* name? Where do *you* come from?"

She ran a hand up through my pomaded hair, sniffed curiously at the toilet water on my neck—again as sweet and uninhibited as a child. I smelled her sour girl's breath along my face, and I was almost undone. I leaned back, docile under her hands, and she swung herself up over my stomach. Pulling the petticoat over her head now, letting it follow the calico dress to the floor. Sitting on me completely, thoughtlessly naked. Bracing herself against my chest with her hands.

"What do *you* like?"

I reached out for her, not sure what to touch first. Wanting to feel her breasts, her cunny, the smoothness of her skin, her face, all at once. Wanting to give her pleasure. Wanting most of all to touch her for my pleasure, that first sublime contact of flesh against new flesh. But wanting, too, to make her feel *something*   to sigh, to cringe, to love or fear me.

Yet she did not. She steadied herself along me as somberly and unconsciously as she did everything else. I took her left breast in my hand—slightly smaller, slightly more rounded than the right one, even the slight difference appealing to me—and then I moved my lips to it, licking gingerly, sucking at the little bud of a nipple. And in that moment I was filled with the desire to treat her as tenderly as I could treat any other human being, to do nothing that would ever hurt her. I believed it was the first genuinely unselfish moment of my life—lying on my back in a brothel, slowly penetrating a street prostitute I had just met.

Afterward she huddled under my arm for a little while, still naked. I tried to cover her with the quilt but she got up, moving around the room again. She stopped and stared at herself in the mirror—turning slowly around, trying to catch a glimpse of her slender back, her bottom, the one place where she had an ounce of extra flesh. I thought again that this was too much, that it must be a performance. Then she turned to me, her face completely in earnest:

"Is there some place I can—"

I allowed her to leave the thought unfinished, threw on a nightshirt, and rang for service. A pair of pretty young women, regular denizens of the house, came in response, Gramma Em apparently having boundless regard for my stamina and appetites. Maddy ran instinctively up to them when they entered, standing on one leg and whispering with her hand over her mouth.

They laughed, and walked down to the hallway of another, darkened room, gesturing for her to follow. She hesitated, and I took her by the hand and walked her halfway down the hall—still naked and oddly trusting. She let go and ran the last few feet to the door, where the older, slightly taller girls greeted her, still smiling, and ran their hands impulsively through her hair, all of them standing there like a trio of naiads or wood goddesses before my rapturous gaze.

I remember her sleeping so soundly in my bed that night. More innocent than ever, her face and her body scrubbed clean, a flowered nightgown tied up around her neck. After her bath I sent down for a ham and some potatoes, and she ate ravenously, then passed straight out, snoring contentedly in my lap.

I lay beside her, finishing a snifter of brandy, tempted to give her an affectionate chuck. Tempted to ravish her again. Every time I looked at her, my desire to protect her from everything in the world grew—as did my cock.

Her name was Maddy Boyle, I discovered, and she lived in the Shambles, that same awful place down Paradise Alley, and just above the City sewer. This was hardly her first time out on the streets, or her first time with a patron. She even had a pimp: one Eddie Coleman, a street thug I happened to be slightly acquainted with, who spent his days drinking and dicing at Rosanna Peers's grocery in the Five Points. She assured me matter-of-factly that he would beat her for not coming home to him, and while she seemed to think little enough of this, I insisted that she stay at Gramma's, at least for another few days.

What I would do with her then I had no idea. Yet somehow the whole prospect filled me with a keen sense of anticipation, almost one of light-headedness. She was mine for the time being—for as long as I wanted, it seemed.

Such a life she had led, already! Such a life they all lead, these children and near-children, begging and starving on our streets. Here, I saw, was a chance to do something for one of them. I had always been fascinated by the great rivers of humanity, the endless, passing scene along our streets. I had passed among them many times, in one disguise or another, for that is what my profession called for.

I just had never, quite, been able to do anything *further,* not even to the point of gaining for myself a wife, a family. Not anything, save in the confines of houses such as the one I was in. Not anything even in the way of close friends, save for the fellow hacks I drank with down at Pfaff's—

But this—this might be something different, I thought. Something I could do for someone else, and for myself. Just outside the window I could see the red-papered Japanese lanterns in the little back garden Gramma Em maintained. Somehow, even in this sordid setting, they seemed to glow with possibility.

That was so long ago—an age, in more than years. Could it be that she was once that sweet, that trusting? Or that I was?

My Maddy. Despite her mockery of me—despite all that has passed between us, her degradation, our awful little games—I still wish to shelter her, to protect her. I wonder if I should go back even now, try to convince her again to come with me, to remove herself from harm's way.

But ahead of me now, from the direction of the East River, I can hear another noise. The tramp of feet, of thousands of boots and low, distant men's voices. An unforgettable sound, one I have not heard since my sojourn down to Virginia for Burnside's campaign.

It is an army of men on the march. Without the discipline of a real army, to be sure, but an army nevertheless. A great tide of men, sweeping north, uptown. *The mob is out, but where is it going?* In any case, they are not coming here, Maddy will be safe enough, plenty of time to rescue her later. I hurry on down the street, running toward the story.

❧ · 14 · ❧

MADDY

She watched him go, through the shutters, running her palm over the smooth, ivory-covered handle of the gun. Gauging its heft. Sighting down its barrel, through the slats, at the women still in line by the Croton pump.

"Let 'em come. Let any of 'em try an' come."

Picturing the men in their stead. All the ones that had come before, and all those who would not come again. Leveling the revolver on them as they came through her door. Her hand feeling blindly along its chamber, then the barrel.

"Let 'em try it."

A new gun, a long gun. A cavalry officer's gun. A sure shot. Made of steel, at least, this one, you would never have to worry about it—

We'll see to your niggers. To you, an' all your niggers.

That voice from the other night, freezing her blood. The one she had locked out on the street. His threats had been spoken calmly, but they felt all the more real for it. Made as an oath, in a voice just loud enough to tell the whole block.

He had been in before. A short, shriveled-up sort of man. Steward or captain of a fire company, she knew the type. Fastening his suspenders with a pair of gold eagles, as proud as though they had been a colonel's epaulets. Unable to raise his hose half the time, that was why she hadn't let him in. Men like that took up too much time. They became only too aware it was a business, pumping away in desperation, an ever-grimmer look on their faces. Then they took it out on you.

All the men and their guns. She had seen every variety since the war, business was booming. Tars in white jackets, up from the blockade with their ships. Zouave officers, wearing their baggy red pants and the funny little fez hats with the tassels. Enlisted men, fuzzy-cheeked boys from Massachusetts and Maine and Vermont, passing through on their way down to the war, recommended by a friend or a cousin who had been this way before. A satisfied customer—perhaps already tucked under the earth, somewhere down in the wilderness of Virginia, or Stone River—

They went on, in their turn. Two or three at least, every night. Scared or excited or drunk or quarrelsome, or dangerously angry. She dealt with them all, sent them on their way, letting them button their trousers in the street if they tried to give her grief.

Yet *he* had come back—this fire captain, this voice—blaming it on the coloreds.

Men were always disappointed with something. That was the first thing to know about them. They were rarely satisfied, and when they weren't, they liked to blame it on something else—a rich man, or a woman. The government, God in His infinite mercy. The niggers. In truth, it was all one and the same, the thing that stopped them. *Best not to be mistaken for it.*

She moved back into the streaked, brown gloom of the house's interior. Rummaging around behind the littered kitchen table, the scraps of last night's meal, bread and cheese, sardines and soured wine, still on the board. *God, it was hot.* She was already sopping beneath the yellow silk dressing gown, the perspiration collecting in little beads along the fine, soft hairs at the small of her back and on her lip. Looking around for where she had put the ladle, and the bucket of water.

She decided she wanted something more than water, and went over to the jug she kept in the coolest corner of the kitchen. There she drew out the plug with her teeth, and took a slow, leisurely slug. Feeling the acid whiskey taste drip slowly down her throat. Wiping her mouth with the back of her hand when she was through, and thinking as she did how much Robinson hated that—both the jug and the hand wiped across her mouth. The look of repulsion on his face when he would smell it on her, especially in the morning.

I do as I like.

Not that it kept him from wanting her. Nothing did. She enjoyed it sometimes, seeing how hideous she could make herself to him, and still have him want her. Leaving herself unwashed and unmade, the house uncleaned until the roaches ran up the walls. Her long, red-brown hair left flat and matted. Baiting him with her tongue.

Nothing worked. Not even the black men who so disturbed the fire foreman. She knew of others, lady birds and nightwalkers, who refused to take any coloreds onboard. She had never cared. It was all the same to her, that pushing and throbbing down there, who cared what color it was. Mostly it bothered the other men, she knew. Jealous as they were of their supposed size, and prowess. Outraged by the thought of it, by the very idea that they might be *spoiled* for white men.

As if there was anything left to spoil.

She hugged herself, scratching her arms vigorously against the memory of Robinson's touch. Her efforts no more availing than all the other touches she had used to obliterate his. The feeling remained. Something deeper, more unnerving than even laying his hand on her sex. *How he would grasp her wrist, pull it behind her back, pull the manacle closed around it—*

The loose play chains that Robinson would put on her. Laughing as he did it—this forced, grim laugh, as if it were a joke they shared, just between themselves. She did not know which was worse, when he laughed or when he did not. For when he did not he would look at her—look right through her—with glazed eyes, his mouth slightly open, breathing hard and unable to say anything.

Robinson had insisted that she like it. He had insisted that she play his game from the day they had first gone to Schaus's gallery, and seen the statue. Starting with the simple band of leather that the sculptor had depicted, but moving, inexorably, to the chains.

She was not sure why. He seemed to like the heft of the fetters, ornamental though they were. Or maybe the way they caught the light through the shutters, gold and silver, or most of all, she suspected, his sense of them against her naked skin. The way their metallic coldness raised the bumps all along her flesh, made her nipples rise when he draped them over her.

It made the hairs stand up on the back of her neck, too, although he did not notice that.

She took another draught directly from the jug. This one went down easier—they usually did, after the first—but her head felt heavy now. She thought to take a short nap, the ivory gun handle still clutched in her right fist.

She opened her eyes without lifting her head from where it lay on the table. *Another rotting dish. Leave it to the roaches and the flies.* There was a dull, roaring sound in her ears, but she could no longer tell if it came from within her head or without.

When was the last time she had eaten? She sat up, considered fetching herself another drink from the jug, but knew it would only make the heat worse. Wondering if it would be worthwhile to get a rise out of him anyway, whenever he came back. *She would be whatever he wanted her to be.* But now she just wanted to get a reaction out of him, any kind of response she could manage. Which was why she still let him put on the chains—

The roaring kept up in her head, and she stood up from the table, moving unsteadily toward the jug, thinking, *At least it will stop that.*

Yet she kept going, past the whiskey. Moving on out into the front room, the roaring growing perceptibly louder as she did. Until at last she stood in front of the shuttered window and realized that it was not coming from inside her at all but from outside, somewhere in the City. The heat pressing down on her chest like an anvil.

"Let 'em come," she breathed.

Wanting them to come, even—but the first sharp stalks of fear already poking into her stomach. Wondering when he would come back for her, then doggedly shaking off such a thought.

"Let 'em come an' try. *I do as I like.*"

· 15 ·

RUTH

"Is he gone, then?"

"I think so."

Ruth peered out the neat lace curtains of Deirdre's house. The well-dressed man was receding from view, moving off toward the East River and the ominous sounds of the mob.

What were men, to go toward such a thing as that?

She had assumed the worst when she'd spotted the man, moving so rapidly down the street. But she saw soon enough that it couldn't be him, that he moved nothing like Johnny Dolan, in the half-crouch she could remember even after all these years.

"Who *was* it?" Deirdre asked sharply, looking over her shoulder.

"Just *him*—just that gentleman of Maddy's."

In all the years she had been on Paradise Alley, they had never learned his name.

"Ah. *Him.*"

Deirdre wrinkled up her face in disgust.

"The thought of it. On our own street—"

"Well, better him than the one who was here the other night," Ruth said.

"Oh, yes. Much better, I suppose," Deirdre said tartly.

It had been another one of Maddy's late-night explosions. Ruth had sat up in bed, listening with that same illicit thrill with which she always liked to overhear things in the street, in this City, late at night. Wild, drunken fights and quarrels, the passionate voices and sounds coming out of the darkness. Listening as she did to the gossip of the other women, and the tales Billy brought back to her—all the joys she had never known before, of living close to other people.

But this wasn't the same. This voice not blustery or winded at all, the way they usually were. Not the usual drunken men shouting to the heavens, but spoken with a purpose, rising just loud enough for the whole block to hear.

"We'll see to your niggers."

The voice sharp and direct as a knife.

"This is a white man's country, an' we'll be damned if we're gonna share our whores with the niggers, too—"

"Niggers? Niggers? *Two* a you couldn't measure up to a nigger! At least a nigger fireman might know how to pump his own!"

Maddy screaming obscenities back at him, as usual. Mocking and taunting him over his manhood and his capabilities, until windows began to open all up and down the block.

"Keep that shite down! We got children in this house!"

"Keep *your* shite down, I got work tomorrow. Your goddamned children can sleep the day away!"

The exchanges of shouts and curses dwindling down to more jokes, sardonic laughter rumbling through the night. Billy shifted in the bed beside her—alert as ever to her slightest movement, mumbling that she ought to lie back down and let him sleep.

But the voice outside Maddy's, still sure and mean and purposeful, repeating its one threat over and over:

"We'll see to your niggers. And to you as well—"

It was something just in the way he said the word. *Niggers.* Of course, Ruth had heard that from the first day she'd set foot in the City. The Know-Nothing gangs, calling her Irish nigger in the streets. Niggers, nigras, black niggers, green niggers—as far as she could tell, it was a City of Niggers.

But this one said it as a careful threat, one that the unseen speaker, the voice out in the darkness, enjoyed making. She could not see who it was—just a short, dark shape outside Maddy's door, repeating it a few more times. Then he had gone away, retreating down Paradise Alley before he disappeared into the fastness of the Shambles.

That had been before she knew that Johnny Dolan was back. But listening to it she remembered nevertheless the way he used to talk, and it sent a chill into her, just coming through her window. The voice even familiar, so that she was sure it must have come from one of Johnny's old companions in the fire station, or the clubhouse. Now risen in the world, to the place where he could threaten whores on the street. The whole incident, sticking in her head, disconcerting her ever since—

She stood by the window, watching the back of Maddy's gentleman recede down the street. Listening to the distant sounds of men marching, still moving steadily uptown.

"Do ya think they will come, then?" she asked, though she regretted it before the words were out of her mouth. It was a foolish question, she knew. The sort of question children asked, just to be reassured. Which was why she had asked it—

"How should I know if those *b'hoys* will come here, or what they'll do?" Deirdre told her.

Still, there was a note of uncertainty beneath her usual fierceness. Her voice lacked its typical tone of command. Something Ruth had never heard from her before.

"They won't come," Deirdre said now, as if to regain herself.

"How do ya know that?" Ruth asked, hoping again.

"They won't come. The government won't permit it," she said, crossing herself. "The mayor won't permit it, the Church won't permit it, now. All that going on in the streets—"

"Ah. Ah, then," Ruth repeated respectfully.

She wanted to ask her: *Just what will they do to stop it?* but not daring—for Deirdre's sake, and her own. For she had seen for herself back in Ireland, just what the government, or the Church, or any of them would do once things went all to hell.

What were any of those things, as unreal as the Virgin or the Holy Ghost, compared to him? Johnny Dolan as she had first known him, looming out of the evening with a knife in one hand, a haunch of meat in the other—

❧ · 16 · ❧

THE YEAR OF SLAUGHTER

That first night they had sat behind the wall of the old *bawn* near Bal-
lykinvarga, and watched the storm move across the plain toward
them. He had made a peat fire there, and roasted the cut-up parts of
dog over it, flipping pieces to her now and then. Smirking, gloating
across the fire at her as she ate up every bit of it—the still-sizzling,
greasy meat, with its thick yellow bile and fat. She had eaten everything he gave her, even down to its liver and its heart, though she had
known even then that he was testing her.

"Better than the flint corn, ain't it?"

She just kept eating, watching him, not sure of what she should say
or even if she should nod.

"Flesh always is."

She kept watching him, still silent.

"Better'n the Cork city poorhouse, too," he went on, grinning at
her with the blackened, goblin stumps of his teeth.

"No meat there. Just cabbage an' turnips, if ya got that."

"They took you in," she said at last, wondering at the luck of that.

They had no poorhouses in Ballyvaughan, or Kilfenora, or any of
the little villages way out at the end of the Burren. The very idea, of
some public place where they might feed you and shelter you. She felt
again the envy she had known, looking at the doors of the orphanage

in Limerick, even though they were latched against the orphans. *Just the idea of it*—

But Dolan only gave a short, sharp laugh that sounded like a bark.

"That's what they did, all right," he said. "That's what they was about—*the takin'-in business*. They took us in one end, and shat us right out t'other."

"But they did take you in. That was somethin'—"

"Oh, they took us in, all right. When we give ourselves up an' admitted we was starvin', they took us right in. First they took us in the boardroom an' stripped off our clothes. Then they had the medical officer look in our mouths, an' the sanitary officer douse us in cold water, an' pour lice powder all over us, an' put us in uniforms like we was common prisoners.

"They took me sisters an' me Ma to the women's yard. An' they took the brother, Patrick, to the idiot ward, an' they took me father an' me out in the back, to break stones an' walk the capstan. And in return they give us a bowl of cabbage soup and a handful of turnips every day, and the bloody flux."

His knuckles squeezed white around the bone of dog haunch he held, his face suddenly filled with rage.

"He was no fuckin' idiot. Just because he was too chary to answer their questions! He should've been with us, he should've been with the Da an' me, it'd been a comfort for him before they carried him up there with the rest of us!"

Ruth leaning back in sudden terror, unsure of what he might do. But the fit subsided, as quickly as it had come over him. Settling into his previous merely implacable anger.

"Not that it mattered. They took us all up there anyway. Took us up to the black gable, one by one."

"But not you."

She knew the black gable from the talk on the road. Every poorhouse had one. It was the room they took them up to when any hope was gone. The dying room—

"Oh, no, you don't come back from the black room," Dolan confirmed, nodding his head vigorously up and down.

Looking very young, almost boyish when he was serious, despite the boils along his scalp, the teeth missing from his head. *But he was young, he must've been very young, little more than a boy,* she would think, whenever she thought about it in the years to come.

"They took us all up. First me sisters. Then me Da an' Ma, then the brother, who was no idiot. Took us all right up to the black gable, when the time come, an' there they laid us on a big wood slide out the window, so they could shit us right into the ground."

"But not you," she said again.

"Oh, yes," he insisted. "Oh, yes. Me, too."

Behind him, far off to the east, she could see the storm moving upon the old cattle fort like an advancing army. Solid sheets of rain battered the empty fields, methodically blocking out the light.

"When all I could do was lie on the ground an' soak me britches in blood, they come for me, too. With a priest to gimme absolution, and a board to carry me on, and a piece a yellow linen for me shroud."

"But you didn't die."

"Sure I did. I told ya, nobody came back from the black room."

The rain audible now, the storm almost upon them. He jumped to his feet, still clutching the grey, half-eaten dog's haunch in one hand, staring out over the mossy, broken-toothed wall of the *bodhun*.

"Shite!" he swore to himself, watching it in disbelief. "What kind of storm is it, blows from the east?"

And in that instant, watching him there along the walls of the ancient fort, the dog haunch in his hand, she didn't know where she was anymore. She didn't know who she was, or if she was dead or alive herself or in some old goblin story of her father's.

The storm swept over them, dousing the fire and wiping out the last, grey light of evening. They huddled back down against the wall. She couldn't see him in the total blackness though she knew his face was just in front of her, could feel his rancid breath along her cheek as he leaned in, telling her the rest of the story.

"When I couldn't open me mouth to say me own name anymore, they come to get me. They got the priest, an' six men to wrap me up in linen an' carry me to the window, an' there they slid me on down into the hole with the rest of 'em."

Her mother's mad, red eyes at the end, shining in triumph. *She saved a potato for her son.*

"But you didn't die."

"But I did. I was dead, an' buried, but it didn't take me any three goddamned days to rise me up. No, I got up that night, before they could put a new layer of lime down, an' I walked 'round to the front door an' banged on it to be let back in.

"'*By the grace of God, who is that?*' they cried. '*Go away, anyhow, whoever you are. We're full up!*'

"An' I said, 'It's me, Johnny Dolan, an' I'm already in!'

"An' they said, '*Go 'way, you're an imposter! Johnny Dolan is dead!*'

"'But it's me!' I told 'em. 'I know who I am, for God's sakes!'

"An' then the officers come to peek out the door, an' they could see the blood an' the shite all over me trousers, an' the lime from the grave pit in me hair, an' the shroud wrapped around my shoulders. Just like Lazarus himself, raised from the dead through no fault of his own.

"'They took all that in, an' then they shut the peephole again, an' I could hear them whisperin' inside to each other an' wonderin' what to do. Then they come back, but all they said was, '*Go away! There'll be a terrible discrepancy if you're alive again!*'"

She could feel him beside her, shaking with hard laughter at his little joke.

"'*Go away, or there'll be a terrible discrepancy!*' And so I did, and so I went, an' lived by me own wits, an' been dead ever since."

The storm swept on past, soaking them to the bone. And when it had passed, the stars came out, and a thin crescent moon, and the silence returned, along the empty and abandoned land.

He made her take off her clothes then, and ran his hands all over her in the dim moonlight. She had been expecting something like this, though she had no real knowledge of it. Later she understood that he did not, either, but still he made her get down on her hands and knees by the old fort wall. Down in the puddles of water and dog grease, and the bones, and he did it to her right there, rutting in the mud like two dogs themselves.

And she felt nothing, only tired and dizzy, as she had for so long now, and went along with everything he told her to do, for fear that he might hit her or snap her neck. All she had been aware of was the smell of the earth under her, the grass cold and slippery beneath her hands and arms. The grey blur of the rock wall beside her, and the smell of the wet peat from the fire, his defecation behind the wall.

Even so, even though she did everything he told her, he slapped her sharply when he had trouble pushing in, fumbling and grunting behind her. He slapped her face, and punched and dug his elbows into her side, below her ribs, and *that* was the first time, too. That was the first time he had laid hands on her, out in the empty blackness of the hill fort.

❦ · 17 · ❧

THE YEAR OF SLAUGHTER

"What good are ye? What good are ye to me, then?"

He told her every night, pushing in at her in the hay, or the abandoned *scalpeen* or the moss bed. Wherever they lay, pushing himself into her—

"You're *useless* to me otherwise. Ye know that—"

After that night, after that first night in the fort, she had walked with him all through the country. Not that she had to. That was the damned thing, the damning thing, that she regretted most of all. She could always have slipped away with the other wraithlike souls treading along the road. Down some alleyway in the blue-slate towns, or even off into some abandoned cabin or tumbledown, while he was still sleeping.

And maybe he would have broken her head like a dog's. Maybe he would have sniffed her out and made her pay for it, but she didn't think so. More likely he would only have laughed and cursed at her: *Go to the devil then. Useless bint!*

Instead he'd said that he would feed her, and he did. He'd said that he had another sister named Deirdre, the only one of his whole family not dead but living away in New York. She did not know if she should believe this—if she should believe anything from him less immediate than the bits of bread or cabbage he flung to her each night as if she were a dog. He told her they would walk to Dublin, and look for some way to get passage money. But mostly she saw that they went where the roads took them, or where he had heard there was food.

She did not even know if he really believed they were all dead—as much as he insisted on it for himself. That hard, crackling laugh—the only time he ever laughed.

"Sure I'm dead. Otherwise there would be a discrepancy—"

Sometimes he would almost seem to slip into a trance, studying every face along the road as they passed. All the caved-in, yellow cheeks and the fearful eyes. Staring back at him, too exhausted now even to look away with the proper modesty. Taking him for only one more driven mad by the hunger.

He kept looking. At first she thought he was after something—but what, from people who had nothing? She thought, too, it might be another one of his quirks. He had many strange habits and obsessions. For all the filth on his clothes and the terrible red boils on his head, he washed himself whenever he could. Making their camp near a stream or a lake. Pouring the water over and over himself, scratching and rubbing himself until he was raw.

She came to understand that he was looking for a particular face. She learned it when she lay beside him at night, those few nights when the hunger didn't cause her to fall asleep as soon as she stopped walking and put her head on the ground. He would gnash his teeth then, and twitch like a dog. Saying the one name over and over: *Patrick. Patrick.* She came to understand that he was looking for his brother, the one taken off to the ward for the simpleminded. Looking into every face he saw on the road for him, for Patrick to still be alive somewhere.

She had thrown it back at him, one night after he had been rougher than ever. Jabbing and throwing himself on her in the dirt, as if he would push her down and bury her there, under his weight. Staggering up afterward, covered in the dirt, all over her clothes, her face and hair. She had looked at him, already eating a haunch of rabbit he had cooked over the fire, and could not hold back.

"He's dead, you know. You know that. He's dead for sure, your brother—"

He had stood up, the yellow bile rising in his eyes the way she had first seen with the dogs. But she could not resist saying it, in her humiliation.

"Not like you, what only pretends to be dead. He is——"

Surprising her, he had even tried to argue it as he advanced on her.

"You don't know that. You don' know that, those fools. He could be as alive as me, which don' say much——"

"Ah, then ye are alive? But you know he's not."

He had hit her then, as he did now whenever he wanted her to do something—move faster, get him something, shut up. He hit her, once on each side of her face, left-right, the fists thrown so fast they seemed to land at the same time. Knocking her back down to the earth, shutting her mouth. But unable to shake loose the triumph she still held, the secret knowledge, to be used against him on some future day.

He is looking for him, I was right——

In the morning, watching him wash himself, scratching and rubbing in the stream, she wondered what he was trying to rub off—the lice, or the lime and dirt from his poorhouse grave? She liked to watch him, in secret, seeing all of his naked, raw self out in the water. Reduced to just that. No banshee or devil but a *man*, with a man's ordinary hands and arms and penis, his red and boil-tortured skin. So ordinary and vulnerable, no different from her brothers. So different from the uncannily swift fists and bulk that attacked her out of the darkness.

Not long after she would take up the same habit. Lowering her lassitudinous, half-dead body into the water. Scrubbing her own skin raw, just as hard as he did his, trying to rub off what she could of him.

The cow pasture lay just off the road, along a hillside. Dolan moving through the thickets in the same quick, crouched, run he had—knife out in one hand. She followed dutifully, not sure if they should be there but driven on as always by the hunger, and by him.

"Just a taste, just a taste——"

Dolan murmuring to himself, over by the cattle. His eyes tracing the pasture for any sign of a herder.

"The red an' the true. Just a taste to keep us goin'."

He scuttled toward a group of three milk cows lounging placidly along the hill. Kneeling down by the nearest one, looking back once more over his shoulder, then babbling something in a low, soothing voice—before he cut the animal, swift and sharp, across its right hind leg. The cow bolting up, kicking out violently. He eluded it easily and kept running beside the creature, sticking a hardened lump of bread against the cut, letting the blood soak into it.

"Here, here, take this," he commanded, handing it back to her.

She did—then held out her own bread and Dolan seized her wrist, and held it to the cow. Sticking it under the dripping incision. She held it there—Dolan's hand still enveloping her wrist, both of them running to keep up with the bolting animal. The deep, red blotches of blood seeping slowly into the bread.

The cow broke away, and Ruth brought the bread up to her face. It smelled almost sickeningly sour, meaty and raw—until suddenly she could resist it no longer and tore into it voraciously. The blood transporting her, the bread now as thick and rich as meat itself.

The last time I had meat in the cabin, when we ate the pig. A feast like nothing I had ever tasted, not ever. Kate and Agnes and Colleen, prattling happily on. The faces of me Da an' Ma, drawn and frightened across the fire. The pig no feast, I knew even then, but a last supper—

She choked down the bread and looked up for more. Dolan had already devoured his own and was still feeding off the wounded cow, nimbly dodging her kicks and the whipping, manure-soaked tail. Pulling directly at the wound with his lips, sucking up the slow drip of blood. She wiped her mouth and laughed out loud, running after him, not even caring about the herders or the sheriffs anymore.

The madness of it—drinking directly from the cow.

Dolan just ahead, holding one calming hand along the animal's flank, pulling his mouth away just along enough to speak, soothingly, as he skipped along backwards. His mouth bent over to its leg:

"Here now, here now, that's a good girl. Let me suckle at *this* tit—"

"Me now!"

They chased the cow up over the top of the hill, laughing and whooping, forgetting where they were in their blood giddiness.

That was when they heard it: a high, squeaking noise, very faint but still musical, and unlike anything she had ever quite heard before. It sobered them at once, dropping them to their haunches. Trying to hide themselves, up there on the hill. But there was no sign of anyone coming, no trace of any human activity at all but that distant, musical noise.

"A hand organ," Dolan said at last, incredulous.

"A what?"

He gave her the back of his hand, rattling her head.

"A hand organ. One you crank. That's what it is."

They looked down the hill across from the farmhouse, toward the ruins of an old abbey that had stood by the crossroads. Its roof was gone, and there was an enormous pine tree growing up over the wall where the choir had been. Just outside the portal, where the abbey steps had once risen, was a little white tent. The sound of the hand organ coming from there, a crowd of people around the tent pushing and edging forward.

Knowing why, now, there were no herdsmen, no farmer guarding the cattle. They watched for a while, then began to walk down the hillside themselves, wiping the blood from their faces.

"All the wonders! Just one penny! All the wonders of the world, for just one penny!"

A sawed-off little man in a grey, grizzled beard and an admiral's hat was pumping the crowd.

"The most stupendous collection of curiosioes ever assembled in the world!" he kept braying, a patch over one eye, hand stuck in his tunic like Napoleon.

"The original Kunstschrank of Philippe Hainhofer himself! Built expressly for His Imperial Majesty King Gustavus Adolphus of Sweden! Brought to you direct from the farthest reaches of Uppsala—"

The people pushed in though they didn't understand a word of what he was gibbering. Elbowing each other out of the way though most of them didn't have a penny to their names. She started to push in with the rest, just wanting to see, felt Dolan's rough hand hauling her back.

"Not now!" he told her, wrenching her shoulder.

That malicious grin splitting his lips again.

"You'll see it all, soon enough. So will he."

The plan already well worked out in his mind, she realized later. *How early? When we came down the hill?*

They waited the rest of the day, squatting in the briars and the wild rosebushes growing up through the floor of the ruined abbey. Only one window was left—the great, rose-glassed eye of God in the nave. Most of the panes put out, the rest glittering like cut and jagged teeth.

She spent the time crawling along the floor, uncovering the mysterious carvings and letters that were chiseled in the stone. The outlines of knights and prelates, the dates of bishops, carved into the smoothed, grey, granite crypts.

Running her hands over the newer letters, too, carved onto the wooden crosses that stuck up amid the briars.

These were the names of dead priests, from the newer wood church across the road—or so he told me, I did not yet know how to read. So helpless.

From what he said I should have known what was going to happen. I should have known, but I went along. That was my sin, the sin of going along.

They waited back in the abbey, listening to the little man's incessant, barking promotion. The sour hand organ grinding out the few circus notes he knew. Until the evening, when the raw wood church across the road from the ruined abbey began to ring its bell for vespers. The crowd moving reluctantly away at last. The enfevered, the starving, and the half dead dragging themselves over with the rest to hear their prayers. The little man in the admiral's hat rolled down his tent flap, moving about the ruins of the church, gathering up scraps of paper and wood to make his fire.

Dolan crawled out through the briars on his hands and knees. Leading her out, trembling, through the tumbled-down walls of the church. The knife in his hand again, cutting a long slit quickly and silently through the back of the little white tent. They slipped inside and rose cautiously to their feet, to uncover the mystery.

And there it was. A cabinet of wonders.

It was like nothing she had ever seen before. Not so much on the outside, no more than a carved wood box, slathered in gold paint. No more than the size and shape of a glassed-in kitchen cupboard, with shelves.

But inside! There were worlds in there, behind the glass.

She could see: the ear of a blackamoor, and the eye of a giant, and a ship in a bottle. A tiny harp the size of a finger, and a daguerreotype of the great O'Connell, and the bone of a monstrous beast. A musket ball, and a giant oyster shell, and a hangman's noose, and a lucifer match, and a broken sword with a jeweled handle. There were pressed flowers, and colored gems, and perfect, tiny paintings, no bigger than a thumbnail, of a raft sinking at sea and an ancient battle. Of lovers walking under the moon, and the most beautiful woman in the world, in all her nakedness, with eyes as grey as a storm and hair like a ring of fire around her head.

All of it, right there. Contained all in that single cabinet, and even he was impressed, I could see it in his eyes. And why not? There was everything you could want in the whole world under that glass, so close you could smash a fist through and wrap your hand around it.

Instead, he turned to me.

He came up suddenly in the firelight, surprising the little studiolo man where he sat at his dinner. Making him drop the pan of rabbit pieces he had been waving over the fire, shoving a hand back into his pack and squawking at the stranger in his hoarse parrot's voice.

"Who are ye? Whattaya doin' out there in the dark?"

Dolan stepped forward, the boils glistening blood red along his cropped head.

"Where did ya get all that, then?" he asked quietly.

The old man wheezed with laughter, fat red cheeks bulging though he kept his hand in his pack.

"I got it off the tinkers, that's all ye need to know. The rest is between me an' them."

Dolan stood where he was, saying nothing, and the smile left the studiolo man's face. He reached for his pan again, snatching up his rabbit parts. In the same motion, he brought his other hand out of his pack, holding a great pistol in it now, trained on Johnny Dolan.

"I just got enough supper for meself. Show's over, come back tomoree if ye want to see—"

"I ain't here for your supper."

Dolan still standing just over the other side of the fire, still saying nothing until the studiolo man finally screamed at him:

"Well? What is it then? *What do ya want from me?*"

"Something else," Dolan said, grinning suddenly. The studiolo man kept his distance.

"What's that?"

"Somethin' you can afford, I think. Somethin' ye'll want to pay for."

Dolan pointed to the man's own tent. On his gesture she stood forward, silhouetted behind the tent flap by the light from his fire.

"What? What is it? How the devil did they get in there?" the studiolo man demanded, squinting at his tent.

"Look—"

At his signal she stood up against the tent flap, began to fold back her dress off her body. Moving into profile to be sure he could see she was a woman, she was so miserably wasted away.

"Well," the old man breathed. Getting up from his fire, the pan of rabbit still in his hand. "Well, now, maybe I can pay somethin' for this."

"Sure now," Dolan told him, still grinning. He raised his voice: "Come on out, now."

She did as she was told, still, coming out of the tent before him. Ashamed in her half nakedness, trying to cover herself with her hands. Dolan grabbed hold of her arms, and twisted the dress up and away from her. Ripping it, drawing her hands up behind her back with what was left of it, leaving her naked before the little man.

"Hmmph!" he snorted. "That ain't so much! I can get better than that in Cork for just a look in the box—"

"Are we in Cork, then?"

"No, no, ye got a point there," the studiolo man considered, looking back and forth between her and Dolan. "What d'ya want for the bint, then?"

Dolan shrugged, as casually as he could, she knew. Ruth watching him, standing there still trembling in the warm night, before the fire.

"You know. The usual. I'll take some a your supper."

"All right. But just half, now. That's all she's worth," the studiolo man said finally, laying the frying pan carefully down between them. "Any more, mind you, an' I shoot an' take the girl anyway!"

"Fair enough," said Dolan. He let go of Ruth and reached down for the pan, still smiling up at the studiolo man the whole time. Reaching carefully around until he had the handle, then flipping the pan up suddenly at his face. The man crying out as the hot grease and rabbit bits hit him, firing his pistol as he jumped backward.

But Dolan was already going for him, the gun discharging harmlessly over his head. He went to tackle him around his knees, but the studiolo man managed to dodge him, running back into the tent. Grabbing up the cabinet though it was nearly as big as he was and bolting off like a hare, into the briary ruins of the church. Dolan chasing after him, his eyes as wide and yellow as a wolf's in the firelight.

Ruth squatted down by the fire in her fear, throwing the torn dress around her. She watched as Dolan jumped through the briars in the ruined church, looking frantically all about him, swinging his club wildly back and forth. Then she spotted him—just a glimmer, creeping over the crypt stones. A glint of firelight on the glass of the cabinet, and she called out despite herself.

"There! There he goes!"

The little man bolted up then, running for his life. But Dolan was on him like a hawk, reaching out and grabbing him around the knees this time. The man cried out, his feet scrabbling for purchase on the smooth, slippery, grey granite. Then he went down, cracking his head against the rock, and Dolan was on him. Clubbing at him in the darkness—once, twice, quick and efficient, as if he were a rat he was disposing of. Then he stopped, and came toward her, the end of the stick dark and wet in the faint moonlight.

"Is he dead?" she whispered.

He only shrugged, and jerked his head.

"How should I know? Hell, he'd better be—"

Retrieving the cabinet of wonders where it had fallen, miraculously unscathed, into the bushes growing out of the church floor. Tenderly folding the black curtain around it. From across the road they could hear a dog barking, they could see a light in the window of the little wooden church there.

"Quick now!" Dolan said, all business again. "You don't know but what the priests are about."

"Jesus, but it ain't right, takin' it off him like this," she protested, looking down at the dark outline of the studiolo man where he lay against the crypt, still trying to see if he was breathing.

He only cursed her.

"There's nothing *right* here anymore. This ain't the country of *right*."

He had started off down the road already, the cabinet of wonders strapped to his back somehow.

"You wanted the money, too, didn't ya?" he said, turning to face her.

"Ah, but Jesus—"

"You wanted to get off this land, too. Y'know that ye did now, that's why ye helped me, an' brought him down like that."

Already retreating down the road with him, step by step, as if slowly pulled along by a rope. Picking her way through the briars— the barking of the dog across the road getting louder now, the sound of someone moving about, of men's voices clear now in the utter country stillness.

"Ah, but Jesus, Johnny, we'll have to see God someday!" she cried as she hurried after him now, shrugging back into her torn dress.

"I hope we do," he snorted. "All the better to curse Him to His face."

18

RUTH

Eight o'clock.

The pretty little brass clock on Deirdre's mantel chimed the hour. Even this sounded loud in the crowded front room, making both of them start.

"I should be back, then."

She peered out the window again, as she had done a dozen times already. She should have been back already, even though she was sure it was fine, sure she could trust Milton to follow her instructions and look after the rest of them. So foolish—she had only lingered because she wanted to be reassured by Deirdre's immaculate house, by her silent, obedient children and her iron control. And now all she knew was that Deirdre herself was scared.

Eight o'clock—and where was Billy? She wondered if it might be his weakness, then was immediately ashamed of herself for the thought.

No, he would know better today. Weakness though it was, he would never do that to her—to them—not today. He would come right home, just as soon as he had his money.

Unless he couldn't. Then she really would be all alone, to meet Dolan. She was friends with most of her neighbors in Paradise Alley, many of them mixed-race families themselves, friends with the Jews who lived on the next block, past the back-lot privvies.

But what could she expect from them if *he* came? She doubted if they could stand against him even if they wanted to. If there was a riot coming on, they would be locked deep in their cellars and back rooms, keeping their heads down. The most she could count on would be Deirdre, and maybe Milton—sweet boy, she could not leave him to go up against the likes of Johnny Dolan—

No. She would have to do it. She would have to think it out herself.

"All right, then."

She went up to Deirdre and kissed her impulsively on the cheek before leaving. Her face so beautiful, held so coldly. Her long brown hair—the very same color of her eyes—tied rigidly back on her head. She looked surprised by the kiss, then embarrassed, turning away from her.

"I got to get back," Ruth said, then couldn't help adding: "I wish your Tommy was here, at least."

It was the wrong thing to say, and she knew it, but there it was. Deirdre looked stunned, then immediately angry and disgusted again.

"Haven't you had enough to do with him, then? Drawing him into your schemes?"

Deirdre's mouth twisting angrily, trying to keep her voice low enough so the children wouldn't hear.

"He did help me," Ruth said evenly, facing her. "He helped me, when no one else would."

19

DEIRDRE

Ruth was gone. Deirdre waited until she had left the house, watching her out the window. Then she went to the bottom drawer of the falling-front secretary, her hands fumbling through it. The secretary was her prize, it had taken them two years to save for it. An enormous thing, carved out of cherry and oak and finished a deep black, with curtained glass doors on top where she watched her own face, terse and drawn, as she pulled out a sheet of the *Tribune* from the previous Friday.

She read the name again, on the long page of names. Crossing herself as she did, every time she read it. The print smeared and worn away by her fingers though she tried to prevent that, loath to rub away any of the names there, as if it were a sacrilege.

The name she didn't want to find was there in the fine type, tucked away in a column in the back pages, under the heading *The Casualties*. It sat there now, like a toad on the page: "In the Sixty-ninth New York . . . O'Kane, Tom. Co. A, leg."

Nothing else — just the bare listing of the man, his regiment and company, and where he had been hit. At least there were none of the dreaded amplifications she had seen before, tacked on to the end of some others: *amp.,* for amputation, or the one she had seen the last time, beside his own name: *chest, severe*. It had almost broken her, last Christmas, seeing that. *Severe*—and nothing else as to where he might be, or what had happened to him since. She had nearly driven herself to distraction, trying to keep it from the children, and get some word of what hospital he was at.

Severe—

She tried to comfort herself, this time, through this absent elaboration. No *severe*. Telling herself it was just a simple little wound, a scratch, a bruise, nothing more. Though in her heart she knew it was meaningless, that men could die from everything, down at the war. She had known more than one woman at the pump who had seen the same simple listing—only to hear by telegraph the next week that he was gone, swept away by an unexpected fever, or a hemorrhage, down in the sodden hospitals where they lay—

She folded the newspaper up, shoved it back into the drawer before it attracted the attention of the children. Her fingers smearing the close-packed print again, wearing off more names despite her care.

She could not bear to think of that—Tom bleeding to death, down in a Washington ward somewhere. His head on fire with fever, and no one to hold his hand or talk to, no one to bring him water. Their second boy, Charlie, had been taken by a fever. Not yet three years old, it was an awful thing to endure—for her, for Tom—but the one consolation had been doing for him. Getting him everything, making him as comfortable as she could right up to the moment the priest had closed his eyes. Knowing that his soul resided with God in Heaven—

Tom had hidden it from her, the hardship, when he had been able to write again. Even then, his letters, when they got through, were so much gentler than she had expected. The first one from the hospital had been in a woman's fine hand, dictated to some volunteer lady when he was barely able to sit up. No mention of her save for the name modestly filled in at the bottom, below his signature: *as to Mrs. Jeremiah Slade.*

She was jealous of the very name, of her presence there beside him, writing down his words. She had asked Tom to send her a picture of himself, once she began to get his letters again in his own crude hand. When he replied she could read his wary surprise between the lines. She was not sentimental, and it was such an expense, what she had requested—with her barely able to keep the children in their clothes, or buy sugar.

Maybee, when Im stronger, he had written back, but she could not wait. Practically begging him in the next letter to have the daguerreotype made. *Let me see you*, she had written him. *I want to see you*—and two months later it had arrived: the picture of him in its brass oval frame. So gaunt, the uniform jacket and winter-issue cape hanging off his frame like old clothes off a scarecrow now. But there, his dear face, under the infantry cap. Almost seeming to smile back at her, at certain angles, the way the daguerreotype shifted—in certain light in the evening, or in the morning when she looked at it on the dresser in their room. The look on his face almost sly, and reassuring.

But now he was hurt again. The thought of it pierced her. She wanted to strike at Ruth, coming into her house to say she wanted him back.

Didn't she just say it herself? Don't I want him back as much as her?

Yet what wrong turn had Ruth ever done to her, save to live on the same block, and try to keep her family and her house together? Even when she had hated her most—for conniving to send her brother away, and getting Tom mixed up in it—Deirdre couldn't really blame her. She had spared Johnny's life, after all, when it would have been a simple thing to have had him hanged, when she herself had first wanted to turn him over to the police.

Ruth had even tried to remain a friend, despite how Deirdre had cut her and despised her, all these years. Always saying hello to her in the street, or at the pump. Even last winter, when Tom had been wounded and she had been so bereft, Ruth had come to her doorstep to tell her how sorry she was—to see if there was something she could do. Even though Deirdre had all but shut the door in her face, disdaining her pity, her help.

But surely that was why Tom had been hurt. For her pride. For her hardness of heart.

Blaming Ruth for getting him mixed up in shipping her brother off. Blaming her, even, for shipping Tom south.

When in fact that was the worst thing. When that was the most damning thing, for it was she, Deirdre, who had really seen to it that Tom was shipped south. *And all because he had let the niggers on the block.*

❧ · 20 · ❧

TOM O'KANE

He couldn't get his mind past how the reb soldier had fallen. Like a thing. Like a bullet or a shell fragment, random and unthinking and blindly destructive.

One moment he had been running across a field, as alive as Tom was himself. Scared but exhilarated, too, once Tom's bullet had pegged off to his left. Trying to remember just what it was he was supposed to be doing, Tom knew, trying to get to a low spot in the farmer's wall.

And then—that lieutenant had stepped forward and he was no longer a man at all. Just a dead thing, falling to earth.

"Did ya see how they came? Did ya see it, then?" Snatchem asked him for the hundredth time that day, still shaking his head in disbelief.

"Yes, I saw it, George. I saw it all right," Tom told him softly, chewing on a straw. Wishing he had a smoke to roll.

That was the thing about the army. Things just weren't to be had sometimes, and usually when you needed them the most. Not like in the City, where maybe you couldn't afford what you wanted but there was always some way to have it, if you wanted it bad enough—

They were sitting in a haystack, a few miles from Harrisburg, in a field outside the operating hospital. Trying to stay upwind from the

stench of the surgical tents, the plague of flies swarming around the
buckets full of lopped-off arms and legs.

*Tom still thinking about the reb he had picked up. Still unable to get his
mind around how the man had fallen. Like a thing. The bayonet in the
man's dead hands ripping through his leg the way he had seen so many
things, so much lead and iron and steel, rip through men and horseflesh—*

"Did ya ever see that many in your life? Did ya ever see 'em come
like *that?*"

"No. No, I never did," Tom repeated patiently.

For the truth was, he never had seen anything like it. The rebs'
charges were usually ferocious, disordered things. That was what
made them so terrifying. The men busting loose like wild dogs, as if
they could not be held back anymore. They would come screaming
and yelling their terrible yell—moving over the ground with incredi-
ble, unnerving speed.

On the last day, though, they had marched out as if they were on
parade. Banners waving high, in one long, orderly wave after another,
some of the officers even on horseback. Moving out silently and deliberately across the road, and down into the fields.

Their own ranks had fallen silent as they watched. Giving over
their jeers and chants for the moment, maddened though they still
were over the bloody fighting of the day before, and all the defeats
and deprivations they had had to endure trying to run down these
rebel sons of bitches for the past two years.

Then the hares had come, streaks of brown and white, running
flat-out before them. How anything had remained alive out there, in
those fields between the lines for the past two days, Tom did not know,
but there they were, bursting out through the wheat and the high
grass. Running in their zigzagging, flat-eared, panicked rabbit way.

A few of the men laughed and pointed to them, making as if to
spear them on their bayonets. The veterans watching more soberly.
Thinking of how the rabbits, and the birds and the deer had burst out
of the Wilderness when Jackson had turned the flank at Chancellorsville, catching them at their supper bivouacs—

The men kept coming out from the trees. One regiment after
another, marching in stately procession. They had been stunned by
the sheer, pointless beauty of it. The rebs had even stopped to dress

the line, when they were still only halfway across the flowing green-and-gold fields. Each man reaching out to touch the shoulder of the man next to him, and drawing up to fill the gaps left by those who had been already cut down. The rebs still took their time about it, even as the cannon balls and the sharpshooters' bullets continued to punch new holes in the line, like a man kicking the slats out of a picket fence, one at a time. Moving at their own, mysterious pace until at last their exercise was complete, their ranks presenting a tidier, better packed target for the canister and their muskets than ever before. And on they came, men moving out of the grass. Men and grass.

"What were they thinking of?"

"I don't know," Tom told him. "I don't know as anyone was thinkin' anything at all, from what I seen of it."

"They could've had twice that many. Twice that many men, an' they still wouldn't a taken a position like ours."

"No."

"Did they think their big guns killed us all, then? Did they think that big noise made us all run away?"

The bombardment before the assault had been endless. More guns than Tom had ever heard before, rattling his teeth. Making the ground shake from across the slight valley and the sunken road where they were lined up, axle to axle, in front of the trees. But nearly everything they fired went high. Spreading havoc in the back ranks, among the general staff and the artillery caissons, but whistling over where *they*, the infantry, lay flat on their bellies, deafened and shaken, but shielded by the low stone wall. Even sharing a smile or two at the distress of their commanders and the artillery men, scrambling and diving for cover, and trying in vain to hold on to their horses.

"Officers," Tom said.

"What?"

"Officers," he repeated. "You saw it at Fredericksburg. Same thing, only on their side. Officer gets some idea in his head."

"But it didn't make any sense!"

"It don't have to make sense. They're just officers, for all their airs. It's like with the boys down the Black Joke. Someone gets an idea goin' an' then the rest go along, whether it's a good one or no. An' then it all gets carried away."

The whole thing had been carried away. *Three days*, out there in the terrible sun, and the heat and the flies. It was a wonder any of them had come through it at all. His face shoved into the loamy, black Pennsylvania dirt, hoping some chance shell wouldn't land on top of him. Thinking how good the soil was, no wonder the neat Dutch farms they passed looked so fine and prosperous. The horses shiny with fat, barns built like Fifth Avenue mansions, the strange, pagan symbols over their doors—

"Willya look at that. Wedged right in there."

Snatchem was worrying over his hand now, the other object of his preoccupation. Picking at it for the thousandth time, the minié-ball fragment lodged in his palm, neat and firm as a diamond set in a ring on the dollar side of Broadway. Stuck in a web of bones, it had had just enough momentum to catch there, spreading the fingers out so he couldn't make a fist, but not enough force to go on through. The surgeon couldn't pry it out, though he had tried with the red-hot pincers until Snatchem was screaming in pain. He offered to amputate the hand, then shrugged and turned away when his offer was declined. There were legs waiting to come off—

They were lucky, the two of them. They both had good wounds. Not so much to really cripple a man, but enough to end their campaign— at least for now. It was the Invalid Corps for them both, and a few months of guard duty somewhere until their enlistment was up. No more chasing Bobby Lee back down into Virginia.

A good wound—though Tom was surprised by how it had hurt. The steel had plunged through the muscle of his calf. Much more painful, at least at first, than when he'd been shot back at Fredericksburg, and the ball had punched a hole out his back the size of a man's fist—

The reb, falling like any other spent shot—

He had heard the veterans talk about it, but he had never seen it himself. Picking out one man on a field. *It wasn't what you were supposed to do.* The officers told them again and again not to aim. What they wanted was massed volleys, fired in time, into massed flesh.

But it had happened anyway. Tom had spotted the man a hundred yards out from the wall, once the rebs' spectacular, parade-ground line had dissolved. The few grey soldiers left had made a final rush for the wall, and Tom had picked him out. Skin burned nut brown from so many days tramping the roads of Maryland and Pennsylvania. A lean man, with a stubborn chin and small eyes. Wearing a pair of purloined red Zouave pants, and the regular grey See-cesh infantry cap on his head. No shoes at all—

Tom had led him, waiting for his shot. The man crossing the last few yards after having come so far, after coming all the way across the murderous, mile and a half of open fields behind him. Running for the waist-high stone wall behind which Tom stood. Running as fast as he could now, not yelling, the way the rest of them had started to, but simply running with his mouth open, with his head lowered and his bayonet held out, belt-buckle high.

The reb had looked up then—and seen Tom there. Tom was sure of it, even through all the smoke from the guns, and their volleys. The man's stride breaking for just a step or two, a dozen yards from the wall, as he spotted Tom's musket lined up on him. *Seeing his own death, standing up right before him.* But still he came on, there was nowhere else to go—

Tom had fired then—and missed him. The shot whistling a little wide to the left, Tom cursing his damned, shoddy piece. The reb pulled up for a moment, then came on faster than ever, reprieved. Tom knew, he had felt it before himself. *The wild, ecstatic hope growing in you that of course you wouldn't die, there were so many other* b'hoys *to die, why the Christ should you?*

Tom was still ready for him, fixing his bayonet. His gun a spear now, every bit as ancient and reliable. Setting himself in a half crouch, behind the wall.

Goddamn all farmers, with their fences and their walls. Hang up a man like he was stuck on flypaper. But they were good things to be behind.

The man went up the wall. Tom waiting, watching as the reb tried to clear it all in one great leap, not quite making it, his feet slipping at the top, staggering, leaving himself wide open. Tom was crouched down a little more, timing his thrust—when the lieutenant stepped up from out of nowhere and shot the man in the head.

Shot him right through his reb infantry cap, and the man toppled down. Falling too suddenly for Tom to get out of the way. The bayonet in his dead hands tearing through Tom's calf, piercing his flesh, staking his leg to the ground where he stood.

Tom was just able to swing his own musket around, knock the dead man's hands loose from his gun before the weight tore the muscle off his leg. Then he had to drop his own weapon, in the midst of the battle, and use both hands to pull the musket out of his leg. Screaming from the pain, directing a string of curses at the lieutenant who had already moved off, oblivious, in the din of the fight. Remembering himself enough to snatch up his own gun again so that he stood there with two spears now, one in each hand, and howling like a dog.

The pain had been unbearable. Afterward, though, what had bothered him most was not the meddling of the lieutenant, or the close thing it had been, or even the wound, painful and dangerous as it was. It was, instead, the way that the reb had become a dead thing all at once, a mere projectile. That was what Tom couldn't get over. The man, alive, going up over the wall, dead before he came down. Transformed into another mindless thing of destruction, a fate, a chance. No more than that.

"Did ya ever see such a thing?"

Snatchem shook his head, asking him again.

"No. No, George, I never did."

❦ · 21 · ❧

DANGEROUS JOHNNY DOLAN

Dolan could hear the screams of the animals long before they got to it. He could smell them, too, the stench of piss and manure, intestines and blood. And then he knew where he was, knew what they were passing: *The Place of Blood*. The roost of slaughterhouses by Houston and Attorney, where his sister's husband, Tom O'Kane, had once gotten him work sweeping the entrails and hooves and ears into the gutter with a birch broom.

There had been something even worse, that he remembered. Not the blood, or the shit—which was, after all, what half the City smelled like anyway—but the smell of fear. The blind, ignorant helplessness of all those goats and sheep and cows, penned in right on top of each other. Waiting and bleating in their own lots, while they could hear and smell the others of their kind being slaughtered next door.

It looked much the same now. The butchers standing outside, to watch the great herd of men pass by. Cleavers and knives still in their hands. Bearded, expressionless faces, arms folded. Their aprons covered with faded red and yellow stains, spread over and over each other like jism stains on flophouse sheets. Some of the men called to them and they came, too, throwing off their aprons and joining in. The thick knives still clutched in their hands, waving them about as if they were off on a holiday.

Dolan walked dully along with them, still in a sort of daze, from the whiskey and seeing Patrick on the street, and all his unfamiliarity still with people. The familiar sight and stench of The Place of Blood confusing him all the more—making it seem like just one more dream from the prison.

He was still ignorant as to where they were headed. He knew it had something to do with the war, from the cries of the men around him, though just what they meant, he could not imagine.

"Three hundred dollars! That's what we're worth to them!"

The war. He had hardly been aware of it before his ship had reached Galveston, and slipped past the blockade there. He didn't bother with newspapers, and on the boat he kept to himself. Bunking alone in a corner of the coal room where it was too hot for the other men. After those winters in the Sierras, he thought he could never be too warm again, not even here, in New York in July. Just like he thought he could never be too full again after Ireland.

It was only too late you learned about anything, and only then through not having it—

After his escape attempt it had taken him fourteen years to get out of the penitentiary. Fourteen years, for the crime of being in a Montgomery Street pool hall at the wrong time. He had taken it all—the beatings from the guards, and the cold and the snow that blew in through the chinks in the stockade in the winter, and the rain that came through in the spring. And when he thought about it, when he could think about it at all without breaking down into a rage, he thought that it was, after all, no worse than the poorhouse in Cork city.

They walked on up past the slaughterhouses, and the sausage-making shops. The putrid barrels stuffed with offal, waiting to be cleaned for sausage skins. Everything in a row, ready for the degradation of the body down to nothing. The tanners with their reeking, green hides hung out to cure in the sun. The fat-rendering plants, where men with long paddles churned piles of bones and hooves in smoking iron pots. Boiling it down to soap and dye and ash—

They passed the Armory, and the Union Steam Works. There was a police guard outside the Armory, which he expected, but also one outside the Steam Works. The mob jeering and yelling, the cops standing rigid and unresponsive outside their posts, caps pulled down low over their foreheads, the brass buttons shining on their blue uniforms.

He remembered the officers in the poorhouse, self-important in their shabby green tunics. Sometimes the other men and boys would trade them turnips for poteen—any food at all being worth more than gold—and then they would climb over the wall into the girls' yard with their clear little bottles. He never did himself, he was always too hungry to give up one of his turnips, even for that. But at night he would climb up and see them at it: the shadowy figures pushing and grunting, up against the brickyard wall.

It was all done quietly, so as not to wake the priest who was in charge of the house. There was hardly any talking, just the rustle of clothes and bodies, an occasional groan or sob. And once he had seen his own sister, Kathleen, up against the wall, the dark shape of a man leaning into her. As he watched she had pulled her head away to the side and coughed. Then she had plucked the bottle out of the pocket of the man who was on her, and taken a long, hard draw on it before she put it back—vanishing back into the blackness of his embrace.

It had been the same thing in the yard in California. The men on their knees, in front of the guards. *He* had never done such a thing, he had sworn to himself he would kill a guard with his knife before he did that, though he knew that was a lie, too. *After fourteen years he would have done anything necessary, anything at all to survive, even that.*

The truth was that no one had ever tried to make him. He knew that he must have seemed too hideous, and he was content to remain so, with his jagged teeth, the old scars crisscrossing his head. Content to ward off trouble just through how he looked and acted, growling like a dog at the guards or the other inmates if they got too close. Trying to keep them off, to keep down the insistent urge to smash, and kill. To keep down the even more insistent need to die before he could get back to the City, and settle what was his—

Then one day it was over. Then some day marked on a calendar, after fourteen years, he was a free man, and they gave him back his clothes—the old jacket and pants he had once worn in New York, now holey and hanging loose on him—and a new silver dollar, and told him he was free.

He had walked on out of the stockade, started back to San Francisco on the back of the sutler's wagon. It had taken two weeks, getting the mules to push through the foothills, stopping at every post and new town on the way. More than once he had considered simply killing the sutler—selling off his goods and eating his damned mules, making his way back to San Francisco with some money in his pocket.

But he was barely able to walk free anymore, after so many years of wearing the chains and wife around his ankles. Not able to trust his reflexes, to even trust himself to think straight yet. Forcing himself to wait until he could get down to the waterfront, get his wits about him, get a ship back east again.

Even then, the night before he was to sail, he had stayed up in his flophouse room, down by the Embarcadero, nursing a bottle of camphene whiskey. Thinking of how long it would be, the sail down to Panama, then across the Strait by mule again, and back up through the Caribbean. The same way he had come—and all because he had thought he was meeting the brother.

All the endless passages, and the waiting—just to get back to the same place.

It occurred to him to just give it up. To sign on with a clipper out to the China Sea, or the Sandwich Islands, where Mose the Bowery Boy himself had gone to set up shop. To find someplace, so far away he could forget all about *her*—and about his treasure, and how they had sold him, and all that he was owed. To find someplace so far away he would have no means of getting back.

Or better yet, to do himself right here, this night, in his flophouse room.

But it was *his.* That was what made him stay up, kept him from touching the whiskey bottle again so he didn't get too black. The cabinet of wonders was still his, and *she* was his, and he was due that, he would have that much coming in this world at least, and if he couldn't have it, there would have to be an accounting.

The crowd kept moving uptown, drifting slowly to the west, over to the Third Avenue. Most of them turned off when they reached Forty-sixth Street, but he kept going, on up to where he remembered that Pigtown lay. *Just as glad to be rid of the mob, almost alone now.*

He wondered idly over just how many blocks there were—over how far the City had moved since he had seen it last, pulling itself up the island like some wounded beast. Many of the streets he passed were still almost empty, a brownstone mansion or a squatter's shack standing here and there, behind cordons of white string that laid out where the next block, the next curb would go. Along the Fifth Avenue there was what appeared to be either the ruins or the beginnings of an enormous cathedral, its great dark stones covered with yellowed, rain-starved vines and weeds.

Just like the abbey outside Cork, where they had seen the studiolo man—

But he walked on, up to Fifty-ninth Street, and there he saw it, just as he remembered. The huge, slate-grey boulder that marked the beginning of Pigtown. His mind reeling just to see it again after so long a time, after thinking about it for so many years. *He had come all the way back.*

Remembering himself, he crouched down behind the boulder, then crawled silently up its side. Thinking to spy it out first, to spy *them* out—though as he remembered, too, the niggers' village was still more uptown, and to the west. *Still, it was better to be careful—*

He climbed up over the rock and saw before him—a lawn. A real lawn, such as he had seen only once before, on a deserted Cork manor he had trespassed on as a boy. The grass green and manicured, looking soft and undulant as a bed. And all around it was a fairy-tale land, like nothing he had ever seen in the City, or even back on that lord's manor in Cork.

It was as if someone had built the land, had laid it out and sculpted it with their hands as carefully and precisely as they might build a house. Everywhere, around the perfect grass, there were gently curving raked lanes, and lily ponds. There were bridges with intricate, crafted iron railings, and charming little shingled sheds, and here and there were planted clumps of slim new sapling trees. And all of it, no matter which way he looked, seemed to draw his eye away, toward a distant green vista opening up to the north. To where there were still more patches of gorgeous new lawn, more trees, more sinuous, raked lane.

Everything else—everything that he remembered—was gone. Not just the gulleys and the dirt tracks of Pigtown—the makeshift homes with stovepipes for chimneys, the scraped dirt yards holding hogs and chickens and the vicious, clamoring dogs. *But the land itself was gone.* The sagging, rock-strewn ground. The bent cottonwood and ailanthus trees, stagnant black ponds of black water. *All gone*—as surely, again, as if some great hand had simply wiped it off the face of the earth.

Dolan did not know what to make of it, wondering if he had gotten it wrong somehow. *But no*—*there was the great, grey rock; the sign for Fifty-ninth Street, no more than a bunch of deserted lots though it was.* He was here, all right, back where he had started from. *But where was here?*

He staggered out over the perfect lawn. Abandoning his caution for the moment, looking for some trace of what had been—something to guide himself by. But it was all gone. And not just Pigtown, with its clumsy shacks—the hogs rooting among the discarded bottles, the broken plates and knives and bones that surrounded each shanty like a fairy ring of garbage. As he walked up one of the meandering lanes with its quaint little cast-iron bridges, he could find no sign of the Nigger Village, either. The whole town, with its neat white saltbox houses, and its two churches—vanished just as completely, replaced by only more immaculate squares of turf and the freshly planted sapling trees.

At every curve and path, he noticed, there were little signs pounded into the grass, and he went to read them, thinking they might provide some clue as to where everyone had gone or at least who now owned this place. Yet all they said was the same, two runic words: KEEP OFF.

Instead he dropped to his hands and knees on the ground. Trying to sniff it out, to smell some hidden indication of what had happened here. To smell *them* out.

But there was nothing—not so much as the corner of a foundation wall. All he could do was get to his feet again and turn slowly around in place, genuinely and completely lost now.

He had thought they might have moved, in fourteen years' time. He expected that they might be gone, if they had any brains at all, but he had always figured that he could find some trace. Some neighbor who remembered them and could pass on their whereabouts, or at least the next place to go, the next track to follow. He hadn't expected *this,* this *nothing,* and as he stood there on the well-rolled lawn, he felt as if his mind were dissolving. It was a numbing, pacifying feeling. One that left him as dumb and helpless as a small child—

Perhaps nothing he knew anymore was real. Perhaps he should give it up, forget about ever finding them. Just stop and lie down, right here on the grass—

There was a flash of movement, and he looked up. A man in a sparkling, blue and gold-buttoned uniform was coming down one of the winding, raked paths toward him, eyeing Dolan suspiciously. The very look of himself, he knew, was always able to attract the scrutiny of a cop.

He rose from the grass and began to stagger back the way he had come, trying to move quickly but not too quickly. He soon realized, though, that he had failed to retrace his steps. Taking a wrong turn at a fork in the winding, serpentine roads. *What did it matter, now?* He walked past a grove of lilac bushes, another pair of towering grey boulders—glad for some cover at least, glancing back over his shoulder for the cop.

When he looked around again, he saw, looming suddenly up before him, a field full of gigantic, hideous creatures. Or rather their bones, whitewashed, and set in terrifying poses. All tooth and claw and jutting bone, like no animals he had ever seen before, but very real. Dolan could not stop walking around them, staring up at their gigantic, bony heads, tapping at the thick leg bones, even though they gave off only a hollow, plaster echo.

So they were statues. But who would ever put up statues of such things—of their skeletons?

Before he could puzzle it out, he saw men pouring into the park. These were some more of the mob, he recognized—rough-looking workingmen like the ones he had come uptown with. Walking slowly but purposefully, right across the well-tended lawns with their little *KEEP OFF* signs. At their approach the lawn cop fled at once, Dolan saw, to his surprise. But the men kept coming, hundreds of them, and he hurried to join them, treading carefully past the giant plaster monsters.

22

HERBERT WILLIS ROBINSON

They are not a mob—not yet. Still more of a holiday crowd, out on a lark. At least five hundred of them now, maybe as many as a thousand, straggling slowly up the East Side, toward the Provost's Office at the Third Avenue and Forty-sixth Street. A captain's guard could stop them now, a single squad of Metropolitans. But there are no police in sight and the crowd grows, in size and confidence, with every passing block.

When we reach the docks of the East River, they call out to their friends. Playing such rough music. Banging pots and pans, any two pieces of metal they can find to clang together. Singing their obscene songs to the longshoremen, wrestling with their crates and bales. The brass finishers and the iron molders, the blacksmiths firing their trip-hammers, the boilermakers flanging the plates in their fiery furnaces.

They drop their work and come out, as quickly as the Disciples must have answered the call of the Nazarene. Still smarting from all the recent strikes—the scabs who had been called in to take their jobs, the thousand other injustices the poor clutch constantly to their bosom.

"We're free men, ain't we?"

"Not some nigger labor they can trade as they like—"

Justifying themselves to each other:

"A nigger, hell! *Three hundred dollars, when you can get a thousand for a nigger!*"

I want to ask them, *What is it that offends you most? The fact that a price is put on your head? Or that it is so low?* But I know better than to press my luck. They are still in their holiday mood, after all. Bawling away at the top of their lungs:

> "*For we'll hang Abe Lincoln from a sour-apple tree,*
> *Yes, we'll hang ol' Abe from a sour-apple tree——*"

They rough up any prosperous-looking gent who happens to cross their path, anyone who looks as if he could buy his way out of the draft. Pushing him back and forth, bellowing in his face, "*Are you a three-hundred-dollar man?!*" They make him swill some of their whiskey or parade along with them, or pledge his allegiance to the Confederacy.

In the end, though, they send their man off with nothing worse than a round of kicks and hoots, even a slap on the back if he's been a good enough sport. It's still all in fun—though that can change in a heartbeat, a cross word, a shot of whiskey.

I am spared any such rough play myself, thanks again to the fatal cave-in and my suit, covered in the dust of men and bricks. Instead, like the crowd in City Hall Park, they take me for one of their own—that is, one of that vast tribe of men without money. I am delighted to play along, secure in my disguise. They offer me free swigs from their bottles and I pretend to accept. Pretending to be as drunk as they are. Swaying along with them, laughing at their jokes and even singing along lustily when they get to my employer:

> "*For we'll hang Horace Greeley from a sour-apple tree,*
> *Yes, we'll hang Horace Greeley from a sour-apple tree——*"

The first trouble comes outside the great Novelty Iron Works, near Tenth Street. Here is where they make the sixty-ton bed plates for the gunboats and the blockaders that are choking the South to death. One of the Novelty's ironmasters tries to stop his men from leaving, running out after them and grabbing at their arms, saying something about meeting their contract.

"Here, we signed up for the job, we have to fill it—"

He is beaten to the ground at once. A big man, a proud man, obviously used to being a leader of men. Stripped to the waist, the furnace-bronzed muscles bulging along his arms. But they knock him to the ground nevertheless, kick and stomp on him until he crawls back into the ironworks he had once ruled, no doubt happy to escape with his life.

It feels to me as if the very air around us has been shattered. A man who had done nothing, beaten to the ground in broad daylight. The ones who did it not running for their lives but standing about, barking their triumph. The others doing nothing to stop them, but joining in, laughing and shouting their own invective.

I have sat through a thousand prizefights, watched men beaten to bloody pulps while the crowd yelled, *Shutters up, there's a death in the family!* I have seen plenty of brawls in the streets of our turbulent City, I have even seen men shot down in battle.

But this is worse, somehow. This feels as if there is nothing to turn to under the sun—not justice, nor mercy, nor simple decency. It feels as if we have all been left to look out for ourselves, as naked and unprotected as the ironmaster was.

I want to do something about it, I feel I must do something—my hand reaching for the pocket where Raymond's revolver was. But of course the pocket is empty now, the gun back at Maddy's. I close my mouth, marching along with the rest, telling myself I cannot do a thing.

Near Dutch Hill we turn away from the East River, and plunge back into the town—past its swarms of half-wild goats and ragpicker shanties, its ash boxes unemptied for weeks and stinking like the plague. The crowd at least five thousand strong now, still singing and banging out their charivari. When we reach Forty-sixth Street, they break into a run, headed straight for the Provost's Office but its door and shutters are still bolted tight, thank God. A rumor goes 'round that they are not going to open all day. I pray that this is true, though I have never before known our elected officials to display so much common sense.

We mill around in the street, unsure of what to do now. Deprived of our target, we start tramping on uptown—the mob gaining still in numbers, but losing momentum and purpose. Past where the sidewalk itself gives out, at Forty-eighth Street. Not far beyond is what looks to be some European ruin: immense white blocks, piled around a long foundation. Already greying with the City's soot and dirty rain, half-covered in weeds and strangler vines.

The mob slows as it passes these blocks, but it doesn't stop. A few of the women cross themselves, and the men remove their hats. This is to be the heart of their faith, the new seat of their archdiocese—for all that they care now. Yet I know it as well to be the last obsession of a dying man.

On Sunday morning, my head notwithstanding, I had gone down to St. Patrick's. *Their* citadel. The sturdy little church at the corner of Prince and Mott, built like a fortress behind its stout, stone wall.

A parish priest I knew from the Sixth Ward, a Father Knapp, had told me he could arrange an interview with Archbishop Hughes. He led me into the archbishop's rectory rooms, right into his bedroom, from where I could hear the chants of the Mass still being celebrated across the yard.

There he sat. Dagger John Hughes, from County Tyrone, propped up in his bed like a wounded hawk. Too weak to man his pulpit but his flashing, blue-grey eyes still as fierce as ever. Working away at something on a little writing table—though when he caught sight of me, he dropped his pen and uttered a single, exasperated word:

"Greeley!"

I nodded, smiling despite myself, and he gestured toward the writing table by his bed.

"I was just trying to finish a missive to your employer. But it's a delicate business, don't you agree, putting words in the hands of a newspaperman."

"Yet that is what I am here for, Your Holiness," I told him, trying to cut short his usual tirades against Horace before I was tempted to join in. "I would like to solicit your views about what will happen tomorrow, when the draft resumes—"

He let his head droop down to one side. Staring out a little window into the churchyard, with its shade trees and high grass, and the narrow red headstones of his predecessors. Twenty years ago, during the Know-Nothing riots, armed men had filled that yard at his beck and call. Dagger John calling in the mayor to tell him that if a single

Catholic church were touched, he would turn the City into another Moscow.

No churches were molested. The City remained unburned—for the time being.

"What do I *think* will happen?" he told me now, slowly turning his most withering gaze upon me.

"I think that the good, Catholic workingmen of this city will go and do their duty by their country. While at the same time I think that *your* young men of society will spend their days wagering on the outcome of the war on Wall Street, and their nights in a brothel.

"That, sir, is not only what I *think* will happen. It is what *has* been happening for the last two years, and I suspect it will *go on* happening for as long as this wretched war lasts."

He broke down into a wracking cough. His eyes clouding over uncertainly, the talons retracting.

So it was true what they were saying. At first glance, he looked enough like the old Dagger John—the same impatient curl around the sides of his mouth, the long, sharp nose poking confidently forward. The face of a great commander, a Wellington or a Marlborough. Enough vanity left that he still wore a half wig, propped carefully up under his skullcap.

Yet, peering closer, I could see how his simple black cassock hung on him, the large gold cross pulling down his head. Gone were the powerful arms and neck, the hickory-lean figure of the ambitious young acolyte who had worked his way through a Maryland seminary as a day laborer, an overseer of slaves, any work he could get. The poor immigrant boy, thirsting for enlightenment—and power.

"You have turned us into cannon fodder!"

His gaze drifting out into the churchyard again. It was not this modest, walled yard he was seeing, I knew, but that lot uptown, along the Fifth Avenue. Where the crowning achievement of his stewardship lay covered in vines and weeds.

"I took the scattered debris of the Irish nation," Dagger John murmured, half to himself. Father Knapp took a step or two toward him in alarm, he suddenly looked so desolate—his face slack and yellowed in the sunlight. Hughes waved him away.

"I was just beginning to make them into a people again," he said bitterly. "A God-fearing, self-respecting people."

It was true, for two decades the commander had bent his church and his people to his will. Took a mob of peasants and molded them

into the faith militant. He had marched their sons into parochial
schools, and brought the Sisters of Mercy over from Dublin, to teach
their daughters how to be dutiful maids and cooks and seamstresses.
Building over a hundred churches throughout the City—

Dagger John Hughes—*more a Roman gladiator than a meek Christian*, Bennett had called him in the *Herald*. Tirelessly writing his letters
to the editor, signing his name with a cross slashed defiantly across the
page. Going in street clothes to Know-Nothing rallies, so he could hear
the enemy's arguments. Speaking for two days and nights—pausing
only for food and sleep—against the City's leading Protestant clerics
and lawyers during the great debate over religious education. Expung-
ing every trace of a brogue from his own voice, so no one could
assume anything by where he came from, but would have to *listen*.

His crowning glory was to be the great cathedral in the Fifth
Avenue. It was to be more than a church—more than the little cathedral just next door to us now, with its humble spire between two slanting towers. This was to be a masterpiece, a monument to *him*, and to
them. Built with the sweat and skill of his own people, financed with
their own pennies in the collection plate.

"And then you had to have your war."

*Stalling all his plans, eating up his pennies and his laborers. The great
piles of granite lying tumbled about their empty lot, like God's very building blocks, abandoned.*

"Am I to understand, then, that you no longer support the war?"

"You may assume nothing of the kind"—staring down his long
nose at me.

He was a shrewd man—but Old Abe was shrewder still. With the
help of Seward he got 'round him, offering Hughes the only thing that
might make up for the loss of his monument. He made him an emis-
sary of the nation, sent him off for a year to defend the Union in the
jaded courts of Europe. It had been too much to resist, a chance to see
Rome again, and Paris—and Tyrone.

"I was rebuffed in Rome by His Holy Father, and scolded by the
Times of London for my unwavering support of the Union," he
informed me, holding up a copy of the *Tribune* from last Friday.

"Yet look what your Mr. Greeley taxes me with. '*Your people for
years have been and today are foremost in the degradation and abuse of
this persecuted race.*' My people! Sir, it is too much to bear!"

There was a glimmer of the old fierceness in his face.

"The Church supports order and authority—even in a *Protestant* country. You may tell your employer what I said from the pulpit last year. The people themselves should *insist* upon being drafted, so as to finally bring this awful war to a close."

He fell back to work on his reply to Greeley, leaning avidly over the writing table again. I was dismissed with a wave of his beringed hand—a streak of gold shimmering for a moment in the sunlight. Dagger John scribbling furiously with his pen, determined to make one last point.

Father Knapp walked me back outside. We paused at the gate of the empty churchyard, listening again to the the Mass still going on inside St. Patrick's.

"So—there will be no trouble?" I asked him.

"Is that what you think?"

"But—what the Archbishop said—"

"His Grace does not see it, he is confined here." His voice trailing off as he gazed back toward the Archbishop's little brick rectory. "He has heard *so many* false things about his people in the past."

It struck me that it was not really Hughes at all who had wanted to talk to me, but Father Knapp himself. He is a short, stocky man, built solid as a cannon shot, but with eyes that look pained from squinting; his dirty-blond hair turning grey at the temples. A truly self-effacing man, with no ambitions that I knew of beyond his parish. Attending the Archbishop now only because he happens to hail from Annaloghan, Hughes's own village back in Tyrone.

"It's an injustice, what's being done to them—making men go off to war because they can't pay their way out of it," he said, shaking his head. "But no matter what, nothing must happen. Justice or no, it'll be a black mark against us that will never wash out."

"What will the church do, then?"

He held out his hands, palms up. It was not so much a shrug as a gesture of despair.

"Everything we can. *Everything* we can. But—you've seen the people, you see how they feel."

"That is all you can promise? It isn't even a promise!"

He looked at me impatiently for the first time.

"And what about you, Mr. Robinson? What would you say to them?"

"Well—"

"Tell me, sir: Have you bought a substitute for yourself? Or are you waiting to see how the draft turns out?"

"I—I didn't have to. I'm exempted. As a war correspondent," I stammered, as idiotic as it sounded.

But if I were not? Brokerage houses have sprung up all over the City now. They advertise in the newspapers, offering to handle the distasteful business of buying a substitute, a man to go to war for you. Everything is taken care of, you don't even have to know the man's name unless you want to.

Meanwhile, other cities have set up booths in our public parks, trying to fill their draft quotas with our young men. They offer competitive bonuses to anyone who will enlist for good old Cincinnati, or Elmira. There are even rumors of certain dens, down in Greenwich Village, or over on West Cherry Street, where bounty brokers drug young men and turn them over to the highest bidder—

Why not? It would hardly be the first time human flesh was sold in this City. Nor the last—

I wanted to explain myself. I wanted to tell Father Knapp that this is what I do. That this is my role, that I observe and I tell—from a distance—just as he dispenses charity and redemption.

But at that moment the Mass finished. The congregation spilling out into the churchyard, blinking in the harsh summer sunlight. Their voices low, and urgent. Looking for some sort of counsel in these times of crisis—not wanting to hear, I imagined, that *they* should insist the government draft them.

"A war correspondent, eh?" Father Knapp said to me, smiling grimly. "Well, you may find yourself back on the front lines tomorrow."

23

HERBERT WILLIS ROBINSON

And so I am, back here on the front lines—if you can call it that. Right now there are no bullets, but monsters loom above us. Immense and skeletal, their mouths open, their claws extended in fury. But no one is intimidated. (This mob has seen worse.) They greet these creatures cheerfully, doffing their caps as they pass. Calling out with the same black humor they displayed at the draft:

"Yer lookin' up, O'Connell!"

"Say, don't that look like Jameson durin' the hunger?"

We have wandered into the new central park, where Prof. Hawkins set up his plaster casts of dinosaur fossils. They are one of the favorite recreations of the City, a place where fathers of all classes bring their little boys to scramble up along the plaster bones, and fight epic battles with the behemoths.

The mob passes them with more cheers and waves. There are thousands marching now, women as well as men, choking the primitive new streets as they stream in from both east and west. They lie insolently along the grass of the new park, scattering their bottles and scraps of food, and butcher's paper, along the immaculate raked paths.

". . . *Lincoln*, this Nero, this Caligula, this *despot!*" some impromptu street-corner orator is already fulminating, perched atop an orange crate. Let these Irish pause for five minutes and one of them will give you a speech.

Yet the crowd begins to gather 'round him, as eager as ever to hear any political blather. I recognize the speaker—a shyster lawyer who moved to the City a few years ago from Virginia.

"Resist the draft! Organize to resist it! Name your leader—and if necessary *I* will become your leader!"

They applaud lustily, cheering, "That's the talk!," and "To hell with old Abe!" There is a call for three groans for the President, and for Greeley, and then three cheers for Jeff Davis, and General McClellan, their perpetual hero.

Like all mobs, they hunger after false idols. I met Davis in Washington, when he was Pierce's secretary of war—a vain, nervous man, hiding his skittishness behind a pompous Bourbon formality. McClellan even worse. I saw him at Bellevue, after I'd come back from Fredericksburg with some of the wounded. He seemed to me a perfect stage general then—puffing his chest out, strutting around from bed to bed. Sticking out a hand to each suffering, jaundiced soldier, and bellowing, "Well, now! What's the matter with *you*, my man?" I pray that he will never be entrusted with any of our armies again.

But none of this would matter to the mob in the park even if they knew it. Like children saying naughty words, they just want to say the most shocking things they can hurl at the Republicans. They flop on the lawn, lolling around as if they were at some Tammany chowder.

Poor rubes. Poor rough, tanned faces from the Five Points and the Arch Block, from Paradise Square and Gotham Court, and Cat Alley and the Shambles. They could be straight out of the Middle Ages, peasants on a pilgrimage, or a crusade. Milling about openmouthed. They never get to such precincts, to Olmsted's wonderful new park with its plaster monsters, its carefully sodded grass and fairy bridges, and tender saplings and scenic rock overhangs.

Maddy's people. They came upon us as a storm—or a plague, brought by boats, as plagues always are. There were always some Irish in the City, just as there has always been some of everybody. Most of them were from Ulster—shopkeepers and shipwrights, carpenters and butchers; hardworking, respectable, Presbyterian and dull.

Then, one day, on the eve of winter, there was a half-naked woman with her baby at her teat, begging in the middle of Broadway. There have always been beggars in the City, but somehow this was more shocking. The leatherheads quickly bundled her away, but the next week she was back, and then there was another, and another. Wild, desperate-looking women, children clutching their skirts as they stared blindly up into the passing crowds, imploring them for a coin, or a piece of bread.

Now they do everything in our City, all the hard jobs, the mean jobs, the jobs that must be done—after they had literally flung the Negroes out of them. They are our stable hands, our draymen, our maids, and our cooks; our hod carriers and brick-layers, our char-women and hacks. The men and women who cut our meat, and cook our food, who sell us our oysters and pour us our drinks. Who build our homes, and unload our ships, and shovel our shit. And they are the men who put out our fires, and keep the peace on our streets.

I sit on the grass among them, now, clinging to my disguises. *Feeling so sorry for them, and wishing they would vanish—*

"And may I be the next glorious martyr upon the altar of my country's freedom!"

The soapbox speaker is still pontificating, but the crowd is bored now. The Provost's office is still closed, and they have no ready victim to attack. They start to drift away, into the vast green beauty of the new park, and I am seized with the hope that we may be rescued after all, that their whole incipient insurrection will simply fizzle out.

Just then some rough beast staggers down one of the gravel paths. He is grizzled and hideous, looking more like a bear than a man. His clothes torn and covered with mud, head covered with terrible red boils that stick up through his clumps of hair. His eyes go wide with fear or amazement as he stumbles upon us, and seeing him the men near me start to hoot with glee.

"Hey, look, it's Mose!"

Slowly, the rest of the mob begins to take it up.

"Mose, it's Mose!"

They begin to crowd around him, laughing and jeering. Their drift halted by this new amusement.

"Keep your old Abraham, here's our *Mose!*"

Christening him with the name of that old stage perennial, Mose the Bowery Boy, hero of the gangs and the firemen. The beast himself only continues to stare at them, his eyes narrowing, but more and more men take up the chant. They offer a whiskey bottle up to him, and some young buck tries to loop a chain with a plank of wood attached to it around his neck, the words NO DRAFT! chalked on it.

Like a bear baited beyond endurance, the creature comes suddenly to life. He swats the *b'hoy* to the ground and seizes the plank at the same time, his movements stunningly fast and effective. He holds the chunk of wood threateningly above his head, and for a moment the crowd falls back.

It is only then that he stares at the plank, as if parsing out the words written there. A small, malicious smile seems to spread across his face, and then he loops the chain deliberately over his shoulders himself, beckoning for the whiskey bottle again. He takes a long draught from it and the crowd cheers and surges up around him again, pushing him to their front.

While they are still celebrating their new champion, a young boy dashes into the park, ducking and dodging around the plaster monsters. He has something dark, dirt or blood, smeared over half his face—could even be the same boy I saw earlier, while stepping up onto the streetcar. Though all these Irish look alike to me—

Grinning up into the sun, as he wiped the blood across his mouth—

"The conscript! The conscript!" he is crying now. "They're startin' it again! The conscript! At the Provost's office!"

At once the mob is on the move again. Still laughing, but marching with a purpose now—their new-crowned Mose leading them on. A smirking young thug falls in beside him, holding up an American flag he has stolen from somewhere, staff and all. On his other side one of the kitchen-pot drummers steps up, banging away with his ladle. The three of them forming a crude mockery of the Spirit of '76, that staple tableau of so many Fourth of July picnics. The crowd gets the joke, they roar their approval as the trio leads them back down along the tracks of the New Haven railroad in the Fourth Avenue.

"To the Provost's!" they shout. "Mose to the Provost's!"

I cannot believe the conscription office has really opened up. *Are they mad?* The mob, so jolly, will turn in an instant once they get to it—

There is the sound of a bell ringing, loudly and persistently, behind us. A sudden surge of hope, and relief. *Can this be—Kennedy's men, come at last?*

But no—it is only the 8:57 from Stamford, pushing its way slowly along the rails. Its prosperous-looking patrons, men and women, peering out the windows in bewilderment at the ragged mob that blocks their way.

The crowd good-naturedly makes way for the cars. Some of the men sweeping off their hats, gesturing grandly at the staring passengers. A few even grab a ride on the cowcatcher, hooting and whistling for their friends to look at them. Still the train keeps moving slowly forward, the locomotive and its twelve cars nearly past—when it comes to the attention of their new leader.

They try to pull him out of the way, afraid for his life, but he swats them away as easily as he did the first *b'hoy*. Standing there now in the tracks so implacably that the train must grind to a complete halt. The engineer furiously clanging his bell and pulling on his whistle—to no avail. The creature ignores him, staring grimly straight ahead. The train slowly cutting its steam until it finally goes dead, the last futile huffs of its engine slowly fading away.

Only then does he walk slowly off the tracks. And now, as the train sits there, building up its steam again, the creature takes a crowbar from one of the longshoremen in the mob, and pries a paving stone loose from the street. Still moving deliberately, completely unhurried—so that none of us, the mob, or the train's passengers, or its engineer can quite believe what we are seeing. Until he hoists up the paving stone—half as long as his arm, cut from solid, Massachusetts granite—and heaves it through the window of the first passenger car.

For a moment we stand there in disbelief. Then everyone is shouting in one ancient voice. The mob prying up more paving stones, grabbing any loose brick or piece of wood or garbage they can find and hurling it at the train.

The locomotive shrieks, and blows its steam, beginning to lurch forward again. But now the mobs stays with it, harrying it like wild Indians, like primitive hunters pursuing some great beast. Bombarding it with stones, and garbage, smashing all its windows. It barely gets away, puffing and hissing on down to the Grand Central Station. And as it does I see its passengers again, now huddled together in the aisles. Peering out from behind the seats at the scene around them, their eyes filled with terror at the alien City they have ridden into.

24

FINN McCOOL

Something had to be done, that much was clear, for they had been meddled with once too often. *Thirty men.* Thirty men drafted from his own fire company on the first day, including the brother, Peter, captain of the Black Joke himself.

All weekend long, he had gone from the bars, to the backroom clubhouses, to the groceries. Talking to aldermen, and committeemen, and the captains of other volunteer companies. Not plotting, exactly. Nobody had done anything like that. They were too good, too experienced as politicians to say anything directly, even in the back rooms of their own taverns and houses.

But they were in agreement—Tammany Hall and Mozart Hall and the independents. *Something* had to be done. Without the men there could be no hands to pull the engines through the streets, or to brawl over the hydrants, or to steal ballot boxes on Election Day. Without the companies there could be no organization, anywhere, and without the organization there was—chaos.

Something had to be done—and it was the machine itself that would do it, which pleased him. It was a fine, modern thing, painted by an Irishman, constructed by Irish carpenters and metalsmiths. It was a useful thing, too, a fire engine. Something absolutely indispensable, unlike the cumbersome new street-cleaning machines that existed only to take a man's job.

He sat before it now, alone in the firehouse. The Black Joke, *Old Bombazula,* as they called it. The great copper engine, enthroned in the middle of its heavy wagon. Two rows of thick piano-pump handles running down either side where the men would stand, working like demons—like machines themselves—as they pumped the water through.

Most of all, though, he loved the images, the shapes and signs that were painted across nearly every inch of the high, black wagon. There were scenes from the life of Rip Van Winkle, and Washington crossing the Delaware, and old Pete Stuyvesant, with his one leg, defying the British. There was the privateer from the War of 1812 the engine was named for, the original *Black Joke* herself, swooping down on an English frigate.

On the back of the hardwood engine case was a painting of a great fire, burning out of control, somewhere out on the Western prairies. And on the front was the company's motto, stenciled in gold paint: *"THE NOBLEST MOTIVE IS THE PUBLIC GOOD."*

Now the wagon was packed with rocks, all around the engine— rocks, and paving stones, and the fragments of brick they had been able to salvage from the construction site, at the old De Peyster place. The hose wagon filled with them, too. When they ran both wagons out to the Provost's office, the leatherheads and the soldiers would never see it coming in time. *But then they would know. Then they would show all the niggers and the nigger lovers they were serious. That you could not interfere with free men in such a way—*

Still, Finn wasn't sure. He walked restlessly around the machine, going over everything. Stopping the draft would mean fighting, no matter how they cut it. Fighting meant having to leave something to chance, and Finn McCool didn't like chance in politics any more than he liked it in the faro games he ran down on Pearl Street; to him chance was the very *opposite* of politics.

But there was no way around it, the Republicans had brought this on themselves. It was bad enough when they had forced the war, and split the national Democracy down the middle. That had only been smart politics, Finn had almost admired it, and neither he nor anyone else down at the saloon or the firehouse really gave a rat's ass about the fate of a few cotton planters.

But this was something else. Now they really meant to kill them, at home and in the field. *Sitting at home on their shoddy profits, while they were sold like niggers down to Virginia—*

"They're comin' out!"

A boy came racing through the firehouse door, shouting and jabbering, fairly bursting with the news he had to tell.

"They're comin' out, all up Corlear's Hook, an' the East River docks! They stopped the New Haven line, too—smashed the express to pieces with the paving stones!"

The boy's face was covered with blood and soot from God only knew where. So dark that McCool thought he was a colored child at first, and he had jumped at the sight of him. But then the boy had grinned—a big, jack-o'-lantern grin, through all the gore, and he had recognized him. *Henry McCarty,* from over in Greene Street. One of the many boy runners the company used, to race out to the fires before them, and find the Croton hydrants.

Finn had posted them all over town the night before—just another precaution to let him know what was going on. He started to question the boy about just what he had seen, but even as he did, more runners, more boys started to come in, faces flushed and excited, telling him all about the broken train, the long columns of men moving uptown along the East Side docks and avenues. He nodded solemnly, satisfied—trying to calculate as he did how long it would take them to get up to the Provost's office, how much of a head start he should give them.

Soon the men of the company began to drift in, as ordered. The volunteers of the Black Joke Fire Company, No. 33. Dressed in their best uniforms, their red shirts and shiny black suspenders and pants, the splendid, black and gold-buttoned jackets they'd worn only for the grand review for the Prince of Wales. Looking only a little the worse for the beer and the lager he had treated them to all weekend, at The Sailor's Rest and other saloons all over the Fourth Ward. Where he had pounded the same points into them, over and over again, at the bar rail:

"They already drafted Pete, our captain, an' you know we can't let that stand. Thirty men—*thirty!*—just from the company—

"And who's to put out the fires, an' save the women an' children, an' babes in arms? You notice, they're not draftin' any of the Metropolitans. Not while there's still heads to be broke, an' families to be turned out of doors—"

Once he had them going about such things, and as to how their wives and children were to support themselves on a soldier's pay, he would pause just long enough before bringing up the price.

"Three hundred dollars, and a man—*any* man, they say—can buy hisself out of the war. Just three hundred and he can hire a substitute to go down an' do his fighting for him."

Pausing just long enough—then bringing out the flier he had gotten, the bill of auction taken off a blackbirder named Flask, a slave trader the navy had picked up off Long Island Sound, and hauled in for trial in the City. The bold print and drawing easily comprehensible, even to the illiterate. The auction block there, and the half-naked colored men and women and tykes in manacles. The cultured gentlemen with their frock coats and sticks looking them over.

The prices, read right out there: "BUCKS—$1,000; WOMEN WITH CHILD—$1,500—"

Letting the bill of auction—which he'd already had reprinted in the thousands—fall lightly to the beer-soaked bar. Before stating the obvious, which was after all, his profession.

"*Sold for three hundred dollars. When—*"

He didn't even have to finish the sentence before they were yelling, all but screaming over the hateful comparison.

Not that he didn't believe it. They would have to settle that score, as well. Saturday night he had gone down there again, to the house by Paradise Alley. Quietly at first, as quiet as he could go on that street full of darkie families, and half-castes, and whores with their children. He had walked around and around the house, trying to see past the red curtains in the first-floor windows. Trying to get a glimpse of her with one of *them,* in the act.

As if he needed to prove it to himself. He knew that she took the colored trade. It enraged him just to think about it, it was one of the very few things that ever made Finn truly angry. *It wasn't right—having to share even our whores with them.* Like fornicating with donkeys, it was a wonder they didn't rip the likes of her apart, the little whore, spoil her for any honest workingman—

That was the limit. They should be above the likes of *them*, at least. His fury had gotten the better of him, for once, the only time it ever did, when he was down there. He had stopped skulking around the windows, and seized with his anger had stood and pounded on the front door until she had answered.

Laughing, right in the middle of laughing. The fine, silken yellow dressing gown clutched up over her breasts and obviously not so much as a petticoat on underneath. Laughing as she had that time, when he had asked her if she did it with such people—with himself hard as an ax handle.

"Are they like us, then? Are they like us down there?"

He was serious, but she had kept laughing—his erection diminishing.

"It don't matter! You men only like to think about your things. But the truth is, one is just like another."

But it did matter, that was the thing. It did matter, they weren't alike at all and she should know it. That should be the least they could expect, even from a whore, that they wouldn't have to share with dogs, or apes—

He had lost himself all over again when she'd answered like that, just in her gown. He had let his anger take hold of him.

"We'll see to yer niggers," he had told her, right out there in the street like that, where anyone could hear.

He didn't know what had gotten hold of him, but he meant it. He meant it now. They would settle with all the whores, and all the niggers, too. For getting them sent off to the war, and trying to take their jobs, and stealing their women, even if they were just whores. *They would settle with all of them.*

The men stood before him now, in their best uniforms, waiting for his word. Finn leaped up on the engine case, above the scene of the wild prairie fire, sweeping over the plains. Holding out his hands to still their chatter.

"Now, men. Now, men," he told them. "It's time to see what you are made of, as true Americans, an' Irishmen, too."

They cheered him to the rafters. Shouting the rallying cry of the engine company, the yell they would give on their way to a fire—

"All Black and Never Been Washed!"

A smile began to spread slowly across Finn's lips, the men smiling back at him.

"Well now, boys, I think it's time we went and paid a visit to the Provost Marshal's office. Are ye with me, then?"

Their cheer was deafening in the little firehouse.

"Burn out all the sons of bitches!"

"The street machines! Burn them first!"

"Then the hotels!"

Finn grinned benignly back at them—though that was the kind of talk that made him uneasy. *That was why you needed the organization, anytime you let men off the leash things were liable to get out of hand—*

"All in good time, all in good time!" he shouted above the din. "But first the Provost's. First the draft records!"

They fell into position around the engine, and the hose wagons—their hands on the harness guides and the organ pumps. Shoving the high black canvas hats down on their heads like so many helmets.

"Look lively now, lads, look lively!"

He called out their drill. The men in their traces. The boy runners jumping and up down in their wild excitement. Cassius Keahny standing in front, his silver horn in hand. Finn McCool held up his right arm.

"All right, then—will you pull, lads?"

"Aye, we'll pull!"

"Will you work, lads?"

"Aye, we'll work!"

"All right, then. Let's paint the old gal green!"

McCool brought his arm down, the older boy runners sliding the front doors of the firehouse open on cue. Keahny out on the street, blowing blast after blast on his silver horn. The rest of them close behind. Finn, sitting up by the engine, calling the pace. Looking down he saw that boy again, Henry McCarty, grinning ecstatically as he ran along, trying to keep up. He could not help but grin back at him as they ran the engine out under the unforgiving sun.

❧ · 25 · ❧

HERBERT WILLIS ROBINSON

"They are coming!"

The cry goes out, wild and hopeful and mysterious. Repeated over and over with no further explanation.

"They are coming!"

The mob is pressed into Forty-sixth Street, before the Provost Marshal's office. Waiting as they did last Friday for it to open up, waiting for—*something*. They are a different crowd now, wolfish and expectant. *Almost a mob.* Methodically prying up more paving stones, tearing up the wood fences around the nearby construction sites to use as clubs.

"My God, they are opening up," a man mutters behind me. I recognize him, a Tammany wardheeler named Eagan. He is not talking to me, simply staring in astonishment at the Provost's office.

Surely he must be wrong. There are thousands of men and women waiting in front of the draft office now, spilling out into the Second and Third Avenues—all of us packed in so tightly we couldn't disperse if we wanted to. Surely they couldn't be so foolish as to open up in the face of that.

But they are. Right on the stroke of nine, the little Invalid guard marches up to the storefront office like the figures on some Bavarian clock tower. The crowd gives a great shout when they swing open the wooden shutters. The sound of blood in their voices, waving their staves and paving stones in the air. The Provost and his men step into the window, their faces pale and concentrated.

If they had any sense, they would close back up immediately. Instead they go on with their duty—the kind of blind, suicidal obedience that a people learn only in wartime. Marshal Jenkins and his assistants, the known blind name picker. The soldiers mounting the great wooden drum back on its axle. Pouring out their names, the thousands of names from the mob out into the drum, while the noise begins to rise all around them.

The Provost has at least strengthened the guard. There are more bayonets, a few more federal marshals crowding the window. Still, he can have no more than sixty men in all. The soldiers keep up a stout front, hands on their weapons, their eyes fixed straight ahead. But I can see the legs of the known blind man begin to tremble, shying away from the drum like a balky racehorse.

Where are Kennedy's police? Can it be that his efficient communications system has really broken down so badly? Or are we betrayed

I try to edge my way out of the crowd. I have some idea of making my way over to the Nineteenth Precinct station house, of getting them to telegraph down to Kennedy's bustling headquarters on Mulberry Street. But it is impossible. The crowd is packed in too tightly to move very far.

"We have to get to the Nineteenth," I whisper to Eagan, who's a loyal Tammany man but clearly as horrified as I am. "We can wire down from there, Kennedy's got the telegraph all set up—"

"I just came from the Nineteenth," he murmurs back, careful to keep his voice low. "They know all about it. They just don't believe 'em downtown—"

"How can that be?"

His lips move, but his words are drowned out. The Marshal has started the drum rolling. The soldiers turn it around and around, its thunder echoing up and down the streets of the City.

Everything is still—the crowd overawed by the sheer sound of the drum, just as it had been last Friday. Then all at once a wild movement begins to ripple up and down the street, everyone being pushed and pushing back at once. I am kicked and elbowed, shoved helplessly into Eagan, and for a moment it seems that the rush has already started.

Then I hear the cry again, overwhelming even the martial thunder of the drum:

"THEY ARE COMING!"

The words rise as cheers. Over them I hear the long, shrill blast of a trumpet and hope that somehow the crowd has gotten it wrong—that it is a company of regulars, or Kennedy's Metropolitans come at last.

"They are coming!

"The Black Joke!"

A fire engine and hose wagon are towed down the street from the Third Avenue. The usual entourage of boys, and a man blowing on a silver trumpet, running on ahead. The crowd unable to quite make way before it—men pushed right through the doors and windows of houses along the block—but the rest of them still cheering it on. The firemen in their red shirts and suspenders, and their black, crested helmets, hurtling the wagons through with their usual breakneck speed.

It is No. 33—the Black Joke. They fall to work instantly. Finn McCool directs them himself, standing over the engine box like some wrathful Irish banshee, passing out with both hands the rocks and paving stones they have brought.

"There you go now, boys. Remember, aim high, ye don't want to hit any of the people here—"

Marshal Jenkins and his men stand transfixed in their window, even as the firemen are handing out their missiles. The great roll of the conscription drum goes silent. The known blind man edging slowly back out of the window—

"There you go!"

There is a gunshot, close enough to make Eagan and me, and most of the crowd, duck instinctively. The guard starts, too—Jenkins and his men flinching back from the window. The blind man toppling back into the draft office with a helpless cry. I don't know who fired, one of the guard or someone in the crowd, but it's followed at once by a rain of rocks and paving stones, crashing through the windows, thumping off the hollow draft drum.

The Invalid soldiers stagger back inside, trying to ward off the stones with their arms and rifles. They try to pull the wood shutters closed—but it is too late now. The crowd surges forward, forcing them open. They pull down the huge wooden drum, smash it on the sidewalk and scatter its names—*their names*—out on the street.

The Provost and his clerks flee out the back—the men of the Black Joke right behind them, scrambling up and through the window. A few soldiers and police try to stop them, but they are beaten mercilessly and tossed back into the crowd, and the rest of the guard break and run. The firemen set quickly about their work, hacking up what remains of the draft office with their axes. It is clear that they know what they are doing, even in this melee, that they have a plan. Pouring turpentine over the floor and setting it ablaze, burning every scrap of paper they can find.

But the rest of the mob is right behind them. They look for any target they can find, however little it has to do with the draft. Within a few minutes they are cutting down telegraph poles, looting a china store next door to the draft office. The sound of smashing plates mingles with the crunch of the flames, and the steady howl of the mob itself. I glare up at McCool, on his engine box, but even he seems a little taken aback by what his men have wrought, his bright, vulture's eyes clouded and uncertain now.

Eagan and I stagger away, toward the Third Avenue—more hordes of Paddies rushing past us to join the fun. Men, women, and boys, their faces as gleeful as the devil's imps, battering at every house and storefront on the block. Others with their arms already loaded down with stacks of china plates, chairs, and cabinets pulled right out of people's kitchens.

I still have some idea of getting to the precinct house, and trying to get another message through to Kennedy. But just as we reach the corner of Third, a carriage pulls up, and out steps the police superintendent himself. He looks much less martial to me now, dressed in civilian clothes and armed with only a rattan cane. His face deathly pale, all the cheery St. Nick confidence and efficiency drained out of it.

"It is madness for you to be here!" Eagan tells him, which is the truth. He has only a single uniformed officer and one of his headquarters clerks with him.

"I had to see for myself," Kennedy says, nodding apologetically. "I had to confirm it."

"You can see it all right from here," Eagan tells him. "Now get back in that carriage and git——"

Instead Kennedy begins to stride toward the mob with his usual briskness. How the surface gestures of men survive even when their inner confidence has died! I cannot say just what he thought he was doing. Perhaps he simply could not believe the scene in front of him. The Provost's office engulfed in flames. The mob beginning to fire the whole block now, flames shooting out through the windows of a dozen stores and homes along Forty-sixth Street.

A group of women who live on the block are trying to plead with the looters. Brave or hysterical, they grab at the rioters' arms, implore them to stop burning their homes. Most of them are Irish themselves— but the men simply jerk their arms away, the mob too intent on their plunder.

I see Kennedy pause for a moment, watching this pathetic scene— then he walks right up to the rioters.

"Where the hell's he going?" I ask Eagan in vain. "You have to get some men up here——"

It is no use, though. Kennedy goes right up to the mob, his clerk and the uniformed officer cursing but chasing loyally after him.

"They'll kill him!" Eagan sputters, incredulous, but most of the rioters seem only bewildered to see this well-dressed gent, with a single policeman, suddenly in their midst. They stop their smashing and thieving for a moment, out of sheer wonder. Kennedy nods gravely to them—and begins to make a speech.

"Fellow citizens! I stand here before you to appeal to your common sense! I will not say a word at present as to the rights of your cause."

He stands there, holding his arms wide open, like any street-corner Tammany man on election day. The crowd—all of us—still looking on with something like awe.

"About the draft: I know you feel you are right. There is no mistake, it is a hard thing for a man to have to leave his home and go soldiering if he does not wish to go, but I can't argue that question now. You probably feel that you are right in what you have done."

"He is mad," Eagan mutters beside me.

Kennedy is completely at the mercy of the mob now. There are no soldiers, no other police left on the block. No one at all, save for another volunteer fire company, the Honey Bee, that came running when they saw the smoke, and now stand around talking with the men of the Black Joke.

Still, it looks for a moment as if Kennedy might actually pull it off. Surrounded as he is by a group of sobbing women from the block, like a scene out of one of those stage melodramas they are so fond of—

"You came here to do a certain thing. You have done it. Now you ought to be satisfied. The draft office is destroyed, and I appeal to you to let the firemen go to their natural work and save the homes of these poor women. I think the laddies here will back me in this appeal, and do their sacred duty. Will you, sirs? Will you put out the flames?"

He holds out his hand with a grand flourish to McCool, still standing astride his fire engine. Shrunken back out of his heroic pose, now—his whole body cramped up with calculation, shoulders rounded, prematurely wizened head sunk nearly to his chest. McCool hesitates—then slowly nods once, raising his hands like a bishop giving his benediction.

"All right then, lads," Finn shouts, echoing Kennedy's argument. "We done what we come to do. Let's put these fires out!"

The mob cheers this as well, even the very men who had been setting the fires. It is as if, for a moment, everything might still be put back in place. The firemen leaping back to their engines, attaching their hoses to the green Croton hydrants. Pumping on the great organ handles to build up the pressure—ready to put *out* the fire now, as they are supposed to.

It is then that the mob's de facto leader intervenes. That strange, grizzled bummer from the park, still wearing the board with *NO DRAFT!* chalked on it. I had not seen him since his moment of glory, when he stood in the tracks and hurled his stone through the window of the New Haven train.

Now I notice him again—materializing out of the mob, right in front of the police superintendent. His eyes as sharp and cunning as a rat's. Before anyone can stop him or even say anything, he goes right up to Kennedy and strikes him a terrible blow on the side of the head with his fist. Kennedy tries to dodge it, he tries to block it with his cane. But the bummer is strong and unnaturally quick. He seizes the thin rattan stick and breaks it like a twig—then rears back and strikes the superintendent again, with his whole forearm this time, knocking him senseless to the ground.

That is all it takes. The uniformed policeman next to Kennedy pulls his nightstick, trying to protect him—but another huge Irisher runs up behind him, and belts him over the head with a wooden fence stave. He knocks the officer to the ground, next to his chief, and begins to strip him of his uniform, raging wildly at the unconscious man while he tears it away:

"You son of a bitch! Now I've got you and I'll finish you!"

The crowd takes up the shout, closing around them, beating Kennedy's clerk as well. Somehow, Kennedy himself manages to get back on his feet again. He begins to run, staggering, down the street—the mob right after him. Chasing the City's superintendent of police through the streets, striking and punching at him when they catch him.

Kennedy breaks free again, running blindly for his life. Eagan and I run helplessly after them all, trying to think of something we can do. The mob on Kennedy's heels baying and barking like so many hounds.

"C'mon, boys! Stick together and we can lick all the damn police in the City!"

"Finish the son of a bitch!"

A man swings at Kennedy with a club of some sort, knocking him down into a construction pit. He goes sliding down, headlong through the yellow mud, and I fear he is finished. But he gets back up at once, scrambling desperately up the far side of the pit as the mob races around after him.

We race with them, Eagan and I, trying to beat the mob to him. And then do—what? I thrust my hand down into my coat pocket—remember again that I gave the big Colt revolver Raymond handed me to Maddy.

It would do little good anyway, against such a mob. The only hope is flight, and Kennedy is already out the other side of the pit now, still running but slowing noticeably. I see his face as he runs toward us—reddened and groggy, mouth slumping open in exhaustion. His face and his neat new suit covered in his own blood, in the yellowed mud from the pit—the chalk of the grave already upon him.

I yell at him to hurry—as if he does not fully understand the peril he is in. Beside me Eagan is yelling, too, even as he looks around desperately for Kennedy's beaten guards, his carriage. God only knows what will become of us all if the mob notices us. But they are too fixed on their quarry—and now they have him. Even as he stretches out his arms to us, imploring, the man with the club catches up again, and fetches Kennedy one last, resounding blow to the back of the head.

It sends him sprawling, a dead weight, right into the arms of Eagan. He holds him there while the mob rushes up, their eyes wide with excitement. Wondering if they have really done it, killed the superintendent of police in the street—

Eagan swings Kennedy's body around to face them. He gropes for the superintendent's pulse—then looks up with an expression of shock and horror, letting Kennedy slip slowly down his legs to the ground.

"He's dead, boys," Eagan tells them, almost in a whisper, standing his ground as the Irish behemoth and his friends rush up.

"You done it. It's all over—"

The mob pauses at the news. Even they, realizing in their maddened state that *this* would have consequences.

"Jesus, but they'll have the army on us now!"

"No use waitin' to see—"

They fall away, their bloodlust sated for the moment. I go up to Eagan, who is crouched protectively over the body.

"I never saw a man more alive than he was last night—"

"Shut up. He ain't dead," Eagan whispers.

"What?"

"He's still alive—the goddamned fool! Get his carriage!"

Somehow, the mob hasn't spooked his horse, and I am able to guide the carriage around to Lexington Avenue. By the time I do, Kennedy's clerk and his guard have made their way over to us, beaten bloody themselves, and stripped to their underwear. Between us we are able to haul Kennedy into his carriage, cover him with gunney sacks from the construction site, and pack him off down to headquarters.

"You should come, too," Eagan tells me before he kicks up the horses.

He is right, of course. I should go back to downtown, to shelter at the *Tribune*. Above all, I should go to Maddy, make her come with me.

But I don't. I have my duty, my vocation. It is what I tried to explain to Father Knapp, but could not. *My job is to see, and to tell.*

All my life I have been too afraid—of my own failings, of the City around me—to really get down to the street and see life as it is. To see what it is that holds me back, that keeps my writings from being anything more than scribblings on a page.

And now I have my chance, presented to me suddenly, serendipitously. That cave-in at the old De Peyster house this morning has given me the perfect disguise. Now I can move among them, these wild Irish, these mobs, even at the height of their frenzy—yet undetected, *unseen* myself.

It is too good a chance to pass up. Maddy will wait, the mob is still far uptown. There will be time, plenty of time, for me to see and tell. I hurry back toward the draft office, and the mob. The whole block is burning now, the thick smoke billowing out at me as I go toward it.

26

RUTH

When she got back Milton had the other children up and dressed and sitting at the table. He went from one to the other, getting them their food, seeing to their needs—as quick and assured in his movements as his father must have been in his trade, she thought.

I would've liked to see him build a ship. I never did see him build one—

Stopping herself then, making herself stop thinking about it as if she would never see Billy again. Instead she smiled at Milton—*her good boy*—and went about getting breakfast. Porridge and milk again, and the babies whining about it, but there was nothing else left in the house.

"I don't *wan'* it!"

"I don' *wan'* it neither!"

Vie and Mana taking turns, their eyes large and teary.

"You'll eat it. We're lucky to have that now—"

Most mornings she might try to baby them into eating. Play a little game, tell some goblin story she remembered from around the hearth.

How strange, how strange not to eat anything laid before you.

She still had trouble herself not eating things that fell on the ground. They rolled right out of the wagons and onto the street, potatoes and turnips and onions, and apples and even sides of meat. She knew that she had reached Heaven when she first saw that, despite her many sins—

But now there was no chance of getting the children anything more, even if she could leave the house. It was impossible to find coffee in the markets for less than fifty cents a pound, sugar for less than twenty. Even then, what she could get wasn't very good. There was sawdust mixed in with the coffee, sand in the sugar; red lead in the pepper and Prussian blue dye in the tea.

"Ain't there nothin' else, then? Nothin' else *at all?*"

They made faces when they tasted the milk, and she picked up the can she had managed to buy the day before, picking out the words PURE ORANGE COUNTY MILK machine-stamped on the side.

She poured a drop of it out into her palm and licked at it. The milk was a queasy, blue-white color and tasted like chalk and magnesia. She doubted the cow had ever come within fifty miles of Orange County. No doubt it was some poor, spavined, consumptive animal. Fed on mulch in the dark stalls of some Williamsburg brewery—

"No, there's nothing else. You can eat that now or go hungry."

Milton answered for her when she remained distracted. Looking down at his little sisters so sternly that they burst into giggles.

Ruth smiled, too. *Her two little girls.* She had so looked forward to having them, so she would not be alone in a household of men. They were lighter-skinned than Milton, though they looked less like her than they did her mother. *Worse luck.* At least they had some of their father in them, too: his broad, strong features. Solemn, intelligent brown eyes.

Sometimes she thought she could feel Billy pondering her through them. That serious gaze leveled upon her, assessing her as carefully as he did everything—a piece of wood, a man, the dinner on the plate before him. The face of a man who had once jumped without looking, and was now more wary. He did not trust, perhaps, but there was forbearance, too. A sadness and a kindness she had always clung to, hoping it would be enough.

Where was he now?

Where was her husband? It was getting too late, she knew, too late even to leave for the ferries, with all these men out in the street. She wondered if they should go anyway—but she was more worried by the thought of him laid out somewhere, bleeding in an alley. Or worse.

No, not Billy. Billy would know better, he would know to lay low, he would not get caught out like that.

But even if he came through the door with his wages the next minute, she didn't know what they would live on, out on the road, with five children, away from all their friends and neighbors. Just to leave, to head up into New England or out into Pennsylvania would eat up everything they had—

But we can't stay here. She tried to set herself to it, telling herself again it wasn't Ireland, this wasn't a starving country. There were miles and miles of farms, and fields full of wheat and corn, and cities like this one.

But what mercy could they expect? A nigger family—black nigger, green nigger—going door to door during this war?

Nine o'clock.

The children ate what they would of the porridge and the brewery milk, and clamored to go outside. Usually by this time the streets and the back lots would be full of their friends, screaming and chasing each other.

Today, though, she would keep them inside—would tie them to her apron strings if she could. Milton took them in hand. Moving them back to the bedroom, inventing games out of nothing to entertain them, and she was grateful for it, but for all that she missed their noise. Rising and falling outside like the sound of the ocean, off Moher. The lulling hush of the waves—

Standing in the grass at the top of the cliff with her brothers and sisters, the other children and their mothers. Waiting silently for the men, despite this chance to talk and gossip. Stupefied by the wash of the waves. The seaweed, when it came, surprisingly heavy, and slippery as eels. The men emptying it out of the baskets they carried on their backs. The children stripping it down—slick and briny, the sea salt and the sand stinging their eyes. Their mothers curling and bundling it with flax, ready to be taken back and spaded into the thin and ungiving earth The long, fishy curls, to be grown into potatoes. To be grown into them, the potato people—

"No, no, no!"

"Yes, that's the rule!"

She heard the cries of the children in the bedroom now, chanting in unison against some decision by their older brother. Milton firmly turning down their appeal. She had to smile, to hear it. *He knew the rules—*

The street outside was still nearly silent. The women in, too, with their men, or waiting for them. Even their laundry pulled in from the empty lines, where before they limply crisscrossed the back lots like so many fallen flags.

Where was her Billy?

By now, most days, she would have started over to the Germans, up at the ragpickers' rookeries. A cluster of slanting wooden shacks, built on the barren blocks between the central park and Jones's Wood. Everything between them—the yards, and the doorways, and the stovepipe chimneys—strung with lines of drying rags, and baskets full of bones. Inside the shacks was stuffed every scrap of garbage the bent old German women could scavenge—broken dishes and legless chairs, bits of colored ribbon and cloth. Pieces of stamped tin and fractured lamps, buckets of cinders and burned-out coals.

Anything and everything they could find that might conceivably be twisted and glued together into a toy, a doll. Leaving only enough room on the floor for the ancient German women, Mrs. Krane and Mrs. Mueschen, to shove their skinny beds together. Ruth worked there each day until her fingers ached. Wrapping and pinning cloth around old mutton bones, polishing and shining, cutting and trimming. Creating bright, society dolls out of whole cloth. It paid four dollars a week, but she had had worse jobs. At least the German women didn't bother if she brought her children to sit and play amid the hills of garbage, and they let her talk with the other women as they worked by the hearth, heads down over the bright and putrid scraps in their aprons.

It gave her a chance, too, to slip a finished doll into her pocket from time to time. She took home only her best work—the pretty little maids that she created from the best patches of felt, the shiniest bones she could find, squirreled away discreetly into her pile. Polished a dark black from the coal pieces, so they shone like their father's lovely face.

She had to take some care about it. She had seen the German women strike other girls who had stolen from them, resenting the theft of even the least bit of garbage they had picked up from the ash bins. Their eyes were always hooded and watchful behind large, round spectacles, constantly appraising their kingdoms of garbage. They kept their sharp sticks near the door, in a salvaged umbrella stand—ready to beat back the stray packs of Irishwomen who came agitating during the bad times, demanding they throw all the coloreds out of their shop.

Mostly so they can pay us all less, Ruth knew. During these brawls they hid in the back of the shed with the others. The colored women not wanting their faces to be seen at all, knowing the fury the mere sight of them would raise. Ruth and the other whites keeping hidden as well, for they knew there would be retribution should they be seen to work in the same shop with coloreds—

It was the best job she could get, though, and she feared losing it, if only because of the chance to make the dolls for her honeys, her girls. They were her daughters' greatest pride. The black-faced figures—or coffee-colored, exactly the shade of their own, a color gleaned from rubbing old tobacco across a knot of wood. *Unlike any doll the other children on the alley might have—*

It was Ruth's greatest pride, as well. Just knowing she could make them—could sell them, even, in the great stores, and earn the money when Mrs. Mueschen counted it out, into her palm every Friday, in two-bit pieces. Knowing she could do it, could do something to provide. That she wasn't useless—

She heard the church bells ringing, and she jerked her head around sharply, distracted from the sound of her children.

Ten o'clock—and where was Billy?

27

BILLY DOVE

He liked to leave for work early in the morning. It was cooler, in the summer, and there were fewer white people on the street, and some days he might make it all the way up to the Colored Orphans' Asylum without hearing something that would make him want to turn, and put his hand on his knife. Sometimes he could walk the whole way without being called a nigger to his face.

They called him Billy Dove, for all the places he had been, but he always came back. *My Billy Dove, one day you will sail off and go far away from me.* He had shipped to London and to Le Havre, to Barcelona and Marseilles, and the Golden Horn. *But he had always come back.*

It was over three miles from Paradise Alley to the Asylum, at Forty-third and Fifth, and he could do it in an hour most mornings. Leaving before dawn, legging it up there with the broad, rolling, seaman's stride he had even after so many years on land. Early in the morning he could still get some sense of the world outside the City, could catch a sudden whiff of trees or grass—or the sea—coming from somewhere. Enough, in the warm weather anyway, to remind him of mornings back in Charleston—the smell of red camellias, and azalea blossoms, down by the docks along the Cooper.

Not today. He could see that as soon as he had reached Broadway.

The streets were filled with men—unusual for so early on a Monday morning. Many of them looked as if they had never gone home from the night before—staggering down the avenue boisterous and loud, and yellow-eyed with drink.

"Must be the heat. Heat always brings out the vermin," he muttered.

Thinking of the cockroaches that came wobbling out of every crack and hole of his home, when the heat got this bad, no matter how much he or Ruth or the children stomped at them with their bare feet, or thrashed at them with the birch broom. *That is what I have given you to live among. These roaches.*

A smothering, yellow cloud of heat had already lowered itself over the City. It was worse even than Charleston sometimes, the way the heat could descend on this City. *Worse even than the Guinea coast—*

He was sweating freely, the perspiration running down from under his shapeless, broad-brimmed hat, pricking him under his burlap shirt. He tried to stay out of the path of the lurching white men, to avoid their gaze at all costs. Yet before he could get to Fourteenth Street, he had been pushed bluntly off the sidewalk a dozen times. The leering, hateful faces pushing up into his.

"There you go, nigger!"

"Hey, contraband! What makes you think you can come up here t'take a white man's job?"

He pivoted away, saying nothing, leaving them reeling behind him. They were not in earnest yet—not quite yet. *Up all night drinking on a Sunday.* There was something going on, he realized—and he walked still faster, even more anxious to get up to the Asylum, to get his money and get back again.

"Shoulda gone already," he said to himself. "Shoulda gone a long time ago—"

Feeling ashamed of how he had argued against Ruth, when she had said the same thing the afternoon before. When they had first heard that Johnny Dolan was back in town.

Go where? And to what purpose? Only to be hunted down by him—run to ground like a wounded animal.

No, it had made sense to stay. At least it had before they were forced to leave Seneca Village and move down here to the Fourth Ward. They had had a home, friends, a whole village around them then, to keep them safe from the blackbirders and anything else. He had still had his hopes of gaining a position in a shipyard, somewhere.

And after that—after the whole village had been knocked down and plowed under overnight, so that not even a board of it showed anymore—after that he had been worn out with running, and was no longer sure in which direction to go.

They called him Billy Dove for all the places he had been, but he had always come back. Until he hadn't.

He walked as fast as he could now, nearly running as he crossed over to the Fifth Avenue. He would run—but he knew that the sight of a black man running anywhere would only draw a cop, then a crowd that would take up the chase. At best he would be grabbed, beaten, thrown into jail before he could get out a word of explanation—at best. There were the streetcars and the omnibuses, but as a black man he wasn't allowed on most of the lines, and anyway, they were bulging with more men and gang *b'hoys* just looking for trouble.

At that very moment, one of the yellow omnibuses passed him and a bottle flew out. Just missing him, smashing on the curb—the sour, acid whiskey splattering over his shoes. The sound of raucous laughter trailed back down the avenue, but he kept walking. Head down, hands in his pocket. Turning around the next corner just in case they decided to leap down from the omnibus and come after him, disappointed with the response he had given them—

"One hour," he repeated to himself.

An hour to the Asylum with its boys in their plain, thick wool pants and shirts. The girls, whirling about like so many dazed butterflies in their long, flowered skirts and padded Chinaman's smocks. The thought of them always made him smile. Running their hoops along the blue-slated, fenced-in back courtyard. Their faces always so grave, so serious.

It wasn't a bad place—the clothes warm, the beds good; the food often better than what he had to give his own children at home. The place was kept heated in the winter, and well-scrubbed all year 'round. The old white ladies who ran it were very serious but kind enough. There was time for games and lessons, and for learning work that they could make a living at, once they were outside.

But the faces of the children were still so serious. They knew where they were, regardless. Most of them not even really orphans, which only seemed to make it worse. Waiting, and wondering when they might be returned—

An hour, each way. Maybe. A few minutes' talk and dickering for his wages in between. He debated briefly with himself whether or not to tell the old ladies he was going away.

No—no sense to that. The grave, erect, grey-haired women who ran the Asylum might take that as some reason to withhold his money, in order to assure his return. You could never tell with white people. Better to claim a sickness in the family, promise to be back before noon. He thought he could look desperate and harried enough for *that.*

Two hours, then, there and back—two and a half at the outside. Then all they had to do was pack up and go. Ruth would have it ready, he knew, he could rely on her for such things. Of course even then it would take them at least another half hour, maybe even an hour to make it to the ferry at Fulton, or Desbrosses Street. To get across the wide, slow rivers that surrounded this infernal island.

Lucky to be gone by noon. If things hadn't blown already.

He gave up, today, the wide detour he liked to take over to the East Side docks, when it was early and he had time. *Not that it was anything but to torture himself with, anyway.* He liked to walk by all the great shipyards there—Smith & Dimon's, and Brown & Bell's; Jacob Westervelt's and William Webb's. Watching them work on the sleek new China clippers, and the steam frigates, on the men-of-war and the cheese-box ironclads that looked too clumsy and low to ever stay afloat at sea. Watching the shipwrights at their lathes, fitting and caulking their timbers—white oak and white pine from upstate; Long Island locust and New England chestnut; live oak and pitch pine from Georgia. Watching the sailmakers and the ropemakers, the carpenters and the ironmongers pounding at their armor and boilers. The whole busy hive of the shipyards, hard at work at their many tasks, until he could stand it no more and had to walk away.

My failing. Beware my failing.

He knew if he went there he would find himself drawn irresistibly to a Water Street tavern, where anything might happen. And he knew that if he walked along the docks with his head down, ruminating over the fine new ships and his own luck, someone might throw an eel down at his feet. And then he would look up and see the pale, grinning, expectant white faces—

They called him Billy Dove, for all the places he had been, but he always came back. His master had given him the name, as a sign of affection from the days he had first hired him out as a ship's carpenter.

"My Billy Dove," he liked to say, a little sadly, a little theatrically, when he had been at it for a while.

"One day you will sail off and go far away from me."

He had shipped to London and to Le Havre, to Barcelona and Marseilles, and all the way through the Aegean to the Golden Horn. But he had always come back to the fat thumb of land where the Cooper and the Ashley met to form the Atlantic Ocean. He had always come back to Charleston.

He saw no reason not to. He was sure of himself, and good at the work he did between voyages, building ships in the small boatyard along the Cooper. He had yet to find a port where a black man might feel more at home. He was even pretty sure that his master would let him buy his own freedom if he wanted—as grateful to him as he was for all the money Billy had made him.

Yet when he thought about it, there was something that repelled him about the notion of spending his money to buy his freedom—to buy his own self. There were many things he had begun to think about. The long lines of men and women, shuffling through the old slave market in their shackles. The empty lot off Meeting Street, where the Emmanuel Church had stood. The heavy stillness of the town itself, behind the Spanish moss that hung everywhere, like smoke, as if to mask some nameless yet immanent menace.

He had begun to notice how everything—everything of any worth—was done by hired-out slaves, or freed Negroes. It was they who shod the horses in the blacksmith shops, and put the wheels back on wagons. They etched the glass in the porches of the great houses along North Market and Wentworth Streets, hammered out the silver and brass in their dining rooms, carved the furniture in the parlors. Or they sewed the white sails, and planed and fitted the white fish skeletons of ships as he did, every day, down in the boatyard.

He knew he could buy his own freedom, and live like the other freedmen in a little house up on the Neck. That he could save up enough money to buy a watch, a waistcoat, a wife—even black slaves of his own, if he should care to.

But at night he would go and sit under the windows of the prison, and listen to the colored men inside singing their mournful songs. He would walk past the site of Emmanuel Church—before the white mob had burned it, thirty years ago, after Denmark Vesey's rising. Vesey had been a freedman, and a sailor, too, but they had hung him in the prison yard, and burned the church where he had worshiped. Now there was nothing in its place but a jungle of camellias, and yellow magnolias, and azalea blossoms.

He could not trust it. Things grew too fast in this place—the constant growth and rot and regeneration covering everything that had come before. After a time it deceived one about how things were, and how they had always been.

From then on he had looked for anything he could take from the shipyards. A scrap of wood, an awl. A lathe, a hammer. He told the other hired slaves he was taking these things to sell down in Ropemaker's Lane, so he could buy some ribbons for his sweetheart, and they let him do as he pleased so long as they did not get blamed for it by the overseer.

He worked on the boat in any spare moments he could steal, keeping it hidden under a canvas in a far corner of the yard. It was just big enough to carry himself but he built it as he had been taught to build, so that it would be strong and supple enough to breach the open sea. The mast he planed thin from a green upcountry pine, so that it would bend enough to withstand the winds of the hurricane season that was almost upon him. The sails he sewed from burlap bags, and the joints and the timbers he fitted and finished and chinked with tar until he could not fit a cat's whisker between them.

And when he was ready, when he believed his little boat could withstand the ocean itself, he went up to the splendid house with the two-story veranda that the man who owned him kept on East Bay Street. There he sat in the kitchen where his mother and his sister worked. Eating the spare biscuits that they gave him, watching them slip quickly about in their simple white muslin dresses and yellow bandannas, baking ham and cornbread in the great brick ovens. While outside, in the brick courtyard, he could see the thick palmetto trees, the light glinting and shifting as the servants threw open the windows to let the cool night breezes in.

They would be closed again just before dawn, he knew, to trap the night air, and hold it against the heat of the day. But by then he was already on his way, back down to the boatyard. There had not been any need even to say his good-byes, to utter words that might be overheard by prying ears. The women had understood why he had come, looking into his face, taking his hands in theirs. They had held him for just a moment—then slipped a few more biscuits, some more of the salty ham to him. Then he had walked down to the docks and casually pushed the little vessel he had made out into the river—so that all the other workmen in the shipyard and the white overseers thought Billy Dove had only gone to test another boat, the way he did all the time before handing them over to their new owners.

Only this day he had kept right on going, sailing on through the mouth of the harbor, past the great palmettos along the Battery. Past Fort Moultrie, and the five-sided brick citadel of Fort Sumter, its big black cannons trained out to sea. He kept sailing, past the oyster boats and the shrimp trawlers and the fishing schooners. Going all the way out to the limits of the harbor, then past. Watching the blue water of the open sea as it skimmed along beneath his rudder, looking back toward the harbor with its forts and its big, wavering trees, and all its fine pink and white and grey houses. Knowing that he would never see them again from the prow of a sailing ship, coming back from across the ocean, proud and happy and full of stories.

The first day out he sailed down to the Sea Islands, where he could stock up on water and hide in the high sweetgrass of the marshes until it was dark. After that he turned north. Sailing always by night, guiding himself by the moon and the North Star the sailors had taught him to pick out of the night sky. Staying close to the shore but not too close, for he had no charts—threading his way up through the barrier islands around Hatteras, and past the Tidewater. Eating as little as he could from the handful of oranges, the rounds of cheese and bread he had brought, anxious to beat the hurricanes up the coast before he had to go to land again.

But it took too long. He had to move carefully, even at night, looking out for liquor smugglers or some blackbirder running with no lights, and all too delighted to pick up a young, skilled runaway to add to his catch. After a week he thought he might have made it far enough north, but he couldn't be sure. He had heard too many stories about runaways who had planned and provided patiently for years, and followed this star and that river until they were sure they had reached Philadelphia—only to come out of the wilderness and find themselves nabbed in the slave towns of Richmond or Baltimore, or Washington City.

After another week the food ran out, and he was down to a day of water in the little cask he had filled in the Sea Islands. The boat had begun to leak, for all his work, but he was still too chary to put into a port. Instead he went to shore along the loneliest beaches and estuaries he could find. Spending more precious nights running inland, deep into unknown country to steal from some stray farmhouse or another. Hoping no dog would sense his presence out by the sheep pasture, by the chicken house or the hog pen, or the root cellar.

He still could not risk sailing by day, so he would take down the frail detachable pine mast, pull the boat up in some stagnant cove. There he would find a hole, in a cave or under the roots of a dying tree and heap the dead leaves and vines up over himself as he slept. As if he might burrow right down into the earth, hidden from any wandering boy or dog. And in the morning he knew that he must look like some part of the forest himself, some half man, half spirit, crawling up out of the ground, covered with leaf and earth.

"Free or not free," he would mutter to himself, crouching there on the wilderness floor, worried that he could hear someone, something, wandering far from the habited fields. Wondering about what he would have to do if it were a man, a woman? A child?

Free or not free?

He had decided in the end that having possession of his own self meant being free to drown if he so chose. He had set back out to sea, and hewed again to the North Star. Determined now, no matter how much he thirsted or hungered, that he would not turn back to land until he had reached free soil.

At first his luck held and he made good time. But then one afternoon he could feel the first of the hurricane winds, just tickling the back of his neck. Only a breeze still, no more than enough to rustle the palmetto fronds back in Charleston, or sweep the first leaves off the well-rolled lawns of the great houses.

Behind them, though, he could feel a greater force, like the punch of a man's fist. The storms he had seen himself, building off the coast of Africa, picking up momentum as they swept across the Atlantic and up through the Islands—

All the rest of that afternoon, he turned his back to them and ran. Not daring to look back, though he knew the winds were there— shifting and capricious, as alive and willful as he was himself.

For hours he tacked as best he could—telling himself that at least he did not have to worry about the blackbirders, that nothing else would be out in weather like this. He even allowed himself to sweep in toward land when the winds called for it   close enough sometimes to see the little white-steepled towns, the redbrick houses, the men harvesting their fields.

It would be so easy still to turn in. To steer his boat to land, walk in among these people. Pay with his own money for shelter, food, warmth. Except that he could not. There would be no shelter for him anywhere along that land—and he turned his boat back on out, below the ravening clouds that had overtaken him.

The rain came first, falling in solid, suffocating sheets and threatening to swamp him at once. He had to rip another small hole along the rail, to let the water run through. But then the wind came up, fooling him, so that it almost pitched him out of the boat before he was able to haul in, then tie his ankle to the mast—tying anything else he could to himself, to the boat, with what rope he had managed to smuggle out of the yard.

He looked back over his shoulder again, though he thought the better of it—and there was the storm. The black clouds spreading over the sky, pinching out the sun. The ocean around him was suddenly quiescent—but there, on the horizon, he could already see the foaming water, the whitecaps racing after him like so many wild horses. There was a low boom, then a sound like a woman's shriek, and the storm was upon him.

He was plunged at once into total darkness. Riding the ocean now only by feel, the lurch and turn of his stomach, as the small boat swept wildly up and down the vast peaks and sloughs of the sea. The wind blowing out his little sail, and threatening to tear it off, cracking the green pinewood of the mast. But when he leaned over to fold the mast in, a breaker took him instead—tossing him into the sea as casually as he might brush a fly off his cheek.

He floundered in the water, held to the boat only by the rope around his ankle, praying that the mast would hold. A wave smacked him back against the hull, battering his ribs and chest, then yanked him away, twisting the rope until he was sure his ankle would break. The next one smashed him into the boat again and only just failed to knock his brains out, his shoulder banging heavily against the stern.

Feeling his way along the side, he managed to grab hold of the rail by his fingertips, barely heaving himself up over the side before the next wave hit. Still, it smacked him flat on his face, sending him scrambling down the deck. Something cracked hard against his head, and he clung to it, keeping himself on board. *The mast,* he thought, though he could not tell for sure. There were only rough surfaces beneath his hands, and he no longer knew where anything was—where the boat ended, or where the water began—until he cried aloud in his futility, into the ravaging darkness.

Somehow, the boat stayed afloat. He clung to his mast and the rope through the night until at last the storm abated—the ocean becalmed as quickly as it had risen up. It wasn't the hurricane yet, just an advance squall, though when the sun rose, he could see that his boat was listing badly to port and the thin, whiplike mast had been beaten and snapped past any permanent repair. He trussed it up again with rope as best he could—deciding that wherever he was, he had to head back in to the pencil line of land just visible against the northern horizon.

That was when he had spotted the sail, between himself and the shore. It was a sleek brig, sharp as a hatchet blade, fighting its way south. Even as he watched it picked up a small southwesterly breeze and flew by him, not more than a hundred yards away. There were no flags, no pennants, not even a name that he could see. Just two square headsails and a gaff sail aft of the mizzenmast—all of them the same dingy, grey color. Sails so dismal that they would be nearly invisible at night, barely stood out even in the day against the grey fall skies.

A slaver?

He stared straight ahead as the ship passed, trying to seem as dis-interested as possible, and after it went by, he did not look around for a long time. *Just some local nigger, out with his marster's boat—*

They worked their way up the inland waterways, he knew, once they got up from the Indies and the slave markets in Havana. Trying to dodge the navy—and at the same time seeing what they could find. Prowling for runaways, maybe even snatching up a few dozen slaves from some coast plantation, if their master was not wary enough.

He would be a good catch.

He sneaked a look 'round under his armpit, while pretending to fiddle with the sail some more, hoping to see the grey sails receding on the horizon.

Instead, the brig had tacked about. She was coming directly toward him now, riding on the swift northerly winds. They would catch him within the hour, unless somehow the winds died down.

But the shoreline was receding, giving way on the port side to some broad bay or inlet. *But where?* Was he in the North? Or a slave state still, like Maryland or Delaware?

He would have to risk it, he knew. At least there would be a chance he could get to shore, get himself hidden before they put out a small boat to grab him. He tried to steer in toward the land—but the crude rudder he had fixed up was all but useless, smashed beyond repair dur-ing the storm. As long as he clutched the mast in place, he could keep ahead of the slaver for a little while more, but he could not get in toward the shore.

He tried to think what to do, searching for his knife. But it was gone, too, lost in the storm, and he began to curse. Knowing, then, that he had nothing that could make them kill him. That his only course if they caught him would be to leap into the ocean. Swimming down so far and so fast into the depths that there would be no way he could ever recover himself, could ever come up, even if he were weak enough to want to—

Or he could let them take him. Sell him off somewhere, and hope sometime, someplace, he would have the chance to escape again.

Free or not free?

The first grey fin cut through the water, just fifty yards off the port bow. It was just visible above the waterline, as grey and sharp as the slaver's sail, still coming on relentlessly behind him. He flattened himself instinctively on the deck, as close to the middle of his small boat as he could get, following the fin with his eyes until it submerged as suddenly as it had appeared.

It is just looking, he told himself. But as he watched, another fin broke the water, then a third, and a fourth. He had been afraid of that, he could not remember ever having seen only one shark. Wherever he had sailed, there had always been a brood of them at once, snapping and lunging for anything that went over the side. Fighting each other in their eagerness to rip it apart, scraps of salt pork from the mess, but also whole buckets and glass bottles. Grabbing at anything in their frenzy—

Even now, the first shark he had spotted resurfaced, its open jaws snapping at a small barrel in the water that Billy hadn't noticed before. The barrel disintegrated at once, no more than a few staves left bobbing along the water, the shark submerging again with whatever his prey was.

But in its wake Billy saw that the water was full of debris. Besides the barrel there were smashed crates and lengths of rope, old fruit peels and moldy bits of bread, bones and crab shells. A small flock of gulls circled overhead, diving and picking carefully amid the sharks. *Of course, it was a current*—

He hadn't noticed it before, in his preoccupation with staying ahead of the slaver, but there it was—clearly marked by its refuse. A current that excursion boats and steamers, yachts and merchantmen must regularly pick up, and follow into land. That was what the sharks and the gulls were following, looking for whatever they could snatch up from the wake of the boats. It didn't matter that his one poor sail was all but shredded, held together only by his bare hands. All he had to do was follow it in as well, and he could beat the brig to the shore, get in fast and close to the beach, where they would founder if they were not careful.

But how? His rudder was gone. The current was only a few yards away, not more than a hundred feet, but he had no means to steer to it—

There was one way. Slowly, reluctantly, forcing his feet and hands to move for him, Billy crawled to the end of the little craft. There he perched along the stern, gazing back at the grey-sailed slaver. It was still coming, already it had closed more than half the gap between them and there was nothing else for it.

He slipped into the water, holding the rope from the mast in one hand. A little canvas bag, in which he had wrapped up all the money he had saved, tied tightly around his thigh. The water surprisingly warm and gentle against his skin.

Slowly, hand over hand, he made his way up the starboard side. Cleaving to the boat, trying to make as little noise or commotion as he possibly could. Pulling the rope with him as he did, hauling his small boat slowly around and pointing it toward the current. Trying to maneuver the sail from where he was, in the water, pulling it around.

A shark zigzagged quickly past him, so close it nearly bumped his shoulder. Prowling restlessly through the sheath of the water, punctuated by more fins up and down its long, honed body. Billy froze knowing that that wouldn't do any good if it went for him. Waiting for the first touch, the bite, wondering how much it would hurt. *Like a knife? An ax along his foot, his calf?*

But there was nothing, just the warm caress of the water—and looking back over his shoulder, he could see the brig, bearing right down on him. He began to kick and paddle again, trying to make his movements as slow, as easy and natural as he could, and still stay ahead of the slaver. He was almost to the current now, he could see the flotsam floating along on its tide, all the bits of garbage glinting in the faint afternoon light. *Almost there*—

Another shark swept by him, and he forced himself to be still again, watching as it flashed by. This one did not swim on, though, but circled once around his boat. He lost track of it for a few minutes, had figured it was gone—when a flicker of motion made him look down and he saw it there, growing bigger and bigger, rushing up at him from the depths.

He did not have time to react, even if he had been able to. Instead he could only watch, paralyzed, while the creature streaked up through the surface just beyond him—its ugly sharpened head near enough for him to reach out and touch. When it broke the water, it rolled over almost playfully. So close that Billy could stare right into the gaping pink mouth, and all the jagged rows of teeth there—the new ones already encroaching upon the old, as if the ancient, voracious urge that drove the creature could not still itself even for a moment.

The small, dark eye stared out indifferently at him as it swept past. Ducking back down under the next swell, as suddenly as it had surfaced, back to its ceaseless hunt.

The boat lurched ahead, nearly pulling the line from his hands— and Billy realized that he had finally reached the current. He swung himself back up over the side as fast as he could, murmuring a small, swift prayer of thanks as he did. Holding tight to the whippet mast with his bare hands. The water shooting him on ahead now, flying him in toward the shore.

He looked back and saw the brig almost seem to hesitate, the grey gaff sail fluttering loosely. It was already too late for the blackbirder to cut him off from the shore, he was certain of it. All it could do was tack and come after him, along the same current, but who knew where that led? It would be easy to run aground, so close to land. And if there were a navy cutter in whatever port Billy was being swept toward, the slaver could lose her whole cargo—

He felt the sea tickling the tops of his bare feet   and realized that the current was beginning to slow. He had been so intent on the slaver, on holding the battered mast together, that he had not realized the boat was taking on water. Quickly, his eyes swept over the little deck. The ash planks he had caulked together so carefully still held, even after the squall.

But there—a space, no bigger than a man's finger, where the rudder had smashed against the boat. Another one directly across the deck, like a hole poked through a folded piece of paper. Desperately, he looked back over his shoulder at the slaver, which still seemed to linger by the head of the current, almost becalmed. He was in too close now, probably, for them to catch him—but they could still send a small boat out, manned with six good rowers, to run him down.

The water was almost at his ankles, the little sloop's speed slackening steadily as it settled. There was nothing he could stanch the holes with, no time to do it effectively even if there had been. Instead he simply began to bail, scooping up handful after handful of the water, dumping it over the side, wishing he still had his hat.

It was not enough. The water was still rising, close to swamping him already. The brig was still hovering by the current head, but at least the water kept carrying him in, little by little. There was a beach unfolding off to the starboard side now—a few hundred yards away, close enough so that he could make out figures on the sand, casting into the surf.

This was it now, he realized. This was as close to the shore as he could expect to get—though he did not know who the men there were, or where he was. There was no getting around it, though, the boat was all but sunk. He would have to try to dive as far as he could, then swim his way out of the current and to the beach. Yet there was an obvious danger here, too, if he could not fight his way out of the current; if it proved too strong for him, he would simply be swept along. Then the blackbirders could easily put out a boat, row him down before he made it to any land—

It would have to be tried. He said another swift prayer of hope and stood up—the water sloshing around his shins. After that he did not hesitate, but went to the starboard side and dived out as far as he could. The water glinting beneath him, the air ripping past his ears so that it seemed for a moment that he was propelling himself halfway to the shore.

Then he came down, still in the current. The water tugging at him at once, trying to drag him after the boat. He kicked out, and pulled for shore. He had always been a good swimmer, but the current was strong, very strong, and he felt nearly exhausted now, his ribs aching where he had been banged against the hull during the storm.

He kept kicking, kept pulling—the current yanking him down the length of the beach. It looked yellow, almost gold, from where he was, the sand mounds behind the fishing men. He kept pulling, the current slowly, grudgingly letting go, pulling loose of it like a man kicking off a tight boot. His breath rasping, pounding in his chest as he kept trying to shake it off.

Then it was gone—and all he had to contend with was the rough surf. Letting it throw him on toward the shore, barely able to lift his arms anymore, but tumbling down, sputtering and gasping as the waves tossed him about. Finally driven down into the sand by what felt like a pile driver, hearing what surely was another rib cracking. Rising up unsteadily—the next swell nearly knocking him over again. Staggering directly toward the nearest fisherman—*no chance of evading them, they were posted up and down the beach, as regular as sentinels.* Going right up to one, trying to make his face as relaxed, as accommodating and blank as he knew how from long and bitter experience.

Free or not free?

"I got swept out in marster's boat. If you be so kind—tell me how I might get back—" he croaked out—careful to keep his eyes down, looking at the sand, only darting small, surreptitious glances at the man before him. *Wondering if he could take him.* He was a little shorter than Billy, with a belly protruding through his coat, and a pair of high boots on. An unlit spray-soaked cigar clutched tightly in his teeth, his hands and his eyes still on his fishing pole while Billy tried to talk to him.

"What the hell should I care?" he snorted. "This is New Jersey! You can go to the devil, but see ya don't foul my line!"

Billy stood before him there on the beach. The yellow sand around him glinting as the clouds shifted restlessly above. Shivering a little, as he remembered how late it must be in the season, his wet, shirtless chest swelling up into goosebumps.

New Jersey. A free state—he had made sure to learn the free ones, before he left. He looked up toward the horizon where he could just see the brig—its grey sails moving away now, making for the South. His gaze shifted, over to the speck of his own little sloop. Billy could barely make it out, but there it was, still being borne along the current. He watched as it settled into the sea, satisfied with it—with himself— for the job he had done. Never thinking, as he watched it disappear, that it would be the last boat he would ever build, the last time he would ever put hand to lumber in a shipyard.

28

BILLY DOVE

By the time he made it to the Colored Orphans' Asylum, the sweat had soaked through even the thick burlap of his shirt. He turned in at the iron picket gate, past the huge weeping willow trees that stood like two enormous upturned mops in the yard. The building itself was three stories high—built like a Southern manor house, of all things, complete with a portico and six pillars over the front door. The only thing missing, the slave cabins out back—

At least the two Yankee ladies who ran it let the colored staff come up through the front, with the white schoolteachers and the philanthropic directors—

You are employees, same as the rest of us. Stern grey eyes flashing, that unbending New England sense of justice prevailing at all times, for better or for worse.

Yet it was different this morning. He could sense it as soon as he walked through the doors, though everything looked and smelled as immaculate as ever. The bleached white halls had all been scrubbed down, and the whole building was suffused with the smell of lye, and boiled soap.

But there was something different. *Something off.* The long, echoing halls were quieter than they should be, though he could hear the children outside already, playing their usual rhyming and skipping

games. Rolling their hoops along the blue slate flagstones of the courtyard—

*Just get the money. Get the money and get out. Three hours at best, the
streets already crawling with drunken white men—*

He went directly to the office—but both of the Yankee ladies,
Miss Shotwell and Miss Murray, were already ensconced inside, the
door locked and the thick green shade pulled down over the window.
Billy hadn't expected this, and all he could do was to linger outside in
the hall. Calculating, for lack of anything better, how much he was
due, and how far it would take them.

*Two weeks' wages was six dollars, plus the fifty cents they owed him
for the hammer. Six dollars and fifty cents—*

Even with the five that Ruth was sure to have—that she would
have put away somewhere—it still would be barely enough to get
them to Providence, much less Boston. Better head the other way,
down to Newark. Take the ferry over from the Chambers Street slip—

*And what then? How are we to live? That is the real reason why we
never went before, I could not provide the means—*

He looked up at the clock, above the Yankee ladies' office. It
slowly ticked away the minutes, loud in the empty hall. *Just past eight
now. Give them till eight-thirty, that was as long as he could risk it. No—
eight-ten, with men already in the streets. With that maniac God knows
where—*

He would have to push his way in then, even if such impertinence
cost him his position. *Why not now? Why wait at all?* He moved for the
door, then stopped. *What if they refused to give him the back pay?* He
could not picture the Yankee misses being so unfair—but who knew
what people would do, on such a day.

He sat himself down on the little visitors' bench just outside the
office, where he had seen so many of the parents come, the aunts and
grandparents, older sisters and brothers. Sitting there in their best
clothes, waiting to hear if the Asylum would take their child. The
children themselves sitting preternaturally still, their eyes taking in
everything. Aware of what was going on, not daring to speak for
fear that would break some spell, the only tie they still held to their
family.

Billy hated it. He hated everything about the orphanage, or at least he told himself he did. It was the only job he had ever held in the City. He hated his dependence on it, and yet he hated to leave it, too.

When he had finally reached New York, he had gone straight to the water. He was sure that he would be able to get some kind of position, once he saw the forest of sails around the harbor. There were more ships than he had ever seen in Charleston, or Rotterdam, more ships than he had even seen in London, and his heart leaped at the sight of them.

He was sure that he would get something. Applying at all the Manhattan shipyards, busy as anthills, that ran from South Street up to East Twenty-third. There must be something for him—maybe not his old position of authority and responsibility, not right away. He was a sensible man, he knew that no one started at the top in a new place—but *something*.

But there had been only white men. And when he told them what he wanted, and that he had not come to dance for pennies or sell them their lunch, they cursed him to his face and told him to leave, and threatened to call the slavecatchers out on him. He went back the next day, to another yard, but got the same answer there. It was the same again the next day, and the day after that, and not only from the Irish workers in the yards but also from the Germans and the Americans.

He tried down in Red Hook, in Brooklyn, and up the river in Greenpoint, and even over in the Hoboken yards, but it was always the same thing. At one site, a small yard by Corlears Hook named McPherson's, he had even gotten the owners to agree to hire him. In his desperation he had grabbed up a stave and shaved and planed it right there before them, so expertly and instantly that they had agreed to hire him at a new man's wage.

But as soon as he had gone down into the yard, as soon as the men realized what he was there for, each one of them put down his tools and walked out. Refusing to listen even when the owners threatened to fire them all—uttering the only thing he had heard everywhere, half law and half threat:

This is a white man's shop. This is a white man's waterfront.

Before much longer his money had run out, even in the dilapidated lodging houses for black sailors he had been able to find along Roosevelt Street. After that he had given up on finding a position in the yards and gone looking for anything he could get. Asking for work on the construction sites that seemed to sprout up on every corner overnight. Applying to shovel coal at the huge gas works, reeking of ammonia, that loomed over Fourteenth Street—even begging to sweep the entrails and the shit and the hooves off the floor at The Place of Blood.

Yet there was nothing for him. And he began to notice that all the other black men he saw were doing no more than pushing wheelbarrows, at best, running errands, hauling sacks over their shoulders like donkeys. Nothing steady. They were not even allowed to carry hods with the lowest of the Paddy construction teams. Their black faces, nevertheless, guarded and furtive at all times. Looking away when he met their eyes, as if to protect what little they had.

Down on the docks, by the fish markets in Fulton Street, he had even seen grown black men dancing for eels. One man tapping his foot in time and flogging away at a harmonica or a banjo. His partner performing the blindingly fast steps, the aloof, loose-limbed jerks of what they called a breakdown. The white fish sellers grinning and nudging each other with delight and unable to keep their own feet from tapping. Condescending, from time to time, to throw out a still-flopping, twitching eel at the feet of the dancers.

What the white men didn't know—what Billy saw—was how the dance was really a mimicry. A subtle, mocking caricature of how the bowlegged white sailors, and the Paddy laborers, carried themselves so importantly along the dockside—especially when they encountered a black man.

A fine little joke, just between the performers, the two black men. But what did that matter to *them*, the white men watching and smirking?

Only the black sailors Billy saw around the boardinghouses seemed to him like full men. Their blue navy jackets and white pants were clean and pressed, their flat sailor hats worn at a jaunty angle. They laughed and spoke as boldly as they pleased, and he considered trying to ship out with them, bound for Brazil, or Peru; Veracruz or Santo Domingo or Havana. But when he went down to the South Street docks and tried to talk to them, they only grinned, and spoke rapidly at him in their own tongues, and it occurred to Billy that he would have no idea what it would be like on such a ship, that he would have no idea of what might happen to him.

As opposed to this City—

He had walked on over to the bustling shipyards again. Trying not to think about how he was out of money now, or the hole in his stomach that seemed to pull his whole self down into it. Watching the carpenters and finishers, laying out the skeletons of their ships like so many fishbones. The start of something fine, that would build methodically and precisely, until it was ready to take the wind and sail around the world, holding a company of men safe against the waves.

That was when he had started. He had turned away from the yards and walked right into the first saloon he saw along Water Street, a leaning wooden shack that called itself The Sailor's Rest. He knew the chances were good that he would not be served—that he might even be robbed and beaten as soon as he set foot inside the swinging doors—but he walked in anyway. That was how desperate he had been, to spend his last nickel on something, anything, that might serve to cloud his mind.

But he hadn't been beaten, or thrown into the river, as he might have expected. He had even been granted what might have been considered a privilege, though he knew that it was not. The white men stood sucking on rubber hoses that ran up to barrels of whiskey behind the bar. But the barman had produced a glass for him—the foulest, dirtiest glass he had ever laid eyes on, to be sure—and poured his whiskey for him.

"Here!" he had barked, grinning sourly at Billy but perfectly serious. "We can't have ye drinkin' from the same hose as a white man, then."

Billy had stood there looking at it for a moment, unsure of whether to laugh or walk out. Instead he had picked up the glass and tipped it back into his throat, swallowing the whole shot in one quick slug. It was the worst thing he had ever tasted, swelling and searing the back of his mouth and his throat, until it felt as if it would burst through his head. Yet filling him with everything he had needed, with bitterness and courage and stupid pride.

"That your last nickel?" the bartender asked knowingly.

Billy blinked dimly back at the man—already made stupid, his every reaction, even the blink of his eyes already dulled and slow.

"Course, if ye want to go to the Velvet Room, there's a whole bowl of the creature for ya. On the house."

The bartender nodded toward a red curtain at the back of the room. God only knew what lay behind it—a covered room in a waterfront bar—but Billy actually considered it. *A whole bowl of the stuff, more than he would ever be able to afford. Already wanting so much of it—*

Very slowly, with a tremendous effort, he made himself shake his head. Sensing, even instantly drunk as he was, that it would be better not to take the bartender up on his offer. *Nothing was offered for free in this City. Somebody offered you something for nothing, you had better run—*

He pushed himself away from the bar. Staggering out into the fetid, running streets, the barman still calling after him, entreating him. Billy kept going, trudging through the yellowed horse manure, and falling everywhere as he walked. All his beautiful rage and bitterness and courage, falling with each step he took through the yellowed leavings, the shit-once-oats already fading and separating back to oats. Falling with each step he took away from the bar.

He stumbled back down to the wharves, walking blindly. His Dutch courage already falling, too, and only the emptiness in his stomach remaining. Wishing he had kept the nickel now, to buy a roll, a piece of fish. Begging silently for a job, any job, just out of pity. Just to sweep the shavings off the dry docks—

Something hard and wet slapped at his feet, so loud he took a jump back. *An eel.* The creature still alive, still trying to wriggle its way off the dry stones, back to water. He looked over to see a pair of red-faced, thick-armed white men, grinning expectantly, and he wanted to grab up the slimy creature and hurl it back at their heads.

"Hey, Juba!" one of them called, the grin tightening at the edges of his mouth. "Hey, Juba, give us a breakdown!"

He almost walked away, some little defiance left in him still, from the whiskey or maybe just himself. But then he looked back down at the eel, still fighting for its life. Humping its way blindly along the dock, trying to find some path back to the water. Still not giving up, the blind and hopeless thrusting toward life—

He picked it up in his hands, wrung the head of its slick, shapeless body until it stopped wriggling, and stuffed it into his shirt. Looking up again, he saw that the white men had begun to hoot and whistle impatiently—more of them gathering now, tars and shipmakers and mechanics, striding proudly down the wharf. And slowly, methodically, carefully studying their every move, he started to dance.

29

BILLY DOVE

He paced up and down the hall of the orphanage. Not even daring to look at the clock above the directors' office. Staring instead out the window at the children—trying to distract himself by the sight of them, spinning and running in their separated courtyards.

Boys and girls. Their own yards and their own beds. The day scheduled down to every last minute, from when they were awakened by the ringing of the matin bell, to when the monitors doused the lights. A good enough life—though what a shock it would be when they had to go out into the world again, the larger City that still awaited them.

The Colored Orphans' Asylum. An asylum it was all right, at least for the time being. He thought of the name, chiseled proudly above the pillars outside. Worrying that on this day it made the place a target—

He had his first thought of the iodine then, kept up in the medicine cabinet. Of the bottle of peach brandy, locked in the kitchen, its level marked off with niches, cut by one of the Misses' rings. They were temperance, the Misses, but they were also practical Yankee women, *acute* Yankees, as his master used to say. They kept something on hand for when a thirsty donor might come by, but marked the level with the cut of a ring. Of course that was easy enough to fix, just add a little water or cut a new niche, the ladies would not notice—

No, he stopped himself—even as he recalled the beautiful russet color of the brandy, three quarters of the way up the bottle.

No, it does not control you. You *control* it. *My failing*—

Yolanda came around the corner just then, rattling her tin bucket behind her. One of the charwomen, a small, sinewy Island woman, skin bronzed almost red by the Caribbean sun. Eyeing him suspiciously as she toted her mop and pail.

"Ya, what're you malingerin' out here for?" she asked, in her high, lilting, ironic voice.

"Never mind, woman," he told her impatiently, but she only snorted.

"What d'ya mean, *me* never mind? I got to mind. You got to come back with me after I do the hall, get breakfast for the children. The cooks ain't in today—"

Standing up to her full height, not more than five feet from the floor in the thin Island sandals she liked to wear in all weather. Bright yellow cloth wrapped defiantly as a flag around her head.

"The cooks didn't come in."

"That's what I *said*—"

Yolanda shrugged, crooking her head at him as if she were trying to figure out the angle of some corner confidence man.

"And the other women—"

"I'm the only one. Why'd ya think I asked you? No cooks, no teachers—nobody come in today. It's just you, me, Old Bert, an' the Misses. Bert's out mindin' the children right now, I got to clean—"

Billy turned away from her, looking in supplication to the green-curtained office. *Now he would never get his money. They would never let him go, not with the rest of the staff out*—

The office door opened, and Miss Shotwell and Miss Murray came out. Erect and grey as ever, the grey in their eyes and their hair and even in their long, straight, faded-purple dresses. A police captain followed them out, bowing apologetically. Broad, red Irish face looking down and away toward the floor as he made his way out.

Billy went up to them as soon as the captain had left, though he could see they barely noticed him, their own faces grim and distracted.

"'Scuse me, Misses, but I got to ask you about my wages," he began. "You see, my wife is sick. She needs a doctor—"

Miss Shotwell turned her gaze fully upon him then for the first time. Her hard, grey eyes filled now with real concern and even pity—so much so that he knew what she was going to say and he hated it.

"Oh, Billy," she told him, in the same soft voice she used for the orphans. For those orphans who had parents, to tell them that they would not be coming this month and they would have to stay over again.

"Oh, Billy, perhaps we can send a message down. There are doctors I know who will see her for free, though I do not know if they will go out today—"

"I don't need it for free," he told her, trying to speak slowly and respectfully, and keep the rising exasperation out of his voice. "If I can get my wages, I can pay 'im myself. I just need to get back down there—"

"But that's impossible."

He saw then, too, a glint of fear in her hard eyes. Then she looked away—down the hall and out toward where the children were still playing.

"No one should be out today," she said urgently. "The police say there are already men in the streets."

"I know that, Miss. I know, I saw 'em, but I got to get back, she's sick—"

Knowing already it wouldn't do any good—

"I am afraid we could not pay you, in any event. The messengers have not come from the bank with the payroll. I doubt very much if they will come today."

Six dollars. Surely you must have six dollars here, somewhere. The pink russet color of the brandy, three quarters full—

"It's out of the question," Miss Murray cut in, sounding exasperated. "We have two hundred and thirty-seven children to take care of—children of your own race! None of the staff came in today, none of the teachers!"

"They're my race all right, but they ain't my children," he told them as bluntly as he dared. But neither lady was listening anymore.

"Maybe we should move them."

Miss Shotwell was thinking out loud.

"Maybe we should move them. Right now."

"Oh, Anna. And take them where?"

"The police cannot spare anyone. You heard what the captain said."

"But where?"

"Take them up to the park, maybe. Into the trees."

"How would we keep them together? How would we *get* them there?"

Billy found himself looking at Yolanda while they argued, her eyes narrowed into wary slits. Thinking, he was sure, what he himself was thinking—that it would all come down to them. *I and I.* Bert, out in the yard, was a grizzled old man who walked with a limp, barely spoke at all—

"It's just us," he said to himself. "Just us."

He went, then, leaving the Misses still arguing in the hall. He walked rapidly back down the halls to the grand entrance under the portico and pillars, with only Yolanda's plaint pursuing him.

"Where're you goin'? Where you goin', you get *back* here—"

He went out through the front door, thinking one thing: *To get back downtown.* Get back to his family, even without his wages, and see if they couldn't do *something.*

Never should've left. A mistake, another mistake.

He went out into the door yard—but stopped well before he got to the iron picket fence, falling back into the shadows of one of the giant, bent willows.

Fifth Avenue was already full of white men. All of them streaming uptown—cutting him off. Carrying crude pieces of wood, pulled out of the trash heaps on every corner, or torn off of fences. The cruder words cut or burned into them, with knives and matches. *No Draft* and *No Draft No Niggers No War* and *No Niggers.* Their eyes hard and unforgiving, and yet also full of dreadful anticipation.

Oh, to be invisible. To be a shade, moving over water—

He shrank back behind the trees, stumbled into the asylum where he could hear the Misses still arguing, Yolanda still calling after him. He had to get back. But it was impossible, now. He stumbled back, into the orphanage, thinking again of the pink-russet color in the brandy bottle, three quarters full. Thinking of the iodine.

30

HERBERT WILLIS ROBINSON

King Mob.

The charivari is fully under way. Unchecked, the mob forces its way back downtown—still baying and shouting, banging on its pots and pans. There is a new sound now, thousands of running feet, as more and more men, women, and children come running from all over the City to join us.

They spread out over the blocks and avenues, weaving back and forth to the East River, then over to the Fifth Avenue, and Broadway. Looting whatever they can, especially saloons and jewelry stores. They sack the old Bull's Head Inn, and the Croton Cottage, and even the Palace Park Hotel. Smashing in the plate-glass windows and running out with bottles of port and champagne in their arms, clutching thick handfuls of Havana cigars.

It is a little game they play. The cry goes up that the draft records have been hidden in this hotel, or that house, and they force their way inside. There they hurl everything they can out the windows— papers, mattresses, whole desks, sheets and bedding billowing up like sails as they fall. Once it is in the streets, they turn it all into a bonfire. They even switch on the gas pipes, set fire to the green store awnings out front.

Hardware stores are a particular favorite, for it is there they can find guns. Remarkably, some of these even open up for the mobs. I watch as one enterprising merchant in Fortieth Street moves his whole inventory of firearms, keeping his Colt leveled on the mob with one hand while he takes the customers' money with the other. He sells them everything, right down to his stock of black-market army grenades. Then, once the mob is fully armed, they train their new guns back on him, force him to hand over all the money he has just made, along with his watch and boots.

Soon they begin to loot the better houses along Lexington and the Fifth Avenue. Always spurred on by some cry that they belong to Republicans, or abolitionists—that they are owned by Greeley himself. On Forty-fifth Street, I watch them attack a pair of three-story townhouses. Even as they smash in the front door and windows, a covey of women and children go running out the back, flushed from their home like so many quail. They hurry across the yard, the women lifting the children over the back fence, then vaulting over it themselves as best they can in their long skirts and corsets, running on downtown.

The mob lets them go. They are too busy throwing everything they can out the windows—books and plateware and silver; carpets and oilcloths; chairs and mirrors and tables, even the drapes and the tablecloths.

"It's Washington! For God's sake, don't burn Washington!"

Some drunken bummer stumbles out of the next house, clutching to his chest a fine oil painting of our Founding Father. A second thug pursues him with a razor, trying to cut the portrait out of its frame so he can steal or burn it, but the other looters chase him off and set the portrait reverently against a street lamp. There the mob gleefully takes up the drunk's imprecation:

"For God's sake, don't burn Washington!"

The portrait remains against the street lamp, while they finish sacking and torching every other house on the block. When they are done the drunk carries it off—another icon to lead their host. Behind them, the townhouses are left burning and desolate—doors and roofs caved in, their window eyes put out.

Where are the police?

Maddy was right, they would not come, not even to protect the homes of the richest and most prominent citizens of the City. Not that they spare the homes of the poor, or the middle classes. I follow them into a new tenement, off the Second Avenue, where they bang on the stairs with their homemade clubs, laughing and shouting.

"Turn out, turn out!"

"Turn out or we'll burn you out, goddamn you!"

They pull the terrified families out of their homes, and rifle through what little they have. An old woman begs them to let her keep a watch her mother gave her, her only possession. They push her aside, take it anyway. Another, younger woman tries to face them down, standing outside her apartment door.

"Damn you, get out of the way!"

They slap and beat her, then toss her over the third-floor railing. She hits the banister, and lies moaning helplessly in the first-floor hallway. A couple of her neighbors drag her outside to safety, before the mob sets the house on fire.

The looters stagger back out, still laughing. Their arms full of whatever they can find—bedclothes and linens, bundles of clothes. Most of it so obviously old, so threadbare and worthless they simply throw it on the ground, start up another bonfire. A man from the tenement, balding and bowlegged, skips around the flames, gingerly trying to pull out his meager possessions. The mob seizes and beats him, too. Yelling wildly—*"Throw him in the fire!"*—before he is just able to run off with his life.

I try to look into the faces of the men who would do such things, stealing glances at them as inconspicuously as possible.

But there is nothing. That is the damning thing. There is no demonic cruelty, nothing in their faces to reveal the sort of cruelty they are capable of. They look only mildly amused, mildly drunk as they go about their business. No more entertained than they would be at a bull-baiting, or a game of base-ball.

I can barely stand to watch them, even though there is a horrible fascination to it all, like watching an omnibus crash in the streets, a steamboat wreck out on the Hudson. But what else can I do? I don't have Raymond's pistol anymore. I try to search out some help, some relief somewhere. But even the nearest precinct house is locked and deserted, the Metropolitans off fighting the riot on another block—I hope. I wander back, helpless. My words to Father Knapp now like a curse in my head: *I watch and I tell.*

The sky above is a completely corrupted yellow now, the air thick and dank as bile. *When will it rain?*

The mob begins to look for new targets, all out of houses for the time being. They find one in the Fifth Avenue at Forty-third Street—the Colored Orphans' Asylum. The only wonder is that it has taken them this long. They rush up the plantation-house steps, smashing in the front doors—no longer merely clamoring for loot now.

There is no sign of the orphans themselves. *Could it be that they have escaped? But how, and where would they go—now, in this City?*

Soon a thin trail of smoke begins to rise from the upper windows of the building. If any of them are still inside, they will surely be trapped, burned and smoked to death, if the mob doesn't find them first.

Where are Kennedy's damned police?

Instead there is the sound of another fire bell, the laddies rolling an engine into the grounds and right up to the steps of the orphanage.

"Make way, make way!"

I wonder what fresh mischief this can be. But it is only the Honey Bee company again, one of the oldest and fastest fire companies in the City. The familiar gold-plated hive swinging between its brakes. John Decker, the chief engineer of the fire department is with them, and he pleads for the crowd to stand back and let them put out the fire.

"They're all gone, all gone inside!" he cries out, and I can only pray it is true. "The wee children're all gone, let us put out the fire before ye burn the whole City down!"

By now, though, the mob is not even willing to listen. Decker is slugged at once, and they chase off the rest of the Honey Bee—turning over their fine engine and pulling it to pieces. Many of them treating even this—even the burning of the orphanage—as one more great lark. I spot a little girl, no more than ten, hopping and skipping through the smoke, playing her games under the shadow of the burning building as obliviously as if she were playing hopscotch back on her street.

"There she goes!"

A plume of flame bursts through one of the upper windows. There is a great cheer, and the crowd rushes the offending building as one person—ripping off its wood paneling, hacking at it with axes and hatchets and knives, even tearing it apart with their bare hands. From the upper stories more of the looters throw down the pitiful possessions of the orphans—tiny white dresses and trousers, a few scattered photographs and other keepsakes. All thrown in the fire.

"Look out, look out!"

The cry from above is too late. A whole chest of drawers comes hurtling down, and there is a terrible scream. It has fallen on the little Irish girl that I just saw, skipping and dancing around the fire. Men hurry to pull it off her, but it's too late, the girl dies gasping in agony. The rest of the mob tearing at the orphanage all the more furiously, as if it is to blame. Shouting, as they do, "*Revenge! Revenge!*"

· 31 *·*

BILLY DOVE

"*They're here,*" he told the Misses. Standing uneasily in the door of their office, hat in hands. Barely daring to breathe the words.

"What?" Miss Shotwell said, still uncomprehending, rising from her desk as if affronted.

"They're here, Misses. The mob. I just seen 'em out in the Fifth Avenue."

"They're out there *now?*"

"Goin' by. Most of them looked like they were headed uptown."

"Well, then," Miss Murray said, relieved.

"We still have to *go,* Misses. We got to get the children out," he told them, as forcefully as he thought he could.

"But if the mob is only moving past—"

"They'll be here again, soon enough."

"But *how?*" Miss Shotwell asked, her voice fluttering slightly, though he could tell she was making a great effort to speak calmly and slowly.

"If the mob is out on the street, how do we move the children?"

"I don't know, Misses. But we got to."

"Perhaps if we simply sit quietly, close up the gate and the front doors," Miss Murray tried. "Shut the window, so it looks as if nobody is here—"

"And if they still come then, Misses, what do we do?" he tried again. "If they try to burn the place, what do we do?"

Both women were quiet then, concentrating. Having absorbed the worst, trying now in their practical Yankee manner to think what had to be done next.

"Mr. Dove," Miss Shotwell said, very formally, the way she preferred to talk when she was giving out serious orders. "Mr. Dove, go up to the cupola, please, and see if you can make out where the mob is headed now. Before you go, kindly have Bert and Yolanda bring the children in from the yard. Miss Murray and I will assist them."

"Yes, Miss."

But we still have to go, he thought, taking long, rapid strides down the hall. Thinking of the peach brandy again as he went past the kitchen. But he kept moving—going to the back stairs and climbing them rapidly, three at a time with his big stride.

He was glad for the chance to move freely, at least. Feeling the spring in his legs, despite how hot it was. The heat made him feel loose, and resilient again, like a good piece of wood. He never minded it, not like the Yankee ladies, or Ruth, who all but wilted in it.

Ruth. The thought flickered across his mind like the shadow of a bird. He had to get back, but how?

There was nothing for it but to see where the mob was. He kept climbing, past the sleeping halls on the third floor. Looking in at all the small, iron bedsteads, lined up in perfect rows. Each one made up straight and neat as a pin, the children responsible for keeping the spaces around their own beds. It was easy enough, most of them with no more to their name than the clothes on their backs and a few pretty ribbons, some curio picked up off the street. Maybe a daguerreotype, or a photograph of their mother or father, if they were very lucky.

He went on up through the attic, then pushed open the trapdoor and crawled up into the cupola. It was barely high enough for him to crouch in—musky and stifling, and full of dead flies. He dropped to his knees and wiped the thick dust from the panes, looking out over the Fifth Avenue.

There were thousands of them now. Still moving uptown, all right—most of them wandering north, then east, toward the Third Avenue.

But why? What was there?

It came to him slowly, through remembered patches of conversation—from the talk of white men on the street, or overheard through saloon doors. *It was something that they never understood. How black men and women paid attention to everything they said. How we have to, since our lives depend upon it.*

They were going to stop the draft, that was the talk. That must be where they were gathering, at the Provost Marshal's office. They were going to stop it, and break the wheel, and burn all their names. If they succeeded at it, Billy knew, they would run wild, doing whatever they pleased. And if they didn't—they would take it out on whatever they could find.

That will be us. A house full of defenseless black children.

His house. He thought again of Ruth and the children, waiting for him back in Paradise Alley. *And what were they supposed to do?* Waiting for him with a mob loose in the streets—with Johnny Dolan somewhere in the City.

Ruth would not leave without him, he knew. They would wait for him, no matter what. *But how to get back?* He would be lucky if he lasted ten blocks, even taking the back lots, and dodging in and out of alleys.

And even if he could, what of his responsibilities here?

He twisted around, looking down through the cupola glass at the fenced backyard of the asylum. The Misses and Old Bert had formed the children into neat lines now—boys and girls, all of them lined up two by two. No sound at all drifted up from the yard now. Like all orphans, he knew, they were especially sensitive to the adults around them, attuned to the slightest shift in mood.

There was a commanding clap of hands from one of the Yankee ladies, and the lines of children moved forward at once, into the house. They were good children, obedient and well-trained, but he knew that if the worst happened, Old Bert and Yolanda and the Misses could not help them. The Yankee ladies would be swept aside, Old Bert and Yolanda lucky if they weren't lynched themselves—

And what could he do, exactly? If they had to run?

Billy did not know if he could do anything at all—but he slid himself back out of the cupola anyway, moving quickly on down the stairs. The decision all but made for him. He couldn't get back to his own home, not through these mobs. *Better at least to try to do something here than to be run down on the street like a dog.*

Besides, it was the orphans who had saved him. He had to admit that, much as he had always hated the work. It was the orphans who had gotten him a steady job, and kept the weakness from overwhelming him.

He had come to it by chance. Wandering far uptown one afternoon, after another morning spent scrounging for what errands and day work he could get around the docks. When he could no longer bring himself, even drunk, to dance for another fish or eel. He got what work there was to be had draining the dregs from the tavern barrels for the bucketshops, or mucking out cattle barges, or running messages when no white boy above the age of six was available. Standing on the Coenties Slip with all the other black men who would not stoop to dance, holding out their hands in silent supplication.

And we were the proud ones.

He had started to walk uptown, thinking to walk all the way off this damned island, if he could. He had walked and walked, vowing not to quit until he had found some rail bridge, or some ford he could swim or wade.

Instead, past the end of all the rail tracks and the omnibus lines— past all the mean-looking Irish shantytowns, and the stills and the rendering yards, hidden away amid the trees—he had come upon a whole town, full of free black men and women.

It was the place he had always known must exist, ever since he had stolen off with himself in his little boat. It was only two neatly raked dirt streets, with crude, square, whitewashed houses, and vegetable patches on each side, and a church at the head of each street. But everywhere he looked there were men and women of his own color— nodding their hellos, and regarding him without surprise or apprehension, a black man in a black town.

They called the place Seneca Village, and he discovered that it was made up mostly of escaped slaves, though there were also some old Negro families from the City, and a few whites, and half-Indians who had married in. He had soon discovered, too, that they still had to work in the white City, or scrape out a living on its edges. There was no black shipyard, no shop he could work in.

Free but not free—but still he stayed on. Boarding with one family or another as they would have him. With scarcely a word exchanged for his board, no money or anything else expected, though he would go out and chop wood for their fire, or till the vegetables for them. Doing what carpentry he could, though most of the village didn't need anyone with his ability in order to bang together their own rude shacks and houses.

Instead he mostly occupied himself with putting up his own house. He had marked off a half-acre lot from the woods, and borrowed what tools he could to chop down the thin, tough trees, and dig out the stumps and roots. Their wood was no good for building with, but he had gone deeper into the woods, to cut down the biggest pine and oak he could find, and trim them into boards.

It was slow going, working with the poor saws and hatchets and axes he was able to procure, but he didn't mind. He took his time at it, delighted to do real work again—and even better, to work for himself. Working the way *he* wanted to—carefully, precisely shaving and chinking every board. Asking for help only in putting up the roof and then covering that himself, with shingles he shaped and cut out, one by one. Until when he was finished, looking over his little house, he could say that this, at least, was his own.

It was the Reverend Betancourt who had put him into the job at the orphans' asylum. Coming to visit one Sunday afternoon, after spitting out another one of his furious, uncompromising sermons from the pulpit of the All Angels Church. Stumping silently all around Billy's new house on his short legs, before confronting him directly.

"What kind of man is it, builds a house before he has work?" the minister had asked—glowering at him until Billy shrugged and looked away.

"A man who plans to stay, that's who!" the minister answered himself. "If you're going to stay, you need a way to make a living!"

He had taken him over to the orphans' then. Ushering him into the Asylum—the biggest building he had ever set foot in before, smelling then as always of boiled soap, and starch, and fresh whitewash. He had introduced him to the abolitionist Yankee ladies, already starting to go grey. Miss Shotwell, the taller one, formally shaking his hand and calling him mister—the first time any white woman had ever done such a thing.

"It's a good job for a man who can use his hands," the Reverend Betancourt had told him. "A good job for a man who likes to build things."

But in fact it was mostly nursemaid work. Minding the children as they played outside. Helping the cooks to fetch meals and clean up afterward. Cutting and hauling wood for the fires, and water from the well, and putting the orphans to bed at night in their dormitory rooms.

He had accepted it, at first telling himself that it was steady wages—that it would do until he could find a real position, somewhere in the shipyards. He had stopped spending any money on the drink, using every penny of his wages, beyond the barest necessities of food and clothing, to buy new tools of his own, like a real workingman. Preparing himself for the day when he would find a position in the shipyards.

Yet even as he did so, he had begun to understand that that time would never come. That there would be no job for him along the waterfront, or in any other profession in the whole City that paid a white man's wage. That there was no place where, the moment he walked on the premises, the white men there would not simply put down their tools and fold their arms, waiting for him to leave.

He had kept the job at the Asylum. Wiping the children's noses, and pulling their blankets back over them. Sweeping and raking out the yard every evening, cutting crude, square bats from the scrub pine for their games of base-ball. Doing whatever he was asked to do.

But he had given up buying new tools with his wages. He had tried going back to the few saloons he could find that would tolerate black men, but they were a long ways away now, and they changed all the time. The whole City was like quicksand for a man of color, shifting constantly beneath him.

He tried to buy himself a bottle of real whiskey—but drinking alone, he only became obsessed with the bottle itself. Watching it carefully as it slowly diminished from three quarters full—down to a half—then to a third. Taking another drink—and assuring himself that it was still mostly full, that there was still plenty left for him. And so on, down and down, until he could stand it no longer, and drained the last drop with a bitter sob.

He preferred to go out, to where he could at least talk to someone. Looking for the stills, up in the wilderness of brush and old trees just to the north of Seneca Village—even though he knew he was taking a great risk, with all the slavecatchers who loitered constantly around the outskirts of the village. He had seen them from a distance—lean, restless men. They prowled around with manacles and whips on their belts, would steal a black man right off the road in broad daylight if they could get away with it.

The men who ran the stills were dangerous enough. Billy sought them out by the smell of the wood, the burning sugar. Making sure to move slowly and loudly into whatever thicket they were holed up in. There would always be two of them, standing over the pot. One of them stirring it slowly, the other standing by him, sure enough, with his hand on a rifle. Watching Billy balefully as he walked into the clearing, already holding out a coin in his hand.

They would take it, all right—still without a word—and hand him a battered tin cup of whatever they were brewing. Billy would drink it there, slowly taking swallows from the sweet, new, warm liquor. Squatting in the clearing, talking quietly with the other men, black and white, around the still. Exchanging hard-luck stories of how they couldn't find work. Repeating his own plans, when he got drunk enough, to go out West, maybe even to San Francisco, where it would surely be easier for a man to get real work—to do something besides wipe the noses and the arses of abandoned children.

But he had never gone anywhere save for back toward his cabin. Aware of his diminished capacities, and how vulnerable he was. Trying to walk as quietly, as lightly as possible. Looking out for anyone who could be trailing him—a blackbirder, or just a cutpurse, following him from the still.

This whole City, a place of hunting and evasion.

He loped back down the stairs from the cupola, passing the long lines of orphans moving past him, up to their dormitory rooms. They had been instructed by Miss Shotwell to go up and pick out one thing they might want to take with them. *What a useless thing to do, when they had to run for their lives*—but he couldn't blame them. It mattered all the more to them to take something when they had so little.

"I have instructed the children to be prepared to leave."

Miss Shotwell and Miss Murray stood at the foot of the stairs, erect as ever, but the fear in their eyes undisguised now. Yolanda and Old Bert behind them, their faces grim.

"They will assemble back down here, then we will see whether it is necessary to leave the asylum."

"*If* we can, Misses," Billy said, as gently as possible. "*If* we can."

Even from where they stood, inside the building, they could hear the rising noise of the crowd, somewhere to the east. He went around with Yolanda and Old Bert, making sure that all the doors were bolted and the windows were shuttered, until they were dripping with sweat inside the airless, sweltering building. *For all the good it would do against a mob—*

The children filed dutifully back down to the first floor. The older ones guiding the very young, holding them by the hand. Lining up again in the dining hall, as the Yankee ladies indicated. Dressed in their bulky traveling jackets and knee pants; the girls in their long, fanned skirts. Alert for their next instruction, each of them clutching the one small possession they valued the most.

Not more than one in three was literally an orphan, Billy knew. They were the children of workingmen and women who had died from the cholera, or the consumption, or who had simply fallen over one day from exhaustion. But they were, as well, the children of whores, and of pickpockets and vagrants, their mothers now in the workhouse on Blackwell's Island. The sons and daughters of maids, and the young masters of their houses. Children who had been found abandoned on the streets, or whose parents simply no longer had the means to feed them. There were even a few who had made it up from the South on their own. Running with some larger group from a plantation splitting up when the adults had been killed or recaptured, but still going on. Miraculously washing up, half-starved and spooked and silent, in this City.

These were likely to be their best years. He knew that, too. It was almost cruel, he thought, how they were being educated now— taught their manners, and how to read and write, and to figure. Trained in some useful skill or another before they were returned to their parents after a few years, or were apprenticed out to work as domestic servants and farmhands—most of them—once they turned twelve years of age.

But there were precious few homes in the City now, even among Republicans, that would hire black servants. Even fewer farms in upper Manhattan, or Long Island, that would take on a colored hand. Those that did were usually looking for someone they could pay next to nothing, and treat as they liked. They were unlikely ever to have something like this again, a place where they would be assured of enough to eat and a warm room to sleep in, and people who cared about what happened to them.

And my children? Billy tried to picture them here, moving up and down the stairs in accordance with the asylum bells. Walking silent and solemn, sitting where they were told. Until they were pushed back out into the City—

Especially the boy, Milton. He would be bored here, seeing how well he read and thought already—much as he would like helping with the younger children, taking on some responsibility.

He was something fine—Billy knew it, though that only made him go harder on the boy. Trying anything he could to toughen him up, make him a man as soon as he could. This was a City that hated fine things, it liked to grind them down and break them to pieces, the finer and darker they were, the better—

The children waited, sweating in the dining hall, for their instructions. Billy waiting with them, trying to ease their minds as much as he could while the Yankee ladies talked over what they should do, where they should run to.

"We're just taking a little trip, a little walk up to the woods—"

He tried to make it sound as if they were only going on a picnic up to the new park, or one of the other rare excursions they got to take. But he knew he wasn't fooling any of them. They gazed back at him, as serious and quiet as deacons. Listening to the sounds of the mob, growing steadily closer now—

"But where *can* we go? Which way is safe?" he could hear Miss Murray whispering too loudly behind him.

There was the sound of fire bells, and what seemed like cheers, very close.

"Mr. Dove—please—see what that is," Miss Shotwell asked him, but he was already moving down the hall to the front, and folding back one of the window shutters.

There was precious little he could see from there, looking out on the Fifth Avenue. A few white men running, the shouting louder than ever. Soon, though, he could smell something through the heavy summer air.

Fire. They had already set it going—

A soldier came stumbling down the Fifth Avenue. Then another, and another. A few of them dragging their muskets by the barrel, the rest empty-handed. An officer futilely waving a sword about. Some of them staggering, bleeding from the head, helped along by their comrades. All of them moving as fast they could down the avenue, glancing fearfully behind them.

So—the soldiers were routed already. And now the mob would be coming. Looking out for something else to wreck, someone else to chase.

He went back to tell the Yankee ladies what he had seen, whispering the news to them. They took it with a show of calm before the children, but he could see the desperation on their faces. What *were* they to do now? They should head south, he supposed, toward lower Manhattan, but that would only be walking them right into whole wards full of drunken Paddy workingmen—

There was a loud rapping at the front door. Billy and the Yankee ladies looked at each other—all of them plainly wondering if this was it, if they could be here already. Slowly, Billy started down the hall again.

"That's all right, Mr. Dove. I'll go," Miss Shotwell said hurriedly, starting after him—but he would not let her.

"No, Miss. That's all right." He paused, trying to find the right words. "Now, you know enough to *move* with those children, if you don't see me come back. Go south, and west, I guess—as fast as you can!"

He hastened on down the hall, not waiting for an answer. Figuring that at least the bolt on the door would delay them. There would be time enough for him to get back to the ladies and the children, start them out through the backyard. *And then?*

The rapping at the front door persisted. He sidled up toward the window shutter he had opened, trying to stay out of sight. Thinking he could at least see whoever it was before they could see him.

A face popped up before him, so close and sudden he jumped back. It was low to the ground, where he didn't expect to see it—a terrible sort of goblin face, wide and grinning and smeared with blood and soot. The face of—*a boy,* he saw now. A young white boy, tapping just as insistently at the window as he had at the door. Before Billy had really thought about it, he had the door open, letting the child in, assuming he must be in some sort of trouble himself. But the boy had only stood there, still grinning at him.

"They're comin' to burn ya out," he said. "They done burned down the draft office, an' broke the wheel. Now they're comin' to burn ya out here."

"When?" Billy asked, squatting down.

The boy just standing there, at his ease, like some terrible messenger bird. *And where had he gotten that blood on his face? And the ashes?*

"Anytime, I figure. Soon's they finish burnin' the block. They're already talkin' about it, sayin' let's go over an' burn the nigger orphans."

"How will they come? Do you know? Down the Fifth Avenue?"

"Sure. An' the Fourth Avenue—any way they can, I guess."

"Uh-huh."

That decided it. They would have to leave now, head south and just hope they could outrun the mob.

"I know a way past 'em," the boy said, matter-of-factly.

"What?"

"Over to the Twentieth Precinct house. I can take youse there."

Billy looked at the child closely, wondering if he could be part of some trap. But he seemed completely at his ease—and besides, they would not need a trap.

"The Twentieth is uptown," Billy quizzed him. "How do we get up *there?* Past the mob?"

"Through the back lots," the boy told him. "It's easy—if you know how."

The back lots. Anything that might keep them off the streets, as out of sight as possible. That way, even if they were found out, the children would have a chance to run for it, hide themselves away in cellars and coal chutes and outhouses—

He stood up then, listening. He could hear what sounded like drunken singing—still a few blocks away, but moving unmistakably closer.

"All right," Billy said, putting his arm around the boy's shoulders and leading him back down the hall. "All right, we'll try it your way."

They started out the back door of the Orphans' Asylum, once again in perfect formation. Two lines, girls in one, boys in the other. The older children carrying the smallest ones on their backs.

The Yankee ladies, Yolanda, and Old Bert each carried one of the younger children themselves—Yolanda puffing and fretting peevishly as she moved—"*That mob's comin' from uptown, I don't see why we're goin' uptown.*" The Misses all but silent with fear, but insistent on bringing up the end, checking for any stragglers.

Billy himself carried two little girls, one in each arm. Walking at the head of the column, to keep up with the white boy who was guiding them. Still unsure of whether to trust or believe him at all, but wanting to at least be in a position to warn the others, if it was a trap.

Also so that he could kill the boy with his bare hands, so help him God he would, if it was a trap—

They moved quickly and quietly through the backyard. One child—a beautiful little Martiniquean girl named Anik—starting to break loudly into a hymn, used to the singing they did whenever they marched anywhere.

> *Then sings my soul*
> *My savior God to me—*

"Stop that now! Stop that noise!"

The other children shushing her before he could. They were fully aware of what was going on, he realized. The sound of the crowd just outside in the Fifth Avenue now—chanting something of their own.

"This way."

The boy grinned up at him, proud to show off his secrets. He unlatched the back, latticed gate, and they marched calmly on out of the back courtyard. As the last child passed through, Billy could hear the mob on the other side of the building, gathering outside the iron gate.

"Wait! Wait! I forgot it!"

At that moment a tiny boy they called Tad broke out of line, bursting back through the gate and into the asylum before Billy could stop him. He had no choice but to hand the two girls off to Old Bert. Yolanda cursed a blue streak at him, but he told them to go on and he would catch up to them—racing back into the house after Tad, swearing under his breath the whole way.

Billy followed the boy up the stairs, toward the dormitory. There he found him, by his bed, pawing through an old cigar box until he found what he was looking for. *A horse.* The tiny, tin figure of a horse.

A small ring attached to its back, part of a key chain once—maybe something that had once belonged to his father or mother. He held it up triumphantly—but Billy was already on him, swinging him up from the floor.

"Is that it? Is that what you want?"

Might as well be sure now.

"Yes," Tad breathed, and Billy scooped him into his arms, rushing him back toward the stairs.

There was the sound of glass breaking, somewhere very close, and despite himself he flinched, and looked out the window into the front yard. There was the mob. White men and women, and children, too, filling up the front yard like a puddle of grease. Some already hurling bricks and dug-up paving stones at the front of the Asylum, others pulling and pushing down the iron fence out front. More of them hurrying down the Fifth Avenue, even as he watched. Whooping and laughing, and chanting something—something incomprehensible at first, that slowly became clearer to him:

"Burn the niggers' nest! Burn the niggers' nest! Burn the niggers' nest!"

Some men came striding up to the front door, crowbars and mechanics' wrenches in hand. Then he was flying—back down the stairs, to the first floor, just praying that no one had slipped around to the back door already. *They hadn't—thank God for that at least.* He went through the back gate in an instant—pausing to latch it, even so. Trying to keep from doing anything that might give them ideas, point them in a direction.

He ran on up the back lot, up the alley where the others had gone. Orphans quickly coming into view before him—Billy relieved, and fearful at the same time that they had gone only so far. Tad gazing happily on his talisman, the tiny horse, in his hands. Seemingly oblivious to the growing chant behind them.

"Burn the niggers' nest! Burn the niggers' nest!"

32

RUTH

Noon. She was sure now, he wasn't coming. All she could hope was that he wasn't stuck in a barroom somewhere.

They would get him there. Surely he would know, even with the creature in him, that they would get him in such a place.

But where else could he be? Would the Orphans' Asylum be any better? Would anyplace in the City?

She felt a new lump of fear in her throat, but fought it down. Billy had been through worse. He was smart and resourceful, except when he had had one too many, and there were alleys and back alleys, culverts and back privvies; roofs and cellars, the rear doors of saloons and stores and stables. A thousand hidey holes, for a man run to ground like some kind of game. Billy would find one of them, she was sure of it, she had to be.

She tried to get her mind off it, to fight down the impulse that seized her sometimes like a pair of choking hands, to just grab the children and bolt. Instead, she joined Milton for a few minutes, playing with the younger children. He had improvised some sort of card game, made up from bills of handling, and labels that he liked to soak off empty crates he found in the streets. She found herself staring at their pretty lettering and pictures. The scenes of half-naked women and tropical lands, that tomatoes and bananas and rice came from. The faces of somber, bearded merchants, advertising the integrity of their goods by the seriousness of their own cloaked faces.

The game itself was too complicated for her, though the other children seemed to understand it easily enough. She smiled, watching them at their play. Pleased at the thought: *Five children, and each one smarter than she was.*

They would know better than she had how to get out of a trap. How to get off an island when everything went to hell—

Milton passed out the bills and labels again. She tried to follow his system: blue beat green, green beat red, red beat plain black and white. But it was the distance of the destinations listed on the bills that were trump: Troy over Yonkers, Hartford over Elizabeth. One bill he had found from San Francisco, over everything

"How far away is it?" she asked Milton.

"That's thousands of miles," he told her. "Thousands of miles, maybe three, four thousand—"

She already knew—wanting to reassure herself. *But what does it matter? He came thousands of miles once, he could do it just as easily again—*

She got up and moved away from the table. The other children happily playing still—Milton following her with his eyes, she knew. It was impossible to hide anything from him completely. She walked over to the window again, looking out, over the wooden shutters. The street wholly deserted now, not so much as a pig abroad. They were smart creatures, would get off the street when they sensed a storm coming, or some other trouble. *Smarter than her.*

She moved back from the window, back toward her children. Glad, then, for one thing. Watching them all, so intent over their game, Milton presiding so sternly over them. *Glad that he didn't know about then—that none of them knew who she had been before, and what she had done.*

33

THE YEAR OF SLAUGHTER

I went with him. I didn't want him to leave me behind. I didn't know how I would live if he did and that was my sin, I wanted to live still—

Along the road Johnny Dolan kept the box wrapped up tight. But at night now they made their camp as far from the highway as they could, and he would open it up, and stare at it until the light faded.

There was everything inside, behind the glass. There were tiny mirrors and gemstones, glued to the back, so the whole size and shape of the thing seemed to shift, every time they looked inside. And they could always find something new. There were the embryos of small animals, and insects floating in jars, and feathers of strange birds, and the bones of the saints. There were miniature charts of the seas, and the constellations, and the compass of the navigator, and the tools of the apothecary, and of the barber and the surgeon—

At first Dolan hadn't wanted to look at it at all. He had kept it wrapped up, as if his looking at it too much would diminish it. Warning her not to let it come uncovered, not to say a thing about it.

"That's our passage off this island," he liked to tell her as they moved up to Dublin. "That's *not starving*, right there."

But then one night he began to look, and after that he would look until the sun went down, and even longer, keeping the fire going even when it meant scavenging for wood for an extra hour. Dolan didn't seem to care—and she was just as glad herself. He stayed off her now, at least most nights. Looking at that thing, and wondering over it afterward.

"An' what d'ya think *that* is, back there? What d'ya think that does?" he would ask as they peered in together by the glow of the fire. Begrudging her even having a look at first, still fearful she would use it up—but preferring to have an audience, for all his speculations.

"D'ya think we can see everything in there? D'ya think we can see everything there is?"

The people moving along the roads were a river now, flowing faster and faster toward Dublin. The families hauling all they owned in carts and barrows. The grim faced men with their spades and their hoes, carrying the tools of their trades, though there was no work anywhere.

There were bodies everywhere. Lying out in the fields, and fallen in the doorways of their cabins. Bodies lying by the road, their mouths rictured open and green inside, from trying to eat the grass and the nettles.

They only glanced down, and moved on. Stopping for nothing, now, not even to look in the cabinet. The fear growing more palpable, more frantic the closer they got to the city. Ruth watched a woman as she dragged the naked corpse of her daughter out of her *scalpeen*. She was nearly as big as the woman herself, but she dragged her out by her heel—covering the body with rocks, out in front of her *scalp*, then crawling back in under its tumbled walls again.

I turned to Dolan, wantin' to see if he had seen, to see what he thought. But his face was only set ahead, toward the road before us.

Once they reached Dublin they kept to themselves, Dolan making more certain than ever that the black dropcloth stayed tightly wrapped around their treasure. Even he was unnerved by the size of the place, the crowds along the streets and the quickness and verve of the people. It was the first town they had seen where food was still displayed in the shop windows—chickens and pigs and chains of sausages hung from the butchers' hooks, fine cakes and tarts in the bakers' trays. The houses still gracious and bright along their avenues, painted in brilliant light blues and yellows.

Down the alleyways, though, they spied heaps of mud and garbage, and the bodies of men and women—dead or alive still, they could not tell. Children stood on every street corner, holding out the skin that sagged from their arms in order to demonstrate their hunger. The hair had fallen out of their heads, but a downy fuzz had grown in along their cheeks and foreheads, so that they looked like monkeys. Muttering their pleas like a benediction and response:

"*Ta sinn ocrach*"—"We are hungry."

"*Tha shein ukrosh*"—"Indeed, the hunger—"

Dolan rented a room, in a sailor's boardinghouse along the Liffey docks, and at his insistence they took turns, standing guard over the box. Rarely leaving the room at all, the city unlit and even more threatening at night.

Yet everywhere they looked in the day, there were signs, directions, advertisements. Shop placards banged and fluttered above their heads—giant boots and hats, kettles and pigs. Abandoned storefronts were pasted with rail tables and patent-medicine advertisements; auction bills, and legal notices from the Poor Law Commissions, and whole sheets from the penny journals, their columns blazing with descending headlines. Clusters of men perusing them, chewing over what they might mean, if anything:

THE LIBERATOR IN ROME!
DANIEL O'CONNELL TO MEET WITH HIS EMINENCE; GRAND
SCHEME TO FEED THE NATION!
His Grace Promises to Aid His Flock in Holy Ireland, Savior of the Church!
O'Connell Said to Be Restored by His Audience with the Holy Father

Dolan read them all, the patent-medicine stories and the bills of attainder, and the penny dreadfuls, as if they could provide some idea of what they should do next, or where they should go. But most of all he preferred to look in the box again—sitting up in their room and staring at all the wonders behind the glass.

Finally, one afternoon, he had her take it with them, down to the *gombeen* man. They had hauled it in, and set it down on his counter, and Dolan had asked the man for ten pounds, right off.

The *gombeen* man just laughed at them at first. A fat little pawnbroker named Murphy, with a shop in Thomas Street that was filled to the ceiling with things snatched for nothing. There were tea sets and kettles and plates, watches and watch fobs, mandolins and zithers and banjos hanging on strings from the ceiling. All raked in from those desperate enough for the head money. The good wedding linen, and the thick quilts, and the lovely brooches and cameos and hair combs, and all the other possessions saved and hoarded over a lifetime—over three lifetimes—now come to hang up in a Dublin pawnshop for anyone who cared to pick them over.

"Look at this here!" Murphy laughed, pointing at all he had. "And not one of 'em will get you ten pounds. Nothing in this world is worth ten pounds!"

Dolan, to her surprise, did not lose his temper. Instead, all he said was, *We'll see*, and threw back the curtain on the cabinet of wonders. And when he did even the *gombeen* man had to gasp.

"It's all here!" he muttered, his eyes flicking back and forth over it. "It's all here!"

Dolan pointed out everything to him—as if it needed any explication. All of the little mirrors, and the fine paintings. All the hidden corners, and labyrinthine tricks they had discovered on the road—the hidden compass, or the surgeon's knife; the phrenologist's chart, and the graphic illustrations of the one hundred and forty-four ways of Hindoo love, and the hidden compartments that sprang open to reveal a music-box dancer, or a desiccated orange, or the skeleton of a toad. The *gombeen* man's breath coming in short rasps as he looked it over, repeating his same, awed cry.

"It's *all* here!"

After that he caught himself enough to turn them down—but even Ruth could see, with her simple country eyes, that Dolan had the hook in him.

He only thanked the man, and left. Acting as if he didn't mind at all, though they were in fact close to starving again by then—the last of the pennies Dolan had pulled from the studiolo man's pockets gone to pay for the room.

But sure enough, when they brought it back the next day, Murphy had leaped down from the stool by his ledgers, as if he had been waiting for nothing else—nothing from the whole world that came to his door.

"Five pounds!" he cried. "Not a shilling more. I hate to offer that much, I swear, I'll have t'carry every junk dealer in Ireland on my back!"

"Ten," Dolan told him.

He lifted up the cloth again, just enough so that the man could see—the jeweled, broken sword handle; the tiny dynamo. The picture of the most beautiful woman in the world in all her nakedness, with her brown eyes like the sea and the ring of fire around her head.

And again he did not buy that day—but Dolan brought it back again the next day, and the day after that, and the day after. Until at last the *gombeen* man put the ten pounds in his hands without another word, and ushered them out of his shop.

"He couldn't stand to lose it again," Dolan said, outside on the street. "He couldn't stand to see it and lose it all those times. No man could."

Dolan made himself wait the rest of the day, and that night, and the day after that—before he broke into the shop through the rear window, and stole it back. That was as long as he could stand it, she knew. And when she asked him if they could not be hung for the theft alone, Dolan shrugged and told her that, after all, the *gombeen* man did have the thing to himself for a day and a night.

Once they had the money, Dolan went out every morning to look over the ships, to kick at their timbers and count the number of water barrels they had onboard. For he had heard all the stories of the boats that had broken down or wrecked or vanished altogether before they reached the St. Lawrence, or New York City—about the *Katie Calhoun*, out of Waterford, which had sunk just outside the harbor with the loss of all hands, in full view of their friends and family still waving from the dock.

Ruth couldn't picture that any of the ships before them would do better, worm-eaten and shabby as they were, their sails patched and repatched. The long, grey wharf rats running freely up and down their lines. But Dolan kept looking until he found a schooner he liked—the *Birmingham*, out of Liverpool—and took her over to book passage.

The broker's office was a narrow triangle, with only a shellacked loaf of bread in the window. Outside, on the wooden sidewalk, two more begging children stood—heads bald, the downy, simian fur creeping across their brows. Unable even to beg, their jaws hanging open so that whenever they tried to say something, their tongues sank into the soft roofs of their mouths.

Inside was a solitary desk, the broker perched behind it on a high stool. He wore a crumpled stovepipe hat on his head, scratching fervently at his well-cropped beard as he worked. They handed over their money and the man began to energetically stamp and scribble away at whole sheafs of paper.

"What's the ship like?" Dolan demanded.

"Don't ya know yourselves? You're the ones who're booking passage on her! Why would ya get on a ship that wasn't no good," the broker drawled—breaking off when he looked at Dolan's face.

"Oh, she's a fine ship, a swift ship! All up to inspection, just like it says in the regulations. There's a gallon of water a day, an' you get a stirabout in the morning. Herring and a whole loaf of bread for supper—just like the one you see in the window."

He pointed at the bread with his pen, and they stared at it covetously—the permanent, varnished loaf, sitting there so temptingly. The broker finished his stamping and pushed the thick packets of paper over the desk to them.

"There's papers. Now all you got to do is go see the medical officer."

There was a line of men and women a block long, winding their way into another narrow storefront next door. But it went quickly—as quickly as the half-starved people could move. The inspection consisting as it did of sticking out their tongues, one after the other, while they filed past the doctor. He looked openly terrified, sitting behind a window cut in the wall, his head held as far back as possible while he stared at their tongues. In the end he stopped no one, signing all their papers though there were people in the line obviously in the last stages of the famine dropsy, or spotted fever.

"Cleared! All cleared to sail!" he shouted at them from his window as they passed—clutching at each other's arms, leaning on each other in their hunger.

"Cleared, oh please God, you're cleared to get out of here!"

Afterward they barely had enough strength left to stagger over to a grocer's and spend their last two pounds on biscuits and salt cod, and lemons and cured beef. Ruth thought they might need the money for New York—but once she saw the food, she could not help herself. She would have wolfed all of it down right there, but that Dolan cuffed her on the back of the neck.

"That's enough then! It's a long trip!"

"But they said there was going to be food on the boat!" she remonstrated with him, remembering the lacquered loaf of bread at the passage broker's.

"Oh, aye," Dolan sneered. "You go ahead an' believe them. I'll be damned if I ever take anyone's word for it again when they say there'll be enough food."

The next morning the docks were so crowded Ruth did not know if they could even force their way through, much less find their boat. There were families and even whole villages filling the wharves, holding drunken, teary American wakes for their sons and daughters. Others tried to force their way up the gangplanks whether they had the passage or not, clutching bags and trunks, tumbling into the water. The teamsters and longshoremen cursing at each other as they loaded the black hulls, their teams neighing and rearing on the cobblestones. Newsboys threading their way in and out of the crowds, shouting out their dueling rumors:

"The Liberator is dead in Genoa! Heart taken on to Rome, his body returned to dear Ireland!"

"O'Connell safe in Padua! Rumors of his death a fraud!"

A few men flipped pennies to the boys, grabbed their broadsheets, and bent over the stories. But these were mostly shipping agents, and other officials of the port—the rest of the crowd pushing on, clutching their few possessions and shoving and tripping each other in their haste to get to the boats.

Dolan pulled her on through and up to the deck of the *Birmingham*— holding up the cabinet while he walked ahead, scowling and kicking at anyone who got in his way. He marched them right to their berth belowdecks, where Ruth thought that it seemed as low and dark as it had been inside the scalp with her family. The whole deck was divided into rows of narrow wooden booths. There was a row of single men's berths up by the bow, another row for the single women by the stern—and in between, only a few inches wider, a row for the married couples and families.

Each of the berths was less than half the width of a horse stall, though like horse stalls, they contained only a single water bucket, and a thin yellow layer of straw along the deck. There were no doors, no curtain. Each berth simply opened onto a narrow aisle that ran the length of the ship, a charred wooden cooking settee squatting in the middle of it like a toad.

"Well," said Dolan, his voice uncharacteristically mild and uncertain. The confidence seeming to seep almost visibly out of him, the idea that he knew what he was doing when he was still kicking ships along the quay.

"Well—it'll have to do," he grunted.

Up on deck it was better. She even felt exhilarated there, looking down on the whole crowded wharf below. There was a wind blowing from the east, and the crew was rushing to catch it, clamoring about in the rigging while the clouds rolled past. And some of the other passengers wept at the rail, and waved to neighbors and family on the dock. But most of them had come to the ship as they had, walking in from the country and leaving their dead behind them.

As the ship moved away from the pier, they tried to shake off their grief with the land, and set up a kitchen racket on the deck. Men brought out their penny whistles and their mouth harps, and then a girl brought an old, blind singer up onto deck. He had a country banjo, and he sat down against a mast and plucked out "Fiddler's Green," then swung into a new song, one that she had heard men singing before in the Liffey bars:

> This ship it sails in half an hour
> To cross the broad Atlantic,
> My friends are standin' on the quay
> With grief and sorrow frantic.
> I'm just about to sail away
> In the good ship Dan O'Leary,
> The anchor's away and the gangway's up
> I'm leavin' Tipperary.

It was a merry reel, when she had heard it in the pubs. But now the old man played it as slow and melancholy, as a lamentation. It was not what they wanted to hear—no one dancing to it, though they tried to keep time with their feet and hands, even Johnny Dolan himself.

> And it's good-bye, Mick, and good-bye, Pat,
> And good-bye, Kate and Mary.
> The anchor's weighed and the gangway's up,
> I'm leavin' Tipperary.
> And now the steam is blowin' up,
> I have no more to say.
> I'm bound for New York City, boys,
> Three thousand miles away.

A few children smiling anyway. Peeking out from around their mothers' skirts and arms. Ruth almost as curious as they were. Thinking only, *How did they do it How did they keep them alive*. The patched white sails fluttering and booming out above them as the ship began to move swiftly down the river now.

"*Daniel O'Connell! Daniel O'Connell, dead and gone!*"

The twanging of the old singer's banjo stopped with the words. Other voices shouting them down.

"He lives! He lives, I tell ye!"

But there was the ship, moving up the river toward them. It looked huge and modern, draped from bow to stern in black pennants and crepe, the *Birmingham* swinging sharply to starboard to get out of her way.

"*Daniel O'Connell!*"

The funeral ship came on, thick clouds puffing steadily from its funnel. Its crew, standing ramrod straight at the rail in their best whites. The *Dutchess of Kent*—the name from the paper, right enough—visible just below its bowsprit.

"The Liberator!"

A man smacked his hand against his penny sheet, as triumphant as if he had just backed the winning horse at a county fair.

"That's him, sure enough!"

"Swaggering Dan!"

The man pointed to where their eyes were already directed—the black catafalque, strapped to the center of the main deck, just behind the crew. An honor guard of sailors stood at each corner of the casket, muskets in hand.

"Don't swagger so grand now!"

There was a small commotion, the speaker immediately knocked down, with threats and a curse.

"Daniel O'Connell!"

"They sent his heart on to Rome—"

"Daniel O'Connell! Dead and gone!"

The singer staggered cautiously across the righted deck, temporarily abandoned, in the excitement, even by his niece. Blind, rheumy blue eyes flicking back and forth as if straining to see across the water.

"I heard him speak at the monster meeting on Sidney Hill!"

He fell into a reverie for a moment, as if conjuring up for himself the mass night meeting, when he had still had his sight. Ruth could see it, too. Her father's voice by the hearth, when the banshee cried outside. The monster meeting. The hill and all the roads and the fields filled with people, making torches out of tar barrels, and hogsheads of sugar. Straining to hear every word, the rumble of their approval sweeping back, up over the man only when they could not contain it anymore.

The potatoes, and the wiggin of milk beside it. And all of us, grinning around the fire.

On the hillside, he waited patiently for it to die down, the handsome, fleshy, broad-chested man, his eyes glazed and beneficent in the torchlight. The old blind singer trying to bring to life his marvelous, rolling voice:

"Ireland! Land of my father—Ireland! Birthplace of my children—Ireland! That shall hold my grave—Ireland! Your men are too brave, your women are too beautiful and good—you are too elevated among the nations of the earth, too moral, too religious to be slaves. I promise you that you shall be free!"

The passengers silent as the singer finished. But when the black ship passed, the women gave out with a high, keening wail, their cries echoing across the water.

The funeral ship answered back with the single gun at its bow. Booming the salute as it moved past, around a bend in the river and up to Dublin. The passengers lapsing back into silence only as the last of their own sails unfurled, billowing out against the clouded sky, and the schooner moved down to the sea.

❦ · 34 · ❧

THE YEAR OF SLAUGHTER

In the hold everything was black. There was only the red glow of the men's pipes and their lucifer matches, the coals in the wood cooking settee. The men and women by the little settee bickering and jostling for space—dancing like maddened imps around the fire when the ship rolled and brought everything sliding down on them.

"Watch the cakes, *watch the cakes!*"

The ship rolled again, its timbers groaning like a wounded beast, snapping like old bones. Snuffing the fire, filling the hold with a fresh stench of vomit and filth as it did.

She rolled with it, along the fetid, scratchy straw. Trying to sleep again, so she wouldn't feel the thirst. It wasn't possible, the unchanged straw in their stall, crawling with lice and roaches. *His* thick body there beside her in the crowded stall. She could barely see him but she knew he was there, big and lumpish and unbearably warm. Lying there remarkably still and untroubled by the straw lice.

Could he be dead? she wondered idly. *Could he be dead, an' this is hell we're in?*

We thought it was a good ship, but they cheated us. We thought it was a good ship, but the captain didn't know his business and once we put to sea, we could make no headway.

Before they were three weeks out, they had run through the salt pork and ship's biscuits. After that they were given only broth, a cup of stirabout, and one pint of water each day. If it had not been for the bits of meat and biscuit and fish Dolan had bought in Dublin, Ruth was sure she would have died, but there was still no making up for the water.

She tried not to think about it—tried to lie in her stall and think of nothing at all. But soon her mouth would dry up, and her lips would begin to crack. She would run her tongue over them, but then that would dry up, too, swelling like a dry clod of earth in her mouth—

If we could've eaten the earth. If we could've

When it got that bad, she would take some of the water, but there was never enough. They gave out the pint in the morning, and she would try to nurse it through the day, but that only made it worse. Having to think about it all the time, right there beside her. Worrying if the next turn of the ship would knock it over, painting the planks of the deck with her ration. Or knowing that, if she turned her back for an instant—even if she got up for a moment to walk around, or empty their reeking bucket of slops—one of the children in the hold was likely to be on her cup. Refusing to pull their lips away from it until she had to drive them off with her fists.

Soon she began to drink all of her water first thing in the morning, just to be sure of it. Many of the other passengers did the same, then spent the rest of the day lying in their straw, calling for more.

And people went mad from it, an' threw themselves in the ocean, just to get a drink. It was as bad as it was back on the land, without any food— but at least then you could get up an' walk somewhere, anywhere, even if it was only to the end of the road.

Dolan sniffed around the barrels, muttering knowingly under his breath. Cursing, but pleased with himself, too—pleased to be cheated.

"Goddamnit, goddamnit, I should've known!"

She hovered behind him, where he had commanded her to follow.

"What is it, then? You counted the barrels before we left—"

He didn't answer, but pulled out his knife and pried the top off the first barrel. A sharp, bitter smell stung their nostrils. Dolan cupped a handful of the water to his mouth, spat it back out onto the moldy deck timbers.

"Iodine!" he announced, and cursed again, his face scowling but triumphant. "They packed the water in old iodine barrels!"

He shouldered his way back through the packed hold. The men and women standing motionless by their stalls, unprotesting as he pushed them out of the way. Others lying about, hanging from the hammocks or laid out groaning on the deck. They stumbled over them, Dolan moving inexorably toward the ladder, and up to the captain's cabin. Ruth still dutifully following, despite the weakness she felt already, struggling on up to the main deck.

She staggered there—out in the open for the first time in days, reeling under the litter of stars above. She had not been up on deck at night since the voyage began, and she could only stare now at the sky, at the blackened, restless sea roiling all about them. The wind cutting through the sails and freezing her where she stood   cutting through her, so that for a moment she did not know if she existed at all, if she was anything separate from the blackness all around her.

And I saw it then. I saw how all of us were riding on the tip of the ocean, like a flea on the back of a beast. And I saw then that this was God's own world—beautiful and vast, and empty of pity.

"C'mon!"

Dolan pulled her along the deck after him. There was a tar posted outside the captain's cabin, seated on a barrel, but he knocked the man aside even as he started to stand up. Forcing his way on into where the captain sat, as passive as the devil, behind his charts and a good bottle of brandy. Seemingly unsurprised by this intrusion—

"Iodine!" he spat it in his face. "Goddamn you, if you didn't buy the barrels off some Dublin chemist!"

The captain not even bothering to rise at the accusation. An Ulsterman, his speech thick with the streets of Derry and slurred with drink.

"What of it?"

"What of it? Ye know that yourself well enough! We won't be able to drink a drop of it soon, that's what of it. Ye damned thieves!"

"It was cheapest that way," the captain said. He pointed over to the wall, where a row of brandy and rum bottles were fastened to the shelves. "Besides, if ye get too thirsty, ye can buy some of this, at a good, Christian price—"

Dolan took a step toward the man, but he instantly produced a knife and a belaying pin on the table before him. Dolan only hesitated for a moment—but then the door opened and more sailors came in behind him, armed with pikes and muskets. They grabbed Dolan by the arms, holding him before the captain.

"Had your say? Now get back in the goddamned hold, where ye belong!"

Dolan forcing himself to stop struggling. Glaring instead with murderous satisfaction at the captain.

"God curse ye, it don't matter where *we* are. *You* still have to cross the goddamned ocean with your water turnin' bad in those barrels."

The captain only leaned back in his chair.

"Ah, if that's all that's worryin' ya. I've had experience with this sort of thing. Trust me—I expect the water ration to be goin' up any day now."

The sailors walked them back across the deck, where the sea was shining and turning like a giant black snake, and forced them back down into the hold with the rest of the cargo. And that night she came down with the relapsing fever—lying in her own filth in the stall, listening to the others all around her dying from the *teascha* and the *tamh*.

And every morning I could hear them, slidin' the bodies into the ocean. Sometimes there would be two or three at a time—dropped over the rail without so much as a word said over them, or a stone to mark their grave.

And I would have followed them, were it not for Johnny Dolan. It was he who fed me, an' cleaned my straw as best he could. Without him I should have perished in the belly of that boat. I should have died there, with my soul unshriven, an' my sins upon my head, an' my body tossed into the wide an' trackless sea.

His awful face leaned in over her. The hair finally starting to grow in again in tufts and bunches. The rotted teeth grinning despite himself, whenever he opened his mouth.

"Here, take some stirabout."

He ladled the thin porridge into her, a spoonful at a time. She didn't quite believe it at first—thinking he would hit her when she could not get up off her straw in the morning. She had even thought he might do for her as he had for that woman, screaming for food in the empty village. One more body for the sailors to bump up the stairs in the morning, step by step—

"Here, take it!"

He made her, holding up a half cup of water, to help it past her dry, splitting lips. She took it in as best she could, trying to keep it down. Grateful especially for the water, which she knew must have come from his own ration. She still could not believe that he would sit there and nurse her, uncomprehending and suspicious despite her gratitude.

What does he want?

"Leave me go. It's a judgment upon me, for helpin' to kill that tinker——" she cried. *Yet wondering at herself, that she still did not want to die.*

"A judgment!" Dolan snorted. "If there was such a thing as a judgment, even God would have to pick up his pace."

He put the cup to her mouth again——and after she had drunk, he began to unbutton and slip off the crude dress, the shabby underthings she had worn since Dublin. She tried to resist at first——thinking this was all he wanted, to force himself on her again.

He ignored her, pulling her clothes off easily, and began to wash her down. Clumsily, but carefully as a mother with a child, he wiped down her head and chest, then pulled her clothes back up and rearranged the straw beneath her. She lay down again, shivering helplessly in his arms now.

"Why won't you just leave me go?"

Looking up at him with an irrational surge of hope. *It has to be something. Some bit of affection——*

"No."

His face above her as brutal and dispassionate as ever.

"No. Not with the money I put out on you. I'll need a wife in Amerikay."

For the rest of the passage, he kept her alive, through all the bouts of the fever. That was the nature of the sickness, the relapsing fever. After a week or so, it would break and she would begin to feel better, cooler, her head clearer. Then it would start again, worse than ever. Laying her out in the straw, her heart pounding in her chest so she thought it would burst. Too weak to do anything, even get to the slop bucket.

He cleaned up for her, even found her fresh straw from someplace. He brought the food and water to her, and she couldn't help herself, she took it. Gulping it down greedily——the water tasting cooler and sweeter than before, less pungent with iodine.

"The water——"

A ghost of a smile hung over his lips.

"The captain knew his business. He had no good idea how to sail a ship, or how to provision one, but he knew his business."

"Did he, then?"

"Aye. They slipped the bugger over the side yesterday morning. Ship's fever. The first an' second mate as well. The rest of the crew's holed up in the cabin with their muskets now. They don't even come down anymore, just throw the food through the hole."

He smiled again at the thought of the captain. Yet as he did she saw that his own eyes looked bleary and clouded—felt that his touch on her head was no cooler than her own feverish skin.

"Are *you* sick?" she asked him, almost tenderly, but he shook his head.

"Never mind for me," he said, making her drink the rest. "You just do as you're told an' take it."

She tried to push back against him but she couldn't. Falling down into the straw again, letting the water run into her mouth and crying for her weakness, but not resisting him any longer.

Sometime later. He was gone for the moment, and her hands groped for the cabinet, lifting up a corner of its black cloth curtain. Trying to stare in at all the marvels. She could barely make out their familiar outlines: the blackamoor's ear, and the lovers in the moonlight, and the ship in a bottle. The giant's eye, staring frankly back at her. All of it now, just so many glittering pieces behind the glass.

And from a great distance above, I could see the scalp, too, out on the Burren, an' the whole family inside, with the roof pulled down over them. Brian an' Sean an' Liam—an' the girls, Kate an' Agnes an' Colleen, an' me Ma, too. With the roof pulled over them like a blanket, an' all of them tucked inside, asleep forever in our house.

Except that one of them had got out of it. I could see that one of them—maybe it was Brian—was out, an' crawlin' along somehow. Crawlin' off through the Burren, after me—after I'd left them all to die.

"Jesus, oh Jesus, Johnny, d'ya think any of 'em could still be alive? D'ya think so, Johnny?"

"Christ, what're you on about?"

"We shouldn't a killed that tinker, Johnny. We shouldn't have done that."

"What're ya goin' on about that for? How do ya know we killed
the man?"

Looking around wildly, she saw the eye of the giant, staring back
at her from behind the glass in the cabinet of wonders.

"D'ya think that's true? D'ya think maybe we didn't really kill
him?"

"How should I know?" He shrugged, and turned away. "But I tell
you this: I'd've killed two dozen tinkers to get out of that damned
country."

A bucket of water was splashed upon the fire. Clouds of grey, vine-
gary smoke billowed up from the settee, choking her where she lay in
the stall. Sailors were stomping through the hold, banging on the stalls
with their clubs and gaffes—kicking at the half-dead bodies lying
there. She had no idea how much time had passed in her fevers, days
or weeks or months.

"Up! Up an' out with you, damn ye! This is what you wanted!"

A tar, holding a broad red handkerchief over his nose, stood above
them. Kicking at her feet and at Dolan next to her—alive or dead she
couldn't tell.

"Get off! You're in Staten Island. *Now* ye'll have to learn to do for
yourselves!"

He moved on to the next stall. She felt as weak as a new calf, but
the fever had retreated again, and she nudged Dolan, still grey and
stiff and motionless in the straw.

"We got to get up now—"

"Why?"

"We're here, an' they need to take the boat back to hell."

He opened his eyes and rose slowly from the straw. Skinnier now
than she had ever seen him, even when they were starving on the road.
The skin hanging on him like an old man's. Yet he got to the hatchway
before she was even on her knees, his crab's legs carrying him as fast
as ever toward the small square of light streaming down into the hold.

"Wait!" he said, one foot on the ladder, just as she had caught up.
"We got to go back. We got to bring the cabinet of wonders."

"How?"

"*We have to*, that's all."

They went back to the stall—crawling on their hands and knees now, with no more strength to walk for the moment. The other passengers, those who were left, crawled past them just as slowly. They made it back, though, and she helped Dolan to lift the cabinet up with the last of her strength, and tie it to his back, looping the rope around this chest and stomach. After that they had to rest again, but then they crawled back out and up the ladder—Dolan, carrying the cabinet like a pack mule.

Up on the main deck, the sailors were still yelling and honking at everyone through their handkerchiefs, kicking and pushing the passengers into a line for the small boats. They waited their turn, leaning against the ship's rail on their hands and knees, and looked out at the broad bay before them. All around them was a low ridge of hills. Each of them was brown and desolate, stripped bare of any remaining tree or blade of grass. But at the crest of each one was planted a new white mansion house.

"That's it."

"That's what?"

"Ameri-kay."

"Christ!"

When it was their turn, they crawled down the rope ladder and into the small boats. Ruth going first though she was certain she would tumble off—swaying with dizziness, digging her fingers into the rope rungs until they bled. Sustained by the thought of how ridiculous it would be to die now, bashing out her brains on the bottom of a small boat after coming all the way across.

Yet others did die. Losing their grips, they tumbled into the water like so many lead sinkers. Some of them bobbed up again, the sailors cursing some more and fishing them out with their oars. The rest were lost where they had sunk, too fast for anyone even to mark the spot, a few yards off the shore of Staten Island.

The sailors only shouted at the rest of them to hurry up. They rowed them hastily up the muddy beach—then simply turned them out, toppling the passengers onto the mud and rocks like so many eggs off a henhouse roost.

"There ya are now, Columbus! We got plenty more to move—"

They landed on their hands and their knees—men, women, and children, all too weak to stand—and began to crawl slowly up the beach. Moving toward another white mansion, on top of another hill, the only sign of human habitation. The beach they were crawling through covered with every manner of debris, natural and man-made—empty whiskey and liniment bottles, rags and holey shoes; broken oars, and tin cans, and ship manifests, and spongy masses of kelp and seaweed, and dead jellyfish.

Ruth crawled along beside Dolan, who was still hauling the cabinet of wonders on his back. And as they climbed, she saw a man walking down from the house, toward them. She could see that he was dressed all in black, with a tall, black stovepipe hat upon his head, and with a beard and a face as grim as death.

Ruth thought that he might be coming down the hill to say something to them. She thought, for some reason, that he might be about to offer them his services, or at least to wish them welcome.

But instead the man in the tall black hat walked right through them. He walked right up to the crew at the water's edge, where they were still hard at work, throwing people out of boats, and spoke to the sailors there.

"You fucking English bastards," he said to them. "You'll kill us all, bringing this scum ashore."

❧ · 35 · ❧

THE YEAR OF SLAUGHTER

She lay in the hospital bed, falling in and out of fever. When she was asleep she dreamed that she was still on the ship, and when she was awake she thought that the room smelled even worse, reeking as it did of rotted flesh, and wet molding. Just above her bed there was a hole in the ceiling, and when it rained, which it did frequently, in brief, thunderous bursts, the water would leak down over her feet and pool into an oily slick along the floor.

Her bed was one in a long row of beds, on one side of a long, rectangular room. There was an identical row across the room, facing hers. It was supposed to be the women's ward, but there were men, too—men everywhere, overflowing their own ward, tossing about half naked in their fever. Trying to get into the women's beds with them, arguing and fighting.

Nobody seemed to care. She wasn't exactly sure herself where they were, or who was in charge. Every day, in the morning or the afternoon, some men in uniforms walked through. Tossing stale, wormy biscuits to each of them, picking up their slop buckets and filling the small, round tin pans by their beds with water from a bucket.

The new water was only a little better than the iodine-tainted water on the boat. It was brackish green, the spindly corpses of insects bobbing along the surface. She drank the rainwater when she could, chalky though it was with the taste of plaster, collecting it in her tin pan.

Across the aisle somewhere, she thought, was Johnny Dolan. *If he was still alive—and if he wasn't, she didn't know what she would do, for better or worse.* Once a day, at vespers, the attendants would come back with a stretcher and haul off at least one body that had lain still for a while, quietly stiffened in its bed. He could have been one of them and she would never have known.

"You! You there! Are ya dead or just sleepin'?"

Ruth looked up, at one of the windows across the room, though she could not tell who was speaking, or even if they were speaking to her. The shutters were usually tied closed, but whenever there was a storm they broke free of their tethers, flapping madly about and waking up the whole ward. They were open again now—and through them Ruth could see the high brick wall that ran all the way around the hospital. At night she would watch the moon struggle slowly up over it, and try to judge how much time had passed by its fullness. But she could not remember, she was never sure how full the moon had been when they had arrived in the hospital.

"There! There you are. Look up here!"

Her eyes flickered open again—uncertain if she had dozed for a minute or a week. All she knew was that it was still dark out. She raised her head from her bed, looking for the moon.

Instead there was a face. A goblin face, at least as terrible as Dolan's, but different. It was long and pinched, with a thin nose and bright eyes, and a wide, malicious grin. An oversized head on a wizened body that was, incredibly enough, squatting on the wall outside the open window. She closed her eyes.

"C'mon, c'mon—we got to move now!"

A hand was shaking her roughly. She opened her eyes, expecting to see the face again. Instead it was Dolan—his eyes more clouded with fever than before, no more than black dots in wide yellow ovals. He was throwing the few things she owned up on the bed, telling her to get dressed and come along.

"But you're sick—"

"*C'mon, there's no time!*" the goblin man on the wall was calling in his urgent whisper.

"Trust old Finn, now. You know you won't last in there. There's two more ships already lined up in the Narrows, an' they're just waitin' for the light to land. Stay here an' you'll have the ship's fever again before noon!"

She got up, knowing he was right. Grabbing up her things—noticing that Dolan still had the black-covered box with him, somehow. And as she did, she realized that her fever had broken again. She still felt weak, and a little jittery, but her head was delightfully cool as she pulled on her clothes. She crossed the hospital floor in a trance, and ascended through the window. The goblin-faced man giving her his hand when she stepped up on a newly emptied bed and hauling her on out—turning back then to help Johnny haul the cabinet through.

"Hullo, what's that then?"

The man who called himself Finn plucked inquisitively at the box with his long, thin fingers, still squatting where he was on the wall.

"Never you mind!" rasped Dolan, scrambling up after it.

"What is it, then?"

"It's a cabinet of wonders."

Dolan said it reluctantly, even sounding a little embarrassed, but with a trace of pride, too.

"*Is* it, then? Well, y'know, the ferry ain't free," Finn suggested. "Maybe a wonder or two—"

He pulled up short when he saw the look that Dolan gave him.

"Well, no matter, no matter. There's plenty a time to settle accounts later on."

He peered down the hill toward the Narrows, where two tall ships loomed like wraiths.

"We got to be gettin' on now, 'fore the next batch is in."

The men and women sat in the flatboat in the predawn light. Ruth counted at least a score of them, waiting silently. Their dark shapes hunched forward, toward the bow, as if they were already moving out across the water. The boatman standing just as motionless above them, leaning against the single sail—a thick Dutchman with muttonchop whiskers and a face like a boiled potato, holding the rudder in one hand.

Finn crowded them in, relieving them of their meager possessions as he did, their tied handkerchiefs and bundles.

"Come on now, you won't need that where you're goin'. Don't

burden yourselves with that junk from the old country. It will only
slow ya down—"

He let them take the cabinet of wonders, though. They set it in the
flatboat, as dark and still as the rest of the passengers, also leaning
toward the City. And when the boat was full, the goblin man shoved
them off himself, laughing triumphantly, jumping in as they moved
away from the land and New York rose up across the harbor.

*And it was like nothing I had seen, even in Dublin. All the steeples, and the
masts, and the smokestacks and the chimneys belching their black smoke. It
was only just morning, but the fires were already lit in a hundred thousand
furnaces. The warehouses sitting fat and squat along the river, with their
rows of windows like dark, dead eyes, an' the din already comin' over the
water to us. There was the bang of hammers, and the roll of wagon wheels,
an' the hiss of the whistles an' the steam presses. The cry of a hundred thousand voices, already up an' at work. It was a City full of life, though black
was its raiment—*

"There she is—the whole Frog an' Toe!"

They were silent, and Finn laughed at them from the back of the
boat.

"What's the matter? Ain't you never seen hell before?"

"Is that where we're goin'?"

"'Course it is! Ain't we all fit for hell? All of us that's made it *this*
far, anyway."

The big Dutchman poled them lugubriously on out into the harbor, past a small sandy island with the remains of a rotting wooden
fort on it and a hangman's gibbet—the noose still swinging slowly in
place. The currents moving faster and faster and the river traffic coming thicker now, until it seemed as if the whole harbor were bearing
down upon them. Steamships and paddle wheelers, ferries and
schooners. Oystermen and Dutchmen's wives, brigs and sloops, cat-
tleboats and railroad boats, and the aristocrats of them all, the beautiful clipper ships with a single black ball painted on their sleek sails. All
of them jostling them with their wakes, or cutting like sharks across
their bow, so the boatman had all he could do to keep them afloat.
Clamping down grimly on the stem of his pipe, clutching his pole and
bracing his feet in the bow as he pushed them heedlessly on, past one

certain wreck after another, until at last they bumped up against the slips of the Chambers Street ferry.

At the docks the goblin man hauled them one by one out of the flatboat, propping them up along the wharf. There they were set upon at once by a gaggle of young boys, quick and furious as jackdaws, trying to pick them clean. They snatched up anything the goblin man had overlooked—money, watches, hats, and coats. Grabbing for their watches, for their rings, those that had them—grabbing at their sexes. Grabbing them all, men and women, trying to haul them away, toward the boardinghouses they worked for.

Finn kept them at arm's length until he could parcel out his cargo. Getting a coin for each, before he sent them off, with one runner or another. His charges waiting as silent and passive as cattle, going wherever they were assigned.

"You're comin' with me, now," he said at last to Ruth and Dolan, when the others had all been distributed.

She stood where she was, waiting on Johnny Dolan. It was the first time she had ever seen him not sure what to do. Standing there indecisively, eyes red with the *tamh*. Still clutching the cabinet.

"C'mon now! Time's wastin'!"

The goblin man beckoned to them, holding on to a hack that had materialized somehow. The horse snorting and scuffling a hoof impatiently along the paving stones.

"*Ain't* you comin' with me, then? Where else are ya gonna go—but with good old reliable Finn McCool? An' be sure an' bring that box!"

Dolan hunched his shoulders—and pushed on into the open door of the cab, clutching the cabinet to his chest.

"There ya go!"

Finn boosted her in after him, then climbed in himself. He yanked hard on the leather strap that was tied around the driver's leg, and yelled out the window to him.

"Take us to The Sailor's Rest, by the Peck Slip. Make time now!"

And though the driver flicked his reins, we could go no faster than a man walking, but that was all right. For everywhere we went, there was food. There was whole markets full of fish, and eggs, right out in the open, an' wagons passing us full of beer, and sausages, and bleeding red sides of meat, so close you could reach out an' grab them.

But the best thing was the pigs. They ran loose, right out there in the streets—whole herds of pigs, each of them big and round enough to feed a family, runnin' right out in the streets, for anyone fast enough or sharp enough to pick 'em up. And that's when I knew this was a great country.

The hack pulled up by a wooden building that sagged like a wen against its neighbor. Finn McCool jumped down at once—hauling the cabinet of wonders on inside before Dolan could stop him.

"Hey—*hey,* where d'ya think you're goin' with that?"

He scrambled to catch up with him, Finn only grinning innocently.

"Where're we goin'? Why, to your new home, son—to your new home!"

They stood in the back room of The Sailor's Rest, blinking in the smoky darkness. The room itself was nearly bare. There was a large sooty fireplace, and a bar along the back and a strange red curtain that hung over a doorway in the back. The only furniture, though, was a long table and two benches where a couple dozen men and women were clustered—drinking and eating, smoking and singing, and shouting at the top of their voices over a dice game.

"God bless all here!" Finn cried out.

"Ah, go to hell!"

The table erupted in laughter—then the dicers turned back to their game, ignoring them. Finn pushed Ruth and Dolan on into the room.

"Hullo! Here's two more poor unfortunates, brought to safe haven!" he cried out to the bartender, who was a fierce-looking man with a barrel chest and eyebrows that sat on his face like a pair of crows. He only grunted back in reply, staring at the black-draped box that Finn handed across to him.

"What's this, then?" he asked, turning it over in arms that were as thick as tree trunks.

"A cabinet of wonders!" Finn McCool told him grandly. "All the great wonders of the world—or so I'm assured."

The bartender grunted and flipped a coin over to Finn, who tucked it away in his vest before it had time to glimmer. Then he hauled the cabinet on over to the bar, and stowed it away in a cubbyhole beneath the stairs.

"Damn ye, I never said I was sellin' that!" blurted Dolan, stammering with fever.

"Safe storage for your belongings."

"Safe for who? Gimme here—"

But McCool cut him off, pulling him back toward the bar.

"Safe storage for us all, then," he said, winking at Dolan. "Don't worry, son, it's as secure as the crown jewels! Trust old Finn! This is the best bondsmen's house in the City, it's safer than if it was at the police headquarters, or City Hall itself! Now, Pat, how 'bout a drop of the creature?"

Pat the bartender pulled a dusty bottle up on the bar, and poured out a long shot of liquor the color of a rusty nail for each of them. Ruth watched Dolan watch it for a long moment, the whiskey slowly clouding the glass before him—still casting one eye over at his treasure, in its cubbyhole under the stairs. Then he gave a quick nod and grabbed up his glass, and she followed his lead.

It was the hardest thing I ever tasted. It felt like I had swallowed fire— and as soon as it was down, I felt me head start to spin.

Finn was already towing them back to the men and women hovering around the table, and the dice game there.

"Here, lemme introduce ya to the house's own detachment of the Roach Guards—"

"That's right! You won't catch any Bowery Boys here!"

"True Blue sons a bitches—"

"No, this is a respectable house!"

Their sallow, dirty faces creasing with laughter.

"This here's One-Armed Charlie, an' Kate Flannery, and Slobbery Jim and Patsy the Barber. An' that's Sadie the Goat, and Jack Rat, who makes his money biting the heads off a rats down at Kit Burns's, an' George Leese, also known as Snatchem, who used to be with the Slaughterhouse Gang, but works the fights as a bloodsucker."

The last sport shuffled forward, looking almost philosophical. His hat tilted at a jaunty angle, wearing a vest full of patches.

"I don't know if I would describe meself primarily as a bloodsucker," he informed them. "I would rather be known as a kind of rough-an'-tumble-stand-up-to-be-knocked-down-son-of-a-bitch, if it's all the same to you. Sort of a kicking-in-the-head-knife-in-a-dark-room-fellow."

An' what made them the Roach Guards or anything else I could not tell, save that all the men wore a blue stripe down their pant legs. They looked to me like they would all just as soon cut your throat or lift your purse as look at you, and the only thing you could say for them was that they came from Ireland.

"Ah, there's me own Gallus Mag!" Finn exclaimed, and the tallest woman Ruth had ever seen stood up from the table. McCool gave a little running start and managed to throw his arm up around her neck, and give her a kiss on the cheek. She smiled shyly when he did, showing the dainty, white tips of her teeth—each one sharpened to a dagger's edge.

"Aw, now, Finn!"

"Ah, I loves her, I do! No woman in the world like my Maggie!" McCool insisted, and planted another kiss on her lips, just to watch her blush again.

"C'mon an' have a snort with us, Mag! Let's have some more drinks, an' somethin' to eat, now!"

He jumped up again, banging on the table with one hand and whistling with his fingers in his mouth for the bartender.

"Hey—hey there, Pat! Ain't it time for dinner yet?"

"'S on its way," the bartender grunted, and a red-faced woman even bigger and rounder than Pat himself came out of a back room holding an entire sow up on a platter. She put it right down in the middle of the table—and when she did every man and woman there instantly produced knives from somewhere, and began to tear at any parts they could, including the ear and the tail.

"Here now, you ain't got any hackers," Finn said solicitously, cutting off still more pieces and handing them over to Dolan, and Ruth. The pig was plainly burned in some places, and barely cooked at all in others, and everywhere its skin was as grey and taut as a ship's canvas. But once they smelled it—once Finn had cut them several slices and laid it in their palms—Ruth and Dolan both found that they could not resist, choking it down as rapidly as they could and holding out their hands for more.

"Get away, you!"

"That's mine there!"

The crowd around the table made a fresh lunge at the pig, all at once—stabbing at it so furiously now that the carcass rolled off its platter and onto the floor. It tumbled across the room—all of them chasing after it, still jabbing at it with their knives—until it finally came to rest faceup in the cold fireplace, staring back at them with its bronzed, openmouthed pig face.

That was when Ruth felt her stomach go. Dolan right alongside her, the both of them staggering over toward the spittoons in the corner to vomit. Her belly heaving convulsively, until there was nothing left to throw up, her head reeling in the close, smoky room.

"That's all right, then."

Finn McCool materialized by her side, cooing sympathetically.

"You both been sick now, that's it. We need to get ya a room upstairs, that's the thing. Don't worry, this is the best bondsmen's house in the City—"

She found herself being led up a rickety wooden staircase, along with Dolan. Finn was towing them down a long hall on the second floor, past room after room. They were mere holes, most of them, without doors, and pitch dark inside, reeking of human filth, and sweat, and worse.

He finally stopped at one hole—how he knew which one, she never fathomed—and lowered them both through the gaping doorway. There was no furniture, only a floor covered with straw. Ruth thought dimly that it was not unlike the stall on the boat, though the stink was even worse.

"That's right. You rest for a spell now."

She was trying to catch Dolan's eye, knowing that something was not right. But he looked barely conscious, and she could scarcely keep her own head up. Wondering vaguely what was to happen to them now, in this hole, but too exhausted to care—letting the goblin man's voice soothe her.

"You're in good hands with Finn, now. Nothin' to worry about—"

Sometime, much later, she awakened to Dolan kicking at her legs.

"Get up. Get up, now, if ya want to get out of here alive."

She forced herself awake, crawling toward the gaping doorway. Still not sure she wasn't back in the hospital, or the boat.

"D'ya hear that?"

Dolan stood beside her, listening intently. The darkness around them was almost total, the only illumination a flicker of gaslight from down the hall.

"D'ya hear what they're about, then?"

Ruth could hear nothing, save for the low murmur of voices belowstairs, down by the bar. Her stomach was still turning over and her head was spinning, but she made herself follow Dolan out to the head of the stairs. From there she could look down with him, into the now nearly vacant main room.

The only ones left were Finn, and Pat the bartender—and even as she watched they lifted the cabinet of wonders up, and laid it out on the bar. Whipping the black covering cloth away, leaving its creamy, white and gold frame suddenly, indecently exposed upon the table.

"There it is!"

"The bastards," Dolan whispered beside her. Gathering his strength, girding himself to go down there—but also anxious to have them take a look, she could see. To know how much it was truly worth—

"What is it, then?"

Their voices sounded incredulous. Then Pat the bartender snorted derisively.

"Cabinet of wonders! I seen better wonders any day of the week up at Barnum's!"

"*Bastards,*" Dolan whispered again, this time with rage in his voice.

"All cheap junk. Trinkets an' glass," Finn McCool said sadly.

"An' to think I gave you a shilling York for this! That's one you owe me—plus the drinks!"

Pat shook his head again in disgust, and pulled out a hammer from under the bar. Bringing it down with one fierce, expert blow on the clasp of the cabinet door. A long fissure ran instantly down the length of the glass, but the clasp broke, and Pat flung open the door and stuck his arm inside, all the way to his elbow.

"Junk!" he pronounced it, even as he held up a hand full of its shiny baubles.

Dolan was already down the stairs, going for him before she could do anything to stop him.

"Worthless!"

The bartender's hand still trawled through the wonders. Idly wrecking the carefully staged tableaux, the perfect tricks of light and mirrors and hidden catches, preserved through all those days on the road, and the voyage over—

"NO!"

He shouted like they had pulled his own heart out. An' I thought then, I don't care what he says, he ain't a dead man.

Dolan was on the bartender before he could look up, wresting the hammer away from him in an instant. The first blow caught Pat between the eyes, sending him staggering into the bar. The second broke his nose, and turned him around. There Dolan grabbed him by the back of his collar and began to pound his head into the bar, over and over again.

"*Worthless*, is it!"

He kept pounding away at the man, unrelenting in his rage, until Finn laid the barrel of a pistol very firmly against his temple.

"But that's enough now. You're *murderin'* the man."

Dolan stopped then, though he still hovered over the bartender. Gazing at Finn and his pistol out of the corner of his eye. *Still thinking about it,* Ruth could see, from where she stood now at the foot of the stairs. But Finn saw it, too.

"Don't be daft! I'll put a ball through your brain. Take your damned box an' get out!"

Dolan continued to gaze at McCool out of the corner of his eye for another long moment. Then he stood up, and closed the broken clasp of the box as best he could, and pulled the black cover back over it. After that he walked slowly out the door with Ruth following, the box clutched tightly to his chest again. Pat still lying insensible along his bar, his face a ruin.

"Oh, but you are a darlin'," Finn called after them, chuckling— though he kept the gun pointed at them. Dolan looked back at him from the door, but said nothing.

"Oh, don't look at me so," McCool called out, still laughing. "It's only to say that a man of your sensibilities could go far in this town— with the proper handlin'. Be sure to come back and I'll teach you to make some money!"

They had walked north, and west, all through the night, away from the endless forest of masts at the bottom of the island. Exhausted and feverish, forcing themselves on. Amazed at how crowded the streets still were, with both people and vehicles—their feverish, leering faces hoving before them.

She followed though she had no idea what he was hoping to find, in the middle of the night, in a strange city. They walked past saloons filled with wedges of dim yellow light, and riotous laughter, and screams pouring out of the back door. They walked past sagging tenements, and boarded-up mansions, and new brick factory buildings that pounded and trembled—the furnaces still burning, the smoke still rising from their chimneys even in the middle of the night.

They walked until the blocks themselves began to thin out, along with the people. The houses dwindling, but getting larger and grander, until there might be just one to a block. Then there were no houses at all—just a low, scrubby marshland with a dismal odor. Yet still Dolan walked them on, until at last he came to a huge, grey rock, looming out of the darkness at them.

He insisted on climbing it, as if this had been some sort of real goal he had been marching them toward. And there, on the other side, he could see the shanties of Pigtown, sitting on the floor of a hollow like so many toadstools. Homes that were no more than crude shacks, rigged up out of a few loose boards and bricks. Each one with a small fenced-in yard, a dog howling and baying like a mad thing—and a pig. It was there that he finally put the cabinet down, to look over the site of their new home.

"This'll do," he told Ruth—and much as the look of it dismayed her, she was just as glad to stop for the night.

They washed their faces in a cloudy pool of water, even though the dogs were howling now as if the Dark One himself had come walking by their homes. The only sign of their new neighbors were one or two who came out to whack at their dogs, and to shake their fists at them, before going back inside.

Dolan and Ruth paid no attention to them. Instead they settled down on a patch of grass to rest themselves for a few hours. Lying right out there, under the stars, until it would be morning and they could start to build their new home.

36

DANGEROUS JOHNNY DOLAN

He did not know why he had hit the man, except that he'd felt like it, and that it had given him the first real satisfaction he had had in four-teen years. He had nothing against him, but he knew the man was giv-ing a speech and then things would stop. Dolan wasn't even sure what he had been saying, he could barely make out what people said at all anymore. Ever since he had gotten out of the prison in the Sierras, it was as if he was underwater, only half able to hear or understand what anyone said to him.

But Dolan knew what he was doing from the faces of the people listening. The men looking a little shamefaced at what they had already done. The women's faces glistening with tears. He couldn't grasp it exactly, but he knew that something the police superintendent was saying would make it stop, and then the fires would be put out, and the whole street put back like it was, and he would be alone again—trying to make his way through this City that he had come back to, three thousand miles on a fool's errand.

So he had hit him. He knew when he did it that it would set every-thing going again. That was all he could do now. He could set things off.

For that they had made him their leader. Pushing him on ahead of them, down the Third Avenue. The block of wood hung around his neck—so natural by now he had almost forgotten it.

.   .   .

He had a distant recollection of the time a mob had carried him off on their shoulders, after a prizefight. *Dangerous Johnny Dolan.* How he had loved that name! Just as he had loved everything else about fighting. *The sweet fulfillment of hitting a man, and being hit in return—*

It was the afternoon he had gone fifty rounds with the great John Morrissey, on a flatboat anchored in the Hudson, off Yonkers. A day much like today, with the taste of blood in his mouth. The July sun turning their backs and chests a painful, glowing pink. The rabbits and gamblers watched from the surrounding steamers and rafts, shouting and waving their money—ducking down out of sight, then bobbing back up with each ebb and swell of the river.

He had had no chance to win. Morrissey was a bear of a man, solid and muscled as a blacksmith. Cold, green eyes staring cannily out of his massive, bearded head, catching everything. Dozens of his Tammany braves were on hand to cheer him, and from the moment he came out of his corner of the raft, it was clear that he meant to finish Dolan as quickly and thoroughly as possible. *To murder him, if that's what it took.*

He could not even hope to foul him. Right off the opening bell, Dolan had tried a trick he had learned from other raft fights, suddenly jumping at Morrissey and landing as hard on the deck as he could, hoping to throw him off balance on the rocking craft.

But Morrissey was too large to budge. Instead he saw Dolan's move coming, timed it so that he hit him with a tremendous uppercut just as he landed. It sent him reeling to the deck before he knew what was happening. The sports on the boats cheering and stamping their feet with pleasure.

"Shutters up, there's a death in the family!"

Morrissey giving him a small, hard sneer of satisfaction as he went back to his corner, his look plainer than words: *Is that all you got, then?*

Dolan dragged himself back to his stool. The rules of the bout being the same as on land—each round ended when a man went down and the fight went on until one man or both could not answer the bell. Nicky Ward, his manager, swabbed him down with water pulled directly from the Hudson, while Snatchem the bloodsucker looked over the back of his head.

"Jesus, but you're already ripped open back there, ye'll have to watch it—" Snatchem implored him, dabbing at the wound with iodine before Dolan pushed him away impatiently.

"I'll try not to turn me back on the man."

They had circled each other around the raft for the rest of the afternoon, and into the evening. Dolan was faster than the champion, able to get in under him with his low, crouching stance. But there was always a price to be paid. Morrissey hit him harder than he had ever been hit in his life, worse than anything he had endured at the hands of Yankee Sullivan, or Bill the Butcher, or even Tom Hyer—and hitting Morrissey in return was like hitting a buffalo. Dolan's fists bounced off the man's head, the furrowed bone above his eyes. By the time he came back to his corner after the twentieth round, his fingers were like chopped meat, so many bleeding, stubby worms.

"You're gonna break both your hands, goin' at him like that," Snatchem admonished him again. Holding them out professionally, then carefully sucking the coagulated blood and pus out of his bare knuckles. Spitting each mouthful into the bucket, then rubbing them over again with flour.

"I don't care," Dolan told him, surprising himself with the words. *But they were true, he didn't.*

Up against some other fighter, he might have used his torn-up knuckles to his advantage—have Snatchem paint them over with iodine or salt, let them sting and blind his opponent. But he knew if he tried any such thing now he would never get off the raft alive. Morrissey's Tammany braves, with their knives and their pistols and their heavy bets, would dispatch him on the spot.

He had no choice but to keep wading in, taking his beating—*and he liked it that way.* The old, uncaring exhilaration building up in him. The more he was hit, the more he needed to hit. Boring in, heedless of the blows raining off his head, his ribs and kidneys. Every punch only driving him on to hit again.

The fight went on through twenty-five rounds, then thirty—then forty. Each round ending with Dolan on the raft's deck. The sun burning his back and shoulders so badly by now that he wanted to scream every time he threw a punch. The chalk-outlined square heaped with sawdust between the rounds, but both fighters still sliding and slipping along the deck, slickened with their own sweat and blood.

Like the floor at The Place of Blood, covered with gore beneath his broom. His brother-in-law, Tom O'Kane, had gotten him the job, but he had not stayed long. Preferring to be somewhere—anywhere—that he got to do the killing—

The forty-first round had ended when Morrissey had slipped and fallen on his own accord, and Dolan wondered for a moment if he could actually be worn out. But he was back for the forty-second, battering him quickly to the deck, and after that Dolan gave over any hopes of winning once and for all.

Yet he kept moving right at Morrissey. Past any thoughts of self-preservation now, only curious to see what he had in himself. Here and there, Morrissey's own proud face showed the marks of his effort. A throbbing mouse along each of the granite ledges above his eyes. A few cuts on his nose and cheeks, his Viking's beard flecked and matted with blood.

Most of it his own, Dolan knew. He had some idea of what he looked like from how Snatchem and Nicky Ward recoiled from him when he came back to the corner. He had already spat out two of his few remaining teeth, and the rest were wobbly. He could not feel his nose at all, there was a constant ringing in his head, and his vision had narrowed to two blurred slits, through which he could just make out Morrissey advancing on him once more.

Yet just before the fiftieth round began, Dolan realized that the crowd was yelling *his* name, now. Slapping down more coins and banknotes, the action on how long *he* could go. In his corner Nicky was begging him to quit, telling him he would be blinded or killed if he went back out.

"What, d'ya have money on the next round, Nick?" he grunted at him, and went swaying back out.

Who the hell were they to worry if he lived or died? Besides, he was dead already, they had said so at the workhouse gate—

But this would be the last round. He could not fight anymore even if he wanted to—his knuckles gone, his hands and fingers broken and useless. He had never been knocked out before in a fight. Wondering what it would be like to be beaten into oblivion. *Wanting it, craving it.*

He walked out to the middle of the ring and threw a wild, looping right at Morrissey, intending to miss. The champ stepped inside and landed a short left to his chin that left him woozy but on his feet. *You still have to earn it.* Morrissey moving in on him again, deliberate and implacable as a man-of-war. Dolan only dropped his hands, and then—in a moment they would talk about for years in the clubhouses and the stuss dens—had spat out a tooth that bounced tauntingly off the champion's chest.

"C'mon, ya fat bastard. What the hell're ya waitin' for?"

Morrissey stared at him curiously, suspecting a trap—or unable to make out just what Dolan was saying through his broken mouth, he never knew which. Then he came on   feinting once with his head, professional to the last. Dolan did not see the left coming, a straight, hard jab, remarkably accurate after so many rounds. The right following at once. A perfect combination, hitting him so hard that Dolan felt as if something had popped in his skull, and he was out before he hit the deck.

When he came to the crowd already had him up on their shoulders. The rabbits and the gamblers gleefully carrying him around and around on the raft and the steamers, strewn with their holiday bunting and pennants.

Dolan was so dizzy he thought he might be sick, but he couldn't summon up the energy to puke. Instead he stared dully across the ring, at Morrissey being sponged and rubbed down by his Tammany seconds. Still standing erect and unbending as an oak, staring back at Dolan and giving him a small, respectful nod that was obviously supposed to be some kind of acknowledgment of the fight he had put up.

Dolan had spat out a stream of bloody phlegm in his direction. Morrissey frowning and turning away   not understanding that he had failed in his job. That he was supposed to have pounded him until there was nothing left, until the thinking stopped, once and for all—

But it was too late. He was awake again, and the drunken sports kept circling him around and around the ring until he fainted, and had to be laid flat out on the deck, and doused with river water until he revived yet again, madder than ever to still be alive.

37

HERBERT WILLIS ROBINSON

The City lies split open on its back, like some broken beetle on the pavement. The mob springs up instantly, on every block. Men, women, and children, swarming into the street, looking for something to vent their fury or their pleasure upon. Shouting and screaming themselves hoarse, waving any crude weapon they can get their hands on—sticks and fence posts, shingles and stones, pressing irons and skillets.

They sack everything now, abandoning any pretense of looking for draft records. Looting hotels and restaurants, groceries and pawnbrokers, tailors and clothing stores and jewelry shops. The whole order of the City, broken down in the course of a morning. Down in the Fourteenth Ward, I even saw an alderman leading the mob.

I fight my way back downtown, desperately trying to get some word to somebody. But the Metropolitans are nowhere to be found. Most of their precinct houses abandoned now, or held by skeleton shifts—some of the stations even fired by the mob already.

I have to go all the way down to the police headquarters, on Mulberry Street. What a difference from when I was here just the other night! Kennedy's smooth efficiency is gone now—along with Kennedy himself, fighting for his life in the hospital. Everything is in an uproar, bruised and battered roundsmen and sergeants, wandering in and out, messengers pouring in from all over the City, fearful and angry citizens demanding that something be done.

I manage to push my way through to Commissioner Thomas Acton, from the Police Board, who is supposedly in charge. He sits behind Kennedy's desk, his face red with fury, trying to make some kind of order out of all the chaos. Breathlessly, I tell him about the burning of the Colored Orphans' Asylum, and how I have heard some members of the mob talking about storming the Armory. But he only nods grimly:

"Yes, yes. We're aware of all that!"

His attention is taken up instead by the constant reports brought in by the messengers, or on the wires from those scattered neighborhoods where the telegraph is still up.

They are beating Negro waiters at Crook's Restaurant. . . . A troop of Invalids has been routed by Grand Central Station, their rifles seized. . . . Men are trying to fire the Harlem River Bridge, and Macombs's Bridge. . . . The mob is throwing up barricades in the Ninth Avenue. . . . They are attacking Negro homes in Baxter Street and Leonard Street, they are burning Negro boardinghouses on Roosevelt Street. . . .

"My God, man, but have you *seen* it out there?" I can't help blurting out at him, thinking that he cannot really understand, cables or no.

But Acton has a plan. All day long he and Inspector Carpenter—the highest-ranking officer left at headquarters—have been pulling men off the streets. They are trying to put together a strike force to send against the mob, and they must have gathered a hundred and twenty-five officers at headquarters, overflowing the muster room.

They are also gambling the whole City. Already the police are stretched nearly to the breaking point, just guarding the vital arteries of the town—the telegraph lines and rail tracks and bridges, the shipyards and docks and banks, their own precinct houses. Many of the roundsmen they have gathered are already bloodied and bandaged from the fighting this morning.

Meanwhile, Sergeant Burdick and the men from his Broadway Squad stagger back into headquarters. These are thirty-four of the biggest, toughest men in the Metropolitans, usually employed in the merciless, rough-and-tumble business of clearing the traffic on

Broadway. They were armed with Colt revolvers and breech-loading carbines, ordered to hold the Armory at Twenty-first Street and the Second Avenue.

Instead they ended up squeezing out a tiny bolt hole in the back of the Armory, and running for their lives. This is the worst news yet. Even as the flying squad forms in the muster room, the mob is presumably arming itself—smashing open all the boxes of brand-new guns and ammunition they have captured. With this sort of fire-power, they will be able to outgun every cop, every soldier left in the City.

Even now, in the muster room at the Mulberry Street headquarters, we can hear their orgiastic shouts and screams drifting through the windows. The mob's moving steadily closer. The policemen twitch and shuffle their feet restlessly, unsure of what to expect, of what they are to do.

Dan Carpenter stands before his men. Ramrod straight, his brow furrowed but his eyes gleaming above the thick tangle of his beard.

"Form up! Form up, men!"

They come to attention, instantly transformed. Looking on eagerly now as Tom Acton steps forward to give Carpenter his charge.

"Will you go now, sir?"

"I'll go," Carpenter replies, in a voice like a ten-pound gun. "I'll go—and I won't come back unless I come back victorious."

The headquarters erupts in cheers, drowning out the mad ravings from the street. *The Irish will fight.*

"What should we do with prisoners, sir?" a Sergeant Copeland asks.

"Prisoners? *Prisoners?*" Acton glowers, snorting like a warhorse. "Don't take any! *Kill! Kill! Kill!* Put down the mob. Put down the mob. Don't bring a prisoner into this room until the mob is put down!"

"Men!" Carpenter booms. "You heard your orders. We are to meet and put down a mob. We are to take no prisoners!"

They are still cheering wildly, their bruises and their weariness forgotten as Carpenter leads them out into Mulberry Street.

"Follow me, boys! And when you strike, strike quick and hard!"

They march out singing, moving four abreast through the ravaged, burned-out blocks:

The Union forever,
Hurrah, boys, hurrah!
Down with the traitor
And up with the star—

I go along with them, telling myself I don't care about the danger. Wanting to see if they can save the City. Just wanting—craving—to see what happens next.

We are marching right at the mob now. We can hear them coming, drowning out our song as we approach Amity Street. It is a terrible noise a mob makes—like the progress of a great conflagration, methodically crunching and smashing everything in its path.

First comes a wild flutter of refugees, driven before the mob like so many flushed doves. Negroes and women, mostly, but also whites, entire families—*citizens of an American city*—running for their lives. They nearly break our ranks in their panic. Desperately toting whatever possessions they were able to salvage, their little handcarts and wheelbarrows bouncing over the paving stones.

"Hold, men, and let them pass!" Carpenter orders—the policemen parting to let them through, their faces paling at the sight.

But there is no time to panic. Right behind the refugees comes the mob. They are swaggering now, full of confidence, filling all of Broadway for as far as the eye can see. There must be at least ten thousand of them, shouting and jeering as they come. Waving their crude clubs and stones and knives; their poles and grappling hooks, muskets and pistols—even a few swords they have stolen from somewhere.

When they spot us, they send up a wild, lusting cry. Far from retreating, or giving up, they run straight at us, roaring like a locomotive. The Metropolitans halt again, and the song dies in their throats. I can sense that they are ready to break, to run before the rioters, and I can barely fight down the urge to flee myself.

But Carpenter leaps out ahead of his men, deliberately turns his back on the mob. He waves his locust-wood club over his head, then begins to tap it rhythmically against the cobblestones—the universal rallying call of the police. The men pick it up at once, rapping their own nightsticks along the street until it becomes a steady, pounding beat that is heard even over the yelp of the mob.

The crowd slows at the sound, but they are less than a hundred yards away, and still closing. A giant Celt hod carrier runs out in front of the rest, waving a huge American flag he has stolen from some hotel.

"*At 'em, boys! They can't stop us now!*" he bellows, and races straight at Carpenter, swinging the flagstaff itself at the inspector's head.

But Carpenter runs out to meet him, his own club at the ready. He ducks easily under the long swing of the flag—and hits the Celt so hard it sounds like a man smashing a pumpkin. The behemoth staggers back a step, blood trickling from his temple, and falls dead in the street. The mob behind him pulls up abruptly, stunned by this show of resistance—while two roundsmen run out to grab the flag before it hits the street.

"By the right flank!" Carpenter coolly barks out his order. "Company front! Double quick! *Charge!*"

With a single shout, the men raise their nightsticks and charge. They tear through the mob like a wheat thresher. Arms rising and falling, rising and falling, their locust-wood clubs smashing down with each stroke.

The mob quivers at their impact—then gives way. They unleash a hail of bricks and stones and fence staves and some of the cops fall, but more move up at once to take their place. Their arms still rising and falling, rising and falling, cutting a swath clean up Broadway.

Carpenter is still in front, his eyes gleaming like a demon's as he leads his men. All of a sudden he is face to face with that creature from the park—their leader—still carrying around his neck the block of wood with the *NO DRAFT!* sign chalked on it. The two men grapple hand to hand, and for a moment it looks as if the creature might be able to overwhelm even Carpenter. Then Sergeant Copeland and another officer come up from behind the man and beat him with their nightsticks until he is lying prone on the ground. They pick up his inert body, hurl him right through the front window of a saloon.

The phalanx of police moves on, still smashing anything that dares to stand in their path. I follow right behind, like a man riding the waves out at Coney Island—miraculously untouched while men are falling all around me.

It is a harrowing, primitive fight, fought with the most elemental tools, rocks and clubs and spears. But the street is too narrow, even on

Broadway, for the mob to bring its numbers to bear. Soon they panic, and break before our onslaught—stumbling and tripping back up the avenue, leaving hundreds of the dazed and dying in their wake. Carpenter's men look barely winded, only a handful of them seriously injured. But there is more still to be done.

"On men, on!" he urges, spurring them toward the Armory.

It is a formidable building, four stories high and built of solid brick, with small windows and a heavy, solid oak door at the top of a steep front stoop. An easy place to defend—and we can only guess what kind of reception we will get there, now that the mob has had plenty of time to fortify it, and break into the weapons.

But they have been slow about it, thank God, the way that mobs always are when they have no opposition to concentrate their minds. The oaken door still hangs open off its hinges, where they first broke it down. Most of the crowd is preoccupied, sacking the nearby dry-goods stores, and saloons—a few rioters only now beginning to pull the muskets and carbines from their packing.

We are on them before they know it, surrounding the Armory, trapping the looters inside. Any who try to flee are beaten, and pitched down the stoop as soon as they step through the door. We can hear the rest of them inside, though, still shouting their hatred and defiance at us. Carpenter draws a pistol, and leads his men in.

"On them men, *now!*"

He shoves the ruined door back with his foot. The rioters stand before us, leaning over some rifles—the crates crowbarred open, but the guns still uncleaned and unassembled. The Metropolitans are on them like dogs on a rat, beating anything that moves. Those rioters who can, leap right through the window glass, desperate to escape the flaying clubs.

A few turn to fight. Carpenter's men push them slowly back across the floor and up the stairs—stumbling up the steps, cursing and snarling as they go. They cannot stand against the relentless, machine-like advance of the police—*those arms still rising and falling, rising and falling.* I watch as Sergeant Copeland knocks a five-foot pole out of a man's hands with his nightstick, then pitches him, flailing, over the banister. Another brute tries to take a swing at the sergeant with a longshoreman's hook—but Carpenter, still up in front, shoots him point-blank in the face.

The police push them up to the third floor. Once there, though, they barricade themselves in the drill room, where most of the carbines are kept. We can hear them in there, hurrying to unpack the guns, and even Carpenter hesitates now, unsure of what to do. If they get the carbines working, they will have us easily outgunned—could burst out and turn the whole tide of the battle.

"We have to have the door down!" the inspector orders.

But that is when we smell the smoke, rising slowly up through the musty, gap-planked floors of the Armory. Some accident—or some fool—has set the place on fire. The flames are already racing along the second floor, eating up the dusty old crates and pilings—moving relentlessly toward powder and ball. Carpenter orders his men out and they go, as fast as they can run.

"Fire! Fire in the hole! Get out while you can save yourselves!"

Behind the door we can hear them laughing and cursing at us still.

"Damn your eyes! What kind of fools d'ye take us for?"

We are just able to make it out before the first explosion. There is a muffled thud, then a tower of flames shoots right through the Armory and fifty feet in the air. A shower of balls and bullets comes ripping through the once-sturdy brick walls, sending even the mob screaming for cover, and peeking out from behind the warehouse across the street, I steal a glimpse of hell. The floor under the drill room has given way, and now the men inside hurtle down into the flames, shrieking and burning as they fall.

A few of them manage, somehow, to stumble out the door. They are on fire, or badly charred—some of them still blindly clutching the carbines in their hands. Carpenter walks up to the stoop and shoots them as they emerge, one after another, as easily as he might shoot rabid dogs.

"At least this saves us having to haul the guns back," he says, casually holstering his pistol again. Then he leads us back down to headquarters, the Armory still burning behind us. Not a soul daring to stand in our way now. The men marching along jubilantly, bellowing out a new song now as they go.

> *Thy banner makes tyranny tremble*
> *When un-der the red, white, and blue—*

I would like to say that I am capable of maintaining a certain objectivity, a certain professionalism in the wake of all this. Instead I must admit that I am jubilant. They have crushed the men who wrecked my City, and I find myself even singing along with them, as they swing back downtown:

When un-der the red, white and blue—

❧ · 38 · ☙

RUTH

Evening.

She could hear the vesper bell ringing at St. Patrick's—the sound of it reassuring after so many restless and frightening noises throughout the day.

Yet it was almost worse, with Billy still not home—

She gazed at their children, where they were slumped around the kitchen. It was impossible, now, to hide from them that something was going on. By the afternoon they had become so pent up, so wild with frustration that she had let them out on the street, provided they did not stray from the very front of the house.

But even there, they had noticed it. The emptiness of the street. The sound of distant, muffled shouts and explosions, the smell of smoke. Before long their play had grown listless, and they had retreated, back inside.

They sat there now, slumped silently in their chairs, Mana on her lap and Elijiah by her feet. Their eyes closed, even Milton dozing with them. *Her emblems of Billy.* His color or his face, stamped on all of them, at least a little. And her own self blotted out, she was contented to see, submerged beneath his.

No, he must be alive still. He has the brains to stay out of their way—at least when he's not drinking.

All day long, the news had been bad. One neighbor after another had darted out furtively across the street, making sure to let her know it. Mrs. McGillicuddy, in particular, bringing her the news of the fighting in this block or that one, another story of a colored lynching, always with a half smirk on her doughy, red face.

There was nothing about the Colored Orphans' Asylum—but still she could not help thinking the worst. The thought of it all but overwhelmed her. *All his beauty gone, just like that.* She remembered the first time she had spied him, walking tall and straight, back through the fields to the coloreds' village. His work clothes old and frayed but his face glistening and high-boned in the sun. *The most beautiful man she had ever laid eyes on—*

She was still living up in Pigtown with Johnny Dolan then, near what was now Fifty-ninth Street and the Fifth Avenue. It was just a boil of a village then, a hollow of shanties made out of wood and bricks scavenged from demolitions, and caulked with mud and grease. The men went out to work in the morning on the construction sites, or in the fat houses and the bone boilers, the butchers and leather dressers a few blocks away. Staggering back in the evening after a stop at their stills, bone-tired and drunk, and mean.

She was already working for the ragpickers then, in their rookeries over by the East River, and at the end of the day she could barely stand to go home at all. She would stop when she got to the lip of the hollow, then strike out across the rutted and barren fields. Not really caring where she was going. Hiking up her skirts to cross over the crude, fallen stone walls and fences, thinking, *How far they have fallen. Don't even know to put up a proper stone wall—*

That was how she had found the Nigger Village. She had never come across it before, though she knew every other inch of the scraggly woods and meadows up to Haarlem, and she had found many things on her walks. More hidden Irish shantytowns, and neat little German villages. A chapel and a school for young ladies, run by the Sisters of Charity up in McGown's Pass. A crazy-quilt of gardens and goat pens and pretty little fields, all put up behind an elaborate brick wall by some eccentric German burgher from Moenchengladbach, who announced himself with a sign that read, *Jupiterville, Jupiter Zeuss K. Hesser, Prop.*—though she did not know that yet, being still unable to read, and could only run her hands wonderingly over the fine, chiseled letters.

Then one day she had come over a small ridge near the Bloomingdale Road, a mile or so to the north and west of Pigtown, and there it was, unfolding before her like a vision. A whole, long trail of *them*, walking together two by two. The women first, then the men walking after. Most of them without shoes, but dressed completely in white, down to the sashes tied around their waists, and the scarves the women wore over their heads. Chanting some sort of hymn that she did not know and did not understand, following the man whom she assumed must be some sort of nigger priest. He held a shiny brass cross out ahead of him—the embroidered yellow mantle he wore over his shoulders the only break in their all-white raiment.

But their skin. She could not keep her eyes off it. That was the real color. They were no two of them the exact same hue; some tan, some coffee-colored, some almost yellow, or an off-red, or even nearly as white as herself.

But more of them were a true, deep blue-black. Their color standing out all the more brilliantly against the clean, white linen pants, and shirts and dresses.

She had seen people with such skin before, in the streets downtown—mostly sailors, in their tars' white jackets and striped trousers, speaking some foreign tongue. *But here! And so many together!* There were dozens of them, walking so close to where she lived, so eminently reachable and human. She moved in a trance after the procession, once they had passed. Desperate to see them, to study every detail of them. The way their faces looked, and their hair, the bare feet—to see and know every difference in them.

And I wanted to jump up then. I wanted to dance and laugh then, just to see them. Just to see there were people like that in the world—anyone, anyone so different from all the shite I knew.

She was left standing in the road, still gaping after them, as the priest led the procession on into the village. It was no more than a few dozen simple plank houses, built around a pair of dirt roads, with a church at the head of each one. Poor enough, she knew, maybe even as poor as Pigtown. Yet its houses looked like real houses, and the land around them was divided into neat little gardens, and cultivated fields, where squash and wheat and spindly stalks of corn were growing, so that it seemed to her they could be marching into Paradise itself.

She wanted to follow right then and there, to walk down the road after them, but she could not bring herself to do so. She started, then retreated—started again and then went back, until she was doing a virtual jig in the road. Unsure of what she would say to them, what she *could* say to them, or what they would do.

It was then that she had seen *him*, coming across the fields. Wearing his blue work shirt and pants, a shapeless straw field hat on his head. *And his skin.* His skin, too, was as black as coal, tinctured with only the lightest sheen of red. Hands thrust deep in his pockets, head down as if he were studying the ground.

And yet, she could tell, still watching—still aware of everything around him. His head coming up just a little, almost imperceptibly with every sound he heard. His stride not straight, but weaving a little. His feet still adroit nonetheless, still nimble, barely seeming to touch down on the swampy earth, as if he were having a dance with himself.

The whole village, moving through the fields to dance at the crossroads. The women with ribbons in their hair, and the men carrying fiddles, and jars, walking softly so as not to awaken the priggish priest—

He was, she was sure, the most handsome man she had ever seen—and she could not help but run then. Even though she was mortified by the noise she made, crashing through the thin underbrush, the old leaves, like some animal in distress. Hiding herself among the scrawny trees, covering her face and head with her arms but still unable to keep from looking at him, from dropping her hands and looking at his face, his beautiful head. Until he had passed on into the Nigger Village, having given no sign whatsoever that he had heard *her*.

She had lingered constantly around the village after that. Crawling through the bushes on her hands and knees. Feeling the brambles scratching her legs, the smell of dirt and the crumbling leaves in her nostrils. At first, before they knew who she was, they would set the dogs on her. They were swift, quiet animals, trained to be on you

almost before you knew they were there, and she had all she could do
to get away from them—hearing their panting, the padding of their
paws in the underbrush just behind her.

Once they got used to her, though—once they had ascertained she
was not the sheriff, or a blackbirder skulking up there in the woods—
they left her alone. Assuming that she was just another white woman,
like all the rest of the white folk from the City, men and women and
children, who liked to dally around the Nigger Village, *Seneca Village*, as she came to find out they called it. Come to gawk at a whole
town full of black people—or for something more.

She would creep almost right up to where they were working in the
fields, crouching down, crawling through the bushes on her hands and
knees. Watching them march into one of the two clapboard churches
on Sunday morning. Wanting to ask if they knew *him*, and what he
was like, but not only that. Wanting to ask them, as well, how they
came to be here, to be tending these little plots of land, unbothered by
the rest of the world. Wanting to know how it was that they came to
be left the hell *alone*.

After that she usually saw him in the evenings, on his way home. He
gave Pigtown a broad berth, she noticed, swinging all the way over to
the rail tracks in the Fourth Avenue. That was where she would pick
him up most nights, coming back from her job with the ragpickers.
She would follow him up along the half-constructed, mostly deserted
streets. Making sure to keep her distance until he turned to the west,
up around Sixty-fifth Street or so, then plunged into the scrubby
woods and fields that led to Seneca Village.

He walked much faster, once he was among the trees. Moving
almost furtively, his strides lengthening so that she could barely keep
up. But even then she followed him, running after him as fast as she
could, just so she could get a closer look at him. Embarrassed and
ashamed of her need, more ashamed to be crashing through the
underbrush so clumsily.

She would lose track of him sometimes, he moved so quickly. One
evening, at dusk, she was even sure that he had gone off the path, into
a deep thicket of trees and bushes. She could not imagine why he
would, but on an impulse she went after him anyway, into the thickets.

Once she was in there, she thought that she must be mistaken. She floundered about in the curls of briar, and the vines and groves of ailanthus trees, unable even to find her way back to the path in the growing darkness. Until at last she pushed past another bush—and found herself face-to-face with him. Looking just as surprised as she was herself—his left hand held up, as if to ward something away. His right hand still at his waist, holding something.

A knife, she saw. Yet she still felt no concern, alone with him there—only embarrassment. Blindly making to push past him, further into the thicket, but he stayed in her path.

"You don't want to go that way," he told her, looking down, as if he were ashamed of something himself. She could make out, then, the sound of men's voices coming from behind him now, the smell of sugar burning. His breath smelled familiar, but somehow not as bad—not as sour or sickening as Johnny Dolan's did, when he had been at the creature.

She stepped back, looking at him, his eyes impenetrable in the nearly total darkness now. Then she had turned and run back toward Pigtown.

After that she tried to look for him in the mornings—to see where else it might be that he went during the day, and what he did with himself. Thinking over their encounter in the thicket. Telling herself, *He did it to protect me, for no gain of his own. He did it just to help me—*

One morning in the late spring, she got up even earlier than she usually did, and slipped out of the shack she shared with Johnny Dolan. She got dressed in the darkness, leaving Dolan still snoring—then ran out, barefoot, across the muddy yards and the high spring grass around Pigtown. Letting the dogs howl as she passed, not caring who might see her but just glad to feel herself running.

She waited by the large grey boulder Dolan had climbed, the first night they had come to Pigtown, until she caught sight of him. Coming through the fields where she thought he might be, though she had noticed that he never took the exact same way twice. She followed him then as she did in the evening, only in reverse—moving out through the fields and the tangles of wood and brush to the east. Taking his same, wide detour around the Irish of Pigtown, all the way to the Fourth Avenue railroad.

After that it was easier, she could get a little closer, behind the other men and women making their way down to work from the uptown wards. She tracked him back to the Fifth Avenue, then nearly a mile downtown—to where he suddenly turned in through the tall iron gates of what seemed like a manor house, sprung up miraculously on a nearly empty new City block.

There were some words over the gates, but of course she could not read them. She wondered if he might be a servant in the big house, if colored people did such work—but then she realized that she had no idea at all of what the people of Seneca Village did, besides tilling their own small vegetable plots, of how they made their living or earned their bread.

She wanted to follow him right inside, but she didn't dare to go up to the door of such a great house. Instead she went around to the back, which wasn't hard. There were only another couple of houses scattered around the desolate block, and her main fear was that he might see her from the windows of the house. But there was, at least, a brick wall that ran around the back courtyards of the big house, and she was able to shelter behind that, making her way along until she got to the wooden back gate.

She screwed up her courage then, and peeked in through the planks—to see two whole courtyards, filled with colored children. Boys and girls both, in the same uniforms, all dressed in thick, padded shirts and trousers, and dresses. Whirling around with hoops or skipping ropes or playing ballgames—though she thought, too, that most of them seemed very grave for children, almost as grave as the children she remembered in Limerick and Tipperary, begging and starving by the side of the road.

At first she was stupefied, wondering if the house were somehow a part of Seneca Village, or another Negro town all on its own. *All these colored children, living in this fine house!*

Then she saw him again, just walking out into the backyard, with its blue-slate flagstones. He was moving differently from when she had seen him going through the fields. Looking more at ease and less watchful—but also devoid of the light-footed swagger she had liked so much. He seemed, instead, to walk in a perennial stoop, bending over or kneeling constantly, to button a coat for a little girl, or patch up a cloth ball for some of the boys. Moving from one to another of the grave children in their funny, padded clothes—wiping their faces, and stopping their tears, tending to their scrapes and bruises.

There was the sound of a gong, and the children hurried to line up—boys and girls, each in their respective courtyards. They stood there in perfect order, more silent and grave than ever, until a tall, grey-haired white woman appeared at each of the doors, and they could vanish inside the house.

She understood it now, she thought. The mansion some sort of a school, perhaps; a workhouse, or an orphanage. *The cartload of orphans in Limerick, outside the poorhouse door. Sitting there with their mouths open, like so many baby birds.* Now that they were gone, he unbent slowly and walked around the courtyards, picking up anything they might have left behind—balls and scraps of ribbon, a small sweater. Taking them all carefully inside with him, then coming back to make sure the gate was shut, and bolted. She had to jump away when he did, swinging back to make sure he did not see her—but she was still close enough to hear him, even to smell him. The sour, liquor smell gone now, just the scent of him—a man's smell of soap and coffee, bacon and tobacco   on the other side of the gate. Making sure that the latch was secured, then the back doors, too, before he disappeared into the orphanage himself.

That night she had raced down the streets from the German ladies', wanting desperately to catch up with him on his way home. Unable to stop thinking about the sight of him, with the children, the whole day in the rookery. She had plunged into the copse near Sixty-fifth Street—and nearly ran straight into him again. He was stopped dead in the path ahead of her this time, his head turned slightly toward the south, as if he were listening intently to something.

"Be quiet," he said, without looking at her. His voice a whisper now, and she had not dared to so much as breathe.

There was a distant sound, almost more the suggestion of a sound, a very faint clinking of metal or glass—and he suddenly turned and clutched her shoulders with both hands. Before she could cry out he swung her around, pushing her down through the bushes into a little gulley. The branches blinding her, scratching at her face and eyes and his much larger body swinging roughly down over her, pressing her into the earth. He clamped a hand over her mouth—the other one drawing the knife she had seen before from his boot, the blade held just inches from her throat.

She lay there, half under him, trying to make herself stop trembling, and prepare for whatever would come next. But still, somehow, even in her immediate, physical fear and trembling, she could not believe he would really hurt her. Then his mouth was by her ear, his breath warm on her cheek.

"You make a sound an' I'll cut you," he whispered. "I swear to God!"

She did as he said—and in the ensuing silence she could hear the men. There was the same faint clinking sound from before, much closer and more distinct now, almost right on them. She moved her head slightly to look up—his hand still over her mouth—and then she saw them.

There were two of them, moving almost soundlessly along the path. They were lean white men, wearing broad-brimmed hats and long white dusters, and bent sharply forward at the waist, as if they were tracking something. Each of them had a curled bullwhip and a pistol on his belt, clearly visible through their open coats.

"—thought I saw him come in here—"

Only when they were nearly on top of them did she realize that the men were talking to each other. Their slow, Southern voices less than a whisper.

"—was sure of it. Does most every night."

"I know. I seen him, too. You figure he's by us now?"

"I don't know—"

They stopped in the path, no more than three feet above their heads. Close enough now that Ruth could make out the short lengths of chain looped around their arms, the manacles gaping like open hands. *That was the noise,* she understood now. It occurred to her, too, that if she could see them, they might see her—her pale white face glimmering through the underbush. She ducked down toward the ground, her brown hair melting into the dusk.

"He could've gone in here somewheres—"

One of the slavers swung a hand out over them.

"Uh-huh. You want to go in after him? If he's seen us?"

"Ah, hell, he ain't seen us."

"Why'd he go in there, then?"

"I don't know. To take a piss. We'll catch 'im with his pecker in his hands."

There was a pause. Ruth listened for it, her face to the ground—

waiting to hear the first crunch of their feet on the dead leaves. Wondering what *he* would do then.

"He's bein' awfully quiet, for a man takin' a piss. Hell, what if he ain't in there at all? We could spend half the night thrashin' around in there—"

"All right." The first voice sounded relieved. "All right, we could go on, then. Sniff around the village—"

She heard the voices receding, their footsteps making almost no noise at all. Still she waited, though—not trying to turn, or get away, or even lift her head up. Trying to show that he could trust her, waiting for him to take his hand off.

"You all right?" he said, removing it at last.

She nodded, looking at him as directly as she dared. But even now, his face was a blank, cryptic and unyielding.

"Tell me somethin'," she said. "Was you really gonna cut my throat if I made a noise?"

He stared at her for another moment, then almost laughed out loud. A long smile spreading slowly across his face, despite himself, and she thought that it made his face look much more tender, and almost boyish.

"No," he whispered, looking down. "No, that would've taken too much time. I'd a had to go for them, first."

This time she laughed.

"Why, I suppose that's so! I suppose that's the truth, now!"

He chuckled, too—then stopped, and looked down the path in the direction of where the slavers had gone, over toward the west, and Seneca Village.

"I should go, now." He looked back at her. "You should, too. With them around—"

"I'll go with you," she said, on an impulse.

"What?"

"I'll go with you. I'll walk before you. That way I can let you know, at least—if there's anything. If they're waitin' for you."

He stood there, looking at her while he thought it over, his dark, handsome face still revealing nothing.

"No," he said finally—the disappointment washing over her. "No, it's not right. But you can walk behind. You see anything happen to me, you run to the village, get anyone you can. Will you do that?"

She nodded emphatically.

"Yes, I can do that. No one in particular?"

"No, tell anyone, first person you see. Tell 'em what happened, and to come quick, an' bring the dogs. You understand?"

She nodded again.

"All right, then."

They started off again, with him walking a good ten yards out in front this time. She picked up the hem of her dress, moving at a half trot. It was a cloudy night, and she was afraid that she might lose him, ahead of her in the darkness. Determined to do her part, to run and give the alarm—but not sure if she really could leave him, if the slavecatchers did jump him. As they drew closer to the village, he held up his hand and slowed, and she stayed dutifully back. Trying to make her eyes bore through every shadow, every possible hiding place behind the low bushes and rocks that dotted the land.

The whole village, walking through the fields, as softly as possible.

He walked on a little ways more, Ruth following, then he stopped them once again. She could see the lights from the village now, the fires flickering through the windows of the square, white, little houses. *Almost there.* But he stood stock-still in the dirt road, so much so that he almost seemed to blend into the darkness—the trees, the rocks, the clouded night. Until Ruth had nearly the same feeling that she had had that night at the old fort with Dolan—that none of this was real at all, and she was out in the darkness all on her own.

He stood there, listening—and then took a half step back, as if he'd heard something. There *was* something. She made out a sort of slithering sound, like someone cutting through the grass, very low. *Could they be trying to crawl up on them?* But just then she heard him chuckle again, reach down to something.

"There, all right. *Napoleon!* Now we're all right."

He was patting an enormous yellow mongrel, one of the many dogs she had encountered before from the village, swift and silent, and smart as a pig. It started toward her, baring its teeth, but he grabbed it back by the fur of its neck, restraining the animal.

"No, it's all right, it's all right, now. There, Napoleon. She's a friend—"

She felt herself warm to the word, from his lips, though she knew it was just for the dog.

"Your dog?"

"No, my neighbor's."

"You ought to have a dog, in this place."

"Maybe."

They walked down the rest of the path to the village together, Napoleon trotting smartly out in front. She could not picture that any-one, not even the slavers, would molest them with such an animal by their side. When they reached the first houses of the village, he looked at her, as if expecting her to go now, but she did not. Instead she stayed right by his side, pretending to be oblivious. Following him right to the small whitewashed house—straighter, and better made, than the rest—that was obviously his home.

She went right up with him to the door, even after the dog had bro-ken off, and gone back to its master's yard next door. She went right up with him, though she had no real idea of what she was doing, until finally he stood before her, in front of his own house, as if to silently ask what it was that she wanted.

"All right," he said at last.

"What is your name?" she asked him, but he only looked away, his hands on his hips.

"All right, then."

Still not answering her, waiting for her to go.

"Let me stay," she said then, because it was the only thing she could think of to say—the only way she could be sure that he would not leave her, and go inside, and she would never get this close to him again.

"What?" His voice was startled, but not disgusted, which was something.

"Let me stay. For the night," she said again, blushing and ashamed that this was all she could think of to do—that she had no conversa-tion, nothing to offer that he might find enticing but willing to beg him, just the same.

"It's a small house," he said at last.

"I don't need much room."

"Small house, small bed."

"I'll sleep on the floor, then. Just a blanket on the floor," she said—then surprised him again: "Do you have a regular woman?"

"What?"

"Don't worry, I won't disturb it for her. I won't lie in her bed, just put a blanket down, an' let me stay beside you for the night."

"No," he said with a sigh, still not moving from the door. "No, I don't have a regular woman. Do you have a man?"

"Yes."

"Your husband?"

"No, but a man. A hard man," she told him, as honestly as she could.

"Where is he now?"

"Away. On a buildin' job, over in Hoboken. But I would never say a thing to him or anyone else about you. You can trust me on that, I think you know that by now," she told him, nodding back toward the fields and woods, the darkness where the slavecatchers still hid themselves somewhere.

But he still did not move, and she blurted it out in desperation.

"I seen you," she told him. "I followed you before."

"I know," he shrugged.

"I seen you with the orphans."

He said nothing, but she thought she saw him flinch, as if from an unexpected pain.

"I seen where you go," she went on. "I seen you take care of the orphans. I know you're a good man, a man who can take care of his own, an' shield them from others—"

"What do you know?" He cut her off, his voice full of bitterness. "What d'you know about anything?"

"I *know!*"

He didn't say anything more to that, and for a long moment she thought that he was going to simply open the door, and go inside. But then he slowly pushed the door all the way open, and held it there for her.

Inside the little cabin, when he struck a locofoco match and lit the lantern, it was everything she had imagined it to be. It was only slightly bigger and better furnished than her own shack, back in Pigtown, but much cleaner. *The home of a man who kept himself in order,* she thought.

It was just the one room, with two windows, the privvy and pump out back. The only furniture was a single bed, and a chair; an old

Franklin stove with a pipe that was obviously patched and pounded together with salvaged bits of metal. But there was a washbasin, and a bright, orange-and-blue rug. Yellowed pictures of sailing ships, cut from the newspapers, were tacked up along the walls, and there was even a small, neat shelf lined with books, even if they were battered, cheap editions, backed with cardboard, and with titles she could not read.

It was the home of a person—of someone who was still living, and trying to make some little mark upon the world.

She was more embarrassed than ever about herself, then. She was usually ashamed—of how she looked, and how ignorant she was. Embarrassed to be so dirty, and thin, and unlovely; so foolish and so poor.

"Put out the lantern," she told him, when they moved over, and sat on the bed. Embarrassed even to be naked with him in the light, though she still could not help wanting him.

Instead he left the wick burning, and kissed her. She thought she saw something that actually resembled affection—or perhaps pity—on his face, and he kissed her very gently on the mouth, and put his large hand on her cheek, and she could not help but lean into it, and kiss him back. When he took off her dress, the poor, muddled shift she wore, she was embarrassed again. But he only held her to him, and pulled her into the bed, under the scratchy wool blanket with him.

It was nothing like what she had known with Dolan, he was so leisurely and gentle. Afterward, lying in the bed beside him, she had adored every part of him. His face, his eyes. He had beautiful hands, she thought, *a craftsman's hands,* like those she had seen on the best seamstresses in the ragpickers' shops. Knotted and calloused from the work he did, but sensitive and clever, with long, tapered fingers.

"What's your name?" he asked her, looking over at her in the flickering light from the lantern, his face cryptic and remote again.

"Ruth. My name is Ruth," she told him, and it occurred to her that she had never said it to anyone she loved before. "What's yours, then?"

He swung his legs out of bed without answering. Pushing some kindling in through the grate of the Franklin stove to start up the fire, though it wasn't very chilly, with the two of them in the small room.

"It's Billy," he told her at last, looking into the stove as the fire slowly built, then sputtered. He shoved the end of a stick at it, stoking up the sparks. "Billy Dove."

"That's a lovely name. *Billy Dove*," she repeated. "Why d'ya hate it, then?"

"I don't hate it." He looked at her sharply. "I don't hate it."

"But ya do."

He gave the fire a final poke, and climbed back into the bed. She stretched an arm over his chest, nestling by his underarm, and he pulled her tightly to him.

"It was given to me," he told her.

"So? Ain't all names given?"

"It was given to me by a man who assumed he owned me. Besides, it's somethin' I was then, what I am not now."

She could feel him shrug uncomfortably against her in the dark. His hands behind, under his head, looking up at the ceiling he had built for himself.

"What were you, then?"

"I was a sea-going man. I was a man knew how to *make* ships."

She could hear the bitterness—and the pride—in his voice again, though she still was not sure that she understood. For herself she could not think of any better job in the world than the one she had seen him at, with the orphans.

"You don't know what it's like, to build a thing like that," he told her, almost accusingly.

"But you get to take care—"

"A black man, a black woman in this town is always taking care of someone. Black children or white children, his own or someone else's. That's all it is, takin' care."

"But what's wrong with that?" she asked him, her voice so obviously ingenuous, so sincere, that he had answered her.

"But what do we get to keep, what's any man like me get? What can I store up, an' lay down for myself? What's the use of all this takin' care—for what?"

She wanted to say, *For me, then*. She wanted to say that, but she didn't dare.

"A man works his whole life for something, a skill. He learns it— but then he can't use it. I don't want anyone else's name for me. I'm bound down here now, I don't want their names for what I'm not."

He pulled her under him again, and she was so glad, despite his anger. Opening herself to him, holding him as tightly as she could. For the rest of the night, they dozed and talked and made love, until she had faded slowly, sublimely off to sleep in the early morning. Recognizing, despite herself, that she would not be here, that he would have nothing to do with her if he were a master shipwright, and she was what she was.

After that she stayed with him whenever Johnny Dolan had a job in New Jersey, or up the North River, anything that would take him out of the City for a night. And even on the other days, when Dolan was home and she could not stay, she would come over for as long as she dared after work, and they would lie together, or hold each other on the bed and talk.

Sometimes, too, when he was late coming home from the orphans, she would let herself in past the simple latch. She liked being in his home, though she was never more ashamed of herself then. Embarrassed by the tattered bits of ribbon that were all she had to put in her hair. The cracked shoes that she wore, just as glad to fling them off and go barefoot most of the year. She would stare at her face in the shard of shaving glass he had tacked up to the wall, wishing that she were pretty. That she had some power to hold a man, instead of being half-starved out, a permanent hole in herself. Not even able to read, to help him with her head, bring him luck, fortune, prospects.

She tried to make things as nice as she could, at least, though the truth was, there wasn't much to do. She might scrub the floor, or bring in flowers from the fields, or bits of bright cloth she had scavenged from the German ladies. Once she had even sewn him curtains for the windows—the same yellow color she had sewn for their curtains at home, right under Johnny Dolan's nose, pretending she was making just enough for them. Reveling in that small deception—

Yet he kept all of his things so orderly that there was little she could do even in this line. She would always remember the time she had found his tools, the new tools he had bought with his first money from the orphans. Still oiled and preserved and kept so carefully in their small kit, hidden in a trapdoor just below his bed. There was his treasure, but she knew they had never been used—just as splendid and shiny as they were the day he had bought them.

She had felt his hurt again, then, and felt all the more badly that she could not do anything for him. Thinking of the men she had seen, carpenters and mechanics, workingmen returning from some construction site downtown. Singing, *We won't go home till morning*. Walking proudly in their leather aprons, their tools in a bag thrown over their shoulders, walking in their workingman's strut, like a man who knows he is considered to be of value; bowlegged, as if there were too much to contain it all—

She did not see the same swagger in him. There was instead some resignation, something lost—something that, perhaps, even accounted for the gentleness in him. *Not a complete surrender*. She could also feel the lingering frustration there, the bitterness and confusion that rubbed like a burr beneath the skin. What it was that accounted for the brandy or the whiskey on his breath. What it was that kept him, too, walking carefully, lightly across the woods and fields every morning and evening. *What it is that keeps him coming home to me*.

When she was with him she thought of nothing else, but in the daytime she was afraid that Johnny Dolan might find out. Fearful that some of their neighbors might notice the nights she did not come home.

She had no friends among them, and she knew that Dolan preferred it that way. Nearly everyone in Pigtown kept to themselves—wraithlike figures she saw in the murky morning light, going out to relieve themselves, or staggering home at dusk. Still, she did not know who might be watching, and she tried to deceive any unseen eyes. Making a point of coming and going after she got back from the Germans. Leaving the house repeatedly to gather wood, feed the pig, do some other chore—before she slipped off to her Billy.

She didn't know if she was fooling any of them. Soon she came to realize that it didn't matter, for her man was not the sort of man people told stories to. No matter what they suspected, no one was about to regale Johnny Dolan with tales of how his woman was spending her nights with a handsome man from the Nigger Village.

And Dolan did not seem to suspect a thing, himself. She watched him closely, for she knew he was clever enough, and kept things close to his vest, but she could see no sign that he knew. He would make baseless accusations when he got home after a job, ask which of the neighbors, or the laddies on his fire company, she'd been keeping time with. But she knew this was mostly to give him the excuse he wanted to push and slap her around their shack—shoving and kicking at her, calling her a whore and a nightwalker, until he had calmed down enough to eat the meal she had waiting.

It was always the same when he got back to the City, often the same if he had just been downtown, or had only been sitting around in the yard all day, brooding and nipping from the jug. It was worse, she noticed, when he came back from a fight than from a building job, though she would have thought he'd had enough of fighting on such occasions. He would come in with his face a mass of purple-red bruises, ears swollen like cauliflowers and his nose pushed in, until she could barely stand to look at him herself.

But it only seemed to excite him, to get his blood up for it. Going into his boxer's stance as soon as he came in, knees bent, arms held up rigidly. Bouncing back and forth on the balls of his feet like some mad, mechanical doll. Taunting her with repeated, vicious slaps, too quick for her to dodge or return.

"C'mon. Tell me what you been up to," he would hiss at her, goading her still through clenched teeth. "Tell me about your day. C'mon."

Until at last, boxed into a corner of the shack, by the stove, she would have no choice but to grab something—the broom, a loose slat of wood, anything at hand—and lash back at him. She would try to get a good shot in—for he would take that moment, that inciting her past the point of all forbearance, to let loose.

One full punch was all it took. She would let it be enough, smashing into her chin or stomach, all but paralyzing her. Her arms and legs suddenly useless—flying back helplessly against the wall of their shanty. And after that, usually, he was satisfied enough to have his supper.

Billy noticed her scars and bruises, even in the dim moonlight that came through the windows of his house. Running his fingers questioningly over the splotches along her jaw, the tight, round, red circles on her stomach. A new one usually forming before the others had faded, so that he got to see her wounds at every stage as they blossomed and turned, and finally subsided—these malignant flowers, water stains upon her body.

"Why do you let him do that?" he asked, his turn to interrogate her. And: "How do you take a punch like that?"

"I got no choice."

"You think he won't kill you, one day?"

His voice full of a concern—she realized with a deep and abiding regret—that was more kindness than outrage.

"D'you want me to do somethin' about it, then? About him?"

She was a little flattered, at least, by the offer. Thinking that he might do it, too, just out of pride. She could see him walking into Pigtown with the big, rusty pistol she knew he kept on the shelf behind his Protestant Bible—walking right up to the shanty, and shooting down Johnny Dolan like a dog.

But then what would happen to him? What would happen to her, to all of them in the village?

"No, no. I can handle him," she told him.

She could hear his rich, bitter laugh, even if she couldn't fully see his face in the gathering darkness.

"Oh, you're handlin' him, all right. You handle him any better, darlin', you'll be dead."

"I can take it," she insisted grimly, though she was not sure at all she was speaking the truth. "He won't ever go too far, he knows he needs a woman."

And why shouldn't he have one? Why shouldn't he have me, do what he wants to me? After all, I would've starved without him—

Still it tormented her, every day, to have to go back to the shanty. To face Dolan again. Trying to humor him, trying to just avoid him. Nothing worked. Standing up to him was the worst of all, he only seemed to welcome the challenge. Sometimes—sometimes she almost sought to bring it to a boil, to get it over early and relieve the tension. Hoping for one good smack, and then it would be over. At least for a little while.

She let it drift while she tried to think it out. Afraid she could no longer think very well, afraid she would not be able to think at all soon, the way he knocked her head into walls. And afraid, too, that her Billy Dove would fly away again, on to one of the other, far places he liked to talk about. To Portugal or the Windward Coast, down to Brazil or the Tortugas, or around the Horn to Peru.

When they were together now, neither of them said very much, as if everything were frozen in place by the changing weather, the slow turn into winter. They saw each other less and less, the colder it got. To be sure, it felt all the better to sleep warmed by him, in the bed by his stove. It was darker, too—easier to hide in the early evenings. Easier to sneak home, with even the dogs of Pigtown tied up inside their homes, lest they freeze and deprive the shantytown of their incessant baying, come the spring.

Yet with the winter the building stopped, too. The City lay dormant, under the ice and snow, its writhing, ceaseless making and remaking of itself stilled for the season. The construction sites shut down, and there were few prizefights, the sporting men asleep over their cups by the fire, pursuing their other entertainment in the brothels.

Dolan was home nearly all the time now. Spending most of his days brooding by the stove in their shanty. Puffing on his pipe, looking into the tremulous little flames that licked at shreds of newspaper and scrub pine. Away only on night jobs with the river gangs, that he did not talk much about.

She was never sure exactly what these were. At night, sometimes, there would be a sudden thump against the wall of the shanty, rattling her so that she would drop her sewing. He would gather up the mysterious tools he had collected, then—wedges of iron, and long knives, and one, a copper curlicue, no bigger than his thumb and shaped like a pig's tail—and walk off into the night, another shadow accompanying him across the snow.

The rest of the time she was stuck there with him, in the abandoned shack of salvaged planks and railroad ties he had moved them into. Glued like one of the few ornaments, the few trinkets still left along the shelves of the cabinet of wonders. He had never tried to repair it, after that night at The Sailor's Rest, had not so much as dared to but kept it as a damaged relic, still covered, in the corner. He did not even peek under the black cloth anymore, she knew; it gave him no more pleasure, although he remained convinced of its immeasurable worth. Grumbling, sometimes, through the winter months, about how he was tempted to trade it in for his fortune, and a grand house somewhere.

"It's a treasure," he would insist, when he was far enough along into his whiskey. "They was just too small to know it, down there. They just wanted to trick me into givin' it up to them."

He spoke of taking it down to Barnum's, or of displaying it on his own, but he never did. She had even thought of repairing it herself, with what she had learned from working at the German ladies', but she knew that he would be outraged by her presumption, might even murder her over such a thing. Though some nights she could barely prevent herself. Some evenings, too, stuck in the shanty with him— the box sitting black and remonstrative in the corner, silent reminder of their original sin together—it was all that she could do to keep from grabbing it up and smashing it to pieces.

After Christmas was over the orders from Stewart's and the other grand stores dwindled off, and the German ladies had let them all go for the season. Some days she would pretend she still had work, and sneak back over to Seneca Village, but she was too afraid to do that very often. She feared that Dolan could sense her desperation, her need to be with Billy, when they were cooped up so long together. Even when she could find good reasons to leave, to buy food or sell the things she sewed, she thought that he did not trust her. She would return to find him standing in their yard, watching her as she came back down into the hollow. Supposedly out cutting firewood, but watching her and saying nothing, the ax gripped in both hands, held level at his thighs.

It was worst at night. She could barely stand it, now, when he forced himself upon her. Punching and fumbling at her, pushing into her in the darkness. Having his way with her until he lay there panting, then snoring, over her. His weight shoving her down, burying her now in this new place, this next bare, uncovered grave he had staked out.

She told herself it did not matter, that Billy did not truly want her anyway. That she was as good as dead, as good as buried here herself. But still she grieved for him the longer they had to be apart. Still she wanted to be with him, even if they could not spend the night together in his bed, even if they had no time to make love. She longed for just the sight of his small home again, for the gentleness of his voice— willing to put up with anything so long as she could have those things just now and again.

Before the winter was out, though, she noticed that her monthlies had stopped. This did not surprise her at first, for she had barely ever had them. There had been no blood at all during the long, starved months along the road. Even after she had come to this place, they had always been spotty, inconsequential—what blood there was, it seemed to her, weak and thin, confirming her belief that she was not really a full woman at all.

But then it had stopped, and one day sneaking off to see Billy, she had found herself vomiting by the side of the Bloomingdale Road. To her disbelief she had watched her belly start to grow—barely perceptible yet, but a definite swelling, until she knew she could put it off no longer.

If it were Billy's, she knew, Dolan would as likely kill her as not, right there, the moment the brown baby came out of her. Most likely kill the child as well. Yet she was even more sickened by the thought that it might be *his*. That Billy would have to see her walking the fields with Johnny Dolan's child clutched to her breast—a constant reminder of what she was, and where she came from.

For a few days she even thought of killing herself, and the baby— of weighing herself down with stones, and breaking a hole in the ice on the North River. She remembered hearing from a priest that expectant mothers who took their own lives were doomed to wander hell for all eternity with their unborn and equally damned child, and she liked that idea. To drift about forever, with his babe constantly by her side—forever mother and child, having nothing to do but to look out for it, and provide for it.

But she thought then that it would be Billy's as well, and the thought of keeping that from him, of depriving him of his child, was more than she could contemplate.

There was nothing for it, then—she would have to tell Billy. She picked up his track in the snow one evening, on his way back from the orphans. She was sure of it—from the size of his foot, the lightness of his step. It was just the barest impression on the crisp, new layer of snow, weaving a little crookedly, back and forth.

She began to follow it, walking beside his footprints at first. Then walking in between them, until their feet were intertwined. As if they were two lovers making their way across the icy field—arms around each other, each steadying the other against the uncertain footing. Until, suddenly realizing, she had turned and looked back at the trail she had made across the open land, and had run back and tried to smudge it out with her shoe, smearing their footprints together. Panting in the cold as she worked, the icy snow numbing her feet through the shoddy patent leather, shivering in her thin coat.

She went on, smudging out even his solitary footprints as she walked—though it was almost completely dark by now, the winter night having fallen as abruptly as a curtain. The only light a stern, white half-moon. Moving almost silently through the woods, even in her condition, the dead leaves buried under the snow now. *No longer some big, clumsy forest animal but a sylvan fox, carefully skirting the trees and bushes.*

It was by the moon that she tracked him to the little rise above Seneca Village—a small, rugged promontory, scattered with bare white birches. He stood with his back turned to her, facing toward the village, and the North River well beyond. And as she watched he drew a small, brass flask from his pocket, unscrewed it, and took a short draught. Still looking all the time toward the water, where the furled white skeletons of ships lay, awaiting the spring or the icebreaker's passage.

She waited patiently until he had finished, and walked down to his village below. Then, still without saying a word, she had climbed up the little hill to where he had stood.

She looked not at the water, but at the half-moon above, and the swath of cold, clear stars. Then down, toward the dozens of tiny, amber gaslights and red fires from the town below. Picking out his figure as he made his trail down to Seneca Village, following him until he reached his home and lit a lamp inside.

She kept watching, ecstatically, until all the myriad little lights seemed to revolve around her. Just as the stars had out at sea, that night on the ship's deck when she had first had the fever. It was the same wide world she had seen on the ship, yet not the same. Not quite the beast, immense and dazzling and pitiless, but a place where *he* existed, and where she might come in and lie by the fire. And she knew then that she would have to figure some way through this.

❦ · 39 · ❧

RUTH

After that she had considered whether to kill Johnny Dolan herself. It would not be so hard, she thought. Find something to put in his food, or his poteen. No one would look into it too closely. They were on their own in Pigtown, not even the leatherheads came up there unless something especially ambitious had gone missing.

Of course, that would mean store clerks who might talk, lingerers on the street corners who had seen her buy the package. She had heard of such things before, of witnesses in famous murder trials. She thought of doing it more *directly,* a blade or a shovel to his head, or even the ax he used to cut their firewood. If she didn't succeed the first time, there would be hell to pay—but she didn't figure she would have that problem.

It would be simple enough, to wait one night until he had fallen deep enough in his cups. One good, hard swing, and then she could bury him in the fields, where the men had already started excavating for the new park. Let them pull his skull from the ground, speculate on what ancient murder it must have been—a casualty from the Revolution, or a slavecatcher crept too close to the dogs of Seneca Village. She would already be well away with her lover, ensconced in the next Negro shantytown, where nobody came looking too closely.

She tried to tell herself that it was impossible, that Johnny would be missed. But she knew it wasn't true. He was a solitary man, even at his jobs—even with the other fire laddies. They never visited, and he never took her out to see them, or down to the firehouse chowders that she knew the wives went to. Chances were, knowing how little he liked to share his business, they were not even aware that she existed—did not even know where he lived. They would just think, when he did not answer the call to the next blaze or the next dance, that he had moved on. Gone out West, or over to Newark, or fallen in the river coming back drunk one night from The Yellow Man.

No, there were only two people, she knew, two people in the whole of the City who would ever miss Johnny Dolan. That was the sister, Deirdre, and her husband. And in the end they would be just the ones to help her.

It was Ruth who had found them, when he could not. *A good Irish girl, named Deirdre, working as a maid or a cook*. She knew how laughably common it must have sounded in this City, with only a hundred thousand or so women to fit that description.

It was impossible, but she had her job at the rookeries by then. Wandering out after one of his beatings, as far as she could to the east. Wanting to see the river she had heard was there—unsure, just yet, if she would throw herself in.

She had found instead the hills of bones. The mountains of scrap, of garbage, of every possible remnant of cloth, of leather, of broken furniture and busted plates. Of everything the great City chewed up every day in its endless appetite, all its most wretched refuse, washed up here, to be painstakingly remade, restitched, transformed in the shops of the German ladies. Mrs. Krane and Mrs. Mueschen, as they told her they were, though she could not imagine either one had ever experienced anything beyond a Boston marriage. Lean and tall and bespectacled, peering over their vast piles of junk. How they had acquired them, she never knew. An inheritance, sheer luck? Through their own endless accumulation?

When she asked for work—wanting something, some excuse to get away from him even for a few hours a day—they had sat her down, shown her their own crude dolls and trinkets. The inelegant but serviceable little figures they sold downtown at Macy's, at Chesler's—at Stewart's, with all its handsome young blond men behind the counters, its exquisite marble floors.

"Do this," they had told her, twisting cloth around bone, ribbon around cloth. *"Do this,"* and she did it, and they looked pleased, even through their dour, enigmatic German faces.

She did it even better than they did after a few turns, a few days, and she had been so happy to know there was *something* she could do—something at least, even if she would then have to do it over and over again, the same thing for the rest of her life.

It was there at the rookeries that she had asked every woman she met about Deirdre. Asking the other women she sewed and twisted the dolls with by the fire, or any women who came into the tiny shop, selling still more junk. That was how Ruth had found her, asking everyone she could for weeks and months, though much good it had done her with Johnny Dolan.

Deirdre was already living in the house by Paradise Alley then, with her husband, Tom O'Kane, and their children and all their nice things. When Ruth and Johnny had finally gone down to visit with them, she had been so intimidated by it all—by Deirdre, by the house. By all the grand pieces of furniture they had crammed into the front room, the fall-front secretary, and the reclining couch, and the square piano squeezed into one corner. Even the light had been different—wonderfully clean and clear, white light from an Argand lamp, with its expensive oil.

And Deirdre herself hovering over the tea table, in a real day dress made of green-striped taffeta, with puffed sleeves, and embroidered muslin cuffs and collar. Ruth had shrunk from her scrutinizing gaze. Struggling with the tea, trying to shove her fingers through the tiny cup handles, having all she could do to keep from spilling it on herself. Trying to sit on the sofa, without her cheap shift creeping up her legs—

She had seemed so formidable that Ruth had actually been surprised when Johnny Dolan told her the rest of the family was dead and Deirdre had cried. Dropping her head straight down in her hands and bawling like a child. Sobbing inconsolably, turning away even from her husband, Tom, when he had half-stood from his chair, and tried to put an awkward, comforting arm around her. But when she brought her head back up, Ruth saw that her eyes were dry again.

She had seen, too, how Deirdre disapproved of her brother. How furiously she would frown whenever Ruth came into her home with a fresh bruise, or another shanty on the glimmer. She suspected him for exactly what he was, and lectured him on his responsibilities.

"You ought to live like a proper Irishman, and give up shaming yourself before your people and your God," she would scold him.

Deirdre had disapproved of her even more, she knew—looking upon her from the beginning as the agent of Johnny's degradation. Her scorn turning to abhorrence when she discovered that they had never been properly married—

But then there was the husband, Tom. *There was always a man*. He had a soft word, and a little joke for her, whenever he saw her. A quiet man, gentle in manner and voice—but a former butcher and a fireman, with arms as wiry and strong as cables.

There was always a man, to get one in or out of trouble.

She saw how he would wince when he noticed the bruises on her. The marks of her martyrdom, making their claim upon him as *a good man*. A plan starting to form in her head even before she had any real plan—even before Old Man Noe was murdered, and Johnny Dolan had come home with his face covered not with lumps and bruises, but with deep, bloody scratches.

She might have put it down to some dockside whore. But when Dolan took off his coat, she could see that his whole vest and his white linen shirt were streaked with blood. Still no more disheveled than he might have been after some regular dockside fracas—but more agitated than she had ever seen him, pacing back and forth around the shanty. Peeking out through the door, and the badly caulked planks, as if he expected someone to be coming after him, across the snowy fields.

He had the walking stick half-concealed under his coat. A black oak shaft, crowned by the golden head of a dog that looked more like a jackal, with a long snout and erect, pointed ears. Trying to stand it quietly in the corner behind the cabinet of wonders—his corner, where he also stashed his tools and any money he might have, everything else that was most valuable to him.

"But what's that about?" she had asked without thinking, surprised.

He had come at her, shaking his fist.

"Ya want to say anything about this? Huh? I guarantee ya, if you do—if you say a word to a *soul*—I'll see to it ya hang with me!"

Bringing the fist right up to her face—but not, she had noticed, actually hitting her.

"Sure now."

"Good thing, then." He had paced across the room, still flinging hollow threats back over his shoulder. "Good thing for *you*."

She had dropped her eyes and her hands back down to the sewing in her lap, pretending not to watch as he removed more items from the inner pockets of his vest and coat. Secreting them back there, behind the box that was the greatest of his treasures.

Once he was through he went outside and got more firewood. Cursing as it sputtered in the stove, still cold and wet from the snow in the yard. When at last he had the fire going, he stripped off the shirt and vest, feeding them frantically into its mouth.

"There! The proof's all gone now. So it wouldn't do ya any good to talk about it anyhow."

He stood over her, bare-chested, hands perched belligerently on his hips.

"No."

"So nobody'd believe ya anyway."

She kept her head down over the sewing, until he put on his night-shirt and climbed into bed, still yelling at her. His voice sounding shrill, and futile—

"Shut that light! How's a workingman to get any sleep?"

"All right, then."

She blew out the putrid oil lamp by which she was working, and sat there in the dark. After a few minutes she could hear him snoring, as she knew she would. He always fell asleep fastest when he was most agitated, most rattled by something, and she rose soundlessly as soon as he did, and went over to his cache behind the cabinet of wonders.

The only light in the room was from the dull embers in the stove mouth, but she didn't need much. She faced the bed where he lay, and squatted over the chamber pot, so that she could have an excuse in case he awoke suddenly, sitting bolt upright, as he sometimes did.

Reaching behind her back, she felt out the tin strongbox he used, clasped with the expensive new lock he had bought down on Broadway. She picked it at once with her hairpin, then worked over its insides with her fingers. Feeling out the newest treasures he had brought home. A fine, silk handkerchief, glorious to the touch. A watch wrapped

inside it. She moved a thumb over the cracked face, and down the
smooth, metallic casing—the instrument still running, throbbing like
a small bird's heart in her hand. Her fingers working so precisely over
the inscription on the back that she might have read it by hand, if she
had had any letters.

She moved on—to the watch fob, and a pair of cufflinks. A tie pin,
perhaps. Thick paper that might have been a wad of banknotes, or
even bond coupons. Nothing out of the ordinary. No more than any
other robbery of a drunken fop, some rabbit sport, in one of the war-
ren alleys along the waterfront.

Then she felt it—the cold, copper twists of that curlicue he carried
around. Like a corkscrew, but no bigger than a pig's tail. She had
always assumed it was a burglary tool, but now there was something
different about it—something loose, even slimy coating the top of it.
Blood, perhaps?

She ran her thumb over it again—but it was slippery, and evasive
as an oyster. She finally picked the whole corkscrew up very delicately,
in two fingers. Realizing only later that she had figured it out before
she held it up to her face. Had known it from seeing the same thing, so
many times in the cabinet of wonders, so that she did not jump or yell
or do anything to awaken him when she finally saw it for herself,
unmistakable even in the dim light—

A human eye.

❧ · 40 · ❧

RUTH

She started awake, still not fully aware that she had dozed. The stark, winter stars and the half-moon were gone. It was summer again—and now the night sky had an apocalyptic, orange hue. There was a heavy smell of smoke in the air, even where she was inside, through the clasped shutters.

"Hullo! Hullo!"

There was a banging on the front door, so loud and heedless that it frightened her at first. *The troops in front of their cabin, bayonets glinting in the sunlight, while the land agent read his bill of ejectment—*

"Hullo! Are ye *thera*, then? Are ye still in there? Hullo!"

It was Deirdre, the impatient, peremptory voice unmistakable. Ruth began to unbolt the door—casting a look around the room as she did at the children, still sleeping where she had left them, slumped on the floor or about the chairs. *Worrying even now what Deirdre might think, to see them still up—*

"Hullo! Ruth, can ye hear me?"

"Yes, yes!"

She pulled the door open hastily. Surprised to see the look of concern across Deirdre's face—even as it changed at once back to annoyance, to the usual impatience with anything having to do with *her*.

"You're here, then. Did you fall asleep? And these children—awake still!"

Milton was already gathering them up, ushering them into their common bedroom. They went passively, walking in a trance, not even crying to be so disturbed. She watched Deirdre watch them go with her usual expression, something between exasperation and astonishment that any children could be such a color, and still talk and cry and smile like real babies.

"What is it, then? Did they take the town back?" Ruth asked.

Knowing it couldn't be true, or Billy would be back. Wishing again—

"No. It's worse than that," Deirdre told her in a low voice, waiting until all the children were out of the room. "The word is, they took the Armory. Maybe the Steam Works, as well. They got all the guns they want, now—"

"I see." Ruth said. Her mind going blank as she waited for what she thought Deirdre was about to tell her.

"They burnt the Colored Orphans' home," she blurted out, then grabbing Ruth's arm, adding quickly, "*Mind you,* there's no word of anyone dead. Leastways, there was nobody there when they got in— they know that for sure. The great bravos are walking all up and down the street, regretting that the place was empty, and bragging about what they would have done if it hadn't been."

"All right. All right, then," Ruth said, taking a breath, determined not to let Deirdre see her cry—not to let go of herself now, with the children to be taken care of still, and worse to come.

So he was out there, somewhere, with all those poor children. If he really was still alive. Maybe it was even proof he was alive. After all, someone had to take the orphans out, get them away from the mob—

She forced herself to think, to talk.

"All right. So what's there to do, then?"

She could scarcely credit it, in the gloomy light through the shutters, but she could have sworn that she saw a look of admiration flicker across Deirdre's face.

"Not much—not much to be done, at that. They say they're burning the whole town. There are fires everywhere—"

"Can we still run for it, then?"

"It would be folly, now. The mob's all over, attacking people in the street. But I was thinking . . ."

She let the sentence trail off, looking down for a moment at the floor Ruth had swept so fervently that morning, thinking that she would walk away and never see the place again.

"You could come with the children to our home. For the night. It'd be safer that way. From the mob and from *him*—"

"No, I couldn't do that," Ruth told her—though to her continuing surprise, Deirdre actually seemed anxious for her to accept. "Your own family would be in danger. It wouldn't be right—"

"Since when has *my* family had a thing to fear from such street rabble?" Deirdre scoffed, contemptuous again.

"This is different—"

"Nonsense! Respectable white people in a white house—they wouldn't dare to disturb us."

"But Billy—when he comes back, how'll he find us? How'll he know where to go?"

"We'll keep a watch for him," Deirdre told her briskly.

Milton had just come back in the room, and to Ruth's surprise she even acknowledged his existence.

"Sure, it will be you and me, and your oldest boy. And maybe my Liza—her eyes are good enough, when she's not watching a stew. As soon as Billy takes a step down the street, we'll pull him in."

Ruth hesitated— *But surely it would be better for them at Deirdre's. It was the thing he would be most pleased with her for, to keep his children safe.*

"All right," she agreed—and Deirdre was all efficiency again, hustling them about the house.

"Let's get your things. You're packed? Good, then. Let's wheel it over through the back lots. There's no reason for everybody on the block to see our business."

They peered out the back door, into the impenetrable night.

"All right, now. It's just three houses. Liza will be at the door—at least she's supposed to be, or I'll tan her backside for her," Deirdre told them. "Knock twice, and she'll answer—"

Ruth could just make out the slumping roofs of the privvies, the air reeking with their odor. Beyond them were the backs of the houses on the next lot, their shutters closed and their lights all out—save for a single, solitary prick of light from one window. *The Jews' place,* she recognized. *God only knew how they were faring over there, on such an evening—*

"All right, now. Go on with you!"

The children looked at her for confirmation, and Ruth nodded.

"Go! Now!"

They scuttled their way like rats down the back lots. She and Deirdre taking the youngest ones by the hand, while Milton pushed the barrow holding all their possessions. Every turn of its wheel seemed to squeal and echo, up and down the alleyway. It was not thirty yards down the lots to Deirdre's house, nothing but the back of their own houses on the one side, the stinking wood privvies on the other. But with every step, she was sure that she could see a pair of feet, the edge of his coat, waiting in the shadows—

How real he still was, even after all this time. She could see the white-knuckled grip of his fists, the rage in his face, right in front of her—

A head jutted out from the privvies, wild and unshaven—red eyes staring through them. Ruth almost screamed to see it—but it was only a local bummer, a deserter from the army who hung around the back lots. The tattered remnants of his blue Union coat still hanging from his back. He took a step toward them, perhaps threatening, perhaps imploring.

"Get out of here! John Kaehny, you miserable old layabout!" Deirdre shouted at him, and he bolted off at once, back down between the privvy shacks.

They raced the last few yards to Deirdre's house, reaching her back door breathless and terrified. They rapped twice—and Eliza opened it up at once. The rest of Deirdre's children standing just behind her, looking worried but silent—a wince of envy going through Ruth, even then, to see how neatly dressed, how clean and obedient they were.

Deirdre shut the door at once, and bolted it behind them. Smiling as best she could at them all. Trembling a little, Ruth could see, as she was herself, but still in command.

"Come on, now, I'll get someplace to sleep made up. And Ruth will get cocoa for you children, you'll like that."

Ruth went gladly to do as she was told, not even minding the order. Marveling as always at the tidiness of Deirdre's kitchen. Sure enough, looking in the pantry, she found a tin of cocoa, though she knew it must have cost nearly as much as gold these days. There was a bucket of real milk, too, from the O'Kanes's cow. They were the only ones on the block to keep one, renting a stall from a livery stable on Oliver Street.

She moved about the kitchen, getting the mugs of chocolate ready, and trying to keep from smiling too much. Trying to hide how exultant she felt—*now that Deirdre would take care of everything*. She still could not quite understand her sudden kindness, or, for that matter, how unnerved she had been this morning. But she was unable to submerge her delight in the moment, even with Billy still out, and Johnny Dolan himself, somewhere in the City.

It was all right, Deirdre would set it right. Feeling now as she never had before, save for lying in Billy's arms in the old house, up in the central park, or listening to her father's stories, half-drowsing through the smoky, winter afternoons in their cabin out on the Burren. Her belly full, and her head against her mother's knee—the small, rustling noises of her brothers and sisters all around her as they burrowed in with her around the hearth, safe in the company of her family.

41

HERBERT WILLIS ROBINSON

Night—and through the ruptured City all sorts of creatures slip.

This is the creeping season. Thieves pick through the shattered storefronts. Cabs stalk slowly up the side streets, and back alleys. They are drawn by horses with muffled hooves, their drivers charging fifty, a hundred dollars to sneak the families of bankers and merchants out of the City.

Up from the wharves and the Five Points come others, with no intention of fleeing. These are the professional gangsters and the river thieves, the housebreakers and crimps and killers. They have no quarrel with the draft. They never planned to go anyway, their names unrecorded in any barrel, any census. Now they swagger through the streets, brazenly hold up the cabs at gunpoint. Robbing men in the City at gunpoint, committing all sorts of other outrages—

The boy in the street, playing in a puddle of blood. Smiling up into the sun as he smears a hand across his face—

I creep through it all myself, still searching. At last I have fulfilled the original assignment that Greeley gave me, what seems like so many years ago this morning. I have tracked down the seat(s) of our government, located now at the St. Nicholas Hotel, corner of Spring Street and Broadway.

The St. Nick is one of those perfect middle grounds that spring up in any good war. Not quite so elegant as the Metropolitan with its ladies' sky parlors, or the Fifth Avenue with its perpendicular railway, but perfect in its own, enormous garishness, its gigantic chandeliers and candelabra, its silver service and Sheffield plate, its six hundred rooms.

All sorts of men gather here—drummers and spies and the aristocrats of shoddy; journalists and generals and politicians. They jam the lobby, alert, feral eyes squinting to see how they might best exploit our national calamity for their own gain. Arguing and cajoling, entreating and seducing. Gulping their iced smashes, their daisies and juleps, excitedly dipping in their fresh, green blades of spearmint. (They would not gulp their drinks so rapidly, perhaps, if they knew that the spearmint comes from the roof boxes of Baxter Street tenements—plucked by the hands of tubercular children, fertilized with pig excrement gathered from the street.)

The place is more jammed than ever tonight, even as wild rumors sweep the lobby. *The whole City is burning. The mob is on its way here.* Mayor Opdyke has his headquarters upstairs, as does General Wool, and there is a martial feel to the whole establishment. Uniformed messengers storm through the lobby, officers in gold braid strutting urgently about.

Meanwhile, the Union League holds the bar like a fortress. Here is the real backbone of the City. My Gramercy neighbors, George Strong and Dudley Field. The Reverend Morgan Dix from Trinity Church, and Bellows, up from Washington. Professor Gibbs and Charlie Brace, and President King, down from Columbia College.

Men of steel, in the Street and in the pulpit. They sit around a side table, imbibing nothing stronger than sarsaparilla. Casting suspicious glances at the dead-horse contractors all around them, while they browbeat our poor mayor.

"Where are the Metropolitans? What is Acton doing?"

"He has the situation well in hand. I have every confidence in him," the mayor replies.

"*Oh?*" George Strong asks, cocking an eyebrow. "May I inquire then, *why have you abandoned City Hall?*"

George Opdyke mops his brow, drenched in sweat, his suit crumpling in the heat. *(It will never rain.)* He is a dry-goods merchant turned reform politician, a man who likes to write scholarly papers on colonial economics—and who thought it would be a good idea to be mayor at the outset of the Civil War.

"One should take precautions—" he tries.

"You should march back to City Hall at once, and read the Riot Act to the rabble!" the Reverend Dix informs him. At the start of the war, Dix raised the American flag over Trinity Church and it has flown there ever since, above any cross, joining God and the Union for eternity.

"Where is General Wool? What is he doing?"

"Upstairs, hiding in his suite!" snorts Charlie Brace.

Wool is the commander of all federal troops in the City. He is a stern-looking man but ancient; an old Indian fighter who made a name for himself running helpless Cherokees out of Georgia.

"General Wool has no more than five hundred men he can put under arms—"

"Impossible!" Strong exclaims. "If that is really so, we must telegraph Secretary Stanton at once!"

"I'm told it is a crucial moment, if Meade is to catch Lee north of the Potomac," Opdyke tries to demur. "If he can, the whole game may be up—"

"*Nonsense!*" Strong bolts up out of his chair. "It doesn't matter what happens out in some Pennsylvania wheat field! The war is *here!*"

As always, these men understand the heart of the matter. Just two years ago, at the start of the war, our then-mayor Wood proposed that the City should actually secede as well, and start our own nation— thereby promoting himself to president (emperor? grand vizier?). Other men of the Street were all in favor, looking nervously to their Southern debtors—terrified that they would simply refuse to pay, and bring a ruinous crash down upon us.

Not the Union League. They have money at stake, too, but their ties to the country are almost mystical. Their whole ideal of themselves—their dour, unwavering Yankee superiority—is bound up with the Union. If they are not the merchant princes of a divinely blessed people, of the world's coming colossus, then what are they? Just more stock jobbers, grubbing for money like everyone else in this town?

It was they who made sure that Secretary Chase found the money to finance the war. Made sure that we remained the Empress City of the West, advancing toward our certain, glorious destiny. They don't mean to turn back now, no matter how much blood darkens the fields of the Southland—or the streets of our City.

"We must do something. This afternoon it took a *priest* to talk them out of burning down the college!" President King of Columbia protests, unclear as to what was the greater humiliation.

"What we need are *gunboats,* gunboats *ringing* this island," Dudley Field insists. "*That* will put the fear of God in them."

The island of Manhattan surrounded by floating machines, girded with iron. Ready to belch fire until the whole of the City is destroyed, if need be—

"We must *at least* declare martial law."

"I don't know about *that*—" Mayor Opdyke equivocates—but George Strong has had enough. He stands up with a dismissive wave of his hand, headed for the St. Nick's convenient new telegraph room.

"I shall wire President Lincoln for more men. We will save this City yet!"

He strides off, ignoring Opdyke's protests. But soon he is back, his face contorted with indignation.

"It seems that the lines are down, all over the West Side. I am going down to wire from my office on the Street—if *anything* is still working in this City!"

I decide to go with him, curious to see how Wall Street is holding up—and what will happen next. As angry as Strong is, I can see that he, too, is disconcerted by this latest turn of events. The previously unthinkable idea is growing—that now, with our communications cut off, we might actually lose the island.

Out on Broadway, the night is more stifling than ever. A corrosive, burning smell is everywhere, filling one's nose and throat. Dozens of fires can be seen, turning the night sky orange. It is our only illumination, now that the street-lights have been extinguished, the gas cut off by the mob or the authorities.

"Your house is still standing," Strong tells me abruptly, and I almost laugh to hear him say it, knowing how hard it is for him to make conversation. He is an odd man, my neighbor. Haughty and aloof but strangely idealistic for a businessman, engrossed in his ideas about what the Union, or religion, or what our civilization should be.

"They have not touched the Gramercy Park—not yet, anyway,"

he goes on, trying something like humor. "We got up a squad of vigilantes. Marching around the square with bird guns and dueling pistols, trying to grimace sufficiently at every young Celt we could find. But they never attempted it."

In truth, I had forgotten all about my home on the Gramercy Park for hours. So Maddy would have been safe there, after all—

Maddy. The day's fighting has carried me back and forth past her little house, but no closer. Paradise Alley, the whole Fourth Ward, lies behind the lines of the mob now. It will be dangerous for me to venture there now, after dark, even in the disguise of my wrecked suit. But I must try it, as soon as I file my story—must talk her into leaving. *Stubborn, foolish girl—*

It is a harrowing enough walk down to Strong's firm. Near Canal Street we pass roving gangs of gang *b'hoys*—skulking about, looking out for their chance. A solitary roundsman comes up the street, tapping his locust club in his hand. He does nothing, though—*can* do nothing, one man alone—and he and the gangsters simply eye each other warily and move on.

Those who can, defend themselves. On Maiden Lane the jewelers patrol in front of their stores, rifles in hand. Ironworkers hold their forges, conductors their rail cars. Lord & Taylor's has armed a hundred of its clerks, and the nice young men at Stewart's Iron Palace now offer to shoot you on sight.

Somehow, we are able to make our way down to Wall Street without being shot by either robbers or vigilantes. Strong goes off to his office, but I wait for him below, preferring to see what I can see, here in the heart of our nation's money capital.

The Street and the blocks around it are bustling despite the hour. Here are most of Wool's regulars, along with sailors from the ships in the harbor, setting up Gatling guns at strategic positions. In the Sub-Treasury Building—the very spot where Washington first took the oath of office as president—clerks stand guard at every window. They are armed with hand grenades, and bottles full of vitriol, and a hose has been run down to the basement boiler—ready to blow scalding steam into any mob that should breach its massive, bronzed doors.

Even so, sailors are lugging chests shaped like coffins down the steep steps of the Sub-Treasury. They toil under the blackened statue of Washington, gesturing disdainfully toward the West, grunting and struggling with the huge, heavy chests. For a moment I wonder what they could possibly be moving—then it comes to me.

Even the gold is fleeing the City. They are hauling the caskets on down to the Battery, and out to the ships in the harbor. The nation's gold reserves, taking flight—can the rest of us be far behind? The capital trembles in its citadel—

Just then I hear a burst of noise, and wonder if the mob could have sneaked 'round our defenses. But no—it is coming from the offices of an ancient and venerable firm, just across Liberty Street.

What mischief is this? Have thieves broken in? The door and shutters of the building are locked—but I spy a penumbra of light around a basement window, and crouch down to peer inside.

There I see a remarkable sight. Some of the most renowned traders on Wall Street, some of the richest men in the nation and therefore the world, are acting like lunatics. Even as I watch they jump in the air, and gesture frantically, standing on chairs and tables, cursing and laughing—and *singing.*

I realize that I have stumbled upon the Gold Room. It is the biggest open secret in the City, save for Madam Restell's abortion parlors. Trading in gold has been banned by federal decree, since Old Abe became exasperated by the wealthiest men in the Union wagering every day on whether it would survive.

But he only succeeded in pushing it underground. Now the greatest financiers in the country gather every night in a different office, to bet America up and down. They huddle around the wires, and it is said that they have spies in every major telegraph office, and both armies, to send them the most critical information before Lincoln himself gets to see it.

Each side sings when the war goes their way. When the tide shifts in favor of the North, those who have bet on Secretary Chase's shinplaster money bellow out "The Union Forever." The goldbugs sing "Dixie" whenever Lee wins another victory, or now, as the City burns around their heads:

> *"I wish I was in the land of cotton,*
> *Old times there are not forgotten,*

> *Look away,*
> *Look away,*
> *Look away—*
> *Dixie-land!"*

They are in full voice, singing ecstatically, even as the gold they worship flees town in a coffin. When they reach hell, I have no doubt, they will sell the devil short.

42

HERBERT WILLIS ROBINSON

By the time I make my way back to the *Tribune,* there is a feeling of utter desperation inside. Over in City Hall Park, the mob has grown larger and louder than ever. The revolutionary barber from Christadoro's is still egging them on from his soapbox. *Can he really have been there all day? Or did he go back to work, shave a few faces in the afternoon, then come out again for the evening show?*

Across Park Row the *Times* is lit up like a Christmas tree. Clerks and reporters showing themselves in every window, with pistols and carbines in hands. Henry Raymond and Leonard Jerome themselves are standing behind enormous Gatling guns, just waiting for the mob to try something.

Greeley, meanwhile, will allow no one to bring so much as a dueling pistol on the premises. All he has allowed is for the windows to be barricaded with bales of water-soaked paper and cotton—a precaution that has left everyone nearly prostrate from the heat, and has only added to the general despair.

Everyone, that is, save for Horace himself. Our leader stands behind his desk, fielding telegraph messages and dispatches with aplomb, Sidney Gay and James Gilmore working grimly by his side. Teddy Tilton, who edits the *Independent,* is here as well and looking even more grim. Come to keep a supper appointment, he has found himself trapped in the middle of the maelstrom.

"Ah, Robinson! What do you have for me?" Horace greets me with a paternal smile, as if I have just come from a meeting for Sabbatarianism.

I know what he is about, playing dauntless captain of the storm-tossed ship. Adding to The Legend That Is Greeley. Besides, as a newspaper man he is in his element.

"Such days we are living through!" he exults, looking over my shoulder as I rough out for him the first lines of my report. He thumbs again through the thick pile of wires on his desk, gleefully reading me stories of this depredation, or that valiant defense.

"It seems that Mother has put a keg of powder in the cellar," he marvels, shaking a message from his wife at me. "With a trail leading up the stairs to the living room, so that in case these curs come to Chappaqua she can blow the whole house down on them!"

He leans back against his desk to consider this, his eyes wide with excitement. Not least, I suspect, over the possibility that The Irrepressible Conflict will blow *herself* to kingdom come—

There is a rattle of something against the front of the building, like hail falling on a tin roof. From below comes the sound of breaking glass, the heavier *thump* of bricks and stones glancing off walls, and we rush to the windows. The mob has begun to move. Even as we watch, they stream out of the City Hall Park, hurling everything they can find at us—still exhorted by their radical barber.

"Come on, my laddies, come on! And we'll have the life of that damned Greeley!"

Blocking their path are no more than four or five roundsmen, posted at the front door of the *Trib*. They will be swept away within seconds; it is a wonder they do not run already. Yet, unaccountably, the mob stops before them, only hurling more insults at us.

"*Down with the* Tribune!"

"*Down with the old white coat, what thinks a nigger's as good as an Irishman!*"

"This is not a riot, it's a revolution," Mr. Gay says, peering down at them.

"It looks like it. It is just what I have expected, and I have no doubt they will hang me," Greeley agrees, sounding rather satisfied.

"We must *do* something—"

"Well, I for one intend to have my dinner." Greeley makes a great show of consulting his watch, then clicks it shut again and nods back toward the mob below. "Let them burst their throats bawling at me. If I cannot eat my dinner on time, my life is not worth anything, anyway. Theodore?"

Tilton nods and swallows like the condemned man, called from his cell, allowing Greeley to hook an arm in his and guide him on downstairs.

"*At least go out the back way!*" Mr. Gay cries after him—but Greeley only waves him off, still clutching poor Tilton's arm.

From up in his office, we watch wordlessly as Greeley walks him right out the front door and pushes their way through the mob.

"They will hang him before our eyes!"

I can't say there is a man among us who would not be at least intrigued by such a spectacle. But the mob seems frozen by his appearance. Even the ranting barber is stunned into inaction by the sheer gall of it. Before they can think to so much as raise a hand against them, Greeley is able to steer Tilton right through their ranks, down the street and into Windust's restaurant.

"It's true," gulps Gilmore, into the awed silence in the room. "God *does* look after children, and the simpleminded."

"Which is Horace?"

"Both!"

But the mob still seethes outside—their rage redoubled, now that they have inexplicably let Greeley himself pass through their fingers. They surge toward the door again, the desperate policemen trying to link arms against them.

"Here they come!" cries Gilmore.

They sweep the police out of the way, pulling the nightsticks out of their hands, beating and pummeling them as they go. They kick down the front door—and all at once they are inside, grappling with the reporters and clerks on the first floor. Breaking up the furniture and the composing boards, heaping up everything they can find in the middle of the room.

"Burn it! Burn it all!" the barber is shouting maniacally in their midst, emptying bottles of camphene along the floor, starting small fires everywhere.

We run downstairs and someone takes a wild, drunken swing at me. I jump back, and it only glances off my chest—still, hard enough to send me sprawling. In the whole day of fighting, this is the first time someone has actually laid hands on me and I lie where I fall, temporarily stunned.

"Up! Up, boys, and at 'em!"

Carpenter and his flying squad come charging up Nassau Street on the run, and fall on the crowd from behind. Just like this afternoon, nothing can stand before them. They beat down everything in their path like the human thresher machine they have become, and the mob is broken at once. They flee back out into the darkness, while the rest of us stamp out the fires—the barber last seen running off up Broadway, still swearing his vengeance upon Greeley.

It is over within minutes. The composing room is a wreck, full of broken chairs and half-charred desks, as if a tornado or a hurricane has swept through it, everything covered in camphene or water. Nothing is damaged beyond repair, though, and before Carpenter and his men leave, Raymond and Jerome send over sixteen *Times* men with rifles, and yet another Gatling gun.

"But Horace said no weapons," Mr. Gay protests half-heartedly.

"He can go hang!" snorts Gilmore—though no one is sure the mob hasn't done that very job already, in all the confusion.

"Where is he? Where is Horace?"

The staff searches frantically through the offices, sends runners out to Windust's, which the mob has also sacked. We peer out the windows—half-afraid that we will see his famous white duster swinging slowly from a lamppost. There are rumors that he has indeed been hanged, that he fled the City—that the waiters at Windust's hid him from the mob under a table.

There is no word, though—until suddenly he appears in the door some two hours later, like an apparition. Patting his perfectly rounded child's belly. He strolls through the composing room barely seeming to notice the smashed furniture and charred woodwork, his mind no doubt on some great Greeley scheme or another. The rest of us watching openmouthed as he makes his way to his desk.

Upstairs he only pauses for a moment before getting back to the next day's editorial. Running his hand mournfully over the Gatling gun that James Gilmore has pointedly set up just outside his office.

"I don't know how I can work with so many guns about," he says wistfully.

. . .

I sit upstairs, at a desk in the hall outside Greeley's office, and write down my stories. My new street scenes—all the terrible things I have seen and heard today. From time to time Greeley emerges, and looks at my leaves, and hums with something I take for approval.

Yet my mind wanders, and I have to strain, and force myself to finish the article. *How can Maddy be faring through all this?* She should be all right. She is one of their own, an Irisher, it is true. Yet she is so pigheaded, and liable to provoke them—

My Maddy.

I should have made her come with me, deposited her in my house in Gramercy Park. Instead I hurried out to see what was going on, as I always have. Trying to find some story, some glimmer of truth, out in the City. Instead there is simply depravity.

I finish my copy and go up to the roof of the *Tribune*, to see if there isn't some way I can scout a path, back to the house I rent for her. Much of the staff is already up there, trapped the same as I am from reaching families and loved ones. The reporters and editors silently smoking their pipes and cigars.

Down below, we are still under siege from the mob. They have set bonfires all around Printing House Square—and throughout the great, blackened City before us. Only an hour or so after the first attack, Inspector Carpenter and his men had to intercept another horde at Frankfort Street, as dead set as everyone else, it seems, on marching down to the *Trib* and hanging Greeley from a lamppost.

God only knows why they hate us so—and why they are so intent on turning the whole City to rubble. There are shouts and cries in the darkness, little hedgehogs of torches moving through the streets. Here and there, a new building bursts into flames, shooting up into the night like a firework—

There is a boom, and a sound like many rushing feet, and for a moment we all brace ourselves, up on the roof, thinking that the gunboats have finally opened up, or that the mob is making another rush. But no. The boom sounds again, then crackles and rolls. It is only the benign intercession of nature, a spectacular, rolling thunderstorm— the kind that once used to terrify us so badly in the City.

The rain has come at last. Even as we watch, the storm forces its

way over the Hudson, smudging out the fires below like a giant
thumb. Forcing the mobs from the streets where nothing else could.

I seize the moment to set out for Maddy's at last. Walking quickly
through the cover the rain provides, not caring if it drenches me, it is
so blessedly cool. Yet soon it subsides to a trickle, the water gurgling
down through hundreds of drainpipes and gutters.

The City is almost numinous at such moments. Even the pigs have
been driven from the streets. The paving stones glistening, the sound
of draining water receding until the town is nearly hushed.

I reach Paradise Alley and move cautiously down the middle of
the street. I am more visible here, I know—but less likely to be taken
with a slung shot, or a garrot, out of some house shadow. When I
reach Maddy's house, I tap quietly at the door, trying not to make too
much of a commotion. But the only sign of human existence that I can
see is a hooded figure at the far end of the block, one so distant and
surreptitious that I cannot even tell if it is a white or a Negro, a man or
a woman. He or she seems to be locking a door, ready to flee with a
wheelbarrow full of possessions. When it turns in my direction, the
wraith freezes in place, and seems to give me a long, scrutinizing stare.
Then it finishes locking up and hurries off toward the west—grabbing up a pig as it goes, the animal squealing pitifully.

"Maddy! *Maddy!*"

My voice tinny and unconvincing in the empty night—the rain
beginning to pick up again. I bang harder now, and even clang the outside bell. Almost frantic, afraid for her, afraid for myself—

Then I spot her face at the second-story window, peering through
the curtains. No longer mocking me, but troubled and pale as the
moon. We hold there for a long moment before she moves away, starts
downstairs to let me into the rented house I have kept her in for all
these years.

43

RUTH

The rain fell like a barrage, rattling like grapeshot on the tin and wood roofs of the neighborhood. It woke her youngest two, Vie and Elijiah, who on finding themselves in a strange house in the middle of a storm, immediately began to cry.

"There it is," Deirdre said to Ruth, sitting across from her in the front parlor, a tone of vindication in her voice. "There's the rain at last, praise Jesus and all the saints. That will drive even the likes of them inside."

"Aye, it will for tonight," Ruth agreed, though she was not sure even that much was so.

She had seen what men would put up with for what they wanted, be it rain, or snow, or rivers of shite.

She went to her children where Deirdre had put them up, three to a bed, in the back and the upstairs rooms. Deirdre went with her, again, much to her surprise. Helping Ruth to calm them, shooing her own children back to bed. Ruth felt the tears welling up in her eyes, and she brushed them hurriedly away. Yet she could not help thinking that this was what she had always wanted, ever since she had moved onto the block. *The two of them like sisters, moving among beds full of babies.*

She rubbed their backs and fetched them each a ladle of water from one of the buckets in the corner. Gazing out the window as she tended to them—the sky all orange now, and luminous, the clouds reflecting back the fires burning all over the City.

Humming a lullaby, she made the children lie back down in the bed while she ran a hand over their heads. Vie felt warmer than she should, so Ruth went back into the parlor to find a cloth she might wet down, and lay over her brow. She did not want to bother Deirdre, still in with her own children, so she began to search on her own, looking through the looming, ebony secretary first.

She pulled open the top drawer—and found the newspaper. The name popping right out at her. Her reading was still such that she almost never looked at the papers, intimidated by their cramped, tiny print, and the multitude of words. But his name came up at her immediately. She sounded it out to herself, lips moving silently as she read the column where the page was folded:

"WOUNDED:
    ... O'Kane, Tom, 69th New York, Co. A—leg"

Ruth stepped away, dropping the newspaper in the drawer as if it had been something hot or sharp. Deirdre came in holding a pan of water in her hand, and she turned to her at once. Embarrassed to be caught so, looking through her things, but full of pity for her nevertheless.

"Oh, Deirdre," she said. "Oh, you poor girl. How long did you know, then?"

Deirdre said nothing at first, carefully placing the pan of water down on a chair. Then she lowered her head before Ruth, and held out a hand to her.

"It's a judgment against me," she said, and began to weep. "A judgment on the hardness of my heart."

"A judgment?" Ruth repeated, confused. "But what've you ever been, Deirdre, but a good mother an' a virtuous wife?"

"The Lord knows, I should have taken you in already," she only insisted, wiping at her eyes, her hand still squeezing Ruth's. "I should have took care of you years ago, you and your family. It's a judgment on me that I did not."

She lifted her head—her face still distraught, and so contrite that Ruth could only hold her and try to comfort her.

"There now, there now. It must've been a shock to ye. Is there nothin' else? No other word on Tom?"

"Nothing yet."

Deirdre began to cry again, muffling her sobs in Ruth's shoulder while Ruth patted her hair and back.

"Well, that's good, then," Ruth said, determinedly, trying to ignore how the bottom had fallen out of her own stomach. *Trying not to think about Billy.* "It's not so bad as the last time, anyway, when he was gone missing. He lived through that, didn' he? An' the fever in the hospital, an' all the conditions. This won't be but a scratch to him, big, strong man like he is—"

Though they both knew how many ways there were for a man to die from a scratch, down in the Washington hospitals. They had heard all the stories from the other women in Paradise Alley who had lost husbands, sons, brothers. *They died from legs that went bad, and the littlest wounds, that turned to gangrene. They died just sitting in camp, from the consumption, or the bloody flux. Leaving whole families of six and seven, to fend for themselves on the streets of New York—*

"But I blamed you for it. I blamed you for everything," Deirdre told her. "I blamed you for Johnny, even though I knew what he was, and then I blamed you for getting Tom to help you. God help me, but I blamed you for the war, too, you and your coloreds. For taking Tom off—even though I knew it was me that talked him into going."

Deirdre lowered her head before her again.

"But how could ya help it?" Ruth told her. "You had a respectable home. God only knows, the way me an' Johnny must've seemed to ya—"

"But I should have helped you! I should have made my home your home. I should've done that much for you, at least."

Ruth felt the tears in her own eyes, despite herself. Trying to think of something, anything she could say to Deirdre. Then she was crying, too—so hard that the two women had to sit down together on the sofa. She gripped Deirdre's arms there, trying to show her that she forgave her. Trying to hold her so she would not think any more on those years, on all the times she had stood like a beggar outside Deirdre's door.

It's done now. It's all done, anyway.

"But I blamed you for everything, and for Johnny, especially after the business with Old Man Noe," Deirdre insisted, when they were able to talk again.

"Ah, now. It's all right."

"I blamed you for all that. The night you came to the house—"

"I know, I know. But the thing was, you wasn't so wrong."

The sky had been orange that night, too. It was snowing, but there were distant claps of thunder, and the boom of the ice floes as they broke and smashed in the North River.

She had pulled the bell, then pounded at the front door. Knowing how Deirdre would consider it unrespectable even to acknowledge a caller at such an hour. Persisting, knocking and knocking, until Tom had answered the door, and pulled her on into the parlor.

Such a pleasant hour it looked in there. She was still jealous, she had to admit. Deirdre in her chair by the clean and odorless Argand lamp, with some book of devotional stories. Tom in his shirtsleeves, a copy of the *Tribune* still in his hand and a pair of reading spectacles hanging incongruously from his nose. The children already tucked into bed, the two of them reading bits to each other.

Ruth had felt the cold ripple of spite running through her. Knowing that she was come to overturn it all, this whole, perfectly arranged world of Deirdre's.

She had brought the cane with her, though she knew it was taking her life in her hands. Dolan would kill her for such a thing, and had she been stopped by a nab, she did not know what she would have done. She had managed to find a sheet of canvas from a construction site, wrapping the cane up with some sagging, discarded chimney brooms around it. Walking it all the way down from Pigtown, too fearful even to take an omnibus or a streetcar.

Dolan had thought to keep her ignorant about the crime. Daring her to ask about it, trying to overawe her into thinking it was just another of his mysterious jobs. But Ruth knew it was something more. He had stopped going out at all, even to fence the goods he had brought back. Prowling more and more restlessly around the shanty.

As soon as she had an excuse to go out, she had spent a penny on the *Herald*. Running it over to Billy's as quickly as she could. She had not wanted him to have anything to do with it, but who else could she ask. She told him to read the whole paper to her, refusing to say what it was she was on about, and he had made his way through it slowly, suspiciously, sneaking glances at her as he did to gauge her reaction.

But it was right there on the front page. She knew it at once: *A Mr. James H. Noe, prominent brush manufacturer, found bludgeoned to death at a new factory he was erecting on Greenwich Street.* The *Herald* ran through all the grisly details, both real and rumored. How Old Man Noe was thought to have put up a fight. The body robbed and mutilated, one or both of its eyes gouged out. His walking stick, crowned with the gold head of a dog, gone missing—presumed stolen by the murderer.

There were plenty of eyes in the City that needed putting out. But only that one walking stick.

Ruth had all she could do to keep from leaping up when Billy read her the story. Fighting hard to control herself, to keep any sign of her emotions from showing. And when he was finished with the story, Billy Dove lowered the newspaper, and looked directly at her sitting on his bed.

"So he was the one who did it."

After that, she had had to confess everything—even that she was with child, and she did not know if it was his. Bursting into tears to have him know anything about it at all. And Billy had listened to everything she said, without showing any expression, until she finished and he nodded and said to her:

"How should we kill him, then?"

She would not let Billy do anything like that. She could keep him from that much, at least. But striding back across the fields she had felt exultant. The feeling undiminished even as she approached the shanty again, and she could feel Dolan eyeing her through the boards. She knew she would have to be especially careful. That he would be watching her all the time, and she was careful to hang her head as she got closer, slumping her shoulders. *Trying to blot out her triumph, and remember the way she felt, returning to him every night. Making herself forget that was all about to end.*

Dolan did not leave the house again the next day, or the day after. Growing more and more jumpy and morose, when he wasn't drunk. No longer bothering to shave or clean himself at all, only peering out the door and the cracks in the walls at the frozen, wintry fields.

On the third afternoon, she returned from the markets to find that he had buried the walking stick in the yard. It was hidden under the snow, down in the fissure of another huge grey split of rock. The hiding place cunningly disguised, heaped up with snow again. But she could tell where it was, she had scoured every inch of their tiny patch of yard for the past year, if only longing to be away from it.

Back inside Dolan was more agitated than ever, stomping about the shanty and rubbing his arms like a madman—his eyes as red as live coals.

"We should clear out," he told her. "We should get out now, while we can. Off this goddamned island."

"Why don't we, then," she had said carefully.

"*No, goddamn ye!* They'll sell me, sell me's soon as I take a foot out the door. We got to burrow in here. We got to stay inside, till the winter's out."

She had to wait for hours, until he calmed himself with the jug, and finally fell asleep across the bed. Then, when the winter sun was already beginning to set over the North River, spreading needles of purple and orange light across the pitted fields, she had gone out and dug up the things he had buried.

She had pulled up the cane and all the rest of his stash, bundling it up with the canvas, and the chimney brooms she had found. Walking all the long way down to Paradise Alley in the Fourth Ward. Not even willing to ask Billy to accompany her, for fear of what the sight of them together, a white woman and a black man, might arouse. Petrified as it was that Dolan should awake, or that a roundsman should stop her.

"What're you on about? What do you mean, bringing those into my house?" Deirdre had said when she stepped into her front room with her bundle.

Standing up from her chair, a look of defiance but also growing fear in her face, as if she already had some presentiment of why Ruth had come. Her voice rising until it was nearly hysterical.

"*What do you mean, bringing that in here?*"

At first she would not believe it, even after Ruth had produced the jackal-headed cane. The story, the details of the crime were in every paper in the City by then. But Deirdre kept insisting that it must be a mistake, that her brother had been framed, or was keeping the loot for some friend. Until at last Ruth had produced the one other item from his stash, which had ended all the argument.

Deirdre had not so much as flinched to see the thing, she had to give her that. She had even wanted to turn him over to the law, right then and there. Insisting that if her brother had done such a thing, they must give him to the police like anyone else.

"Now, lamb, you don't want t'do that," Tom had soothed her. His big hands on her shoulders—sending more spasms of envy through Ruth. "You don't want to do that, you'd never forgive yourself for it."

In the end Tom had convinced her to let *him* take care of it, to find some way to send Johnny Dolan out of the City. Deirdre had finally agreed that it was the just thing—though even then she had burst into one last, tearful protest.

"Ah, it's not him, it's not him! It must be from seeing them all die like that, that's what did it. From having such companions!"

Her eyes searching Ruth's face, with an expression both beseeching and full of hatred.

It was Tom who had known how to arrange the rest of it, through his old friends from the Black Joke company, and on the floor at The Place of Blood. It was he who had set up everything, with Billy's help. All Ruth had had to do was to rebury Dolan's stash in the rock—and then to get him outside. Tom had offered to help her with that, too, but she had refused, knowing that this was the delicate part, and that it was for her to do alone.

"Are you sure you'll be all right?" he had asked her, again and again. But she had assured him that she would do it.

She had made herself wait for another three days, while Tom finished preparing things. Even though she could barely stand it, her nerves nearly as raw as Dolan's. Waiting for somebody to sell them both to the police. Watching Johnny Dolan pace endlessly around the shanty, drunk and raging, or simply sitting on the bed, opening and closing his fists, over and over again.

Then Tom had sent word up that everything was ready, and Billy had met her on the little outcropping overlooking Seneca Village, where, unbeknownst to him, she had watched him that winter. He held on to her there, once he had delivered his message, drawing her to him and making her look him in the face.

"You sure he don't know?" he had asked her.

"I'm sure at that," Ruth told him evenly, sure of no such thing, but just glad that he cared enough to ask.

Billy looked over in the direction of Pigtown.

"You *sure?* I could just go there an' kill the man. I could."

"*No,*" she told him. "I won't put that on your soul, or mine. He don't know a thing."

"I'll follow ya, then. Anything goes wrong, you run to me, you hear?"

"Yes. Yes, I hear," she had said, and held on to him tightly for another few moments.

Ruth had taken her one, grave risk then—staying away from the shanty for half that night. Not even telling Billy about it, knowing that he would not allow it. Yet it had to be done. She had roamed the streets, and the fields for hours, walking fast to try to keep off the cold—walking until she was half-exhausted, and knew that she looked it.

Only after midnight had she come back in, as quietly as possible. Acting as nervous and unsettled as she could manage, though in fact she found herself filled with a deep and inexplicable calm.

Dolan was on her at once.

"Where you been? Sellin' me to the leatherheads?"

He bounded off the bed and grabbed her by the throat before she could say a word. She hadn't counted on that.

"Got you," he had breathed, his eyes, inches from her own, rheumy and yellow with rage and fever. "Before you could tell me your lies about where you been tonight. Got you, goddamnit, but I ought to snap your neck right now, you worthless, traitorous bitch."

He had paused then, his powerful hands still wrapped around her throat. Ruth could only try looking him in the eye, unable to get so much as a sound out. Knowing that to strike out at him, to try to get away was useless. He was too strong, and he was as likely as not to kill her even if she did manage to break his grasp. It was too late even to scream or shout for Billy Dove, whom she knew was waiting close by, outside.

All she could do was keep staring into his eyes. Hoping to convey something, anything to him that might stay his hand.

It had worked. Dolan had relaxed his grip—the thumbs still digging into her throat, but letting up just enough for her to speak.

"*Your . . . brother.*"

She choked it out, wheezing and gasping.

"What?"

He pulled his hands away from her neck altogether then, and flung her back into the corner of the shack, where she flopped with that same humiliating helplessness. But he was on her right away again, pulling her up, slapping her across the face.

"What? *What?* What did ya say about *my brother?*"

"That he's alive!"

She had just managed to get it out through her raw throat, over the edge of her lip already swollen and bleeding.

"You're a liar. You're mad!" he barked at her.

But she could see, even then, the look of vindication, even through the alcoholic sag of his face. *He still believed it.*

"You're a lyin' bitch—"

"No, but he's alive!" she cried, talking as fast as she could. "I just been down to Deirdre's. She an' Tom's with 'im now, down at Coenties Slip."

His hands gripped her arms so hard she feared he would break them. But she forced herself to go on, taking one more breath and spinning out the whole tale now, figuring it would work or he would kill her, and one way or the other that would be all.

"Ya got to be careful. He's heard you're in a spot, an' he wants to help you get out of the City for a spell. That's why he come. Deirdre figures he'll take ya over to Hoboken, or maybe up to Providence."

Dolan walked away and sat back down on the bed, looking bewildered now. Trying to think it through, she could see—but failing. Asking none of the obvious questions, about how his brother would know anything about him, or why he would help him with this. *Still wanting to believe.*

"My *brother?* Here?"

"Aye, an' he wants to help ya, Johnny. As best he can—"

"So he *was* alive. The whole time he was alive. Those sons a bitches in the black gable—" He snorted and looked up, something almost like a smile on his face. "T'think, they put him up in the idiot's ward. I *knew* he was no idiot. An' now he's here, you can *see* he's nobody's fool."

She watched him scramble about the shed, gathering up his few things. All but unable to believe he had bought the whole tale. *So far.*

She had not been able to dissuade him from taking his stash with him—the jackal-headed cane, Old Man Noe's money, the cufflinks and watch. Or the other thing, which he shoved quickly into his pocket. Plenty to get them both hung, should a leatherhead stop them.

Yet he had left the cabinet of wonders where it stood, in the corner. She had noticed it there, and almost suggested that he take it, too, having to bite her tongue, for fear that would give the game away. *After all, he was just supposed to be going for a few days.* As it was, before they had left he had grown suddenly suspicious. Some vestige of his base, animal mistrust returning.

"If this is a trick. If you're sellin' me—" he said, putting one hand on her shoulder and squeezing so hard she feared that her collarbone would snap.

"No, Johnny," she had stammered—just managing to think of something at the last moment. "If I was tryin' to sell ya, Johnny, why would I try to tell you not to bring the stash? Why wouldn't I want the evidence on ya?"

He hesitated for another, long moment—then pushed her out the door ahead of him.

"We'll see."

When they reached the paved streets, and no squad of roundsmen fell upon them, he seemed to relax a little bit. They were lucky enough to wave down a hack, ambling along after dropping off a fare at a new Fifth Avenue mansion, and they took the long, slow drive down to the docks. Rolling past the brimming Bowery theatres, and through the Five Points, past the city hall, and the humming, throbbing newspaper presses under the ground. Working their way through the side streets by the river, choked with their express wagons, and the wobbling drunks from their taverns.

And all the while, she kept a look out the windows of the cab for Billy. Thinking that perhaps she had a glimpse of him from time to time—a dark figure in a high overcoat. Walking fast, the collar pulled up around his ears. She wasn't sure, it was a murky, moonless night, but she wanted to believe it was him, trailing behind them in the crowded streets.

They paid off the driver at Coenties Slip, and alighted from the cab by a crooked, reeking excrescence of a bar called The Yellow Man. There was a sullen fog just beginning to roll in off the East

River, and the place seemed very quiet for this time of night—something that almost made Dolan shy from it at the last moment.

"You sure he's here? You sure it's *him?*" he asked her, in a voice so uncharacteristically pathetic that she nearly felt sorry for him.

He peered through the deepening murk. The fog not so much a real fog, but an oilier, more tangible thing, a sort of merging of the dark and the smoke, and all the foul vapors drifting up off the river.

"Where is he?"

"He's comin'," she promised. "Oh, he's comin' to ya."

They waited in the saloon, sipping whiskey at a back table. Dolan holding the glass in his hands, letting her have a drink from it from time to time. The awful liquor helping to steady her nerves. The only other patrons were a couple of seamen and a few drunks, standing against the bar. The barman staring at them with cold, sunken eyes.

There was noise and Dolan sat up, listening—though she noticed that his eyes were cloudier, and more unfocused than ever.

"Is it he then? Is that him?"

"No. No, not yet."

He turned restlessly about in his chair.

"You wait an' see what we do together. There won' be a thing what can hold us, now that he's back."

His words were beginning to slur.

"That's the truth."

"D'ya think he'll hold it ag'in me, though?" he asked her, suddenly fearful. "That I went off like that, wit' him still alive?"

"No!" She tried not to be too emphatic—the whiskey affecting her, as well, though she had had no more than a mouthful. "How could he? It was t'same t'ing wit' you. They thought he was dead an' slid 'im out, an' how's he supposed to get back to the livin'?"

"Aye, how could he get back? How could he even know I was alive?"

He said nothing for a long moment—then slowly, awkwardly, put out his hand across the table and patted hers. Ruth had to use every muscle in her body to keep from jerking it back from him.

"Don't think there won't be somethin' in it for you, too," he mumbled, looking down at the table. "Don't t'ink we'll forget ya now, we'll send for you—an' for the cabinet!—soon's we're settled someplace."

"You'll be needin' someone to do the duties of a wife."

"Tha's right," he nodded, missing the dryness of her voice. "Tha's right. You been a good girl, arrangin' all this. Ye'll get yer due for this, don't worry."

His words sent a small, dreadful chill through her body. But then the door of the saloon swung open, and she pulled her hand back. Tom stood there, looking grim. He gave them a quick, furtive nod from the doorway and they followed him back outside into the dark—Dolan all but marveling that it was really coming true.

"So he's 'ere! So he is. I knew I could always count on Tom. An' Deedee. She's a hard woman, but you can rely on her—"

Tom walked to the edge of the pier, signaling for them to wait back in the shadows of the bar. She let Dolan talk on, though it flayed her nerves. *Dangerous Johnny Dolan.* Wondering that this could be the same man she had met in that village, able to kill vicious dogs with his bare hands.

How had he ever been able to survive in such a place for so long? Full of nothing but the dead. And come out looking so strong and healthy still, when even the dogs had been half-starved—

"There he is!"

A dinghy appeared in the river, with a single man rowing it, a dark, indistinct figure in the fog, his overcoat pulled up nearly over his ears against the cold. A single lantern hung from the bow, and as they watched, the man locked his oars and covered, then uncovered the lantern with a cloth—two, three times.

"That's the signal!"

"Is 'at him? Is it really him?"

She had never seen Johnny Dolan so eager, even half-drugged as he was. The man in the boat raised a gloved hand and gave a single, beckoning wave.

"Is 'at him?" Dolan tried to squint into the night. "It looks taller—"

"No, that's just the man with the boat," Tom said quickly. "Your brother's out in the harbor. Come now—we have to look lively!"

The boat dropped from sight below the wharf, and Tom walked him down toward it, bustling him along.

"Come on, now. It's time."

He went at once, Ruth noted, without so much as a word or a backward look, which she remembered with both relief and a last, bitter resentment. He walked eagerly out to the end of the pier with Tom, even with his legs wobbling, then the two of them vanished. The boat reappearing again, with three figures sitting in it this time. Tom in the bow, facing Dolan, and Billy behind him. Both of them rowing steadily out into the harbor while Johnny Dolan sat, docile as a child, in the middle. *Not looking back even then,* as the boat slowly, silently receded into the oily night.

· 44 ·

TOM O'KANE

They finished cleaning their rifles in the twilight, Tom going over every inch of his with the brushes and rags, the lens-cleaning kit he had bought in the camera shop back in Washington City. It had cost him five dollars but he was willing to spend it; he had learned the value of having a reliable weapon in the field. He gave it a complete going over at least once a week, whenever they were in camp. Oiling the barrel and the trigger mechanism until it shone. Dry-firing the Springfield two, three times before he was satisfied.

Even that wouldn't tell him enough, he knew. The gun pulled to the left no matter what he did, and it was better than many. Just as much depended upon the ammunition, the cartridges they were given. The shoddy contractors liked to spike it with dirt, or saltpeter, as much as they could get away with, or more. It would cause the flash to sputter out—or, worse yet, explode in a man's face, tear the barrel right off the stock.

Nonetheless, he liked how the Springfield felt in his hands, something real and substantial to defend himself with, or at least to hang on to, out in the chaos that was the battlefield. He was almost sorry to stack it at night, in front of the tent with the others. Fearful that he would pick up some other fool's Enfield in haste the next morning, have the damned thing misfire on him when he needed it most.

Yet that, too, was a delusion, he knew. Only in the rare fight did it ever come down to anything like that, one man against another. War was mostly one dim, distant line arrayed against another. A stray shot or a shell fragment tearing into you before you could even see where the enemy was.

War was marching, and making camp, and marching again, until the soles of your shoddy boots were worn through. And war was all the time in between. Before, he hadn't known that so much time could exist. Time to be filled up with songs, and puffing around the camp-fires — and tedious practical jokes, and sheet-iron crackers, and drinking, and shivering with fever in your tent.

At least I'm out of it for now, he told himself, sitting around the field hospital while the rest of the army lumbered south after Bobby Lee. *Maybe even for good.* He would not be back in the line anytime soon, and he was due leave, and then they would most likely go into camp for the winter. *Surely, the war couldn't last much longer than that.*

Three masked figures rose up before him in the summer dusk. He stacked his rifle and looked up, unable to keep from smiling. It was Snatchem — George Leese — and Danny Larkins, and Feeley, looking much better from his wound. Grinning back at him behind the dark cloths they had tied over their faces like highwaymen.

"Faith, if it ain't the ribbon men, come to steal the landlord's cattle."

"C'mon along. We're off to requisition a fat German goose from some fat German farmer," Snatchem told him.

"No, no, it won't do for me to be gallivantin' around the countryside with this leg."

"It'll be an easy thing," George insisted. "These farmers'll be so glad we come to save 'em, they'll throw in their daughters besides—"

"I doubt it," Tom said, trying to keep a straight face. "Better you should see you don't find yourself on the business end of a shotgun, like what happened up at Newburgh."

He saw George's face moving beneath his mask, laughing silently. Then he was laughing with him. They had all signed up together— Snatchem and Feeley, and John J. Sullivan, and Black Dan Conaway. The only *b'hoys* from the Black Joke who had enlisted. *More fools us*—

He and Snatchem went all the way back to when they had both run with the Break o' Day Boys, when they had actually stolen an entire schooner from the East Side docks. They had taken to sailing it up the

Hudson and raiding the little towns along the river there. Breaking into farmhouses, grappling with the farmers' well-fed daughters over their kitchen tables. Smashing the eggs and overturning the sugar, just for the hell of it. Some wit had even gotten hold of a skull and crossbones and they had hoisted it from the mainmast, as if they were regular pirates.

Of course, it had been too brazen to go on for very long. After a couple of weeks, the farmers had been waiting with their shotguns and pitchforks. They had had to run for their lives back to the boat, with the whole country raised behind them, the church bells ringing out the alarm.

"—an' then, when we was all back an' ready to shove off, there comes George! Runnin' hell-bent for leather, with a big, Dutch farmer right behind, wavin' his blunderbuss—"

"Oh, but Jesus, the thing must've been from the French 'n Indian Wars!"

"But here comes George—still tryin' to hold on to the chicken he's got under one arm, an' the pig under t'other. An' he's almost there, he's runnin' down the bank, slippin' an' slidin' in the mud, but he's still got a hold on that pig an' that chicken. An' just then the farmer fires that blunderbuss—"

"Ah, but it must've been brought over with Pete Stuyvesant!"

"—an' he fires it an'—*boom!*—a great cloud a black smoke comes out, an' little enough otherwise, but by Jesus the sound throws Georgie off his footing. He goes slidin' down the riverbank on his face—*I swear to God!*—slidin' right through the mud, so when he gets to the bottom, he looks like he does right now, like he's wearin' a mask. But—he still has hold of that chicken an' that pig!"

The both of them were laughing so hard with the memory of the thing, and with relief that the battle was over and that they were still alive, that the tears rolled down their cheeks. Snatchem had to pull down the mask to wipe his face and his eyes.

"You sure you won't come with us, then?"

"You go on with yourselves, ya topers. I got some sow belly with the tits on, an' I'll make meself some skillygalee. Good luck with yer gobbling, though to be sure I shouldn't wish it for ye."

Snatchem smirked at him, then pulled his mask back up. Stalking off into the gloaming with the others.

. . .

Tom watched them go, then started his small fire. He threw a bit of pork fat and some salt into his skillet, then pulled the thick chunk of hardtack out of the mess tin where he had been soaking it in water all day. He fried the cracker in the pork fat until it was browned all over. Then he brewed himself some coffee, black and thick as pitch, and crumbled up another tablet of hardtack into that—making sure to skim off the weevils that bobbed instantly up to the surface.

"Though God knows why I shouldn't eat ya, you'd be more meat than I've had all month!" he told the struggling insects as he tossed them away.

He ate the skillygalee slowly, savoring the substance of the meal, though like all army rations, it was mostly tasteless. Thinking of Snatchem out hunting down a shoat.

The war was another sort of game to men like George, Tom reflected. *One more scheme.* Back in the Five Points, he had always had a dozen things going—stuss games, working the fights as a bloodsucker. A little moll buzzing and house cracking on the side. Once in the army he had settled immediately into new schemes, new games. *Requisitioning* what he could from the quartermaster, and the local farmhouses. Taking other men's pay with crooked dice and marked cards.

He was no worse than the rest. The sutlers and mule sellers who cheated them blind. The manufacturers of shoddy, churning out their rotten rations and rottener shoes, guns that didn't fire and uniforms that fell apart. The politicians, getting themselves commissioned officers so they could curry more votes.

What was some farmer's fat goose, to all that?

Tom sat thinking by the tent for a little while longer, watching the twilight turn to night. The insects already beginning to swarm, insects and flies, thick as soup. *God knows, I must have been bit by every creature that flies or crawls in God's creation—*

But all across the encampment now, he could hear the sounds of the wounded men settling in for the night. Their voices genial and good-hearted, knowing there wasn't going to be a fight the next day, or anytime soon.

It was almost pleasant, the war, at times like these, when the weather was warm, and there was no hard work to do. Listening to the birds

gather, twittering and cawing loudest just before the dark silenced
them. He didn't know what they were called, he had never been a
country boy, but he knew them by their calls now, after so many
months marching about with the army.

A few men, here and there, were singing, too, the quiet, sentimental evening songs of the camp:

> *Hard times, hard times, come again no more;*
> *Many days you have lingered around my cabin door,*
> *Oh! Hard times, come again no more—*

He roused himself, and lit the candle in the small lantern that hung
from the top of the tent pole. From where he was he could see hundreds, maybe thousands, of other lights, campfires and lanterns and
torches, flickering across the rolling fields. *Men announcing themselves
upon the land.*

Rummaging around in his pack, his hands felt their way over the
contents he knew by heart—his mess kit, and his gun cleaners, and
the small water bottle he carried instead of the heavy, metal canteen,
discarded long ago down some dusty Virginia road. There was a Bible
and a devotional book as well; his one change of underwear and two
pairs of socks, and his housewife—the small mending kit he had
become adept at using over the past ten months.

At last he found the lead pencil and a few leaves of paper he had
been able to bum from a hotel back in Chambersburg. Clamping his
white clay pipe between his teeth, sucking at it dry while he tried to
concentrate on the writing.

Before he began, though, he pulled out the locket he wore at all
times, on a chain over his chest. Popping the clasp and gazing at the
serious, beautiful face of the woman there, her eyes large and luminous even in the daguerreotype. Deirdre. His wife, the mother of his
children. The woman who had saved him.

How he had hated her.

He thought now, as he often did, of the last time he had seen her.
Up in that wretched camp, by the central park. Everything filthy, the
water seeping in everywhere from the swampy ground. The men
drunk all the time, brawling and bickering, rolling around in the
mud like so many hogs. They'd had to post a provost's guard,
twenty-four hours, with orders to shoot any deserters. There hadn't

been enough tents for all of them, or enough wood to make cabins. The flimsy Brooks Brothers uniforms and shoes falling apart in the first good rain—

Every morning, parading out across the muddy ground, he had thought of how it had been her idea. The whole City, with his home and his family, still just there, below him. Practically visible, behind the scrawny trees, and the dismal, rocky hills. He had not been able to restrain himself, had said it straight out, the first Sunday she had come to visit:

As if life wasn't bad enough.

He had watched her face fall when he said it—looking more hurt than if he had hit her, which he would never do. Which had been just what he had wanted at the time, he had wanted her to feel the misery that he went through every day.

As if life wasn't bad enough already. And always what she said it should be. Getting up every day to trudge off to the job, hacking and digging at the land. Worrying day and night if he would make enough to keep up the house payments. And hardly a drop of the creature—never any relief at all but the Sunday mornings sweltering in a pew, watching the back of a priest.

Yet even then he had been softening, he knew. Even before he threw his words in her face, he knew that she understood. Seeing her look over the camp, taking in the way they lived. *Realizing what she had done.* She had gotten herself up in her finest dress for him, even better than her usual clothes for Mass, the cut-velvet gown with black Chantilly lace that she had bought with her own money, and worn only for their wedding, and the children's christenings. A matching hat, and ribbons tied through her delicate brown hair.

Such a beautiful woman she still was. All but untouched by age— those large, serious brown eyes the same color as her hair.

How troubled she had looked, too, for a change. The pride, the unbending confidence gone, for once, back in that camp by the central park. Realizing the mistake she had made, how her blind faith had gotten them both into this. Doubting herself for the first time since he had known her, but most of all looking sorry for him. Seeing that, he had felt his anger already beginning to crumble—

The tattoo sounded, but he ignored it. There was little discipline enforced in the hospital camp, so long as the men didn't get too drunk or take to fighting. He continued to stare at the daguerreotype, in the light from his candle and the dog-tooth moon above. Her face seemed to flicker and move in his hand, as they did in such pictures. So serious and somber at first, now seeming to smile ruefully back at him. He sucked at the clay pipe, staring at her image in the wavering light, then licked the pencil and began to write a love letter to his wife.

> *My darlin girl*
> *Dont worry Im all right—*

He had seen her for the first time when she walked into the church-yard, bringing water to the men, the defenders of the faith. Her face was already as beautiful and grave as a saint's, and he knew right then and there that she could have anything she wanted of him.

"Look, it's 'Mollie Maloney, the wicked colleen'!"

She was with the Sisters of Mercy, bringing succor to the motley army assembled in the walled yard of St. Patrick's. A long line of nuns, the sisters in their habits and wimples. The young women they had taught to be chambermaids and cooks and scrubwomen, trailing after them—heads bent, eyes cast down in the true spirit of Irish womanhood. *The handmaidens of Judah.* Deirdre walked among them, her back held straight, her eyes looking straight ahead. He never knew her to carry herself any other way.

"Oh, but will ye look at that one!"

"Jesus, but ain't that a proud thing!"

They had been sprawled out among the grey slate headstones of the yard, where Dagger John had summoned them. No more than a bunch of *b'hoys* and fire laddies. Carrying whatever they could find, a few old muskets and horse pistols, knives and pikes, but still spoiling for a fight. The Know-Nothing mobs and gangs had been in the streets for days, even pelting the bishop's rectory with rocks, and there were stories that they had burned down every Catholic church in the city of Philadelphia, and that the state militia had been called out.

But nothing had happened. The Protestants had never shown themselves, and they had sat all day by the tombs and the headstones, gossiping like fishwives, and ogling the girls who came to bring them food and water. The other chaste maids from the Sisters of Mercy gig-gling and smiling behind their hands. The Magdalenes, and the Peni-tents, and the poor orphaned girls of the Preservation Class—some of them actual reformed whores, and others who had only been trying to get enough to eat. Just pleased to be out among so many brave men. The *b'hoys* joking and flirting, trying to get a rise out of them—

"Would there be any whiskey in there?"

"Is this already changed to wine, then?"

She had stopped their blather with a look. Giving out the bread and dried haddock, pouring out the well water the sisters had brought. The men getting to their feet as she approached, standing about awkwardly with their weapons. Trying to act like the defenders of the faith they were supposed to be.

"Thank ye, missy."

Bowing and nodding to her as if they were knights.

"Thank ye kindly."

Her head up, eyes straight ahead, more rigid than any soldier on parade. They snickered at her, incredulous, once she was past.

"Oh, but there's a hard one!"

"All beauty has its thorns."

"Don't be daft! A woman like that, she'll have ya singin' the Murphy hymn before the wedding breakfast is over."

But Tom had followed her, moving away from the rest of the men lounging in the tall grass. Trying to get in front of her. Trying to get her to *see* him, though he knew how he must look—dirty and insignificant, in his gang boy's soaped locks, his greasy vest and striped pants. He was suddenly ashamed, just to think of himself. *Only another smirking Paddy.*

He stepped out before her anyway. Determined to get her to look, at least.

"Accost me on consecrated ground, will you!" she spat out, radiant brown eyes spinning with indignation. "On this day!"

"Anything ya want, miss," he whispered, trying to hush her but overawed by her beauty at the same time.

The perfect, smooth skin of her face, the long brown hair that matched her eyes. Her voice still filled with righteous rage.

"We are here at the Bishop's request—"

A hard woman, too. He had no doubt but that his friends were right. *His salvation.* He spoke to her again, more sincerely than he had ever said anything in his life.

"Anything at all. You just name it and I'll do it for ye."

.　　.　　.

He had been working as a butcher's boy then, up at The Place of Blood in Houston Street. Wading through piles of entrails. Spending all day slitting the throats of pigs and cows.

Of course, he had had to work his way up to cutting throats. From sweeping the floor—the unbelievable gore there, the entrails to be kept aside from the manure, the bits of brain and eye, the hooves and long trails of spine. All of it had a use, to be separated for some purpose or another. It was a process as mysterious as the Trinity, though he did not doubt its reasons.

Once the thing was dead, the butchers and their apprentices could strip a bull's carcass in a matter of minutes, swarming around it like flies. Slicing off the best cuts for the table, the filets and ribs, and the flanks and rounds and shoulders. Cutting off the hooves and the tail for stews, and pulling out the tongue, and the brain for head cheese, and the heart and the liver. The blood was caught in a drain pan, and the intestines pulled out for the sausage stuffer's, and the hide for the hide curer's, and the bones for the rendering shop. Everything to its use, even the shit that was left behind, wheeled off to the vast manure pile that rose above The Place of Blood like a mountain. Until there was nothing but another fast-drying blotch, a stain upon the floor where the living animal had stood not twenty minutes before.

It wasn't enough for them. On Friday nights the other butcher boys would go up to Bunker Hill—the remnants of an old fort, abandoned since the Revolution, on a little rise above Grand Street. There a proprietor from the Fly Market had arranged hundreds of long benches in a circle, and planted an iron pole in the middle. He would chain a bull to it, and charge them all a penny to watch. All the butchers and skinners, and the butchers' boys and mechanics' apprentices, and all the other workies—still wearing their white paper caps, the leather aprons tied around their waists.

Tom would go with them, for the company. That was his failing, he recognized it. He confessed it each week at St. Patrick's, though the old priest behind the latticework barely understood.

It is natural for man to be with others. These are not impure thoughts, are they?

Bless me, Father, but I hate it.

He went along because he liked the company of men. Still dirty, and bloodstained and sweat-soaked from their twelve hours' work. He liked to be around them, to hear them cursing and guffawing, even to smell their rankness near him. He liked the company of men—but not what they liked.

The bull was always as fierce an animal as they could find. The rare kind they would get every once in a blue moon at The Place of Blood, that did not seem stunned or panicked into submission by the very sight of the slaughtering yards, or the smell of fear from so many of its fellow creatures, but only the more fearless and enraged for it.

Yet for all its bravery, its fate was always the same. The bull holding its own at first, huge and thick-chested, but Tom knew better. When they let the dogs into the ring, it wielded its head like a pair of swords, skewering them on its horns whenever they dared to lunge in too close. The butchers and the skinners and the apprentice boys jumping up and yelling in their excitement. The workies throwing down their bets, their few pennies on the bull.

But the dogs were half-starved, and canny, and the smell of the bull before them drove them to work together. Becoming a pack before their eyes. They darted in, one after the other. Tearing out the tendons in the bull's back legs until it stood immobilized and exhausted before them. Still chained to its pole, staring out at them with yellowed eyes, filling up with blood. When they had tired it enough, the dogs would run in and tear out its belly, and its throat. The butcher boys cheering louder than ever—as if they did not see enough of this, every day of their working lives.

That was what had convinced Tom to go and find her. What had convinced him that there must be something more than this, what he did and what he ate, and what he sat through for entertainment every Friday night.

He liked the company of men, but not what they did.

He had gone up to Gramercy Park, where he had heard she was working as a cook. Wearing the best coat that he could get hold of, borrowed from Feeley, at the firehouse. He had walked up from the Five Points on a Sunday, arriving there near the evening on a warm spring day, while all the servants were still taking their long promenade around the park.

He only watched them at first—how slowly they walked, as if trying to extend their last few hours of freedom. *Wondering what it must be like, to belong so completely to another man.* Moving around and around the park itself, the rectangular patch of flowers and trees, and the pretty gravel paths, all locked off behind a high, iron fence.

There were women strolling in pairs, and courting couples. A few solitary men such as himself, walking with their heads down. Some of them still in their domestics' uniforms, their maids' hats and aprons, and carriage livery. Sniffing—with their hands carefully behind their backs—at the daffodils and magnolias, and the lilac bushes behind the fence. The last few moments of the evening air, before they had to go back inside—

Tom walked out onto the slate-blue slabs of the paving stones. Joining them, trying not to look too conspicuous. Sneaking glances at the house where he knew she worked, across from the west side of the park. On his third time around, he saw the servants' door open, under the long wooden porch—but only a pair of girls ran out, still in their maids' uniforms, giggling furiously.

The next time around, though, she was there. She had changed from her cook's apron and was wearing a simple, blue-grey dress, almost the color of the slate paving stones. The delicate brown hair pinned up, covered by a modest black shawl.

Even here, she looked the furthest thing from a servant. Walking as she did with her back straight, and her head held high and proud, just as she had in the churchyard of St. Patrick's.

Like Mollie Maloney, the wicked colleen. Like Joan of Arc herself, walking like that—

The slow, steady stream of domestics divided at once to make way for her. She walked quickly past them, paying no mind to the men who half-bowed, or put their hands to their hats. Rushing on in her own course around the park. Tom hurried to catch up—memorizing her figure there before him, tall and unbending. He wanted to get in front of her, to show himself to her, but he couldn't find the gumption, not even in Feeley's good Sunday coat. Only able to follow her around and around the perfect, empty park, until it was nearly night.

She stepped back across the street, then. Turning back into her master's yard, walking down to the servants' entrance on the side, under the veranda. Away from him for another week, at least. Perhaps forever—ensconced in the home of some Gramercy Park Yankee, impenetrable as if it were a castle.

Yet somehow, she had managed to leave the gate unlatched, he saw when he came up to it. Tom had crossed the street as casually as he could. Putting a hand on the iron gate, only meaning to close it. But then something had gotten hold of him. He took a quick look for the roundsman stationed on the corner, making sure he was looking the other way. Then he slipped inside the yard, clicking the gate quietly shut behind him.

He still had no good idea of what he was doing. Padding quietly on down a flagstone path to the side of the house, under the wooden porch with its lovely trellis full of roses. Hoping at most—if he had thought about it at all—of getting a quick glimpse of her, in her home, her kitchen.

Yet the side, servants' door was open, too. Tom stared at it for another long moment, wondering what it was she could have been brooding on so to have left it ajar. Not quite certain—yet—that he ever wanted that sort of concentration turned upon himself, but curious anyway.

He pushed the door open the rest of the way and stepped inside. Knowing that it could be a serious charge if he were caught here, even without having taken anything. A crime that could get him years in the Tombs—

He went in anyway. His every footstep seeming to echo down the hall of the servants' quarters. There were no other sounds from the house, everyone out, or at their duties somewhere else.

Except for her. He could hear the sound of her voice then, coming from a room just down the hall. *Talking to someone?* But no—there was only a familiar, quiet, whirring noise, and the sound of her singing.

"Was there ever a sweeter colleen in the dance than Eily Moore?
Or a prouder lad than Thady, as he boldly took the floor?"

Singing to the wheel. Unable to help himself any longer, he looked around the door into her room, and the sight made him stop his breath. She sat there at the spinning wheel, singing as she spun her yarn. Her voice soft and barely audible over its steady hum and click, but he recognized the air, from back in Tipperary, when his mother would sit and spin in their single room there. Yet Deirdre's voice was even softer than his mother's. Her hands moving expertly over the spinning cloth, as if she were playing a harp to accompany herself:

> *"'Lads and lasses to your places, up the middle and down again.'*
> *Ah! The merry-hearted laughter ringing through the happy glen!*
> *O, to think of it, O, to dream of it, fills my heart with tears—"*

He had backed quietly down the hall, not wanting to frighten her. Worried about what she might think of him, a man who walked right into people's houses, and spied on them in their bedrooms.

But from then on, he was determined he would have her. The next Sunday he had been bold enough to introduce himself, and ask if he might walk out with her. Tom would never forget how she had looked at him. Her face as grave and beautiful as ever, but also unsurprised, as if she had expected just this thing.

"I am sincere," he had blurted out, thinking that she was about to reject him, that she must get such offers every week. "I am sincere. I want to be led into a life of mercy."

And she had looked him up and down then, as if making some final decision. Her face still grave and unsmiling. Though he would never forget, either, what she had said to him:

"All right."

And that was it, just that. *All right.* From those two words, she had changed everything in his life. She had made him give up his bad company, and running with the river gangs, and cutting throats at The Place of Blood. She had taught him to read good books, and even to write a little, and how to dress and conduct himself like a respectable, God-fearing Irishman. She had brought him to the Church, and married him and given him children and a fine home, all with the assent of those two words.

All right. He echoed them now in the letter he wrote, by the waning, yellow light of the candle, and the Pennsylvania moon. Wondering if she had seen the account of his wound and hoping, in the hard way of lovers, that it had hurt her just as much as it had after the first time—after Fredericksburg. But glad, too, to relieve her mind. His hatred having dissipated in all that had passed since he had last looked upon her face. Scribbling down the words, *Im all right,* before he went to bed in his field.

DEIRDRE

She had seen from the start that she could make something of him. The awkward, big-eared boy staring at her like a calf in St. Patrick's yard. Even then he had been in arms, dutifully clutching a huge, rusted musket someone had given him. *A soldier for Christ,* as they had called them, she and the other volunteers for the Sisters of Mercy. Giving out food and good, clear water to the men there—scandalized that they could want them to give out something more, even when they were assembled for such a cause.

She did not think that she was naive—a young woman living alone, earning her own living for years in the City. She had some idea of what men were, she had just expected them to be transformed by the cause, at least for the moment. *To be soldiers for Jesus—when else would they ever have such a calling?*

Instead they had used the call to arms, the call to defend the Church and the Bishop as one more excuse to wink and paw at the girls. *Not with her.* She had stared them down—giving out the bread and dried fish from her basket and looking right through them. Daring them to so much as say a word to her—until she had seen him, staring at her there like such a calf. His face hopelessly open to the world but serious, too, she could see. Great big, overgrown boy, holding carefully to his musket, his charge. She thought it right away, here was someone she could do something with.

She was already working at the house on Gramercy Park. Cooking for a rich Yankee in the big, brick home he kept there, complete with trellises and porches, and a garden in the dooryard. He lived alone, amid all that, with just a small household to run the place. Another member of the codfish aristocracy, with bundles of money he seemed to have scooped up from the ground, the way they all did. Patronizing and supercilious, joking smugly with the help.

At least he kept his hands off them. She had been in too many positions where there were such goings-on. From the time she had first started, not yet fourteen, she had had to fight off men. Not just the young men, back from school or a day's riding and drinking with their friends, but the masters of the house as well. Carefully setting their traps. Waiting until she was upstairs alone, changing the sheets or dusting a mantel, when they would just happen to wander into the room. Trying to corner her behind a bed, or a chair. Rarely even bothering to say anything, simply grabbing at her, or throwing her skirts up over her head.

She had learned that pulling at the roots of their hair was a powerful dissuader. There was hardly a man alive, she had found, who would persist in having his way when she was halfway to pulling his scalp off. Of course, she had to be careful—often enough the hair came right off in her hand, leaving her holding some shabby horsetail wig. Others liked to unbutton themselves first, and come at her with their thing front and center. She had found this was actually helpful, once she got over her incredulity, seeing what looked like a chicken's neck emerge from a man's pants. At least it gave her a good target. All that was usually required was to take a good, healthy swing at it with the most harmless of items—a mere dust cloth, or a pillow case—and most men's would immediately shrivel right up. Once that happened they were usually too morose to try for anything more.

"But you Irish are supposed to be so free with it," one householder had told her, in astonishment, even as they wrestled on a couch.

Sometimes, for her chastity, she received a shanty on the glimmer or a bloodied lip, a mouse along her high, exquisite cheekbones. She tried to keep these hidden. To a perceptive mistress they were a sign as clear as a shingle, and she would be unlikely to remain in such a household. Yet even when caught out, she would insist, if questioned, that she had walked into a door, or banged her head while mucking out the fire. Knowing that her future employment depended on this unspoken pact with the lady of the house—her ability to get a reference, and go on to be the sport in some other home.

But himself left them all alone, in the house on Gramercy Park. Always speaking respectfully to *her*, seeming to sense her disapproval. He had a mistress somewhere, she was all but certain. He spent too many nights away to believe his mumbled excuses, stumbling home in the morning, that he had passed the night at his club. His collar smeared with rouge, his clothes reeking of port or brandy. Or maybe he spent the night at a brothel—though it seemed to her, when she was still the upstairs maid and hauling down his shirts every day, that they always smelled of the same flowery scent.

She found herself thinking of him at odd times in the years to come, though she was angry to have such idle thoughts. Wondering what had become of himself, while she was cleaning her own home. A grey, trudging man, gone to fat. Breathing hard to climb the stairs. Combing his hair over, adjusting his silk stockings and the edge of his trousers in the hall foot mirror.

He must be dead by now, she assumed. *And his fine house? What had become of that?*

She had liked it there, as much as she'd liked any home not her own. She got to run most of the staff the way she liked, all save for his valet, and the place ran like a newly wound clock.

She had a room of her own there, too, up on the third floor, her reward for having finally worked her way up to cook. She spent her nights reading the old common school grammars that she had found, bought for one bit down in the Chambers Street shops. Or her copies of *How to Read Character,* or *Whom to Trust?* Stories of miraculous conversions, with titles like *The Path That Led a Protestant Lawyer to the Catholic Church,* or *How a Universalist Lady Came to Christ.* Or even, once in a rare while when she wanted to treat herself, some collection of sentimental stories, *A Basket of Chips,* or *Bits of Blarney.*

On her night off she would join the grand parade of servants around the iron-gated park. Walking proud and alone most of the time, she couldn't help it. Sometimes, particularly near the end of the month, she might walk with the O'Looney sisters, Ellen and Sharon, the young serving girl and scullery maid who worked under her. A

Sheelahs' night out, the three of them walking arm-in-arm, Deirdre trying to talk some sense into their silly, girlish heads. But if they had anything left at all from their wages, both O'Looneys preferred to go see a shillelagh drama, or a blood-and-thunder down on the Bowery. Running with God knew what sort of company—

Deirdre went back to thumbing through her pamphlets. *Whom to Trust?* Whom indeed?

She had always been able to do for herself. From the time she was still eleven years old, back in Cork. She had gone to see a cousin get married, and after the wedding feast the whole party had walked the couple back to their quarter acre. There she had seen her cousin's new home—literally, a ditch by the side of the road. A hole as deep as a grave, with a little thatch thrown over it, and surrounded by potatoes.

They had all stood there—the fiddlers playing and everyone waving and wishing them luck—as the cousin descended slowly down, into her new hole, until only her head was still aboveground, smiling bravely back at them. Within the year they had a babe as well, all living and rutting in the ground like so many animals.

Deirdre had decided even then that she wanted no part of such a life. She was still young to leave home, but her father had been just as glad to lose the cost of a dowry. She had gone first to the Sisters of Mercy, in Cork city, to learn a little sewing and some needlepoint, and ever since then she had been able to do for herself—had always been able to stick her ear in anywhere and get a job. It had been hard leaving her family—the younger brothers and sisters she was in charge of, even her parents, as shiftless and conniving as she perceived them to be. It would have been even harder to stay.

In New York she had been guided to a rooming house when she'd first arrived, still only fourteen years old. There she had been locked up in a room for two days with no food, until a man came in to tell her what a great bill she had run up, and suggested there were other ways to settle it.

Yet even then she had been able to make her way. She had talked and bluffed her way out, fulminating that her uncle was a sergeant in the star police. The proprietor had believed her just enough to have his doubts, and once she was finally free she had gone at once to buy a piece of bread and a cup of milk. Walking around the Five Points, eating and giving thanks to the Virgin Mother for her deliverance. Feeling almost giddy with triumph, and excitement, even though she had almost no money left.

She had learned the skills as she went, faking them when she had to. Working her way up through the households, taking an almost ferocious pride in what she could learn to do. Keeping up her appearance and working steadily on her letters, on learning how to speak and deport herself properly. Putting aside nearly all of the seven dollars a month she made in wages.

Putting them aside for what? Deirdre had listened to the older, married women in their gossip over the washing. *"If I had it to do over, I'd never marry"*—spoken with a bitterness that always startled her. Most of them even sounded wistful for the days they had been in service. Making their living now as best they could, running groceries and grog shops, selling baked pears and matchboxes on the street. Their husbands useless idlers and drunks, pontificating in the saloons. Or they were hard, silent, equally bitter men—coming home from their twelve-hour shifts shoveling coal at the gas works, or loading raw meat onto a boat, and just waiting for somebody to try and say something.

Yet as much as she reveled in her independence, she was not sure how much longer she could stay alone in the world, and feared lest she fall into error. Getting up every morning before dawn, shaking the O'Looneys awake, the lazy, torpid beasts that they were. Making her own bed, straight and tight as a sail, while they got the fires started— then going downstairs in her starched, spotless apron to get the master's breakfast. Taking her inventory of the larder and the pantry. Going out to the fishmarkets and the meat stalls and the vegetable groceries in the wide, bustling City. Keeping herself in hand, walking with her head up along the dollar side of Broadway, just as proud as the ladies.

But always alone. Sometimes a whole day passed without her uttering a word besides an order, or a reprimand. Turning out her meals, keeping a stranger's house. She prided herself on being a decent cook, on working on meals again and again until she got them right, but she had no real flare for it—no love of foods or flavor. She made what she needed to make, then ate in silence in her kitchen. Chasing Ellen and Sharon around until she was satisfied they had scrubbed it clean.

Then—it was back up to her room. To wash her hair with soap and cold water in her basin, and go back to her reading. That was all. Trying to get through her true stories of miraculous Protestant conversions, her grammars and her pamphlets on how a proper Catholic girl should comport herself.

She tried writing home, but she had learned it was futile. Her father had some letters, but he would not write back, claiming that he could not afford the postage, or the paper, even when she sent him the money. Sooner or later the priest would write back for him, letting her know in bland, general words what had happened since to her family, who had been born or who was ill, passing on supposed greetings from her mother and father. It had only made her feel worse, thinking of her father standing before the priest, hat in hand, telling himself, no doubt, *Let the Pope take the expense.*

The Church was her one consolation. She went to Mass every morning she could, stopping in at St. Patrick's or one of the smaller parish churches on her way to the markets. She loved the cool, darkened interiors, awash in the smell of candles and incense—kneeling there, sanctified already with the holy water from the door.

Yet she was proud even here, though she tried to fight it in her heart. Slipping out her small, black, devotional book, while the other women around her simply prayed through their rosaries. Following carefully along with the priest's devotions, soothing and calming her, as they always did:

Judica me, Deus, et discerne causam meam de gente non sancta—Judge me, O God, and distinguish my cause from the nation that is not holy: deliver me from the unjust and deceitful man.

Yet when she found herself in the confessional, she could not help but blurt out her sin, before she hardly knew it.

"Bless me, Father, but I think sometimes that I might do anything, just to feel the touch of another upon me."

The priest's small, discomfiting silence above her, behind the screen. She was sure that it was Father Knapp, who had recently come to the parish. A stocky, humble, nearsighted man, with a touch of Tyrone on his tongue and a tendency to look down at his feet. A man she trusted for his unease, and his obvious humility.

"Have you given in to these temptations?" he had asked.

"No, Father, I never have. But I fear that I might. Just for a touch."

"It is time that you should marry, perhaps."

"I know, Father, but I dread it."

"But you should marry rather than submit to wickedness. Come to see me after Mass."

That morning the reading of the gospel was from the Book of Matthew, and she thought that the Father looked at her when he crossed over to the pulpit and read the English:

Come to me, all ye who labor and are heavy laden, and I will give you rest. Take my yoke upon you, and learn from me; for I am gentle and lowly in heart, and you will find rest for your souls. For my yoke is easy, and my burden is light.

Afterward she had waited shyly outside the sacristy door until Father Knapp had emerged—escorting her just outside to the rectory, where he had given her another, slim book.

"I know that you can read, Deirdre, and that you are a wise girl," he told her. "Read this, and take it to heart, and I will answer any questions you may have."

She had looked at the title curiously—*A Guide for Catholic Young Women, Especially for Those Who Earn Their Own Living*—before sliding it into her marketing basket. That night, when all her work was done, she had studied it in her room. Sorting through all the varied advice on marriage that it contained—wondering just what it was the Father wanted her to read, until the words blurred and swam before her eyes.

"*Marriage is a state of life instituted by God Himself,*" she had read. "*Do not be too hasty in making a decision.*"

The writer, who was a man, apparently thought it as proper as Father Knapp did that she should marry. Yet he wrote page after page of warnings about what could happen if a good Catholic girl hurried into it, or married the wrong man. She worked her way through it, thinking of the women she knew, while she wondered if she might ever find the right man, or how she should marry at all.

"*Who is that bloated, coarse-looking woman who has not apparently combed her hair for a week, with a lot of ragged children bawling and fighting and cursing around her in her miserable, dirty hovel? That was, a few years ago, a pretty, modest girl, who was innocent and light-hearted, earning an easy living in a quiet, pleasant family, and attending to her duties regularly and with great delight in her soul."*

Then the next month had come the disturbances. The Protestants running loose in the streets, burning down churches in Philadelphia, and the Bishop himself had put out the call to protect the cathedral. She had gone with the Sisters to offer what help she could—though the men gathered in the churchyard had seemed less than pious, and more like men everywhere, leering and whistling at her as they did on the street.

"Where are ya off to now, darlin'? To serve the priests?"

"Forget it now, Pat. The three hardest things to teach in this world are a mule, a pig, and a woman—"

She had walked through them with her head held high, not so much as acknowledging their jibes or their laughter. But then she had seen his face. *So young and so open, the stupid moon calf. How had he survived so long in this City, with a face like that?* Yet daring to come up to her, to approach her alone. Having the impertinence to tell her:

"Anything. Anything ya want, miss."

Silly, boyish thing to say. And from himself, who didn't look like he had two coins to rub together in this world.

Yet throughout the rest of the afternoon, she had found herself looking back at him, where he stood among his comrades. Noting how many friends he had, though he always conducted himself in a dignified and civilized manner. Catching him sneaking looks at her.

Whom to Trust? Looking at his open, handsome boy's face, she thought she knew, then, what she was supposed to do—what Father Knapp and the book were directing her to. That if the right man were not to be found, perhaps she would have to make him. She would have to shape and mold and steel him to the world herself.

When he had shown up on the square, she had taken it as a sign. Moving around and around the slate-blue sidewalks with the usual parade. She had noticed him when she was heading back to the house. That broad, open face, following along behind her, like some common footpad. She was surprised to see him there, startled by the effrontery of it. But noticing, too, the good coat he had bothered to wear, his combed hair. Understanding the trouble he had taken to find her.

She had decided to take another loop around the park, waiting for him to approach her. But he hadn't—something that pleased her as well, that he was so overawed by her. Yet realizing that something had to be done, or else they might walk around the park forever.

She had let him see her, then. She had improvised it all on the spur of the moment, from some inspiration that she was sure must have come from the Virgin Mother Herself. Knowing that the O'Looney girls, all the other servants, would be out for a while more. Turning in when she got to her house again, but making sure to leave the dooryard gate unlatched—leaving the door to the servants' quarters open as well, just to be sure.

She had sat down at her wheel, then, and begun to sing. Berating herself for a fool, at first, when he still did not appear—sure that he must be upstairs, stealing the silver and murdering the master. But hearing, then, the first, tentative footfall in the hall outside her room. Loving the very timidity of that step, his unsureness, his gentleness, even as he followed her. She sang a little louder:

> "I've left Ballymornack a long way behind me
> To better my fortune, I've crossed the big sea
> But I'm sadly alone, not a creature to mind me,
> And faith, I'm as wretched as wretched can be—"

Letting him come in, and see her there, singing to the wheel. One old song or another, it didn't matter which, just so long as it was in her best voice. Her mind hardly even half on it, just making sure that he could see her there, before they went on.

✦ · 46 · ✦

RUTH

She went on back at last with the wet cloth to Vie and Elijah, groping her way through the strange and darkened house. When she got there they were already asleep again, but Milton was up. Sitting at their bedside, where he had gone to comfort them himself. *Sweet boy.* Looking up at her with large, questioning eyes when she came in.

"It's all right," she told him. "Things'll be all right, now the rain's here."

She sat down on the bed next to him. Running a hand over the brows of her younger children, glad to feel they were cooler.

"Why are we here?" Milton asked her, in a whisper.

"Me an' Deirdre figured it'd be easier, if anything happened. You never know, with the disturbances."

Not wanting to tell him they were hiding out in a white family's house so the mob would not attack them. Knowing even as she tried to put him off that of course he would reason it out on his own.

"Is it that they're coming after us? Is it that they're out after the coloreds?"

She tried to keep doing what she was doing, tucking Deirdre's pretty sheets up over her children. But her mind stuck on that word.

The coloreds. How quickly he had made that separation. And just where did that put her?

"No, no. It's the draft they're on about. It'd just be safer in one house or t'other. You know how Deirdre is about her house."

Trying to bribe him with this little, adult confidence. But Milton only leaned in stubbornly, whispering again in her ear.

"Where's Daddy?"

"He's all right—"

"How do you know? How do you know anything like that?"

Sitting on the edge of the bed before her. His black, serious face nearly impenetrable in the darkness. But still, she knew, unconvinced.

"No, no, he'll be along now, with the rain. We have to wait for him here. An' you have to help me."

Appealing to him openly now. *Her good son.*

"With lookin' out for him. You have to help like you always done."

His face softening. Boyish again, a little sheepish but pleased by her praise. *He was still, after all, a boy.*

"Come now. Come have a look out for him."

"All right," he said, nodding seriously. "All right."

They stayed up in the front parlor together. Milton sitting straight-backed and rigid as a sentry, in a chair by the window. His neck and head thrust forward, staring vigilantly out into the street through the half-opened shutters.

Outside the storm lessened, then stopped, almost as abruptly as it had begun—a curtain yanked back open on the town. The City smelling almost clean, the way it always did in the first few moments after a rainfall. There was a sudden and startling quiet, Ruth even daring to hope, *Well, maybe that did do it. Maybe it is over now—*

The quiet was broken by the sound of footsteps—half-walking, then running—and Milton stood up from his chair. Deirdre and Ruth rising as well, going over to peer out through the cracks in the shutters, full of both hope and alarm.

They could see a lone figure hurrying down the street toward them. It was no more than a vague silhouette in the dark, with the gas unlit now. The three of them watching without a word, until it was nearly up to the house.

Only then could they see for sure that it was not Billy—or Johnny Dolan. It was a man, his face clearly white, though besmirched with what seemed to be soot, or dirt. His clothing was also dirty and tattered, but too good for anything Johnny Dolan would have—a coat and what looked like a real silk vest, and yellow linen trousers.

He hurried quickly on past the house, down to Maddy's door, where he clanged the bell, the sound echoing up and down the deserted street. He banged on the door with his fists when she did not come down, shouting her name. Ruth could see the light from candles begin to flare up behind the other shutters up and down the block, until at last the door opened, and he was taken in.

"It isn't him," Milton said, the disappointment plain in his voice.

"No, it's that man of hers," Deirdre said disdainfully. "Oh, but men are desperate creatures!"

They settled slowly back down, into their places around the room—Milton leaning alertly forward again at his post. Staring out into Paradise Alley as if his eyes alone might burn a hole through the night, and bring his father back through it.

Ruth leaned back, into the rosewood reclining couch. Its shallow frame so uncomfortable when she used to visit Deirdre—though now she felt herself sinking into it, wavering on the brink of sleep. Deirdre herself sitting back in her chair, her eyes nearly shut.

Already, though, Ruth could hear the sound of more feet running through the streets, of shouts and voices from somewhere, far away. The City—the mob—gathering itself again. Regrouping in the saloons, and at the street crossings. Preparing itself for tomorrow.

Tuesday
July 14, 1863

Our holy and beautiful house,
where our fathers praised thee,
is burned up with fire;
and all our pleasant things
are laid waste.

ISAIAH, 4:11

HERBERT WILLIS ROBINSON

It is hot again. It is still early morning, but already it is even hotter than yesterday, as if the cooling rains had never come. The sun a merciless, red eye above the top of the shutters—

But inside, Maddy snores gently on the pillow beside me. How angelic she looks now, sleeping by my shoulder. How like our first nights together!

She has aged, but not badly—not nearly as much as I have. She is no longer girlish, but if anything her face is now fuller, and more sensuous. Even with her hair unwashed, and disheveled, as it always is these days, she looks more beautiful than ever to me.

Last night, after I spied her face in the window, she rushed to let me in. Running down the stairs, flinging herself into my arms with gratifying haste.

"I heard them. I heard them out there, all day," she admitted, still clinging to my neck. "There's been nobody around. None of the women out on the street. Nobody come up to see me!"

I sat her down at the kitchen table, held her gently in my lap. *She is still so small—as light as a girl*. There was no game now, on either of our parts. Instead it felt like our earliest time together, all needing and unguarded. I held her tightly to me, stroking her hair while she spoke.

"I was alone all day," she told me, pushing her face down, nuzzling into my neck. Still unbathed, dressed in the same, decrepit yellow gown I saw her in that morning. Both of us must have been quite a sight—me in my filthy suit, ruined by the construction dust.

It did not matter. I kissed and touched her everywhere, my caresses moving down over her arms, her breasts, her belly. I stood her up and undressed her lovingly, right there in the kitchen. Shucking the unspeakable dressing gown off her, pinning her hair back up as she stood naked and docile before me.

"My good girl."

I led her upstairs by the hand, to the fine oak bed I bought for her years ago. And when we made love she clutched at me, as if she could not make me out, between the total darkness of the room and the hard rattle of the rain again on the windows, shutting out all other sound. When it died down, we could hear distant shouts and laughter, and breaking glass, and she had clung to me all the tighter.

So why? Why is it that I should ever leave her?

I am a hack.

That is the heart of the matter. Oh, I do not say it to insult myself. I even take a certain pride in it.

I am a hack, a writer. It is a trade much like any other trade, no more or less honorable. I write about everything that I know, and much that I do not know. I write about dogs and guns, and horses and birds. I write reviews of books I have not read, and plays I have not seen, and firsthand descriptions of places I have never been. I have even written poetry.

I have written for the Republicans, and for the Democracy, and for the old Whigs, and the Anti-Masons, and the Temperance party. I have written miraculous conversion stories for the One True Church— *How a Protestant Lawyer Saw the Light,* and *How a Universalist Lady Came to Christ.* And I have written Know-Nothing pamphlets about the dreadful carryings-on in papist convents and monasteries—*Awful Revelations or, The Confessions of a Lascivious Nun.*

I have written shilling shockers for a nickel, and thrilling stories for a dime. I have written *The Blue Avenger of the Waves,* and *The Red Revenger of the Plains,* and *The Black Revancher of the City.* I have written for *Harper's Weekly* and for *Harper's Monthly;* for the *American Museum,* and *American Monthly,* and *National Era;* for *Brother Jonathan,* and *True Flag,* and *Flag of Our Union,* and *The Starry Flag.* I have written for *Godey's Lady's Book,* and *Petersons' Ladies' National*

Magazine, and *Ladies' Companion;* for *Burton's Gentleman's Magazine*, and *Mrs. Stephens' Illustrated New Monthly*, and *Frank Leslie's Illustrated Newspaper*, and *Ned Buntline's Own*. And I have written for *Country Living and Country Thinking*, and *Musical World and Times;* and for *The Scorpion* and *The Congregationalist*. I have written.

It was never something that I planned to do. I was—like Greeley—the sudden spark in my family. The prodigy, in my little New England village. Reading and writing and doing my sums so adroitly as to attract the notice of a distant uncle. He became my patron, at least to the expense of sending me off to boarding school, then to his old college out in the gentle, rolling hills of western Massachusetts.

After that, I was on my own—and as poor as ever. My immediate, old Yankee family was so unambitious that they did not even move on once the meager soil of their farm ran out, content to slowly decay into impoverished gentility.

I came to the City instead, turning my back on them. Looking to do something, anything, that did not require capital, or the sort of insane risk my countrymen are so fond of taking—fighting Indians, growing corn on a prairie, crossing mountain ranges to hunt for gold. Tinkering with boilers, and steam pressure all the day.

Then I saw it. People reading, everywhere—poring over books in social libraries, and reading rooms, and on the streets. Only then did it strike me, once I was in the City, though I had perused the written word since I first could walk. Only here, where it was altogether, did I see it. Printers and their presses on every other block. Turning out mountains of paper and words; of books and newspapers, and yearbooks and handbills, and any old leaves stuck between two cheap pieces of cardboard.

I knew then I had found my calling—my commodity. Do not think me too cynical. Like any craftsman, I took pride in what I could do so easily, just through the weight of my experience, and expertise. In how I could put my hand to anything—any public event, any passing fancy, any work of another writer (preferably one in Europe)—into something that people would *read*, would spend their hard-earned money and—even more!—their time on.

And I made a living. Enough to make my way, even in this most damnably expensive of all cities. Relentlessly pushing my name (and my many pseudonyms) out before the public, until I could afford finer clothes, finer restaurants than I had ever dreamed of bothering with before. Until I had acquired the fine house in Gramercy Park, bought off the doddering scion of an old Dutch merchant family as decayed as my own.

Still, it was not enough. It was almost like a disease, a mania. I went on, writing and writing, until I was drawn down into the newspapers. There was something to write about every day—something right out on the street before me.

Surely, there was something here I could gather to me. *Something greater.* That was my secret dream, the longing that lies in every hack's heart. The desire to do something, write something of lasting worth. Some song I could cobble together, as bearish old Whitman did with his intemperate, pulsing odes to everything. I looked for it everywhere, out in the great City.

Yet my *Street Scenes* proved hopelessly stuck. I tried everything. Once I even set myself in the upper window of the *Tribune* for a whole day. From there, I vowed, I would take in the whole scene along Broadway, and write down everything I saw, every jot and line of humanity.

How I loved them all—watching them from such a distance, unobserved as I was myself. The flower sellers dickering and laughing, hanging their goods along the fence posts by St. Paul's Chapel. A proud and beautiful cook, striding along, her head held high as a bishop's. The businessmen and the gang *b'hoys*, both idling along, eyeing her and any other woman they saw. The society women shopping with their maids, the politicians slapping shoulders and talking, talking. The teamsters pulling up and prodding their thick horses on—

I believed there was some greatness here, but it was in the City and not in me. I could make nothing of it, even of my day in the aerie, not even a story for the *Tribune*'s readers. I battered and flailed at it, like a sculptor smashing at some unyielding block of stone, trying to cut out some truth, some greater story from it all.

It would not emerge—and I fled, out into the City. Plunging up one street and down another, shouldering my way through the mobs along the sidewalks. Taking reckless chances, cutting across the avenues just in front of the cabs and the wagons and the yellow omnibuses. Willing to risk being cut in half, just to get across the street a moment sooner.

I discovered that I was not alone in this. That there were hundreds, perhaps thousands of my fellow New Yorkers racing along with me. Their feverish, anxious faces, always at my shoulder. Restless as sharks, we darted this way and that. Moving, always moving—always hoping to bury or unearth something in the great bulk of the City.

I would walk until I found myself bound, as always, by one river or another. And there I would stop, panting for breath, and then I could hear it—the steady, dissonant drone, rising up all around me.

I thought I was going mad at times, but I could hear it. I cannot say just what it was   the whine of the new machinery, or the babble of a million voices; the unceasing tramp of feet and hooves along the pavement. Perhaps it was all of these, and more, joined into that awesome, senseless hum. The City as a living, breathing, conscienceless thing, all around me. Yet I could make nothing of it.

I am, as I mentioned, a hack.

Then I found Maddy. I kept her at Gramma Em's, in the Seven Sisters, for a few more weeks, then I paid off her pimp and rented this house. I went with her, to fetch her things and her mother from their home up in the Shambles. It was a terrifying climb, through almost total darkness, along a staircase almost as steep and narrow as a ladder. On every step, beneath my boot I could feel the soft squish of filth, animal or human I could not tell. Other dark figures, reeking of whiskey or cabbage, smashed blindly into us and were gone, cursing and grunting as they fought their way down the stairs.

Maddy led the way, surefooted as an Indian. It seemed to me that the new red frock I had bought her was the only glimmer of color in that place—leading me up and up the stairs as if it were a lantern, to the decrepit cubbyhole where her mother lived, on the top floor. There the old woman sat rocking back and forth in a chair, before a cold fireplace, sucking on a corncob pipe. Maddy shouted greetings a few inches from her head—her mother's face clearly oblivious to what she was saying but a smile forming along her toothless mouth, gnarled hands reaching out to stroke her daughter's cheeks.

Maddy gathered their few belongings, then patiently led her back down the steps, though the old woman seemed nearly as surefooted as her daughter. I, on the other hand, stumbled across some protrusion by the threshhold to the Shambles—and to my horror my foot plunged right through the cobblestoned paving of Paradise Alley. The loose stones plunging into a dark and pungent torrent, suddenly revealed below.

"It's the City sewer," Maddy explained blithely. "The Swamp Angels and the Break o' Day Boys like to cut holes in the culvert. They hide their treasure down there."

"You go down there?" I gaped at her.

"All the time. We never found any treasure. You had to be careful, though, even if they found ye lookin' around, they'd just as soon cut your throat."

"Down there," I repeat, staring down into the raging tempest, pouring all of our accumulated filth, day and night, out into the East River.

"Of course!"

And just like that, she swung down through the hole I had inadvertently pushed through her pavement, and into the reeking sewer below.

"Maddy!"

For an instant I feared that she was gone. I peered frantically down into the darkness, expecting to see her small body being swept off into the river.

Instead, she smiled up at me—her exquisite little feet balancing along an upper ledge no wider than my hand. There she strolled along, as easy as a mountain goat. Oblivious to the effect the blackened walls must have on her new red frock, walking through the bowels of the City.

"Come down!" she called to me, still smiling up at my horrified face. "Come on down—I'll show you where to walk!"

But I could only cling to the rim of the culvert, watching Maddy. She walked on her toes, executed a pivot on the slender ledge, as graceful as any tightrope walker, dancing on the edge of a cesspool.

After that I did everything I could for her. The house was only a start. I hired tutors to teach her how to read and write. I retained dancing masters, and music teachers to school her in the harp and the piano, in drawing and decorum. I opened up an account for her at Stewart's, along with the services of a knowing widow who could instruct her on what to buy, and how to wear it. In short, I gave her everything she needed to become an accomplished, finished young woman.

When her mother passed away, I even paid for the funeral—

complete with a marble headstone and a black-caparisoned team, a glass coach and paid mourners to follow it out to the Green-Wood Cemetery. A fine funeral—something that always seems to mean so much to *them,* after the mean lives they lead on this earth.

It had surprised me, I admit, how much she had cried at the cemetery. Keening like those Irishwomen in their shawls, in the pit of De Peyster's old house. I tried to be especially attentive to her after that. My companions among the literati down at Pfaff's Cave noticed my absences, how I slipped away in the early evenings now. I tried to lie, and tell them it was a case of gout, but they saw through me.

"Don't you see?" George Arnold had cried out. "It must be his secret passion!"

"She must be very beautiful, for him to keep her from us so," Clapp, the Oldest Man, said, smiling at me through the smoke that always wreathed our back table. Then he surprised me, turning almost serious.

"But you should be married! When are you going to marry, Herbert?"

Why should I? We had, as it were, a perfectly workable facsimile of a marriage. Better, even, than the real thing. Any evening I wished, I could simply stroll by. Listening to Maddy play, or sing for me after our supper. Enjoying whatever else I desired afterward (she never denied me anything). There were no scenes over my smoking or drinking. No objections when I took myself off for a fortnight of hunting down in Jersey, or fishing in the Adirondacks. There were no demands of any sort made upon me. *How dreary it all was!*

Then I discovered our little game.

It started when I took her to see a show at William Schaus's gallery. I hadn't expected much, just some more of the *"Ruth-mania"* we were still enduring then. Endless paintings of Ruth, sketches of Ruth, sculptures of Ruth, gleaning in the fields of Boaz. Cooper's frontier Ruth, dragged off to live with the Indians in *The Wept of Wishton-Wish.* Ives's bust in every home, with its demure, chaste, womanly features—the one symbolic grain of wheat tastefully arranged in her hair. Ruth the dutiful wife, the dutiful daughter-in-law, clinging to her new people.

But what I found was something else again. Schaus had only a single exhibit on display, executed by some self-taught sculptor Hamilton Fish had found upstate. The work was called *The White Captive*, and according to the literature at the gallery, it was supposed to have an uplifting moral purpose—"*to show the influence of the Savage upon Christianity.*"

The influence of the savage indeed! After I put down our four bits, Maddy and I were swept up in the mob as if by a riptide at Coney Island. We were carted almost bodily down a narrow hall, until I thought Maddy would be crushed, and my nose would be broken from being jammed so repeatedly into the back of the gentleman before me. Then, finally, we were shot through into the gallery, and there she was.

It was the sculpture of a young woman. A young, pioneer girl, pulled from her cabin in the middle of the night by marauding savages. Stripped of her nightdress, she stood naked now, and tied to a tree stump. The whole work was a blatant steal from *The Greek Captive*, Powers's old sensation—but this was much less classical, almost lifelike in its feminine, sensuous roundness.

Schaus even had a halo of tinted gaslight over the piece, so that her skin looked almost as real as flesh. A mechanic stood by, laboriously turning a crank that rotated her pedestal slowly around and around, so that the crowd could see all of her. Her legs, her buttocks—the leather strap where it bound her hands together behind her back, and tied her to the tree. Her nightdress strewn over the stump, as if to remind us again of her soon-to-be-lost innocence. So helpless. So terrified that she could only stare blindly ahead, ready to do whatever she was bid—

Greeley—with his usual boundless capacity for self-deception—wrote the next day that "in her nakedness she is unapproachable to any mean thought. The very atmosphere she breathes is to her drapery and protection. In her pure, unconscious naturalness, her inward chastity of soul and sweet, womanly dignity, she is more truly clad than a figure of lower character could be though ten times robed—"

In a pig's eye. The women in the room knew better. They huddled fearfully together in the corners, holding up their fans and arms in front of them, as if to ward off an assault. Meanwhile, the men in the crowd stalked relentlessly around the piece, the mechanic with his crank still not fast enough for them. Schaus was wise not to put anything else on exhibit; they would have smashed it to pieces in their frenzy. Banging heedlessly into each other, swarming around the statue like so many sharks. There was no talking—no buzz of words, excited or bored, that rise up inevitably from the crowd at every exhibition. Only the constant scuff and creak of men's shoes, moving back and forth over the carpet and the floorboards.

Gazing upon her I maintained my equanimity for as long as I could. Then I took Maddy home and ravished her. Making her take off every stitch of her fine, new clothing before me, tying her hands behind her with my own belt. She took it all with as much passivity as the white captive. Seemingly frightened and overwhelmed by me now. Reduced again to her most primitive nature—to the wild savage I had first encountered upon the streets of New York.

Yet it was more than lust—it was literature. I had, I now discovered, the key to my *Street Scenes*. Why shouldn't a good story, a tale of moral reform, have episodes of wild and lascivious adventure in it? *The influence of the Savage upon Christianity*. Well, why not? What better way to discern which was which?

I set to work again at once. My long months of stagnation broken. Retitling my tale as *Paradise Alley, a Tale from the Streets of New York*, to give it more of an air of social reform (and, of course, depravity). Taking as my subject—Maddy herself.

Of course, it had to be changed, improved upon. Her father—and her mother—now were both drunks. The father falling into the bottle first, through a series of misfortunes, and bad company, then dragging the mother down after him. Maddy was still a hot-corn girl, but a pure, virtuous thing—every night fending off corruption, and still selling her wares. Beaten not by her pimp, but by her very own parents when she returns to the Shambles. No longer a lone child now, but blessed with a younger brother. *No*, a younger brother *and* a sister, whom she shields from one travail after another of the streets, and from her dypsomaniac parents—

It all fit so perfectly. An adventure full of one peril and pitfall after another. Lending itself naturally to so many conversions and reversals, rescues and deathbed scenes. Of course there had to be a little tragedy, a few depictions of truly depraved places. Perhaps even a few social statistics at the back of the book to give it weight, make sure it was regarded as important literature. And for the main character—the much-put-upon hot-corn girl—I had the life model right there before me.

My editors down at Harper and Brothers were ecstatic. It went so

well that I started to map out my little book's successors as soon as I
sent it off to the printers. There might be something with Five Points
in the title, or the Cow Bay. I need never run out of depraved neighborhoods, not in this City—

It was soon afterward that she came to my home on Gramercy Park. I
remember it was an evening in autumn, just at that turn in the season
when the days become noticeably shorter. The street lamps lit earlier,
glowing against the orange leaves, and the blue slate sidewalks that
ring the park.

She simply appeared before me. I had walked back from the *Tribune,* was about to turn into the gate of my home, when there she was.
Wrapped in a cloak and hood, moving across the street so swiftly that
I stiffened—thinking she must be a beggar woman, or some particularly brazen nightwalker.

Then her face was in front of me, lovelier than ever. More defined
now, the first, delicate lines of full womanhood beginning to sculpt
her cheeks. Framed there against her hood, her hair pinned into careful, artificial curls. Her eyes no longer so frankly ingenuous but knowing, seeing me now.

She had come to tell me that she loved me. I moved her nervously
in through my dooryard gate, shielding her under the elm tree there.
Wanting to get her out from under the eyes of my neighbors but not
willing to bring her into my house. Holding her hands, trying to
smile—I could feel the trap closing on me, the long-delayed extortion
coming at last.

"What are you doing here?" I asked, disbelieving. Wondering what
had finally made her restless. *The death of her mother? A new opportunity? Or simple boredom?*

"You are welcome to keep the clothes. The piano, too, if you like.
Even the harp. As to cash money—"

Her eyes flickered down, away from mine, for the first time since I
had known her.

"I love you."

"I don't understand," I said, astonished. Half-smiling, thinking
that this must be some ploy.

"I love you," she said again.

I had to admit then what I already knew—that it was no game. I
knew that she meant it.

"You are still grieving for your poor mother. You are distraught——"

She turned her head, looked with some little wonder now at the gracious redbrick house where I lived, the long porch with its trellises and vines out front. The wages of hackdom.

"This is your home."

"Yes. How did you know?"

I said this tersely, and she looked down again.

"Look, if it is the condition of not being married that bothers you   " I tried. "I could situate you in a shop, perhaps. Or another home, where you are unknown. You could even say that I was your guardian. It would not be hard to arrange a match, now that you have become so accomplished——"

That only made her angry, and she looked at me with an expression of sudden hatred that I had never expected to see in her.

"Now who is talking about money."

Such a woman. She had learned to speak.

"It is impossible," I said, shaking my head.

I looked toward the house this time, afraid one of the servant girls might be looking out.

"No. It is just not possible."

Her eyes bored into mine, full of hurt and frustration.

"I love you."

I was reduced to muttering, under my own elm tree.

"Not possible. Not possible."

❦ · 48 · ❧

HERBERT WILLIS ROBINSON

There is a shout from outside, then the sound of a bottle breaking, and Maddy stirs against me. Untangling her legs from mine, unsticking the soft, wet flesh of her inner thighs. I put out an arm, and pull her back into me. Breathing in the sweet, musky night sweat of her underarms. She burrows her head into my neck, murmuring, her eyes still closed—

There is another shout, some incoherent cry, and we both sit up. A faint smell of smoke seeps into the room, and peering out through Maddy's bedroom shutters I can see that the sky is powdered with a dull, red grit.

They are back out again already. The riot is not over.

We rouse ourselves, both of us silent, still surprised and a little embarrassed by our anxious, clinging passion from the night before. Even tender with each other as we climb back into our clothes, and hurry through our morning ablutions.

I wash myself a little in one of the stale buckets of water she hauled in yesterday. Not *too* much. Not even brushing my disgusting clothes before I dress again—not wanting to look anything like a three-hundred-dollar man. After all, the riot is on again, and I shall have to go back out there.

And again—why?

I should have gone home last night, I suppose, to stand guard over my property in Gramercy Park, along with George Strong and his troop of vigilantes. Instead I seem to have come completely adrift in the City. Staying where I will, doing what I want—

So why here?

Down in her sodden kitchen, we chew away at some old bread. Trying to find something to fill the void in our stomachs, to fill the awkward silences between us. *Maddy.* She looks so pretty, so *familiar* at the table across from me, has even put on a new red dressing gown. *For me?*

I go to the door, though, having said almost nothing to her. *What is there to say now?* When she came to my house, to tell me she loved me, I only told her that it was impossible. Preferring to have her under me. To tie her up in little chains, so I could look at her—

There must still be a way to put this right—for me to redeem her. I turn back from the door to entreat her. Wishing to have her by me or simply fulfilling my responsibility, I am not sure any longer. Only knowing that, as ever, she will do as she likes.

"Maddy, I have to leave now. I want you to go to my home in Gramercy Park."

"To your maid's room?"

"To wherever you wish!" I snap at her, instantly angered again, trying to fight down my temper. "Sit out on the porch, if you so desire. You cannot stay here. It is hot, and they will come."

"Why should I fear a thing from them? *You* should be afraid!"

She tries to look defiant again—but I can detect some indecisiveness, some uncharacteristic hint of fear in her face. Something has spooked her, at least a little. Is it the growing cries of the mob we can hear now? How silent and deserted the street was yesterday?

"*Please*—go there. For your own sake. And for mine, too."

There, I have said it. She hesitates for another long moment, looking me over, as if trying to see if she can trust me.

"All right—perhaps!" she says at last. "If you take me there!"

"What? Why?"

There is too much to do. I must get back down to the *Tribune*, then out to the streets again—

"You must take me there. Make sure the servants let me in, make sure they treat me right."

She holds her chin up, intransigent again. But it will take up half the morning, for me to escort her all the way up to Gramercy Park, then get back down to Printing House Square. I must get back out there, to see the struggle for the City at its most critical hour—to see it, and write about it. It is crucial for my career, my need to write something of lasting worth—

"I can take you someplace else," I tell her. "Just for a while, a few hours. Then we could go—"

"No. To your house."

"It is *impossible*—"

That word again. She puts her head down, crosses her arms over her chest and looks away.

After she came to my house the first time—from that moment on— she looked for any opportunity she could find to defy me. She sent away the tutors—the geography instructors and the music masters, and the dancing professor. When I asked her why, she only gave me a long, deliberate look.

"I will do as I like," was all she would say.

That became her standard refrain. Whenever I tried to get her to accompany me somewhere, to take some excursion up the Hudson, or over to the Elysian Fields in Hoboken, she would level that same, baleful stare upon me—"*I do as I like.*"

Soon she began to turn away my gifts. The only thing she would take from me was clothing, on the account at Stewart's. Even there, though, she defied me. Dismissing the knowing widow, choosing whatever colors and fabrics she might, however vulgar. Having the seamstress cut them in the most lewd and garish patterns conceivable. I began to buy her finished dresses myself, which she accepted—only to cut these, too, as she liked.

"Are they mine or ain't they?"

"Yes, they're yours, all right—"

"Then I will wear them as I please."

I thought then that she might leave me. In my more honest moods, I hoped for it, looked forward to the relief. But nevertheless I continued to ply her with more gifts, more entreaties.

To my surprise she did not go. She continued to sleep with me whenever I wished. We continued to play my little games.

Then one sunny Saturday morning, I arrived in time to see a Negro tar from Trinidad walk out her door. He gave me a gap-toothed grin, tipped his hat to me, and said something obscene in Spanish while I stared at him, stupefied.

For all that I treated her like one, until that time I had never really understood that she was a whore. Or should I say, more accurately, *a public whore*. I flung the term at her one night, but she took it coolly enough.

"It was you what made me one, when you decided you did not love me."

"You have so many other loves now. Perhaps you should see if they will foot the bill."

A mistake. (How is it I could be so constantly outwitted by this unlettered girl?) She took down the plain silver necklace she wore around her lovely neck, the one piece of jewelry she had not refused from me.

"If you like. You can have this, too."

She laid it in my palm like a limp thing, a handful of worms.

"You can sign the lease over to me, if you want. Otherwise, I can just go. If you got someone else in mind—"

"That won't be necessary!"

I continued to pay the rent. I continued to visit her, too. Rutting at her with some resurgent, wanton desire, even after her other lovers— her other *customers*. Writing down *their* stories, too, as she told them to me.

I kept going back even after her little visitation. She had never been pregnant before—not by *me*, at least that I knew. And truth to say, I never much concerned myself with it. When I thought on it at all, I simply assumed that she was utilizing some womanly art passed down by her mother, or some older girl at Gramma Em's.

Now, suddenly, she was as fecund as the rest of her race, breeding in each tenement rain gutter. She acted unabashed about it—implying she would get rid of it herself, or even have the child if I chose not to help her. Even speculating to me as to whom the father might be— a Nassau tar, a German or a Sicilian, or maybe even a Jew. As if the whole world had suddenly come to drop on my doorstep—

I took her up to Madam Restell's lonely marble palace on the Fifth Avenue and Fifty-second Street. Trying to make the visit as quick and discreet as possible, sweeping up in a covered hansom, the curtains drawn. Pulling Maddy, as fast as I could move her, through the side visitors' door.

Everything was handled with impeccable discretion. Maddy issued into her waiting rooms by a bowing male servant. Scarcely a word spoken or any acknowledgment of our names, beyond the aliases I had chosen: *Mr. and Mrs. White.*

Still, it was grotesque. Even Maddy was jolted by it. The siege of boys chanting, "*Madam Killer! Madam Killer!*" and "*Your house is built on babies' skulls!*" every time a carriage pulled in or out of her gates.

And inside, the endless halls of tessellated marble one had to walk through to Madam Restell's examining room, footsteps echoing flatly along the walls. Everything furnished in vulgar shades of red; the windows hung with scarlet satin curtains. Worst of all, the hall lined with huge gilded French mirrors, so that with every step we took, we looked back at ourselves. A frightened young pregnant woman, on the arm of a furtive-looking man slipping into middle age, his face half-obscured by his high collar.

I only saw Madam Restell herself by chance, at the end of their interview, when she held the door open for Maddy. She had a disconcerting way of looking right through me, a frank, chalky English face for all of her French airs. The face of the Gloucestershire shopkeep she was, measuring me exactly.

I bundled Maddy up in her cloak, whisking her back out the side door and to the rented carriage as quickly as I could. Laughing softly to herself, head down, as we drove back out through the horrible boys. Then turning to look at me, still laughing. Saying, *Well, that's it. I can't have any more*—

What had I done? Should I have let her have her child—*my child,* perhaps? And if it wasn't?

But strangely, after that afternoon at Madam Restell's, there was no question of us parting. Maddy still saw her other callers, still did as she liked. More bitter with me than ever after that, more sharp-tongued, but there could be no good-byes now. I had seen her through the whole span of her youth, and we were bound now as closely as husband and wife, with all the appropriate grudges and resentments, and the binding hatred.

Of late we have done almost nothing between us, not even the silly game, the chains. We have become as quarrelous and chaste, as dependent on each other as some elderly couple. Looking at her standing before me—sleeping beside me upstairs—I know that I might even love her. That at least I have loved nobody else.

So why didn't I marry her? She was below me, certainly, but that hardly mattered. There is no City on earth, probably, where it matters less. New York is full of men and women who crawled up from God knows where, telling the world anything they wished. Madam Restell, with her French name and her English fishwife's face. Building her marble abortionist's mansion just two blocks from where Dagger John's beloved new cathedral still molders.

I could have changed Maddy's name, her past, her grammar. Brought her to my house in Gramercy Park. It wouldn't have made that much difference, save at the tables of those most ancient families of the City—who wouldn't have me anyway, on account of my profession.

So why?

Because I am a hack, after all. Only wanting to see my name in print, to revel in the praise and adulation of those I do not know. Wanting to watch the crowd, and write of it, but not to be part—not to be part of anything, in this great, dangerous, devouring City.

It is not too late to change, for both of us. *Is it?*

"All right," I tell her. "All right, then. Wait for me here. I will not be long. Wait for me here, open the door to no one save for myself. And I will come back and take you to my home."

She looks at me, her arms crossed. Still suspicious, but hopeful. *Still afraid, of something.*

She says nothing, just gives me a quick, short nod, and I turn again and go out the door. Back out into the blistering street, looking for a story. Telling myself it will not take long.

❧ · 49 · ❧

MADDY

She watched him go, out into the street again, wondering if he would be back. Not sure if she wanted him back, hoping to God he would be.

She hadn't expected him the night before. She had finally fallen into a shallow sleep, with the help of the whiskey, when she had heard it— the quiet tapping on her own door. A sound both closer and more sinister than any of the wild cries she had heard from outside all day. There was just that small, insistent knock, in the middle of the night— as if someone were testing the door, testing to see if she were home.

She had sat up in the darkness, unable to move. Expecting next to hear the sound of the knob being twisted, the door frame beginning to splinter. Finally she had grabbed up the revolver and run to the window. Peeking out from behind the curtains at first, her palm tightening around the pistol. Feeling the sweat as it cooled on her naked back and neck.

We'll see to your niggers—

By then, though, Robinson had started to ring the bell. She had let him ring, listening with some pleasure to him calling her name out in the street. Then she had rushed down the stairs, pulled him eagerly inside, in her relief and desperation.

It had been like that when they were first together. *Without the game, without anything.* The two of them clinging to each other, against all the terrors of the City outside. Afterward they had listened to the rain, and he had held her, and talked about all the terrible things he had seen, and how worried he was for her. And she had held his head against her chest, and let him.

Yet now he was off again. Promising to return, to finally take her to his house. He had even sounded sincere for a change, though she tried not to believe him—to believe that she needed him at all.

I do as I like.

But she didn't, not now. She had let him go, even though she didn't want to. Already, she could hear it starting up again. The same distant, roaring sound. The mob on the move again, somewhere. While she sat and waited for him to return.

In the beginning he had been much more fun. It was a more straightforward transaction; she had no illusions about it. She was used to the hands of men on her. She was even used to the hands of men raised against her—was more than willing to trade that in for a real bed, in a private room, with clean white linens and a mirror to see herself.

In the summer he would take her out to Coney Island for a week, to wade in the sea, and stay in a hotel, and dance around the midnight bonfires with the other guests. Or at night he might take her to see one of the blood-and-thunders, or a Mose play on the Bowery—*Mose and the Gold Rush*, or *Mose in Bleeding Kansas*. They would sit up in the top galleries, with the newsboys and the street sweeps, the ragpickers and the cinder girls. Stamping their feet and whistling, chanting, "*Hoist dat rag!*" along with the rest before the curtain came up. Drinking whiskey from a flask and eating fresh-roasted chicken wrapped in a newspaper, tossing the bones down on the fat German mechanics and their wives, sucking on peppermints and pink lemonade in the stalls.

Afterward Robinson would take her to the Atlantic Gardens and there, amid all the crowds and the pandemonium, they might have still more fun for a while. They would perch on a bench inside the enormous beer hall, ensconced in the continual din of the drums and bass fiddles, the pianos and harps, and the shooting-gallery rifles, and the men slamming down their dominoes and dice.

They would sit there, wedged together, the whole commotion so loud they could barely talk to each other. And she would look over at him, and see his gaze slide away. Taking in the scene around them, as if trying to fix it in his memory. Looking for some interesting character to shout back and forth with. Robinson's lips smiling at her, but his eyes moving away restlessly, evasively, whenever she tried to look at him.

It was around then that she had tried to become what he wanted, even though she had no good idea of what that might be. It was then that she had let him move her and her mother to the house he had rented for them. When she had begun to take the lessons that he pushed on her—learning to read and to figure; to dance, and to play the square piano that still sat in the corner, its case unopened for years now. Learning how to dress, and to carry herself.

She had not asked him for anything, content to take what he thought she should have. Grateful to him for providing a decent home for her mother, a dry, warm room for her in the winter. An ailanthus tree out the back window, where they could watch the birds lighting in the summer, just as they had back in St. John's Park when they were still a family. Sometimes, when Robinson came over for supper, it felt almost like they *were* a family again—the way it had been when her father had been alive, the three of them laughing and eating together around the kitchen table.

And when her mother died Robinson had hired out an enormous hearse, with a great glass-box wagon to mount the coffin in, and horses with regal black plumes on their heads, and a carriage for them to follow in. She had relished the looks from the other women on the block as he'd helped her up into her seat—dressed in the fine black crepe-trimmed bonnet and dress he had bought her, complete with an actual veil. She knew how much her mother would have appreciated such a funeral for herself, how much it would have meant to her. And when, three blocks from Paradise Alley she had begun to cry compulsively, she could not help but lean in to him, and let him comfort her.

She supposed that she was in love with him by then. Or at least, she had wanted him to see her, to really see her now. Watching herself in the mirror every morning, smoothing out her fine new clothes, her green-striped taffeta day dress, or her mantilla wrap, embroidered with red and brown velvet. Barely knowing herself, how different she looked. Thinking that this must be the start of it, that Robinson must be changing her into what he wanted, what he could love.

She had been through this before. Dressing up for the men down on Broadway, and the Bowery. Putting on the checkered shawl and the ragged dress of the hot-corn girl, and taking off her shoes. Playing at something they wanted, though she barely knew what that was, either. Yet they had come around, circling her avidly, and she had realized then that men would accept almost any disguise.

Robinson had come, too—and she had sat in the house he rented for her, waiting, patiently shaping herself into what he wanted. But there had been nothing else. Still she had waited, trying to impress him with her newly acquired skills. Engaging him in what conversation she could on the day's events, or a book her tutor had had her read. Playing for him on the square piano.

He had only sat in a chair in the corner, sipping his brandy and blowing smoke rings from his cigar at the ceiling. She had not understood it at first, because she was not allowed at the sort of evenings he attended. She could not accompany him to the society dinners and the musical soirees, the seances and nocturnal tappings, so only gradually did she begin to get the idea. Able to glean it solely from his manner and his tone of voice, his expression and his half smiles and all the other little hints she now paid so much attention to. Not until then did she understand that what she was turning herself into was just what he was used to, and was already thoroughly bored with.

Then had come the show at Schaus's. She had not quite understood that, either—the men circling all around a statue, with a halo over it like the Virgin Mary. Some solid, well-fed girl, with an expression Maddy recognized from the women at Gramma Em's brothel in the Seven Sisters, staring off impassively over the heads of the men perusing her.

Nonetheless, she had let him take her home after that, and stood before him and let him tie her hands as the statue's had been tied. Her new maroon frock laid out over the chair beside her. Standing before him, in the parlor of her little house. His breath coming in short, shallow draughts as he watched her there. Letting his hands move over her—while she stood there helpless, unable to touch him in return.

He never seemed to grow bored with the game, had even moved on to real chains. They were light enough, discovered in God knew what brothel, or maybe even custom-made by some discreet blacksmith. *It was not hard, in this town, to get a chain for anyone.* Fastening them eagerly about her hands, sometimes her ankles as well; draping them about her shoulders, her breasts.

When the weather was good, he might take out a carriage. Driving them out on Broadway, then far up the Bloomingdale Road. Past all the little squatter villages of Irish, and the Negroes up there, the small plots of corn, and wood stills and crude rendering plants. All the way up to some isolated thicket of woods, past any remaining dribble of civilization.

There he would have her go through the whole game. Taking off her garments one at a time. Laying them over a tree branch or a stump, until she was completely naked. Watching her every move—then walking slowly up to her and snapping the chains on while she stood there waiting, trembling. Intensely aware of every sound of the birds and the smaller animals in the brush around her—the farther-off sounds from the City of whistles and hammers, the tremble of the New York and Harlem rails to the west—

One afternoon there had been an especially loud rustling in the trees, more than a dog or any other creature might make. She had thought something was wrong the moment she heard it, but before she could even get to her clothes, the men were walking out into the clearing.

There were two of them, leering openly as they looked her over— trying to cover her nakedness as best she could, but restrained by the chains. They wore long traveling coats, covered in red dust, and broad-brimmed slouch hats pulled down over their eyes. They had irons themselves, slung from their belts, and coiled bullwhips at their hips. She had seen men like them in the City before, and she realized at once what they had to be, skulking around in the woods so close to the coloreds' village. *Blackbirders*—

"I see ya got one already," the first one out of the woods said— grinning and winking at Robinson where he stood, rooted across the clearing from her, his face perfectly expressionless.

"Looks like ya been poachin' on us."

They turned their back on him, and moved toward her. Their pink faces nearly identical under the black hat rims, lined with dirt and scraggly, red-brown hair. Round, feral eyes looking her over.

"She's just a little green niggah anyway. Brown 'er up in the sun a little, we could take 'er right back with us—"

"She already got the irons an' everything!"

They walked up to her, and she tried to hold herself perfectly still. Meeting their gaze, their eyes like those of dogs she used to see on the streets. Staring right into them, hoping they would back down—

"All right now."

Robinson had spoken quietly from across the meadow. Pulling back his duster to show the pistol he had in his belt. *Of course he would take precautions,* she thought with a small tug of relief, but resenting him for it as well. *Thinking he might need such a thing, he had brought her anyway.*

"All right."

They ignored him, moving in on her, until Robinson pulled the gun and clicked the hammer back. This did make them pay attention, though they still did not move away from her.

"You've had your joke now. Go on back to whatever Carolina shit-hole you came from."

Still they did not back off—and she could see now that they, too, carried pistols on their belts, tucked just behind the bullwhips.

"*Wait*—" she started to say, but she couldn't get the rest of it out. Fearing that they would kill him, and her, too. *While if he just let them do her* . . . It wouldn't be nice, but that would be the end of it, nobody would get killed. Besides, they would do her anyway—

The first one turned his grinning face back to her.

"Ah, now, ya see, boss? She just wants a little taste."

The slaver slipped suddenly behind her, sliding an arm across her waist. She could feel his hardness, pushing into her buttocks, and she began to tremble despite herself.

"Whatta you gonna do now, boss? Don't wanna hurt your little honey, here."

The man ran a hand up over her right breast, his thumb and fore-finger squeezing at her nipple until she cried out in pain.

"I'll shoot your friend here first," Robinson said, calmly training his pistol on the other blackbirder, who took a quick step backward but was still several paces from the trees.

"Then I'll come over there and see about you."

"I reckon you'll see, all right!"

"I reckon you'll have to let her go to get to that pistol in your belt. And before you do, I will put a ball in your brain."

"Cass, enough a this nonsense. Let her go now!" The other black-birder spoke for the first time, the nervousness plain in his voice. But the man who had his hands on her still hesitated, his grip tightening around her waist.

"Ah, what's he gonna do, Chance? Swing for some little tart like this?"

"It will be a year at least before they find you up here," Robinson said. "If they do, they will just blame it on the local Negroes—a couple of dead slavecatchers. Chances are the coloreds will make sure nobody *ever* finds you, just to save themselves any trouble."

Maddy could feel the one behind her shift. Those feral eyes looking over the forlorn plot of earth around them, the tangle of scrub woods. He took his hands off her, complaining as he did.

"Jesus, mister, what kind of place is this?" His voice actually sounding hurt, even as he backed slowly into the woods with his partner.

"Shoot a white man over some little whore!"

Robinson kept the gun on them, his lips just barely peeled back from his teeth.

"This is New York, sir. We will shoot a man over almost anything."

When their footsteps had receded into the brush, she ran over to Robinson, and he threw his duster over her. Grabbing up her clothes, running her on back to their carriage without pausing to so much as dress her, or take the chains from her body. He whipped the horses back down the Bloomingdale Road, driving them at a breakneck pace until he was sure he had outpaced any man.

Only when he was certain they were well away did he turn the carriage down a deserted lane. Pulling up there, and turning to her where she sat, back on the leather carriage seat—still wearing the duster over her helpless shoulders. Running a hand down her cheek.

"Are you all right, then?" he asked her. She only nodded—still chained. Feeling his hand tremble against her face now.

He threw his legs on over, sliding down into the seat beside her. There he held her face in his hands, kissing her all over her face and neck, moving his hands inside the coat. Caressing her breast where the blackbirder had bruised her, as if to soothe it. His hand moved lower then, and she had let him, pushing herself against him, letting him take her right there in the carriage, even still in the chains. Thinking that this was what he wanted and willing to be that, too, willing to be whatever it was he wanted.

But it wasn't. Nothing was, it seemed. She had put up with all that. She had even gone to his house to tell him she loved him, only to have him keep her out there under his elm tree, mumbling that it was impossible.

Until now. *Was he really going to come back for her?*

She doubted it—but she went over to her closet anyway, to get ready, just in case. Pulling hurriedly through all the fine clothes she had there—

It was another strategy she had used to repulse him, dressing in slovenly, stained gowns. But the fact was that she could not bear to use her best things. Hoarding all of her fine dresses, her best robes and bonnets, endless pairs of gloves and stockings and ribbons. Yet still buying more, with his money or what she earned herself. Packing most of them away in balls of camphor as soon as she got them home from the milliner's. Saving them for some occasion, someday when he broke with her, once and for all.

She had let him pick her up, right off the street. And he had taken her to a brothel. But to shelter, nonetheless—

There was a noise from the street, and she broke off her search through the wardrobe, stumbling over to the second-story window. Below she could see the women of Paradise Alley, beginning to emerge from their houses and tenements again. Mrs. McGillicuddy, Mrs. O'Connell, Mrs. Buckley—all the ones who put on such airs, just because they were white and married to white men. *Broken legs and laced mutton, the lot of them.*

She was surprised that she couldn't see Deirdre O'Kane, out there among them. Deirdre was the only woman on the block Maddy was a little afraid of, always immaculately dressed and clean, head held as high as the archbishop's. Crossing herself whenever she passed Maddy's house.

"I'm as good as you are yourself!" she had yelled at her one morning, not wanting her to think that she didn't see her.

Any of the other old morts and mollies on the alley would have scuttled away, or pretended they didn't hear. But not Deirdre O'Kane. She had stood her ground, stopping right where she was, and turned her head slowly in Maddy's direction until she had fixed her in the window there. Eyeing her so coldly and deliberately that it was only her own pure stubbornness and the whiskey she had already imbibed that morning that kept Maddy from throwing the shutters closed.

"Our Maker and our Savior, the Lord Jesus Christ, will be the judge of that, Miss Boyle," Deirdre had replied, in a voice that made the pigeons fly away. "In the meantime, I suggest you stop advertising just how good you are to the general population."

It had almost made her laugh out loud, once she'd gotten over the shock. Deirdre had had fewer airs, she'd noticed, ever since her man had gone off to the war. The others, the coloreds or the race women, weren't such bad sorts, either. Like Mrs. Derrickson, or that one, Ruth, who had been fascinated with her gun at the pump the morning before. She seemed like a simple thing, worked to the bone, but always nice to her. Married to that big, good-looking Negro who walked like a sailor. She would have done *him* for free—him, or that son of theirs, just as dark and nearly as handsome. So sweet in his youth, his cheeks still barely bearded.

Someday, perhaps, he would come to her.

The only ones on the block who could ever afford her were the young men. Butchers' boys and mechanics' helpers, and apprentice sailmakers, just starting on their first jobs, with no household to support yet. Or their fathers would bring them over, if they could find a way to hide their first week's wages from their mothers. Anxious and impatient to learn—yet too embarrassed and ashamed to look her in the face.

Ashamed for her, in the end. The father patting the son on the back in her parlor afterward, both men going out the back door without another word to her. A few moments later she would hear them laughing as they had a piss together, out in the back lots.

Would it be like that with him? With that beautiful boy?

Or would she last that long? What would she do when the war finally ended, as all wars did? When her price came down, with no more hordes of farm boys passing through, eager to stick it in once before they went to the killing. Would they all be able to have her then—all the men in Paradise Alley?

She pulled one of the new red silk dressing gowns defiantly out of the closet, and wrapped it around herself. *What was she saving it for, anyway? He wasn't coming.*

On the sill by the upstairs window she found the gun, where she had put it down the night before. *At least he had left her this much.* Sticking the gun in her pocket, she ran downstairs—checking the front door, then the back and the windows, making sure they were all locked.

Of course he wouldn't come back for her, she was just a whore.

She pulled out the pistol and shoved its barrel repeatedly through different slats of the shutters, trying one angle, then another. Outside, just across the street, she could see the white women gathering like so many geese. Talking avidly to each other, and gesturing, she was sure, toward her—toward her house. Her finger caressed the trigger, pretending to knock them off, one by one, like so many tin targets at a shooting gallery—

Then she heard it again. The dull roar of the mob, like the sound of a locomotive in the distance, slowly rising as it came closer. She stumbled back into the kitchen, cursing him as she did. Looking for the jug.

Offering to let me be his maid. Just another whore. Just another Paddy.

✦ · 50 · ✦

RUTH

She awoke slowly, unsure of where she was at first. The heat pressing down upon her chest like a steam iron, and the first, conscious thought skittering across her mind like an insect: *My God, it's even worse than yesterday—*

There was the sounds of footsteps outside, moving quickly, and she got up from the chair in Deirdre's parlor and went over to look through the shutters. But it was the same man—Maddy's man—who had come so late the night before. Hustling away again already, looking nearly as frightened and disheveled as he had when he arrived. A little man, in his dirty yellow trousers, with a gaudy red handkerchief sticking out of his vest pocket now. Whistling tunelessly through his teeth—glancing back over his shoulder from time to time as if he were fleeing something. He walked rapidly to the corner, then was gone.

What creatures men are! Always hurrying back and forth. Spending and replenishing, until the mere facility of motion seemed to be enough for them—

She turned back to the room. Deirdre and Milton sat slumped where they had fallen asleep the night before. Milton, with his usual instinct for her, waking just moments later and sitting bolt upright. He looked bewildered for a moment, then stared wildly around the room.

"Did you fall asleep, too? Were we all asleep?" he asked.

"Yes—I guess," she answered, without thinking.

"Then we could've missed him!"

He started to go for the door.

"You're not to go out there!" she cried, all but throwing herself at him.

"But if we were all asleep, how do you know we didn't miss him?" he insisted, his voice rising. "Maybe he came home, and we weren't there. We have to go out now, we have to *look* for him!"

"*No*," she said, trying to reason with him. "Your Daddy's no fool. It was a good thing we stayed up so long as we did, just in case, but he'll know enough to call here when he finds we're not home—"

"He would have to, just to ask where you had gone," Deirdre said, rising from her chair now. Her voice as clipped and practical as ever, even as she pressed futilely at all the new folds in her dress. "That would be his first concern. You can see that, can't you? He would look first to see where you'd gone, and he would have to come over here."

Ruth watched, silently grateful for Deirdre's quick thinking, as Milton nodded slowly.

"But still he might've come home last night," he insisted after mulling it over for a moment. "He might've come back, and decided to wait out the night. We've got to look for him back home, at least."

"That's fair enough," Deirdre told him quickly, before Ruth could raise any further objection. "But let me do it. That way I can just go in and out, down the back lots, and nobody will be the wiser."

"Because you're white," Milton said. His voice suddenly resentful.

"Yes," Deirdre agreed. "Because I'm white."

"All right," he agreed cautiously. "All right, then."

Ruth could tell from her son's face that he was still not completely assuaged, but she hurried him on into the kitchen.

"You can come help me with the others," she told him. Hating to have Deirdre go out there for what was her husband, her family—but willing to do almost anything to keep Milton safe.

Was that how it was, then? You sacrificed what you had to?

"Is it all right, then?" she whispered to Deirdre, ducking back out of the kitchen. "If ya don't want to—"

"I understand," Deirdre said, waving her off, already heading out the back door.

Didn't she have babies, too, a husband—

Ruth tried not to think about it anymore, setting out breakfast.

Trying to maneuver around Deirdre's fine, spotless kitchen. Glad, even with everything, that she had given her own abandoned place a last sweep—

She could remember how it had felt, to have a proper home around her for the first time, even if it was only rented. How it had been when she'd first come on the block. It had been Tom who had set that up as well, so many years ago—though Ruth was certain that he had not told Deirdre beforehand. Tom who had seen to it, after he had come up to Seneca Village with the rest of his work crew, to tear down the roof over their heads.

Ruth had been living in the village ever since the night they had made Johnny Dolan disappear. She had loosed the dog that Dolan kept, kicking at his haunches and hurling rocks at him until at last he'd moved off into the fields, growling and snapping. Then she had slaughtered the pig; cut it up and salted it herself, taking it off to Billy's in a burlap bag as a gift. *Her dowry, as it were.* Slamming the door behind her when she went, leaving the shanties of Pigtown behind her forever.

Billy had insisted they get married, and she had been very pleased, though she had never asked him for it. Before the wedding the Reverend Betancourt, the same little Protestant priest she had seen the first day she had ever laid eyes on the village, had come to indoctrinate her in the practices of her new faith. She had looked forward to his visit, as willing to trade her faith for any other, but when he did come to see her in Billy's house, she had burst into tears.

"Look at me, Father, I am not a fit person," she had told him. "You can see, I have been with men. And I have done worse things, sinful things, Father, just to keep alive."

"Arrogance!" he had thundered at her. "You think that you are the only one here who has not done terrible things just to live?"

He was a small man, but he looked much larger now. His eyes swelling and burning—staring past her to a random point somewhere along the wall above her head. Gesturing toward where the City lay.

"And out there, too! They think their lives have been so blessed by God they do not have to sin. But they are wrong!" he declared—speaking more calmly now, but still in the great, orotund tones he used from the pulpit. A trace of the same Island lilt that Billy had in his own voice.

"They are wrong, for there is no sin too low for man. You know that truth, at least, and you are so much closer to God because you know it."

He stood up abruptly, proclaiming from the Bible, though she scarcely knew what he was talking about:

"As it is written in Joshua, 'And they utterly destroyed all that was in the city, both man and woman, young and old, and ox, and sheep, and ass, with the edge of the sword.' "

Then he sat back down, just as suddenly. His voice all but indifferent now, his eyes looking smaller in his head. The wild light gone out for the time being.

"You know your sin, now you are ready for your redemption," he said matter-of-factly, waving an empty cross over her, and sprinkling oil across her brow. "All you have to do is learn your lessons, renounce the wicked church of the pope in Rome, and you will be anointed."

A few weeks later she was baptized in the Hudson. The little minister grasped her firmly around the back and clamped his hand over her nose, then he dipped her abruptly backward, into the freezing spring water that swirled and tugged at her ankles.

And afterward, that same day, she was married in the little clapboard church—wearing her own white robe now, flowing out over her swollen belly. A wreath of wild flowers and strands of wheat in her hair, woven for her by the other women in the congregation, although she barely knew them.

She had been unsettled by the strangeness of the service. The whole church standing and booming out their sonorous Protestant hymns. Shouting back their call and responses to the minister. She had been filled with a sudden terror that she might be losing her soul once and for all—as battered as it was—by abandoning the True Church for this strange and heathen ceremony. But she had stood up nonetheless and married her Billy Dove, as she knew she should have if it had been required that she become a Jew or a Muhammedan, or if she should have gone to hell directly.

And when they were married she had done everything she could for him, in her condition. Whitewashing the little house, or tilling the square of vegetables he kept out in the dooryard. Trying always to surprise him with some treat, some little improvement. She rose early in the morning to cook for him, and before he came home in the evening she walked out into the fields to cut a wildflower, or a sprig of lilac to put by his plate. Though it occurred to her, sitting there watching him eat, that she would have liked to have decorated him in flowers, he looked so beautiful.

He was very pleased with her in those days. His hands were on her constantly, caressing and holding her. Grabbing her up and tickling her when he came home—the hour when he was formerly at his most moody and discontented, and had already had a few drinks on his way back from the orphans. Now he was usually sober, or at least had only had one. Rubbing his hands over her stomach, insisting on lifting up her dress even if they were outside.

"A big boy for me. A child with a mother and a father," he would say, running his hands over her taut, bulging flesh. "A boy who can truly learn to sail, to go where he might."

She had waited patiently for her time, for she knew that she was not likely to live through it. She saw it in the looks the other women gave her, wrapping their hands around her skinny arms, frowning and shaking their heads. Murmuring, *Too thin, too thin,* to each other, trying to fatten her up with pieces of fatback, and cornbread soaked in the grease.

It did not bother her much. She was only grateful for their company. She had been afraid that she might be lonely—*as if she could be more lonely*—living in the village. But she made friends easily enough—walking down to the Hudson in the morning with the other women, black and white, to wash and beat the clothes against the rocks. Standing up to her knees in the deceptive, swift-running water. Culling through the played-out beds of Stryker's Bay for a last stray mussel or clam. Letting them teach her how to fish, casting the crude hemp nets they used out into the current, and hauling in striped bass and weakfish.

It was such a country of abundance. Like some miracle in the Bible. Put your hand over the water and you shall have all that you want.

And afterward, waiting for the clothes to dry, they would take their ease for a little while in the long, summer afternoons. Lying or squatting under the trees by the river, gazing across at the Jersey shore and the Palisades. Some of the women smoking cob pipes, or tobacco they had rolled in sheaths of newspaper. Laughing and waving at the trains on the Harlem line when they came chugging and clanging down the track behind them—the engineer and the firemen blowing the whistle and waving, grinning lasciviously back at them.

Just before it was time to go, at the very heat of the day, they would wade back in and bathe once more in the Hudson. Then they would return to the shade for a few more minutes, letting themselves dry there, away from the sun, cooling themselves for the evening. The life growing inside her keeping Ruth pleasantly, drowsily warm anyway. All worries about her time to come dissipating as she thought how nice it would be to die like this, breaking up and drifting helplessly, painlessly off over the broad, grey river.

When her confinement did come, the women had made her take to the bed in the tiny house. Coming in to sit with her in teams of two or three or four. Bringing their own chairs, knitting and talking quietly by the foot of her bed, one or another of them constantly running a wet cloth across her head, and arms.

She lay there, hearing them whisper still— *Too thin, she's too thin.* Glad only to be facing a clean and certain death, after all the times she had encountered it in confusion—fleeing along the roads, or lying in the hold of the ship. *Feeling the first, cold pull of it, like the currents of the Hudson tugging at her ankles.*

Even so, the pain of the first contractions took her by surprise. She had known pain before—the ache down in her bones when she had had the relapsing fever on ship, or Johnny Dolan's hands on her, or the pain of her stomach, seven days without food. But this was different. It was a harsh, ragged feeling at first, as if she was being split open by gigantic hands, and it only got worse. Going on for hours, the pain endlessly elongating the time. Leaving her too helpless to do anything but watch the agonizingly slow progression of life all around her. The flies crawling along the walls, the summer sun retreating second by second across her windowsill—

And just when she felt almost accustomed to it, when she thought that she could nearly accommodate it without being ripped in half, it changed. The pain no longer ragged and searing but a dull, grinding thing now, worse than anything she had ever felt before in her life. Pressing against her back and her spine like some wild creature, trying to burrow its way ever deeper inside her.

"You got to push. You got to push again' it," one of the women was saying, crouching down by her legs.

Ruth looked down and saw her bare white knees—so terribly pale against the faces of most of the women in the room. All of them here now, it seemed, standing against the walls like the choir in the church.

Some of them moving about urgently, doing things, although she could not imagine what they were. More of them praying or just staring at her. Their faces cringing, or drawn with foreboding, depending upon their own age and experience.

"You got to push it out. Ain't comin' out any other way, you know. Ain't any other way *for* it."

But the thing inside her only seemed to burrow deeper, as if it were about to burst out her back, and she cried out—screaming in the small, cramped house. Hearing herself, surprised that she could still make such a noise. Thinking, *Of course it would not be that easy, not even to die—*

Then she spotted him in the doorway. Her eyes spun wildly around the room again, and there was Billy, head and shoulders above the women. His handsome, copper-red-and-black face more solemn than she had ever seen it—his eyes wild, and red with fear.

She saw him there, and wondered at it. Then the pain had gripped her again, the wild thing still trying to get deeper, and the woman above her knees had shaken her head, her brown face grimacing.

"You must push it past. *You must,*" she insisted.

But it would not come out, whatever it was. It preferred to stay inside and eat out her innards, grinding her backbone to powder. She pushed and she pushed, but she could not dislodge it, and then she let herself sink down and that seemed to ease the pain. Her senses going now, sinking back into her as well, so that she felt herself to be blind, and nearly deaf. She could no longer see the women around her, could barely hear them calling on her to *Push,* and other such fantastical demands.

Instead, she could feel it very close now, the cold currents of the river rising up around her legs. Engulfing her the way they had when the minister dipped her backward, and she welcomed it, she sought to sink deeper.

"Dear Christ Jesus, take her in Your hands—"

She opened her eyes again, to see the little minister by her bedside. Waving the barren cross over her, his pupils burning red again at the imminence of death. *And not even with a real priest, to say a proper prayer over me. Still, it was better than the ocean—*

She swung her head back over, toward the other side of the bed—and saw Billy still kneeling there, his face etched in grief. She could smell the familiar scent of the brandy on his breath—but with such a heavy, deeper sadness in his face now, something beyond the usual tragedy of the drink.

"Don't go," he whispered to her, his voice barely audible across the pillow. He said it over and over again, a plaintive little whisper, but the most heartfelt words he had ever addressed to her. "Don't go, now."

She stared at him, amazed that he might actually care if she lived or died. He went on like that for hours—whispering all the usual, desperate things that she had always imagined him telling her. Muttering that he loved her, and that he wanted her to live, and not to leave their boy without his mother—

It would make him unhappy, she thought, still astonished. *It would make him unhappy, to have me die.*

She decided that she should try to live, though she was not sure if she could now. The pain only increasing, somehow, growing worse than anything she could ever have imagined.

There has to be some end, she thought. *Let's find it.*

She pushed back against it—and screamed and screamed. The women leaning hurriedly over, pushing Billy's face out of the way. Running a cloth soaked in laudanum over her lips.

"Here now, here now. Just a little a that, but you got to push."

"I know," she said, and the sound of her voice seemed to surprise them.

She pushed again—and the pain was worse yet, reaching whole new parts of her being. Yet she thought she had it now, she thought she understood. The creature in her was hurting, too. It wanted to get out, and she had to help it, she had to ease it out to help the both of them. Pushing slowly, carefully, rolling her body a little. Trying to nurture and comfort it, to enfold it in herself. Giving it one soft push, then a harder one. Trying to coax it, to lure it on out. Pushing again, then halting, then screwing herself up for one great push that hurt so much she was sure it would kill her.

But it didn't, and she started all over again—another little push, a bigger one. On and on, until at last Ruth felt the burrowed creature, the great fist smashed against her backbone, begin to recede. Her spine springing back into place, so that she was able to get a grip on the wild creature now—to push more firmly and easily, reassuring it all the time in her mind. Until at last she could look down and see there, between her gawky, skinny white legs, the midwife holding up her baby.

A boy, Billy was right. As dark-skinned as his father, black against her pale white legs. She cried to see him as they gently wiped him off with a cloth and laid him on her chest. *So pretty and sweet and black—* and with Billy still beside her, whispering things into her ear. So that she could not help but cry, and wonder how it was that she should have lived to see this.

RUTH

That was the best time between them, those next few years in the village. It was nearly the only time that she could remember not having to try to get away from someone or something.

How any one time, any span of years or months, could be the best time of one's life and then end—

It had taken her a long while to convalesce fully from the hurt, from the tears in her body, but after a few weeks she was able to limp around the house, doing what she could. When she was well enough, she went back to tilling the vegetable plot, and helping to harvest the wheat field. Walking down to the river with the other women again to do the washing, the musseling and the fishing in the shallows with their hemp nets.

There was cider and beer to be made in the autumn, and syrup in the winter; evenings bottling preserves and salting meat, and quilting at the church house. She knew how to do almost none of this, they had been too poor even for such homely things. Learning it from the other women as she went along, abjectly grateful for their help, their instruction—realizing all over again how ignorant she was. She knew almost nothing of value besides the sewing her mother had taught her, and how to haul the kelp and plant potatoes. Glad now to learn everything she could, even happy to stand and sing the strange hymns with the rest in the African church.

Best of all, Billy was delighted with her, with the son she had given him. He liked to see the child whenever he could, to look in on him when he was sleeping, and spy on him playing out in the fields. Jiggling him on his knee when he came home from the orphans', laughing at everything he said and marveling at what a bright boy he was. They had him christened in the clapboard church, the Reverend Betancourt dunking him rather harshly, she thought, in the baptismal bowl, so that he sobbed and sobbed. But his father was beaming, naming him Milton after his own father, who had made the middle passage.

"He's smart like him, smart enough to get away," Billy told her, with that practical fierceness she had seen in him before, and that always frightened her a little. "One day he'll leave here, never see us again."

The child had also given Billy the chance to build another room on the house. Glad to have the chance to pull out his carpenters' tools, salvaging the wood from old abandoned fences and houses up past the northern fields. The money was tighter, but they were able to get by with her job at the German ladies'. Carrying Milton along on her back—surprised and disturbed though she was by the shouts of derision they suffered from any passing Irish and German workmen, or the conductors on the Fourth Avenue rail line.

"*Whore! Whore! Nigger-lovin' whore!*" they would call out from the railing of the last car when she happened to pass behind it.

"Get yourself a real, honest workingman, ya lousy gooh!"

Ruth was amazed at their ferocity—the trainmen only having glimpsed her for a moment from the moving car, already receding down the track toward the Grand Central Station. She was baffled that they could be so different from the men on the Harlem line, who still waved and whistled to the women as they lay out in the grass.

Mrs. Krane and Mrs. Mueschen, at least, had been delighted with the baby. Letting Ruth hold and nurse him as she worked—so long as she did not stop turning out the rag-and-bone dolls for them. And Milton was always glad, even then, just to be close to her. He was an almost unnaturally amiable child, his head coming up, a broad smile across his face whenever he heard her voice.

When he got older the German ladies let him play in his own piles of scraps, and imitating his mother he would put together remarkably adroit—and saleable—toys and dolls of his own. Ruth marveled at his dexterity, and told herself that he must have his father's skills.

"Someday ye'll build a ship yourself. A ship like none they ever saw," she would croon to him, holding him tightly to her.

When she could she took him down to the docks and the shipyards along the East River, to see the boats building there. And when she did—when she saw the marvelous, white keels taking shape—she had some understanding of why Billy felt such a pride in the thing, and why its loss wounded him so.

Yet she did not take Milton back. Before she had gone a hundred yards down the docks, she discovered that she was fair game for any men there, the sailors and shipbuilders and longshoremen, sailmakers or boardinghouse runners alike. They grabbed at her with every step, calling out their obscene threats.

"Hey, girlie, what's that nigger doll ya got there? Put him down, I'll give ye a better one—"

"Come here now, Molly, I'll give you the hair a *that* dog!"

Groping brazenly at her breasts and her buttocks, trying to jostle and shove her down blind alleys, or in through doors of the saloons. Ruth was unnerved by their ferocity, thinking at first that it must be something in the nature of their profession. Soon, though, she understood that it was the fact that she had the boy with her. Mortified that she had not figured it out before, that she had put her baby in such peril.

That was what the railmen had been on about as well. It was the child that enraged them. Their righteous feeling that any woman so desperate and depraved as to diddle a nigger should be happy for their trade—

She was thankful, at least, that they were tucked way up in Seneca Village, among their own. They would lie in bed at night and hear the sounds of twigs breaking in the woods, and the low growl of the neighbor's dog, and she would know that the menacing shadows outside were real. The slavecatchers still loitering around Seneca Village, to see what they might find—

She had clutched her baby tighter to her chest, knowing that even he could be taken. The blackbirders had no compunction about who they carried off, whether they were escaped slaves or freed men, children or adults. The people in the village, black and white, kept an eye out for each other, but all it took was one slip, one moment, and they might vanish into the trees, never to be seen again.

And if we did not think on Dolan more, if we did not worry about him as much as we should have, it was only because we knew we were already as safe as we could be anywhere else. Besieged up there, in the Nigger Village, for better or for worse.

Before long she found that she was pregnant again. She was not so apprehensive or so fateful about it this time—knowing what it meant now, the pain she would have to expend. She was even able to put on a little bit of weight, which Billy liked to tease her about. Not enough that she wasn't still skinny—the possibility of any true fatness having been burned out of her once and for all, back on the Burren, and the road—but that she did not look as if she were actively starving, and he would call her his big woman, his Mother Rock.

And this time it did go easier. She did not feel the cold tide creeping up her—though she knew it was still there, abiding, just out of reach. This time only half a day was required before she gave birth to a girl they named Lillian. She was longer and skinnier than her brother at first, her skin a shade or two lighter as well, as all the others would be. And Billy had been delighted in the girl, too, she was relieved to see—not quite as ecstatic as he had been with his son, but still very happy.

A few weeks later, on a Sunday off from the orphanage, Billy had tracked up into the woods again, looking for lumber he could use to rig yet another room up to their spreading house. He came back with a load of fine, first-rate boards along his shoulders, but a wary look on his face.

"From the German place," he had explained. "That man up there with the goats."

And she had known exactly what he meant. The little estate with its meticulous German brick walls. Its unswerving, orderly lines of vegetables and fruit trees had been as permanent as anything they knew, up in the still undemarcated wilds of Bloomingdale. The eccentric name that he had read to her once, chiseled into the bronze plaque on the wall: *Jupiter K. Zeuss, Prop.*

"An' he didn't mind it?"

"He's all gone. All he took was his goats an' his furniture. An' no one else moved in to claim it."

"Well, maybe he passed suddenly," she said, though she could scarcely credit it herself. If there was one thing she knew, it was that real estate did not go wanting in New York. "Maybe that was it, poor soul—"

But soon the word got 'round that the German had been evicted, so that at last the City could build the new park, and a sense of foreboding settled over the village.

There had been rumors about the park for years, and stories in the papers, but no one had thought it would ever be built. It had seemed too absurd an idea, even for the City. *To tear down people's homes and gardens, just so other people could walk around in the grass and the trees, and breathe the open air.* Everyone had just assumed it was politics, and that if it were built at all, it would be over in Jones's Wood, or down on the Battery, where the codfish aristocracy preferred to take the air.

Yet less than a month after Billy found the German's place deserted, a man had come from the sheriff's office, to speak in the churches. Ruth had recognized him at once. It was the same little man with a too-big head who had perched on the wall outside the hospital on Staten Island, and tried to steal Dolan's cabinet of wonders. The man with the terrible goblin face, *Finn McCool*—

He had come up in the world since she had seen him last. Looking very important now, with a wide red sash across his waistcoat and the colored cane that the City leaders carried on official business. Telling them with the same easy grin she remembered that they, too, were to be evicted, and that all of their own homes, and the little schoolhouse, and both the village churches were to be torn down, and plowed under to make way for the landscaping of the new park.

They were shocked into silence at first—by the grin on his face, by the matter of factness of his tone as much as anything. Then the whole church had erupted in protest, the men and women both, standing and shouting at him in their pews. Other men tried to rush the pulpit, and push their way past the burly shoulder hitters he had been prudent enough to bring along. Even the Reverend Betancourt was shouting, she could see—slapping his hand down repeatedly on his Bible, as if trying to prove a theological point.

McCool had stood his ground where he was, above them in the pulpit. Still grinning and raising his hands for silence.

"Now, now! No property owners will be evicted without payment!" he cried out over the tumult. "Anyone what can produce a legal deed for their property will be compensated to the full extent, thanks to the generosity of the Common Council!"

This announcement only stayed the congregation for a moment. Then they were shouting again:

"A deed! *A deed!*"

"There never was no deeds! This was swampland—this was just the woods!"

"Shame! Shame!"

Finn McCool only shrugged and grinned again, climbing spryly on down from the pulpit and pushing his way quickly out the back door of the church, with his shoulder hitters. The villagers still raging, though they soon subsided, and filed numbly out of the church when they saw that they had only each other to appeal to.

"Do ya have a deed, then?" Ruth had asked Billy, as gently as she could, when they walked back to the house. Already knowing the answer from the look upon his face.

"No. Nobody ever needed any deed before. Nobody even said a *thing.*"

His voice baffled and bitter but not quite outraged, like that of a man who had been done terrible wrong before and expected no better from the future.

Ruth had been carrying Lillian in her arms, and Billy had Milton riding on his shoulders. They had walked down the rest of the lane in silence, and stopped in front of the little white house he had built, and added on to so carefully for them. She remembered looking at it in the dusk there, and thinking that this was how the time ends—

The steely thicket of bayonets. The land agent reading out his paper while they blinked like moles in the sunlight.

Though when they did come, there was no need for a guard of soldiers, or even a policeman. The whole village gathering up its few belongings, and walking away in still-unbelieving silence. Only a handful of them were armed with any valid deed, and entitled to compensation—the rest of the inhabitants of Seneca Village simply wandering slowly off down the Bloomingdale Road toward the City, without a complaint or a look back. All of their friends and neighbors, a whole village, simply drifting away, so that there would scarcely be a trace of them left by nightfall.

All it took were a few of the sheriff's men to oversee the whole business, waiting patiently enough to turn them out of their homes. A contingent of surveyors, led by a nearsighted, diffident man in spectacles and a little student's cap, who ignored them altogether.

And a work crew—much like those she saw all over the City, tearing some new hole in the street. Leaning and squatting against the side of the now-abandoned and desanctified All Angels Church. The workmen quietly working their chaws of tobacco and spitting from time to time into the churchyard lawn. Not intending any disrespect by it but merely killing time, as they always did, while they waited on their betters.

Tom among them. In charge, even, as far as she could make out, wearing an official blue City tunic with another bright red sash across it. He walked over to her looking abashed, taking off his hat as he approached.

"I'd forgot you were here," he said—his voice apologetic, even ashamed.

"Sure, but it's not your doin'," she had told him.

But he had continued to stare at her there, holding Milton by his hand and dangling Lillian on her hip. Eyes widening a little at the sight of them. Looking at her with that mixture of pity and protectiveness that made him a little bit in love with her—and she knew it.

"All the same, I'm sorry to see you in such a way," he had said, fingering the band of his official hat and looking down. The last, straggling line of the villagers moving out of sight, heading down to the City. *A life of forty years' duration, vanished in a day.*

Tom scuffed his feet again, rubbed the rim of his official hat.

"I'd forgot you were here—"

It was Tom who had found them the little house on Paradise Alley—out of his infinite generosity and, she hoped, his quiet, brotherly love for her. Even loaning them the rent for the first month, on the ground-floor apartment. Though he had suggested, squirming and blushing as he did, that perhaps it would be better if she did not tell Deirdre about it.

That was nothing Ruth had not surmised already—certain though she was, too, that Deirdre must have already known. Nevertheless, she had determined to try to stay out of her way for as long as possible, even timing her trips outside to hang the wash and fetch water from the green Croton pump so as to avoid her.

Yet Deirdre had surprised her, showing up unexpectedly on her doorstep one morning. She had brought a fresh, iced flour cake on a plate, and Ruth was so startled she did not know what to say—though the sight of it sent Milton, following behind her skirts, into paroxysms of joy.

"Oh—oh, look at it, Mother! Look at that!"

"This is to welcome you to the block," Deirdre had told her, her diction and manners, as always, so rigidly, Yankee perfect. Ruth had mumbled something back—still mesmerized by how beautiful she looked. *How such a face could be so hard—*

But Deirdre was looking down at her son where he stood in the doorway, still gazing up in wonder at the cake.

"This is your oldest," she said, as a statement, not a question.

"Yes."

Ruth had smiled automatically, assuming that Milton would brighten any heart, the way he brightened hers.

"How old is he, then?"

"I—" Ruth started—then stopped abruptly, realizing the trap she had fallen into.

"I thought as much. You were taking up with him when you were still with my brother."

"Billy's my husband," Ruth had said defensively, pushing Milton back inside so he would not hear more. "We're married now, which me an' Johnny never was—"

"Oh, aye!" Deirdre spat out. "Married in a proper, nigger church, I'm sure."

She leaned in now, her face filled with still-unabated rage.

"You're on a respectable block now. You'll have to learn to live among respectable white people. Not like you did up in the woods, running around with whatever you chose."

With that she had thrust the cake into her hands and walked off, and after that Deirdre had had nothing to do with her, though Tom would still sneak over sometimes, to share a cigar or a pint with Billy. When he did he always brought a gift for her, some little thing, a new pot or a ribbon, or a toy for the children. And when he was gone, they were always sure to find money hidden somewhere around the house, a nickel or a York shilling or two bits, stuck under a frying pan or on the mantel over the fireplace. Ruth had picked them up silently, without even telling Billy—knowing that Tom did not want to offend their dignity by offering it to them openly.

She was grateful for the money, and the gifts—grateful for the house, as well. The block was not so bad, though the ash boxes overflowed on the corner, and the blood swelled up from the gutters whenever it rained. It was much longer for them to get to work, making the walk uptown. But Ruth was able to make friends with most of the women, and there were more and more race families moving onto the street. *They would not simply be living with white people after all, Deirdre's admonition notwithstanding—*

Yet Billy was tetchy all the time, she noticed, stopping for a drink more and more often on his trip home from the orphans'. She knew that he did not like living in houses that were so close together—that they prevented him from seeing what might be coming. He was mistrustful of the white neighbors, and when she tried to tell him that the slavecatchers were less likely to come down to the Fourth Ward, he still would have none of it.

"At least up there you could see who's with you an' who's not," he liked to say, moodily tapping his fingers on the kitchen table. "At least in the nigger village, nobody called you a nigger."

But their old friends and neighbors were all scattered now—living at best in a few houses together on the Arch Block, and down on Roosevelt Street, and Baxter, and along York and Lispenard Streets in Greenwich Village. Paradise Alley was as safe as anyplace for them, and she had thought, *Well, it's not so bad. At least we got a roof over our heads, an' enough to eat, how bad could it be?*

But before their first summer on the block was out, Lillian had come down with the wasting sickness. Ruth had seen right away that it was serious. She had stayed home from her job with the German ladies to nurse her. Giving over most of her own dinner to the child, plying her with whatever sweets and fats she could lay hands on. But it was hard to get good, clean food or water anywhere in the ward, and the only milk came from the brewery cows.

Despite everything she could do, Lillian would not stop vomiting, would not stop shitting out whatever they fed her. Ruth watched her growing thinner, every day, starving in front of her eyes. *Just as they had all been, back in the cabin. Down in the dark of the cabin, huddling under the thatch.* Her daughter screaming with pain as her little limbs convulsed with the cramps, unable after a few days even to keep any water down.

Billy could not get too close, having to go to his job at the orphans', but he did whatever he could. Giving over every penny they had, borrowing more just to get good milk from a real stable he knew of up on the West Side, above Fifty-ninth Street. Walking the whole five miles back home with a bucket in each hand, every night. He had even hired a real physician, one Dr. Sloper, a self-confident, elegant young man from Great Jones Street, only to have him inform them that their child had the cholera morbus and advise that she be quarantined before he fled, back uptown.

Ruth had stayed by her bedside night and day, doing whatever she could for her. She had patted her brow with a wet cloth, and tried to force what food and water she could into her. She knew, though, that she was only wearing her child down all the more, as she threw it all up, and the realization of that had made her frantic—sending her running out into the street blinded and crazed with helplessness. Only the thought that her baby might die alone forced her back in, back to her bed to watch the final, merciful death throes.

That night she had stayed up and washed her child, and dressed her in the best clothes she could find. Getting her body ready for the picture she wanted from the daguerreotypist in the Second Avenue. She had seen such pictures before, displayed in his window. The deceased child always looked so peaceable, so lifelike and tranquil, as if she were only sleeping. Dressed in her best clothes, a solemn brother or sister at her side, done up as well in their meeting clothes.

She had seen that and wanted it, so she dressed Milton up the next day, too, while she sent his father out to hire the daguerreotypist. Milton, who had eaten and drunk everything she'd given him during his sister's illness, and only grown bigger and stronger. So that for a while she had hated even him, although she had forced herself not to show it to the child. Realizing now, as she saw him so somber and obedient, standing a little perplexed by the body of his sister, that she loved him more than ever, loved him just for surviving, as well as for everything he was. Waiting calmly, as peaceful as she had been in weeks, for Billy to return.

He had come back shaking his head, though—telling her kindly but firmly that the picture was too much. That it was impossible, they would be better off spending the money for the funeral, and to make a better life for their son. And she had wailed like a madwoman, and raged against him to hear this. Clawing at him while he held her gently against his chest, and comforted her, until she realized that he was right.

"Leave the dead for the dead," he had told her, but so gently that she knew he was right, that there was nothing more she could do for her daughter, but that she would have to get back to the dismal business of living.

They had buried her in Brooklyn—with the help of Tom, again, who knew a digger in the fine new Green-Wood cemetery, and had forwarded them another bit of money. This not even Deirdre had begrudged, nodding to Ruth curtly but with as much sympathy as she had been able to offer the next time they had crossed paths on the street, telling her with a quick, sharp intake of breath, "*Sorry for your loss.*"

Ruth had been somehow comforted by that, as much as she supposed that it should have made her hate Deirdre all the more. And also by the fact that her little girl was to lie out in Brooklyn—far enough away that she could not visit her there often. Glad, now, that Billy had stopped her from having the picture done, to be able to remember her how she was—and not to have some permanent record of that chiseled, hunger-wizened face. *To not have any picture of her boy, standing next to death.*

A few months later she had been pregnant again, and she would be again after that, and they would go on with things, such as they were. But it was never the same for them, there on the block. There was nowhere else they knew of to move, and nowhere else they could afford, but it was never the same for them, or between them. They still went off to their jobs uptown, Billy going up to the orphans' everyday, and she to her German ladies. But it was the end of that time and they knew now that no better time was going to come, that there was nothing more to expect than that they would go on, living on the block.

❦ · 52 · ❧

DEIRDRE

She rattled the key noisily in the back door of Ruth's home, opening it as loudly as she could. She had considered trying to slip in, to steal into the house as quietly as possible, but she thought that might only alarm Billy, if he were indeed back—or any bummers inside, trying to loot the place.

And if her brother were there, she knew, it wouldn't make any difference anyway. She would be as good as dead before she got across the threshold—

But there was no one. It was quickly apparent in the few small rooms that no one had been in at all—not Billy, nor Johnny Dolan, nor any of the looters. The narrow house was all but emptied out—only the stove and the furniture, rough and unfinished and scarred with use, still remained. That damned box of Johnny's standing in the corner like a covered gravestone. *Like some black effigy of Johnny himself, mocking them yet.*

Everything else was thoroughly swept out and washed, cleaner than Deirdre could ever remember seeing it. Even now, though she tried to be charitable, she could barely keep from showing her repugnance for how Ruth kept her house, and raised her children. It was not to be helped, she guessed, considering the money they had. At least they were cleaner than most of the children on the alley, and that oldest one, Milton, was smart as a whip. Yet Deirdre could not stop herself from thinking, deep down, that somehow she could have at least *tried* a little harder.

She had disapproved of Ruth right from the beginning, when her brother had first brought her 'round to their house. Mooning at her like some dumb creature, like she had never been in a proper home before, and Deirdre could not help then but hold her at least partly responsible for what had become of him.

All those years, as the famine had taken hold, she had thought of her family with a growing sense of dread. Reading about the deaths in the Irish papers; the coffin ships, and the starving people walking the roads like living scarecrows. She had tried to get word—but this time there was no reply at all. Even the letters she sent to the priest came back, with a note that the parish church had been closed on account of the typhus, the families all scattered or holed up in their cabins.

She had sent Tom over to the Corcorian Men's Association, though he was a Tipperary man himself, to see if he could find anyone there who had heard anything. But all he could come up with was a friend of a friend of the family, who thought that they had gone to the work-house.

"At least they'll be fed there," Tom had said, trying to ease her mind. "At least they'll have a roof above their heads, and two meals a day. Soon as we hear, we'll bring 'em on over."

But she had read about conditions in the workhouses, and when she wrote next to the one in Cork city, she got no reply from there, either. He was a good man, Tom, but she thought that he tended to be a little too hopeful about such things.

In those days they were still renting an apartment in an old brown-stone on St. John's Park, and Eliza was already on her way. She had made him quit running with the Break o' Day Boys, and the other gangs on the East River—had made him quit all his old associations with men, save for the fire company, the Black Joke, because he had convinced her that it served a valuable public function.

She got him as well to go down to the clubhouse, and start attending the political meetings, until he had been hired as a lamplighter for the City. He had been a little ashamed of it at first—a fawning, beholden political job—and his friends had made sport of him. But it paid better than a butcher's apprentice, and he didn't come home anymore stinking of blood and offal, or have to stand over the sink for half an hour before he could unbend from the pain in his back and shoulders.

And in the evenings they would read together. She had taught him to read her inspirational tracts, or the proper Catholic newspapers and journals, not just Mr. Bennett's *Herald* and the other penny dreadfuls. His arms around her, stroking her hair and laying a hand on her swelling stomach—treating her at all times, in the bedroom and without, with respect and adoration. And at such moments she thought that this was everything she had always wanted, and how wise the priest was.

She made sure, in her turn, to follow the rest of the advice in the *Guide to Catholic Girls Who Earn Their Own Living*. Going to great pains to keep herself up—to comb her hair out, and scrub and clean herself and her home more fervently than she ever had, even when she was well along. Not that she was really earning her own living anymore, having left service and the house in Gramercy Park behind after they were married. Still doing some needlework and spinning at her wheel, to speed along the purchase of their house—

She would have given it all over, though, every last penny of their savings, to know that her family was safe from the hunger and the workhouse. To have had any word from them. Certain as she was on some nights, lying in bed, that the worst had happened and they were all dead. Trying to banish such thoughts even as she had them, to preserve her baby. On other days, scrubbing the floor or doing the dishes, she would tell herself that they had emigrated, to England or Amerikay, or even to Australia. That maybe even now they were in New York, and trying to find her. Once a month or so she sent Tom to the docks and the rooming houses, to inquire if anyone had shown up. But none of them ever did.

Then Ruth had appeared with her brother, like some damned storm crow. Coming around when they already had the new house by Paradise Alley, and Eliza, and she had all but given up hope for them. Telling herself, *Well, they were in Dublin or in Heaven, it was all the same, and she would see them in the next life*. She had all she could do to keep from weeping when she learned that Johnny was not only still alive, but in the City.

Yet she had thought right away that he looked so different, so hardened. Back in Cork, he had been her little man. He had been no more than a child, still, when she had left. A headstrong and reckless boy, capable of being as ruthless and cunning as the devil. But tender, too—she had taken care of him many days when her Ma was out in the fields, and she had loved him like her own son. Playing at being a mother, before the hearth. Feeding him his milk and potatoes, and wiping his face. He was a wild one already then, he would not hold still for her, but she knew he had loved her.

Now, when Deirdre saw him again, he seemed changed beyond the natural hardening of a man. The only likeness was a certain determination in his eyes—something that was so like her, and which she took an improper pride in. But there was a queerness even in this. There was a mulling restlessness in him, more like that of a loose dog than a man. He would look right through her, she noticed—through Tom and the baby, the new house and the furnishings. As if, like a half-starved dog, he was only ferreting out what he might batten on.

When Johnny had told her about the rest of the family, she had burst into tears, surprising even herself with her sobs, her inability to hold on to herself. Crying like some drunken washerwoman out in the street. Yet crying as much for Johnny as for them, she knew even then—this wreck of a man before her, who had had to witness it all.

And the girl he had brought with him—half wild herself, barely able to pull her dress down over her knees. Bewildered and unlettered, some mad child out of the West. *God only knew what temptation she had put before him*—

Deirdre had determined, then, to save him—to bring him back into the fold of God's mercy. Getting Tom to work on him, to invite him into the Black Joke company. She had thought that he might be her work, her sacrifice for the blessings that had been bestowed upon her. *Offering it up to Jesus*—

All it would need was her hammering at him enough, she was convinced. Yet to her surprise, he resisted her. He had joined the Black Joke readily—willing enough to carouse over lamb pies and ale—but otherwise all he had done was to take up with Tom's old, bad companions. Insisting on living up in Pigtown, among all the heathen niggers and the shanty Irish there. Doing God knew what to make his living.

The trouble must be the girl, Deirdre decided—especially when she learned that they were not married. *Why else would any woman want to live up in that wilderness, save to hide her own shame?* and she had decided that shedding himself of her might be the first great step toward his salvation.

But she could not ignore the black eyes, the split lips and the bruises that Ruth came to sport. The two of them showing up at her house like a traveling pair of prizefighters, they were so marked up. She saw in Ruth's eyes the sort of crazed wariness that she saw in the faces of other women on the block who felt the back of their husband's hand. And when she saw it she wanted to throw them both out of her house, she was so angry.

She had tried to tell herself that this, too, must be Ruth's fault somehow. *For any woman to let herself be hit like that.* She must have no self-respect at all. Goading him to it, somehow. Driving him to it with her own sluttish, godless ways, tormenting him with his own weakness.

Yet when Ruth had come to their home that night, to tell them it was Johnny who had killed Old Man Noe, she knew it was the truth. For all that she had cried and screamed at her, Deirdre knew that she had suspected it all along—had known that something had gone out of her brother. That of course he had done it, of course he would be capable of even worse things, just like all the rest of the human filth she walked among, head held high, on the streets of this City. Ready to kill or fornicate or sell their souls for a dollar, another drink, a good suit of clothes. Seeing each other as no more than the next grist for the slaughterhouse, the herds of pigs and goats and cows shipped in each day by flatboats. No more than another one of the butchers, her brother. *Her brother.*

And even then, too, she had another sense of Ruth's worth. This ignorant, half-wild girl coming to them, already having worked out a plan. Getting her Tom involved in it, for which she could not forgive her. Wanting Ruth to keep her hands off him, imagining God knew what terrible things that she might draw him into—working along with that drunken Negro she had found, no less.

Beneath it all, though, lay her fear that she might draw Tom himself away—a girl this resourceful, this hardened herself, at such an age. *Hardened just as she had been, making her way alone in the City, as no more than a girl.*

She had hated it worst of all when Tom, without her knowledge, had brought Ruth down to live by the alley—along with her new colored brood, and the Negro husband. Offended just to see them there, every day, following her down the street. All those halftones—and the oldest boy, jet black as his father, the devil's own color. All of them living on her block, defying all her efforts to mold it into—to *think* of it, even—as a respectable neighborhood.

Living here, in this house, only a few doors down from her own.

Deirdre backed silently out of Ruth's deserted home. Locking the door again—the hairs on the back of her neck pricking at the empty house behind her, though she had looked into every corner. The house where Ruth's family had lived for so long, and what had she ever done for any of them? Only resenting, endlessly resenting her for it all—that she had ever dirtied Tom's hands with her business, and sent her brother away. Not even confessing it, but harboring her resentment through the years.

When Deirdre got back Ruth was busy at work in her kitchen, feeding her children along with her own, glancing shyly up at her, amid all the commotion, for her approval. Her heart went out to her at the sight of it. Seeing the doggedness in her now, the tenacity beneath her seeming confusion, her ignorance.

How easy it was for all of her hatred to fall away. How hard it had been to keep it in place for all these years! Wondering if this was how it was for all those stories in her inspirational books—the Protestant lawyer, or the Universalist lady—to finally come to Jesus, and the True Church. All those saved souls who had finally let their resistance fall away, like shedding an old garment.

She had had some presentiment of it when Ruth's little girl had died. Her anger fading a little even then, as she saw every day what it had taken out of Ruth—having to watch while that child wasted away from the cholera. Fearing for her own children. Remembering how she had felt when she had lost the two in childbirth. *The little babe coming out blue, and not breathing, strangled by the cord, its very lifeline to her.* Or dead already, in the other case—carried about dead inside her, as she had already suspected for over a month, for one of God's awful, impenetrable reasons.

She had felt her hatred, her fury begin to recede even then. But she had pushed it back into place, holding it there for all those years more. Keeping up her hatred like her street face, though there was no reason for it.

"So—nothin' there?" Ruth asked her now in a whisper, wiping her hands on her apron. Her face already sure of the answer, composed and unaccusing.

"No."

Ruth had turned and looked at Milton, shaking her head. Including him, sharing him in their adult council, above the heads of the other children. Smiling at him as he frowned, softly calling over something to allay his fears as best she was able:

"To be sure, he's all right. Like any sailor, he knows to put in at a storm—"

Making it a virtue that his father was still missing, maybe strung up from a lamppost somewhere in the City. And doing it so convincingly that Deirdre wanted to weep at the effort, at her own hardness of heart.

How could she have held herself aloof from this woman for so long? It was one thing that had always bothered her about the inspirational books, all the wondrous conversions. Weren't the writers of such stories the more embarrassed by their past sins, when they saw the light at last? Didn't it make them feel all the more remorse—all the more *foolish*—for the years lost in darkness?

At least they had the glorious revelation of their conversion, the sheer joy of the scales falling from their eyes, to carry them through. Deirdre had yet to come to her own full reckoning. *It was one thing for her to forgive Ruth, and to take in her children.* But then there was Tom—still out there, wounded again, undergoing God knew what agonies. And she had sent him there. She had sent him out there, she knew with a knowledge that all but crushed her, because he had brought the niggers on the block.

"It is our Christian duty," she had told him, and he had gone and done it. *What was her duty?*

After she had read the casualty lists from Fredericksburg, last December, she had wandered around in a trance. Keeping it in her glove, the scrap of paper that was part of him, against her. The announcement that time. The tiny lines of type from the *Tribune*, under the usual, plain grim heading of *The Casualties:*

THE KILLED AND WOUNDED IN THE IRISH BRIGADE.
COLONEL NUGENT, OF THE SIXTY-NINTH NEW YORK
FURNISHES THE FOLLOWING LIST OF CASUALTIES FROM
PERSONAL RECOLLECTION.
IN THE SIXTY-NINTH NEW YORK WERE WOUNDED . . .
. . . *O'Kane, Tom, Co. A, chest, severe.*

It was she who had started taking Horace Greeley's *Tribune* in the first place, trying to emulate the Protestants. Not their heathen worship, God knew, but how they thought and lived—and how they made money. For the longer they lived in Paradise Alley, the more Deirdre had wished to live somewhere else.

The urge had only grown and festered as she had watched the City moving lumberously uptown   the new blocks and homes springing up everywhere in the open fields, the airy new blocks to the north. They had not been able to go with it. Tom had made a slow but steady rise through the clubhouse, from lamplighter to a City watchman's job, to foreman of his own construction crew, digging out the central park uptown. Yet they were barely able to keep up with the babies she turned out, one after another, like clockwork. Never getting enough ahead to move, particularly with the war now raising the price of everything.

While Paradise Alley and the blocks around it in the Fourth Ward grew more crowded every year. Still dirtier, still busier. Still more full of race families and now even whores like Maddy Boyle, with their fancy men and black tars—

"It's a sin to wish too much for the things of this world," Father Knapp had gently chided her in one of the talks they had in the rectory study at St. Patrick's.

But she knew that he was wrong. It wasn't a material wish she had, but a wish for all that was respectable and good. Wanting to live like decent people in this pit of a City, just as the Archbishop himself admonished them every Sunday. Wanting to live like *Americans*.

It was in the *Tribune* that she had read the accounts of what slavery was like, and life in the South. About all the miscegenation, and the race mixing, with the white planters and overseers imposing themselves upon the Negro women. Spawning still more halftones, who were then impressed into slavery. White women having to live every day with slaves who were in reality their half sisters, and stepdaughters, and cousins. *But of course men would do such a thing. Of course they would do whatever they pleased, given that sort of power—*

She had been so appalled she had even asked Father Knapp about it.

"Is it right, then, Father?"

"The Church teaches us that slavery is not an *unmitigated* sin," he had answered her slowly. "It is the next life that matters, and if slavery should bring any poor heathens to Jesus, no matter how inadvertently—"

"Is it a Christian thing, then, Father?"

It was the first time she had ever seen him look embarrassed. Staring at the floor as he drew one foot across the worn rectory rug.

"No," he said softly, meeting her gaze then. "No, no, it isn't a Christian thing a'tall."

"It is your duty," she had told Tom.

He had argued about it, though he never argued with her on anything in their marriage. Standing his ground on this, though he spoke to her quietly and reasonably enough, seated at their kitchen table in his shirtsleeves.

"It ain't that I'm afraid. You see that, don't you? It ain't that I'm so afraid as to shirk me duty."

Just to remember that, alone, made her blush with shame. *That she had forced such a man to defend his honor—*

"But what will the rest of you do, then? To go down to Virginny an' fight for the poor colored peoples, when me own wife an' babes go hungry—"

"We'll manage," she told him. "If it's your duty, God will see to it that we get by all right."

"Ah, Dee, but it can't last much longer. Just wait awhile—"

But soon after that recruiting posters had gone up all over town for Corcoran's Legion, announcing that *A Few Good Men Are Wanted*, and the Archbishop had proclaimed that if there were not enough volunteers it was the people's duty to rise up, and demand that the government draft them.

"It is our patriotic duty. The Archbishop said so himself—" she had told him to his face, and he had given in then, and gone down to sign his name.

Yet she knew it was a mistake as soon as he had joined. It had been a dismal scene, down at the striped enlistment tents the Provost Marshal had erected by Castle Gardens. The gang *b'hoys* standing around, sneering at the recruiters and trying to talk men out of enlisting. Rival tents set up by towns and cities from upstate, or as far away as Ohio, trying to draw recruits in with better offers, so their own sons and husbands would not have to go and die.

She had realized what she had done as soon as he stepped out of the tent, and put $129 in greenbacks and a fat clutch of relief tickets in her hand.

"There it is," he had told her. "That's the whole of the enlistment bonus. Best you should keep hold of it as long as ye can."

Hating her already, it was clear in his face. She had wanted to stop it then. She had wanted him to go back into the tent, and hand over all the tickets and the ridiculous green gobs of shinplaster money, and take his name back.

"It's too late for that," he had said, as if he could read her thoughts, or her face. *Just hating her.* "It's too late for that, so why don't you go on home now."

His coldness astonishing and dismaying her. Thinking as she turned and left him without another word, *What have I done?*

She had been further appalled when she'd gone to see him up at the mustering ground in the central park. Stunned that the government would let its soliders live in such a way—seeing for herself all the long lines of dirty white tents, pitched in a sea of mud. An open ditch for a latrine.

"You look starved. I'll bring you some more food," she had told him, fingering his blue tunic, pitifully light and shoddy for the weather, already. "I don't know how they expect you to get through the winter in this—"

"Yes. That would be good."

His hatred already banked somewhat by then, he was that good a man. *Much better than she was.* He had only seemed very sad, which made her feel all the worse—already looking so much thinner and older, with his beard growing in. His eyes staring past her, as if he could only get through by keeping himself very contained and distant. He put a hand on her shoulder, and she had thought of him then as he had been, coming to see her in Gramercy Park. His young face so open and innocent, so obviously hopeful. *What have I done to him?*

She went back to visit him as often as she could, though she hated seeing him there. Unlike the first year of the war, there were no grand parades or reviews now. Sometimes on Sunday the regimental band would play forlorn camp songs that already sounded like dirges. Otherwise she would meet him on the same desolate, muddy lane by the camp—waiting there with the wives and the sweethearts, the prostitutes in red velvet sauntering back and forth, looking for their customers. Trudging back alone afterward in the gathering darkness, walking for a mile before she could even catch the horse cars for the two-hour trip downtown.

It felt as if she were visiting him in the Tombs prison, and she feared that she could not stand it much longer. Yet it was even worse once he was shipped down South, to the war.

The City had become a strange and dismal place by then. Everywhere there were picket lines. The strikers standing along the sidewalk outside the gasworks, the shipyards, the iron foundries. Their hands shoved deep in their pockets, shivering and coatless in the winter. The construction sites standing idle, the boards around them plastered with handbills calling for rallies for or against the war, denouncing the Copperheads or the Niggerheads.

She saw men being arrested on the street every day, usually deserters picked up by the Provost's guards. There was a whole stockade set up for them in the park by Broome Street, the men led out to use the latrine behind it in shackles.

Even the pigs had thinned out. Small wonder, with any meat, even mutton, impossible to have for less than fifteen cents to the pound. She spent all her time now tramping the streets, trying to find decent food for her family to eat. She did not even try for coffee anymore, saving the money for what sugar she could buy for the children. The prices rising still higher—the shopkeepers eagerly sticking their new, marked-over signs up in the window each morning.

She took in any sewing and washing she could find, but there was only so much time, with all the hours she had to put in shopping, and the measles and the mumps running through the younger children. She had gotten Eliza a job at the counter at Macy's, and she had found their oldest boy, Henry, a position as an apprentice clerk, though he was barely thirteen. Even so, she had had to empty out the account at the Bank for Savings they had built up so carefully over the years.

If it is your duty, we can manage.

She had even given up the *Tribune*. Instead she got hold of whatever sheets she could scrounge, blushing as she bent down to pick up a copy from the gutter or the ash box, but still needing to *know*.

It hadn't been so bad at first, checking the daily casualty lists. Tom had just missed the bloody fight at Antietam, and when it got to be December, the other women on the block, the ones who already had husbands and sons in the war, told her there would be no more campaigning until it was spring again.

Then had come news of the fight at Fredericksburg. She had barely been able to pick up the paper for the next three days. Thinking, *It isn't fair, it isn't fair, there isn't supposed to be another fight!* Her stomach sinking each time she saw the heading for his regiment— *New York 69th*—and the long columns of names underneath it. Knowing they had taken the brunt of the fighting. Reading through them all with her heart in her mouth, and falling to her knees to thank God and the Blessed Virgin as soon as she was through.

Until, on the third day, she had seen his name. *Her name. O'Kane, Tom, Co. A, chest, severe.*

She had heard her children's feet in the hall—and not knowing what else to do, she had ripped out the line of type, sticking the rest of the paper hastily in the kindling pile. Unwilling to simply throw his name into the fire, but slipping the scrap into her hand, hiding it in her glove, as if she were holding him there.

She had picked up her basket then, and walked out into the streets. Intending to get something, to do something, but mostly just wanting to get away from the children until she had composed herself.

Outside there was a constant drizzle, the wind lashing the water into people's faces, and she had wandered aimlessly through the streets. Past all the shooting galleries that had sprung up since the war, blazing and pinging away on the Bowery. Gazing dully up at a free-

and-easy hall near Grand Street, its huge, red banner flapping in the cold breeze: *Who Complains of Hard Times?*

Who indeed? If it is your duty, we can manage—

Near Tenth Street she had noticed a small crowd gathered around a shop window and wandered over to see what they were staring at. There, in the window, was a remarkably small, grey felt cap. Shaped so much like the one Tom himself had been wearing, the last time she had seen him—

"Cap of a Secession Officer," she had read on the sign beneath it there—and then, just above the bill, slightly off to one side, she had made out a little, drunken circle, like the hole a cigar might burn through it.

Most of the crowd turned away without saying anything, lowering their eyes. A few hard cases exclaiming, *"Good!"* or *"Thus ever to traitors!"* But Deirdre had kept staring at the little, wobbly hole, no bigger than her thumbnail.

"Heaven be his bed," she had murmured at last and crossed herself, plunging back into the hueless streets.

She had spent the rest of the day walking, in a fog. She could as easily have ended up in the river, she thought later on, and she was sure that it was only the love of her children and the intervention of the Blessed Virgin that had sustained her. *That—and the hope that he might still be alive.*

She had just gotten inside when there was a knock. There on her door stone was Ruth, her face lined with worry and pity, obviously having heard the news from someone on the alley. Deirdre was touched by the gesture—but still suspicious, even then, of her concern over Tom.

"Oh, Deirdre. Oh, I'm so sorry to hear it—" Ruth had started to say. "Have ye heard anything—"

"No more than anybody else on this block," Deirdre had told her, despising her pity. Unwilling to let Ruth claim any part of her Tom. *There is nothing, nothing at all you can give me. Not even your sympathy.*

"Well, then." Ruth had shuffled her feet, not knowing what else to say. "Well, if there's anyt'ing I can do to be of help—"

"Thank you very much. Very much obliged, I'm sure," Deirdre had told her. Shutting the door as abruptly as she could.

Blaming her, blaming Ruth for it still as much as herself. For getting Tom mixed up in all that business. For bringing her halftone family down to this block. For getting rid of her brother—

Hanging on to her pride still, despite all the prayers she had said on the way home. Blinking back the tears, but with her head unbowed and her back straight as she went in to tell the children. Feeling the little scrap of paper in her glove, hanging on to Tom, in the palm of her hand.

53

TOM O'KANE

"The whole City's on fire, that's what I hear."

"I heard the rebs snuck a regiment up, rose in the middle of the night—"

"You know the North River's full of gunboats, just waitin' to open up!"

Tom listened dully to the soldiers' stories as the train rocked slowly across the bridge to Camden. Sitting jammed against one wall of the boxcar, without enough room to so much as stretch his leg out. The car reeking of its last inhabitants, which he guessed from the smell of them would have been pigs.

"There won't be a *thing* left standin', once those boys let 'em have it!" a private exulted.

"*Shut* it, will ya," one of the veterans told him.

"What?"

The man's voice sounding hurt. *A Westerner,* Tom guessed, from the sound of it. *And young.* Some farmer's boy, from the plains of Iowa or Illinois, blown all this way east by the war.

"I was just sayin' what would happen when the gunboats open up—"

"I said, *shut it.* Just stop yer puffin'."

The second voice—the voice of the veteran—was more familiar. Many of those in the car, Tom knew, were drawn from New York regiments—his own 69th, and the 88th, and the 63rd, all of Meagher's Irish Brigade. Thinking of their own homes, now—just as he was worried to distraction over Deirdre and the children, stuck in the middle of whatever the hell was going on up there.

It makes a difference, in your own yard. Tom felt a stray jolt of sympathy for the rebs, fighting nearly the whole damned war over their own fields and homes. He had seen what an army could do to a town before, when they had encamped across the river above Fredericksburg last winter. After a few weeks the place had barely been inhabited. Whole blocks shelled into smoking ruins. Bummers and deserters, looting everything they could find. Citizens shot on sight by patrols that took them for reb snipers—

But now it was *his* home. He had hardly believed it when the muster sounded, just a few hours ago, though it seemed like months. The morning in the Invalids camp proceeding at its usual sluggish pace. The wounded settling in for another blessed day of just trying to stay out of the sun. Serenading the sick-call bugler with one of their typical, mocking songs:

> *Are you all dead? Are you all dead?*
> *No, thank the Lord there's a few left yet,*
> *There's a few—left—yet!*

Minutes later had come the call to arms. Snatchem looking at Tom in amazement, he and the rest of his little raiding party, Feeley and Larkins, still bleary-eyed, and bloated with fresh chicken and sweet potatoes roasted in the crossroads the night before.

But there was no mistaking the call. They had gone scrambling for their Springfields and haversacks, some of them still pulling up their pants, thinking that Bobby Lee must have doubled back and was about to descend upon them. *Nobody wanting to end up in a Confederate prison camp, they had all heard enough stories of what that was like—*

Instead a potbellied little colonel with his leg shot off below the knee had stumped back and forth before their ranks.

"The whole town of New York is gone up in rebellion," he told them, nodding his head in sudden, rooster-like movements. "Which of you fine Invalids wants to put down a mob?"

Tom had stepped forward at once, Snatchem right beside him.

Followed quickly by Feeley, who had taken a ball through his shoulder but could still steady a rifle in his elbow, and Larkins, who had only been shot in the foot. *All the fellas that was left from the Black Joke, shot to hell though they were.*

Most of the other New Yorkers had stepped forward as well—those who could still limp along, at least, and shoulder a piece. Instantly clamoring to get back, to find out what was happening to their wives and children and parents.

"Discipline will be maintained at all times," the colonel had warned, mistaking their enthusiasm. "There will be no goin' off on some spree of your own, or usin' this duty for leave!"

They had ignored him. What the New York men wanted was to see their families, and know that they were safe. Talking about it quietly among themselves, as the train wound its way slowly east and north from the country junction where they had boarded. Trying to assure each other it was overblown, that the rubes didn't know what a riot was.

But at the station in Philadelphia, Tom had watched as the 26th Michigan, and the City's own 7th New York, boarded the train. No Invalids, but crack regiments, pulled from the line, and the chase for Lee.

It must be serious, he had realized then. *They must be worried, to pull back troops when they have a chance to end the whole war.*

Followed by another thought—one that he had had so many times already but that came home to him with renewed force now, stuck in this boxcar.

What was he doing here? Why wasn't he home already, where he belonged?

They crossed the Delaware into New Jersey at Camden. The train chugging its way slowly across the low coastal plains, past salt marshes and cranberry farms, and dense forests of pitch pine and shortleaf and cedar. The soldiers knocked holes in the boxcar sides to get air, but that made things only a little cooler, and in no way dispelled the reek of pig.

Near Toms River the gauge on the line changed, and they had to get off and climb into a new boxcar—this one used most recently by cattle. From there they were shunted onto sidings again and again, making way for supply trains and troop trains that rambled past them, on toward the South. Once he even saw a regular passenger train from the Lackawanna line rocking slowly on by. The men and women inside gazing incuriously back out the windows of the parlor car. They looked prosperous and well-fed, their eyes complacent—as if there were no war, anywhere, much less in the nation's greatest city.

Just like the army. Shipping soldiers back and forth, right past each other. Such a terrible crisis that we have to make way for the shoddy merchants and their wives.

At a water stop they were allowed out to stretch their legs, and eat a quick ration of fat pork on hardtack. George had foraged some sugar from somewhere to smear on the pork, so it wasn't too bad. Sitting along the rail embankment, Tom could see a gaggle of officers up by the engine, hovering over the latest telegrams passed down the line, making agitated gestures.

So the elephant really has hit town. And again: *What am I doing here?*

Back inside the boxcar grew steadily darker, streaked with hazy bars of afternoon sunlight as they chugged up the Jersey coast. Moving through small, white towns that ignored them, no one so much as looking up as the train passed by. The air was still as thick as chowder, most of the men nodding in and out of sleep despite their anxiety. George lay next to him, his head fallen on his shoulder. Feeley and Larkins snoring loudly, their mouths tilted toward the sky.

Tom might have slept himself but his calf muscle cramped up again. He rubbed at it with both hands, feeling the new matching scars on either side of the leg. *No worse than what a man could do dropping his razor in the morning, and just as straight.* Even the scar below his breast, from Fredericksburg, no more than a puckered hole now, the size of a nickel—at least in the front. A good deal bigger in the back, where the ball had exited, he knew—but still not nearly the size he would have expected, for all the damage it had done.

It don't take much to kill a man. Just a little hole, big enough to let the air or the blood out.

He had seen it often enough. Men who had an artery nicked, or were shot through the lung. The life just seeping out of them. *And the question again—why should he have ever taken part in such a thing?*

Deirdre Dolan, singing to the wheel. He remembered the old proverb: *A whistling woman or a crowing hen was never good for God or men.*

He had stood on a street corner, that fall before the war, watching in silence with the rest of the ward as the Wide-Awakes paraded up the Fifth Avenue. Ten thousand of them, at least, tramping through the crisp October night. Each one carrying a torch, dressed in identical black-and-silver military capes and hats. Marching up the avenue in lockstep, like some dreadful, inhuman machine.

They were thuggish young rich men's sons, most of them. Their cheeks flushed and their eyes blurred from the drink. Rabbit sports he had seen a dozen times before, on their slumming expeditions, picking fights and retching in alleys along the Bowery. Bellowing out their marching songs now, as if daring anyone to object:

> *Hurrah for the choice of the nation,*
> *Our chieftain so brave and so true,*
> *We'll go for the great reformation,*
> *For Lincoln and Liberty, too!*

It had been a nervous, agitated time, that October. Men were marching all over the City, and there was a feeling that something was bound to happen—the same feeling that the fire companies got when there was smoke in the air. A week later the Democrats had had their own parade for Douglas, and all the workingmen and women from the lower wards had turned out—three times the showing of the Wide-Awakes' parade, going on until well past midnight, with everyone carrying lanterns, and the *b'hoys* shooting off Roman candles.

By far the biggest parade that fall, though—the biggest sensation in the City—was to celebrate the visit of the Prince of Wales. All the fire companies had taken part, six thousand men in all, with their machines in tow. Singing "Solid Men to the Front" as they passed the balcony of the Fifth Avenue Hotel where the prince stood—a slim, elegant figure in his Coldstream Guards uniform, smiling or bowing graciously in response.

Tom had never seen such a spectacle. The paint job on every engine or hose wagon touched up for the occasion, with fantastic new scenes added by Professor A. P. Moriarty himself, the finest of all the fire-engine painters.

There had been the Old Honey Bee, with an illuminated gold hive swinging between the brakes. The Silk Stockings, with their silver dolphin fittings and their painting of guardian angels hovering over a sleeping child on the hose reel. Shouting out their rallying cry, *Come, ye Old Silver Nine!* as they passed.

There was the Old Turk with its tantalizing harem scene, and the snooty Yankees from the Amity Hose, with their red running lamps shaped like pineapples and mounted in solid gold. There were the Quills of the Oceana—a company of merchants and clerks who kept notably ponderous minutes of their meetings—and the Old Blue Box, with its depiction of Jefferson signing the Declaration, chanting *True Blue never fades!* as they came. There was the Niagara, with its painting of the falls, and a volcano at sea; and the Lafayette, with Rip Van Winkle wandering out of the Catskills after his long sleep. The Iron Horse and the Man-Killer, and the White Ghost, which always maintained it was the fastest engine in the City when in fact it never was. The Shad Bellies, and the Dashing Half Hundred, and the Bean Soup and the Mutton House and the Live Oak, and the Old Sal and the Old Jeff, and the Mazeppa company with its hose reels that featured nothing less than a depiction of Hope, and Washington's camp at Valley Forge, and incidents from the life of Mazeppa, and a fireman at his hydrant, and the City's coat of arms, and the New York Institution for the Blind.

Tom was there as well, marching with the Black Joke. Engine Company 33, *Old Bombazula.* Dressed in his proud red shirt, and black cap, pants, and suspenders, the black ribbons hanging from the back of his tarpaulin hat with "33" etched in gilt on the end. The wagon with its shimmering new coat of black paint and gold stripes running the length of its sides. Professor Moriarty's proud picture of the privateer *Black Joke* on one side of the box, and a great prairie fire, ripping across the plains, on the other. And on the front was their motto—*THE NOBLEST MOTIVE IS THE PUBLIC GOOD.*

He had thought that even Deirdre had been proud of him that night. Watching the parade of the fire companies wind its way through the cheering crowds—more thrilled by them than by the prince, or even the looming prospect of war, so excited that they had pushed past the lines of police and militia trying to keep them on the sidewalk. The Black Joke was the one thing that Deirdre had let him keep at, the one thing of his old life he had still been allowed to continue. He had convinced her that it was a public service and thus worthwhile—although she suspected that it was no more than another excuse for drinking and carousing, and Democratic politics.

Most of all, he knew, she distrusted the position of Finn McCool as assistant foreman of the company. That was something he could hardly blame her for, since he did not quite trust Finn himself.

Yet Tom also saw how much she enjoyed the Saturday night chowders at the firehouse. The evenings of music, with the chowder pot thick with eels and clams and lobster, chicken and duck. Or the annual Amity Hop, given by the Amity Hose in the Apollo Rooms, with Jerry Go Nimble, and Jack Diamond playing the hornpipe and dancing his breakdown, and Jack Ballagher, a huge black man with an earring and a red kerchief like a pirate, playing on the fiddle like Old Scratch himself.

And on such occasions Tom was sure, even beyond a husband's natural pride, that her beauty and her grace outshone all the other laddies' wives and sweethearts. He thought that Deirdre had known it, too. He had seen her smile and blush with pleasure behind her fan, and she would dance half the night away with him, much as she disapproved of it herself.

There was nothing he had ever wanted more in this life than to run with the machine. They had all been mad for the fire companies, Tom and every other boy on the street. When the tocsin sounded they poured out of the tenements like bedbugs, just waiting to see them go by.

First had come the runners—no more than boys themselves, most of them, dashing down the street trying to sniff out the fire, and find the nearest pumps. Then there would be another, older boy, blowing a long silver horn as he ran. Then the company, thirty or forty men, maybe more, in their black tarpaulin hats and their red shirts and galluses. Running the engines along by their tongues and handles, moving the great machines so fast that their wheels barely touched the pavement. The crowd along the sidewalk breaking into spontaneous cheers and whistles and yelps of pure pleasure, just to watch them come.

As boys they had dressed up in the red flannel shirts and the colored suspenders of their favorite companies. Lingering around the firehouses, drawing water and building up the stove fires for the men. Polishing the machines and even their boots until they shone. Those who could afford it, whose fathers had a few extra quarters, even pitched in to buy the companies new signal lanterns, or a brass band to strap around the engine.

But it was not enough. You still needed to have pull, just to become a runner. A brother or a cousin in the company, at least, and Tom had neither.

What he did have, as it turned out, was Finn McCool. It was Finn who had sponsored him for the Black Joke, just as it was Finn who made him a citizen, and a loyal member of the Democracy.

It was Finn, too, who had taught Tom the old molasses trick, the very first day they had met in the Five Points. Pulling him over to a brand-new grocery—this one not just a front for a saloon, the usual mound of rotting vegetable mass out on the sidewalk, but a *real* grocery, with fresh-caulked barrels of flour and sugar, and kegs of molasses along the walls. The proprietor—some poor Yonkers rube— standing behind his counter in a spotless white apron, a sharp new pencil behind his ear.

"Oh, lookit him, lookit him, lookit this hen! Dumb as an oyster!"

Finn whispering behind his ear, his prematurely wizened face almost up against Tom's as he pushed him forward. Announcing grandly as they came through the door of the shop:

"Me friend here an' I got a bet. Him an' five dollars says you can't fit a gallon a molasses into my hat. I says you can."

Throwing the high, plug hat he wore onto the counter with a flourish.

"Be a good man, will ya, an' fill it up."

Even the grocer, balking at such a suggestion. He was a solid, square-shouldered man, and Tom would have started edging toward the door but that Finn's hand below his shoulder blades held him steady.

"You want me to fill up yer hat? With molasses?"

His voice incredulous.

"Sure, it's just an old topper. I can buy ten of 'em with what I make off of this rabbit!"

Flipping a dollar piece casually onto the counter, after the hat. The grocer scooping it up, gnawing contemplatively on the coin's edge.

"Just go on with yas an' fill it up, I'll make it good outta that."

The counterman shaking his head but grinning a little now. Think-ing he was safe so long as he gripped the solid dollar in his hand. He

drew the gallon measure from the nearest molasses barrel, Finn making a great show of watching as he poured the oozing, green-black
molasses, cement-thick, into his hat. Carefully trickling out every
drop until Finn's hat was filled almost to the brim.

"There! You see!" Finn picked up the filled hat, pushed it triumphantly under Tom's nose. "That's five dollars, fair and square!"

Tom inadvertently helping him, looking completely lost. The grocer leaning over the counter, grinning at what he thought was the joke.

"He's got ya there, I can attest—"

Before he could complete the sentence, Finn had flipped the hat
over with one deft move. Pulling it down, hard, over the grocer's
head, all the way to his ear lobes.

"Here's a *test* for ya!"

The grocer staggered back, making strangled noises as he tried to
push the thick, glutinous molasses off his face. Finn was already over
the counter, pulling open his change drawer and scooping up as many
coins and banknotes as he could gather in both hands. He was back
across the counter again before the grocer had the hat off his eyes—
the green-black gobs oozing down his shoulders and shirt and the
once-spotless apron, still blinding him.

"Now, boy! *Out!*"

Finn had pushed him on out the door, thrusting as much of the
money as he could down into his pockets, shoving more at Tom—
making sure to grab up even the original dollar piece that the grocer
had dropped back on the counter. They bolted around the corner, had
vanished down Orange Street and into Bottle Alley before the first
police whistles sounded. Finn McCool slowing to a walk then, taking
Tom's arm in his own, heading back out onto the streets and the
anonymous crowds.

"Now there y'are, boy-o. More than you make in a month, I'll
wager—if you want to wager. An' if ya do, I know a good stuss
game, what ain't even halfway crooked—"

He was right—it was more than he made in a month, or sometimes two. Tom ran his fingers over the money in his pockets, not daring to bring it out in broad daylight. Suspicious immediately, though,
of what Finn might want of him.

"No, no, it's nothin'!" McCool had waved him off. "Just your vote,
that's all. An' what's a vote off a man, anyhow? Less than a flake of
skin, less than a bit of his fingernail!"

He had taken Tom over that same afternoon, to meet Captain Rynders at the American Club, and get his citizenship. The Captain setting up on a small platform, looking down his large nose at them like a hawk. When Tom went up to him, his piercing, gambler's eyes had raked across him once, then he had taken Tom's hand in his own— greeting him as if they had known each other for many years and slipping a small, convenient square of paper into his palm:

To Whom It May Concern:
Please naturalize the bearer.
Cap'n Isaiah Rynders

Finn had snatched up the piece of paper and towed Tom on over to Judge Pietr Brinckerhoff, a decrepit old Dutch magistrate in the Sixth Ward who sat up at his bench receiving an endless line of Irishmen. They approached him like a marriage procession, two by two, some wardheeler or another shoulder to shoulder with each supplicant, handing up little notes like the one Captain Rynders had given him, now wrapped around a coin.

No part of Judge Brinckerhoff moved in response, save for his hands, and these worked like a particularly well-balanced machine. Scooping up the paper, pocketing the coin. Scribbling a few words on another, official-looking piece of paper, then bringing down his gavel.

"Done!" was all that he ever said, and, "Next!"

That was it—and then he was a citizen. Finn had walked him back out of the court, holding the new, larger paper with its official seal, its mysterious flourishes of eagles and Indians and Dutchmen, windmills and sailing tackle.

"Oh, my boy, that's the thing to have!" he had congratulated him, pounding Tom on the back. "That's the ticket, all right. Oh, you'll make some money off a *that!*"

That was how it had been. That was the part of it, the story of how *men* got by in the world, which Deirdre had never quite learned. It was Finn he had gone to, as well, to get a job with the City, once Deirdre had decided that he was too good to work as a butcher anymore. It was Finn who had made it possible for him to work his way steadily up the organization, rising—rising just as she had wanted him to—from lighting lamps to running his own digging crew, in the grand, new central park they were building.

And in return, Tom had only had to go to the Tammany nominating meetings when Finn said to, voting for whoever it was he wanted him to vote for. Never telling Deirdre any of this. Knowing how important it was that she think it was she, and she alone—save for the advice and counsel of the priest—who had made him rise.

It was Finn, too, who had told him not to go to the war. When it had finally come, many of the laddies had been ecstatic. Transforming themselves instantly from fire companies into companies of ninety-day volunteers—the Fire Zouaves, and Billy Wilson's Boys, and Kerrigan's regiment. Replete with colorful new uniforms, and regimental banners full of harps and shamrocks, and the Irish sun bursting through the clouds.

They remembered how it was, those lads who were old enough. All the grand parades, and the honors and the banquets the men had gotten when they'd come back from the Mexican War.

"Only it ain't Mexico, and it ain't goin' off to fight Santy Anny an' that bunch, is it?" Finn had groused. "It's fightin' other Americans, in America, an' good Demmycrats, at that!"

Finn the real force in the company, anybody could see that. His brother, Peter, the captain—a strong, vain, handsome man, with a head of marvelous blond curls, and not enough sense to pound sand in a rathole. Finn was hoping to run Peter for the Forty Thieves, and he wanted to discourage the idea of any potential voters departing for the South. But it was more than that, Tom could see, he truly disliked the whole idea of the war.

"It's *their* war, the Republicans. They'll use it to crush us if they can, you wait an' see."

"But Jesus, Finn, don't ya believe in keepin' the Union together, then?"

"The Union!" McCool had scoffed. "Oh, the Union, is it! Sure, I believe in keepin' the Union. I believe in keepin' the union between me neck an' me shoulders. You watch: If the war comes we'll fight it, an' they'll profit by it."

But then had come all the new parades down to the docks as the volunteers marched off. The whole town strung with American flags, and green crinoline for the Irish regiments. The crowds like none that Tom had ever seen before, even for the Prince, with boys hanging off every tree and lamppost just to get a look, and the girls running out to throw flowers under the men's feet, and kiss their faces and place garlands on their heads. Dodsworth's famous band serenading the new soldiers as they marched down to the Battery—

So we gave them hearty cheers, me boys,
Which was greeted with a smile.
Singin' we're the boys
Who fear no noise
We're the Fightin' Sixty-ninth!

And Deirdre was caught right up with the rest of them in it. For the life of him, that was what he had never been able to get over. Reading her Republican newspaper, always worrying about being respectable and doing the right thing. She had shown him all the abolitionist tracts, about the horrors of slavery, and they were horrible all right, but he did not know what he was supposed to do about it.

Hadn't he been doing, already, everything that she required? Going off to work each day to the diggings in the new park. Putting his back to the shovel for ten hours a day, and keeping watch so his team of men didn't go off and lie down under a tree somewhere, which they would do in a heartbeat if they didn't fall in a hole first. Stuffing his ears with wax, as they blasted out the huge stones, hauling whole, new great boulders up from the docks—something else that he never understood, why some rocks had to be blown up for the new park, while others had to be shipped in.

Nonetheless, he had done it. Even enjoying it, he had to admit, seeing the whole thing, the perfect, landscaped park, take shape before him. On Sundays he would take the children up to play among the plaster fossils of dinosaur bones Prof. Hawkins had set up there, watching them climb all over the great, white monsters. And back at home, after they were asleep, he would sit by the fire with Deirdre and tell her of all the work they were doing, building the new City, and watch her eyes flare up with pride.

But somehow, it wasn't enough. Deirdre had kept on about it, especially after the Archbishop had called on every good Catholic to *ask* to be drafted into the war. Confirmed in her faith—and in her great, Protestant respectability. Telling him it was his *duty* to sign up, to go down there with the rest.

His duty. His duty was with his wife and family. By God's grace he should be with them now.

It was nearly nightfall, the boxcar completely dark. Peering out the open door, though, he could tell that they were almost there. The train plowing through the Jersey meadowlands, the high, yellow stalks of marsh grass waving beside the track. Soon, he knew, they would cross Newark Bay, then on over to the Hoboken station along the river. From where the ferryboats would take them across to the City—

The same route he had traveled to the war, in reverse. Coming back now, even, with three of the men he had signed up with, Snatchem and Feeley, and Danny Larkins. Black Dan Conaway left back on Marye's Heights. John J. Sullivan shot down in the wheat field at Gettysburg, by some bastard from Mississippi.

And now come back here, to fight in our own streets. Jesus, but it didn't make sense. Fearing all over again what could happen to Deirdre, and the children. Surely no one would harm her, a respectable Irishwoman with five kids. But you never knew what could happen in a war. And then there was a special provocation on their block.

Ruth—and that black husband of hers, and their half-caste family. That would bring the mob down on them like nothing else.

It was his own fault, too, Tom knew, what had come between him and Deirdre. It was just that he had felt so sorry for that child, coming into their home, week after week, with her black eyes, her jaw and cheeks bruised and discolored from his beatings. So ignorant and helpless. *Or so it had seemed, anyway.* Deirdre had never taken to her, for reasons he didn't quite understand—though he had to admit now he hadn't understood his own feelings for Ruth. The queer pang that he got whenever he saw her, helpless and battered. *Something more— and less—than pity.*

He had liked her husband, Billy, too, as much as he had ever liked any colored man. *A quiet sort, always brooding about something. But he had been quick and reliable enough when it had come down to it—when they had had to take care of Deirdre's brother—*

Johnny Dolan. *Dangerous* Johnny Dolan, as they had it on his fight cards and his handbills. He knew that Deirdre still lit a votive candle for him, once a month. Insisting on keeping his daguerreotype on their bedroom dresser.

Jesus, but that was a face to see, first thing in the morning with your pants half on.

Deirdre had treated him almost like a child of her own from the moment he'd shown up, and Tom couldn't blame her. He had gone ahead and gotten Dolan in the Black Joke, as she had asked. He had even gotten him some work with the road crews downtown, fixing the streets.

Yet Tom had known from one look at the man that there was something wrong there—something that no job, no fire company was going to fix. The rage floating just below the surface, ready to spill out over almost anything, like ashes bubbling up through the sewer grate.

How he had struggled in the boat that night! Tom hadn't thought that they could hold him, even with the sack over his head, taken by surprise. He had fought like forty cats, and if Billy hadn't subdued him with that grappling hook, he didn't know but he would have capsized the boat. Then there would have been the devil to pay—

Deirdre had never forgiven him for it. When Ruth had come to them that night—when she had *shown* them what Dolan had done to Old Man Noe—and proved it beyond any doubt, Deirdre herself had insisted that they hand him over to the law, whether it meant hanging or not.

Nevertheless, she had not forgiven him—

Or was it really that? he had always wondered. *He had never been sure—was it that he was the one who had taken her brother away? Or was it because of Ruth?*

It was a little after midnight when they finally pulled into the Hoboken station. The men slowly unbending and staggering over to the cattle-car doors. Those who had come the farthest, the men from the Michigan regiment who had come from Meade's army, dropped down to sleep right on the platform.

Tom tried to let himself down easy, but his wounded leg still crumpled beneath him when he hit the ground. He limped on out of the train shed, swearing quietly and punching at the muscles as he tried to get the feeling back. Wandering after Snatchem and some of the others, to where they were standing now, just outside the station, by the edge of the Hudson River.

There he could see the great City again. His heart welling up at the sight of it, more affected by it than he had anticipated—longing to be home at last.

Yet he thought that the town looked scarred, too—even in the darkness, even from where they stood, so far across the broad river. They could see buildings burning, all along the West Side wharves, and plumes of smoke trailed across the moon. The rest of the night sky was lit up a bright red color, as if it were dripping fire into the City below.

"What's happening? What's going on?" Tom said agitatedly, to nobody in particular.

There was no answer, the other men as amazed and stupefied as he was, watching the stricken City.

"We got to get over there—"

54

HERBERT WILLIS ROBINSON

A funeral train reels its way down the Bowery. Eight drunken *b'hoys*, hauling a black coffin. The epitaph chalked on one side:

Old Abe's Draft Died Monday, July 13, 1863

But the carnevale spirit is gone. It is too hot, and there are too many dead. There will be no more delicacy about saving Washington's picture now. The pallbearers themselves, surly and grim in their drunkenness. In Astor Place I watch a pair of Irish laborers haul down the colors and tear it to pieces, shouting, *"Damn the flag!"*

All over the City men are throwing up barricades in the streets. They are tearing up the rails in the Third and Fourth Avenues, uprooting the Hudson River and the Harlem lines, in the hopes that the government will not be able to bring in more troops. All of them arming themselves, in any way they can, grabbing up not only guns and knives and slung shots, but even adzes and axes, clubs and pikes.

Wherever I walk I can hear sounds in the air above me. I look up, just in time to see figures scuttling off along the rooftops. Dodging around behind the chimneys, plotting God only knows what new mischief. I can barely bring myself to put a foot down, for fear that the sidewalk will crackle into flames beneath me.

This is no city to take Maddy abroad in. I would not dare to walk a woman one block through these streets—though certainly there are plenty of them out now, the red-faced harpies, plunging into the loot-ing and calling for blood even more rabidly than their men.

Paint the town red.

From lampposts all over the town, now, there hangs a particular shame—worse than anything I have ever seen in the City. The bodies of black men, and black women—even Negro boys—hanged and cut open, mutilated and tortured.

Many of them have been there since last night, even yesterday afternoon. The mob chases off anyone who tries to cut them down. Their children even play under these awful effigies, running up to tell me all that they have done, while I nod and force myself to smile. Lis-tening to everything, *seeing everything*.

Over in the Ninth Ward, there is a black tar named Williams. He came ashore from the transport *Belvedere*, looking to buy a loaf of bread. Somehow, no one had told him what was going on in the City, or maybe he simply did not believe it. At the corner of Leroy and Wash-ington Streets, he asked a schoolboy where he might find a grocery. The boy only stared at him, and a white man came out of the liquor store on the corner, to ask what it was that he wanted.

"Why, just bread, sir."

The white man looked at him, and nodded. Then he hit him in the face. Knocking the sailor down in the street, and jumping up and down on his chest.

The rest of the mob was on him at once. The mob that assembles all at once now, from everywhere and nowhere—white men and boys, even women and girls, streaming out of the saloons, and the groceries, and the tenements up and down the block with terrifying speed.

They held Williams down while the first white man, leaning on a friend's shoulder, kicked over and over again at his eyes. They dropped stones on him where he lay in the street, still wearing his country's uniform, then they strung him up. Slicing open his arms and legs with knives, then pouring oil into his wounds and setting them on fire. Even a white tar, a shipmate from the *Belvedere*, ran up and plunged a knife into Williams's back while he hung there. The crowd watching eagerly, cheering as he twisted and burned.

"Vengeance on every nigger in New York!"

. . .

In West Twenty-eighth Street, they have hanged a man I knew by
sight. Everyone did, he was a longtime resident of the neighborhood,
an elderly, crippled black coachman who went by the name of Abraham Franklin.

It seems that they have murdered him for his name. The mob
shouting *"Abraham! Abraham! Tell us your name—if ye dare!"* over
and over again. Then they hanged and burned him from a street lamp,
and gave three cheers for Jefferson Davis. A hulking Irish butcher's
boy, still in his teens, cuts down the body and strips it, pulling it along
the street by its genitals. Still wearing his butcher's apron, he cuts
pieces from the old man, and tosses them to the mob for souvenirs—
before hanging him back up from the lamp, the way he might hang up
a sheep's carcass.

It is a stunning thing, almost beyond comprehension, to see someone you once knew—if only a nodding acquaintance—actually cut to
pieces like a piece of meat, a *thing*. At least poor Abraham the coachman is dead. Elsewhere, they subject the living to every humiliation
they can. In Thirty-third Street I come upon a young black mother,
dazed and beaten, wandering along the sidewalk along with her little
son and daughter—all of them as naked as the day they were born.

This has become their special humiliation—stripping any Negro
they can catch in the street. Some of the mob inform me that they have
to do this, after they caught a Negro man trying to board the Brooklyn
ferry, disguised in his wife's clothes. (How dare he try to evade being
tortured to death!) But there is more to it than this. I listen to them as
they taunt the shamed mother, shouting and leering in her face:

*"What's a nigger need with clothes? What's a jungle nigger need with
clothes, anyway?"*

I try to get the poor, stunned woman inside to shelter—though
even to do this much is to risk the wrath of the mob. No one will so
much as open their doors to her, no doubt afraid the crowd will burn
their house to the ground. I am told that even at the Infirmary for
Indigent Women and Children, the white inmates demanded that all
patients of color be put out, lest someone fire the place.

I finally manage to get the woman and her children some horse blankets, from a looted stable, but that is the best I can do. The Negroes have

been all but left on their own, as if they were strangers among us. The
mob attacking them anywhere they find them. Avenging themselves
upon them for the war—for the crime of being below them in society.

In the Minetta Lane some of the coloreds have managed to arm
themselves, and hold off the mob at gunpoint. Mostly, though, they
are too scattered around the City, too vulnerable to do anything but
flee. They take refuge wherever they can, in churches, and in the
homes of a few brave abolitionists; in the British consulate—even on
a French warship tied up along the West Side docks.

The police do the best they can to protect them; they have sent out
a whole flying squad under Inspector Dilks, to rescue any Negroes
they can and take them to shelter in the precinct houses. But as it is, the
station houses themselves are being fired now—the 22nd Precinct,
then the 23rd, the 10th—all up in flames. There aren't enough men to
hold them now, and when the mob approaches, they hand over weapons
they have to the Negroes, then wish them Godspeed and flee back
downtown with them through the burning, smoking streets.

I go with them, back to the police headquarters on Mulberry Street.
Trying to find out *something,* anything I can. Is the City about to fall?
Is the army finally on the way? Should I take Maddy back to my house
in Gramercy Park—or try to flee this wretched island altogether?

There is indeed more information at headquarters—all of it bad.
The key continues to chatter away in the telegraph room:

*The mob is firing the Negro sailors' boardinghouses along Roosevelt
Street and Water Street . . . They are looting the private homes of col-
oreds up in Baxter Street and Pell . . . attacking the Metropolitan Gas
Works . . . firing the town of Harlem . . .*

Our resources are stretched nearly to the breaking point. General
Meade still has yet to send any troops from Pennsylvania. General
Wool is still huddled in his room at the St. Nicholas Hotel. Only
General Brown, Wool's brigadier, has been able to wrench a few com-
panies away from guarding the shipyards and the Sub-Treasury
Building. A detachment from the 11th New York Volunteers is form-
ing out in front of police headquarters now, under the command of
Colonel Henry O'Brien.

Meanwhile, Commissioner Acton paces back and forth in Kennedy's office, haggard and infuriated. Swearing and barking out orders,
dispatching his beleaguered forces wherever the next crisis erupts.

"They are always ahead of us!" he rails. "Striking wherever they please—while all we can do is react. At this rate they will burn down the entire City!"

An aide rushes in with another message, his face and clothes covered in dust and soot now, like those of everyone else in this City. Acton studies the paper he hands him, his own face reddening immediately.

"They've chased the guard from the Union Steam Works," he tells me, and swears bitterly. "If they take that they'll be armed to the teeth!"

He turns back to the aide, orders him to have Inspector Carpenter's flying squad and O'Brien's troops sent up to the Steam Works at once. I tell him that I will go, too, and he pulls open his top desk drawer, revealing a row of shiny, new Colt revolvers.

"Do you have a weapon, then? No? Take one of these—I have three more in the next drawer!"

I pocket the piece immediately, grabbing up a box of shells as well. Acton shakes his head ruefully, plopping a pistol in one of his own pockets.

"This town is lousy with guns!"

Dan Carpenter's roundsmen reassemble in the muster room. Most of them are sporting plasters by now, or bloody red rags wrapped on their heads and limbs. No longer, quite, the merciless threshing machine they were the day before. Now they lean and even sit against the walls of the muster room, nearly exhausted now from a full day and night of almost continuous fighting.

This little space, this room, they have made their own. It is hung with testimonials and presentation swords, and the names of long-gone companions—with prints of Emmet and Daniel O'Connell, and the Bonnie Prince and the Wild Geese, Tyrconnell and Tyrone. Hanging here, too, now, are the battle flags from the Irish regiments at the war, shot through with holes. Gold harps on green fields, the sun bursting perennially through the clouds. Beneath them the old, romantic legend: *RIAM NAR DRUID O SBAIRN LANN*—*Who Never Retreated from the Clash of Spears.*

"Up, men, up!" Carpenter calls them into line. "We still have a job to do!"

Tom Acton yells after them, frenzied now with lack of sleep and bloodlust.

"Quail on toast, boys, quail on toast! Quail on toast for every man of you, if you put down the mob!"

But they ignore him. They do not fight for such as that. Not against a wild mob that outnumbers them a hundred to one, and includes so many of their friends and neighbors.

Inscrutable race. *What do they fight for, then?* For the love of this country, this City that despises them for being poor and Catholic? For the love of dear old Ireland, then? Or for this room—this little place that is theirs?

"Form up!"

They rise and fall into ranks. Not exactly springing up but still willing. Tapping their nightsticks on the pavement again as they move out into the street, beating that policeman's proud tattoo.

55

HERBERT WILLIS ROBINSON

We should have seen the ambush coming.

Carpenter rushed his men up the Third Avenue on the few street-cars the mob had left intact, trying to spare their strength. I tag along with them, watching breathlessly as they drive the mob back from the Steam Works. Fighting just as hard as they did yesterday, their arms and the locust clubs attached still rising and falling just as pitilessly.

But this time the mob breaks much too easily. It gives ground whenever the police approach. The rioters no longer fleeing blindly for their lives but taunting and baiting us, chanting obscene songs and insults as they retreat slowly up the Second Avenue, toward Murray's Hill.

Carpenter pushes his men after them, trying to crush the insurrection right here and now. He waves his nightstick in the air like a sword, yelling to his officers above the fray:

"On! *On!*"

They spring their trap as soon as we pass Thirty-fourth Street. All at once we are surrounded. A whole new mob pours out of their hiding places, the houses and bars all up and down the street. Surging into the avenue behind us—cutting us off.

Suddenly, the rioters who had been retreating before us stand their ground—the men brandishing their axes and spikes, and sending up a raucous, triumphant, bloodcurdling cry. They have chosen their spot well, trapping us between Thirty-fourth and Thirty-fifth Streets. It is a finished block, one with no empty lots to escape through—only tenements four and five stories high, looming above us like canyon walls.

I hear a familiar scuttling sound above me and look up. They are scampering along the rooftops now, crouching by ready piles of dismantled chimneys, and uprooted paving stones. More of them stand in the windows with rifles. Their women and children, even with babes in arms, right beside them, come to watch the show. Crowing down at us exultantly:

"You'll be killed like rats before you leave the ward!"

The Metropolitans hesitate now, beginning to lose their cohesion, as trapped men often do. I can see their eyes darting around for some way out. The maddened crowd roaring wildly, waving its pikes and axes.

And there, at their front—still alive somehow, even after being hurled unconscious through the window of a tavern—is that hideous creature from the central park. I would not believe it could be him, but there is no mistaking it. *Their Mose.* Still wearing the same ludicrous chunk of wood they decorated him with, the crude sign reading NO DRAFT! Looking more hideous than ever now—ugly red slashes, from where the Metropolitans put him through the window back on Amity Street, ringing the top of his brow. The dried blood streaked down his face, more puncture wounds along his wrists and hands.

He rages and spits his defiance at Carpenter's police. A club in his right hand, his left hand beckoning: *Come on, come on—*

A shot lands in our midst—the soft, lead ball splintering on the granite paving stones. Fragments fly up into the shin of a roundsman, making him howl with pain. More balls and bricks begin to land among us, and the Metropolitans waver—pulling back into a tighter circle all around me, bracing themselves, but with a hint of fear in their eyes now.

"At 'em, men!"

Carpenter comes roaring to the fore, refusing to accept that he is trapped. Urging his men forward still, despite the odds—

"At 'em, now, and take no prisoners!"

They charge ahead—arms still rising and falling, rising and falling. Breaking one head after another, pushing the mob back at first by sheer will. Carpenter has his revolver out again, firing carefully, trying to cut a swath through the mob for his men. He hits one rioter directly in the chest, a bright bloom of red bursting through his shirt. Another man doubles over like a rabbit, shot in the stomach, then still another goes down—

But a blizzard of bricks and bullets is falling on us now. Somehow, Carpenter himself remains unscathed—but as I watch, a paving stone hits a roundsman in the shoulder, knocking him to the floor and breaking his collarbone. Another cop beside him falls, this one shot through the back. He tries to rise, but spits out a stream of dark red blood, falls back in the street again. More bricks and stones fall on men's arms, their shoulders and legs and heads. Knocking them down, sprawling them out in the street—

I look up, the gallery of mocking faces spinning before me in the upper-story windows. All of them watching as avidly as they would any blood-and-thunder at the Bowery. The faces of toothless old men, and gawking children, of women not that different from Maddy. They wave their aprons and handkerchiefs, screaming and cursing. Hurling down anything they can at us, urging their men on with their bone-chilling cries:

"Die at home! Die at home!"

Carpenter's policemen struggle up again, still fighting desperately—fighting for our lives now. But they can make no further headway against the mob, trapped as they are by the sheer weight of the people jammed into this one block. My own arms are pinned to my sides, unable even to get to the Colt that Acton gave me, and I realize that I could actually die here, in the Second Avenue, of all places. Wondering what Maddy will do then. *Will she mourn me? Think that I have forgotten her?*

There—at the head of the crowd—I spot that creature with the NO DRAFT! sign again. I am sure that I must be dead now, and descended into hell. Somehow, he is still charging into the police like some sort of berserker, snarling and laying all about with his club. He sends one cop sprawling with a blow to the head, throttles another one with his own locust club—the roundsman gagging and sputtering horribly.

He fights his way steadily closer, threatening to break through the line all by himself. Moving relentlessly, right toward where I am standing, watching his progress with a morbid, frozen fascination. *He is coming to kill me—*

"Hold, men! Hold and give 'em hell!" I can hear Carpenter still shouting—but his voice sounds hoarse and desperate, even the bravado stretching thin.

"Hold!"

Abruptly, as if in response to his shout, the mob that came up behind us begins to waver. Just a little quiver through their ranks— but enough to make even the grizzled creature from the park turn around, to see what is going on.

Then we can hear the drums. A solemn, martial roll, calling troops into the line. Looking downtown, we can see something else through the mob—a long, dark patch of blue, formed across the whole width of the Second Avenue.

"Disperse! *Disperse,* damn ye!"

It is Colonel O'Brien's men, the 11th Volunteers. Unable to find another streetcar, they have followed us uptown by forced march, arriving just in time. Some of the mob turns to face them now, taunting and mocking—expecting to put them to flight just like the Invalid Corps troops they routed yesterday.

But these are able-bodied men, veterans, most of them, who have seen battlefields from Antietam to Fredericksburg to Chancellorsville. They hold their ranks, impervious to anything the mob can throw at them. As I watch they form quickly into two regulation volleying lines, one kneeling, the other standing behind them, both straight as a ramrod. The muskets of the soldiers clearly visible—pointed at us as well as the mob.

The mob starts to break then, some of the rioters running for cover. The creature who is leading them, though, refuses to budge, standing his ground only yards from the guns.

"It's just blanks! It's just blank cartridges!" he insists, and the rest of them begin to rally to him. They move slowly in on the soldiers, shuffling and spitting, shouting their defiance. The women in the windows above echoing their every cry:

"Go back to the war! We ain't some bunch of Southern rabble!"

"Go to hell, ye bunch of Invalid shirkers!"

"Die at home!"

But Carpenter is yelling, too—at his men, at the rest of us— exhorting us to get out of the way of the volley: "Down! Down! Get down!"

"Disperse!"

We drop flat on our bellies. The mob no longer engaged with us, all of them turning back to face the troops. Peeking up from the paving stones, I can make out O'Brien, standing beside his men as straight as a lead soldier—a tough little terrier of a man, with a bristling black mustache. He brings his unsheathed sword up to his shoulder, the silver blade flashing in the sunlight. Then it sweeps downward—and a row of fire erupts along the line.

"Get down!"

The mob staggers backward to a man. Throwing up their hands, pushed back by the very blast from the guns—stumbling and even falling, staring down at themselves.

Only to find that they are whole. For a moment, we all stare at each other, police and rioters alike, wondering what is going on. Then I hear fresh screams and wailing from the windows above us, and look up again.

There, in one of the third-story windows, I can see a woman holding up the limp body of her young daughter. A boy stretched out over the next sill, a red stain growing on his shirt. The woman holding the child begins to scream, and from the windows across the street more women begin to scream back, until the whole block is filled with the same desolate Irish keening I heard at the cave-in yesterday morning.

O'Brien has had his men fire high, to make sure he didn't hit any of the police in front of him. Instead their volley has raked the houses and the roofs, all up and down the street, hitting many of those who were hurling stones and their invective down upon us—and the children. Now the mob in the street, finding themselves mostly unharmed, turns on the troops again, their rage redoubled. Many of the men gesturing at their own chests, as if daring them to shoot. But the soldiers hold their line—

"Murderers! Butchers! You long-necked Yankee killers!"

"Disperse!"

The second line of troops fires now—and this time bodies begin to fall along the pavement. There is another volley, the mob reeling and breaking, and O'Brien orders his men to fix bayonets and charge. All around me, Carpenter and his men are already back on their feet, hitting everything they can see with a renewed fury.

.   .   .

The rioters break, and run at last, fleeing into homes and taverns all along the block. Within minutes, the block is cleared, and suddenly quiet, the mob all fled, or in hiding. Some Metropolitans grab the wounded boy from the window—who is still alive, miraculously enough—and his mother, and bundle both of them off to the hospital over her vehement protests and curses.

The woman whose daughter was killed, meanwhile, makes her way down to the street, still carrying the body of her dead child. She no longer screams, but her eyes look dazed and blind. The soldiers and the cops turn away from her, embarrassed, one of them crossing himself as she limps past. She is barefoot, I notice, like so many of them, a dirty red shawl wrapped around her head, her dress a crude patchwork of bright cloths, yellow and red and green. She stumbles on across the Second Avenue while the soldiers form ranks beside her, to begin the march back downtown, and leave her to her dead girl.

I linger behind on the block. Wanting to see—what, exactly? What is left now, but the woman weeping over her dead daughter? Pushing the story on, through one edition after another. *And then? And then?* Wondering if it makes any sense at all to bring Maddy out into such a City—

Across the street I spot my friend Father Knapp. He is making the sign of the cross over the back of a man who lies motionless along the curb. When I approach him he looks up at me with a numbed face, his collar and cassock stained with soot. Wearing the stole of his poor parish around his neck—white on one side, penitential purple on the other. He finishes his duties and accepts the arm that I offer him, rising stiffly from the pavement, but ignores all my entreaties that he find some food and a bed for himself.

"Have you seen what is going on?" he asks me, his voice so hoarse it is little more than a whisper. "Have you *seen* it?"

"Yes. Yes, I have seen it."

He shakes his head, his face haggard and dazed.

"They will never forgive us. *Never.* D'you know the mob tore down the Colored Orphans' Asylum? Wanted to burn the university—"

"Is there anything the Archbishop can do?"

"The governor asked him to give a speech." Father Knapp shakes his head. "A *speech*. There are priests out all over the City, tryin' to stop them. It doesn't matter. *They will never forgive us—*"

There is a commotion down the block, and both our heads turn toward it, wondering if the troops have returned—or the mob. Then we see him, wheeling a wagon up to his house. It is Colonel O'Brien of the 11th Volunteers himself, returning to the same street where he had led his troops a few hours before.

I will never know what has led him to return. He owns a house in Thirty-fifth Street, and some claim he came back to see that his family is all right.

But why like this? Whatever has made him think he could come back in full uniform, without any kind of escort? Did he believe that, once the street was cleared, it would stay that way? Cleansed and subdued, properly restored to civilization. Or is it the other way around—that he simply could not believe, despite what he had seen with his own eyes, that his friends and neighbors had all become savages in the course of an afternoon?

Whatever it is that is driving him, he brings his wagon right up to the door of his home. Pulling the horses up with one quick, deft tug, jumping down smartly from the wagon seat. Maintaining his soldier's bearing at all times, his pressed blue uniform still unmarred, gold buttons glimmering.

"It's him!"

They recognize him at once—just as they had a little while ago, when he returned to his block with two companies of soldiers. The voices rising steadily along the street, sounding astonished.

"It's him, all right! What shot Ellen Kirk, an' Mulhare's boy!"

"There's the man!"

Their cries angry now—and eager. They are moving before his feet touch the ground. The mob reassembling instantly, emerging from the houses and the bars, and all the secret places they know of. Before we can so much as shout a warning to the man, a brick thunks off the side of his wagon, then another one. Three large men emerge from a saloon across the street and make straight for him—a whole crowd at their heels.

O'Brien stands his ground, and fights them off. *He is a strong man, that will be his undoing.* He draws his sword as soon as he sees them, cuts one man's arm to the bone, slashes the next one across the face. These are just warning swipes, but expert and effective. The third Celt brute manages to close with him, mauling at his face. He is a big, brawny man, a butcher's apprentice, the bloody apron still wrapped around his waist. But despite his size O'Brien is able to get one hand free, knock him senseless with the hilt of his sword.

By now, I think, he understands the mistake that he has made. He straightens up and pulls his tunic down, still erect and unbowed. Yet his face is already bleeding, and his eyes look a little wild from the ferocity of the attack he has just endured. He glances about for his wagon—but the mob has it surrounded. Already, they are unhitching the horses, wheeling the flatbed away. The women and girls moving out in the street to hiss and scream at him.

"Butcher! Killer!"

"How dare you come back here—*how dare you!*"

"After you killed that little girl!"

He should have just run then. He should have turned, and run as fast as he could back downtown, and maybe he would have made it to a station house or an army patrol before they could catch him. He should have just turned and run, at least he would have had a fighting chance.

Instead, with great dignity, O'Brien turns on his heel and strides across the street, into Von Briesen's drugstore there. Incredibly, he stands inside at the counter, getting some iodine from the proprietor. *Thinking, maybe, that his only hope is to face them down now?* We can see Von Briesen, his friend, talking to him, helping him to paint his cuts but all the while glancing fitfully back out at the mob gathering in the street.

"He must leave here. He must go at once," Father Knapp is telling me.

But Colonel O'Brien continues to stand in front of the counter, his sword sheathed, as if oblivious to it all.

"Murderer!"

"A little girl, no less! An' right on 'er own street—"

It is almost inevitable then, a chunk of rock goes sailing through Von Briesen's window. There is another stone, then another, knocking his displays to pieces.

O'Brien flinches, as if startled. Now, at last, he puts down the little stick and the bloodied rag he had been applying to his face. He draws his sword and a revolver, and walks out of the shop, straight at the mob.

How brave you are! How little good it will do you here. Another man might have tried to talk his way out of it—to reason with the mob or claim he is not really who they think he is. But O'Brien says nothing, only advancing upon them. And when he moves out onto the sidewalk, they actually begin to give way, while still spewing their hatred.

"Killer! *Bloody killer!*"

Unbeknownst to O'Brien, one of them has gotten into the drugstore now, from a door on the other side. He moves stealthily up behind him, through the shop—and I see, to my horror, that it is that creature from the park. The killer. *Still alive,* somehow, even after the battle in the street, when he stood and beckoned at the soldiers to shoot him.

Now he carries the huge clump of wood with the words *NO DRAFT!* scrawled on them in one hand, holding it as lightly as a stick. He moves with startling speed through the store, too fast even for Von Briesen, the large, placid German shopkeeper, to see him and shout a warning in time. Not too fast for Father Knapp, who tries to at least alert O'Brien.

"Watch him there! *There, behind ya, son!*"

But it makes no difference. O'Brien hesitates but does not turn, afraid no doubt that this is some crude street trick. He only starts to look around when he hears the drugstore door open, and by then he is too late. The creature from the park is already bringing his block of wood down, hard, on his head.

It should be a crushing blow, a killing blow. But O'Brien is a strong man, and somehow he stops himself even from falling all the way over, only drops his pistol on the sidewalk. He leans down to get it—and the creature hits him again with the lump of wood, knocking him senseless this time.

"Oh, God!" Father Knapp repeats his lament, one long wail directed futilely to me. "Oh, God, you know what is going to happen now!"

"Yes—"

He wades into the mob even as it begins to encircle O'Brien. Waving his hands in front of them, speaking at the top of his voice, as if trying to wake a somnambulist.

"You must stop! As your pastor I forbid it! *For the love of God!*"

They only pick up the priest and move him bodily away, solid as he is—as firmly but gently as one might move a toddling infant out of danger. He tries to push his way back in to O'Brien, but some of the bigger louts only shove him on out again, until at last he turns to me, red-faced and openmouthed in his desperation.

"We must *help* him. We must do something to help him!"

"Yes, Father," I tell him, gripping the gun in my coat pocket that Acton gave me at police headquarters. *Armed again—but what a deception it is.* The six shots in the revolver might cut us through to O'Brien, but he is still lying on the ground, unconscious, and what would we do with him then?

I clutch the revolver, thinking, somehow, that maybe it will not be so bad. O'Brien is one of *them*, after all, an Irishman and a Roman Catholic. I can see the crucifix around his neck when they tear open his tunic. The little silver man, spread out upon the cross. *After all, his skin is white—*

But the whole block must be out by now, and many other blocks as well. The women, in particular, cursing and kicking at him. More of them looking simply bemused, like a teenage girl I notice, gawky and freckled, and big-eared. Caught halfway between her adolescence and womanhood, still wearing an apron tied around her waist. Her mouth is slanted open in wonder, as if she is seeing the circus elephant for the first time. As the both of us look on, they tie a rope around his arms and legs, and drag him up and down the street, his head bumping help-lessly along the uneven paving stones—

"We must help him! We can't just stand an' watch!"

Father Knapp clutches at my coat, nearly knocking me over. His renewed cries jolting me back into action. I wrestle him a few more feet away from the crowd, where I hope they cannot hear us—though already I can see several gang *b'hoys* looking in our direction.

"There is nothing we can do here, not by ourselves!" I hiss at him, trying to make the man see sense. *Trying to ignore the revolver in my coat.* "We have to go look for help, the both of us. You start for the west, I'll make my way downtown, try to find any cops or soldiers you can—"

He sees the sense of my plan, nods and sets out at once. I do as well, running down the streets toward the south. Wondering if I should return to this accursed block at all—if I should not simply make my way back down to Maddy's, hide myself away in her bed-room there—

No, I must find help. Here is something for me to do, at last, something real, and at first I am even exhilarated. Scurrying around to the nearest precinct houses I know of. Running toward the sound of any fighting or looting, thinking that I am sure to find some troops, or Carpenter's Metropolitans there.

But there is nothing. Most of the station houses I take myself to are on fire, or already burned to a crisp. The only two I find that are still intact are manned by the usual skeleton crew of a couple police sergeants, with orders to hold for as long as they can. They could not help me anyway—silently standing aside to let me see the houseful of refugees behind them, the frightened, brown faces of women and children, peering out at the smoking streets.

I even go back to my own block, to Gramercy Park, around its pristine, fenced-in square. Looking for Strong's squad of German vigilantes, hoping to convince them to save O'Brien. They refuse, too—afraid to leave the park even for a few minutes, afraid their intervention will bring the mob over in force.

They may well be right; I can hardly blame them. I stand on the sidewalk for a moment, staring up at my own home, before I have to scurry off again. Everything here still untouched, as quiet as the grave, despite all the smoke and the shouting coming from the greater City all around us. Wondering what it would be like, to have Maddy there, in the silent house, to be in there with her.

Then I must go on. But the fighting, Carpenter's flying squad, and the troops, are always somewhere else. I consider trying to make my way down to the headquarters on Mulberry Street again, but it is too far. Surely O'Brien will be dead by the time I can make it there and back, and I do not know if they even have any men to spare.

At last I make my way back up to Murray's Hill, hoping that somehow it may now be possible to steal him away—that the crowd has grown tired or ashamed of their sport, as they did with Superintendent Kennedy.

But they have done no such thing. Instead they have tortured him throughout the afternoon. There are bloody smears now on the paving stones from where they have dragged him, and they have broken all his teeth, flattened his nose and cheeks by dropping stones and brick on him.

Now they push small wads of paper into his hair and under his nails, and set them on fire. After that the women begin to do their work on him—kneeling around him in the street, grinning fiercely at one another. They slice through his uniform pants, into the pale, white skin beneath. Pouring in the oil when they make a deep enough cut.

Worst of all, he is conscious again. Awakening to the nightmare, trussed and tied helplessly before them. But he will not cry out, will not scream or beg for mercy—at least not before they set the oil on fire. And even when he does, then, it is only a low, rasping, grudging sound, all the more wrenching for being barely human anymore.

It brings him no respite. The women hovering over him only kick and spit at him all the harder. Still screaming their insults and justifications:

"You killer! You damned killer! How could you come back here an' show your face—"

"That's what you get for killin' Ellen Kirk!"

"That's what you get for killin' babies!"

They will not let anyone so much as move him. Von Briesen, his friend the druggist, tries to bring him a cup of water. Lowering his sweating, white-shirted, German bulk down over the pavement— "*Please—please, just a little water—*"

They snatch the cup from his hand, dash it through his already fractured shop window.

"Did Ellen Kirk get a glass of water? Did she, then, before they killed her?"

They demolish what remains of the German's store. Tearing down his shingle and looting the change drawer. Smashing the lovely apothecary bottles behind his counter, the tonics and balms in all their amber and rusty hues. Von Briesen gives a sorrowful little shrug, walks prudently away down the street.

The teenage girl I spotted earlier begins to scream when they castrate him. She was probably a domestic, I thought—a scullery maid, or assistant cook. She edged her way into the women's cutting circle, kneeling down in the street with the rest of them, smiling shyly about herself. Someone pressed a knife into her palm and she began to slice through the blue wool leg of O'Brien's uniform, as diligent and industrious as if she were peeling her mistress's potatoes.

But then, as they cut into his actual living flesh, her face begins to fall, her jaw going slack. When they mutilate him she struggles up, and runs around in a little circle. Then she runs back toward them—

to where he lies—screaming at the top of her voice, screaming and waving her hands at them.

"Stop it, stop it! Oh, do stop it, for the love of God!"

Several of the women rise up indignantly, slapping at her face.

"Who is she? Who is she to speak to us like that?"

Seething with indignation, they kick and bully her down the street and off the block. Then they go on into the boardinghouse where she lives, drag out her meager possessions and set them on fire in the street—no more than a couple of threadbare linen dresses, and the wicker chest she brought from Ireland, the inevitable copy of her *Guide for Catholic Young Women, Especially for Those Who Earn Their Own Living.* As the flames grow, they rekindle their fury:

"What care did she have for little Ellen Kirk, that's what I'd like to know! What care did she ever have for any of us?"

Yet behind the indignant women, the street is quieter, almost philosophical. Men and women sitting on their stoops, smoking their white clay pipes, staring dully at O'Brien where he lies on the sidewalk, still alive.

They watch the small boys as they take turns parading with O'Brien's shiny silver sword, trying to wrap their fingers around the jeweled presentation handle. Passing around the other souvenirs they have pulled from his pockets—his paper and ring, a few bits of shinplaster money. A locket containing a picture of his wife and children, who had already fled to Brooklyn this morning.

"What was he doin', comin' back here like that?"

"Still, he's a brave Irishman—"

"Don' waste a thought for him. Shot them down, just like they shoot anyone they please!"

"On his own block, too. His own block!"

Father Knapp has returned at last, with no more success than I have had. I can only shrug helplessly when he looks at me, trying to pull him away. He will have none of it. His face swollen with rage, his neck bright red, he plunges right in again, trying to beat his way through to O'Brien.

It is no use—the best they will let him do is to give the dying man extreme unction. In the street he opens up the small wooden box he has brought with him. There is a miniature altar inside, candles and a crucifix, a tiny silver spoon and patina; clean linens and a little bottle of oil, and the holy water and silver chalice. When it is all set up, he turns his stole back over to purple again, and leans in to hear the dying man's confession.

O'Brien struggles to raise himself up on one elbow, grabbing hold of the priest's cassock. As he does I see that they have cut the ring finger off his hand—no doubt for another souvenir. His arms and his legs are still smoking from the oil, his body nearly naked now. His face is blistered from lying out under the sun all afternoon, his lips swollen and cracked. Nonetheless, he is still alive—still able to murmur something in the priest's ear, while Father Knapp nods and cradles him in his arms.

"Does he repent the murders, Father? Does he?"

The crowd leans in.

"He goddamned well better—"

"If he don't, then no last rites!"

The priest ignores them, and grants the dying man absolution. Giving him the communion, the host out of the thin, silver patina. Chanting to him the prayer that he must repeat.

"O Lord, Who hast mercifully provided remedies for all our necessities; grant me Thy grace—"

"O Lord—"

". . . give me that true light, by which I may be conducted through the shadow of death . . ."

When it is finished he drizzles the holy water over O'Brien, then offers him the crucifix to kiss with his torn and blistered lips.

"Adjutorium nostrum in nomine Domini . . . ex hoc loco accessus ademonum, adsint Angeli pacis, domumque hanc deserat omnis maligna discordia—"

Next he opens the little bottle of oil and begins to anoint the dying man. Dipping his thumb in the holy oil, then making the sign of the cross on O'Brien's eyes, his ears, his nose, his lips; his hands and his feet, and his groin. Any part, any orifice that might give offense to God, here in this wretched, oozing boil of a City.

"Kyrie, eleison.
"Christe, eleison—"

O'Brien releases his grip on the priest's cassock, slumping back to the sidewalk. Father Knapp blesses him, finishing the sacrament—

and then, with the last words of the rite, makes one last try to save the man, throwing himself over his body.

"Please—leave him to me! For the sake of your own souls! He can't do a thing to you now—"

But they only pry Father Knapp loose again, carting him bodily over to the sidewalk where he can't interfere with them.

"Finish him! He's had his last rites!"

They drag him into the backyard of his own house. The women kneel over him once more, looking to finish him off. Grunting and cursing like savages as they pound and stab away at the man.

I clutch at the pistol in my coat pocket, looking down at them, my head spinning at the sight of their cruelty. Thinking still, *There must be something I can do—*

I start to stagger away, to try to go somewhere, do something— when I find myself looking into the face of Finn McCool.

He was standing directly across the street from the women, with a brace of his hulking shoulder hitters in tow. Something else, which should have given me pause—he was already looking at me. The look on his face baleful, even reproachful. As if to say, *See, I told you I had no authority over them—*

I walk toward him, nevertheless, thinking that somehow I would get him to stop them from killing O'Brien. When he sees me coming, he holds up an arm, almost as if frightened—as if he were trying to ward me off. But I am as stunned as a rabbit by the awful things I have seen, the heat. I keep moving toward him, at least until I see his gesture has changed. He is pointing at me now, his eyes almost feral in the light from the growing fire.

"He's a spy! A spy for the police! For Greeley!" he is bellowing now, loud enough to be heard for two blocks over.

I stand frozen to the spot. Stupidly holding out my hands, as if to appeal to him. Everyone looking up, the *b'hoys* around McCool eyeing me now. Suddenly my disguise—my disheveled, dirty, yellow suit— has been peeled away.

"Search his coat, he's got a notebook in his pocket! Takin' down the names of everyone on the block, for the police!"

McCool's *b'hoys* begin to move now, running across the street toward me, their mouths spread in slack, malevolent grins.

"Get him! A spy!"

I turn, and bolt. *What else is there to do? Let them find the note-book—the police-issue Colt?* Instantly, I am a refugee. Running, now, as I watched poor Kennedy run—

"A spy! A spy! Stop the spy!"

The cry goes up behind me. I rush past a blur of men and women—some smiling, some grabbing at me. Their faces turning, one after the other, to see what all the excitement is about. To see *me*.

"A spy! Stop him!"

"One of Greeley's spies!"

All it would take would be one well-placed stone, one leg tangled in my shins, and I would be down—as helpless as Colonel O'Brien was, clubbed down by that creature. Reduced to an object for their sport

"Get him!"

I keep running. Looking for an alley, a doorway, for anyplace to duck into where I might be safe. My legs are as heavy as blocks now, after all my exertions during the day, my breath beginning to give out. My pursuers driving me steadily toward the south, and west, until I am near the Ninth Avenue now—only a couple of blocks from the river, the very edge of the island.

And still, behind me, I can hear the sound of running feet. Muffled laughter, too—as if whoever is pursuing me revels in the chase.

Who would ever pursue me such a distance? When they could have their fun on any street corner tonight?

Could it be that monster—their Mose from the park? It must be him, who else would laugh in this pursuit?

The streets and avenues are strewn with makeshift barricades now. Furniture and carters' wagons, lampposts and dead horses, and bales of contraband cotton, and twisted-up railroad ties—anything that can be thrown across the street.

But the battle has already come this way, the barricades broken, even charred by fire. I can still hear the sounds of fighting, the shouts and cheers, and men singing and screaming, both in the streets above and below me.

I run on toward the waterfront, all the way to end of the island, and the Hudson docks. Still looking for some refuge. Fumbling for my pistol in my jacket pocket—

Just across West Street there is one of the new street-cleaning machines the mob has been at, broken and abandoned now. I squat down behind it, gasping for breath, unable to run any longer. Besides, there is no place to run to, here at the edge of the City.

The footsteps draw closer behind me. I am sure I hear them, even against the distant, constant roar of the riot. The steady, dissonant hum of the City, rising louder than ever now—

Behind the broken machine, I hold my pistol up. Ready to kill him—ready to kill even *him*, that awful, unkillable creature, should he come upon me here.

The footsteps keep drawing closer—real noises, I am sure of it. They start to slow, then stop altogether—as if he is feeling me out, listening for me in the deserted night.

It must be him. Who else among them would have this sort of intelligence? The discernment of a preying animal, which has learned through long experience not to fall for the lurking snare. Instead he waits, somewhere in the shadows of the long, low warehouses down the next block. Listening, watching—

I hold my pistol up. Ready. Ready for him.

❧ · 56 · ❧

MADDY

Maddy tried to sit as still as she could against the heat, listening to the breath rising and falling in her chest. Unsure of what time of day it was anymore. The whine of the cicadas growing steadily higher from the ailanthus tree out back, the one her mother had liked. *A China-man's tree*, they said. They could grow anywhere—wiry, misshapen things, emerging even from the unspeakable muck around the back lot privvies.

They had grown in the back lot behind the apartment in St. John's Park. That was when her father had still been alive, and they had lived in two rooms, on the second floor of a brownstone. It was the nicest place she had ever lived—before Robinson had rented the house for her, here in Paradise Alley. Maybe nicer, even, though they did not own the whole of it. *But then, she owned nothing of this place—*

It had been just the three of them, before her Da had fallen off the scaffolding, and even though her mother had lost the other babies, they had been happy enough. In the summer evenings they had eaten their meals by the back window, with the tree there close enough to touch, as if they were living up in the branches. She had never seen anything like it again until Robinson had installed her over the back-yard of that brothel in the Seven Sisters, where she would look out her window in the twilight and gaze on the red and yellow Japanese lanterns, dotting the trees—

He would bring it back. He would put it right. That was what she had started to believe, when Robinson had first begun to buy her things. He would put it right. She had even started to pray again—the first time since she had prayed to the Virgin as a little girl. Thinking that this was the purpose in it, to make it come out like it had been, before her Da had fallen.

After his death they had had to move to the Little Water, and then to the Shambles. Her mother had tried to keep track of her, but she had had to spend most of her time taking in all the sewing and washing work she could get, or scavenging junk off the street to pay the rent. Maddy had been left to explore the sewer culverts, and all the labyrinthine alleys of the tenement houses—

That was how she had met up with Eddie Coleman, her pimp. He had offered her twenty-five cents to go out on the streets as a hot-corn girl and she had leaped at the money, it was enough to let them eat for a week.

Still, she had been frightened by the busyness of the streets, out on Broadway and the Bowery, and down on Park Row. The avenues jammed with onrushing omnibuses and carts, and drays and street-cars. The pavement beneath her feet shaking from the roll of the newspaper presses. The spectral faces of the men sweeping past her—peering blindly, acquisitively out of the darkness, seeing what she had to sell. Then circling back around her—

Maddy had learned to give them what they wanted—whatever it was. Shivering and flirting, begging and teasing them. And at the end of her first week, Eddie Coleman had taken her into the back room of the grocery and taken off all her clothes. Running his hands over her as coolly and professionally as he might have handled a load of fenced silks from the docks.

When he discovered she was a virgin, he had auctioned her off to some rabbit sport. A drunken young man, not much older than herself, down to shoot dice in the Five Points for the night. The sport had brought a retainer—a big-shouldered man with a scar on one cheek and a neddy in his pocket—so instead of simply rolling the boy, Eddie had sold her off to him.

The sport leaning her over a rough table, in a workshed just down the alley. It smelled of machine oil, and damp sawdust, the sport smelling of gin and toilet water. He had humped and pumped at her back there, so that

*it hurt a little, then she felt something wet on her thighs, and that was it.
He was already gone, back out in the alley buttoning his pants, and she
went home to her mother.*

That was all. She had not asked for anything more, she had not
expected it. Making her way as best she could, out on the fast, change-
able streets. Trying to keep from being run over by an omnibus, trying to keep her ears of corn away from the pigs.

She liked it when she could bring a little money home. She didn't
like it when Eddie hit her, or when he chose to take her back to the
shed and saw away at her himself. She tried not to think too much
about what she had seen him do to his other girls, when he was in his
rage. She tried not to think about the things the other girls told her,
over a glass of gin at Rosanna Peers's. Stories about men who had a
strange look in their eyes, and wanted them to go someplace deserted.
Stories about men who looked perfectly normal—and then, when
they were alone down some slip, suddenly produced a razor, or a knife
in their hand—

She didn't think much about the future, or putting anything right.
She didn't think much about anything except trying to help her
mother, half deaf and bent double with the rheumatism by then.

And then her gentleman had come by. Like something out of a storybook, like the religious tracts she read sometimes, handed out by the
Protestant missionaries, where girls who were rescued to a life of
virtue married stalwart young men, and were intent on improving
themselves.

Not that she had ever believed them. Things did not get put
right. People fell off scaffoldings, and were bent low by the misfortunes
of life, and slashed to death by strange men in alleys that smelled of
cats' piss. Besides, you had to become a Protestant for things to work
out—

Then he had come, her prince. And whisked her away to a brothel.

She had tried to be whatever he wanted her to be. Standing before
him in her chains, during his game, letting him see her as he wanted to
see her. And nothing had happened.

At last she had gone to him, unable to believe that he did not love
her in return. She had gone up to his house in Gramercy Park, and
stood under the tree in his yard, and asked him if he loved her. And all

he had been able to do was to stand there, muttering that it was impossible.

After that she had tried to make herself as miserable to him as she could. It was then that she had started taking on other men. It had begun with a sailor, wandered up Paradise Alley from the dockside. He had seen Robinson leaving and had gone up to her door, assuming it was a brothel. And she had thought, *Why not*, and taken him in.

The rest had soon followed. His shipmates, and sailmakers and carpenters from the docks; innkeepers and draymen, and barbers and bootblacks. Black men and white, just so long as they could pay what she asked.

She didn't care. She didn't care what the other women on the block thought, they already believed her to be a whore. She only made certain that *he* knew about it.

But even that had not driven him away. He had kept coming back, day after day, week after week, wanting to play his little game, wrapping the chains around her. Although he was even tiring of that—she could see the signs. The eagerness in his eyes fading, his breathing less ragged. Small hints of boredom, of distraction creeping in. Certain he would tire of her altogether—

Still, she had gone on with it. Letting him back in, even when the touch of his hand made her cringe. Filling her wardrobe with the clothes he bought her, but not wearing most of them. Hanging on to something—hoping somehow that he would see her again, past the chains.

Then had come the baby—something that had never occurred to her before. She took her precautions, learned like so much else from the women at the brothel in the Seven Sisters. But she had never been so much as a week late, so she figured that it would not happen, had gotten lax about it—

But there it was, after so many years she had found herself with child and she had had to tell Robinson, knowing he would take care of it. She had let him take her up to Madam Restell's and the small, inner room in her garish mansion—the one he never saw. The shades all pulled down, and the walls and even the floor painted red, in case there was too much blood.

And after it was all over, she had laughed and told him that it was impossible for her to have another. Wanting to hurt him—wanting him, she realized, to guess that it had been his. For him to want more than anything that they should have another.

But he had not. If anything, he had only looked relieved to be rid of one more burden. *One more Paddy.* Just as glad to have snuffed it out, and to go on seeing her as he liked.

And what would she do, then? With no boy and no girl to take care of her? What would she do when he finished with her, without a child of her own and no friend in the world?

There was a noise from the street, and she roused herself, and shuffled over to the shutters again. *The bitches were all out there now.* Every one of the white women from Paradise Alley, plus some who must have come over from other blocks. Cackling and gesticulating among themselves, gathering something up in their skirts and aprons—

Rocks, she saw at last. Pried-up paving stones, and pieces of loose brick and masonry, scavenged from the construction sites. *Was the riot that close, then?* She tried to concentrate on it, to think what she might do. Try to make her way through the streets to his house on her own? Stay and wait—knowing he would be back?

Or that someone else would be back first. She thought again about the threat that the wizened little man had made a few nights ago: *We'll see to your niggers—*

She sat back down at the kitchen table and looked at the jug. Wondering if she should pour herself a glass—wanting one, but wanting to be presentable for him, when he came back to fetch her to his house.

To take her right up inside, as if she was his own wife, almost. That was something. She had not expected even the riot to draw such a thing out of him—some abiding affection, at least. If, that was, he meant it. If she still didn't end up working as his maid, his scullion, while he took some younger bride up to his bed—

It was when she had found the book that she was sure she hated him. It was only another novel she had found in a street stall along the shilling side of Broadway, run by a courtly, greying Negro vendor who liked to call himself Peter Bookman. Maddy stopped there sometimes when she could not stand being in the house any longer and had to go out for her walks. Moving as fast as she could in her long skirts, paying no attention to the people who stopped and stared to see a well-dressed woman walking so fast. Roaming obliviously, all over the

City, until she could see clearly again, and the throbbing in her head had died down.

Then she might take something home to read. This one was a popular novel, no more than four bits, bound in a simple, brown pasteboard cover. The title stamped in gold on the front and the spine, *Paradise Alley, a Tale from the Streets of New York*. She had no idea it was his, a pseudonym printed on the title page—*by Dr. E. C. Argent*—only later had she learned what the pun meant.

She had taken it home and started to read. Barring the door, and turning away all visitors as she went on, though it was an excellent night to make money. Becoming steadily more engrossed in it, reading on through the evening as the usual commotion from the streets outside slowly died down. Reading into the small, quiet hours of the night, although the City was never completely quiet. The sound of some drunken revelry, some cry of dismay, even a scream, still drifting up to her from somewhere. *Some other poor soul, learning something in the middle of the night.*

The book had been all about her, she had figured it out quickly enough. The names had been changed, and the events, of course. That was to say, the whole thing was a lie. Her life—made into some lesson on the evils of drink, and being poor. Her father was a drunk, and her mother as well. It was they who had put her out on the street, selling her hot corn. It was they who had benefited from her ill-gotten gains. Beaten her when they thought she hadn't brought enough home. Fed her whiskey for dinner, to get her through the night.

She had a brother, in *his* version of her life, a boy they put to thieving, though he didn't want to. A younger sister, as well, an angelic sort with blue eyes and blond hair, who tried to get to the Protestant missionaries at the Old Brewery. The evil parents beat and starved the sister to death—though she died still looking quite angelic, according to the plate next to the deathbed scene.

And then there was herself. *Maddy Boyle, now Mary Boggs.* Described to a fare-thee-well, right down to the birthmark on her cheek. There was no mistaking it. Nor, for that matter, was there any mistaking his typical asides and turns of phrase, his sense of humor and little jokes. *It had to be him*, she had discerned before the end of the first chapter.

And it had to be her, his innocent girl. In the end she was left alive—he had the good grace to do that much for her, at least. Packed off to a good, Protestant home up in Pelham. Not only redeemed, but redeeming others, making her parents see the light. *Though if her real parents had done such things she would have redeemed them with a grappling hook—*

She had read it all through the night, finishing just as the first birds had started to sing in the ailanthus tree, and when she was through she had wanted to weep. Knowing, then, that he had never really seen her at all. Knowing that he had always regarded her, right from the beginning, as no more than his model.

No more than his hot-corn girl. His White Captive.

But even worse than this fantasy, this *book*—worse than his gross distortion of her life, his disregarding of all that she ever was and all that she had ever felt toward him—was how bad it was. How tedious, how lacking in sensibility. *How poorly drawn the characters were, how weak the dialogue, how offhand the descriptions—*

She had been mistaken in him, she knew it now. *He had never seen her. And she had not seen him.*

And now what was there for them both, save for the time they had put in? Hanging on to each other, for no better reason than the past— against the usual frightfulness of the wider City outside?

She looked around for a glass, any glass. Pulling the cork out of the jug with her teeth. *He was not coming.* There was little light left in the house now, but instead of trying to light the gas, she had simply gone to the front windows and thrown open the shutters. Pouring herself a long drink of the whiskey. Convinced, now—*He's not coming.*

The day already slipping rapidly toward late afternoon and evening. She had been mad to think he would be back, to take her back to his house. *He only wants to see me as his captive, shut away here—*

She was still standing there, having her glass and looking out the unshuttered window, when they threw the first rock. It was half of a paving stone, thick and grey, and she had watched it tumble end over end, unable to believe even as she watched it that they would hurl such a thing at her—

Then it had smashed through the parlor window, and she had screamed, and thrown her hands up over her face, shielding herself from the flying glass. Listening with even greater shock to the jibes and laughter, coming from her neighbors out on the street.

Another heavy stone slammed against her front door. Then another, and another—rocks and bricks and granite paving stones, raining down on the front of her little house. They smashed through the rest of the parlor glass, cracking the slats of her shutters.

She ran to the door, tugging it open and staring out in disbelief. A fragment of brick the size of her fist hit the door frame just above her—showering her with red dust, sending her reeling back inside. She peeked out again, but there was no mistaking it. The white women were holding their stones in their aprons as they advanced, shouting for her as they heaved them at her home.

"Come out, come out, where'ere y'are!"

"Come on out, ya whore! Ya cheap molly bit!"

"Come out an' face what you got comin', ya nigger's whore!"

To her own surprise she had felt the tears welling up in her eyes when she heard them mocking her. Then she had the revolver in her hand, storming back out the door. Unsure, now that she'd had the drink, of how to use the thing, but not caring. Charging on out into the street—

"Here I am! Here I am, ya bitches!"

She waved the gun wildly, trying to fiddle with the hammer, the trigger. Grinning with satisfaction as she saw the other women retreat at first, back across Paradise Alley.

"Here I am!"

But they had regained their courage quickly, as they watched her fumbling with the gun. More rocks and bricks bounced off her home— one whizzing just past her cheek. The women advanced again—laughing at her, gesturing at her to come on—

A stone struck her in the head—a glancing blow, but enough to send her scrambling to her knees. The pistol skidded out over the pavement ahead of her and she crawled after it, cursing to herself.

"The bitches. The goddamned bitches!"

They laughed and shrieked like crows now. Moving still closer, picking up more stones.

"Where are your niggers now? Eh? Where's your Yankee gentleman?"

"Take our sons, willya!"

She moved after the gun, feeling another brick strike her side. Realizing only now what they were doing to her, through some dim recollection of a Biblical story—

They are stoning me.

RUTH

All that day they heard the wild, animal cries again—the sounds of things breaking or burning, off in the distance. But not so far off now. It seemed to Ruth that it was drawing slowly in on them, from all sides. She knew that Deirdre noticed it, too—saying less and less as the day wore on, her lips drawn steadily tighter.

The white women held the block now. They ran back and forth in the street like schoolchildren. The pale, pinched faces excited, even gleeful, as they informed her that Horace Greeley himself had been hanged, or that a whole regiment of infantry had been massacred in the Arch Block. Mrs. McGillicuddy had even come by to tell them they should leave now.

"You best get out while the gettin's there for ya," she advised, her statuesque figure swaying a little in the doorway, her breath sour with whiskey. "Otherwise, ye'll see, they'll lynch all your children, the poor darkies, right before your eyes!"

Deirdre came into the front room, her face chiseled in anger.

"Missus Mack, you best go find a better use for your teeth and your tongue."

"But it's true! There's a hundred thousand Irishmen on the way right now. They're marchin' down the Bowery, burnin' out every nigger they come across—" She leaned in toward Deirdre, pointing a thumb toward Ruth and talking as if she could not hear her:

"Me cousin Seamus already seen her husband swingin' from a lamppost in the Fourth Avenue, near the little niggers' home. Everybody pokin' an' cuttin' at the body, an' puttin' it to the oil—"

"Go on with you now!"

Deirdre gave the larger woman a furious push away from her door, shoving her until she was halfway back across the street.

"You know as well as I your cousin's been cowering in your kitchen the last two days, Mrs. Mack! He wouldn't know about a thing beyond the end of your apron strings."

"Not hisself, no, but someone said—"

"No, but you're willing to come over and say that it's so, once you've drunk your courage up."

Mrs. McGillicuddy's face hung sullen and spiteful.

"We know that she's here, she an' her nigger brood," she said now, in a voice that slipped like a knife through Ruth's ribs. "We'll take care a them, all right—an' that other one up the street, what trucks with the black sailors—"

"Get off, I said!"

Mrs. McGillicuddy moved on reluctantly, retreating from the promise of Deirdre's wrath but still mouthing her threats over her shoulder.

"Don't think they're safe here. Don't think ya can get away with it, just because they're under your roof!"

"But she's right, we'll put you all in danger," she told Deirdre as soon as Mrs. McGillicuddy was gone and they were bolted back in the house again. "We can't stay—"

"Don't be daft. Where would you go—and you have to wait for Billy—"

"But it's your house, what you done so much for."

"Go on now," Deirdre said dismissively. "It's a house, that's all."

She hesitated then, looking more closely at Ruth and lowering her voice.

"You know she's lying, don't you? You know she doesn't know a thing she's talking about."

"I know."

"Not her, or a hundred of her Seamuses—"

"I know. I know it's a lie," Ruth said softly.

The picture of Billy, hung from a lamppost, piercing her mind anyway. His beautiful person, degraded, mutilated.

"Whatever you do, though, don't tell the boy—" Ruth asked her.

"No, of course not!"

"Please don't tell him. I wouldn't want him to hear it, even though I know it's a lie."

"Of course it's a lie. 'A hundred thousand Irishmen, marching down the Bowery!'" Deirdre snorted loudly—for her benefit, Ruth knew. "When did you ever hear of a hundred thousand Irishmen able to do anything together—"

There was a sound like hail out in the street, and they went to the window shutters. The women were throwing rocks and chunks of loose brick at Maddy's house now. Standing out in the street, screeching and crying like so many gulls or jackdaws—

"Whore, whore, dirty whore!"

"Come out, come out, the niggers' whore!"

There was the sound of breaking glass, and the women yelped with glee. Then, to their amazement, Maddy came running out into the alley—wearing only a red silk dressing gown, and waving her gun above her head.

"Get out of here, all of yas, before I blow your brains out!" she was screaming, holding up her pistol.

The women only laughed and screeched at her some more. One of them threw a stone that glanced off the side of her head, knocking her down and sending the gun sliding along the gutter. Maddy crawled after it on her hands and knees, still screaming and cursing, tearing and muddying the dressing gown as she did. But another stone hit her in the ribs, then another and another—the women in the street screaming in triumph with each hit.

"Jesus God, but what's this block come to!"

Deirdre was already throwing a shawl over her shoulders, running instinctively out into the street. Ruth followed behind her—thinking they were going to be killed, but following her nonetheless.

When they reached Maddy, though, the stones stopped. The women were still mingling about across Paradise Alley, but Deirdre was able to stare them down as she helped Maddy—brushing off her fine gown as best she could. Not knowing what else to do, Ruth leaned down and picked up the pistol where it had fallen, holding it gingerly.

It looked very different from the gun she had envied earlier, at the Croton pump. This one seemed very new, with a pearl handle and a fat, shiny, revolving chamber. *A gentleman's gun,* she thought.

"God's shame upon you for Christian women!" Deirdre was yelling across at the other white women. "I would tremble to think what the Father would think if he could see this!"

"Ah, go on back an' tend to your niggers!" one of them jibed back at her, and there was another gale of laughter. But they moved grudgingly off down the street, averting their faces from Deirdre's wrath, at least for now.

"Where's me gun?" Maddy had asked, as soon as they had her inside, and down on Deirdre's fine reclining couch.

She had seemed nearly unconscious out in the street. Now that they had her inside, though, she was full of fire once more.

"*Where's me gun?* I can take care a all a those cows an' kisses with that—"

"Never mind about that now!" Deirdre commanded, holding her head while Ruth washed out her wounds with a cloth. "There'll be no shooting going on from this house. And you'll manage your tongue, there are children here."

"I do as I please! That's what I told him an' I'll say the same to you!"

She jerked away from the wet cloth.

"I don't need *you*—"

Ruth thought that she seemed like a wild Indian, or some other half-savage creature. Sitting up on Deirdre's couch, dripping blood over her embroidered yellow slipcover. Her arms were wrapped defensively around her knees, her legs tucked up under the now-shredded red silk gown like a child's.

She was still very pretty, Ruth saw. There were some lines around her eyes and mouth, her face a little dissipated. But undeniably pretty—even with her hair unwashed, the dirt ground into her skin from well before her fall outside. *Pretty enough so that any man would still want her—*

"As long as you're in my house, you will do as I say," Deirdre told her, in her sharpest, most obedience-inducing voice.

"I'll go, then!"

Maddy jumped up from the reclining couch, her tangled hair falling wildly over her face.

"I didn't ask to come here, an' I won't take it from you, or anyone else. Where's me gun?"

She began to stalk about the room, looking frantically for her pistol—even though it was in plain sight, where Ruth had stuck it inside the glass cabinet of the falling secretary.

"I ain't afraid of those bitches. I know them an' I know their husbands, an' I ain't afraid of either one!"

"They'll beat you to death in the street."

"Let 'em come an' try! They want to run me out, let 'em come an' try—"

She lurched suddenly over to the window at that thought, staring out through the shutters.

"They better not be into my house. The cowards!" She looked at Deirdre and Ruth very earnestly then. "My man'll see to them. He's a real American, not like these shiftless Irish sons a bitches. He'll see to it they get theirs—"

"I thought you took care of yourself."

"I can, all right! Just gimme my goddamned gun, I'll take care of it!"

Maddy charged for the door at that, but it proved surprisingly easy to stop her. Through her gown she felt almost hollow to Ruth, her arms and legs mere sticks, and as soon as they stopped her, she gave up.

She let them lead her back to the couch, and patch up her head and the scrapes on her knees. Ruth fetched her some lamb stew from the pot they had cooked the night before, while Deirdre kept watch over her. Maddy eating the stew up ravenously, even though it was still cold.

"Thanks for the food. Now give me the gun, an' I'll be on me way—"

"Why don't you get your man to take you off this block," Deirdre suggested, ignoring her demand. "Doesn't he see it isn't safe for you here?"

"To hell with that!" Maddy cursed, sitting up straight again. "These mabs don't scare me, I can take care of 'em. Let 'em try to come burn me out—them or any of their men!"

"Enough of that talk now, no one's going to burn you out!" Deirdre told her sternly—but Ruth remembered the threatening voice from a few days before. Familiar, somehow, but strange in its hardness. *A voice that meant what it said.*

We'll see to your niggers—

"I'll talk as I like! I do as I like, an' I go when I like, too—"

"*Enough,* I said!"

Maddy struggled to get up off the couch again, but Deirdre pushed her back down easily, and Ruth helped to hold her there.

"What's it to you, what's it to you!" she screamed, at the top of her lungs, until the children came and stared fearfully into the parlor.

Yet after a few more minutes she ceased to struggle. Sitting quite still now, wiping her nose on her sleeve as she looked around herself.

"This is a nice place," she said softly, suddenly docile again, admiring Deirdre's parlor. "I had a room like this once. My man got it just for me. Just like he got me the house."

She gave a long, openmouthed yawn then, and curled up on the couch, as casually and comfortably as if she were in her own bed. Within minutes she was sleeping soundly, even snoring, and Deirdre put a blanket over her.

"Look at her there, the little darling."

"It's all right, once she calms herself."

"Yes. If we can just get her out of here without killing us all in our beds, we'll be doing all right."

Watching her, Ruth remembered how beautiful Maddy had been when she'd first come to live on the block. Her clothes still well-kempt, and her mother living with her. There had never been any doubt as to what she was, the well-dressed gentleman accompanying her, then vanishing back into his carriage. Yet she had acted genteel and exotic enough for them to almost believe some mysterious foreign lady had come to live among them.

By then they had settled into their lives on the street. Billy was still working up with the orphans, and she was still walking all the way up to the German ladies and their ash piles every day. Every two years or so, there was another child, Mana and Frederick, Elijah and Vie. And Milton, all the time growing like a vine stalk—bigger and taller than his daddy, and nearly as handsome. And so smart, reading everything he could find, after only a term at the common school they had sent him to.

Ruth had even accepted a little Bible from the Protestant missionary man at the Old Brewery, who had naturally assumed she was still an idolatrous Catholic. She didn't disabuse him of the notion, but took the small book with its red, false-leather cover for Milton, enfolding it in her dress lest any of their neighbors see.

He had been so pleased with it. Going through the whole thing— then reading the religious stories, and moving on to the patriotic histories of Washington and the Revolution. Then after that, the nickel and dime novels that he consumed more avidly than anything else— *The Black Revancher of the City,* or the *The Green Redeemer of the Hills*—so that she worried they were not of the highest morality. But she could not bring herself to forbid him, he seemed to love them so.

He would read night after night by the light from the fire, while his father grumbled from his chair about how he wanted him up and ready in the morning. Even though it was Billy who had insisted that he go to the common school, and would bring him anything he could find to read from his long walk home, all the scraps of newspaper, and journals. The discarded books he discovered lying in alleyways, and chucked in ashboxes, and selling two for a penny in the back of some liquor grocery—abundant as everything else in this country.

And Milton, in turn, even taught her to read some of them—even taught her to read *The Black Revancher,* which she found was an exciting story despite herself. Their moments together were the only times of real joy she had anymore—when she would lie down on the floor next to him, by the fire, after all the labors of the day were finished. She had to be up before it was light, getting Billy his breakfast and then getting the other children up and off to the common school. And afterward there was the long walk uptown to her own work, then home to clean and get the supper, packing the rest of the children off to bed in their one crowded room.

Billy was worse, then, too. She knew that he still brooded over Lillian, the girl they had lost on this street. Not showing it much, for that wasn't his way, but lingering over it as one final, unpardonable insult from life. She thought, with time, that they should consider themselves lucky to have lost just one, with how many children died on the block every year, from the typhus and the measles, the *tamh* and the cholera.

But he would not accept this. Hating the long walk up to the orphans', she knew, through all the white neighborhoods. Bored and insulted by the work once he got there. He would come in later and later, despite the looks Ruth gave him—knowing that even a whiskey or two on the way home would be more than they could afford. Weaving over to the table in the way that she hated now   hated the children to see, to smell the queer, sour scent upon his breath.

He would vow to reform. He would wait until they were both in bed, and she could not see his face in the darkness, and then he would speak to her in anguished self-accusations, and swear that he would do better. Astonished to find he had failed again, he swore that he would curb his weakness, that somehow he would find them a better place to live, even outside the City.

And Ruth would lie next to him, and rub a hand silently over his back and shoulders, listening to everything he had to say. Knowing as well as he did that there was nothing to be done. That there was no place to go, no work in the City or out, no work anywhere in this country where he might find a better position.

For a few months, then, he might stay away from it. Forcing himself to come home in better spirits, cavorting around the house with the children. Rooting up what carpentry work he could, from other colored families on Dover and Oak Streets, to make a little money on the side.

But it would always come down. He would wander over to the boatyards, or simply walk by a construction site, and he would be through the doors of the next saloon. Coming home that night with the sickly-sweet smell of the brandy, or the whiskey on him again, and the weaving—*how she hated that weave now, what she had once thought of as his nimbleness and grace.* And how the drink slurred his speech, and made him seem stupid and groggy, until she wanted to choke off all her own pity for him, her husband.

Her only remaining delight, then, was when she stretched herself out on the floor by the fire, and studied the dancing, teeming symbols in Milton's book or leaf of newspaper. There were so many signs, and so many combinations that could be made of them, that she marveled to think that her own son could keep them straight in his head. She loved to simply lie there, and let him explain it to her. Enjoying his sweet, earnest voice, taking such pleasure in it that she did not learn nearly as much as she should have. Listening to him until the tiny, insect-like symbols began to spin before her, falling asleep before the fire.

Billy would have to rouse her—angry with her, though he could not admit to it. As angry with her as if she had actually done something wrong. As angry as she got when he drifted off in his chair from too much drink after dinner, snoring so loudly it seemed to make the whole house shake, and the children laughed and smirked at the noise.

"You never care what I want for the boy!" he would admonish her. "Keepin' him up late, keepin' him tired, learnin' things that ain't no use for a colored man in this City!"

"Where is he? Where's the boy?"

"I already sent him to bed. He needs to learn to mind *me*. You need to learn, too—"

She would get up and go silently to bed, hurt not so much by the unfairness of what he said, but that he could talk to her at all in such a way. Later, in the darkness, he would be repentant again, and sad, and even ashamed. But Ruth thought that so many apologies were only like water after a time, pleasant enough running through her hands but leaving nothing behind.

Maddy, at least, had brought some excitement to the block. Breaking up, for the moment, life's weary circles of penance and decline. The other women, Ruth knew, regarded her almost as royalty at first, and she had felt much the same way herself. Looking to catch a glimpse of her, of the man who kept her, walking down the alley in his elegant silk waistcoat and gloves.

But after a few years that had changed, too. There were others now, ringing freely at the bell in front of Maddy's house, day and night. And after her mother had died, and been taken away in the splendid, glass-walled hearse her man had bought for her, Maddy had begun to appear among them more often. Trudging out along the alley to haul water from the pump or to go to the market—as often as not wearing no more than one of her elegant dressing gowns and nothing else.

They still talked about Maddy in breathless voices, as if it were all they could do to keep from peeping in her windows. Exchanging threats of what they would do to their husbands if they ever caught them going over there.

They had little to worry about, considering Maddy's price and the proximity. Men, Ruth had noticed, felt free to do their foulest things far from where they lived—at their jobs, or across town, on someone else's block. Even so, she had worried that Billy himself might be tempted. Fretting over how old and haggard she looked whenever she saw herself in a glass, a shop window—the cracked and darkened reflection from *his* cabinet of wonders, when she dusted it.

But Billy never seemed to have an eye for Maddy so much as he did for the colored sailors who came to visit her. They were bold, confident black tars, strolling down Paradise Alley with their rolling gait, and she saw how intently he watched them. Laughing and joking among themselves in some foreign sailor's tongue, before they disappeared into her house. She was always aware of how much he wished he could be away with them.

It was worse, once the war had started. Billy had taken to buying the freedmen's paper, the *North Star*, whenever he could, scouring it to see if they had started a colored brigade yet—complaining bitterly when they hadn't.

"They got a Irish brigade, and a German brigade, and a regiment for Poles, an' one for the Bohemians!" he would exclaim, stamping around the house. "Why not a colored brigade? What's wrong with us, we ain't even good enough to die for them!"

She had refused to say anything—though he must have known how much the whole idea of his leaving hurt her. *To go off to war, and let the rest of them live from hand to mouth.* Perhaps not to come home at all, or with an arm, or a leg off, like the men who had begun appearing on street corners all over the City, replacing the hot-corn girls. Leaning their crutches against a wall, or hopping about with a begging cup. Men with a folded-up sleeve, performing small miracles of agility to roll and light their own smokes, or make change for the newsie.

What were they to do then—if, God forbid, such a thing should happen to him? Live on what she made from the German ladies? Have Milton fill in his position up at the orphanage, and forget about any better life?

But instead of the wreckage and the limbless, he saw only the brash young sailors and soldiers who came to Maddy's in greater and greater numbers, full of their own confidence and insouciance.

When Tom had up and joined the Fighting 69th it had only gotten worse, she knew—without even him to come over for his occasional smokes, Billy's only real friend on the block. He had brooded more than ever after that. No longer stopping at the shipyards on his way to or from home—but pausing instead to watch the levies of soldiers marching down to the wharves.

Until one day just a month before, when the summer had first started to close its sudden, heavy grip upon the City, Billy had gotten up especially early, earlier even than he usually did for the orphans. Going out without telling her, but returning earlier than usual, so that he had already been home for some time when she got back. Cold sober still, but without the reticent, awkward dignity he usually had about him—the small gleam of pride he had whenever he managed to refrain from the drink.

Instead he seemed exhausted, more tired than she had ever seen him, holding his head in his hands as he sat at the table. She had wanted to ask him what it was but he made it clear she should not approach him. Barely touching any of his food before he retired to his chair, the rocker he had made himself. Smoking and rocking silently there, while she started to lie down by the cold hearth, and read with the boy. But as she did, he had suddenly pushed himself forward in the rocker and forbidden it.

"No, no more books!" he had exclaimed, standing up—his face sweating profusely, a fiery, red-black color in the light from the candles they had lit. "No, you need to shut your eyes, like any working-man! No more of this foolishness."

Ruth had started to protest, but he had turned such a ferocious look upon her that she had stopped at once. His expression like something she had seen before only on the face of Johnny Dolan, in its most pure and agonized desperation. Though Milton, being less experienced with the ways of men, had only looked his father carefully up and down, then resumed reading the installment of the *Black Revancher* he had before him.

"You want to stay up?" his father had shouted at the uncomprehending boy. "All right, then, c'mon!"

Billy had swung him up with one rough hand, as big as Milton was—his carpenter's arms still powerful, even after all the years at the orphans'. Pulling his son up, scattering all the flapping pages below him like some rousted bird. Catching up the book, too, and flinging it against the wall, toting Milton along with him over her outraged and bewildered cries.

"C'mon, now—I said, c'mon!"

The other children wakened out of their beds by the commotion, coming into the front room and bursting into tears. The lights, Ruth could see, flaring up in windows across the narrow street. *This time they were causing the racket*—

"Only one reason a workingman's still awake at night. You come with me!"

Billy shook his son like a rag doll when he tried to pull away, gripping his shirt in his fist. Ruth prying at his hands, repeating his name over and over again, as if that might bring him back to his senses, but he ignored her.

"C'mon, I'm gonna make you a man. We'll go pay a visit down the street, you an' me. A hollow leg—father an' son—how about it?"

He had yanked open the door, hauling Milton down the street with him in the darkness. Dragging him toward Maddy's—and no doubt he would have gotten there, his progress slowed only by Ruth still clutching at him, Milton trying to dig his own heels in, but nearly frozen in fear and astonishment by his father's fury.

"No, not there! No!"

She had feared that Billy might actually do it. She had already seen how Milton had begun to notice Maddy's house, watching the men there himself. Too shy and smart to ask either her or his daddy about it—but watching. Watching Maddy, too, with new eyes, she thought, whenever she emerged into the street. So far just *wondering* about it. And though she knew his first encounter with a woman would likely be someplace similar, maybe worse, still she did not want him to go there. *Especially not now, with his father.*

"Here! Here!" Billy was still shouting. "What's the matter? You think I can't pay for it? I can pay for it. Here, here!"

He thrust his hand into his pocket and pulled it back out, a small array of gold coins in his palm. Ruth wondering, despite herself, where he could have gotten so much.

"There, now, whattaya think? That's my wages, the wage of a workingman!"

But he was crying by then and he let them stop him, still short of Maddy's house. Milton running off, back down the street, into the house and the children's room. Ruth could hear the doors slamming behind him. But she had stayed where she was, with her husband, trying to hold him there in the street as he continued to hold out his hand, weeping uncontrollably.

"Here's my wages! Wage of a work-ing-man!"

And afterward, when she had at last gotten him back into the house, he had talked to her for a long time. And she had held on to him, and let him cry in his shame—and could not help but wonder, with all the genuine sorrow she felt for him, if this was what her son would become. If this was what her Milton would come to, crying for his pride at the doorstep of a whore.

❦ · 58 · ❧

BILLY DOVE

They sat in the cellar of the precinct house, trying to listen for the tumult outside. The children huddled up against the walls, tucked up into themselves, arms wrapped around their knees. The basement was not big enough for them, as small as they were, and their every breath was labored in the close, hot space.

At least they had got here. That wild child, the white boy with blood on his face, had been good to his word. It had seemed like a game to him, Billy was not sure right to the end but that he wouldn't betray them to the mob. But he had done what he'd said he would, leading them stealthily up back-alley lots, behind fences and new houses. Having them duck down behind privvies and into unfinished foundations. The boy even going on ahead, sticking his head out to make sure it was clear whenever they had to cross a street.

The mob had gone streaming blindly past them, bent on the destruction of the asylum. The children moving fast, the older ones carrying the youngest on their backs. Dropping immediately to the ground when they were told; waiting silently in the newly dug basements, knee-deep in standing water.

At last they had reached Fifty-first Street. There they had to bolt out into the open, and go east for a few queasy blocks to where the Twentieth Precinct house was, in the Third Avenue. A pair of big, grim cops were standing guard out in front, tapping their nightsticks

in their hands, revolvers tucked conspicuously into their belts. Billy
told the orphans to run, and they did; he grinned as he saw the cops'
jaws drop, watching two hundred and thirty-seven black children
sprint toward them. All they could do was to stand aside and fling
open the doors, letting them run on into the station house.

They made it, Billy thought, almost unable to believe it still. *We made
it.* What he owed to the children and the Asylum settled now. He was
already planning how he would get back downtown, back to his own
family. Maybe they could even give him a pistol, though he doubted
that.

*If nothing else, he would go himself, now, with just his own two
hands—*

As soon as they were inside, though, his feeling of triumph had
evaporated. The precinct house was empty. It was filled with the usual
cop odors of tobacco and boiled beef and potatoes, all right. A layer
of lye poured ineffectually over the still-pungent jail smells of sweat
and vomit, and blood.

But there was not another man left in the whole building. No one
at all, save for the two sergeants standing guard out front. The regular
complement of Metropolitans already ordered downtown, to fight the
riot.

"It's just me an' Sergeant McCluskey left, ma'am," the other
sergeant, a man named Murphy, had told the Misses. "We're tryin' to
put on a big show out front, but you know it won't fool 'em forever."

"Sergeant, we have over two hundred children in our charge.
What can we do?" Miss Shotwell had asked him, standing erect and
dignified as ever—a slight tremor rising in her voice despite herself.

"The mob's liable to burn the place to the ground, ma'am, they
can't stay here—"

"They can't *not* stay here," Billy had spoken up then. He had never
talked in such a way to a New York City policeman in his life, and
Sergeant Murphy had looked him over coolly, as if deciding whether
to knock him to the floor with his nightstick then and there.

"They can't run no more," he had continued anyway. "They don't
have a chance out there."

He turned toward Miss Shotwell, as if he were addressing his
words only to her. She looked at him intently as he spoke, her jaws

pressed together so tightly that she might have been trying to break a walnut in them. Then she nodded slowly.

"Very well, then. They will have to stay."

Sergeant Murphy had shrugged, helpless.

"We'll do what we can, ma'am—but I can't say what that'll be, the two of us against a mob."

His tone was sharp, and not a little bitter. They all knew, the officers might be allowed to leave a bunch of hardheaded Negroes and orphans to their fate, but they could never abandon a couple of Yankee ladies.

And just what good would two men be against a mob—against a mob of the size and ferocity Billy had seen clogging the Asylum yard? Even their guns would be no good, would probably just enrage them—

"You'd better get 'em below to the basement, then," Sergeant Murphy told them, gesturing toward the stairs. "No use in advertisin' 'em, at least."

They had been in the cellar ever since. Like the basement in every station house, it was one long, open room. There were a few cells in the back, but most of it was an empty floor, where in the winter the most destitute families in the City could come and sleep, if they did not prefer to freeze on the street.

Now it was hotter than an oven and pitch-dark, save for a single candle the Yankee ladies kept lit. The green shades pulled down over the windows. Throughout the night and the morning, they had all tended to the children as best they could—waiting until it was dark, then taking them out to the necessary behind the station house in groups of two or three, hoping that no one would notice them. The sergeants, meanwhile, had brought them down water, and what little bread and meat they could find around the precinct house.

Some of the younger children had begun to whimper from the heat, and their hunger, but most of them remained still. Sitting huddled up against the wall, their small, solemn faces glistening with sweat. Looking up, attentive, when any adult went by. *Nothing like an orphan to understand the gravity of a situation.* Billy noticed Tad, half-hidden under the station-house stairs—the boy who had gone back for his little tin horse, whatever it meant to him. He smiled at him, and Tad smiled back, still fondling his horse.

But the whole time he was thinking, *He had to get back*.

It had been over twenty-four hours since he had told Ruth he would return with the money. He had stopped even asking for the time anymore, it seemed so pointless. Wondering what his wife must think had happened to him, if she assumed he was lying dead drunk, in an alley or a barroom somewhere. Or if she thought worse, with the riot sweeping back and forth over the town.

Never mind what they think of me, I know that I am safe. What about them?

He tried to tell himself that at least that lunatic, Johnny Dolan, could not possibly have found them through all this. But he knew that he could not count on any such thing. If the mobs downtown were anything like the one he had seen in the Asylum yard, it would be all the easier for a man to go in where he liked, do what he wanted.

He knew, too, that if Dolan came, the boy, Milton, would fight for his mother as long as there was a breath left in him. And that Dolan would kill him, too, as easily as he might kill a dog. It had been a long time, but Billy knew enough of the man. The way Ruth's face had looked, how he had battered her about, a woman—

He had to get back.

Upstairs, he could hear the precinct telegraph clatter to life from time to time, tapping out dispatches. One of the sergeants would come down every so often to tell them what they knew. In this way they learned that the orphans' asylum had been looted, and hacked apart, and burned to the ground, Sergeant McCluskey conveying it as gently and apologetically as he could.

Miss Murray had made a small, sad groan at the noise, thinking of the wide, handsome house. Miss Shotwell, by contrast, had sounded defiant, a touch of iron in her voice still.

"We have the children out safe, that is what matters!"

Do we?

After they had given the children what breakfast they could, Billy had stepped out into the alleyway behind the precinct house. Looking up and down the narrow alley before he did, then stripping the rough, itchy shirt over his head. He soaked it thoroughly under the pump there, ringing it out until it was no more than a hard, roped knot in his hands, then soaking it again. *His hands.* He flexed them out, under the water now, splashing some up over his face and chest.

Could these same hands have ever done what they once did? Build a boat? And what could they still do now?

He thought of that bottle of peach brandy suddenly, back in the cool closet in the asylum, and laughed to himself. *He should have finished it, after all*—hoping at least that the mob had burned the place to the ground before any of them got to sample some. It occurred to him, too, that there was probably some whiskey, somewhere, around this deserted Paddy station house—but he made himself put the thought out of his mind.

No. He could not be drunk now. They had to do something about the children. And he had to get back.

He had almost struck out for his home the night before, during the thunderstorm. Telling himself that he could move like a shadow through the City, a dark black man on a dark night, shielded by the rain. He had even thought he might get that strange white boy to help him, tell him some secret way—but sometime between when they had arrived at the station and when they had all been herded down to the basement, the child had slipped away again, as easily as he had come. Off no doubt to some other part of the vast game he had created for himself, in the midst of this riot.

Even without him, though, it would be easy enough. All he had to do was tell the Misses that he was going to the outhouse, then just run off. Padding down the streets through the cool, invigorating rain.

But how could he abandon all these children—to a pair of helpless old white ladies, Old Bert and Yolanda, the police sergeants? He thought, too, about what would happen if he did not make it—bushwacked and disposed of somewhere between the precinct house and Paradise Alley. He would be of no help to anyone then, here or there, it would be as if he had simply disappeared into the night.

He had stayed. *But for how long? How long could they hold out here—or before they were discovered by the mob?*

When the morning had passed with still no sign of relief or the riot abating, Miss Murray had gone out to find help. Cleverly letting her hair down first and covering her head with a black shawl—anything to make herself seem more like some Irish widow. They opened the front door to let her out—and Billy could hear the sound of the riot, like breakers against the shore, a regular rising and falling, the sort of sound he had once found so reassuring. There was the smell of things burning, too—so strong it seemed as if it must be coming from the next block.

Yet he knew that Miss Murray had the easier task, even walking out into all that. Unless she was hit by some stray shot or lunatic, she would be all right—a grey-haired white woman with a shawl over her head. It was the rest of them who would face the worst, and they knew it. Sergeant Murphy had even come downstairs and shown him where the gun case was in the precinct basement.

"If they get in, go ahead an' smash the glass, take what you want. You can give one to the old feller, too—" He had hooked a thumb toward grizzled Old Bert, waiting patiently in the far corner. "Hell, give 'em out to the women an' kiddies, if it comes to that."

The sergeant paused, sounding almost apologetic, his voice low in the stuffy room.

"I saw what they done to the draft office—"

Yet the mob had not come. And more hours had been lost—hours when he should have been moving, back to his family. Instead he was here, in this trap.

Going from one trap to the next. The Orphans' Asylum to this basement. Back to—home.

It had always been like that. Doing everything he could, taking his life in his hands to get out of one place—only to find it just as bad, if not worse, in the next. *Is that the lot of a black man in this world—or is it me?*

No. He had seen something else—the village, up there in what was now the central park. Small and circumscribed and incomplete as it was, ringed in by its enemies. Just two lanes, two churches, a few little houses, but a *place*—a black place, for black people, and whatever whites wanted to join them.

Like Ruth. But why had she gone to him there? And why had he let her?

He had thought about it often enough over the years. Why he had never married any of the Negro women in the village, despite the Reverend Betancourt's efforts to thrust different prospects before him. He had always wanted to wait, to have something he could offer a wife—a real job, a decent wage. Something he could respect himself for. The truth was, he had had precious few women at all in New

York, even prostitutes. *The very idea of how little he had, how little he had done shriveling him up inside.*

He had never intended to have anything to do with a white woman. He had seen how mixed-race couples were treated in the City, even in the Five Points where they were common. Their very appearance drawing the rage of white men much more than even the ordinary sight of a Negro, and he had wanted nothing to do with that.

But there she was, this skinny little girl, standing out in the road, waiting for him, and what was he supposed to do with her? She had not screamed when the slavers came. She had not balked or quailed, or asked him for anything. Only coming to his home and begging him to have her, and what was he to do?

That small, indissoluble strength, evident even then. Beaten and battered as bad as she was, ignorant, unlettered girl. Still coming back for more. She had been able enough to figure out who could help her when she needed to get rid of Johnny Dolan. She was willing to do whatever she could for him, too, never shirking from it.

Was it courage? he wondered. *Or just the blind, burrowing urge of existence? Going on and on, breeding and surviving, no matter the point.*

Before he knew it, he had married her. And thank God, too, he supposed, for when the village had been plowed under without warning he had been able to go back with her, down to the white wards of the City. To live on her block, with her people—

Another trap. The village pulled out from beneath them. A lot of white talk about legal deeds, and property rights, all to take a man's land away from him. It was gone just like that—the ramshackle houses they had so painstakingly jimmied together, and the two streets, and the small, whitewashed churches, and all the people. Scattered down through the fetid, noisy tenements and alleys where it was decided they should live instead. All the green niggers and the smoked Irish, mixed in together.

He had never liked it down in Paradise Alley. They had lost the first girl, Lillian, soon after moving in, and he had always blamed it on the place—on how close and foul the air was, the pigs running wild on the street. And down there he had always had to look out for the slavecatchers, especially at night. It was so much easier for them to get close to a black man along the dark, narrow streets—even a freed

man, or one who had never been a slave in his life. Slug him or drug
him, and bundle him off to the docks before anyone knew he was
missing.

Living there, he had thought for the first time that he might just
disappear. He had never felt quite that way before, not even at the
very depths of his existence, dancing for eels on the waterfront. He
had begun to stop in at The Glass House and the other saloons more
than ever, even though he knew how dangerous it was. Even though
he knew his children needed every penny of his wages, and he could
not stand to see the look in Ruth's eyes when he came home drunk in
the evening.

The thought had occurred to him that it would be easy enough to
make himself disappear. Ruth would not even blame him for it. She
might suspect—but she could put it down to the slavecatchers, or
some river gang, trawling the docks for bodies. He might even go
back, after a while, if he had gotten any money together. Say he had
escaped again, or been shanghaied off to Peru.

*He knew Ruth would take him back, even then. She would hold him,
and feel sorry for him, and welcome him back in without question. Maybe,
if he found some other, good place, he could even send for them—*

But he could not leave her. He could not say for sure if he had ever
really loved her, but they had a bond between them by then. He had
helped her to take another man, and bind him over to Egypt, and then
there was the family they had raised together. He could never forget
how she had cried when he came back and told her that they could not
afford a daguerreotype of Lillian. She had accepted it, she had not
even held it against him, but he knew what she must have been thinking. How any expense could be spared for the fleeting pleasure he
drew from a bottle, but none for a picture of the child—

*Yes, they had a bond. The usual bond of long-married people, forged
out of matching grudges and animosity, as much as anything else. And
yet, maybe he did love her.*

He had stayed on. Still going to his job every day, looking after the
orphans. Collecting his wages, and trying not to drink them all up on
the way home.

The war had awakened him again, for a while. *It would even give
him an excuse, a good, brave excuse to go.* He read the *North Star,* and
the *Anglo-African,* and the *Ram's Horn.* Eagerly searching for any

word of a Negro regiment, and dreaming of going off to the fight. Listening in rage whenever he heard some street-corner Tammany orator go on about the perfidy of his race.

"Not a black man in the Union lifts so much as a cook's spit to help defend our liberties—"

But the colored regiments had never been called. He could not even fight. It didn't make it any better, knowing that he should not go even if he could. That he had too many obligations here—Ruth, and the children, and the debts piling up, with everything costing more and more in the City since the war.

Then had come the strike, just a month ago. There had been strikes before, some in the very same shipyards that had rejected him, but he had never answered the call for strikebreakers. Telling himself that no matter what he was, he would not take another man's job, take bread out of the mouths of his children—not even a white man's.

But the longshoremen had walked out, and the strike had spread all along the waterfront. The ship joiners and the caulkers, the carpenters and the sailmakers and the mechanics, and he could not resist the idea of building a ship, at least once more, just to see how it felt again. Handbills had gone up, calling for men—even for skilled Negro workers—and the next morning he had risen even earlier than usual, and gone down to the waterfront with all his fine, unused tools.

The wharves along the Hudson were in a tumult. Even before it was light out yet, the Irish and German strikers were jamming the surrounding streets—setting smoky fires in the ash bins, screaming and grabbing at the scabs. Pummeling any black man they could get hold of, yelling out their old refrain:

"This is a white man's waterfront!"

He had had to go through an empty warehouse he knew about, dashing across the street to the dock where the handbills said to report. He had just made it, at that. Along the piers a large contingent of soldiers, with fixed bayonets, was barely holding the strikers at bay. The troops had had to pull him almost literally out of the hands of the mob, and on into a small wooden shed on the dock. There he had huddled inside, at the end of a row of white drunks, reeking of bad whiskey and body odor. One other colored man, dressed in his best clothes, squatted on the other end of the line—carefully avoiding his eyes.

"*Name?*" the hiring agent had asked—a burly, bearded Yankee working a toothpick around with his teeth. Two more uniformed soldiers, also with rifles and fixed bayonets, standing just behind him.

"Billy. Um, Billy Dolan," he had said, holding on to his own name, out of some last hope that he might need it again.

"All right, Billy *Dolan*," the hiring agent had snorted. "Tell all your friends in County Cork you can bring 'em over. Two dollars a day, twenty-five cents for overtime."

"Two dollars?"

"That's right. Take it or leave it. More, *maybe*, if you can do skilled work."

"But they're only asking for one seventy-five a day," he said wonderingly, gesturing back toward the howling mob outside.

The hard, acute Yankee's eyes glinted with amusement.

"Well, don't worry, Mr. *Dolan*. It ain't like it's gonna last."

He had gone ahead and signed his name—his made-up name—and the Yankee agent had dribbled his signing bonus, a few small gold coins, into his hand. Then he had walked back out on the slip with the other scabs. Some thirty or forty of them now, all told—himself, and the man he had seen in the shed, the only Negroes.

It was a white waterfront even now—even for scabs. But then what were the strikers yelling about? Did they see only the black and tan?

A leaky, moss-covered barge was poled up alongside, and they were ordered onboard. There they waited—for what, nobody bothered to inform them. Instead they simply stood in the boat, a steady, drizzling rain beginning to fall. The water pooling up in greasy puddles around their feet, in the shallow bottom of the barge. They could see the mob, up along the wharf, still shaking their fists and screaming at them, just held back by the soldiers.

"*Dirty scabs! Dirty scabs! Dirty, dirty, nigger scabs!*"

Niggers? He looked at the white drunks on either side of him—

"*You'll never live to spend it!*"

A hail of rocks, and thick clods of dirt, and horse manure came pelting down upon them. One of the rocks hit the man standing next to Billy—knocking him down, cutting a bloody divot in his head. He fell, and Billy and another man helped him back up, looking toward where the rock had come from.

Billy studied the faces of the men above them—pinched and

hollow-cheeked and dirty, cheering viciously at the blow they had landed. Their eyes gleaming with hatred. They jabbed their hands around their necks, to imitate a noose.

"You'll never live to enjoy it!"

A steam sloop chugged slowly up, fastening itself along their starboard side. A long line of soldiers clamored over into their barge, the strikebreakers silently falling back to make room for them. *Protection at last,* Billy thought—but then he saw that the soldiers were all unarmed. Many of their faces were slack and sallow, their uniforms loose and ill-fitting, some of them with arms still in slings. Then came another group that had to be helped over by the rest of them—five or six men at a time, and all chained to each other by their ankles.

Invalids and convicts, he realized. *That's who we're fit to work with.*

He had stood there watching them slowly fill up the boat, with his satchel of shiny, still-new tools in one hand and the rain soaking through his hat. The chained men, clinking and shuffling slowly onto the boat, the water rising up their ragged blue pants.

He had climbed up off the barge then—moving quickly before he could think anymore about what he was doing. He had hoisted himself back onto the wharf with one arm, tucking his precious tools up under the other. *Still unused.* Not that his repentance would do him any good, he knew. He had to sprint back into the City as fast as he could—the men from the mob on the dock chasing after him at once, seeking to vent their rage on whoever they could get hold of. Billy's lungs pounding in his chest, the jeers of the mob trailing after him.

And afterward, he had gone back to his house, and tried to hold in his rage. Ruth had been understanding, though she didn't even know what it was all about, and he had appreciated it, and loved her for it. But the truth was, she still did not know, she still had no good idea of what it was that he had lost—

There was the sound of shouting, and running feet, suddenly very loud and near. Billy listened to it in the torpor of the basement, not understanding it at first as anything more than the same sounds of the riot. Then Sergeant Murphy came running down the steps.

"Pardon, ma'am, but they're very close now," he reported to Miss Shotwell.

"What? What's that?"

She blinked and pulled herself up straight—as much in a trance as Billy was from the heat.

"The *mob,* ma'am. There's a bunch of the bummers just outside now. Sergeant McCluskey an' me have been watchin' 'em. They brung a keg a whiskey they been enjoyin', but now they're eyein' the precinct house. When they drink up enough courage, you can expect 'em to come."

Miss Shotwell blinked at him.

"I see."

"Sergeant McCluskey an' me thought you should know, ma'am," Murphy went on—the urgency clear in the man's voice, beneath his cool, deferential words. "We'll stay as long as we can, but you got to get the children out. By the back, if you can—"

"Thank you. Thank you for your help."

Miss Shotwell repeated the words dully, as if she did not quite understand them. She stared around the cellar at the orphan children, crouched in the shadows, the recesses of the basement.

Like a child's game, Billy recognized. Trying to fade back into the corners, the dark places. Just trying to disappear.

But it wouldn't work—not if they burned the place. Fire worked its way into every corner, that was its terror, its usefulness as the mob's weapon. They could try to stay out of the way as much as they liked, it would not work with the white folks.

Another trap—

He stood up—seeing the children's eyes swing over to him. As alert as ever to any movement—to danger—despite the heat. Fully aware of what was going on, just waiting for their next instructions.

How they trust us, just because we're adults. As much as that trust has been betrayed.

He saw Miss Shotwell's face, looking strained to the point of desperation now. Still willing to go on—but where? What chance did they all have, so many of them together, with the whole City on fire?

"Don't go anywhere. Don't go anywhere, *yet,*" he told her quietly, making sure she understood, and headed for the stairs. Pausing for a moment by the banister when he saw Tad there, crouched under the staircase. Staring silently up at Billy, his face blank now—still clutching his tiny tin horse in his hands.

Trying to be even smaller than the rest, tucked away in an even darker corner.

"Don't you go anywhere, neither." He smiled at Tad, running a finger over his talisman. "I don't want to have to go look for you again."

He got a brief, involuntary smile from the boy. Then he was flying up the stairs, after the sergeant, running up to the first floor. Murphy staring at him as if he had lost his mind—his lips flattening into a knowing exasperation. *He thinks I am going to run out—*

"It's no good, son, there's too many of 'em out there," Murphy started to tell him. A serious young Irish face beneath his high Metropolitans hat, a thick, red-brown mustache creeping down to his chin to make him look older. His eyes, at least, betrayed a certain sympathy—a sympathy for them all, trapped as they were in his basement.

"You'd never get through, not even alone. Best try to make it out the back, with the others. We'll hold 'em off so long's we can—"

"I'll be right out here," Billy Dove told him.

Reveling in his freedom, now, knowing what he was going to do. *Is this the only real freedom you get? At the end?*

He bolted on out the front door, before either of the sergeants could stop him. A little woozy in the sudden glare of the sun, the sharp taste of smoke in the air, after so many hours down in the cloistered dark. Forcing himself to walk straight, at least at first—not wanting the white cops to think that he was afraid. *Still possessing that much pride, at least.*

Yet he did feel fear when he saw how many they were. Three or four dozen of them, at least, standing and crouching around their keg, just across the street from the precinct house. They looked blooded, too—reeking of smoke, their coats sooted. Smoking their pipes, laughing a little too loudly as they held their cups up to the tap.

Like so many other, bitter groups of men he had seen, crouched around their stills. But freed now—just like him—to do as they pleased. To take out all their bitterness on whoever they chose—

He had thought that if worst came to worst, he could fight, or flee—pull them away from the precinct house. But seeing their number now he realized they could easily tear him to pieces right here, and there would be nothing he could do about it. Nor was he sure yet of just what he would do—letting the inspiration of the moment drive him on. Moving into the trap this time, at least, with the full knowledge of what he was doing.

Free or not free—

He put the tremble back into his legs as he approached them. Not as if from fear but from inebriation—a condition he knew much better. Starting to weave and stumble as he walked toward the white men, letting his mouth fall into a slack, drunkard's grin. Remembering what he had learned, back when he used to dance for eels along the dock.

He was only a few feet away before they even noticed him. Crowding around the whiskey keg, a name stamped on it. *Spelman's*—no doubt the establishment they had taken it from. They were still making wandering, drunken, self-important speeches to each other but they fell silent, one by one, when they saw *him* coming. The amazement etched plainly across their faces as they watched this drunken black man walking straight up to them.

"*Hail, all ye bummers!*" Billy shouted out at the top of his voice, waving a hand dramatically over his head in salute. His audience completely, dangerously silent now. Stunned and uncertain but still just watching him, like dogs deciding whether to sic. *It would not do. There had to be something more.*

He braced himself, and made a sudden, wild leap, landing right on the head of the whiskey keg—just praying that it did not cave in, or fall over. Making sure to balance drunkenly, nearly falling over one way, then the other—holding on to the surprise.

"*Dislike me not for my complexion, fellow bummers!*" he shouted again.

Alone there among dozens of the white men, closing in around him. Their coats covered with blood and ash, still wide-eyed and silent. Yet even as they moved in, he could see some of them start to snicker. More showing their teeth, their mouths pink and jagged—

"We live in a happy day, oh my bummers! And I am happy to be able to address so respectable and intelligent an audience as that now before me."

There were more snickers, some outright laughs—a few suspicious looks as well. The white men seemed just like those at the docks, who used to watch him dance. Suspecting, perhaps, that they were being made fun of but unable to admit to any such thing. Unable to see him as anything more than a crazy, drunken nigger, for if he *were* anything more—if he were able to actually mimic and abuse them so faithfully—then they would require some restitution beyond what even their knives and ropes could give them.

"We, fellow bummers, are the foundation of New York City! And if the foundation moves, you know, the structure falls!"

He had them now, the men laughing despite themselves. Actually giggling—these gang *b'hoys* and hod carriers, laborers who toiled all day in the construction pits or the stockyards. Taking him for what he wanted to be, for what *they* wanted him to be. Shouting back to him as they might shout the familiar responses to a Bowery minstrel show.

"It *is* falling!"

"Bully for you! Go on, darkie!"

He tottered above them, unsure of just what to say now. Unsure of what he *could* say, of what he could get them to do. He tried to think of what there was, and what he might lead them to, way up here, on the rim of the City. Longing for the quicksilver, slippery way his brain worked when he had lubricated it with alcohol. Yet knowing that it was just as well, that he could not afford a single slip—

"Hey, c'mon now, Juba! Don't stop now. Give us a little breakdown!"

The voice belonged to a particularly tall white man, who had pushed his way to the front. He had cold blue eyes, and a goatee cut in the minimal, affected style of the French emperor. Billy thought that he detected a drawl. The man was smiling, at least showing his teeth, but there was no real mirth in his face.

"Let's see it now, bummer! Breakdown!"

"Yeah, a breakdown!"

The others took up the cry, and slowly, awkwardly at first, Billy began to go into the dance he had last done so long ago, down on the docks. Slipping into the old steps—the bowlegged squats and kicks that the white men had never understood as a mockery of their own, self-important struts.

The same, humiliating dance that he had hated, so many years ago, that had made him swear he would just as soon throw himself in the river if that was all he could do. If he could not walk off this damned island—

Only making sure this time to exaggerate it even more—keeping in mind that he was supposed to be drunk. Weaving back and forth as far as the barrelhead would allow. Wobbling on the very edge, nearly falling off a dozen times—until the whites below him were actually rushing to the edge to catch him. Cheering and clapping and hallooing with each new twist and bend he made.

"Go it! Go it, boy!"

The cheering and laughter kept up until at last he wound down. Admitting desperately to himself that he still had no idea of what to do next, knowing only that he could not dance anymore. He moved slower and slower, until he finally stood, wobbling—truly exhausted—on the edge of the keg. The Paddies still cheering him. But he had nothing else to give them and here they still were, just outside the precinct house and all the children tucked away in its basement. The blue-eyed Southerner standing directly below him now. His mouth still smiling, but not his eyes.

"All right. All right, now," he drawled. "That was pretty good. Jump on down here now, boy, let us stand you to a drink."

He made to climb down—but the Southerner stopped him with a hand.

"No, no. I said *jump*. Go ahead an' jump, we'll catch ya. Or don't ya trust a white man?"

"Jump, jump!" the rest of the men right around the barrel began to chant, picking up the idea. They stood before him, their arms outstretched as if they really would catch him.

"Jump, jump!"

This wasn't good—he was letting them call what he should do now. Billy could see the Southerner sneaking little smiles, and winks and nods to the other white men—some hint of real amusement on his face for the first time. But there was nothing for it now. Billy struck another exaggerated pose, holding his nose as if he were about to dive into water.

"Jump, jump!"

He let himself go then, falling forward, straight off the keg—the gauntlet of grinning, jagged faces coming up at him fast. At the last instant, though, just as he had suspected, they all pulled away—leaving him to fall face first onto the pavement. The street struck his face and his body with brutal force and he felt something in his nose and mouth crack, a wetness spurting up along his cheek. The fall had nearly knocked him out—which he knew would be fatal. As it was he had to lie there for a long moment, prostrate with the pain, fighting to retain consciousness.

"Aw, we missed you!" he heard the Southerner's voice boom above him. "How'd *that* step go, niggah?"

There was a fresh burst of laughter—but harsher this time, more raw and violent. Billy still struggled on the ground to get his breath. Realizing, stunned as he was, that now that they had hurt him—that the first blow had been struck—they would be all the more willing to finish him off.

The mood of the mob swinging at once, and he had already been reduced partway, from man to bleeding thing. He knew that he had to say something—

"My fellow bummers," he managed to croak out with what little breath he could gather, hoping they could hear him. Forcing himself up to his hands and knees—and forcing a comic grimace. Deliberately spreading his mouth as wide as the faces he saw on the posters for minstrel shows, curling back his lips from his teeth—

"My fellow bummers. The foundation has *indeed* moved. And the structure *has* fallen!"

There was a roar above him—their brassy, exaggerated, white laughter ringing in his ears. Then they were picking him up, even dusting off his blood-splattered clothes. The blue-eyed Southerner, he noticed, receding from the crowd right around him. The rest of them hauled him on back to the keg and filled up a tin cup with whiskey, pushed it into his hand. Standing, grinning, around him, as he sat on the curb. Knowing he could not refuse their hospitality, he put it to his mouth, lapping eagerly at the liquor.

"How's that, nigger? The best damned whiskey you ever had!"

They crowed above him, their laughter still echoing painfully in his head—and he had to admit they were right. *Spelman's* must be a first-class establishment. The whiskey went down smoother than anything he had ever tasted, like fine wine compared to what he was used to from the woods stills, or the block-and-fall joints by the river. He wanted to spit it in their faces.

"Hey, Juba—whattaya say? Come with us!"

"Yeah, come along with us! We'll keep ya safe —"

"First we'll burn that frog shop, over there—"

Pointing to the precinct house across the street

"—then there'll be plenty more to bum an' drink!"

"Burn the *police* house?!" Bulging his eyes out, minstrel-like, as if the very idea filled him with fear.

"It'll be easy! If it's like the others we seen today, there won't be more'n those two cops in there—"

Pointing toward the sergeants where they stood, watching them, just in front of the station-house door. *So they knew. Knew it was defenseless—even if they did not know the children were in there—*

"Oh, no, oh, no thanks, boss," Billy told them, putting up his hands. The fine whiskey hot and cloying on his tongue—but trying to talk, trying to *think.*

"I just got outta there, *as is.*"

They laughed again, and he tried desperately to come up with something they might like, something else he could offer them. His mind wandering to the orphans, sitting with their legs tucked up, in the shadows along the wall, trying to be as small and inconspicuous as possible—

They were beginning to stroll on out into the street. A few of them already shouting things out to the sergeants, who only glared silently back from the door. More of them, back in the crowd, feeling around on the ground for loose stones. *All those children down there, trying to shrink into the wall, to shrink away from the fire.* Tad, clutching his tin horse under the stairs—

Then he had it. What was it that the Irish would love above all things?

"My fellow bummers!" he said, staggering up to his feet. Adopting the portentous, minstrel voice he had used before. Holding his hands up over his head as if he were testifying, and they stopped—at least for a moment they stopped, grinning slackly. Wondering if more fun were in store.

"My fellow bummers! Why should we risk our bodies to injury— to the outrageous fortune that may be visited upon us by those gentlemen over there?"

He nodded in the direction of Murphy and McCluskey, standing in the door like two blocks of granite. There were a few more snickers— but a hardening of the laughter now, in anticipation.

"Oh, 't'ain't gonna be no injury, Juba. They'll run like rabbits, always do."

"C'mon, whattaya scared of, uncle?"

"Nay, bummers, why should we distress ourselves when we do not have to? Why should we even walk—*when we can ride?*"

That got their attention.

"What's that? What's the darkie on about?"

"Horses!" he bellowed at them. "I know where there's enough horses for all of us!"

That stopped them in their tracks. Each man of them, the poor earthbound Paddies, thinking what it would be like to ride, like a real lord. Their eyes betraying their eagerness as they turned to him.

"Where is this now, ya say?"

"Ya better be talkin' for real, nigger—"

"I *know,*" he repeated, thinking of the stagecoach line stables he remembered, up by Fifty-ninth Street. Far enough away from the precinct house.

But he had no idea whether they would still be there, or if the stage line had already removed its stock. Not even positive he could remember just where the stables were—

"To *ride.* Enough horses for *everyone* to ride."

That had done it. The white men veering instantly away from the precinct house, moving uptown, as he directed them. And as if in reaction he also felt a hand on his collar, the breath of a man scored with whiskey on his neck. He was not surprised to catch the hint of the pointed, imperial whiskers out of the corner of his eye.

"You better be tellin' the truth now, nigger. Just where are these horses, anyhow?"

"Ah, go easy on 'im, Langdon!"

"If he knows so much about it, let him take us to 'em. That way he can explain if they ain't where they're supposed to be."

The voice as cold and unyielding as the man's blue eyes. But it was exactly what Billy had wanted—what he had wanted all along, even as he pretended to tremble and quiver under the white man's hands.

"Sure," he told them, trying to make his mouth sound dry. "Sure, I'll show ya."

They marched him on up to Fifty-ninth Street then. The Southerner with the Louis Napoleon beard frog-walking him the whole way, one hand on his collar, the other on his belt. Digging his knee deliberately into his thighs and joints from time to time.

Billy took it all, making sure to moan and tremble from time to time. Resenting each breath of the man—just hoping that the stables would still be where he thought he remembered them. The horses—any horses—still inside. Thinking of how even if he survived this he still had to get downtown, to his family. And yet at the center he was calmer than he thought he had ever been.

He had got them away from the orphans. At least he had done that much. It was vital that he still get away alive, that he get back down-

town—get back to Ruth and his children, the boy, Milton, waiting
for him there. Strong and willful as a two-year-old colt, but just as
innocent.

*What would he do without his father? Without someone to guide him
through these streets, here in this City where one misstep could kill him—*
Yet still there was that spreading, impenetrable calm at his center.
Untroubled by any obstacle ahead of him, by even this stranded,
drunken old slavecatcher or overseer pushing him up the avenue.
Maybe it was just the fine whiskey in him. He had had this same invulnerable feeling before when he was drinking—just fleetingly, just for
a few moments before the liquor took its inevitable downward lurch.

But still—he had done this much. He had gotten them away from
the orphans. That was something, anyway. Terrible things might still
be done to him, he knew he could still end up screaming for his life or
screaming for them to kill him—but there was nothing he could do
about that. Being marched uptown, up the island that he had once
tried to walk off, he understood, now, that he could never have left
them. Not Ruth, or Milton, or his other children. Not any of the small
black faces, staring up at him from the dark as he had gone up the
stairs.

It was a trap, all right.

They reached the stage-line stables. They were still there, at least,
right where he had remembered them, at Fifty-ninth Street and the
Fifth Avenue. The doors were chained shut, though, a large, flaking
cardinal painted across them, over the words *RED BIRD STAGE
LINE.* There was no indication of any remaining horses—no sign of
life at all about the stables.

"Sure, horses for all of us," Langdon, the Southerner, sneered
behind him. "What were you tryin' to get us *away* from, nigger?
That's what I want to know. What were you lookin' to distract us
from, with all that Juba act?"

Maybe it wasn't enough. Maybe he had won nothing, after all. The
thought beginning to seep through him like bad water. Billy could feel
the man starting to bend down, certain that he had a knife in his boot
he was reaching for. He would wait until he had bent all the way down
for it, when he was most vulnerable. Then he would shove an elbow
into the man's face, wrest the knife away and do him, right there. He
would try to run off north, leading the rest of them farther away from

the precinct house. But even if they caught him, they would still be distracted, entertaining themselves tearing him apart—

There was a heavy knock from inside the stables. Then another sound, like a muffled sneeze. The white men hurried up to the door, pulling and tearing at the chain with whatever knives and spanners they had with them.

"Hey, c'mon, Langdon! Maybe there's somethin' to what he's sayin'—"

The Southerner suddenly straightened up, releasing his grip on him. Pushing past, as intent on the prospect of horses now as the rest of them. They had the chain off, and were peeling back the wide, heavy stable doors. Revealing there a pair of sparkling-new red stage-coaches—and the horses.

There were more than even Billy could have hoped for. Dozens of them, horses of all colors, bay and chestnut, and white and black and even palominos. All standing jammed into their stalls, sometimes as many as two or three in one partition—the drivers and stablehands apparently having shoved them in and fled after the start of the riot, leaving their stock to fend for themselves.

"Horses!"

"Enough for our own goddamned Black Horse Cavalry!"

The Paddies ran to them as if it were Christmas morning. Tearing down the stall doors, leading their mounts out into the street. Climbing up on them at once. A few of them bothered to throw bridles over their heads, but the rest simply clutching their manes—all of them riding bareback.

"Horses, god*damn*it!"

They were mostly big, heavy animals, bred for hauling wagons and coaches, slow-looking and lugubrious in their stalls. But once they were taken out onto the street and subjected to the touch of the Irishmen, they began to rear and bolt—racing off suddenly, throwing their riders into the street or leaving them holding on for dear life to the reins.

The men didn't seem to care, shouting and laughing as the horses carried them away. Scrambling back up and throwing themselves over their wide backs again and again, even after they'd been dumped on their heads along the pavement. He saw Langdon, the Southerner, clinging to a pale horse that bolted across the street and went smashing right through the windows of a deserted saloon there. In another moment it was back out, bursting through the swinging doors—Langdon still with his arms clutched around its neck for dear life.

Another man, who actually seemed able to control his horse a little, came riding out on a chestnut mare, blowing on a long brass coach horn he had found. He looked down on Billy, where he was trying to dodge the immense animals careening and clamoring all around him, mouths already foaming at their bits.

"G'wan an' getch yerself one, Juba! You earned it!" he shouted, waving at where the remaining horses were now kicking the bejesus out of the stables, and the remaining stagecoaches, slamming one Irishman after another against the walls.

Billy looked up at the man and smiled appeasingly. He was already backing away, ready to bolt back down to the precinct house. The horses were carrying the rest of the mob off, on up Manhattan, or over into the new park, or away to the west. The Irishmen still roaring with glee, chasing after their runaway steeds. The horse bolted under the man with the horn as well, pulling him away even as he blew out more trumpet blasts.

"G'wan!" he called back over his shoulder to Billy. "Ah, but isn't this the day, when niggers will ride!"

❦ · 59 · ❧

JOHNNY DOLAN

In the summers he had made money killing dogs. The Board of Aldermen paid fifty cents for each dead stray, and there were always thousands of them on the street. Mad from the heat, fighting the pigs for the garbage in the gutter, foaming at the mouth and biting anyone who got in their way—

Yet they always seemed to know when the dog killers were out. They melted away, into the back alleys, and the tenement courtyards and cellars, leaving only the pigs, who were far too valuable to kill for sport.

He had to smoke them out, club in hand. Learning how they thought and moved, cornering them before they smelled him coming.

The same way he had snuck up on the officer as he waved his sword out on the street. Going in through the back door. Moving swiftly across the room of red and amber light, reflected through the apothecary jars. The mob's noise muting his footsteps.

He had taken the sign in his hand, and knocked the officer to the ground with it. Then he had put it back over his neck himself—the mob swarming in on the downed man—

There was usually a crowd when they went to kill the dogs, too. Half of them would be gathered around some boy or his mother, screaming at him not to kill the beloved old family pet. The other half rooting against the animal—hoping to see some kind of spectacle, at least a death.

He dispatched the dogs the same way he had the officer, with his club. One sure whack across the head. A grunt of triumph, then he had walked off again, uninterested in what the mob might do to the man. *Only looking for what was his.*

He had been content to shelter in the mob. Absently fingering the sign that had been hung around his chest—the one he had hit the officer with. From time to time, when it seemed right, bellowing out the sentiments engraved there like a wounded bull.

"No draft! No draft! No draft!"

The men and women all around him absorbed in their destruction. Pulling apart houses, hotels, bars, streetcars along the Third Avenue. Pulling up lampposts, and the streets themselves.

Ripping it all up. Ripping it all up, picking it apart. Somehow, surely, this way he would find where they were hiding—

He had wandered along aimlessly with them. Sleepless and light-headed in the heavy, wet heat, his very senses betraying him. Hefting the paving stones, which felt now light as a loaf of bread in his hand—hurling them effortlessly through the windows of the shops, the train cars.

And when the cops had attacked, or the troops had leveled their rifles, he had found that he was not afraid at all. Eager to come to grips with them, to smash and kill, and see the worst that they could do to him. Even when the troops had fired at him, point-blank, he had not been afraid, had not tried to move out of the way. Somebody trying to scramble back down the street had fallen into him, pulled him down just before the volley whizzed over their heads.

He had gotten back up—the block of wood still secured around his neck, the flag still over his shoulders. Trudging on with the mob, watching their looting and marauding with indifference.

Just ahead of him now, two black men were pulled bodily from the basement of a boardinghouse. As he watched they were beaten to the sidewalk, robbed and stripped of their clothes. Still struggling to preserve their modesty while ropes were thrown around their necks. One of them was able to break free, sprinting down the street for his life, cutting his feet on the sharp paving stones, the broken glass with every step, but still running.

The other one, not so lucky, was lifted up to a lamppost, a fire set under him. Still kicking his naked legs, still struggling. Dolan turned away, brooding—

Ruth. She had betrayed him for a black man. He had to find her just for that, if nothing else—

That was who the darkie in the boat must have been, the night he was shanghaied. *Her nigger lover.* He had figured that much out, over the many years, though he had not seen it at the time. Going on like some poor ben about seeing his brother again. Noticing only at the last moment, in the boat, how nervous the brother-in-law, Tom, was acting. Only then had he understood how unlikely it really was that his brother had survived, that he might actually be waiting out in the fog-shrouded harbor for him, to help him escape. *How he had fooled himself*—

Before he could move, the nigger behind him had thrown the burlap bag over his head. *Bagged like a quail in the bush.* Had it been his plan all along, then? It did not seem possible that it was Ruth, her brains so addled before he had ever laid a hand on her. *But to be outsmarted by a nigger*—

The one thing he had never been able to figure out was why they hadn't simply sold him, and collected the reward money for Old Man Noe's murder. They could have seen him hanged, and had the cabinet in the bargain. *That would have been the smart play. So why?* Some sort of gratitude for his having saved her neck in the first place? A woman's sentimentality?

Unless it wasn't either one of them. Unless it had all been Deirdre's idea from the start.

She would not have minded seeing him disappear. *Not quite dead, but gone, that would have been her way.* They had always been getting him jobs, Tom and Deirdre. Working on City road crews, or sweeping the floor at The Place of Blood. Getting him into the Black Joke company.

He had never stayed with any of it for very long. Preferring to make what money he could killing dogs or fighting, working construction or running with the river gangs.

What did she care—she or the church she took refuge in? Leaving them all back there, to starve in the workhouse. Leaving him and his Da to walk the capstan, and his sister Kathleen to take it up against the yard wall and their brother, their poor brother Pat, stuck in the idiot's ward. Until it was time to be brought up to the black gable, and slid down into the earth.

He had seen the way Deirdre frowned, the few times he had been
prevailed upon to bring Ruth over. Tom, too—both of them staring
at Ruth's bruised face, her cut lip. Dolan had always made sure to dec-
orate her real good, before they went. Sitting her down in their parlor,
just to challenge them, to see if they would say anything. *Here we are.
What are you going to do about it?*

Deirdre had never understood it. Nor Ruth herself, quaking when
he came in after a fight, never fathoming how much he still wanted to
hit and be hit. Trying not to provoke him, to stay out of his way—as
if that were possible. *She had never understood anything, it could not
have been she who shipped him.*

Or couldn't it? After all, she must have been the one who had
found his swag. Old Man Noe's watch and fob, and that dog-headed
cane, and another thing or two of a more delicate nature.

He should never have taken that off the man. It was a desecration—
and besides, it had ensured that the newspapers would never let the
case drop. He had done it out of pique, his wrath over the old man's
Yankee presumption, trying to have him arrested. Instead of simply
giving him a good crack and running away, he had had to finish him
off—but even that had not been enough. The old bastard lying still
and broken beneath him, but he had had to pull out his thumb
gouger—

He had been scouting the new brush factory in Greenwich Street
for weeks. Three stories high, the frame and the brickwork completed, but the inside still unfinished. The firm name already lettered
just under the eaves: *Noe's Industrial Brushes, Est. 1848.* Dolan had
cracked the casa easily enough. It was a Sunday morning, the quietest
time of the week on the street, and he had broken the lock and chain
across the door at his leisure, then strolled up the temporary carpenters' staircases.

Yet it had been slim pickings. None of the mammoth black brush
machines were bolted to the floor yet. There were no fixtures or furniture, or anything of glass, the floors not even finished.

It was only when he had reached the roof that Dolan had seen
something worth the taking. They had already lined the gutters with
lead, but it hadn't been soldered down yet. It was an easy enough
proposition for him to take the short crowbar, the one that fit in his
jacket for just such jobs, and pry it loose. Knowing he could get a good

price for it, selling it to any of the construction yards along the West Side—

He had already pulled out half the curved lead sections from the front gutter when he felt the hand on his collar. Dolan had let it jerk him to his feet, thinking it must a cop. So intent on his work, so secure that he had never even heard the steps approaching. It was the workmen's day off, and there had been no watchman in sight, he had made sure of that. He could only think that it had to be some ambitious new beat cop, looking to land himself in a meatier precinct.

Instead he found himself looking up at a white-haired man in a high silk hat and a frock coat, holding a walking stick menacingly over his head. Old Man Noe himself. The face clenched and livid—not unlike the portraits of General Jackson that hung in every Tammany clubhouse and saloon. He clutched Dolan's collar with surprising strength, shaking the walking stick at him.

"What are you about here, you scoundrel?"

"I just come up, sir, to correct me work from the week," Dolan pleaded as meekly and fawningly as he could manage. Hoping the brush manufacturer would not be able to tell one of his workers from another. Yet even as he tried to look his most imploring, his eyes had stuck on the glint of Noe's golden, dog's-head cane. The ears like that of a jackal—

"Work!" Noe had sneered at him. "You don't work for me, lad, that's for certain! I've never hired a thief and a liar like you in my life. You're up here trying to steal my gutters!"

"All right, all right, just leave it," Dolan had told him in his regular voice. Trying to work his collar loose from the old man's grip. The red, unreasoning anger beginning to rise in him when he could not.

Another few minutes and he would have had a good score to peddle. Now he had to listen to this old man, this factory owner, tell him about work.

"Just lemme get outta here an' you can have the damned gutters—"

But the old man did not loosen his grip, instead yanking Dolan around and toward the roof door. Pushing him back toward the stairs.

"The hell you say! You're not getting off this one, you miscreant! I'm takin' ye straight away to the precinct house!"

Trying to keep the red rage down while he let the old man march him down the makeshift stairs from the roof to the third floor. Still talking at him all the way.

"Tearing up a new factory, for your own pocket! D'ya know how many men a place such as this employs? But that's all your sort thinks about, just what you can steal from it—"

So he would just take him off to prison now. After the workhouse, and that damned boat, drinking water out of iodine barrels. After all that he had put up with, to live even after he was dead. They would wall him up in a prison, and make him work just for them. Damned if they would.

"You'll see, they'll set you to it up in Ossining! No easy job tearing up gutters there! They'll have you breaking rocks, and walking the capstan—"

They were starting down the stairs to the second floor then, and on the next step, Dolan stuck out a hand, grabbing onto the wobbly carpenters' banister. He pivoted about, drawing the crowbar from his coat at the same time, and struck down hard—snapping the arm Noe had on his collar in one swift, satisfying blow.

The old man staggered back, and Dolan watched as all the color drained from his face. His eyes widening with fear behind his spectacles, truly understanding for the first time what he had caught.

It was too late. Noe tried to bring the walking stick down on him but Dolan was already moving under it, the cane falling ineffectually on his back and shoulders. He brought the crowbar up again, smashing Noe across the chin, and he fell back over the top stair, landing hard on the floor—but still conscious, still flailing out with the cane. Dolan cursed as it whacked into his shins, nearly knocking him down, and then the old man was scrambling to get up, panting as he tried to lift himself.

But Dolan stayed over him. Before Noe could rise he stomped a foot down on his chest, pinning him to the ground. He went back down with a small, tired sigh, and Dolan hit him again with the iron bar. He was still trying to squirm away after that, so Dolan held him in place with his foot and hit him again, then again and again. Sending the walking stick flying across the floor, knocking the spectacles off his face—breaking his other arm and smashing away at him until at last the old man lay still beneath him.

"Whatta you know about work? *Whatta you know about work?*"

Noe's eyes unshielded now, still wide with their final realization.

Seeing the monster before him. Dolan had the thumb gouger out and in place before he even fully knew it. Digging in at the left orb, feeling the tendons stretch before the dull, awful pop.

That had been enough, finally. He left the other one, still staring up at him, just as horrified and senseless. Its twin, safely ensconced in his gouger—looking out at the world with a new and rounded objectivity.

Still, he had to do something about what remained. He had untied the red handkerchief from around his own neck and knotted it around Old Man Noe's head—around both sockets, empty and filled. Ready to leave, now that this task was completed—with no stomach to go back up, finish tearing out the gutter. *Besides, what if someone had heard?*

Yet he realized that, throughout the whole struggle, the old man had made no sound—did not scream or yell, or cry out to anyone. *He must've been alone, with no chance of rescue.* Those eyes, reflecting the full horror of the mistake he had made. Thinking himself, as a brush-factory owner, invulnerable to such a fate.

Take him off and make him work. Breaking rocks, walking the capstan. Damned if he would.

He had rifled through the old man's pockets. Pulling out the watch and fob, and chain. A diamond tie clasp and gold cufflinks, a small wad of banknotes, and a little silver. Then he had fled. Noticing only at the bottom of the stairs the dog-headed walking stick, where it had rolled.

He picked it up instinctively, twirling it even as he carried it out of the factory. Whistling tunelessly, forcing himself to seem as unconcerned as possible for whosoever might be watching—might have noticed a man with a stick go into the factory.

But Greenwich Street had still been all but deserted as he strolled away, the church bells ringing all over the Village. He had sauntered up the street—belatedly making sure to conceal the head of the cane, at least, under his hand. Knowing he should have simply left it with the old man's body but unwilling to let it go, enjoying the heft and elegance of it in his hand, the open, leering mouth of the dog, caught in gold.

It was only when he was on the corner, waiting for the omnibus, that he realized James Noe's left eye was still on his thumb.

TOM O'KANE

He would have liked to sit down, and rest his leg, but the large, vaulted waiting room in the Hoboken station was filled with refugees from the City. Most of them were Negroes, their black and brown faces like so many others he had seen down in Virginia. *The contraband, fleeing to the Union lines from their households and plantations.*

Yet those faces had at least been full of hope, exhausted and half-starved as some of them were. These in the station looked only despondent, and infinitely weary. Many of them battered in some way or another; cut and bruised, the women and children—even the girls—as well as the men. Most of them without anything save for the clothes on their backs, and some without even that. He saw men and women clearly naked but for the rough horse blankets the railroad employees had given them to wrap around themselves. They sat themselves anywhere they could, slumped over the waiting benches, cross-legged along the tiled floor—as if waiting for something, something that was never going to come and could hardly suffice if it did.

Snatchem came over to him, having made his usual reconnaissance, his face grim.

"Sounds bad," he said, abandoning his usual loquaciousness. "More than some Dead Rabbits riot. A regular fight in the streets, wit' rifles an' pistols."

Tom swore.

"We got to *get* there—"

The officers and sergeants were bellowing at them not to walk away, to prepare to fall in at any moment. But that was only more army puffing. An hour had already gone by since they had detrained, and there was still no sign that anything was happening, or that anything ever would.

"The boats is all over the East River still," George told him. "They got 'em movin' all the gold over to Governor's Island."

Of course, they would get the gold off first—

His leg was still throbbing, but he could not sit still. At least he was able to find a tobacconist in the station, packing his clay pipe full as he wandered outside by the docks again.

Unable to look at the burning city anymore, he stared up the river at Hoboken this time. It was a thriving, compact little town of mechanics and shipbuilders, homes and factories. Neat, square shapes in the darkness, wedged into a mile of land between the heights and the river. A few grander homes of ship captains and factory owners, up along the water, encroaching on the grounds of the Elysian Fields, the pleasure park.

So much the same as the last time he had seen it, heading down to the war. Nothing had changed but them.

They had been shipped South in irons, out of fear the men would try to desert and enlist under another name, in order to get the bonus all over again. Tom was chained up to Snatchem—who had been hoping to do exactly that. Their manacles were not removed until they disembarked in Washington City, from where they were marched on down to Virginia, and the war.

It was coming on to the end of the year when they arrived, and the army had already been encamped on the hills above Fredericksburg for weeks. The veterans sullen and clannish, cheating them at cards and filching food and money from their tents. *The Fighting 69th.* No more the boys who feared no noise, they sensed another disaster in the making. Staring at the river below, and the empty, gutted town that their artillery was slowly, uselessly reducing to rubble, trying in vain to drive the reb snipers out. The generals still waiting for the swollen Rappahannock to go down so they could cross —while every day the rebs brought in more men, digging in still deeper along the heights on the other side of the town.

At least some of the boys from the Black Joke had signed up with him—George, of course, and Feeley, and Black Dan Conaway, and Danny Larkins, and John J. Sullivan. They looked out for each other as best they could, and it provided a certain comfort. Shivering in their tents at night, barely able to choke down the meager rations of hard-tack and salt horse. Soaking the meat in water for hours before they could get enough of the brine off to choke it down.

There wasn't much that even Snatchem could requisition down there, resourceful as he was. The country was desolate by then, picked over as it had been by one army or another for more than a year. There was little enough for them to do, save to sit by the camp-fires, arguing over whether there would be another fight before the spring.

"They can't be serious," George had insisted around the campfire. "It *can't* be they'll try it now, not with that many rebs up there."

It did seem mad. The rebels were dug in along a slanting ridge, half a mile or more past the town of Fredericksburg. Just to get at them, the Union troops would have to come down from their own positions along Stafford Heights, cross the Rappahannock on pontoon bridges, march through the town, and only then charge the bluffs at their highest point—with the rebs able to track them every step of the way.

"That's right," John J. had joined in. "Another week or two, they'll have to throw it in, go into winter camp."

"Won't that be a pleasure!" Feeley had snorted—but then Black Dan Conaway had interrupted their speculations.

"Don't deceive yourselves," he had told them, as doleful as ever. Black Dan had the face of a young clerk, or a schoolmaster—smooth round cheeks and spectacles, a sparse red beard and mustache. Yet his youthful appearance was always belied by his nature, bleak and pes-simistic to the point of madness. Back in the ward they would have shouted him down but here, in the darkness of a Virginia December, they all fell quiet under his words.

"Haven't ya seen enough of it already? This is the army. There ain't a thing they won't consider, so long as it only means killin' some more of us."

.   .   .

Sure enough, the next morning the engineers had started laying down the pontoon bridges. And soon after that the army had bestirred itself and begun to move slowly out of its bivouacs and toward the Rappahannock, like an old dog poked away from the fire with a stick.

It took them all day to actually get across. The reb snipers, still lodged in the town, started picking off the pontoniers even before dawn, firing at any sound in the dark. It only got worse once the sun rose—Tom watching as one man after another on the pontoons suddenly gave a little cry, then toppled over into the ice-filled water. When the firing got too hot, they simply gave it up and ran back to the Union bank. Then all the work would stop until the officers rallied them again, and led them back out to the bridges.

Only after nightfall were they finally able to cross, and make their camp on the other side. The tents had not come up, so they were left to forage lengths of board from the ruined town and lay them over the muddy ground. Covering themselves as best they could with their thin blankets—glad, for once, for the new overcoats they had been issued and that hung like a hundredweight on parade.

"Still, we got over easy enough," Larkins had pointed out that night, trying to see the bright side of things. "Maybe they're just bluffin' us."

"That's right, how can they stand against such an army?"

All night long the columns of Union blue had kept coming across the pontoons, so that it seemed as if a whole city had been moved across the Rappahannock. They had all been impressed by their own numbers—all save for Black Dan.

"They want us to come, you'll see," he told them. "Gettin' back won't be so easy."

At dawn the next day their blankets were covered in frost, and a glowing, white fog lay over their whole encampment. It was so thick that no one could see more than ten feet ahead of himself, and despite the cold their spirits were high as they went about getting their breakfast.

"We'll be on the rebs before they even know we're comin'!"

All along the riverbank, Tom could hear the hum of the enormous army as it made its preparations. The noises disjointed but comforting—a huge, invisible host, hidden in the fog.

"We ought to go now," Conaway had told them. Even Black Dan's mood had lifted somewhat when he awoke to see the fog. Now he sat with his jaw clenched tight, watching it slowly dissipate.

"Ah, Dan, I thought we shouldn't go a'tall," Snatchem teased him, but Conaway only shook his head vehemently, and stared off in the direction of the rebel fortifications.

"No, we're goin'. An' since we are, we ought to go *now*, before those up there can see us."

But the generals seemed to be taking their time as usual, and before much longer the fog had worn away. In its place was left a bright, brisk day, the sun gleaming off the rebel rifles and guns above them.

"We can take that. We can! One good rush—"

"Why aren't they shelling us *now?*" Conaway only asked. "Why aren't they, answer me that. It's because they want us to come—"

They ate their breakfast and mustered in the ruined town with its two jutting church steeples, its ruined courthouse and homes. Father Corby came up to hear confessions, and give them communion and extreme unction. Even the priest looking uncomfortable before the men, knowing as they all did that their commanders had already blundered.

"'*Take, eat, this is My Body*—'"

Tom knelt and let him place the Host on his tongue. Still wondering if he had even given a true confession. He had had to rack his mind for the smallest, venial sins, partaking of stolen chickens or gambling at cards. *Not knowing how to tell a priest, at the start of a battle, I have come to hate my wife.*

Opening his eyes he saw above him the two red-skinned observation balloons floating high above the church steeples, directing the Union fire. The big guns back on Stafford Heights beginning to open up, making the ground tremble beneath them.

"Jesus God, but let us go out and die already," Snatchem was saying softly, crouching down beside him.

The other men in the company made their own preparations. The more superstitious among them tossing away their cards and dice. Writing out their names and addresses on little scraps of paper, pinning them to the insides of their tunics.

Tom thought that he should do something, too, but he could not. It was all he could manage to squat with Snatchem and a dozen other men behind a ruined wall. Emptying their bowels, their fetid, liquid shite swirling together before it began to freeze along the ground. The smell of the shit, and the fear, reminding Tom inexorably of something: *The Place of Blood*.

The bugler sounded the call to arms, and they formed their ranks. General Meagher riding down the line just before they advanced, seeing to it that each man was given a green sprig of boxwood to put in his hat.

"Is he the May queen, then?" snorted Snatchem.

Meagher of the Sword, founder of the Irish Brigade—a big, impressive-looking man, with sunken, piercing blue eyes. The rumor around camp just the week before was that he had been so drunk he had almost fallen into a fire. Now he trotted up to the head of his men, wearing a dazzling new uniform stuffed with gold braid—and dismounted, waving them forward with a grand flourish of his sword.

"What, ain't he comin' with us?"

"Shut up there! Form your ranks!"

The little fife and drum boys struck up "The Wearing of the Green," and they began to march, moving up through the town, and singing to keep down their fear.

Oh, I met with Napper Tandy and he took me by the hand,
And he says how's poor oul' Ireland and how does she stand?
'Tis the most distressful country that ever yet was seen,
For they're hangin' men and women for the wearing of the green—

Tom could feel his gut tightening like a fist. Glancing around himself at the ruined town of Fredericksburg, the neat little wood and brick houses smashed open by their artillery. What the guns hadn't wrecked, the looters had, spilling broken mirrors and chairs, disfigured family portraits, even women's underclothing, out along the muddy ground.

They felt more or less sheltered, at least, in the narrow streets of the town, though a few rebel shells were already whizzing over their heads. Tom saw one land in their ranks, a few hundred yards ahead. It blew ten or twelve men up in the air, and he ducked down instinctively. So did every man around him, but he felt humiliated anyway—resolving to stay up, to not so much as flinch when the next shell hit. Yet when it did he ducked again, nearly dropping to his knees this time.

"Hold your line! Hold your line!" the officers bellowed.

They marched on out into the bare, trampled fields beyond the town, and the whole battle opened up before them. It was a spectacle so vast and grand that Tom lost all sense of equilibrium watching it, and would have fallen had not Snatchem grabbed his arm.

The top of the heights they had to take was already obscured by white smoke. The noise deafening, the ground shaking beneath their feet from the cannonade. But there, before them, they could see rank after endless rank of the men in their thick blue overcoats. All of them marching grimly toward the bluffs, moving with the utmost solemn precision and determination, and watching them, Tom was certain that they could not fail.

His regiment halted at the edge of town, to await their turn in the assault, and load the heavy Enfield .69s they had still used then. All those hours of drill coming into practice. Tom, moving solely by rote, tearing off the paper head of the cartridge, stuffing it down the barrel, placing the firing cap on the nipple under the hammer. Doing it all as naturally as breathing, an exercise he could not possibly have performed in any other way by then, in that place.

Then they were moving again—double-time now, across the open ground and toward the rebel positions. The advance suddenly bolting forward at last—

Yet almost as soon as they did, it went wrong. Right away they had to pull up at some sort of canal—a straight ditch, thirty feet long and six feet deep. The only way across it was over three small bridges, but their planks had all been removed, leaving them to inch their way over on the stringers.

"Sweet!" Snatchem shouted beside him. The officers themselves swearing bitterly about the scouting, the men trying to hurry across as best they could, the veterans sure of what was coming next.

Within minutes the reb guns had begun to range in on them, still straddled over the canal. The shells and cannonballs tearing freely through their ranks now, the men moving frantically, yelling, "*Hi! Hi! Hi!*" as they swung themselves over. Some of them even preferring to jump down into the icy water, to try to climb on up the other side. Running on past the dead and wounded men who littered the field before them.

Once they were finally across the canal, Tom and the others from the Black Joke ran up to a small hillock, which at least gave them a little shelter from the guns. Pausing there, as they reformed and gathered themselves—not four hundred yards from the reb lines now.

"Still drawin' us," Black Dan Conaway muttered next to Tom as they waited for the order. "Still drawin' us in!"

"Now, men!"

They leaped up over the top of the little hill, running full out toward the guns above them. It was only then that they spotted the sunken road, the stone wall and the entrenchments thrown up across the crest of the heights. The grey and butternut figures crowded behind it.

"Oh, Jesus, oh, Jesus!" Snatchem was chanting beside him. "Oh, Jesus, so that was it!"

The rifles along the stone wall flashed as if a match had been struck along the whole length of the line. Every blue-coated soldier Tom could see ahead of him went down at once, as if they had fallen into a ditch. He ducked his head involuntarily, and saw the ground beneath his feet moving, as if it were alive, and teeming with insects. Realizing only later that what he was seeing was a hundred more reb balls and bullets, ripping through the mud and the sparse grass.

"I knew it! I knew it!" Black Dan was yelling, just to his right— shaking his head, but with an expression almost of pleasure on his face. He pushed on a little ways more, then suddenly spun around— blood from the hole in the middle of his forehead spewing out over Tom and George Leese before he dropped.

Tom took a step back—and something that felt like a great wind picked him up and pitched him over on his side, tearing the knapsack right off his back. He struggled back to his feet, feeling over himself but finding no wound, only Dan's blood upon him. Staring dully at the small crater the shell had dug into the ground behind him—

"Get back, get back!"

Snatchem was pulling at his elbow then, tugging him back behind the small hill they had advanced from before. Tom realizing that they had not advanced more than a hundred yards or so—the ground they had just covered now a writhing mass of blue-clad bodies.

"*Sixty-ninth, New York!* Up, men, up! Show 'em what you're made of!"

They ran out again. Tom had lost his gun when the shell hit, but he stooped and picked up another Enfield lying on the field a few feet out

from the hillock. There were plenty of them to be had now. The same
storm of concentrated reb fire smashing into them again, men dropping all around him.

"Lie down, men! Lie down and fire!" an officer was yelling, and
they did as they were told. Tom threw himself down into the mud,
operating by rote again—loading and firing as he had been drilled, as
if he were become a machine. They were able to get off a ragged volley, enough to keep some of the rebs down, and get back to the cover
of the little rise again. Snatchem panting with exhaustion beside
him—the two of them looking at each other with something like
wonder.

"Jesus. Jesus," was all George could say.

"Up, men, up!"

The officers stringing increasingly meaningless, inchoate words
together, exhortations and threats, and any appeals to what they were
supposed to be.

"For the Union, men. For your wives an' sweethearts! *Sixty-
ninth!*"

"For New York, men! *For Ireland!*"

Tom did not know how they could go out there again—but one
man did and then another, and then it was Feeley, and he and George
were running after him.

They got farther, this time, until they were no less than forty yards
from the stone wall, and the sunken road. There was a sudden lull in
the firing, when Tom, still running forward, could hear only the sound
of his own breath, the screams of the wounded men on the ground.
Some of the smoke blew off—and he could see the next firing line
already drawn up and reloaded, waiting for them. So close, now, that
they could hear the rebels' taunts as they came.

"C'mon, blue belly!"

"Bring them boots an' blankets, now! Bring 'em here, blue bellies!"

Their voices not quite the usual slow drawl they heard from the
rebs, but something more familiar.

"Oh, Christ," Snatchem breathed beside him. "They're Irish!"

The reb line burst into flame again. Tom saw a color sergeant, just
ahead of him, to the right, take a ball that shattered his leg. The man
stayed up on his knees somehow, waving the flag at the rebs. He was
hit by at least five more bullets in rapid succession—another sergeant

grabbing the flag as he went down—falling under still another swarm of bullets himself.

Yet somehow, they were there. The regiment, still making its way up to the wall. Every man in the ranks now, right down to the drummer boys, shouting at the top of their lungs against the insuperable noise of the battle.

"Fire!"

Tom brought his Enfield up, stopped, and squeezed off a shot. The men all around him stopped to fire as well, their bullets tearing through the stone wall and the entrenchments. The first line of rebels falling back, going down.

But then they were done. Another line of the butternut uniforms had already moved up, raising their rifles. Their volley shattered the point of the charge, stopping them in their tracks. Men were going down everywhere around Tom, as if struck by a great wind, and the next thing he knew they were running for their lives again. Tripping over bodies, falling into the mud and scrambling up again, crawling back toward the hillock.

"Oh, Jesus, oh, Jesus!"

They had made six charges in all before the early winter darkness covered the fields. It would become the stuff of legend. He would hear teenage boys talk about it in awe, because of what they had read in the *Herald*, or the *Irish News*. Yet at no time did they get within a hundred yards of the stone wall, and the sunken road again.

Tom had been hit on the last charge. Still moving toward the wall that he had seen all day, like a recurring dream, whenever the smoke had cleared. Then the reb ball had passed through the left side of his body and on out his back, and he fell flat on his face. He tried to get up at once, but his legs buckled beneath him and he fell back down, completely helpless, unable even to crawl back behind the hillock now. Watching from the ground as the last charge crumbled around him, and his friends and comrades ran back past him, trying to save their own lives.

❧ · 61 · ❧

TOM O'KANE

He had lain out on the frozen mud for a day and two nights before the armies had finally concluded a truce and sent out the stretcher details. He was able to stanch the wounds with the folds of his overcoat, at least—the hole in his chest no bigger than a nickel, though the exit wound in his back was large enough to swallow his fist. He managed to steal a blanket, and a canteen of water from the dead men around him, though he was afraid to move even that much—even at night— for fear of the body robbers, or the bored reb sharpshooters, firing randomly into the bodies still on the field.

He listened to the sound of their shots, thudding into corpses all around him, and wondering when one would hit him. The ceaseless moaning and pleading of the other wounded men tearing at him— yet diminishing steadily as the hours went by. The bodies of the dead swelling up, their eyes bulging and their skin blackening as they rotted.

By the second night he was racked with fever, and all but delirious. Still lying on his chest, staring up with the one eye he could turn freely to the heavens. There, spectacular, glowing, red and blue streaks of color began to appear, spreading out across the entire night sky as he watched. Tom assumed that they were due to the fact that he was delirious, but still he watched them in awe. His mind wandering back to the night of his greatest triumph with the Black Joke—the night he had found the fire, and saved the butt, and first proved himself to be a full-fledged member of the company. *The night they had washed the Big Six.*

It had been a night much the same as this one, in the deep of winter. The week between Christmas and the New Year, when the City was at its darkest and most mysterious. The sky full of luminous orange clouds, a high, crisp layer of snow covering the streets.

Tom had been nearly alone in the firehouse. A couple of older men were half-dozing around the big Franklin stove in the common room, hiding out from their wives. A few more bachelors upstairs, sleeping it off, everyone else with their families for the rounds of parties and suppers that ushered in the new year. He would have liked to have been with Deirdre, and Liza, and the new baby, but he didn't mind too much. Happy to have the chance to prove himself, even glad to be out of the house for a night, if only to sit around the stove and faithfully read one of Deirdre's inspirational tracts, and try to stay awake.

Then he had heard the alarm bell—distant but distinct, through the uncommon stillness of the City. It was past vespers, he knew, and it could be nothing else. Ringing twice, then stopping—then twice again. *A fire in the ward.*

He was on his feet at once. The older men rising reluctantly—but Tom was already in his boots and red shirt. All he had to do was pull down his coat from the wall and he was out in the street. The night air instantly cold and bracing, sweeping away the cobwebs in his brain, the drowsiness from the stove.

He had squinted toward the tower of the Tombs prison, a pointed shaft of darkness within the dark. *There*—he could just make it out. A single lantern was being shimmied out at the end of a long stick. He could picture the runners from half a dozen other companies, already off and running, but he forced himself to wait—and sure enough, another light appeared. A second yellow lantern, swaying and dancing along the signal pole.

Then he was off, his boots crunching through the snow, moving toward the river. The two lanterns meant the waterfront—but where? When there were other runners at the station house they would split up and look, but tonight the responsibility was his alone. *To find the fire, find the closest Croton hydrant and hold it for the company—*

He stopped at the end of Catherine Street. Sniffing the cold air, trying to feel out the fire. Peering into every doorway and alley. He was certain that he could already hear the runners from other companies racing down the snowbound streets behind him, but he forced himself to wait again—knowing that he had to be careful. Any stray *b'hoy* from the river gangs, he knew, would be just as glad to lay him out, and then there were the Old Maid's Boys. A gang of hundreds, men and boys, who liked to set fires just to ambush the volunteers, beating them up and leaving their engines smashed and useless, in the gutter—

He ran out along the docks as quietly as he could. The ships' furled masts covered with ice, jingling quietly as they jostled in their moorings. The forest of bare branches looming white and spectral before him. He ran on down along the waterfront, past where it curved in near James Street—and there was the fire, dead ahead.

It dazzled him at first, a geyser of red light, erupting out of an old tea warehouse. He stood there staring at it. The smell of the burning tea fragrant with chicory, and cinnamon—

Then Tom had spotted the first, other figures, wobbling toward him from the saloons along South and Front Streets. *No time, now, to stand and admire the flames.* He ran desperately up and down the block, trying to find one of the pea-green, wooden Croton hydrants. *That was the whole game—to get there first, find the hydrant for the company.* He had almost given up when he fell over it—halfway down the street, all but covered by the snowdrifts.

But how to hold it against the others before his company arrived? Across the street he spotted a hard-cider barrel, providentially abandoned in the gutter. He snatched it up, planted it over the hydrant— and sat down upon it. Folding himself into his coat, trying to look as inconspicuous as he possibly could on the deserted street.

Soon he could hear the sound of dozens of running men, and the rumble of the engine wagon rolling and sliding down the street. *The machine!*

But there was something wrong. He could tell it right away, just from the sound of the wheels—the wagon much bigger, heavier than the Black Joke's pump. He put it down to the snow at first, but then he heard the trumpet, louder and deeper than theirs. More men running with the machine than the Old Bombazula had ever had—

Another company, it had to be. But who?

Tom was tempted to stand up and look. It sounded like an army now, coming around the corner of Peck Slip. But he made himself stay where he was, on the barrel, guarding and hiding the Croton hydrant. Willing himself to shrink down, to look as inconspicuous as he possibly could. *Dead, perhaps. Frozen where he was, wrapped up in his coat.* Listening to the cheers going up from the boys along the street and the men coming out of the taverns, whole families leaning out the windows of their homes to see the fire. His blood turning colder than it already was, once he could make out what they were shouting:

"Big Six! Big Six!"

It hove into view—the Americus Engine No. 6. The huge, piano doubledecker, with its suction engine and a gooseneck pump. *The Big Six.*

He barely dared to lift his eyes up to see it. The Black Joke was a double-decker, too, but there was nothing like the Big Six. It weighed more than two tons—a huge, bold, red machine. Its lanterns glowed like two amber eyes in the darkness, and between its runners was painted the head of a snarling Bengal tiger, looking as real as life now, in the light from the flames.

There were at least seventy-five men pulling the engine along by the handles, or running beside it with military discipline. And directing them from up on the engine box was the foreman, Bill Tweed himself—decked out in his long white foreman's coat, arms crossed over his belly like a great pagan idol.

"It's here, it's got to be here! There's at least one on the street!" he was shouting fiercely. "Where is she? Where's the plug, men?"

It took Tom all the courage he could muster to hold his ground. The Big Six was the most feared fire company in the City. It was made up entirely of enormous, burly men—the only ones who could work the brakes on such a monster. Most of them were over two hundred and fifty pounds, and lightning boys with their fists, plucked from Tweed's old Cherry Street gang. They were also the Black Joke's most hated rival, ever since the Big Six had been awarded their old firehouse, following an unfortunate Christmas Eve incident that had involved the firing of a loaded mortar at another company. Yet they had never quite dared to take them on—

"Get away, get away there, ya old rummie! Is that the hydrant you're sleepin' on, then?"

Discovered. One of the boys came up to him at last, but Tom made no answer. He could hear another trumpet now—one that sounded very much like the Black Joke's, just around the corner. Sometimes as many as five or six companies might converge on the same fire, and then the fights for the hydrants alone could take hours. Tom had seen whole buildings burn to ashes while the firemen pummeled each other senseless with pistols and knives, iron spanners and slungshots—then go out to a saloon together afterward.

But such a turnout was unlikely, now, in the last week of the year, with half the town off to its balls and parties. *He had to last on his barrel until the lads could get there.* The runner from the Big Six shook him again and he groaned like an old drunk—the boy's face twisting in disgust. He was younger and slighter than Tom, and he knew that he could take him. Instead, he let the boy push him back a little farther, revealing only the grey cider barrel underneath him. The boy saw it, and started to leave—

"There it is! The old drunk's on it, after all!"

He had rocked a little too far back on his barrel—another runner spotting a glimpse of green, racing over toward him. The first boy grabbed for his arm then—and Tom pulled him on forward, hitting him in the face with his other hand. The boy went down in the snow, blood spurting from his nose. The rest of the Big Six runners swarmed him immediately, fighting frantically to push him off the hydrant, but it was too late. The lads came, running the Black Joke down the slip, spotting Tom at once. Before the Americus laddies could move their wagon they had chased the runners off, hooking the butt of their machine up to the hydrant.

Yet they were still outnumbered and outmuscled by the rest of the men from the Big Six. They began to converge on them now, spanners and ax handles in their hands. Tom and the rest of the Black Joke company formed a semicircle around the hydrant, ready to fight for it. The flames licking up out of the warehouse windows across the street—

"We was on the street first! It's our hydrant—"

"The hell you say," Finn McCool had told them, bustling up at the fore of his company. "We got the hydrant, it's our fire. Or are ya too afraid to lose your maidenhead?"

Only the first engine could hook up to the hydrant. If there were no more hydrants, the later wagons would have to get their water *through* the first one—and that was the whole game, their point of honor. If the second engine could not send the water on just as fast as they got it—or faster—it would build up in their own wagon. Building up until it spilled right out over the box, the greatest disaster any fire company could endure. Washing the whole wagon, and ruining whatever elaborate series of paintings and emblems decorated its sides and front. *An indelible disgrace.*

The Big Six was still a virgin. It had never been washed by any engine—and they were all aware that it had washed at least a dozen others in its time. Its big men working the brakes of the huge engine with indomitable ease. Capable of building up such pressure that they had once sent a spout of water sailing right over the Liberty Pole at Franklin Street, during the firemen's Fourth of July rally—a prodigious feat, even if it was later discovered that Tweed had paid a sailor to shimmy up the pole and cut three feet off it during the night.

But they were not about to let them wash the Black Joke, now that they had the hydrant—not even if it meant they had to take a beating for it, or the whole town burned down. Only at the last minute did Tweed come down from his engine box, and step in between his men and theirs. Even Finn McCool looked a little nervous then, in the shadow of the much bigger man, but also no doubt aware of how much he overshadowed him in the Tammany clubhouse. But to everyone's surprise, the big man made a gesture of magnanimity.

"Sure, let 'em have the plug," he told his own company. "It's only fair."

Tweed's face as bland and impenetrable as ever. His small, clear eyes blinking guilessly.

"What harm can they do with it, after all? It ain't like they can wash *us*—"

Transforming the situation at once, making it *their* shame, now, if they could not wash the Big Six. Finn letting his breath out. Tweed's own men falling back to their machine, laughing and smirking derisively.

"What can they do to us, then? What can they?"

"Sure, the pups!"

"Stand by your brakes, men!"

The laddies from both companies ran to their places, by the rows of two-handed pumps. There were twenty on each side of the double-decker machines. Ten up top, worked by men actually standing on the machine, and ten below, worked by the men with their feet on the ground. Pulling the water up from the earth, the pipes running deep beneath the pavement, all the way from the Croton reservoir—

Tweed's assistant foreman from the Big Six ran back with the thick leather hose, ready to connect its riveted copper end to the Black Joke.

"Mind, now, ya don't nigger the engine!" he admonished them.

Sometimes the machine on the hydrant would try to grab a head start. The laddies would get in eight or ten strokes before the other engine was hooked up, so that the water would boil out and wash it almost immediately. Men had been knocked down and nearly killed for such a stunt—or for not pulling the butt out in time when the fire was done.

"Mind yourself! Get back t'your machine, you'll be baptized soon enough!"

The jeers and insults continuing to fly between the two companies as the assistant foreman put the butt in. The men shuffling in their traces like workhorses against the cold, eager to get to work. Tom was manning a brake pump on the ground level, with Snatchem to one side of him and Dolan, who was still with the company then, on the other. He had been surprised to see his brother-in-law there, on such a night, so far from where he and Ruth lived up in Pigtown. But he had said nothing and Dolan—was Dolan, silent and ready, just waiting to release the murderousness that was always coiled inside him.

They looked to Finn, standing up on the machine, to call the stroke. The tension palpable in the air, like nothing Tom would ever know again, save for the moments just before a battle. The fire itself nearly forgotten by now. A crowd had gathered on the sidewalks, and Tom could see that some of them seemed to be the owner of the tea warehouse and his employees—dashing in and out of the burning building, salvaging what merchandise they could. But the rest were there to watch them, in their competition, whether or not the whole of the City went up in blazes.

"All right now. Put in the butt and play away, men!"

Then they were off. Finn gave the signal, and they pressed their brakes down as one man. The laddies on the Big Six pushed their own brakes down immediately in response—and the crowd broke into a cheer as the water spurted out in a high arc against the night sky.

Tom reveled in the feeling of the pump, springing back against his hands. The good, familiar ache spreading at once across his back and shoulders as he worked. Rapidly building up their speed—working in perfect tandem with Snatchem, and Johnny Dolan, and all the other men down the line and above him on the machine.

"Pump! Pump! Work her lively, lads!" Finn sang out from above them. They usually called back in response, like sailors hauling up a mainsail. But this night they knew to save their breath, putting everything they had into the brakes.

"Everyone a ya now, will you *work*, lads? You don't half work now!"

Soon they had built up to their top speed, sixty—then seventy—strokes a minute. The Big Six matching them easily so far, stroke for stroke. The water speeding through their two machines, cascading up through the hoses and out over the burning warehouse. The crowd growing steadily now, men and women running from the taverns and even from fancy parties to join them along the sidewalk.

"Will you *work?*"

Tom felt the nudge of his replacement against his shoulder, and stepped aside. At such a pace, the men worked no more than a minute, a minute and a half, before being relieved. The second shift taking over the top brakes first, scrambling past them, up on the machine. The ground brakes behind Tom coming in next. With a precision born from many long hours of drill, they pulled out of the line, he and Snatchem and Dolan together. Taking a single step back and to the side on the upstroke, letting the replacements move in past them so they did not miss so much as a beat on the change.

"Stave her sides in! *Say* you will now!"

When he shifted off Tom could see that the fire had already spread down the block—darting over to a saloon, and a sailors' boarding-house next to the warehouse. When he was on, all he was aware of was the metal brake before him, putting everything he had into forcing it down, staying in rhythm with the rest of the lads, and Finn's call.

He remembered that George had nudged him once, when they were off, and told him the mayor himself was on hand. He had looked over to see a short, nondescript man in a high frock coat, buttoned to his chin, and a high top hat. Holding in one hand, as if he were the Bishop himself, the official fire staff: a snow-white wand, topped by a gilded flame—

Tom had shrugged, and gone to grab a slice of bread and cheese. The company steward walking up and down the brake line with his bag of food, singing out his chant—"*Eat some more cheese, and a good slice of ham, and wash it well down with another good dram.*"

He grabbed the cup of brandy the man held out—taking just a sip, enough to burn and glow through his chest. He poured the rest of it into his boots, the way he had seen the veterans do it, to keep his feet from freezing. Then he moved back into the line, stepping nimbly, taking care not to let his fingers get crushed by the swinging metal pumps.

"Will you *work* now, lads?"

The battle went on and on, deep into the night. The fire only slowly diminishing. The warehouse a total loss, the tea merchant sitting and weeping on the curb, though the crowd paid him no mind. The saloon and the boardinghouse looked badly charred, but salvageable. The only question remaining—the *real* question—was if they could possibly wash the Big Six.

By now Tom's arms felt as heavy as thirty-pound weights, and he could see the strain on the faces of all the men around him, even Johnny Dolan. But Finn only picked up the pace—and they responded. The company working as it never had before, up to seventy-five strokes a minute. The runners and the neighborhood boys throwing handfuls of snow up around the brakes, making sure that they didn't spark and light the whole wagon on fire, they were working them so hard.

And still the big men of the Americus pumped the water on. Tweed himself working the upper brakes now, letting his assistant foreman give the call. The Big Six jumping and bouncing with every long stroke he made.

"Hey, Frank is coming!"

"It's Frank! It's Frank! Here he is, it's Frank himself!"

A thrilled little ripple ran through the crowd, and Tom watched the great throng part for a dapper, smiling man in an opera cape. *Now he was impressed*—seeing that it was none other than Frank Walton

himself, the greatest of the fire tenors, of whom it was said that when
he sang "Napoleon's Dream" at a fire, even the old Quakers on Henry
Street would weep to hear the sound of his voice.

With a dramatic flourish he loosened the cape around his shoulders, cleared his throat, and began to sing another favorite:

> *Shule, shule, shule agra*
> *Sure a sure and he loves me*
> *When he comes back he'll marry me*
> *Johnny has gone for a soldier—*

His gorgeous voice resounded through the midnight air, and the
crowds grew even greater—nightcaps poking out of every window
Tom could see now. He went back to his brake, thinking that it must
surely be over soon, the fire all out. He did not know how much longer
he could go, he felt as if his shoulders were about to be torn from their
sockets—and meanwhile the big men on the Big Six still looked unfa-
tigued, even if they did seem to be working harder now, thumping
their enormous wagon back and forth.

But a few minutes later he felt a change. A slight but growing resistance, through the brake handle. Tom had helped to wash another
machine before, and it had felt the same—when the wagon ahead was
filling up, coming close to slopping over. Glancing at Snatchem and
Dolan, out of the corner of his eye, he could tell that they sensed it as
well. Finn, up on the box, quickening the call yet again—driving
them up to eighty, then eighty-five strokes a minute.

"Now you've got her!" he cried out. "Now will you *work*, lads?
Paint the old gal green!"

The pace impossible to sustain for very long, all the men in the
Black Joke knew. The danger being that if they tried to keep it up, men
would break their arms, and they would lose control of the brakes. It
was not as bad as being washed, but a disgrace nonetheless—the
water receding to a trickle out of the great leather hose, the fire liable
to flare back up again.

Incredibly enough, though, the men on the Big Six were visibly
laboring now. One of their runners hastened over to the machine's
butt with a spanner, ready to release it on a moment's notice.

"The fire's about out!" he cried up to Finn.

"*Is* it out? *Is it?*" Finn cried. "Don't give me no 'abouts.' You pull that butt before it is, an' I'll come down there an' hook you up to it instead!"

The runner stood where he was with the spanner, looking up at Finn, then back at the lads from the Black Joke—knowing every one of them would back him.

"*The fire is not out,*" a voice blared down the street.

It was the mayor himself, calling out through his black voice trumpet, and holding his snow-white wand in the air as if he were making a papal decree. The crowd sent up another cheer—and Frank Walton launched into an encore, his voice swelling out even over the sound of the flames and the ferocious competition:

> *I'll sell my rock and I'll sell my reel,*
> *I'll sell my flax and spinning wheel,*
> *To buy my love a sword of steel*
> *Johnny has gone for a soldier—*

The men of the Black Joke pumped the brakes as they never had before, up to ninety strokes a minute now, a pace they had never reached even for a few seconds. Tom's arms were numb, the muscles trembling visibly with fatigue. He could see Snatchem struggling, too, though Johnny Dolan was still working like a demon, pounding the brake up and down. Eyes locked straight ahead at the machine, as if there were nothing else in the world for him.

The pressure was building steadily, their job getting all the harder as they felt the Big Six fill up—that was the difficulty of washing a machine. But Tweed's company had lost all pretense of indifference by now. The assistant foreman called the stroke faster and faster, banging on the box for emphasis. The big men giving it all they had, some of them stripped down to shirtsleeves, even in this cold. The gigantic double-decker engine rocking wildly back and forth, its springs groaning under the effort.

"There she goes, boys! She's about to boil!"

"Not yet, not yet!"

There was a sound like a cannon shot, and the Big Six slumped over on its right side—its wheel axles finally cracking under the exer-

tions of the enormous men upon it. The brakes swung back down—
and the axles on the left side cracked this time. The whole chassis of
the machine giving way then, the wheels breaking free and the
machine collapsing, the men flung cursing into the street.

And as it fell the water gushed on up and out over the engine box
of the Americus company. Flowing out over the face of the snarling
tiger, and despoiling all the other, grand scenes, the fine, black running stripes and the red wheel spokes. Tom and the rest of the Black
Joke threw over their brakes in celebration. Pummeling and embracing each other, those who still had the strength to do anything at all
but rub their arms. The crowd sweeping over them, pounding their
backs and picking them up on their shoulders—no one bothering
with what was left of the fire.

When they had recovered themselves, the men from the Big Six
ran over, too, insisting that the butt should have been pulled when
their wagon began to break, and spoiling for a fight. But Tweed was
between them again—still unruffled, even though his heavy mutton
face was pink with perspiration.

"Now, boys, they beat us fair an' square. We can admit when we're
licked, an' give credit to a company of good Americans, an' Demmycrats!"

Even as he spoke, a sailor from the boardinghouse was tugging at
the coattail of Tweed, of Finn, of any fireman who would listen.

"He stuck! He stuck up there!"

An olive-skinned boy—no more than thirteen, at the oldest—
with a heavy Portuguese accent, dressed in the white trousers and
short jacket of his profession, now covered with soot. Most of the
crowd laughing at his frantic excitement.

"My friend, he stuck! It fall—it fall on 'im! He burn!"

He came around the engine, pulling at Tom and Snatchem and
Dolan, where they sat exhausted on the curb. Pointing up to a room,
on the third floor of the boardinghouse. The window and the gable
around it were blackened and charred but any remaining fire appeared
to be out now, and Tom had only stared dully back at the boy, while
George tried to brush him off.

"Well, then, pull him out! What more d'ya want from us—"

"Up there? He's up there?" Dolan had said, grabbing the boy suddenly by the shoulders and pointing up toward the blackened gable.

"*Sí, Sí!* Up there!"

"Show me."

Dolan was already grabbing an ax from the side of the Black Joke engine, running into the boardinghouse after the boy. Tom and Snatchem running after him, though Tom did not know why he should ever care what that lunatic did. He ran after him as he would any other member of the company, he and Snatchem both shouting at Dolan to come back—

"Stop, stop, ya crazy bastard! Ya don't know what's in there! Let 'em find their own friends—"

But Dolan was already inside. They had no choice but to run on after him—pausing again almost as soon as they got past the door, Snatchem cursing fervently.

"He'll be the death of us all!"

They had been to enough fires to know when a house wasn't safe. Even in the hall they could see that the damage to the boardinghouse was much worse than it had appeared from the outside. What was worse, the whole edifice was not really one building but two, the whole thing hastily cobbled together with some boards and bricks, a few slatherings of plaster. The only thing keeping it up at all was how the two sides leaned into each other, but now the fire had undermined even that, having eaten through the middle walls.

The burned side—the half they were in—looked as if it could slide right off and collapse in a heap at any moment. It even *felt* unsteady— the floors and ceiling, the doors and banisters in the close stairs hall reverberating with every step they took. And worst of all, they could detect a whiff of fire, hidden somewhere—and still burning.

But Johnny Dolan was already running up the steps, after the Portagee boy. The whole staircase wobbling with each stride he took. Snatchem looked at Tom and shrugged—and then they both started to run up after him.

"Hold up—hold up for us, at least—"

They slipped and scrambled along—not so much as daring to hold on to the banister once a long chunk of it fell away into ash, crashing down to the first floor. When they reached the third story it was no better. The floor honeycombed now with holes where the fire had burned through, the feeble, cracked slats clearly visible underneath.

They had to pick their way down the hall in nearly total darkness.

Even Dolan moving more slowly now—though the olive-skinned boy continued to race nimbly on ahead, down to the gable he had pointed out. They caught the scent of the fire again, too—very strong now, coming from somewhere just under the floorboards, or maybe the eaves above them.

"Jesus, but we could fall all the way to hell—"

"Here—he stuck!"

The Portagee boy was pointing to where a ceiling beam had fallen across a door, knocking it down and wedging it in place. Underneath it they could see a pair of blackened feet. Snatchem cursed.

"Ah, but your friend is dead already, bucko—"

But even as he spoke, one of the feet moved, and a low groan came from the body underneath the door. Moving closer, they could see a slight figure, not much older than the boy who had summoned them. His feet were not burned, but the deep, coal-black color of his skin. The boy naked under the door that trapped him, still lying on the remnants of the cheap boardinghouse bed he had been sleeping on when the beam collapsed.

He only groaned, and opened his eyes for a moment when they arrived. The boy who had brought them stroking his close-cut hair, while he spoke torrents of Portuguese to him. The boy under the door only groaning some more, until Tom thought that he was making a great effort just to breathe. He was obviously in terrible pain—likely as not a dead man already, his innards crushed under the beam and the door.

But you never knew. He had seen them pull out people with all sorts of injuries. Sometimes those who only seemed to have taken in a little smoke, or suffered a slight bump on the end, keeled right over in their arms and died. And other times men and women who were a mass of contusions, or shrieking in pain from their burns, would come around the firehouse in another couple of weeks' time, grinning the gloating, defiant grin of the survivor. Boasting, *Remember me? Good as new!*, although they rarely were quite that.

"Stuck, are ye?"

Johnny Dolan was looking all around the blackened gable room, trying to size up the situation. Finally he just picked up his ax and struck one, swift blow at the beam. They could feel the entire house move beneath their feet.

"Jesus, Johnny, ye'll kill us all!"

"No. No, not this time—"

He seemed almost to be in a trance, flailing at the beam again with his ax, oblivious to where they were, or to how the floor itself was slanting and slipping away with each blow. Until they stood on it like sailors on a listing ship, barely able to keep their balance.

"Goddamnit, ya fool, it's *useless!* Ye'll knock the house down before ya cut through that log!"

The beam did seem impossibly large, but it proved to be dry-rotted at the core—and after no more than half a dozen strokes it broke in two. The Portagee boy hastening to push it away, and pull the door off his friend. The injured boy's naked form pitifully cut and flattened underneath it—Tom guessing from the look of him that he had broken at least half a dozen ribs and maybe a leg, if he was lucky.

"Easy there! Easy with 'im!"

The Portagee boy was already hauling his friend up. Tom tried to slow him, knowing from experience how damaging it could be to move them too quickly.

But there was a disturbing noise growing all around them now—a sort of rustling sound. That part of the ceiling where the beam had been wedged in place suddenly gave way, a large patch of plaster and dust and crumbling shingles falling through—and with them came thousands of cockroaches, many as long as a man's finger, dropping to the floor and scrambling away.

"Ah, Christ!" swore Snatchem. "It's up there! It must be up above us!"

The fire burst through before the words were out of his mouth, peeling back the rest of the ceiling like the top of a tin can. The five of them already moving back down the hallway as fast as they could go, Dolan slinging the injured boy over his back like a sack of potatoes. The smoke hurtling down the hall after them, then down the stairs. Whole sections of the roof falling past them in flaming sheets, chunks of the floor and the stairs disappearing under their feet even as they ran.

They made it down to the last flight of steps—able to see only a foot or two ahead of them now, and barely able to breathe at all. Hoping there was not some gaping hole before them. The fire was right on their heels, though, and they had no choice but to throw themselves halfway down the stairs—Tom saying a quick prayer to the Virgin that they wouldn't go through to the basement.

The floor held, and they were back in the front hall—but not out of the building yet, still engulfed in the smoke and dust. Tom had heard of firemen who had died in just such a situation, a few feet from safety but staggering helplessly in the wrong direction—

They dropped to the ground and began to crawl toward where it seemed that the door had been. Clutching to the hem of each other's pants—Dolan in the lead, Tom only hoping he knew where he was going. He had no good idea himself, by now—the smoke choking him, making it impossible for him to open his eyes. Trying to keep his head as low to the ground as he could. Hunting for the drafts of cool, clean air to be found there—

Then a dozen hands were on him, lifting him up and out of the smoke, back into the dark, frozen world by the nighttime river. The bright, orange sky wavering above him. He had all he could do to drag himself to the curb next to Snatchem. Still choking out the smoke, gulping down the gorgeous Croton water the steward handed him.

"All that—for a nigger sailor?"

Many of the other firemen still incredulous over what they had done. Not over him, or George so much. That was expected, following another man into trouble, no matter what he did. *But Dolan*. The man had never shown any inclination before toward heroism—a hazardous tendency in any company, particularly when there was a large enough crowd watching. They looked him over warily, none of them able to quite fathom what had gotten into him—and particularly for this boy.

"Still, 'twas a damned bold thing."

"Oh, aye, brave as a robin—"

Tom didn't think he understood it, either. He kept watching Dolan, who was still carrying the boy he had pulled out of the gable. He would not let himself be attended to until he had laid him out on a blanket, along the chassis of the Black Joke's machine. Pulling another blanket up over him, and a fireman's coat. Getting the steward to give him a cup of brandy—holding it to his lips, helping him suck it down.

The boy had trembled and lain still. His eyes still open, twitching back and forth, his mouth opening from time to time as if to say something, though no words would come out. Dolan had stared down at him, as if studying him, for a long time. Then the police had come to take him away to the hospital, and Dolan had turned abruptly and walked off, letting someone drape a blanket over his shoulders.

They had gone to Udell's restaurant afterward, once the engine was cleaned and put away. Finn McCool had had a toast and a good word for every man in the Black Joke, and Tom had been singled out for saving the hydrant, and Dolan for his heroic rescue, and all the food had tasted better than anything he had ever had in his life—fresh coffee, and buttercakes, and hot mutton pies.

Afterward they had sung endless choruses of "Hunt the Buffalo," the strange, slow song that was all the firemen's favorite, played at every hop and chowder:

> Come all ye likely lads that have a mind for to range,
> Into some foreign country your situation to change;
> In seeking some new pleasures we will all together go,
> And we'll settle on the banks of the pleasant Ohio.
> And we'll range through the wild woods and hunt the buffalo;
> And we'll range through the wild woods and hunt the buffalo.
>
> If by chance the wild Indians should happen to come near,
> We'll all unite together with heart and cheer;
> We'll march through the town, boys, and strike a deadly blow,
> And we'll drive them from the banks of the pleasant Ohio—

But the best part of all was when he had gone home. The sun was only just beginning to rise and Deirdre was still in bed, after being up half the night with the baby herself. He had slipped in beside her, and they had made love slowly and wantonly. She had smelled the smoke on him and wanted to know what had happened, but he had only hushed her and held her close to him. She had felt so good, so warm to him after the brutal night air down by the docks, smelling of boiled soap and washing lye, and milk. After a little while the baby had cried and she had gotten up to feed her, but Finn had given Tom the day off from his City job, and he had been able to stay in bed. Luxuriating in its warmth, and the lingering smell of her between the covers—

He had been unsure, at the start, of how Deirdre might be in bed, knowing that she had been educated by the Sisters. He had heard stories of how such girls were, how they would only do it with a sheet between them, and never on a saint's day. He had been uncertain of how to approach her at all, considering how beautiful she looked, and somehow it had still seemed an impertinence even after they were married.

But she had welcomed him to her from their first night together—as grave as she was in all things, but passionate and yielding as well. Unbending as Deirdre could be outside the bedroom, he took refuge in her there. Nestling his head between her breasts in the darkness, marveling over the hardness of her swollen belly, during her many pregnancies.

Their life in bed had sealed the bond between them. It had affirmed his faith in her, to let her make him what she would.

Then how? How was it that she would have wanted him to go away to such a thing as this war? Or that he would have wanted to go?

He could not remember when they had finally come to fetch him off the field outside Fredericksburg. His only memory, hazy at that, was of the wagon on the way back to Washington City, nearly breaking his back on the rutted, frozen roads. Drifting in and out of the relapsing fever for the next four months, lying on a bed with filthy sheets in the overcrowded army hospital.

He did not know how he had survived any of it. The other men crying constantly in their agony. The simpering Yankee gentry visiting in the daytime, peering avidly at their wounds, and praying loudly in the middle of the room. The whores who posed as nurses at night, offering to do all kinds of things, whatever the men could bear and then some, for a few coins.

Yet it was in the hospital that he thought he understood at last. Lying in the bed, with nothing to do but think, in those times when the fever receded—thinking on Deirdre, and himself.

In the end, he knew, he had gone to the war because he had wanted to go. *His own confession, exchanged with her.* He had wanted to see the elephant. To take his leave from working every day, leveling the land in the park, and staying sober save for the beers he could sneak with Billy Dove.

He liked the company of men—

He had to admit that now, he could no longer blame it only on her. And in the end he had only gotten what he deserved, after all, for helping to ship another man into servitude.

Her brother. Johnny Dolan. That was when the whole rift had first opened between them. It had been as Deirdre had said she wanted it, sure enough. She had agreed to it all beforehand, that it was the best way to save Johnny from the hangman—to get him out of the City.

But he knew that she had never really forgiven him for it, and after all, he was the one who had taken care of it all. Going down to The Sailor's Rest, and speaking to some of his old *b'hoys* from the Break o' Day Boys. It had been simple enough, they were always on the lookout for new bodies. Ruth had seen to getting Johnny down there, to the docks. All he had had to do was to get the boat, with Billy Dove, and row it out to them.

He had seated Dolan between him and Billy—hoping desperately that he wouldn't catch on until they reached the ship but taking his precautions just the same. Thinking that it might just work, that Dolan had seemed drowsy from the drugged whiskey at the bar, and all but ecstatic over the lie that Ruth had told him about his dead brother.

"So he's there waitin' for me, is he?" he had yammered. "To help me get on away?"

"Aye," Tom had nodded, tending to his oars, fearful of saying too much.

"And alive all this time! I knew he was, I knew he had to be. To get out a the black gable—that's somethin'. I thought it was only me that could, but he did it as well."

"Sure."

Going on like that, while they searched for the ship through the crowded, fog-shrouded harbor. But inevitably, he had begun to see through it. Maybe it was how little Tom was saying—or the more that Dolan himself talked, the more he knew how unlikely it all was. Tom could see his face change even as he watched him. The realization slowly sinking in that there was no brother, there could be no brother rescued from Ireland, waiting to help him. His words trailing off, his eyes darting, looking out at the water—then right at Tom.

He had just started to make his move when Billy Dove threw the burlap sack over his head. Tom had seen it—Dolan coming off the bench, right at him, while he could only sit there mesmerized. But Billy had caught him by surprise—apparently not figuring that the black man, rowing the boat, would be good for anything but follow- ing Tom's orders. Billy had thrown the sack over him and followed with a short, quick punch to the head, then another one, but still Dolan had struggled—striking out in all directions from under the bag with his fists and feet. One of his blows had caught Tom on the side of the head just as he'd moved forward to help, nearly knocking him out of the boat. Dolan had almost gotten the bag off, when Billy had hit him again with the butt of the grappling hook. Tom joining in then, both of them flailing away at the hard, ungiving form underneath the burlap, loosing their fear and their anger upon him. Smashing away until the covered form lay still beneath them—standing over it even after the bag lay still, letting the boat drift, in case it was one of his tricks.

But there was no other sign that he was even still alive, and they had tied him up with rope that Billy had been farsighted enough to bring along, and shoved his supine form down into the bottom of the dinghy.

Their night had still been far from finished. They had lost one of their oars in the struggle, and it took them a long time just to discover where they were now in the fog-ridden river. Tom checking the body beneath the bag from time to time for breath, or a pulse. Not wanting to have Dolan's death on his soul after all, even if that might have been the best thing for all concerned.

At last they had reached the ship the Break o' Day Boys had arranged, and banged on the side with the grappling hook. The vessel looming dark and sinister in the river, with barely a running light along its bow. Tom giving the signal he had been told—lifting up a lantern and cloaking it, then letting it shine out again. After a few unsettling minutes wondering if they had come to the wrong boat, or if it was a trap after all, an answering lantern had appeared along the gunwales.

But a moment later a broad webbing of rope was unfurled over the side, and two men in pitch-black coats and caps had scuttled down. They were silent and quick as cats, their eyes red and suspicious in the lantern light, and Tom had truly understood for the first time just what sort of a business shanghaiing was.

He and Billy had handed Dolan's shrouded body up to the men from the ship, who still did not say a word. The two of them warily keeping their distance, as far as possible, from the silent men— knowing that they would just as soon take three bodies as one. And when it was done, the covered, still-supine body disappearing on up over the rail, they had rowed away as quickly as they could, putting water between themselves and the darkened ship as fast as they could manage.

It had been the worst night's work he had ever done, shipping another man off to God only knew where. *And she had known about it, and given her approval, but still it had never been right between them after that.* Especially afterward, when he had discovered Ruth and her family up in the park.

When he had brought the niggers on the block. It was not just an affront to Deirdre's airs of respectability, he knew now. More than that, it was a reminder to her, as well, every day, of what Tom had done—of what *she* had done—to her own brother.

He didn't know how he could have been so foolish. But he had felt too bad for Ruth, turned out of her home, up in the colored village. For Billy, too, a good enough sort, colored or no, and for their babies. But mostly it was for Ruth, he knew—still suffering, still pathetically trying to get by. Tom had not been able to help himself, and he suspected that Deirdre had sensed that as well, the way she could sniff out almost anything.

Whatever the case, it had never been the same between them, after that. They had gone on working as always, reading together in the evenings. Having more children. Even so, there had been a coolness, a distance between them that was plainest in the bedroom. He had started to stay out as much as he could. Lingering behind at the job, or at the firehouse, wishing that he could go along with the lads on a spree. But not really—even more miserable outside his home. The taste for the whiskey gone in him, after so long a time. Bored by the idle, silly chatter of the *b'hoys,* after so many years talking about serious things with his wife. *A horse too long in harness to be let loose now.*

And yet, he had to go somewhere. He had taken to stopping over at Ruth's more and more often—supposedly to steal a drop of the creature with Billy Dove, but really to see her. Unable to get enough of the gratitude he saw in her face the moment he walked in. Showing off, blowing about who he knew down at the Wigwam, or in the greater City, insisting on leaving money about the house for her, as if he were as rich as Croesus. Gratified to see how she ate up every penny, every compliment he threw her.

It was a desperate situation, he admitted it. He had even contemplated paying a visit to Maddy Boyle, that pretty little trollop down the street. Pausing in the street once to wish her good day—just to see the surprise and the gratitude in *her* eyes. Wondering what it would be like to visit her in her house, where the sailors and the Yankee gentlemen all went. To see, perhaps, still more gratitude—the bigger a tip he left her, the more polite words he could throw her way—

But he had wished to go even farther, to bust loose of all of it, the whole, straitened world of the block, and his job, and his duties. Tired of trying to please his wife, who would not be pleased. Telling her, remonstrating with her that he did not want to go to the war.

But in the end he had gone. Leaving his wife and children, and all he held dear behind him. Going off to this charnel house.

He had been so glad to get Deirdre's letters, then, when he was in the hospital in Washington. Grateful for her confession, written in the agony of not knowing whether he was dead or alive. Unburdening herself of all she had thought and done—all that he had suspected. He had lain in his hospital bed, still barely strong enough to move, and read over every word.

Writing out his own confession, then. Sparing her the details, how close he had been to dying, though he thought she could guess it. Speaking to her one heart to another, the way they had before. Confessing to her that he had wanted to go, taking the whole blame off her. Even getting the picture made that she said she craved from him, had begged him for.

He had hoped to see her as soon as he could get to New York, on furlough, but then the orders had gone wrong. Mislaid somewhere, forgetting his leave and his convalescence. They had rushed him back to the regiment instead, as Bobby Lee headed north and the whole, enormous army had wheeled around to chase after him.

Tom had had to go back. It was another thing he had learned about war. It did not get any less cruel simply because you had learned something. He had joined his company again near Frederick, Maryland—what was left of it. The Irish Brigade barely even a brigade at all, anymore. The regiments all thinned out, half the men boys from Boston, or Germans from Pennsylvania now. Even Meagher himself gone, resigned in some fit over the most recent debacle at Chancellorsville.

Yet Snatchem and Feeley, Larkins and John J. Sullivan were still there, at least. They had seemed delighted to see him back again, even looking as he knew he did—staring at the picture he had had made for Deirdre, bearded and gaunt and all but unrecognizable. Every one of the lads but Black Dan, remarkably, had survived the fight at Fredericksburg, and Chancellorsville, to boot. They had fattened him up as best they could, stuffing him with extra rations and George's "requisitions" as they marched up into Pennsylvania, chasing Lee up to Gettysburg.

And now he was here, full circle—or almost. Back to the dock in Hoboken, waiting to cross the river to his home. He could hear the boatmen, bringing the flatboats up at last. Dark figures out on the darkened water, ready to take them back over the water, to the burning town. *Back to her.*

"Back to the old Frog 'n' Toe," Snatchem said, moving past him. *No doubt already plotting whatever schemes he could get up.* But even he looked grave, and ready to do what was needed. Shocked as they all were by the sight of the burning City there before them.

The boats thunked up against the wharf pilings, the sergeants yelling and pushing them into line. But the troops were already hurrying down on their own, even though they knew, in the way of such things, that transporting them across the river on the flatboats was likely to take up the rest of the night. They didn't care—already standing on deck and staring over at the City, chafing to get back home. And when they did, there would be hell to pay.

❦ · 62 · ❧

RUTH

For the rest of the afternoon and evening they listened to the white women cavorting about in the street. Staging their own small purposeless imitation of the riot. While the race women of Paradise Alley—the blacks and Creoles and mulattoes, and Indians, and all those women who were married to the same—kept themselves low, hidden away in their houses and cellars. *As she was—but not even hidden in her own house.*

For all that, there were no more assaults. The worst they did was to hurl another stone or two at Maddy's house, or to urge their children to do the same. Yelling some taunt or another that Ruth guessed was meant for Maddy or herself.

Of course, Deirdre insisted on going out twice to refill their buckets, even though they still had plenty of water. Striding defiantly over to the green Croton pump, looking the women gathered across the street right in the eyes—all but daring them to say or do something. Returning to the house triumphant, happy just to have done something.

"*They* won't be causing any trouble," she said, then nodded at Maddy, still sleeping on the couch. "She's right enough about them, the cowards. It's just a matter of getting enough men to clear the streets and it will all be over."

But from what Ruth could hear, she suspected that it would not be anytime soon. At least Deirdre kept them busy with one thing or another—all of them, even Maddy, after she finally woke up. Never allowing them to simply sit and wait for word, but keeping at them to help her clean the house, mind the children, and get the meals—all the while keeping watch through the shutters.

Ruth had helped her to go over all her meticulous preparations, combing over the house from cellar to attic. There was still plenty of food, with the tinned fish and the salted meats she had stocked in. There were veritable barrels of water now, in every room, enough to drink and wash in for days, if need be—or to put out any cinders. Enough milk for the younger children, stored up in the icebox in the cellar, along with roots and bottled preserves and—potatoes. What seemed like a whole year's worth, back in County Clare, stored up on a board. *And never a one to go bad here*

Ruth was glad for the tasks, happy to have something to fill the time. Grateful even for Deirdre's officiousness—filled with awe again by her talents at running a household. Until at last, when the day had finally trickled out and the children had been put to bed, they had gone up to the roof to try to escape the heat. Leaving Milton posted vigilantly below by the windows—Maddy's gun well hidden.

Ruth didn't know that she had ever been so high up before—climbing out on the flat, tar roof, some two and a half stories above the ground. From where she was she could see, just to the west, the slanted grey walls of the Tombs prison, with their mysterious Ægyptian markings. The dark pile of the Shambles tenement just to the north, looming over them as always—the whole, long sweep of the City beyond it. Each block packed full of stubby slanted houses much like her own, along with the longer slabs of the tenements and warehouses, the church steeples sticking up over them all like so many spiky thorns.

And to the south, all around the rim of the City, she could see the ships—their masts and rigging craning up over the roofs. Hemming them in like a stockade, or the spears of some silent, deadly army—marking both the ends of the island, and the way off. She remembered one of the rumors the women on the block had brought—*those white carrion birds*—telling them that the government was bringing in the navy to shell the town.

"Jesus, d'ya think they will come to blow us up?" she asked Deirdre, shivering a little in the heat just to think of it. "D'ya think they'd do it, just to keep from losin' the City?"

"Don't use the Lord's Name in vain," Deirdre scolded her. "But no, no, they'd never do that. The Archbishop would never allow it—"

All around them, she could see the fires suddenly flaring up, through the windows and even the roofs of houses. Here and there, along the darkened streets, she could see tiny, individual lights as well. Moving along together, the luminous insect skitterings of a mob, of a dozen mobs, with their torches. Scuttling up one street, then stopping. Waiting, listening, the very way the cockroaches seemed to listen in her kitchen when she lighted a candle and caught them in the middle of the night.

Then the little bundles of light would fly apart, like so many sparks from the hearth. Or skitter off suddenly in another direction, or vanish around a corner. Accompanied by wild yelps and screams, dying away in the night—leaving her to wonder what they were after, out there.

Something else to loot, to root out? Some poor, trapped Yankee or Negro? My Billy?

She shuddered, and raised her gaze again, looking out toward the north of the island, as much as she could see of it. It made her think of that night she had watched Billy, unseen, on the hillock by Seneca Village, the thousands of tiny, lighted window squares down below her.

But the humanness of it—the order and the warmth—was gone now. Snuffed out in favor of these malignant, glowing insects, bustling about at will. The human world gone out, reverted to the cold, arbitrary world she had seen from the tossing ship's deck. *The beast returned, immeasurably beautiful, and cold, and meaningless.*

"Don't worry. Nothing lasts for very long."

She felt Deirdre's arm around her shoulders, pulling her to her, and she let herself be drawn closer.

"Not in this City. It'll burn itself out. It always does."

"Yes."

"They'll put it down tomorrow, for sure. The Archbishop's sure to be doing all he can."

"Yes."

She wanted Billy Dove back, right now, to sit beside her on this rooftop. She wanted him with her, even if he couldn't stop the mob. Just to know that he was all right, and to have him hold her, and put his hands on her once more. To know that she was not alone, watching the beast.

There was a movement in the darkness, over along the roof by
where the trapdoor was. They both flinched at once—though they
knew it was impossible. There had been no commotion on the street,
there was no way that even *he* could have come up, unheard, through
the whole, locked house. But there it was, the trapdoor opening—and
out came Maddy. She stopped, looking just as surprised as they were,
then walked a little sheepishly over to them.

"I just come up for a smoke," she said, holding up her cigarette of
rolled newspaper scrap as if by way of explanation. Looking submis-
sively toward Deirdre for permission.

"Well, I suppose, why not—"

Maddy grinned—an unexpected, still girlish burst of enthusiasm
suffusing her face—and lit the smoke with a locofoco. A sudden
whoosh of flame before it receded into a bright, red glow at the end of
her smoke—one more glow like the random others, lighting what
there was of the City below them.

She sucked away at it placidly—so different from the wild thing
they had dragged in off the street that morning. After several more
wild, screaming attempts to run out in the street, or retrieve her gun,
she had ended up sleeping through most of the day, there on the
reclining couch where she had first dozed off. And when Deirdre put
her to work she had dragged herself torpidly about the house, but no
longer protesting, or refusing. At supper she had not said a thing, but
had worked through her potato and the salt pork as single-mindedly as
she had eaten the stew earlier.

"It's nice up here," she said now. "Cooler. I never go up on the
roof on my house. 'Course, it's slanted."

She leaned forward, gazing out toward the north with them.

"Lookit all ya can see."

"Yes."

Maddy held out the smoke to them. Deirdre shook her head no—
but Ruth took it from her hand and drew a long, deep drag. Hoping
that Deirdre wouldn't think the worse of her for it but unable to resist.
It was the first smoke she had had in a long time, save for the occasional puff on one of Billy's pipes, and she savored the taste of it filling her lungs and head.

"I wish Billy was here," she said, despite herself. "I wish he was
here right now."

"I wish Tom was here," Deirdre said, to Ruth's surprise.

"Oh, I do, too. I wish he was here, too."

Deirdre stared out over the City, crossing herself as she spoke:

"I'd give anything for Jesus to keep him safe, to hold him in His infinite mercy."

She looked back at Ruth then—her eyes somber in what dim light there was, mostly from the fires raging out over the City. Her beauty clouded, out here in the dark, the wonderful brown eyes no longer matching the color of her hair.

"I'm sure that He will—" Ruth tried to reassure her, but Deirdre ignored her consolations.

"It was me that sent him out there. That's the thing. It's not like with your Billy, may the saints protect him. You didn't push him out there, but I did with Tom. I got him to the war, and anything that happens to him now is on me."

"But surely Tom wanted to go, in the end," Ruth told her. "Surely he thought it was his duty—"

"No. You know how Tom is," Deirdre said flatly—and Ruth had to admit she was right. "He'd never have gone to the war by himself—not some war five hundred miles away. But *I* read about it in the newspaper, and told him it was his duty. And so he went."

"My Billy *wants* to go to the war."

"He's just sayin' it," Maddy said, startling them for a second time. They had almost forgotten about her presence, she had been so silent—sitting there beside them on the roof, with her legs tucked up under her arms in that child's way again.

"He's just sayin' it," she repeated. "Men say all sorts a things they don't mean. Trust me, no man wants to go to a war."

"So why is it they do it, then?" Ruth wondered. "No, no, lookit 'em all down there."

She gestured toward the luminous insects, darting here and there through the streets below them.

"There's plenty of 'em likes a war all right. Even Billy. They might not like how it comes out, or how it goes, but they like it well enough. They like to get in theirs. It's a chance to get back."

"I can bear the thought of him coming back home on a crutch," Deirdre said. "That would be a hard thing, but I could stand it, at least. That would be my punishment, and I would bear it and praise God for His mercy every day, just to have him back—"

"Ah, now, but it won't come to that—"

"But to think of him dead! To think of him dying from the *tamh* in one of those hospitals, with all the poor, suffering souls around him! Ah, me. I don't know that I could take such a thing."

"It just said a leg, Deirdre, that's all it said. It didn't say it's comin' off, or nothin' like that. It didn't say a thing, save that he's alive."

"Yes."

"After all, he survived the chest, an' that was *severe*, you said so yourself."

"Yes, that's true."

They fell silent for a while, listening to the bacchanal below. The wild cries and screams, the sudden, startling reports of muskets and pistols—even a coordinated volley or two, making them jump.

Maddy finished her smoke, and lay back on her elbows. Then she rested her head in Deirdre's lap, just like a child, and Deirdre let her—slowly stroking her head and her tangled hair as she might one of her children's. Ruth leaned in closer, until the three of them were huddled there together, even in the heat. Listening to the wild sounds slowly dwindling below them, watching the torch lights blink out one after another.

"How's for you, Maddy?" Ruth asked. "D'ya wish you had your man here?"

Maddy snorted.

"Not much chance gettin' rid of him. He's prob'ly down ringin' me bell right now."

There was a light suddenly eye level with them—a lantern, flickering along the roof of one of the buildings behind them, across the back lot. *From the top a the Jews' house,* Ruth realized.

"Hullo! Over there!" a voice called softly through the darkness.

They all stood up abruptly.

"How can we be of service to you, Mrs. Mendelssohn?" Deirdre called back—both their voices seeming terribly loud, now, in the quieting night.

"What're you gonna do? If they come tomorrow?"

"Praise Jesus in His mercy, they won't come at all."

"With no disrespect, it's not Jesus that I'm worried about."

Peering into the darkness, Ruth could make out the figure of Mrs. Mendelssohn, hunching forward over her lantern, a shawl around her shoulders. Standing beside her she could see her daughter—Sarah, she thought her name was. *She had a lovely face, but there was something wrong with her legs—*

"What if the mob comes?"

"If they do, I don't think they're interested in the likes of us, Mrs. Mendelssohn."

"But what about the others? The coloreds, an' the like. Or what if they just want to loot?"

"I don't believe it will come to that—"

"But just if it does. You can come over here, you know. If you can get out the back, just come right across. We'll take you in—an' anybody else you know."

"Thank you, Mrs. Mendelssohn, that's very kind of you. And the same goes for you. If they come to your block first, our house is always open to you."

"Thank you," Mrs. Mendelssohn said, sounding relieved and very pleased. "Thank you, I'm sure. Remember, come over!"

She and her daughter turned away, and the little red glow of their lantern disappeared, going back down into their house.

"D'ya think they'll go after the Jews, then?" Ruth asked. "If it comes to that?"

"I don't know," Deirdre said frankly. "I don't know what they'll do, or what they want. I don't know what they think they're doing now."

"They're doin' what men always do. They're takin' it out on someone else," Maddy said sleepily, from her place back in Deirdre's lap—and Ruth felt a pang of envy, wishing that she could be there herself, feeling Deirdre's reassuring hand on her brow and her hair.

"But how long?"

"Until they get tired of it. Until they get sober enough, or scared enough to quit."

"And when will that be?"

"Who can say? There's a building still standing, ain't there?"

"Enough of that talk, now!" Deirdre chastised her, but Maddy only yawned loudly, and stretched her body like a cat's. Her form, still clad in the red dressing gown, lank and unconsciously sensuous.

"I just hope he's all right," Ruth said fiercely. "I just hope he knew enough to go to ground. He's smart like that. He's a sensible man, when he ain't got the creature in him, when he ain't too fed up."

"Oh, aye."

"And I know Tom will be all right."

"God willing."

Down in the streets, the luminous bugs blinked out, or rushed away.

"God willing, preserve all the sons of women tonight."

In Deirdre's lap, Maddy snored.

63

DEIRDRE

Up on the roof, she stroked Maddy's hair where it lay in her lap. Almost amused to find herself cradling the head of the block's whore.

The poor, daft child. And where would she go after this? After the harpies below had finished turning out her house?

Beside her, Ruth was nodding as well, leaning against her shoulder. *Who would have thought it?* But here she was, herself giving sanctuary to the whores and the blacks, and just as glad to do it.

She had been right after all—it was not a fit block to live on. Thinking of the women who had come by the house all day, with their hateful rantings. Their savage faces, creased with joy as they hurled their stones and bricks.

Stoning a girl! On her own block! What has happened to us, then?

Yet her thoughts always went back to Tom. Trying to think of where he might be, and how he was. Mulling over the line in the paper again—the most recent line: *O'Kane, leg.* And before that there had been the *chest, severe,* and how many more would there be after that, even if Jesus granted her prayers and he did live through this one?

At least now we are reconciled. At least now we would have some chance to meet in Heaven, having both confessed.

All through that winter, after his last one—the *severe* one—she had agonized over him. Wanting desperately to see him, to take the train down to Washington and go searching through the hospitals until she found him.

But it was too much of a risk. The smallpox and the measles were raging through the City by then. She could not leave the children, and besides, there was no money for it, anyway. Instead she had sent him all the food she could manage, and spent her evenings writing—writing to anyone and everyone she thought could help. Writing to the Sanitary Commission and to the hospital nurses; to the Congress and the War Department and the colonel of his regiment. Hoping and praying for some word—for some chance somebody might take notice of her husband.

And first of all she wrote to him every night—a letter every single day, though they could barely afford the postage. Going without supper sometimes so she could buy the pens and ink, and candles. Getting the children to write as well, those that could already, doing whatever she could to make sure that he had a letter at least once a day, wherever he was.

It had nearly driven her to distraction, trying to get word, in the first place, as to whether he was alive or not. Suffering all through Christmas while she tried to nurse the children and make some sort of holiday for them.

How good it would have been to have some friend then, she thought, feeling the weight of Ruth's head against her shoulder. *How good it would have been simply not to be alone.*

She had finally gotten an official letter from the War Department, late in January, informing her briskly that her husband was still invaliding at the Bethesda hospital. The note sending her into paroxysms of both new fear and exultation—overjoyed that he was still alive, but fretting over why he was still in the hospital.

Only after another month had gone by, deep into February, had she received the first scarce lines from him. *Im alright now,* written in his schoolboy's hand, but even more wavery and uncertain than usual, as if he barely had the strength to work the pencil. *Im reecovered now and back with me company.* She has sensed the trace of resentment still running through those words, reminding her that he was still in service.

Slowly, they had made it up. Over the course of those first tentative letters, the daguerreotype he had finally sent to her. She had been shy herself, wanting desperately to confess, to debase herself before him, but she was afraid of how he might respond.

To know himself, in so many words, to be married to such a woman— how would he take it?

"I know what I have done," she had written him at last. "And I repent it with all my heart, and all my faith, and would repent it with my life as well, should I think that would be of use."

And getting his reply then—still cautious and unsure, still with a touch of the old resentment running through it. But slowly making his confession as well, with a man's own grudging, prideful slowness. Writing to her in that uneven hand, *But I wanted to go. Thats the truth out I wanted to go.*

The words there, the frankness, sitting between them like some newfound thing. The question still unresolved, the bond still fragile, still tenuous, but restored, at least for the time being. While the war went on.

Then had come the newspaper again, after Gettysburg, with his name there. The whole thing starting up again too soon.

If she could only have seen him. He was supposed to have leave to recuperate but there was some mistake, he had had to report back to the regiment first. Then with Lee moving north, all liberties had been canceled. He had written her, she was glad of that at least. Not wanting her to think he had spent his furlough gambling and whoring in Washington City—letting her know he wanted to come back, to be at home with her and his family.

I kiss you and embrase you. Id be back with you if I could all of you.

Knowing at least from that there was hope, at least from that there was something to pin her faith on. Then had come Gettysburg, and the new line in the newspaper.

O'Kane, leg.

It had stunned her, to see it. Thinking that she had made her peace now, that by confessing she would be forgiven by God as well as by Tom. But there it was—just another battle, another desolation. She nearly lost all the faith she had gathered over it. Knowing it would only go on and on, the battles, the killing, with no reason to it. Until her Tom, too, was killed.

"God does not bend to our wishes, but we to His," Father Knapp had told her—though she could barely look him in the eye anymore, for all of the wickedness he must know was in her now.

"But what good is the sacrifice, then, Father? What does it do for Tom?"

"Jesus teaches us, 'I require mercy, not a sacrifice.' All we can do is wait upon His mercy, and extend our own."

It was not good enough—it was still not good enough. But then she had learned that her brother had come back, and the riot had started, and she had had no time to think about anything else. Making sure to lay in enough water and food, and keep the children in off the street. Forcing herself to think what else, what else had to be done.

It was then that she had remembered Ruth. Wanting to hate her still   but she could not anymore. Her last, residual well of hatred spilling out when she saw how frightened she was, how helpless but how determined. It was then that she had seen God's purpose clearly. That she must ease the hardness of her heart, still unconfessed, for this woman who had wiped away the last of her family. This grudge held so carefully, all these years—but she had given it up willingly. Pleased at last to submit to His judgment, washed of her cares like some thick-headed Protestant lawyer.

Below she could see the last lights going out—around the Five Points, just to the south, and much of the East Side. The City slowly going black, and finally quieting. Wondering what they would do, what *she* would do, if they came back in the morning—if the riot reached the block.

· *Escape over the back lots to the Jews? Try to face down men, as she had faced down those foolish women today?* And what would she do with her brother, if he found them?

She didn't know, it was all in God's hands, and even her most careful preparations could not help with what might descend upon them. She was just glad to be able to do something—to be able to fight, if need be, as he had. Glad to have a duty.

64

MADDY

It was cooler on the roof.

The air was still hot enough, and there was a constant smell of smoke in the air, but it was better up there, and besides, there was company.

She lay in Deirdre's lap, passing in and out of dreams. Cosseted and cushioned, her eyes opening from time to time to stare out at the lights flickering below. Deirdre's hand smoothing through her hair. Embarrassed by how knotted and dirty it must be, but pleased to feel her hand anyway. Pleased to feel any human touch that wasn't methodically probing and grabbing at her.

Her father had smoothed her hair, as she lay in bed at night. Or maybe it had been her mother. It was hard to remember, they had both been gone for so long. She barely had any recollection of her father at all—just the sense of a large, confident presence. The memory of him standing in the doorway with his hands on his hips, laughing at something she had done.

She could never understand what had gone wrong with the scaffolding, casting him down from a height no higher than they were this night. Not too long a drop for a man to survive with a broken leg, a bad back—a shoulder that didn't work quite right for the rest of his life. *He must have lost his footing, got tangled up in the ropes and fallen at a bad angle.*

She had wondered since if her mother had been called to the sight—to see her husband's body lying there, his neck bent like a hanged man's. She didn't know, the old woman had never spoken of it. Maddy could barely remember the day herself. Only that she had come home from the common school and her mother was sitting in a chair, dressed in black, and all the neighbors were over. The wake held that very night—her father in a box, a candle at his feet. His face looking ashen, scrubbed and dressed in his best clothes by her mother and her friends. Maddy had seen him last that very morning, her eyes still bleary with sleep, finishing his tea in the kitchen before he went off to his painting job.

And now, in Robinson's silly creation, he was a drunkard, a brute, a pimp. Selling his children on the street for alcohol, beating his wife. When in life he had been guilty of only one thing—he had died.

Ah, well, that was enough, wasn't it?

Her anger from the day settling into a deep, muddy sediment—though she still flinched and swore to herself when she thought how, even now, the bitches could be looting through her things. Stealing what they liked, and who was to stop them? Half a dozen times during the day she had stood up in Deirdre's parlor, looking for her gun. Determined to run out in the street and settle things, scatter them all like a roost of chickens.

They had gotten hold of her each time, Ruth or Deirdre. Walked her back to the couch, sat her down there, gently but firmly. In truth, she had been just as glad to be stopped, even though she had cursed and shrieked at them, struggled weakly against their hard grips. She was still unsettled by the stoning, the piece of brick glancing off her head. It was a small enough wound, Deirdre already having dressed it up with iodine, but it had rattled her.

She had come out with her gun and they hadn't run. She had gone out there, and they had only laughed at her, and stoned her like a whore—

Which was what she was. That had hurt as much as anything. They saw her as no better, even now, with the war come right up to the block. They really meant all the cuts, all the curses. Stone her in the street and take her things, just as they would the race women's, or Ruth's family's—

She could not fathom why Deirdre had stood against them, though she was grateful for it. At supper she had been sat down with all the rest of them. The children from both families crowded into the table like it was Christmas Eve. Deirdre and Ruth and Ruth's son, that beautiful dark boy, serving up the food and taking care of everything.

And she, Maddy, had been tucked into the table, too. Sitting right between Deirdre's two oldest girls. She had been put right there, like one more member of the family, sat down and served with all the rest. All the trimmings of a family, even if it wasn't really hers.

The meal had cleared her head, for the first time in days.

"Are ya missin' him then, Maddy?"

Ruth, very close, just above her. She opened her eyes and saw her leaning into Deirdre's shoulder. Her face looking softer in the refracted orange light from the sky than she had ever seen it before.

"Who?" she asked—though she knew exactly who Ruth had meant, had made a show of it, and pretended that he was right downstairs, running after her.

"You shouldn't be encouraging her to miss such a man as that," Deirdre admonished her, but Ruth paid no mind.

"D'ya know where he is? D'ya miss him not bein' around tonight?"

"No, not him," Maddy told her truthfully.

She was thinking instead of a scaffolding giving way, a man falling to his death just like that. It had changed everything, but she had done her best, she and her mother. She had never made any apologies for it.

"That's right, then," Deirdre said, misunderstanding. "No need to miss the likes of *that* one."

No—not when there were so many other bastards still to come.

All day long, she knew, she had been waiting, hoping for her lover to come back somehow, and keep his promise. Willing to forgive him even then, for all that he had done to her family in his book—for all of his nothingness. Just on the faith and hope that he would see her for what she was—someone to come back for—rather than what he wanted to see her as, his White Captive, his artist's model.

But she didn't need even him, in the end. If he hadn't wanted to come back, it was just as well that she knew it, at last. She had always gotten by, since the scaffolding had given way. She always would. *It was cooler on the roof.* Deirdre's lap so comfortable beneath her. Almost like a family.

She told herself that none of it mattered—the women on the street, or the fire captain with his threats to clear her out. Robinson and his games. Letting it all drift away from her with the night. All her things, and her love for him, and all the scores and the insults and the outrages still left unsettled. All the hands of men upon her.

She tried to think only of the tree, just outside their kitchen window on St. John's Park, the three of them eating there on a summer's night. Insisting that nothing else mattered—and none of it would ever be avenged, and he would never see her for herself, and her mother and father would be left in peace, God rest their souls.

Only the small voice, restless inside her. Knowing that it did matter, to her, as much as she wished that it did not. Insisting, as she spiraled down to sleep, It's a lie, It's a lie, It's a lie—

65

FINN McCOOL

He stood out in the street, helpless. Not knowing what to do, watching in horror as the mob tortured O'Brien.

An officer, no less. And an Irishman at that.

He was stunned by everything he saw around him now. The drunken, reddened faces. Breaking into homes, smashing and burning everything in sight.

Even the machine, the Black Joke itself. Smashed beyond repair, and tossed into the gutter like so much trash.

Even his own men—swarming over any house they could loot like so many murderers. And those who had remained loyal, who had followed his orders and tried to put out the fires, had only seen his authority overturned. The machine smashed, and its hoses cut. The water, the lifeblood of the City, draining uselessly into the gutter.

They had looked to him, as usual—then, seeing him helpless, had walked away. Back to their own homes, their own wives and children—or off to see what they could loot for themselves.

Everything, beyond his control.

He hung back by the stoops, hands in his pockets. Watching O'Brien writhe in pain before him. Men and women and even girls, now, laughing as they cut him to pieces.

There would be payment for this, he was sure of it. *And how was it ever to be rebuilt?* How were they to have any organization again,

instead of a useless mob of jackals? There had to be some way—
some way to get back out ahead of the crowd again. Some way to give
them what they wanted, without wrecking the whole damned town—

He thought of that tart down in Paradise Alley, from the other
night. The one who had laughed in his face, and locked him out in the
street.

*They would like that well enough. And what was she? Just some whore.
Nobody's house and property—*

He stood up, a plan beginning to form in his head. *That was the key.*
Lead them to what they wanted to do, without bringing on some fight
with the army or the police, a fight they were bound to lose. *Just give
them what they want.*

He noticed the reporter across the street then—Greeley's man, that
damned Robinson. Now he looked as sick as Finn felt himself, watching
them torture poor O'Brien. *Well, he had tried to warn him.* A reporter,
though, that was bad. Taking it all in, writing it down for later—

To his consternation he saw Robinson turn, and notice him in turn.
He had even started across the street toward him, before Finn had time
to turn, and duck away behind his *b'hoys.*

Now he would see him here. He would see, too, how little power
he had here—even worse than if he had blamed him for the whole
riot.

*That was the first thing. They had to put out the eyes of the enemy—
of the Greeleys, and the Republicans. They had to shield the people from
their crimes.*

He gave Robinson a look, tried to warn him off again—the
reporter looking perplexed. *Well, how many warnings could the man
expect?* Finn turned to one of his shoulder hitters, pointing out the
reporter.

"*Here now,*" he told them, already beginning to shout. "*Don't that
look like a spy for the police? Or Greeley?*"

He had all he could do not to laugh, watching Robinson skedaddle.
Trying not to look too much at O'Brien, who was nearly dead anyway, poor man. *His body could be dumped somewhere it would never be
discovered. The whole crime only a rumor.*

He hitched up his galluses, trying to stoke up his confidence. There
were things that had to be done, and he was the one to do them, a
leader of men. He rubbed his hands together, thinking again of that
damned whore in Paradise Alley—

66

HERBERT WILLIS ROBINSON

Crouching behind the street-cleaning machine, I loosen the spigot on its water barrel like a farm boy milking a cow. Greedily lapping up what water is left. Spilling more out into my hands, rubbing them over my face. (No doubt, this is the first time this machine has ever truly cleaned anything.)

Keeping my eye on the darkened corner, the bar, across Ninth Avenue. Listening for their steps—the ones who chased me here. Listening for *him*, that monster from the park—

From my hiding place, I can watch all the ignorant armies as they parade back and forth through the night, their torches raised high. Still set on some original act of destruction, some fresh looting.

It is no easy task. The City is a picked skull, but the maggots are still in the streets.

All I want is to be back home—to be back with Maddy, now. *How I have let her down.* But I do not dare to move—scared of the City, the hum of the mob still. I can do nothing but crouch here, holding my pistol. The footsteps that followed me have fallen away. But I still cannot know if *he* is out there somewhere, just around the next corner, *waiting*.

And what is there to report from all this? What is the *news?* The depredations of man? These mindless cruelties, endlessly repeated?

Hiding behind a street cleaner, I wait in ambush for another man.

·   ·   ·

Across Ninth Avenue now, I watch a large white man—a bricklayer
or a hod carrier, his bulk partly hidden under the eaves of the tavern.
Whenever a black man comes by, he runs out at him, knocking him
down in the street, grabbing and biting at him like an animal. The
black man grappling desperately with him, finally pushing him off
and running for his life, the bricklayer lunging after him. He bites off
part of an ear and a cheek before the next man can tear himself free—
stumbling on down the street, sobbing in fear and pain. The white
man shouting after him.

*"Nigger! Nigger! Nigger! Oh, you better not put any niggers to
work!"*

The big white bruiser finally falls silent, lying prone for a while
where he is, out in the middle of the street. Then he gets up, moves
back into the shadows of the tavern. Waiting to set upon the next
Negro who happens by.

I want Maddy. I want to go to her, to have her with me—even to
take her to my home.

I know I should go to her, to shelter her, God only knows how she
is faring. But I cannot. The night crawls by, deep in the midnight
hours, but I cannot go back out there, into that despicable *City*. My
legs are paralyzed beneath me. I can do nothing but huddle behind this
broken bucket.

I have seen the crowd, and I despise it. I am terrified by it. Knowing, even now, that I will still witness it, write about it, with a drunkard's compulsion. But I will not be bound to it, by anything or
anybody—not even Maddy. I will not be a part of it. I want only to
hide from the dissonant hum, the terrible, meaningless drone of
massed humanity.

I will not be a part of it.

67

JOHNNY DOLAN

It must have been Ruth who had sold him. His wife.

He told himself now that he was sure of it. Figuring it out as he kept lurching around the town with the mobs. The sign still over his chest and still no good idea of how to find her, anyway—

Worse yet, he was sure he had noticed the mobs beginning to abate. Falling away with the goods they had looted. Still drunkenly shouting their ridiculous rallying cries—but no one else came.

"Sold! For three hundred dollars, when a nigger gets a thousand!"

And why not? Three hundred dollars was a good price for a man— more than any of them were worth. No doubt a nigger could do a better day's work.

But before they were all gone—before the police and the soldiers finished them off—he had to find Ruth. *But how?* He wandered away from the crowds, trying to think it through. Walking until he found himself at a river—which one, he wasn't even sure. Aware only of the blood-red sun that hovered above the water.

It must have been her.

Only she could have seen how agitated he was, coming back to their shanty in Pigtown that night. He should have left the City at once, he realized that now. Instead he had lost his nerve, fled back to her, and their home.

She wasn't the sharpest one, but she noticed things. Women always did. He had thought he would be all right, after all, she couldn't even read the newspapers that he had her buy. But she must have had a look at his swag while he slept—must have gotten wind of the murder from the talk on the street.

He should never have let her go out, even to get food. Better yet, he should have battered her head in the moment he had stepped through the door—

Instead he had sat. Too nervous to stick his head outdoors for more than a few minutes at a time. Afraid even to take his loot—the fine watch and chain, and the beautiful dog-headed walking stick— out to a fence or a popshop, from the fear they would be recognized. Afraid some one of his old companions from the river gangs, the Break o' Day Boys or the Swamp Angels, might have gotten word of it, and would sell him for a nickel, just on suspicion.

He knew that he should move. Go over to Jersey, or up to Providence, or even Boston, as soon as he had the chance. But he couldn't, afraid that if they were looking out for him he would surely be caught trying to leave the City. Picked out of a crowd by someone he knew—

So he had sat, and waited. Drinking too much, clouding his judgment by the hour. Until they had everything arranged for him, luring him out with the perfect excuse.

Telling him that the brother was still alive. Jesus, but that was a dirty thing. They deserved to get it in the neck for that alone, if nothing else. How could he have gone for such a thing?

But by then he had spent nearly two weeks sitting in the shanty. Sneaking over every night, when he thought she was asleep, to stare at Old Man Noe's eye, still snugly encased in his thumb gouger. Trying to peer deep inside it, having heard that a dead man's eyes contained the very last image he had seen.

Dolan had always doubted that, figuring that otherwise every murder in the world would be solved—and sure enough, he could see nothing, no matter how hard he stared. The orb before him looking back, dark and blank and perfectly objective. Reminding him of something else—

The box.

Dolan had remembered then, uncovering the cracked and half-wrecked cabinet of wonders. Pulling back its black shroud to see there the very same eye—almost. *The eye of a giant.* That was how the studiolo man had billed it, although in fact it didn't seem even as big as a normal man's eye, now that he had the example before him. What he had stared into for so many nights, on the road and in the belly of the ship—that single eye behind the glass, staring back from its own perfect world. Always tracking him, pitiless and unblinking.

Yet he realized it was not even a real eye at all. For unlike Noe's he could see, deep within the iris, a tiny, wavering image—an image of himself, in the artfully painted glass. Staring back at his own self, haggard and fearful. *The image of the murderer.*

And after that, he had chosen to believe them. After that he had gone along, and let them gull him, get him on that boat. *Out to see his brother. Out to sea, his brother—*

He might as well have believed they were taking him to Heaven. Instead there had been just Tom, and her black man, whose name he didn't even know, in the boat. Throwing the burlap sack over his hat, bagging him like a fine rabbit. By the time he came to, his shanghaiers were well out past Seagate, and when he had struggled they had put the boot in, knocked him senseless again.

The ship was some wormy bucket, worse even than the *Birmingham* had been. Refitted just enough to get it to Panama, with a load full of shovels and mining pans, canvas pants and bags of flours. *Pure gold—* to be sold at a thousand percent markup to the prospectors. His new masters had worked him like a dog, kept him belowdecks whenever they came near a port. He had been sick all the time, the voyage nearly as bad as the Atlantic crossing, and when he refused to work they had whipped him to within an inch of his life.

He had thought about trying to jump ship when they finally got to Panama. But he still had no money and all around him, on the docks at Colon, he could see white men dropping like flies from the yellow jack, lying facedown in the mud. He decided to go on to San Francisco, where they promised to pay him at least. Hightailing it across the Isthmus with the rest of the crew, as fast as the mules could move him.

And then, on the way up the coast to California, he had almost forgotten himself, and enjoyed the sail. The weather was warm, and he had picked up a little seamanship for the want of anything else to do.

Learning the stars, and how to navigate by them. He had even found himself thinking that he might ship out again, once he had his money.

He still did not forgive them. He still wanted what he was owed, his woman and his treasure. But it had occurred to him that he should just keep going. The sailors talking about what the South Seas were like, and China, and the East Indies—

And what would he be when he got to such places? Something different—without a past.

But then they had struck anchor in San Francisco, and the next morning he had awakened to find the ship deserted. Everyone else, the captain and the entire ship's company, had already gone off to the goldfields without so much as letting him know. Their cargo had vanished as well—their ship just one more planting in the forest that all but filled the harbor now. So many abandoned ships lying at anchor—their crews gone off to find their own fortunes—that he had made his way to land by leaping from deck to deck.

But the gold was not for him, that was a ben's game, he was sure. For the next day and a half he had wandered around the waterfront, trying to figure out what to do. *How to get back, or get out, he still wasn't decided.* How to do anything that might gain him a little real money, not gold dust—

That was when he had wandered into the pool hall on Montgomery Street. Not even having any definite plan in mind, he had never had any aptitude for the game. *That was the problem. He was just that—the rube, waiting to be taken.* There had been some argument, a shot had been fired, over just what he still did not know. But the next thing he realized, he was being pulled up before a judge, then shipped off to the penitentiary, from where he had been so foolish as to try to escape—

He stumbled back from the gleaming, red river, still unsure of what he would do. Walking blindly back through the dusk—ignoring the little wars raging all around him, from block to block.

There was a noise—a throaty, guttural sound like something a dog might make in its death throes. He had come upon another mob, gathered around some fresh entertainment, and going up to investigate he saw that they had an army officer stretched out upon the pavement. The man's body tortured nearly to death, but still not dead. His face beaten in with rocks and clubs, his legs and arms cut and burned with oil—

The same officer he had smashed.

He had walked in another circle, only coming back to the block where he had been. *They must have been tormenting the man for hours,* he realized. Some of them still kicking at him, others holding back a priest who was trying to have him moved inside. The women mocking him where he lay, and telling coarse jokes. The children on the street running tentatively up, slashing at the man with knives or scissors, then screaming delightedly and dashing back again.

The officer himself, meanwhile, was unable to speak or even to move anymore, under their blows. Yet still he groaned and twitched from time to time, still alive.

It was so hard to die.

Dolan remembered a man he had rescued once from a fire, in the dead of winter. He hadn't even meant to do it, but the next thing he knew, he was running into a burning building, with an ax in his hand. Tearing up a wobbling staircase until he had found him, trapped beneath a beam.

He had been as dark as the ace of spades. A sailor, as dark as the nigger in the boat, the night he was shanghaied. Yet Dolan had cut him out, without a moment's hesitation. Risking his own life, the lives of the other men from the fire company to save him. Hauling him out of the building just before it collapsed on them all.

The others had been amazed that he would do such a thing. He had been amazed himself. He had simply wanted to cut the man loose, that was all—

He looked down at the twitching body of the officer now, and fingered the blade in his pocket. All it would take was one swift plunge and he would be finished. Let the others raise what hell they might, he would face them down. Then he could walk away. Retrace his steps back to the river, perhaps. *Wade on in and let it cover him. Be off this damned island, once and for all—*

He began to shove his way forward through the crowd. Unbending the blade in his pocket, ready to strike—when before him, on the ground, the officer groaned once more and died. It was over just that quickly. The mob letting the priest through now—bending their necks, instantly as docile as lambs before him again. He ordered them

to take the body into a house and they did as they were told. Six of
them meekly carrying the officer's body away, treating it almost delicately now.

Dolan began to back away with the rest of the crowd. Seething
with envy for the dead officer.

He was already dead himself. That was what he kept forgetting.

They had slid him out the black gable, right into the lime-strewn
soil, but he had risen. He had been stranded out on the roads, with not
a thing to eat in ten counties, but he had walked out. He had been stuck
in the bottom of that boat, with no good water to drink, and then
shipped to California, but he had lived. He had come back, he had
done too much to live again, to simply go off now and disappear without claiming what was his.

His wife. His treasure, and his wife.

She was his, as surely as if they had read out the banns. He had
saved her life back in that village, with the dogs ready to finish her off.
He knew she had resented him, how he had taken her for his pleasure
then, just pushing into her. How he had treated her ever since, coming
home with the blood leaping in his veins, in his fists.

She could resent what she wanted, she was still his. He had gotten her
off the damned island, hadn't he, and away to Amerikay. She only
thought she knew what he had done to live. She had been fortunate
enough just to get there near the end, when the roaming pack of dogs
had come.

He still had to find her. Even now that the mob had ripped everything up, it had not flushed her out—her or her nigger lover. The
answer descended upon him like a revelation, leaving him all the more
livid that he had not seen it before.

Deirdre. She would know where Ruth had gone, if she and her husband were at least in the City still. *Where had they lived? That skinny
little house she was always so proud of?* Somewhere down in the Fourth
Ward, near the river. The names coming back to him now with the
cumulative trickle of memory. A little street, just off Paradise Alley.

*Deirdre would know where his wife was—if she was still there herself.
But he could not imagine she wouldn't be, not with that house.*

He began to move south, trudging down toward the waterfront.
His hand still clenched around the blade in his pocket. Going to get
what was his. *Going to cut it loose.*

DAY THREE

Wednesday
July 15, 1863

It is a kingly thing . . .
. . . city . . .

"THE RUIN"

68

HERBERT WILLIS ROBINSON

The third day. Eight in the morning.

The pigs are back on the streets. No doubt they have discerned, with their quick, feral wits, that the worst is over now. They tiptoe about, feasting on all the new mounds of garbage rotting out in the street.

Between them, men stagger from post to pole — knowing no more landmarks, no schedule or habit. Hungover in the wretched heat, the blood and ash still blackening their hands.

I trudge along with the rest of them. All of us stumbling about. Unshaven and unwashed, and the dead among us still unshriven. Still we march on, toward something, as if we deserve it.

We reek.

There is another short, fierce rainstorm. I think at least that it will cleanse us, but the rain is as full of ash as it is of water, drenching us in splotchy, black cinders from the City's own burning.

Troops are pouring into Manhattan at last, from Pennsylvania and upstate. It is reported that the City's own 7th regiment has already disembarked at the Battery, along with the 152nd New York, the 26th Michigan volunteers, the 74th and 65th National Guard. Those troops who were not too badly wounded at Gettysburg have been pressed into emergency makeshift companies.

The mob has not surrendered, though. The rioters still refuse to believe it is all up, certain to the end that the regulars will not fire on them.

"Not on their own friends an' neighbors," one of them assures me, repeating the common sentiment.

"Not on their own kin. You wait an' see, they'll come over to us."

But in fact the troops are taking the City back block by block, brooking no resistance. They fire full volleys into the crowd when it tries to stand against them, rake the house fronts with canister whenever they encounter snipers.

In West Twenty-eight Street, a colonel of the 8th New York at last orders his men to cut down poor old Abraham Franklin, the lynched coachman. The hulking Irish butcher's boy, who had hung Franklin up in the first place, now tries in turn to pull the officer from his horse. The colonel only draws his sword—and runs him through the chest. The butcher boy falls to the ground with a look of real surprise still on his face, twitching a little as the blood bubbles out of his breast. The mob scatters at once, leaving him to die in the street. The soldiers lay Abraham Franklin's body gently on the sidewalk beside him—the colonel's own handkerchief placed over his tortured black face.

At the St. Nicholas Hotel, Wool's brigadier, General Brown, has cleared out most of the lobbyists now. The hotel is an efficient, bustling, military headquarters—the bar telegraph working again.

Commissioner Acton is there, too, come up from Mulberry Street to coordinate the army's attacks with his Metropolitans. He sends off one wire after another to those station houses that are still left standing.

Kill any man with a club . . . Receive colored people as long as you can. Refuse nobody . . .

He laughs when he sees me—bedraggled as I must be, not only my suit but my face, as well, covered in soot.

"What have you been up to?" he roars. "Taking up minstrelsy, Herbert? Well, you better get washed up. We are winning the town back for civilization!"

All through the night, he tells me, the police have been sheltering hundreds, perhaps even thousands of fleeing Negroes.

"We even have men out looking for them now, trying to rescue them, poor creatures!"

Over in the 27th Precinct, I witness a trio of hefty Irish roundsmen trying to talk a colored man named Jackson out from under the dock of Pier 4. He had been beaten half to death, trying to make his way to the Brooklyn ferry—managing to escape only by burrowing his way deep into the unspeakably filthy cesspool of discarded fish heads and tin cans, dead cats and oyster shells that wash up under the pier.

The police try to get him to come out, but they cannot convince him that they are not simply the mob in other forms. The ferry passengers join in, trying to persuade him, but Jackson only becomes more wary with every insidious new white voice he hears above him.

"C'mon, now, we mean ya no harm," a brawny cop named McClusker pleads, dangling by one arm from the wharf planking. "Ya can see that now, can't ye?"

From deep below in his pier cave comes a disembodied voice:

"I can see nothing. I can see nothing but that you're white."

Finally, in an act of colossal faith—or resignation—Jackson emerges. Cut and bleeding in half a dozen places, his black skin greyed by the harbor mud. His eyes stare off wearily into the distance—the ferry passengers falling back from the very sight of him. The cops bundle him up in a blanket, taking him off to a carriage and then on to New York Hospital.

"Tell me, what made ya finally trust us?" McClusker asks him.

"I just couldn't," Jackson tells him, and begins to weep long, silent tears. "I just couldn't stay down there no more."

Near Chambers Street and Oak, just in back of City Hall, I come across an old Mohawk whitewasher—a veteran of the Mexican War who has worked downtown for years. Everyone knows him. He lies dying on the sidewalk now, in the arms of some other workingmen. The mob, it seems, mistook him for a black man—not that they would have cared very much either way. *Extinguishing one old tribe or another.*

At the African Methodist Bethel Church, on Thirtieth Street, I ask the colored minister if his people have any hope for the future. He looks at me very directly, his lips pursed and his eyes level and unblinking.

"Yes," he replies, "in the next world."

The mob wavers—but incredibly, it is not yet spent, the rioters in many places more determined than ever. They throw up still more barricades in the streets, wage pitched battles against the police and the army at half a dozen points around Manhattan.

Meanwhile, individual looters are still roaming about, brazenly taking whatever they can. In Second Street I watch a gigantic German workman, striding along with two women's hoop skirts hung over his neck while he sorts through the ruined shops for more. Brooks Brothers—which has so battened on selling shoddy merchandise to our troops—lies sacked and broken on Cherry Street, the sidewalk strewn with fine men's pants and suits, vests and hats.

But I have had enough, at last—looking on all of their depredations now with only half an eye. They can all go to the devil, my City, and the quicker the better. I trudge toward Maddy's house through the sulfuric heat. The fears and phantasms of the night before dissolving in the daylight now. Ashamed of myself, almost too ashamed to look her in the face. Wondering if she is still there at all—

And why should she be? Why should she stay where I have kept her? What could she possibly need me for anymore?

Still, I must make sure that she is all right. I must see if she will come back with me—if she can stand to be with me at all, after I have let her down. We must reach some new arrangement, if that is possible.

I am nearly to the Shambles when I see the men. Some forty or fifty of them, at least. Moving swiftly, loping off the block with the look of furtive dogs who have just done something they know they should not have.

Maddy—

I begin to walk faster—then to run—grabbing for the gun. Knowing, as the bottom drops out of my stomach, that there is no more time. *The war is here.*

69

TOM O'KANE

They arrived just before dawn and mustered in Stuyvesant Square, in the pretty little park across from a plain redbrick Quaker meeting house. It had taken the flatboats all night to pole them across to Desbrosses Street, and when they were finally all assembled, they were served a breakfast that was too rotten to eat, even for men used to field rations—wormy beef, and soggy bread and cheese that was covered with fuzzy blue splotches of mold. Soon after that a thunderstorm came up, sudden and fierce, soaking them to the bone before it danced on out over the East River and doing nothing more to improve their disposition.

At last the order came to move out, into the Second Avenue. Their command was made up of the wounded men from half a dozen different regiments, but they were all veterans and they marched with an easy professionalism. The sun was already out again, water steaming off the street before them. They stepped over the gaping holes in the street where the paving stones had been torn out, staring at the burned-out shells of houses, the clothing and broken furniture strewn along the sidewalks. The City so much the same as they remembered but so altered, like a familiar place revisited in a bad dream.

What the hell is going on? Tom wondered, chafing to get back to Paradise Alley already. *So close to home now.*

They got some idea of what they were up against when they

reached Nineteenth Street, and Duryea's Zouaves came streaming
back past them. They had been sent out as the advance guard, with
their howitzers, but now they came limping back, looking shamefaced, and glad to be away with their lives.

Like Sickles's men, tumbling back from the wheat field—

"It was a trap! They led us on, then shot us to pieces from the
rooftops," one of them told Snatchem when he stopped him. *The old
gang trick—one that any police sergeant would have seen through.*

"There was thousands of 'em! They got the howitzers. I think they
kilt the officers, too—"

The man broke away and ran on down the street with the rest of
the Zouaves, their baggy red pants and Turkish harem jackets blackened with soot and powder now. *How fine they had looked in those uniforms, marching off to the war two years ago—*

They opened their ranks to let the defeated men pass—Tom and
the others from the 69th still unmoved. They had seen plenty of
defeat, including their own, and they knew enough by now not to be
spooked by it. Instead, it only added to their slowly kindled anger. *To
be run by a mob, in their own city. They would have to see about that.* They
swung on up around the corner, over to the First Avenue—and there
it was.

The Zouaves were right, Tom saw at once. There were hundreds,
maybe thousands of men and women in the street. Swarming over the
broken, looted homes and stores like so many cockroaches on a chunk
of old cheese—some of them still pummeling the helpless wounded
men the Zouaves had left behind. On the corner, too, they had put up
their shingle—three black bodies, hanging naked and mutilated from
a single lamppost, like a brace of pheasants. Two that had been men
and one a woman, their bodies still smoking, dripping human fat that
hissed like the rain when it hit the street.

"Jesus. Jesus God."

"The sons a bitches," Snatchem said softly.

He could hear the other men—battle veterans, all—swearing
softly, up and down the line. But when the crowd took notice of them,
they began to cheer, recognizing how many of them were from New
York.

"C'mon, Irishmen! There's not a thing that can stop us, if you're
with us!"

"We'll take the whole City!"

"Come, friends, come to us!"

Yet behind the cheering rioters Tom could see others, running back and forth, trying to find anything they could fire from the howitzers they had wrested from the Zouaves. Stuffing the mouths of the wide, squat guns with nails and rocks, chunks of metal and glass, trying to find something they could employ for a fuse.

"*Friends, my arse,*" Feeley muttered.

The drums began to beat, and Tom's company moved down the street, double-time. The artillerymen coolly rolling up a battery of rifled cannon along their flanks. The colonel walking his horse on ahead of them, waving his sword in a slow circle over his head.

The looters dropped what they were doing now. Some of them fled behind a flimsy barricade they had erected across the First Avenue—while others still chanted at them hopefully, even holding out their arms.

"Join us! Join us!"

"Join your friends and neighbors!"

But there were already scattered shots and bricks, from the rooftops, spattering along the pavement by their feet. The soldiers ignored it—marching up to the barricade—nothing more than a lamppost, and a pile of broken chairs and beds, and wagon beds. *Nothing that would stand against veteran troops.*

"*Join us! Join us!*"

They halted and leveled their rifles, ten yards from the grinning, cheering faces. So like the ones Tom had seen his whole life in the ward—some of them the very same faces. Tanned and weathered from so many days of working under the sun, streaked now with soot and ash, from their exertions this morning. Or the night before, or the day before that—whenever it was that they had decided to hang their fellow human beings up from a lamppost and light them on fire.

Still grinning now—still thinking the troops were coming over to them. Not understanding, even now, that this was not another game. Not understanding, for all they knew of the hardness of life, what a war was. Whooping and laughing as they had the day they had first seen them off, with their grand parade to the docks—

"*Singin', we're the boys that fear no noise—*"

Their first volley swept away the barricade as if it was so much litter. The second one cleared the street, sending the mob screaming,
shrieking and crying, down the block, fleeing into any house or storefront they could find. The pavement covered at once with the dead,
and the moaning, bleeding wounded. *Just like every field they had seen
for the last two years.* The rioters howling and cursing as they scattered
before them.

"Damn ye! Damn ye! To do this to yer own people!"

"You're no better than the police!"

Tom spotted one bunch of hard-looking bruisers and went to run
them. Chasing them up the stairs of a brownstone and into the house,
George and Feeley and Larkins right behind him. Even with his bad
leg, he pursued them through the smashed house, the broken crockery
and glass and furniture crunching under his feet.

They chased them right up on the roof, where the men had suddenly turned and thrown up their hands, trying to surrender. Tom saw
that at least two of them were men he knew, from the Black Joke—
men who had manned the brakes just down the line from him for
years. They recognized him, too, and the rest of them. He could see it
in their faces—their eyes widening, a look of relief passing over them,
as they saw that they were saved.

Instead they kept right on coming, their bayonets fixed. The men
they had cornered had kept their hands up, unable to believe they
would actually run through their old mates. Only at the very last did
they understand that they were not going to stop, and jumped off the
roof—landing hard in the street, three stories below, breaking legs
and arms and screaming in pain.

Tom and his men watched them from above for a moment—then
they ran back down, their bayonets still out, to root out the rest of the
mob.

They did not know what a war was.

When he had gone back to the regiment, after his long convalescence,
Tom had been certain he was going to die. Convinced that this was
God's judgment upon him for what he had done to Johnny Dolan, for
selling another man into servitude, only grateful that he had been able
to reconcile with his wife.

All through the campaign, as they churned through the dusty

turnpikes of Maryland and Pennsylvania, he had known he would die in the next fight. It was a feeling the more veteran soldiers talked about, and though he had silently scoffed at such premonitions in the past—having seen plenty of those same veterans who had thought they were doomed standing in front of their tents the day after the battle, their faces filled with wonder—he had had no doubt that he himself was going to die.

And what a fight it had been, as bad as Fredericksburg, and two days longer.

He had nearly been killed on the second day. The regiment had been cut off in a peach orchard, thanks to the usual foolishness of their commanders, and they had had to cut their way out. It had been a desperate, running fight, through the lined trees of the orchard, the air around them fragrant with the smell of dropped peaches. The gaunt, screaming faces of the rebs all around them.

John J. Sullivan had fallen there, shot point-blank by some lieutenant from Mississippi when his head was turned. He never even saw the man, though Snatchem had gutted him immediately, plunging his bayonet up through the officer's kidneys. Tom looked down at him as he ran past—some immaculately tailored college boy, looking as if he had just left his cadet class, the life shaking out of him now amid the fallen peaches.

Before they could make it back to the line, Feeley had taken a ball in his collarbone, too—another reb trying to stick him where he lay. Tom was just able to knock the reb down with his rifle butt, then he and George had pulled him back toward their own guns along Cemetery Ridge. Feeley cursing and screaming with each jolt of his shoulder, the rest of them shrieking like madmen as they ran straight toward the gun muzzles, the cannoneers already setting the fuses—

"Don't you fire! Don't you dare fire yet, you sponging sons a bitches!"

Then they were past, back in their own lines. The guns firing almost immediately, into both the rebs and the still-retreating men from their own brigade. The soldiers from both sides, torn apart in an instant. The guns firing again and again, until at last the charge was broken, the rebs falling back through the bloody fields and the shredded orchard trees.

Later, when the regiment was pulled out of the line, they had helped Feeley off to the field hospital. It was the most gruesome sight

Tom had ever seen, the cutting floor at The Place of Blood not excluded. The surgeons sawing away through arms and legs with terrifying speed and recklessness. Tearing into guts and chest cavities with their fingers and wresting the balls—the flattened, obscene half orbs of lead—out of the living body. The men screaming, anesthetized with only the slightest dose of laudanum or whiskey. The surgeons cursing when their knives and saws became too dull and hurling them to the ground, rubbing off the blood and gore in the dirt before they went back to work.

Tom and Snatchem had helped to hold Feeley down when it was his turn. The surgeon had twisted and yanked inquisitively in his shoulder, until he had tugged the ball out. Holding it up to the lantern light with a passing, professional interest—

"That was a lucky wound," he opined, "the bone stopped it flat. Who knows what damage it might have done, and a clean break, at that—" Setting the collarbone back in place while Feeley ground his teeth and cursed a blue streak.

They had left him to rest then, and walked slowly back to their bivouac. There Tom had sat on the ground, and tried to eat some salt pork, and listened to the sounds of the army recovering itself all around him. The artillerymen, and the thick-chested horses, hauling back the guns. The men cleaning their rifles, eating and talking softly among themselves. The whole, long rustle of bridles and metal spurs, bayonets and skillets, wagon wheels and gun wheels, from all up and down the Union position.

He had felt, then, the infinite faith and sadness of all soldiers, knowing that he was part of this much greater thing, this beast. This mighty *machine* made up of men and animals, plans and orders, guns and powder, all around him. And that, for all its might, it would do him no good. Knowing that he would surely be laid out in a field the next day, and peeled off the great body of the army. His spot taken, and his musket handed to someone else. Thinking how damned lovely it all was. Thinking, *I will endure. I will not endure.*

He had gone to sleep in his tent still possessed of the unalterable conviction that he was going to die. But the next day there had been no mad new charge. The men had been so badly shot up that his company barely existed anymore, and he and Snatchem and Larkins were rounded up by a major, along with some other stray men and moved in to fill a gap along a farmer's low stone wall on Cemetery Ridge.

Even this forward position actually proved safer, once the rebel guns had started to thunder late that morning. They had thrown nearly all their shells and balls high, over the line, and into the officers' mess, and a few artillery caissons in the back. Tom and his friends, meanwhile, had clung to the trembling earth. The noise shattering, even through the cotton in their ears, the worst bombardment they had ever heard. Yet when it finally stopped, hours later, they had risen up from the ground in the ringing stillness, as whole as the souls on Judgment Day, brushing themselves off and grinning sheepishly at each other.

They still hadn't thought the rebs would come, then—not against them, not against the center of the line, strong as it was. The shells had missed their mark, and no bombardment on this earth was capable of driving them from where they were dug in, with their own guns, behind a stone wall.

Tom had been as surprised as the rest of them when he had seen the rebs marching out, in their perfect parade lines. Trying to overawe them with their numbers, their drill—their casual disdain in dressing their lines, even as the Union guns culled and threshed their ranks.

But they all knew, it was they who would be doing the killing this day. The grey soldiers resorting in the end, when they must have known they were almost within rifle range, to their old rebel yell. Shrieking it louder and higher than ever—that eerie, lunatic, hunting cry. Behind the Union lines, a few of the newer recruits had trembled, but the veterans held them steady, disdainful of all their noise.

"I heard women an' children makin' worse sounds in the cabins during the hunger," one of the men near Tom snorted. "Would that I had a rifle in me hands then."

The yells dying out again, by the time the rebs had reached the foot of the ridge. Already shot to hell, most of their officers gone. Both sides understanding that the charge was already doomed, even as the officers gave the command and the blue soldiers raised their muskets to their shoulders. The reversal of their positions so striking that it was immediately understood, on both sides of the wall, when the men on the Union line began to chant their own bitter cry:

"Fredericksburg! Fredericksburg! Fredericksburg!"

The single word reverberating across the field. Until the command to fire rang out, and all other noise was drowned in the sound of their volley.

And how could they know about that? How could they know what war was, these people who used to be his friends and neighbors?

They killed so easily, so thoughtlessly. Hanging men and women from the lampposts, in a Christian city. Screaming for them to join them. Even burning the flag before them, waving the rebels' banner. Yelling to hell with Abe Lincoln, Horace Greeley, the codfish Yankee aristocrats.

How could they know? What he held his allegiance to—

It wasn't for the flag. Or Abe Lincoln, whom he had never seen, except once from a very great distance, when he had come out to inspect the army—a tall figure in a tall hat, riding a little horse. Or to Horace Greeley, whom he had only read in his wife's newspaper and could never make hide nor tail of. Or to any of the Yankees, or the aristocrats. Or the Black Republicans, or the Peace Democrats or the War Democrats or the Copperheads, or anything else like that.

His loyalty was to those other men he fought with, the ones marching beside him now. To his wife and children, here in his City, for whom he would do anything, kill anyone. And beyond that, his allegiance was simply *against* all those who would kill so easily—string up innocent men and women or anyone else, just because they could.

He had seen too much of killing to spare them now.

70

BILLY DOVE

He had to get back.

He lay against the wall in the darkness, and the still-smoldering heat of the ruined Armory. Squeezing the gun in his palm, feeling the pain course through his splinted leg. Listening for any noise above him then, thinking surely that they must be gone by now. He was about to try raising himself up, and looking for a way out, when he heard it again—the mocking call, as hateful and chilling as ever.

"*Nig-ger, oh, nig-ger!* We're still *heeere*, nigger!"

The same words, the same taunting cry he had listened to since the evening before, and all through the night—ever since he had finally been able to leave the orphans, back uptown at the police station. The bastards were too leery to come down after him, knowing he had his gun—but reminding him, still, that they had him holed, here. Letting him know they were willing to wait until he had to come out—until it was too late anymore.

He tried to think of a way around it, though his head was still bursting with fever. *Some way he could get himself up and out of the basement, and back to his home, with his busted leg.* He had tried to think of something all night, when he was not passing in and out of consciousness. There was nothing he could even try, with them right on top of him like that. But still—

He had to get back.

His luck had turned now, he knew. It was bound to, after holding up all the previous afternoon. Soon after he had managed to get the Irishers up to the Red Bird stables and get them all on horseback, he had run upon a priest. A Father Knapp, who was chasing what rioters he could off the streets, running after them as determinedly and with as much effectiveness as a child chasing pigeons in a park.

"Father, don't go after them!" he had warned, grasping the priest by the elbow. The prelate's face looking harried and distracted, barely able to focus on Billy at first.

"They must stop," he had panted at him, all but out of breath, leaning heavily on his arm. *"They will never forgive us."*

Only then had he looked at Billy—seen the color of his skin.

"You must get off the street!" he had urged him. Pushing him into a doorway with surprising strength.

"You must help us—" Billy had told him, hanging on to the man until he could truly focus on him, and pay attention to what he was saying. The priest's eyes finally clearing, though they still looked wild.

"They will never forgive us—"

"They won't even remember it tomorrow. You got to help *me*."

The priest had been able to lead him to a company of regulars just ashore in the City, to convince them to follow him back to the precinct house. Billy had brought them right in past the astonished-looking police sergeants—right to the cellar door—

"What? Who's there?" The voice of Miss Shotwell. *Foolish to say anything,* he thought—*as if the mob would answer politely back*—but knowing that she was only trying to shield the children.

"Who's up there?"

He had lit the lantern and walked out on the top of the stairs. There he looked down at the hundreds of children crammed into the small basement below him. It was a sight that he would never forget— the best sight of his life, save for the first look at his new son, his eldest. Miss Shotwell was standing defiantly at the foot of the stairs— but all around her, all around the walls and under the stairs, and crammed into every nook and cranny of the police station basement, he could see the eyes of the children.

They blinked defensively in the sudden glare of the light, but were still silent—still willing to endure whatever came next. The dozens of black and brown faces staring up blindly—then creasing into smiles, even wonder, as they saw *him* up there. The armed soldiers behind him looking all the taller, like storybook grenadiers, with their rifles and bayonets.

"Billy!" Miss Shotwell had breathed then. "Oh, Billy, you sweetheart!"

His charge completed then. Paid in full. They had arranged for a guard of the regulars to take the children over to the East River. From there a gunboat was to ferry them over to Blackwell's Island, where the army was stowing all the Negroes they were able to rescue. The Yankee ladies, Yolanda, and Old Bert, would go with them.

They would be all right there, Billy had thought, squinting down at the snout-nosed, iron-plated gunboats, steaming up and down the broad river like so many alligators. They were a new type of ship, nearly all metal on the outside. Boats that were no longer shaped chiefly by a man's hand, but tempered in a white-hot furnace.

Not that it mattered. The factories and the iron forges were all white, too, same as the waterfront.

"Why don't ya go with 'em, now?" Sergeant Murphy had asked him, gesturing toward the long line of children, walking doggedly off to the river. "You'd be safe there, till this is all over."

He'd only shaken his head, though he knew the cop meant well. When he had reappeared with the soldiers, the two of them had greeted him like the true miracle, Lazarus come back from the dead—

But it will never be over, he wanted to tell him. *Not in his life, or his boy's life, or any age after that. They would never give it up. Not until the hand of God made all skins black—or cast all men into darkness.*

"Well, then—take these, at least," Murphy had nudged him. "You'll need 'em, with what's still goin' on out there."

He had pressed something into his hands. A new Colt revolver, Billy saw, and a box of shells. He tried to mumble out some words of thanks, but the cop only slapped him on the back again.

"Goddamnedest thing I ever saw a man do, you with those sons a bitches yesterday," Murphy said, shaking his head.

Billy had stared at him wordlessly, realizing it was the first time he
had ever seen a white man look at him with genuine admiration.

"Damn, but it was a bold thing!"

He had let Murphy fill the barrels of the revolver for him. Hiding
both the gun and the extra bullets deep in his pockets, not anxious to
be seen with them, but ready to shoot his way down to the Fourth
Ward if he had to.

"God go with ye," Murphy was telling him.

Billy had mumbled something in reply, not even sure of what he
had said, and started off down the Third Avenue. Ahead of him he
could already see burning buildings, their trails of black smoke curling lazily up into the thick summer air. But then he had heard something unexpected, and glanced back to see the orphans going off, hand
in hand. Most of them looking back at him, waving with their free
hands as they went off. Still singing their hymns as they marched.

> Then sings my soul,
> My savior God to thee,
> How great Thou art,
> How great Thou art—

He wondered if he would ever see them again—once they, and he,
had fled the City. The rows of boys and girls, marching along in their
usual good order. And all around them, the phalanx of soldiers, towering over the children, their rifles held at the waist, bayonets at the ready.

*What kind of City was this, where you needed an armed guard to keep
orphan children from being lynched?*

But there had been no time to think further on it—or how he
would miss them, or even what he would do for his back wages now.
He had another charge. Billy gave them a small, guarded wave in
return, and turned toward the south. Hurrying on down into the
burning City.

He had managed to reach Twenty-third Street before they picked him
up, which he knew was a remarkable run of luck in and of itself. He
had made it almost all the way to Gramercy Park—thinking it wasn't
too far now, not more than another mile and a half as the crow flies to
Paradise Alley, he could be there before night—

Then he had turned a corner and nearly run right into the crowd of white men outside a saloon. It was unavoidable, he had known it from the start, there were too many bars in this town, and he had tried to brazen it out. Trying to dash by before the Paddies outside could recover themselves—

But they had begun to chase him almost immediately, shouting and hallooing behind him as they did, as if they were off on a game, or a hunt. He had tried to just outrun them at first. Running to the east, down a block that he knew was famous for its brothels. Dodging by prosperous-looking gentlemen, still strolling up to the brownstone stoops, who only stepped carefully out of his way.

"C'mere, nigger-nigger-nigger! C'mere, we got somethin' for *you!*"

They were young workingmen, most of them, fast and muscular, and soon they had started to gain on him. Billy felt his legs growing heavy, winded from having already run nearly a mile and a half, with nothing to sustain him for two days, now, save for the short, sweet swig of whiskey the bummers had forced down his throat.

He had slowed then, letting the men come up on him. Clutching the Colt in his pocket, looking back over his shoulder at the lead man. *His mouth dropped open, short brown stubs of teeth leering excitedly in his pink face.* Billy let him draw to within a few feet—then he yanked the Colt out and shot him point-blank in the belly. The man screamed and went rolling over like a ninepin in the street—some of his fellows tripping over him, others stopping to tend to him, shouting with rage.

But it was not enough. The rest of them had kept on, more incensed than ever now, imbued with the courage they had been drinking up all afternoon. When they got too close again, Billy shot another one, right through the lungs this time. But the mob behind him was only growing now—gunshots buzzing past his own head, chipping the stoops and store awnings around him.

He had feinted uptown—then run around the block and turned back toward the south and east. Running on every last breath he could manage now, looking desperately for some alleyway or building he could duck into, maybe hide himself away.

He ran down Twenty-first Street, the mob almost at his heels, right up to the ruined brick hulk of the Armory. It didn't seem to promise much, but it was the only structure left standing on the block. The bullets were whizzing past him more frequently, and Billy swerved inside, pounding up the steps and through the enormous front door that swung loose, off its hinges.

He rushed through the door—and found himself in midair, his arms swinging wildly, trying to find some purchase. Instead he fell, into the still-smoldering pile of rubble just inside. Cutting his forehead open on the end of a beam, his hands burning and smarting on the still-hot bricks.

He was up immediately, nevertheless. Running on through the Armory, realizing even as he did that it had become an empty shell, its roof and interior floors all burned away. Nothing more than the piles of broken bricks and planks and gun stocks inside—

There was no shelter for him here at all. The building's shell was even a trap. He could already catch glimpses of the mob, cleverly dividing, half of them running over to head him off on the other side of the Armory, surrounding him.

Billy stood in the middle of the burned-out building, not knowing what he could possibly do now. All around him, through the holes in the brick, he could see their flitting shadows, could hear the laughing, singsong voices.

"We got you now, nigger!"

"Come out, come out, where e're you are!"

A rifle bullet streaked past his ear this time, and he had crouched down, and scrambled back through the piles of wood and brick, toward the door again. Hoping that maybe he could shoot his way through, get by them somehow. But his foot slipped on one of the loose piles, and he nearly fell. Hopping back up, trying to get his balance, he came down hard on a loose floor plank. All he could feel after that was the ground giving way beneath him, before he was enveloped in the darkness.

He had awakened all at once, though he did not make a move—afraid to give himself away. He had no idea where he was, or how much time had passed, but to his great relief he saw that he was still in the dark.

There was a terrible throbbing in his right leg. Looking down, he saw that it was bent at an impossible angle, a large bolt of wood lying on top of it. He understood, then, that he must have fallen through the first floor of what had been the armory, into its basement. He was lying there now, on a pile of charred beams, and old gun casings. The leg was obviously broken, and he could feel some blood dripping down his calf, wondering to himself if the bone had gone right through his skin.

"*Nig-ger! Where are you, nigger?*"

The taunting, leering voices right above him. A great pile of the rubbish above had fallen down the hole after him, he saw, or the mob would have been able to simply reach down and pluck him out. *God only knew what would have happened to him then.* Above him he could make out orange shafts of light through the planking, and he realized that they had stoked up some kind of bonfire in the rubble of the armory, on the site of their conquest.

"Nig-ger!"

Billy had forced the top half of his body up, pulling gingerly at the wood that lay on him. He was trying to make as little noise as possible but it was a large beam, and when he gave it one last push, it fell over on the stone floor of the basement with a deep thunking noise.

"Didja hear that! Did ya!"

"He's down there, all right!"

He could hear the feet, scrambling like rats through the rubble, toward him. But he was free then, and able to push himself away from where he had first fallen, even deeper into the blackness. Soon, sure enough, he could see a grotesque goblin face, in the orange light of the flames, peering down blindly into the darkness.

"D'ya see him, then?"

Billy reached in his pocket for the Colt—gratified to find it still there, at least. Wanting to fire another round right into the searching, sodden face above him.

Instead he held back. Preferring they stay afraid of what might or might not be down there in the dark. *Waiting with Ruth in the bramble, for the slavecatchers to move on—*

"Where's he got to? He didn't come out—"

"He's gotta be here. Somebody ought to go after him."

"You go on down, then. You go on down an' look for a nigger with a pistol in a dark cellar."

For the rest of the night he listened to them trying to goad each other into it. The heat in the basement was even worse than what it had been in the police station, and when the smoke from the fires

drifted down, it was all he could do to keep from choking and cough-
ing. He had tried to breathe shallow, fighting down the panicky feeling
that he would smother here, right below the mob. *Chased like a dog,
from one cellar to the next—and still so far from Ruth and his home.*

He was able to splint his leg, at least. It was broken, all right, just
below the knee, but it had not gone through the skin, as he'd feared.
He tore his burlap shirt into strips, and used them to strap a stray musket stock to the limb, trying to do it all as quietly and deliberately as
possible. In the end he thought it would serve, though he did not see
how he could possibly run on it, was not even sure if he could boost
himself back up from the basement.

There was nothing more for him to do, then, but prop himself up
against the wall and wait, thinking the Irishers would have to get
bored, or run out of liquor, and leave. But they had stayed right where
they were. As the night went on, the fevers came on him, and he had
drifted in and out of sleep—awakening again and again to hear them
still carousing above, shouting out their raucous songs. Trying to
think of what he could do.

He had to get back.

By the morning, when slits of real sunlight had replaced the glow of
the flames, and the smoke had finally cleared, Billy thought they
would at last have to leave, or sleep. But they were still there. Scuttling
and combing through the rubble above him, looking for some way to
get at him—to drive him out. Back to their old pursuit:

"Nig-ger, oh, nigger!"

He knew then that they would never leave—not until it was much
too late. If he was to get back, he would have to figure out some other
way himself. *But how?* He had the Colt, but the leg still hobbled him.
He could shoot as many of them as he had bullets for, it didn't matter.
Inevitably they would run him down, cut him off; he was like
wounded game to them now.

In desperation he began to hobble about the Armory basement.
Even this was dangerous, he knew—trying to make as little noise as
he could, waiting and listening until he heard them moving about
themselves, before he dragged himself forward again. The old floor
above him was potted with holes, and he never knew when one of
them might look down and spot him. In other places it was sagging

heavily, too, under the weight of all the debris piled on it, and he knew that at any moment he could be crushed like a miner in a cave-in, unable to so much as jump out of the way with his leg.

But he kept searching, painstakingly, around the basement. Looking for something, anything—groping along the walls with his hands, in the darkness. The City, he knew from long experience, was catacombed with tunnels—dug by the gang *b'hoys,* or for abandoned bank vaults, or as secret basements for who knew what ancient purpose. There was a hole in a backyard in Mulberry Street, where everyone knew you could go in, and come back out on Elizabeth Street, two blocks away. It was unlikely, of course, there would be any such passage in the basement of the armory, a government building, constructed to certain specifications, but still—

At last he heard it. Behind the wall he was gripping, there was a sound like rushing water. *An underwater stream? A culvert?* He hobbled along until he found the place along the foundation wall where the sound of the water was at its loudest, almost right against his ear. Yet he could see no opening of any sort there, only more brick and masonry.

He pulled out the penknife he always carried with him, and began to chip and wedge away at the bricks. They were already loosened, obviously damaged by the collapse of the building—though this did not especially encourage him. He knew that he could easily bring the whole wall and the floor above down on himself, smashing him flat. Nor did he have any idea what he might dig through to. The City was full of long-buried streams, swift currents forgotten beneath the pavement, that periodically burst through to swamp basements and spill out over the streets, mystifying the passersby.

Better that, though. It was the choice he had really made so long ago. *Better to be drowned than to stay here, slowly smothering.*

It took him a maddeningly long time to remove the bricks, having to pause and listen to the sounds above him every few minutes. But at last he was able to squeeze his way through the wall, even with his hobbled, throbbing leg. He stepped in—and almost fell into the fast-moving water below him.

The sewer. The dark, swift current below flowing, as he knew it must, in the direction of the river. He was balancing on a thin ledge above it, not so much as a foot wide, and there he hesitated for a long moment, wondering if he could maneuver along the ledge with his broken leg. Knowing that if the rain came suddenly again, the tunnel might fill in an instant, sweeping him away. Knowing, too, that many of the river gangs used the culverts to move about the City, and that he could just as easily meet his death down here.

But he owed her that much. Ruth——and the boy, Milton, and the rest of them. The family he had brought out on this earth. Too long neglected in favor of his yearnings, his bitterness, the grievance he'd nursed against the whole course of his life. He owed it to them to try, exhausted and crippled as he was.

He prepared himself to start, trying to figure out where the culvert might come out. Edging his way out along the ledge, against the flow of the current——refusing to look down at the rushing black water below him.

71

RUTH

"They're coming! They're coming!"

In the morning she heard them running. Out in the streets, and in the back lots. The sound of their feet, their cries racing past the house. Surrounding them already, leaving them no choice but to fight or to hide.

"Here they come!"

Ruth ran out of the back room where she was sleeping with her children. Deirdre moving past her in the hallway already, pulling her dress up over her shoulder as she did. She shrugged into her own shift—feeling the heat wrap around her like a wet cloth, listening to the wild, exultant cries of the women outside.

"Where are they?" she asked, coming into the kitchen where Deirdre was peering out the window, into the back privvy lots.

Deirdre pointed—and as Ruth looked a shadow swept by, then another. *A man,* she saw then, shouting something and whacking a rude wooden club against the side of the house.

They were already in the back. Cutting them off, just like that.

"She's sure to tell them," Ruth swore. "That bitch is sure to tell them—"

"In the front," Deirdre said, running through the house. But when they got to the parlor, Maddy was already staring out through the half-opened shutters.

Mobs of men were swarming in the street. Suddenly, they were there, after the block had been all but deserted for the past two days. The war come to them at last.

The men were not doing anything in particular yet. Most of them were just milling about, talking excitedly to each other. A few of them running aimlessly up and down, as if they were too excited to control themselves. Others reeling drunkenly around in circles, drinking from open bottles of brandy and wine and rum. All of them looking ragged, their coats ripped and shredded, their faces bruised and bloodied and covered in soot.

All that terrible noise, and here it was. Just a bunch of men who still didn't know their own minds.

So far, at least, they didn't seem to have anything in mind for the block. Many of them were already drifting away, looking for fatter pickings, no doubt—a block with a saloon, or some wealthy Republican's house.

Then she saw Mrs. McGillicuddy's head, above the other white women, coming up the alley to meet them. As Ruth watched in terror, she planted herself across the street from Deirdre's house, pointing vigorously toward the window. She could see the men looking over, already beginning to take notice.

"Oh, you damned fool!"

Deirdre had the shutters slammed and bolted at once, rushing them all back into the depths of the house. She shoved through the bolt on the back door, as well, shouting out orders as she did.

"Ruth, get the children from the back. Quick now! Get them up the stairs!"

But Ruth had already rousted them from the back room, was herding them upstairs. Milton, as always, right by her side, already dressed and alert, scooping up Vie and Elijah, in his arms, pushing Deirdre's youngest along with his hand. She and Deirdre grabbing up the rest—even Maddy pulling along Mana as best she could in her skinny arms. They all but flew up to the second floor, pushing and dragging the children two at a time.

None too soon. She heard the bricks begin to thump off the front of the house at the same moment they reached the upstairs landing. The shouts from the men rising outside—Mrs. McGillicuddy and the other white women urging them on.

"The back! The back! Don't let 'em get out the back!"

"What is happening—what is happening to this block," Deirdre was panting under her breath.

"Maybe—maybe we can still beat 'em out the back—"

"No! Too late already," Deirdre said, and looking down from the second-story windows Ruth could see that she was right. There were dozens of men racing down the privvy lots now, whooping and laughing.

"What, then?" she asked, waiting for Deirdre to come up with something.

But what more could Deirdre do to save her than anyone else? She had been saved so many times before, who was to say there should be anyone to save her now—

Deirdre stood where she was for a moment, near the stairs, listening to the crowd, and trying to think.

"The gun," she said suddenly.

"My pistol!" Maddy perked up. "That's it, just gimme the gun. I'll clear out the sons a bitches—"

"No. Milton—go down and get the gun. It's in the third drawer of the secretary, in the back to the right, under the good linens—"

Milton nodded, listening intently, but Ruth interrupted her.

"No! I'll do it. I don't want him back down there."

"All right, then."

Ruth was already flying down the stairs, pulling out the pistol from exactly where Deirdre had said it would be. As she did, she saw the front door and the window shutters beginning to shake. First the door, then the shutters—one after the other, reverberating as the mob pounded against them.

They want in—

She felt the gun in her palm. Thinking what it would be like to see the surprise on the first drunken face as he came staggering through—

There was a new pounding sound, against the back door this time. It startled Ruth back into movement. *Of course she couldn't kill them all. Of course there were too many of them—and even if she did, what would happen to her children?*

She ran back up the stairs, pistol in hand, holding it out to Deirdre.

"All right," she said, grabbing it confidently. "All right, at least this might slow them down."

"Let me have it! I'll show 'em, the bastards!" Maddy bleated, trying to grab it. "It's *my gun*—"

"Now what?" Ruth asked, ignoring her. "Now what'll we do?"

"I don't know," Deirdre admitted, scowling in concentration as she listened to the banging down below. "I don't know. If they get through, they still have to come up the stairs. Maybe if I shot the first couple, that would make them think—"

"Hullo! Hullo!"

They both looked out the open window, over the privvy shacks. There they could see Mrs. Mendelssohn, waving a handkerchief out of her own second-story window, and calling as loudly to them as she dared.

"Hullo!"

Of course—the Jews.

"Hullo, can you come over?" she called, leaning out the window—her daughter looking over her shoulder again, her beautiful olive face staring at them across the back alley. Drained with fear now, but also full of sympathy, or pity.

Is that how people look at you when they know you are going to die?

"I don't know—" Deirdre started to call back to her, keeping an eye on the men, still running about among the privvies. The mob was still oblivious to them, up on the second floor where they were. Focusing their attention instead on breaking down the back door—

"The roof! The roof!" Mrs. Mendelssohn was calling now, pointing upward with her thumb.

She raced on up, through the artisans' attic, and out onto the rooftop. Ruth could smell the fire in the air now. *So hot already, so hot.* All so different from how it had been just a few hours ago, just last night. The fires were very close. She could only guess that when they tired of trying to knock down Deirdre's heavy oak doors they would set her house ablaze, as well—

"Here, here! The line!"

Mrs. Mendelssohn was yelling from her own roof now, her beautiful daughter stumbling up behind her. Moving as fast as they could, running the clothesline over to them.

"It's too thin," Ruth said, distracted, looking dutifully at the double length of rope that ran back and forth between the simple rusted pulleys on Deirdre's roof and the Jews'. *I don't care, I won't put my children out on a clothesline—*

"It's too thin, I don't know as it can hold us—"

"No, no! Look!"

Mrs. Mendelssohn pointed to where her daughter had unstrung the two ends of the rope from their pulley. Now she twisted and tied them deftly around each other, doing marvelous things with her hands. *Much more clever than anything she had ever done herself at the German ladies'.* With a few more deft turns she had looped together a crude sort of bosun's chair out of the line—tying it all together in a seat that looked as if it might well support at least a child—and attached it to the pulley again.

If they could just get the younger children over, at least. But what about Milton?

"Here, we're sendin' it over!"

The rope chair swayed out over the privvies, Ruth yanking it in from her side as fast as she could. The men below still seemed not to have taken any notice of it, for all the squeaks and groans of the old metal, and she looked it over quickly, admiring the Jewish girl's handiwork.

But would it hold?

There was the first, withering sound of wood cracking from below. She clambered back to the second-floor landing, told Deirdre what was going on as quickly as she could.

"But will it hold?"

"I can't say."

There was another crack—the front door slowly beginning to give way.

"But we've got to see."

"Yes."

"Milton—you stay here. With the gun."

Deirdre looked at Ruth when she spoke, making sure that she had her consent. But she knew it was the only thing they could do, much as she hated to leave him even for a moment. *Much as she wanted to weep, seeing her boy standing with a gun in his hand, ready to ward off a mob of men.*

Milton only nodded, as solemn and aware of his responsibility as ever, and Deirdre placed the revolver in his hand.

"You know how to use this, don't you?"

"Yes," he said, his mouth dry. "Yes, I understand."

"All right, then."

They hustled the other children on up through the attic, and out on the roof. Moving faster than Ruth ever thought she could go—moving with the pure dexterity born of panic now, all but throwing and thrusting the children up through the trapdoor. The tar roof already bristling hot, sucking at their feet and knees, liquefying under the broiling morning sun. Ruth tried to make them stay down, below an extra lip of cement that ran along the roof's edge—trying to make sure they were not seen by the men down in the back lot. But they wept and fretted to be so close to the heat. The fear palpable to all of them now—

"The littlest one first," Deirdre said, pointing at Elijah.

"But—"

Ruth hesitated again for just a moment, wondering if this were right. Wondering if they shouldn't choose one of Deirdre's children, since after all it was her roof—

"They're white. You know it," Deirdre said bluntly. "Put your own on first."

She nodded, and worked Elijah into the little rope swing. Telling him to be sure to hang on to the line, and not to kick or fuss as she steadied him. Trying to make herself sound calm.

One at a time. That was how they had to do it, one at a time.

"Are you ready?" Mrs. Mendelssohn called from across the privvy lots—both her hands and those of her daughter ready on the line.

"Wait!"

The palms of Ruth's own hands were sweating—preparing to swing her child out over an alleyway full of dangerous men, thirty feet off the ground. She looked down into the alley once more, making sure the men there were still preoccupied with trying to knock Deirdre's door in.

"All right. Together!"

Ruth tugged at the cord as hard as she could—Deirdre and Maddy pulling on it right behind her, Mrs. Mendelssohn and her daughter pulling them over from the other side. She could barely stand to watch, whispering the Hail Mary under her breath as he moved out through the open air, wondering if he could tip out if they pulled too hard.

But Elijah sped across the chasm like a pea in a current, carried over to the Jews and safety before he could even start to cry. Mrs. Mendelssohn and her daughter gathered him in on the other side, plucking him out of the chair and holding him to them, his mouth still hanging open in shock.

"That's one!" Deirdre hissed triumphantly as they whipped the bosun's chair swiftly back over. But there was the sound of human voices from below now, some of the men looking up to the sky.

"What's that, then?"

"Is the buildin' comin' down?"

They had to wait until the voices died down again, the men speculating on the nature of the shadow that had passed over them. Soon, though, they could hear the pounding start at the door and the shutters again, which was no more reassuring.

"They'll be up any minute," Ruth said frantically, unable to help herself.

And with Milton there to meet them on the steps.

"Hurry—"

They slipped Vie into the bosun's chair next. The little girl too scared to cry—shaking so hard they could barely tie her in. Ruth kissed her head and face all over as she did, whispering to her to look to her brother, still standing on the Mendelssohns' roof.

"See Elijah, see Elijah there. You're just crossin' over to him now."

Ruth was terrified that she might start to scream at any moment, but they yanked her across the gap before she could open her mouth. When they plucked her out, she stood hugging her brother tightly— the two of them staring back incredulously at the height they had just passed over. The chair slithering back over to them

"Listen!"

There was a sudden burst of laughter from down in the back lots, and then they could smell something sharp and familiar.

"What is it?"

They were burning the privvies. Wisps of putrid black smoke began to curl their way up to the roof.

"Hurry now, there won't be much time—"

Mana was hoisted across next, then Frederick. The smoke from the privvies was growing steadily thicker now—so much so that Frederick could not help it but coughed and cried as he went over. They stopped the line in terror as soon as he was safe—but the men below were choking on the smoke themselves, still too busy with their ruckus to notice what was going on above.

"Let's burn *all* the shite! Burn all the *niggers!*"

Ruth shivered on the roof. Maddy beside her was looking down in contempt, forming her mouth to spit before they pulled her back.

"Look at the sons a bitches down there—"

But there was no time. Even up on the roof, tears were streaming down their faces from the rancid, filthy smoke.

"Now your children," Ruth told Deirdre—much as it pained her, much as she wanted to send for Milton, right away.

But what if the line broke under him? And who would mind the stairs?

They swung Deirdre's brood over as quickly as they could, but it still took time, their arms slowing with fatigue. And as it was, the metal pulleys rasped and bent toward the edge of the roof with each new passage. The line sagging steadily lower over the smoke—the children trying to hold their breath or gasping desperately for air. They arrived at the Mendelssohns with their faces and clothes covered with the soot. The faces of Mrs. Mendelssohn and her daughter were just as black, but they stood their ground, the children helping with each pull now.

"Now for Milton!" Ruth cried.

"That's it, now! Just your boy—" Deirdre agreed, as soon as they had pulled her Eliza over.

There was the sound of a great crash from somewhere below, then a muted cheer. Milton was coming up through the trapdoor, running out onto the roof, pistol in hand.

"They broke the front door!" he told them, breathless. "They got the top panel busted in, it won't be but a few minutes before they get the rest of it—"

"All right, then, you're next," Deirdre told him.

"How d'ya know it will hold him?" Ruth asked. *Seeing him plunging, screaming, down into the burning privvies as the rope broke.*

"We don't, but what choice is there? Besides, we'll send him over with the pistol, that way even if he drops—"

"Look, look! It's burnin'!"

Maddy had come forward now, and was pointing toward the line—her own pale face and hair and the tattered red gown blackened with smoke as well, so that she looked fully mad. *But she was right,* they saw at once. Halfway over the chasm between the houses, smoke was rising from the clothesline itself.

"Jesus, no, Jesus, no—"

"It's going, there's no helping it."

The rope was in flames now. The Jewish girl's clever bosun's chair consumed at once, the fire skipping quickly up the line toward where they stood. Deirdre seized the pistol from Milton and began to batter at the pulley, prying it loose and knocking it off before the burning line could reach their house. Across the back lot the Mendelssohns stood on the roof, holding their children, watching helplessly.

"Go on now!" Deirdre called to them. "We'll be fine here. Go on, and get them inside!"

Fine, with the mob downstairs.

Mrs. Mendelssohn nodded quickly—though from her look Ruth knew that she didn't think they would be fine at all. Her daughter was already shielding the children's faces with her arms and dress, limping back with them, away from the edge of the building and downstairs.

"What now? What now?" Ruth cried, looking around at Deirdre and Milton, behind her. "We got to hide him! That's what we can do, where can we hide him—"

"They'll tear up the whole damned place, you know they will!" Maddy yelled wildly. "And if they find him, then—"

"Maddy!"

"Maybe we'd be better off just closing the trap," Deirdre said. "Pray to Jesus they don't come up. Hold them off with the gun if we have to."

"But what if they just burn us out?"

"Wait. Maybe I know—"

Deirdre was already leading them back down to the second floor. There she threw open the window in their upstairs front room. *The mob still downstairs, thank God.*

"Come on, now! Give me a hand with this!" Deirdre called, grabbing hold of anything she could—anything that looked valuable—and tossing it immediately out the window, down into the street below.

But your things, Ruth wanted to say, though she knew there was no choice now. *They had to do something fast or her boy would die.* She could hear the men downstairs, clearing away the rest of the ruined door. Pushing in the parlor window. *Soon they would be clamoring up the stairs—*

"There! Take that!"

She shoved a huge quilt out. Ruth knew it was one that Deirdre had made herself—forty-eight squares, each one depicting a scene from the life of Jesus. It had taken her two years, she remembered. Now it fluttered brightly out the window and into the street. Distracting the men downstairs from their work, at least for a moment—staring at this strange offering from above.

"Come on! More! That won't concern them for long!"

Ruth looked around, still unsure of what she should presume to throw out the window. Then she spotted Milton, standing by the doorway, still guarding the stairs. Trying to look brave—

"Here!" She grabbed a pair of real silver candlesticks, tossed them out the window. "God forgive me—"

They clanked along the paving stones outside, the men scrambling for them. Beside her Maddy threw down a framed print of the Sacred Heart of Jesus—then a pitcher that smashed uselessly in the street.

"Save that for when they come!" Deirdre scolded her, scooping up the good linens from her very bed, tossing them out like sails that blew open and spread above them.

The men downstairs laughed and cheered. There was no sound of them down by the door now—thinking their work was being done for them by other looters, already in through the back door.

"Keep going!" Deirdre yelled at them, gathering up some of her best dresses.

It was working. Ruth didn't know how long it could keep working, but it was working for now. Even Mrs. McGillicuddy and the other white women were scrambling for anything they could get their hands on. A few others working their way down the street, looting any empty home they could find. Ruth almost wanting to laugh when she noticed some men smashing the front of her own abandoned house.

That was when she heard the voice again. It was the same one she had heard just a few nights ago, out on the street, while she huddled in the bedroom with Billy. *Maddy's customer.*

"Where is she? Where is that goddamned nigger whore? We come to settle with her, now that we cleared all the niggers out—"

She could see a new gaggle of men, walking onto the block from whatever mischief they had been up to. At their head Ruth recognized the goblin-faced man. The same wizened head, shrunk down into his chest—the same withered, long-armed body, from so long ago, back at the hospital on Staten Island. No longer smiling his unsettling false grin, but smirking viciously now, his teeth showing. Calling out to the block in the same measured, deadly voice she had heard that night.

"Where is the niggers' whore? We come to take out her debt in trade."

The goblin man was leading the mob toward Maddy's, and for a moment Ruth's heart leaped. But the white women on the block ran along with them—Mrs. McGillicuddy pointing back toward Deirdre's home.

"She run out, she run out! She's holed up over there, along with the rest of the niggers!"

The mob swayed, hesitating just below them. Ruth holding her breath, watching them, Deirdre doing the same. The crowd gazing uncertainly at the ruined door, all the detritus tossed into the street, surmising it must have been sacked already.

"It's thin pickins here—"

"Let's go over to her place, that's the lode!"

"Oh, the dresses that whore wears!"

They felt Maddy moving behind them before they saw her.

"Goddamn them, they think they can run *me?*"

"No, Maddy, don't be mad!" Deirdre shouted at her.

But she was already bursting down the stairs, cursing at the top of her lungs, waving something in her hand.

"Goddamn bummers! Goddamn Irish sons a bitches, here I am!"

"The pistol!" Deirdre said, remembering even as she said it where she had left it last, on the roof, after she had knocked the pulley off.

"Dear Jesus, if she shoots one of them they'll kill her for sure!"

They ran down the stairs after her. Maddy making for the door, Deirdre right behind her—and Milton running right after her, though Ruth screamed for him to come back.

"Get in! Get in! Get back in, they mustn't see you! *Oh, God, they mustn't see you!*"

But Maddy was already down to the first floor, bolting through the ruined door like a rabbit. She ran right out into the street, flourishing the gun under the noses of the astonished men.

"Here's what you want, ain't it? Here's the niggers' whore!"

There was some disbelieving laughter, then a few jeers. Someone threw a piece of brick that barely missed her head, falling on the paving stones behind her. Even as it hit the ground, Maddy lifted the gun and fired.

"Jay-sus!"

Her shot going wild, whizzing over the heads of the men before her and thumping harmlessly into the wooden front of the grocery across the street. The men ducked instinctively, then began to run toward her, laughing and cursing. She fired again, running toward her house now.

"Get her! Get the goddamned whore!"

Maddy dashed inside her house—reappearing a minute later on her roof. Still firing her pistol, screaming down at them in the street.

"Irish sons a bitches! You goddamned Irish sons a bitches!"

A couple of men in the crowd were firing back at her, balls smashing the upstairs windows of her home. They began to kick in her front door, and she turned and disappeared again, dropping from sight, but still screaming at them.

"You Irish sons a bitches!"

But now the rest of them were out. They stood in the street, before the mob, without even the protection of the gun. At least most of the men had run off down the street after Maddy, though, and Ruth tried to grab her son and push him back into Deirdre's house, thinking somehow that the mob might not notice.

"Maybe we can get out the back still—"

But they could already hear Mrs. McGillicuddy, rallying the men again. The cry immediately taken up by the other women.

"Here's where the niggers live! Here's where they're stayin'!"

"Shoot at us! Shoot at us, the little whore!"

"This is where he lives, the big nigger on the block. His whole family's here!"

Men were starting to move toward them now. Deirdre and Ruth took another step or two back into the house, for all the good they knew it would do them, with its smashed-in door and shutters. Ruth with her arms wrapped around Milton, trying to pull him back physically.

"We can go out the back door, maybe—"

"I don't know," Deirdre said, the dread thick in her voice, but trying to stay calm and think even now. "I don't know if we can get past the fire."

They could feel the heat from where they stood—the acrid smoke from out back beginning to fill up the bottom floor of the house, drifting on up the stairs. Ruth started to cough, loosening her grip on her boy as she reeled about, trying to get air.

"Maybe we can go back upstairs—"

"It's no good," Milton was saying.

He pulled away from her—staring toward the front door, the men outside. His face grave and angry.

"No, don't ya do it," Ruth said, reaching for him again through the choking smoke. "No, don't go out there, son, *don't*—"

But he was already shrugging her off, moving toward the door. His young, beautiful face alert and unswerving as a hunting dog's, trained on the mob outside.

"Who're they to come burn us out? Who're *they?*" he murmured, brushing off her hands. "They already killed my Da—"

He was through the door then, walking out into the street before the mob. So quick, so quiet and calm and dignified that they did not react at all—at first. Then Ruth ran out after him, still trying to pull him back. Still trying to get between him and the mob. *Even as she was filled with a terrible pride in him, her son—*

"Get back in! Get back, the both of you!" she could hear Deirdre yelling behind her—but Ruth was already through the door, standing out in the street with him. Not sure of what she could do yet, but determined to do something, to shield him from them. *My boy—*

And that was when she saw *him*. Then she spotted Johnny Dolan, himself out by the front of the crowd—and she knew that she was going to die.

· 72 ·*

BILLY DOVE

He could see the water opening out ahead of him. The dark effluence of the City rushing out, absorbed into the wider, slower currents of the river. *At last, the mouth of the sewer, right there before him—*

It had taken him hours to make his way down the culvert from Twenty-first Street, shuffling painfully along the thin ledge. Again and again he felt himself losing his balance, and had to clutch onto the rough brickwork of the tunnel to save himself. Every few blocks the ledge had been eroded away altogether, and he was forced to swing his broken leg carefully out over the gap—praying that it wouldn't come down upon nothing, and that he would be left to dangle over the dark torrent below.

He had to do almost everything by feel, his hands groping along the bricks like a blind man's. There was no sound but the rushing water, or the stray cries from the street above, and the only light was what leaked through the occasional sewer grate. There were rats that ran along the ledge, too, and he could feel them darting over his feet, even running up his legs before he could shake them off—listening to them squeal, and splash into the water beneath him.

There were men, too, down in the sewer. Most of them passed along the other side—furtive, crouching figures who moved much faster along the ledge than he did. They seemed to take no notice of him, but even so he made sure to keep the Colt at the ready.

Once he had encountered a man on his side of the tunnel. Billy had sensed him before he'd seen him in the dark—smelling the odor of his body, hearing the fumble of his hands along the wall. He had frozen—and when the man heard or smelled him, he had stopped as well. All he could see of him was a dark lump, clinging to the wall; from where he was, he could not even make out the man's color. Just his eyes, watching him in turn, no doubt trying to decide whether to go back or to push on ahead, and knock him off the ledge.

Billy had pulled out the Colt—not pointing it, or saying anything. Just holding the gun up, making sure the other man could see it, in the distant light they had. He watched the man's eyes register it—then saw him begin to move slowly backward, the same way he had come. Billy edging after him—keeping a certain distance, careful not to hurry or provoke him into something desperate. Listening to his grunts and labored breathing, the same groping slither along the brick wall. Only then had Billy moved after him—almost glad for the company, for the small human noises in front of him.

After a few hundred yards, the man had stepped back, into a shallow recess along the wall. He made a quick, curt little wave then, a gesture for Billy to go by him. Neither one of them saying a thing. Billy had pulled the Colt out again, then swung one arm and his good leg past the man. As he did he shoved the pistol deep in the stranger's belly, making sure he didn't take this chance to shove him off the ledge. He heard the man grunt with surprise, but still he said nothing, keeping his hands carefully by his sides as Billy swung his broken leg over. So close now, he could feel his sour breath on his cheek—his eyes staring, carefully blank, into the darkness over Billy's shoulder.

Then he was past, and he jerked the gun back. Still holding it up. Standing still against the wall until he heard the man move off again, in the direction he had been headed in the first place, shuffling and scratching his way back down the sewer.

Billy tried to guide himself by memory of direction, from having decided that the water he had seen first, in the basement of the Armory, was running to the east, and the river. From there, he had inched along down smaller tributary tunnels and streams. Hoping that none of them would bring him up to a dead end, in some tenement basement, or one of the hideouts of the river gangs. Always trying to

move to what he thought was the south and the east—*toward home*—
though he understood that he was just as likely to end up high on the
West Side, that there was nothing to truly navigate his way by down
here, neither sun nor stars nor land.

It was painfully slow work, but he reasoned it was the only way.
He could not move very fast aboveground anyway, not with his leg
busted. Down here, on the ledge, he was at least the equal of any
other creature he was likely to encounter. *While up in the City he
would only be blood in the water, a wounded creature, just begging to be
finished off.*

It was the only choice, he knew it, but still he begrudged every
minute of it. Aching to be back now.

And if he made it, he thought, inching his way along, his face up
against the wall of a sewer, *if he could get home, he would not go anywhere. He would hole up with the gun, if that was what it took, and wait
for Johnny Dolan or all hell to come and find him. It was his home, such as
it was, and he would not run again for anyone or anything.*

His home, and his family. He thought of their faces as he made his
way along the endless, darkened tunnels. His children, his smart boy,
Milton, in particular.

He realized now that he had thought of them as something so
insignificant—in light of what he thought he could have done, the life
he could have made for himself. Just more additions to the vast flocks
of colored children he saw every day, up at the Asylum, with no better hopes for a life than they had. Destined to go through this world as
he had, eaten up by bitterness, by a wanting that could in no way be
assuaged.

He thought how much he loved them, now. Ruth, too, that ragged
little girl he had found standing in the road, mooning after him. *How
long she had cared for him, even when he disappointed her. Giving her
nothing in return, only the most grudging portion of his affection. Not
even able to tame his greatest failing for her, much as he was disgusted by
it himself.*

Well, that would change. He was certain, now, that he never had to
have another drink in his life. He would give it all up, try to put some
money aside. Live a life that she could respect him for, at least, even if
he could not respect himself.

Or maybe they would go, after all—on their own terms. Once the war ended, if it ever did, and the slaves were really free, maybe then there would be someplace for them to go. Something like the little village, now plowed under the earth. Only bigger, maybe even a city, somewhere he could even use his skills again.

They would deserve that much from him, at least—his family. Maybe he would leave for that, but whatever happened he would not leave without them, he would not be separated from them again.

He had to get back.

There was a thumbnail of light before him. At first he thought it was just another grating, but it grew steadily larger as he edged toward it and he realized it was the mouth of the culvert, at long last, opening up before him. The underground stream rushing out into the deceptively passive currents of the river.

There was a gate of metal bars across the entrance to the culvert there, but he knew the river gangs always kept that unlocked. Sure enough, he was able to swing it open easily enough and pull his way back up and outside, into the sunlight again.

He stood there for a long moment, blinking like a mole. Trying to get his bearings—suddenly feeling how exhausted he was, his lips chapped and his tongue swollen with thirst. He looked around—and saw to his vast relief that he had not been far wrong. He had come out right behind the Shambles, and all he had to do was make his way a couple of blocks down Cherry Street, to the end of Paradise Alley, and he would be home.

He paused only long enough to get a drink from the Croton pump. Gulping down the clean, fresh water until his belly bulged, letting more of it run down his head, and neck and back. Trying to wash off a little of the ash, and the grime from the sewers, though he knew what a sight he must look. Shirtless and all cut up, a gun stock lashed around his broken leg. Grinning to himself, to think how happy Ruth would be to see him anyway, and how she would cry.

The streets around him seemed quiet, and there was not so much as a soul in sight. But he did not let that fool him. He could still hear the shouts and even gunshots coming from somewhere, out in the City—could still smell the scent of smoke. He concentrated on the task at hand, clutching his gun, limping his way down the street, dragging himself back to his home.

73

JOHNNY DOLAN

He saw them the moment he came on the block. All of it instantly recognizable again, as if fourteen years had just melted away. There was Deirdre's proud, silly house, under the looming double tenement. Its grandness dented now, the front all caved in—

And there *she* was, even, running out of the house right there before him. *Ruth*. And in front of her—a black boy. Not the husband, no, he was not old enough. That one, he swore he would recognize him anywhere from that night in the boat, and he was nowhere in sight.

But the boy, even better.

Dolan understood at once that this had to be her son. A tall, slender black boy, very dark and still maybe in his early teens. And Ruth was running out into the street, right into the jeering, chanting mob, to protect him.

She must have been pregnant already, the bitch. Pregnant, or just after—

He saw his chance, now, to truly hurt her.

There was some madwoman, running about with a pistol, distracting everyone. He started for the boy—

Deirdre. She ran out of the house, too, after them all. It stopped his heart, slowed him for half a stride, to see his sister. *Still so beautiful, even after all this time.* Her dress and hair still so carefully arranged even now, covered though they were with soot and sweat.

He would teach her. He would teach them all.

He moved through the crowd, in his crouching, crablike run. Coming up on them before they could see him—going for the boy.

74

RUTH

He looked worse than ever, she thought—even worse than the first time she had ever laid eyes on him. *Back in that deserted village, with the dogs—*

His hair was all but gone, the terrible boils bulging along his scalp again. His face grizzled and unshaven, covered with soot and ashes and powder stains. Nearly blackened, now, much like her own face was, much like every face in the crowd was from the fire spreading around them. Some strange carved length of wood hanging down over his chest—

She saw him there—and she knew that he had seen her, too. He was already moving straight for her, toward the broken door of the house. Deirdre hurrying out now. Trying to get between them, speaking very rapidly as she held up her arms.

"It was me that put you on that boat," Deirdre started to say. "It was me that put you on it because I knew you weren't fit to be with decent people—"

Dolan hit her with a left and then a right hand, the combination sending his sister sprawling into the street, on her face. The mob gawking and laughing uncertainly.

"Hey, now, that's an Irishwoman!" the goblin-faced man started to say, coming up, but he didn't dare to actually try to restrain Dolan, and no one else did anything. Ruth was busy, still trying to pull Milton back.

"Get away. Get away, *now*—" she urged him.

But there were no words between her and Johnny Dolan. He simply moved in on her—his face twisted in that same rage she remembered so well. His arm darting out before Ruth even saw it, as quick as ever. He knocked her backward, then flung her away, her head bouncing off the paving stones. Turning his attention to her son—

"*You leave my mother alone!*"

Milton swung at Dolan—his brave child's cry still hanging in the air. He managed to hit him with a wild left—his fist disturbing the soot and exposing a sudden small white mark on Dolan's cheek. The punch put him back on his heels for just a moment—the great chunk of wood banging against his chest. Then, as Ruth watched, Dolan ripped it off and swung it at her son, catching him on the side of the head and knocking him to the ground at once.

She was already on her feet, running toward them. The arms of the mob reaching out to pull her back—

"Easy, now, missus, our quarrel's not with you—"

"Let me go! *For the love of God, let me go!*"

She pulled free, throwing herself at Dolan. He was already standing over her son again, hitting him every time he tried to rise, punching him viciously back down to the pavement. She grabbed his arm, but he flung her off. Reaching down for Milton again—lifting him halfway up off the ground by his shirt front before he hit him once more with the block of wood. Kicking at his head as he fell—

"*Goddamn you!*"

She launched herself at him again. Flinging her arms around Dolan's thick neck, trying to choke him somehow.

"Get off."

The same rough, angry voice, barely able to make a human sound at all. He pried her hands loose, spinning her around to face him.

"Get off now, you got this comin'."

"Kill me," she told him, trying to think of some way to provoke him—to get him away from her son. "Go ahead. Kill me instead. I'm the one ya want to kill—"

Trying to hit at him—

"No." He held her arms in his fists, smirking grimly at her. "No, *he's* the one I want to kill."

"It was me who put you on that boat. It was me saw you shanghaied, me who sold ya—"

"Don't I know it."

He threw her aside again, picked Milton up from where he still lay
on the paving stones. Hauling him up by his neck, like a dog with a rat,
her son barely conscious, his eyes rolling in his head. Dolan ripped off
the boy's shirt, began to work methodically at pulling off all his
clothes.

She yanked him back, going at Dolan's face this time, clawing at
his eyes. Trying to sink her knee into his groin, trying to do something, anything, so that he could not ignore her—so that she might
enrage him into killing her despite herself. He only hit her in her side
with the block of wood—so hard that she heard something snap, and
break within her. She doubled over in shock, and he turned his attention to her son once more, but somehow she managed to raise herself,
and grab him around the legs before he could get to Milton.

This time he pummeled her, raining one blow after another down
upon her head and shoulders. He hammered her to the ground with
his block of wood, hitting her until the thick chunk of wood split in
two, half of it bouncing away down the street.

Then he went back to her son again. Pulling off the rest of his
clothes. Milton trying automatically, even half conscious, to cover
himself, put his hands over his shame. Ruth watching from the street,
trying to get up, the blood streaming down her face. Dolan hauled her
son naked across the street, where a group of laughing white boys had
already thrown a rope up around the lamppost. Others—other men
and women, even from the block—hurried over now with knives,
with a lamp full of kerosene, giggling and shouting.

"Burn him! Burn the nigger now!"

Still more men—grown men, now—brought over a bucket of
water from the pump. They poured it over her son's head—slapping
at his face, forcing whiskey down his throat. *Trying to revive him. Trying to revive him, so he would be sure to feel it when they cut his flesh, and
poured in the oil. So he would provide all the more entertainment for them.*

Milton's eyes opened—but she could see the first veil of death
already falling across them.

She was back up then, moving back across the street. One leg
dragging, her right arm hanging at an odd angle from where she had

tried to ward off his blows. Some of the white women from the block tried to hold on to her—actually looking sympathetic. Mrs. McGillicuddy even put a hand on her elbow, trying to keep her back.

"Ye saved the rest of 'em, after all. It's just the one that you're gonna lose—"

Ruth shook her off. Wiping away the blood that kept running into her eyes, but still moving toward Dolan.

He saw her coming, his lips slightly parted in that same grim smirk. Letting her son slip back down to the sidewalk for the moment. She went straight at him and he braced himself, ready for her—but at the last moment she ducked her head and ran headfirst into his stomach, just under his fighter's stance. Grabbing on to him, still clinging to him even as he punched and shoved at her.

"Do me," she told him again. His face only a blur above her now, through the blood.

He tried to peel her off, but still she clutched to him—knowing, as she did, that if he got her off it would be all over. Knowing that he would kill her son. The other men watching them, hanging back a little now, unsure of what to make of any of this.

"Do me. You know it's me you want. *Do me.*"

"No."

His eyes above her, yellowed and maddened with rage and pain, just as she remembered them.

"No, I want your nigger spawn. I want you to live to see me kill him."

He pushed her off then, flinging her to the ground. She wrapped herself right back around his knees, and when he kicked her loose she clutched onto his chest again.

"Kill me an' you can have your box. I still got it, you know. It's just in the house," she breathed, barely able to get the words out but still trying to think. Trying to somehow make him kill her instead. "That's what you come for, ain't it? Don't you want it 'fore one of these others gets their hands on it?"

He cocked his fist, and punched her left eye as hard as he could. It closed up at once, but still she hung on.

"You son of a bitch," she spat at him. "But you know it's all junk, don't ya? Ya know it's just all useless junk, the man was right. An' you wanted it."

He cocked his fist again, rammed it into her mouth, knocking the teeth back in her throat. *Trying to do as much damage to her as he possibly could,* she knew, but she hung on.

Somewhere in the background she could hear people yelling and screaming, but no one interfered. She wondered dully where Deirdre was, if she were still alive. It was as if they were alone, just Ruth and him, fighting in the street in the middle of the City. And her son.

"You liar," she kept talking at him, as best she could through her ruined mouth. "You lie, you never was dead. You never thought you was dead. You'd do anything to stay alive. That's why you let your brother die—"

"Goddamn bitch!"

He punched at her now with both hands—but she still managed to shrink down, hold him around the waist somehow. She was nearly blinded from his blows, the blood covering her face, but still she turned it up to him.

"That's it. You never did want to die—"

"I did. I was dead—"

"No. No, you never was. You lived—you lived on meat."

"No, it's a goddamned lie!"

He shoved at her but only weakly now—backing up, trying to pull away from her.

"You let him die, an' you lived on meat. You think I don't know? You think I don't know how you stayed alive in that village, after everyone was dead? When all the dogs was skinny, an' you was fat? You think I don't know what you would do to live?"

Dolan made a howling sound then, and shoved her away. Pushing her hands off him, stumbling down the street. She scrambled about, feeling for her son, barely able to see anymore. Finding his poor boy's body, lying naked in the street. She threw herself over him, covering him where he lay. *Still warm, still breathing, she was sure of it.*

Three or four more men crowded in on her at once. They tried to pull Milton out from under her, to get back to their lynching, but she hung on. They kicked and punched at her, flailing at her with an iron cart rung they had brought from somewhere. Hitting at her so fiercely with an ax handle that she screamed out loud.

"That'll move the nigger's whore!"

But still she hung on. Trying to cover her son as best she could with her own body. Trying to keep him burrowed down there below her, shielded from everything else, as their blows came faster and faster. She could feel the cold currents of the river, grasping at her feet, pulling her under. But she held fast to him—keeping him warm, and alive beneath her.

They kept thrashing away at her, more and more furiously the tighter she clung. Hitting at her in a frenzy now, with anything at hand, hitting her with ax handles and the cart rungs, and with their fists, and with sticks and clubs and pieces of brick. But it was if she could feel nothing, now, inured to all their blows. Enduring, holding herself in, holding her son, safe, beneath her. The men still hitting— until at last, they stopped.

DEIRDRE

Her brother's fists threw her back across the pavement, smashing her head into the curb. His punches were harder than anything she had ever felt, but even as she went down all she could think of was Ruth. *How did she take it? How did she take it all that time?*

She was back up as soon as she could get her wits about her, lurching toward him again. Trying to get to Ruth and Milton, sure that Johnny would kill the both of them if he could. She staggered toward them, trying to regain her balance. The taunts and jeers of the other women on the block filling her ears—emboldened now, with the men back on the block. Mrs. McGillicuddy jabbing her arm, gap-toothed mouth wobbling excitedly.

"There! There! Ya see, you're not so high an' mighty now, defendin' the naygurs!"

Deirdre punched her in the mouth, knocking her down on the sidewalk. She shoved past the other women easily enough, for all their fearless, drunken ranting—but she could not get past the men. She ran at them, pounded and kicked at them, but they only hauled her back. They would not let her break through the ring they had formed in the middle of the street—the ring where she knew her brother was killing Ruth and her son.

"Here now! Get on with ya! Be glad *you're* still alive."

She stumbled back, her head still throbbing from where she had fallen—trying to make herself think. There was no one on Paradise Alley who would help her. The women were still jeering and pointing, the men standing with their arms crossed, watching and laughing while he killed them.

Somewhere else. Off the block—

She began to run—still wobbly, moving as fast as she could. Bumping off the sides of houses, and stumbling in the slick gutters. Running for the Jews' place now, around the corner on Water Street—knowing they would help her if anyone could, though she had no idea what they could do. This was nothing that could be helped with a clothesline, or a crippled daughter. *At least they might fetch more help—*

Mrs. Mendelssohn was out on the high front stoop of their house, the beautiful lame daughter right behind her. Running down the stairs to her, already—her face puckering as she noticed the bruises on Deirdre's face, the blood on her head and dress.

"There you are! Thank God, thank God! And where is the other?"

She was already bundling Deirdre back up the stoop, toward the house.

"Your children will be so glad. Where are the rest of them? Are they coming?"

Deirdre clung onto the stoop banister, forcing her to stop.

"We got to help them," she breathed, trying to explain what was happening, what the mob was doing. Mrs. Mendelssohn's eyes narrowing in her almond-shaped face, her lips pursing.

"You have to help," Deirdre repeated. "They'll kill her. They'll kill her boy, and her, too—"

"All right. Jake! Jakey!"

A middle-aged man was already hurrying up the street toward them, from the other direction. He wore a workingman's clothes, with a revolver shoved into the belt, his long, drooping mustache twitching with worry. *Mr. Mendelssohn, the glazier.*

"Thank God you came—" he started to say, bounding up the stoop to them.

"You have to help," Deirdre repeated, as calmly as she was able, trying to get the words to make sense. "He'll beat her to death. I know he will. You have to help—"

Mr. Mendelssohn held her in place, his brown eyes narrowing.

Deirdre knew that she must appear half mad to him—with the blood, with her face and clothes blackened with smoke. She started to explain it to him again, though she knew there was no time, that he would kill them both—

"Ruth! It must be Ruth! You must help her!" the daughter shouted, and then the mother was yelling at him, too. Doors were opening up and down the rest of the block, men and women looking out. More men were walking down the street, the air thick even here with the smell of smoke—

"I have to protect my wife. The children—" Mendelssohn started to say.

"Then give me the gun," Deirdre begged him. "Just for a minute. There's no *time!*"

Mrs. Mendelssohn made an impatient gesture.

"*Go,* Jakey!"

"All right!" He pushed them back inside, kissing her impatiently. "Go back in, go in! Don't open the door for nobody! I promise you, I'll be back!"

Then he was running with her. Other men on the street were calling to him, asking him what was happening, but Mendelssohn ignored them, understanding her urgency at last.

They ran back around the corner—the fire from the privvy lots, the shortcut, too hot by now for anyone to pass through, they could feel it from the sidewalk. Deirdre thinking bitterly, *That would have been a few seconds, that would have been a few seconds at least but for those idiots.* Not even noticing that the whole block was in imminent danger of burning down. The air itself broiling by now, so thick and heavy they were panting for breath after a few yards, the powdery black flakes of ash falling on their heads and shoulders like snow.

They turned the corner to Paradise Alley—and Mr. Mendelssohn pulled the pistol from his belt as soon as he saw the scene ahead, but he kept going. The white women jeering when they saw them approaching, but falling back out of the way when they saw the gun.

"Get away! Get away from there!" Mendelssohn called out angrily.

They moved back, but the men seemed oblivious to them—huddled where they were in the street, mesmerized by what they had down on the ground, still flailing and pulling and shouting, like men at a dice game, or a rat baiting. Mendelssohn had to go right up to them, and yank them back by their vests and collars, pulling them away like a man pulling dogs out of a fight.

Until at last Deirdre could see them—Ruth's oldest boy, lying in the street, naked and senseless, at best. And Ruth still lying over him, still trying to shield him, while the men swarmed over her like so many flies. One of them was even now beating at them with an iron wheel rim, another with a fence post—another simply smashing at her with his fists and boots. Trying anything to get her to move, cursing and beating at her in their frenzy—while Ruth held on to her boy.

Deirdre could see then that she was still alive, still conscious. Turning to block their blows from her son however she could, with her arms and legs, with her own body, until at last Mr. Mendelssohn brought the gun up. Levelling it at the chest of the closest man and pulling the hammer back with a loud click, although even then he had to scream to get their attention.

"*Stop it!*"

The men paused at last. Looking slightly bemused but not at all frightened by the sight of the gun. Still panting from their exertions, crouching down, arms hanging loosely by their sides, their faces and clothes covered in soot and blood.

"Stop it this minute! Get away from them, now!"

Deirdre could see, even in their black faces, that none of them was her brother. None of them was Johnny Dolan. *Where had he gone?* She looked around fearfully, but she could see no sign of him—

"Whattaya you got to say about this?"

One of the men took a tentative step toward them, bringing his arm up. Mr. Mendelssohn turned the gun on him, and he stopped.

"I say it's a shame for you to hit a boy, and a woman like that, that's what I got to say about it. You great big men, to come here an' attack a boy. Why don't you try hitting a man, if you want to fight?"

"T'hell with you, then!" the man who had been beating them with the cart rung jeered angrily.

"You just stop this now an' get off the block," Mendelssohn said, turning the gun on him now. "I swear to God, I'll give you all the hell you like if you don't."

The crowd began to sway slightly now, coming forward. They looked no more worried than they had been by Maddy's gun, and she knew it was only a matter of time before someone produced a pistol, even a rifle of their own. But she was worried more about one man than the whole lot of them, trying to spot him before he could surprise them. Wondering frantically, *Where is he? Where is Johnny*—

There was a commotion at the end of the alley. She thought at first that it might be a fresh mob—but then she saw to her relief that it was the Mendelssohns' neighbors, striding over from their street. Most of them Germans, their faces serious and determined, armed with wooden staves and more guns of their own.

The mob fell back before them, but it still did not give way, the women jeering at the Germans. Deirdre feared for a moment that the whole street was about to erupt in a new battle, and she was wondering how she might move Ruth and her son to safety. But then she heard a new sound, growing, from just a few blocks away. It was unmistakable, growing steadily louder—a roll of drums.

The army was here.

The goblin-faced man who had led the mob onto the block stepped forward. Deirdre recognizing him now—that assistant foreman she had never trusted, down at Tom's old fire company. *Finn McCool, that was his name.* His skin and clothes remarkably clean of any of the soot and gore that blackened the rest of them, holding up his hand to the men around him as if he were in charge.

"Come on, boys, there is no use in standing here any longer! We've done the job. There's another nest of niggers 'round in Leonard Street, let's go clear them out!"

The mob gave three cheers for Leonard Street and began to move promptly off the block, pretending they were going in their own time but moving faster the louder the drums sounded. The Germans standing their ground around Mr. Mendelssohn, watching them go every step of the way.

Deirdre was already beside Ruth in the street, trying to pull her gently back, off her son. Ruth resisting at first, thinking she was still one of the men, no doubt—her grip on the boy like death itself. Deirdre had to get down by her ear, whisper to her that it was all right.

"It's me now, Ruth. It's me, he's all right."

She let herself be moved at last then, trying to look up at Deirdre. But her eyes were closed, and covered in blood, her face beaten almost beyond any knowing.

"My boy," she croaked. "My boy."

"Yes. Yes, he's all right," Deirdre told her, cradling her head in her hands. "You did a fine job, he's all right, now."

"He's safe? He's alive?"

"Yes, he is. You saved him, you did."

Ruth's head lolled back, unconscious, and Deirdre looked up, already barking out orders at the women on the street. They milled around harmlessly now, gawking at what had become of their block.

"Help me move her inside. Gentle, now! And go for a doctor at once, I don't care where you have to go. Help me with the boy now, get a blanket to cover him decently!"

The women complying meekly, helping her to lift up Ruth and her son, and carry them back into Deirdre's house. Moving them very gently, indeed. Their faces were even full of pity, Deirdre noticed, as they went about it. *All back to being people. Just like that, back to forgiveness and righteousness. For themselves, at least. Everything they did already forgotten.*

She got Ruth and her son into beds and set the women to cleaning them up, and washing out their cuts and bruises. The boy, Milton, was unconscious but still breathing, she was surprised to see, despite what she had told Ruth. Deirdre washed him herself, wiping tenderly through the layer of ash to the elegant dark hue of his skin. He was cut and bruised all over his body, but she thought that none of the wounds looked too deep and nothing seemed to be broken. *If he could just live through the fever—*

She knew that there was less hope for Ruth, much as she wanted there to be. Once Deirdre saw the extent of her injuries, she thought that it was a miracle she was alive at all. Her face, even cleaned of blood, was a mass of huge, purple-black bruises. Both of her eyes were still swollen shut, and her cheekbones were smashed. At least one arm was broken, and some ribs as well, and her forehead was already broiling. She lay there muttering things in her fever— Deirdre unsure of just what she was saying, or if she even knew she was there.

"I got him out, then, I got him. Without even the potato."

"Yes, yes."

"I got 'em all out, an' didn't sacrifice the one. I saved him—"

"Yes. Try to sleep now."

She fell into a deeper sleep, and Deirdre left Eliza, who had come back from the Jews' house, by her bedside and walked through the ruined front of her home. Moving obliviously past the remnants of her parlor set and out the broken front door. Grabbing the first woman she could find by the elbow.

"Go find a priest. Tell him it's urgent, a woman is dying, and maybe a child as well. Go, *now!*"

The woman, who had been another member of the mob minutes before, nodded and ran off without another word. Deirdre stood out on the street, surveying all the damage there for a moment longer— the mattresses and bedclothes. The bureaus and dressers, portman- teaus and chests—all her best pieces—smashed or burned, or emptied out where they lay.

Then she saw it—just up the street, in front of Ruth's house. That *thing* of his—the cabinet of wonders. Lying out on the paving stones, its front panels smashed and the glass knocked out. She walked over to take a closer look—staring down into the cabinet, expecting to see it emptied. But it didn't seem to her as if any of the countless gewgaws inside had actually been taken, only jumbled altogether. *A meaningless scramble of junk, lying out on the street.*

She crossed herself, beginning to murmur a prayer.

"Hail Mary, full of grace—"

She was interrupted by a wild clanging noise, like some loose bell rolling down a hill. Turning her head, wondering what new calamity this was—she saw a fire company running its engines onto the block. She watched, incredulous, as the men rushed to fix the hose to the Croton hydrant, pumping immediately at the great piano handles with clockwork drill and discipline. Some of them the same men, their faces still blackened, that she was sure she had just seen on the block, trying to burn it down—

She walked toward them, reading the name and number off their wagons: *No. 6. The Big Six.* The ferocious tiger's head painted on the front of the engine box. The big red machine all but unscathed, some- how, in all the turmoil of the City. Deirdre walked up to one of the firemen as if in a dream.

"What are you doing?"

"Why, we're puttin' the fire out, ma'am!" the man told her, tipping his leather-backed hat but looking at her as if she had lost her mind.

"Why? What for? You started it."

"Ah, now, ma'am, that couldn't a been us," the fireman said, admonishing her with a smile as he hurried, with the rest of his company, to guide the hose around to the smoldering back privvy lots. "Besides, it's orders of the boss hisself—"

She wandered away, back toward her house, and Ruth in her bed. The firemen hustling up and down the block around her. The women slowly fading back into their homes, unshuttering their doors and windows—and the sound of the drums growing steadily louder.

Another company of men came around the corner now dressed in blue tunics, running in a crouch. The bayonets on their muskets flashing in the late afternoon sun. *The soldiers*—here at last. They jogged down the street, looking carefully all around them, scanning the upper-story windows and the roofs. An officer followed on a large black horse—more teams of horses hauling a pair of field guns along.

Deirdre stared at them numbly, at the men and their weapons, moving together as one dangerous being. *Like a machine.* Wishing numbly, devoid of all charity, for them to simply sweep the street clean of any life, to sweep all the streets in the whole wretched City.

And then she saw him. Scarcely able to credit it at first, or to understand. Seeing him there, and whole—moving well enough, with only a slight limp in one leg. His face nearly covered in a beard. Older and more worn than she could have imagined, just in the past few months, but him, unmistakably him. Tom himself, running along with the rest, his eyes looking much more worried than the rest. Until he saw her there—

76

JOHNNY DOLAN

He stared down at the wreckage of the box, where the looters had laid it out. *A cabinet of wonders*—lying along the pavement before him. All of it still there. The painted glass eye, and the broken hilt of a sword, and the tiny engine. The miniature of the most beautiful woman in the world, and the lovers walking in the moonlight, and a ship in a bottle.

All junk. All of it so much junk, worthless even to a rampaging mob. Exactly what McCool and his bartender had said it was, on his first night in the City.

He ran a hand through it, dredging up the jumbled scraps. Letting them roll out into the street.

A delusion. Just like his brother.

He stared back down the street at the wreckage of his wife, still lying on the ground—at the boy, her son, hidden beneath her. The mob, and the frenzy of violence around them.

All smashed, by his own hand. He had not meant to hit them so hard, Ruth, or her boy. No—he had meant to hit them as hard as he possibly could, to smash the life out of them. But it had done so little good.

He looked back down at the junk by his feet, and wanted to bellow out his rage again. *All that.* Traveling halfway around the world and back, just for this junk, the illusion of a brother. *All that trouble, just to live.*

But here he was, at the end of it—still alive. Still breathing, despite everything he had tried. He stood up and walked away unnoticed, off Paradise Alley, over to the waterfront. Looking for a bar, if he could not die.

77

HERBERT WILLIS ROBINSON

She lies out on the street, barely alive. Her face horribly swollen, covered in blood. Moaning over and over again the name of someone, whom I am told is her son. Barely able to get the words out of her broken, bloody mouth, but she keeps asking.

"My boy, my boy . . . How is my boy? Did he kill my boy?"

I think I know her face, even as battered as it is. No doubt from passing her in the street, over so many years, on my way to visit Maddy. And she must then know me, at least, as Maddy's gentleman.

How many such faces do we pass every day in the City? Gaining no more than, at best, a nodding familiarity. Never suspecting that they might know us as something else, something better or worse than how we choose to present ourselves to the world. Never looking at them twice until something happens—the horse bolts, the streetcar shudders, there is shouting—and they lie before you, as this woman does before me, moaning for her child.

The son lies over in the gutter, a few feet away. Beaten bloody himself, his dark, brown body stripped naked. He is unconscious, but still breathing. A sweet, boyish face, bearing the marks now of the same hard fists that pounded his mother. A beautiful youth—or so he was, before the mob. The nose and probably at least one cheek broken, cuts and gashes covering his fine, youthful brow. He is young, perhaps he will live.

They tell me all about it, the people on Maddy's block. This collection of half-castes, and half paupers. White women married to colored men, ragpickers and bonepickers and streetsweepers and whores. From what I can gather, it was the woman's former lover who did this. She having forsaken him to marry a colored man who is absent now, missing since the riot started.

"Do ya know him? Do ya know anything of him?" they implore me about the colored husband. Pulling at my sleeve once I begin writing down notes and they ascertain that I am a journalist. Thinking I know all things; fearing the worst for him, a black man missing in the City—

"They call him Billy Dove. Works up at the Colored Orphans' Asylum. Or did, before t'other day—"

"Ah, would be a shame to lose 'em both!"

"Oh, but the boy'll live, you'll see—"

"That's enough talk out of all of you."

A strikingly handsome Irishwoman takes charge, shooing them away from the woman where she lies in the street. Barely able to contain her rage, she is still as efficient and coolheaded as a great general.

I am given to understand that she is the sister-in-law—trim as an oak sapling, her hair tied back in a neat, tight chignon. Her face is truly beautiful, her eyes the same color as her light brown hair. Yet for all her beauty she has a hard, unflinching look about her.

"What should we do with all this, then?" one of the neighbors lingering in the street asks her.

He gestures toward a broken cabinet, lying out on the sidewalk, and a vast array of junk around it. I can make nothing of it. It seems both archaic and incomprehensible—the junk of the ages scattered randomly along an alley, as it is in so many of the streets of our City.

The woman, the sister-in-law, looks it over with the contempt it deserves. Then she flicks a hand at it, dismissively. The haughty Irish maid, right to the heart, showing the chimney sweeps 'round to the servants' door.

"Get rid of it. Get rid of it all! Or just leave it, it'll get rid of itself out there!"

But then I see tears well up in her eyes—as unexpected as they might be on the cheeks of a marble statue. She turns, and ducks quickly back inside to her sister-in-law's home.

Some of her neighbors linger in the street, wondering what they should do—wondering if the mob will return. Soon, though, a company of soldiers makes its way down the street, posting pickets on the corners. They sweep on through the ward, driving the mob before them. Going door to door to search for stolen merchandise, arresting anyone they find with dress coats or ladies' frocks.

And Maddy is gone. No one knows where she might be. The door to her house yawns open, and there is no one inside. Soon enough I am able to piece together that it was she who the mob came for.

"Shootin' away at 'em the whole time," a woman tells me, with a note of awe in her voice. "Cursin' those men for what they were, an' firin' away like the devil with that revolver."

So, she finally got to fire it after all. And then fled—where? All anyone could say was that she had escaped up to the rooftop, then down the privvy lots. Running back into the City with an empty gun. *Free of me at last—and with no more idea of how to survive than a child would have. The child I first picked up, in Printing House Square—*

Inside her looted bedroom I pick up the dirty, spotted dressing gown she had been wearing. The thing feels threadbare, and almost insubstantial in my hand. The rest of her closet, her wardrobe, is bare, completely turned out and sacked, as is the whole of the little Dutch house I rent for her. I wonder if she will ever come back to it now.

Outside, on the street, I kick through the garbage from that odd, broken cabinet. A few of the soldiers are bending over it, fingering the various curios, then flipping them back in the street. I spot one private—his collarbone in a sort of cast—tuck a lewd etching away in his tunic.

So at least it is good for something. I am about to let it go, and head down to the *Tribune,* when I see something else lying amid all this rubbish. It is that same infernal sign. The block of wood the creature from the park wore all day, a chunk of it, anyway. Their crude demand still chalked upon it: *NO DRAFT!*

I tell myself the mob must have made hundreds of such signs—but there is no mistaking it. There is even the same length of chain around it. The very same piece of wood, discarded right here.

Then I know where I have seen that look before—in the face of the sister-in-law. *That brusque, beautiful woman.* A face as different from that man's as night from day, but not really. Still the same expression in it, the curled disdain I saw when he faced the troops, invited them to shoot him down.

It must be he who has come this way, unleashed all this havoc, all his rage and fury upon that poor woman, that boy. I am up and running at once, asking everyone I can where he went, in what direction, but they are only confused and suspicious. They can give me only garbled, useless answers, even as I keep confronting them. Demanding to know—

"Where is he? *Where is he?*"

78

BILLY DOVE

He limped on up the block to his house. Looking on, incredulous, at what seemed like a celebration ahead of him. Not daring to hope this much, but seeing it all there, right before his eyes—the blue tunics of the soldiers, the men running about with their rifles, bayonets fixed. *There was even artillery.* Surely no mob would even try to stand against the likes of it—

He was not too late then. Billy let the relief flow through him. He could see his neighbors out, all along the sidewalks, greeting the soldiers like conquering heroes. They held out tea, and bread to them, the women curtseying and flirting. One of them was even embracing a man, right out in the middle of the street. *Soldiering didn't seem so bad—*

Only when he got closer did he see the scars on the block. The fire engine pumping water into the smoky back lots. The busted house fronts and the piles of broken furniture, and clothes, all strewn out along the street.

He looked for his own house, saw its smashed-in front window, and door, and he began to move faster. Tangling up with his bad leg now, pitching face forward on the pavement. He pushed himself back up at once, still limping forward as fast he could go, trying to get back to the house.

"*My home,*" he breathed. Pulling himself up to the window, looking inside for any sign of life.

My home—

"Billy—Billy, you best come with me—"

Deirdre was at his elbow now. Saying something, reaching out her hand for him, but he didn't take it. Enraged already by the pitying look on her face, knowing what she had to tell him. Knowing the trick that had been played on him once again.

April 24, 1865

79

JOHNNY DOLAN

He was walking down a dark street, looking for a saloon, when the cop got on to him. Dolan had lowered his head and looked away, but the cop had come after him anyway, the way that cops always did, quickening his step while pretending to be in no hurry at all.

He went around a corner, onto Water Street, where he ducked into the first bar he could find. He took a stool in the back and ordered up a seven-cent whiskey, keeping an eye on the swinging doors up front while he waited to see if the cop would follow.

He nursed his drink slowly, killing time. The whiskey as harsh as he had expected—barely whiskey at all so much as adulterated kerosene. But it seemed to steady him, and he ordered another. Glancing surreptitiously around the saloon as he did, trying to see if anyone was staring at him with special interest.

The place looked vaguely familiar, but then what waterfront bar did not? It was a dusty, sparse room, with a few chairs and tables, a few prints on the wall, and precious little light. In the back was a plush, red velvet curtain that Dolan assumed led to the back door—an incongruous touch of elegance, most likely masking the exit to a piss-covered alley.

He shot a look over at the bartender, as well, to see if he were paying any attention to him. The man's face looked as if it had been drained of every last drop of blood, Dolan thought—so white that it almost seemed to glow in the darkened room. He stood silent and stoop-shouldered, drying glasses in a far corner, coming over only when the customers called for him.

Satisfied, Dolan leaned back against the bar, and soon he had ordered yet another whiskey, then another. There was no sign of the cop, but he could not bring himself to step back outside. It felt too good to finally rest in one place, after the way he had been on the move in the twenty months since the riot. Going back and forth from one waterfront, one bar to another, all around the harbor—over to Newark and Hoboken, and Elizabeth; back to Brooklyn, and the East River. Working here and there on the docks—loading ships, stealing what he could. Trying to steer clear of anyone who might remember him. Drinking whenever he could get two coins together.

He had never been able to bring himself to break away—to go back to California, or down to the Islands. *He knew that he should go, to live.* He knew that if he didn't, sooner or later he would be spotted. Another Big Nose Bunker, or some ambitious police sergeant, remembering him from the reward posters. His name back up all over town, on the walls of their precinct houses now: *Dangerous Johnny Dolan.*

He had even gone back to Paradise Alley. Creeping past the awful, looming double tenement, up to the row of skinny two- and three-story houses one night. Looking down the street for them—any of them.

But he had seen nothing. *No sign of Ruth.* Telling himself what he knew to be the truth—that she was dead, that he was wanted for her murder. But still looking for her—

Thinking that he should not have hit her so hard—

Even then, he had not been spotted. He had passed a dozen men and women, even at that hour, some of them staring right into his face. But his damned luck had held—no one had whistled for a leatherhead, no one had chased at his heels, calling the neighbors out on him. *No luck at all.*

He finished another whiskey, and searched deep in his pocket for some coins. All he could find was a nickel—pulling it out, holding it up before him. An Indian head on one side and a buffalo on the other, bathed in the red lantern light. Regarding it sadly there. *Two cents short of a whiskey.*

He would have to go. He stood a little shakily, and pulled his coat up around his ears, bracing himself for the wind along the dockside, still cold even this late in the spring. Looking out the front doors once more before he left, just to make sure the cop wasn't still around. There was a noise above him and he looked up, at the small wooden sign there, flapping in the breeze: "The Sailor's Rest," it read—a name that sounded familiar to him, though he could not remember why.

The barman appeared before him—snatching the nickel that he still held in his hand, waving off his protests. His drained, sepulchral face actually smiling at Dolan.

"It's all right, sir," he told him. "You been a good customer. The rest is on the house."

He pulled a huge glass out from under the bar—more like a great glass bowl than a cup—and began to pour a punch into it, mixing whiskeys and brandies so furiously that Dolan could not even follow it. At last he finished—a fizzing, swirling bowl of punch, glowing red in the dim gaslight—and placed it carefully before him.

"There ya go."

Dolan was scarcely able to believe it—saloons along the waterfront not known for giving out free drinks, no matter how many one had bought. He stood where he was for a moment, wondering if he had misunderstood in his drunkenness, if there was some price to be paid after all.

But the bartender only leaned over the counter, and pointed toward the plush red curtain that veiled the back doorway.

"If ya please, sir. Over there—the Velvet Room. For special customers only. You're welcome to spend the night."

Dolan walked cautiously over, balancing the precious bowl in both hands. Noticing, even as he did, that the few other drinkers there were in the place seemed to be smiling at him. That puzzled him, too, even as drunk as he was—yet once he passed through the red curtain he saw the bed, and all thoughts of anything else slipped away.

The curtain did not mask an exit, or an alley at all. Inside there was only a small room, with more red velvet cloth covering every wall, a red rug over the center of the floor. The only furniture was a chair and the narrow bed, and he sat down on the latter to steady himself. Sipping slowly from the punch, wanting to make it last—though the liquor in the bowl never did seem to diminish.

He lifted it to his mouth again with trembling fingers, feeling it spread and glow throughout him, much as it looked in the bowl. The drink was really fine, better than any whiskey he had poured down his throat before, and when it was done he would sleep. And then, tomorrow—he would find something to do, something to make him more money, to keep him going. *Something to keep him living.*

He had tried to lift the bowl again, but found it was too heavy in his hands now. Trying to lower his lips down to it, instead—to lower himself to the ground so he could drink—

The red rug slid away beneath his feet. Only then did he see, to his astonishment, the shape of a small door cut into the floor.

It was the last thing he remembered.

80

DEIRDRE

Ruth had lain in the bed in Deirdre's back room all the rest of that summer, clinging to life. Her waxen, smashed face staring up at the ceiling. Her breath came in long, ragged snores they could hear throughout the house, at every hour of the day and night, so that her presence hung over them like a cloud at all times, causing them to lower their eyes and speak softly whenever they came in the door.

Deirdre had waited at her bedside day and night. Soothing her head with a wet cloth, and feeding her what broth she could take.

She had even brought Ruth's children by her bed, hoping they would give her more of a will to live, though, in truth, she did not know how Ruth could possess more of a will than she had already. She wasn't sure if the younger children should really see her in such a state—her whole face still so discolored, her cheekbones and nose horribly flattened. Nor could she tell if Ruth recognized them. She would drift in and out of consciousness, and when she was awake she was usually delirious. Deirdre could not even be sure when she was smiling, her mouth was so twisted and broken.

Yet Deirdre knew that she would have wanted to see her own children at such a time—so she brought them into Ruth's room in their best clothes, trooping solemnly by where their mother lay in the bed. Milton was the only one she had hesitated to bring in. The boy was still wobbly on his legs from the beating he had taken, and Deirdre wanted to weep every time she saw how bruised and scarred his fine young face was. It had taken him weeks before he stopped having dizzy spells, or spitting up blood whenever he coughed.

But he asked all the time for his Ma, and there was no hiding her from him, with her gasps for breath filling the house. Billy had even insisted on it, with a hardness in his voice that made her nervous.

"Let the boy see. Let him see what they did to his mother."

The first time Milton had stood stiffly at the bedside, trying to put his hand in hers. Ruth's fingers had only fallen limply away, her breathing more labored and terrible than ever. Then he had broken down, throwing himself over her, kissing her face until Deirdre and Billy had to pull him off, out of fear that he would hurt her.

Billy himself would hobble into her room on his own broken leg, as soon as he was awake in the morning. He would sit by her side and try to feed her—stroking her head, speaking to her in a low voice. Spending every hour with her, save for those he spent tending to his stricken son, or his other children, or when Deirdre insisted that he get some rest. Talking to Ruth about them, about how Milton was coming along, or telling her that he would never be away from her again.

"We'll go now," he promised her, his voice more gentle than she had ever heard it before. "We'll go to the West, or up in Canada, somewheres, soon as you're well. We'll all be there together, an' you an' the children can be safe."

Sometimes Ruth would raise a hand to touch his cheek, or murmur something back to him as he bent over her. But mostly she just lay there, staring at the ceiling, with that terrible, ragged breathing coming out of her mouth, and Billy would leave the room with his face twisted in rage.

His whole family was still living with Deirdre. Their own home abandoned and unrented, the front door and windows still smashed in. It was easier for her to look after them that way, making sure that the children were all washed and fed, and besides, she liked the company—the more people around her, the better.

They were all but shunned on the street now, though Deirdre didn't care. It was nothing vicious—no more taunts or threats about the colored. It was more as if they simply wanted the memory of that day to go away, as if they associated her family and Ruth's with bad luck, like the crippled Jewish girl's leg. As it was, Billy and his children were almost the only people of color left in Paradise Alley, she had noticed. The rest of the race families had quietly slipped away in the days after the riot, though no one ever talked about that, either.

Ruth had hung on for so long that Deirdre had even dared to hope she could live, somehow, and spent every cent she could raise on a doctor. He had spoken to her of the need to keep the fevers down, of the fear of blood poisoning. But Ruth was able to take in less and less food as the days went by, and soon the doctor had admitted that there was probably something smashed inside her, and nothing could be done.

They were spending all their time sitting with her in the back bedroom by then, Deirdre and Billy and Milton. None of them willing to leave her alone for long, even though it meant watching her waste away before their eyes.

And was this how it had been for the rest of them, over there? Deirdre wondered, thinking of her family. *Was that how it was? No wonder he went mad*—Thinking even of Johnny Dolan with pity, though she wondered how that could be.

It was the worst deathbed she had ever attended, even worse than the ones of young children she had seen. Ruth's poor face was so smashed, her eyes still swollen and half shut from her beating, her husband and son so beaten down with grief. Deirdre could see nothing of the work of God in it, hard and inexplicable as she knew His ways to be.

The last night Ruth's fever had risen so high that it seemed to Deirdre she must burn up like a candle. It would not go down no matter how much water she mopped across her brow, how cool she tried to make her and in the end they had only been able to sit and watch as the minutes and hours ticked past midnight.

Yet Ruth had also been more animated with the fever. She had seemed to know them then, and spoke to them, though they weren't sure what she was on about—talking about saving her brother, or begging with some old women in Limerick during the hunger. Repeating their words, as if they meant something:

"I am descended from perhaps as good a family as any I address, though now destitute of means!"

Billy had tried to keep her with them by sheer force of will. Lifting her hand up again whenever she let it fall, clutching it in his own. Repeating the same things over and over to her, with all the conviction of a rosary.

"Don't you go, now. Don't you leave me alone. Don't you leave your boy alone."

He had leaned in, closer and closer as the night went on. Talking to her as if they were not in the room.

"You fight it, now. You remember how it was when you had him, you fight it like that."

She had seemed to smile then, and clutched his hand tighter, and he had taken heart in that, whispering all the more fervently to her.

"You were the only one I loved. The only good thing I had, you an' the children. Don't you go now. Don't you leave me."

But as the night had wound down, he had lapsed into silence. Still holding on to her even though her hand had gone limp. Milton had tried to speak to her, too, but when he did, he only burst into sobs, burying his head in her shoulder and stretching his arms gently around her neck.

Deirdre had watched them together—wanting to say something herself, to do something, but all she could think of was to keep changing the wet cloths, trying to bring Ruth's fever down. Even that seemed to be futile at the end, and so she withdrew to her chair. Until at last, in the hour before morning, they were all half-dozing in the little bedroom and she realized with a start that the terrible, raspy breathing they had all been hearing for so many weeks now was almost gone—Ruth's breath slipping away.

Just before the very end, she had opened her eyes once more, and clutched at Billy's arm now, speaking directly to him.

"You must help him," she had wheezed out, moving her head slightly toward where Milton sat, across the bed. "You must stay with him and help him."

"All right, all right, now," Billy had tried to assure her, putting his hand on her head. "I will, then. But you fight—"

"Promise me?"

"Yes, I promise. I promise—if you fight."

Deirdre got up to leave, thinking they would want to be alone with her, but Billy had only waved her back—a gesture she would be grateful to him for for the rest of her life. She had leaned down over her in the bed—and Ruth had let go of her grip on her husband for a moment, and run a hand down her cheek. Deirdre had been struck by how rough it felt, the fingers and palms so calloused and worn. The hand of a workingwoman, worn from so many years of twisting together her little dolls out of junk, of grabbing up pots out of the fire, and hauling water from the Croton pump. A hand that was not young anymore—*one so much like her own,* she knew.

A half grin forming across her face. Repeating the words of the Limerick woman again:

"From as good a family as any I address—"

Then Ruth's arm dropped, and she was gone. Falling into another deep sleep, her breath harsher and more rasping than ever. She went on for another few minutes before it stopped, rattling away all at once, and they had sat rigidly in their chairs around the room, looking at each other.

At last Deirdre had gotten up, and shut Ruth's eyes, and walked out to see to what had to be done.

Afterward she had begged Billy Dove to stay on. No longer caring what the neighbor women might think, a black man staying in her home while her husband was still off at the war. Telling him that his children needed him, that the children at the Orphans' Asylum needed him.

But he would not listen. It was all over the newspapers, that they were forming a colored regiment from the City, and as soon as they had buried Ruth and his leg was healed, he had gone down to enlist.

"But you *promised* her. You promised to help him," she had argued with him while he packed his few belongings, unable to fathom how he could break such a vow.

"I promised a dying woman," he had said, his voice cold and remote. "Her problems ain't with the living no more."

"I'm sure you could get hired back with the orphans. They still need you—"

"There'll always be plenty of colored orphans in this City. There's precious little me or anybody else can do about it."

"What about your own children? Don't they need to know they have a father?"

He had turned his gaze fully upon her then, his face a stone.

"*My children,*" he had told her, biting off the words. "What my children need to know is that their mother cannot be killed in the street like a dog. My children need to know that their lives are worth something."

"And what about the boy?" she had asked. "What about him, she asked you to help him——"

His face softening a little, looking only sad now.

"We had a talk about that, me an' him."

"And?"

"We had a talk. He's goin' to look after his brothers an' sisters for now. And when he's feelin' better, in a little while, he'll come down an' join me."

"*No!*"

"Yes, he will." Billy set his jaw. "An' after him, his brother, an' then his youngest brother. Who knows, maybe his sisters as well before it's over. As many as it takes, or can die tryin'."

"No, you can't tell him to go down there——"

But Billy had only shaken her hand formally, and put his kit bag over his shoulder.

"You been a good neighbor to me," he said from the doorway. "I'll thank ye to take care a my children. The boy'll help you however you need. I already gave him my last pay from the orphans, an' I'll send along what wages the army gives me."

"What if I don't, then?" Deirdre had tried. "What if I won't take care of your children at all——"

But it did not work.

"If you don't, then send 'em up to the other orphans," was all he had told her. "They might as well be there, till it's their turn."

Nine months later she had seen his name in the lists, after the terrible slaughter reported at Cold Harbor.

"*In the Twentieth Colored New York, the following were reported missing following the battle:*

Sgt. Dove . . ."

She hadn't known how to tell Milton. Aware that he read the newspapers, too, and that even if he hadn't, he would have heard it soon enough from the other children, even the men and women in Paradise Alley. Finally she had laid it right out before him on the kitchen table.

Showing him the lists because she could not bear to say it out loud. She could not even think of *what* to say, with his name there under *Missing*. At least that was one she had never had to suffer with Tom—

"I have to find him," he had said at once, after he had read his father's name there.

"You can't—"

"I have to go down and find him."

"You can't, you could never find him down there in all that," she had pleaded with him.

Deirdre was never sure what to make of the boy. He seemed to have healed as well as he could. She thought that he seemed quieter, though—more somber, which she could understand. She would catch him thinking on things, just staring out an upstairs window into space. He had nightmares when he would wake up shouting his mother's name, jumping up out of bed, and the whole household would be aroused, all the children crying and screaming before she could get them back into bed.

Yet she did not know what she would do without him. Things were harder now than ever, with so many children to look after, and Deirdre scarcely had time to take in any work. Milton helped her in any way he could, as smart and reliable as ever. Minding the younger children when they were all down with another run of the measles, or the smallpox. Sticking his ear in anywhere and getting what work he could find—

She was aware, too, that he got his own letters from his father. Deirdre had heard almost nothing from Billy, since his enlistment— just a line or two, enclosed with his soldier's pay. But she did not know what he was writing his son, and from the moment he had left, she had worried about this day, fearful that Milton would simply light out for the South.

"I know what you and your Da talked about," she told him. "But I need you here, and you still won't find him. The best you can do is stay and wait for him here, the way you did before, during the riot."

He had nodded then, and excused himself and gone upstairs. But the next morning she had heard him go out early, closing the door very quietly as he left. She had run down the stairs after him at once, throwing a shawl around her shoulders, crying for Eliza to watch over the children.

Deirdre had run all the way down to the Battery, where the recruiting tents were pitched. So afraid that she would lose him. *They took so many his age now,* she knew. *Not only for drummer boys, but to put right in the line—*

She had combed through all the recruiting stations after him, pushing her way past the barkers from the upstate cities, and the taunting gang *b'hoys,* the poor men offering themselves up for substitutes, and the Copperhead politicians stumping against the war. Searching frantically among them all, until at last she had come upon the largest tent in Battery Park—and the long line of Negro men, winding down the promenade.

Milton had looked embarrassed and a little ashamed as she tried to pull him away. Deirdre pleading openly with him, not caring who was looking or what they said.

"We need you. We need you for all those children. Who will look after them, if you don't?"

"I'm a man, now," he told her, but his voice was shaky. "It's not a man's job to look after the children."

"I'm speaking to you like a man, now. Who will do it if you don't? Who will if he never comes back?" she said, though she had not wanted to say it out loud. Crossing herself as she went even further:

"What if my Tom doesn't come back, either? Who will help with them, then? Who will make a man's wages for them to live on?"

Milton had let her pull him out of the line, then. Agreeing to stay on, to help. Looking away from her, as though he were still ashamed—though when he looked back, she saw that his eyes were full of tears.

"I didn't really want to go," he confessed to her. "I told him I would, I would do my duty, but I didn't want to."

"No, no," she said, comforting him as they walked back up the shilling side of Broadway. "We have a duty, too, those of us who just abide."

It was true, too, she did not know what she would have done without him. There were not only the children now, but Maddy Boyle, as well, who was little better than a child. Deirdre had found her in an alley off Pearl Street. She had been sitting up against a wall, covered in filth. Her dress in tatters, barely able or willing to talk at all.

Deirdre was never sure just what had happened to her, if the mob had caught up with her or if she had finally gone out of her head. All she knew was that the great Colt revolver she had delighted in so much was nowhere to be found, and Maddy did not look as if she had bathed in weeks.

Since then she had improved somewhat, at least—though Deirdre felt in her less charitable moments that she was running an invalid soldiers' home. Yet within a few weeks she was speaking a little more, and smiling sometimes, and after a while she could even be trusted to do simple tasks, such as watching the dinner, or minding the younger children.

For all her old pride, though, Maddy would not go back to her house. She even refused to claim what was left of her possessions, only shying away from the windows when she saw the gentleman who had kept her coming down the street.

The man had been bold enough to come to their door, asking about her, but Deirdre had told him to his face that she had no idea where the girl might be. He had looked her over carefully, clearly not believing her; no doubt he had been told something. *Oh, this block.* But she had stared him down, and he had gone on. She knew that he had kept the lease—the house still sitting empty, as if waiting for Maddy. But she would not go back.

Sometimes, too, she thought about Johnny. Making herself pray for his soul, though she could not think that it would do any good. For she did not forgive him.

At first, in the days and weeks after the riot, she had worried that he might come back, still trying to extract some kind of revenge for all that had been inflicted upon him. Yet as the months went by she began to think that he was gone for good this time. She hadn't thought where—*just gone, as if hell itself had opened up, and swallowed him down.*

And then in such moments she would try to think on what it must have been like, with the whole family dying, back in the Cork poorhouse. She tried to think of him again as her bright, wild boy, the child she had cared for when she was little more than a child herself, and to imagine how it was that he had become what he was. But she could not forgive him.

Much more, she thought of Tom. Praying for him, and writing to him every night, even when she was so tired the letters swam before her eyes. They had had such a short time together in the City, after the riot. He had been able to stay with her for only a few nights before he had to go on back to the war, back to his regiment, still chasing Bobby Lee down into Virginia.

It had felt like a nighttime visitation, like something that she was barely sure at times had happened at all. *To be in his arms again, to hold his precious face, gaunt and bearded as it was.*

Then he was gone—and for weeks afterward, she thought that her seeing him meant he was going to die, for certain. Her conviction mounting, through all the terrible battles that butcher Grant had waged over the last year and a half, throwing his men's lives away like they were so many trifles—

Yet she had been wrong again, trying to outguess God. Tom had come home again, on several weeks' leave, though this had been even more painful than his first visitation. Deirdre had agonized over when he would have to go again, nearly as soon as he was home. Seeing it in Tom's eyes, too, the anticipation that corroded every moment between them.

How men went to war, she didn't know. But how they went back, she could not fathom at all.

Yet in the last few months since, she had come to hope again. Trying to think of the words that Father Knapp had read to her—"*I require mercy, not a sacrifice*"—on those days when she could still imagine the existence of a merciful God at all. Her best part of the day had been the afternoons, when she would go out into the street for a few minutes. Checking the post box for the letters from Tom, from the trenches before Richmond. All of them routine and loving now, trying to reassure her. The war still winding down so slowly, agonizingly, during the great, final siege of the reb capital—though she was grateful for that, too, happy that there was less fighting now.

When the end finally came, she had been ecstatic. Her joy was all but undiminished even by the news of Lincoln's murder in the theatre. It was a terrible thing, she knew, she would have to do penance for the indifference of her heart, but all she could think was, *Tom—Tom was finally coming home for good.*

Until, that was, she had gone upstairs one evening to find Milton with an old campaign map he had saved from one of the newspapers. His eyes shining with determination as he plotted his trip down to Cold Harbor, as soon as he could.

"I've got to go find him," he had told her. "If he's still to be found, I will find him."

81

TOM O'KANE

He is coming.

They made Hoboken station at five that morning, the train wheezing and shuffling into the station like an old bull driven into the East River yards. They reached the platform and it sat there for a little while more, huge and black and mysterious. The window curtains all pulled shut, shreds of black crepe still hanging from its sides. The engine puffing white clouds of smoke into the cavernous, copper-green depot before the engineer cut the steam and the brakes let out one last long hiss.

Sergeant Thomas O'Kane shoved open the door of the coffin car and swung himself down to the platform, bending both knees to favor the leg that still pained him from Gettysburg. He shouldered his rifle and stood at attention, saluting Colonel Pennybacker as he came down the car steps. The rest of the honor guard hustling down right after, already washed and polished and dressed for parade, as he knew they had been for hours. Wanting, like the engineer, to make sure they got everything right.

He is coming. He returneth to us now.

It had taken them a long time to come this far, winding their way slowly north from Washington City. Through the Pennsylvania fields, and the Piedmont foothills, the single track across the dismal Jersey meadowlands. Retracing much of the same route Tom had traveled, nearly two years before, on his way to save the City for the Union. Not shunted aside for any passenger lines this time, but stopping at each whistlestop and town. Longer layovers in the cities, at Harrisburg and Philadelphia, and even Baltimore, that Se-cesh town *he* had had to skulk through in disguise, on the way to his first inauguration, the Pinkertons fearing for his life.

Now they all came out to mourn—to *see*, and to say that they had seen. The townsmen at their proud little sandstone stations. The stout Dutch farmers beside their crackerjack barns, and bull-chested horses. The oystermen and the fishermen, by their estuaries in the Chesapeake and the Schuylkill, the Delaware and the Susquehanna. Little clumps of black men and women, standing along the rails in deserted clearings, in the middle of nowhere, as if they might be set upon for displaying their grief too openly even in the middle of New Jersey.

Tom watched them all, from the corner of his eye, standing guard at one corner of the casket during his long hours of duty. Watching openly through the black-draped windows when he was off duty.

There was, after all, nothing else to do. No card playing, or singing, or any of the drinking or the rough, ironic conversation with which they usually killed their long soldiers' hours off the line. No one even smoking, nothing more than a chaw or two to keep them going. Peeking out the curtained windows at the wood and brick villages, the praying Negroes, standing, holding hands along the rail clearings in the middle of the night.

> *We are coming, Father Abraham,*
> *One half a million strong—*

They lined up in parade formation on the platform. Rifles grounded in front of them, legs splayed out, eyes right. The crowd before them filling the station, the narrow platform just inches from where they stood. The good citizens of Hoboken town and their families. Mechanics and merchants, shipbuilders and ironmongers. Dressed up in their best church clothes, gaping up at the murky bulk of the coffin mounted in the last car.

So different from the last time he had been here. And so long. The station filled then with desperate, ravaged Negroes. The City burning, across the river.

And all that had gone on since then. So many more lost. Thinking then, in the days after Gettysburg, that the war must be nearly over. Never suspecting that the worst days, the most bloody and continual slaughter still lay ahead, back down in the fields and trenches of Virginia.

Danny Larkins, shot through the head in the murk and chaos of the Wilderness. Feeley, cut down before the breastworks at the Bloody Angle, at Spotsylvania. And then there was George Leese—Snatchem—doing thirty days in the guardhouse back in Washington City, for stealing a chicken from the backyard of a senator.

And he himself, remarkably still intact somehow. Nicked in the ear by a bullet at the Hare House, his cap shot off his head and another bullet through the fleshy part of his thigh just a few weeks before, during the fight for Sutherland Station. That last wound not even hurting anymore, much to his amazement—having passed straight through his flesh and blood as if he were made of no more than the ether now. *A wound that would not even make the casualty lists,* he hoped.

"All right," Colonel Pennybacker harrumphed now. "All right, men!"

His face pale with responsibility, eyes wide behind his little silver spectacles. Not a year out of West Point. The thin line of his first beard just rimming his chin but already a seasoned veteran, Tom knew, twice shot out of his saddle. All of them experienced and decorated men in the honor guard, soldiers and tars selected from representative states of the Union for this leg of the journey. Yet all of them just as nervous and pale as the young colonel; this was simply too big for any of them.

"Ready now! All at once—"

This was the part they hated most of all. Bringing down the coffin, transferring it to whatever new train or ferryboat awaited. The oaken casket heavy, and long, of course. They had to move the whole catafalque because, after all, they couldn't just set *him* down on the platform. As it was they were terrified of letting it slip and tumble to the ground, the murdered President rolling out before them.

What would that be like?

Old Abe himself, tumbling out of his shroud. They had all seen worse things, of course—much worse. They had seen fields so thick with writhing men that they looked like maggots on a horse's head.

They had seen bodies stacked like firewood, waiting for the ambulance corps to cart them away, and men's skulls blown apart, and whole buckets of severed arms and legs, sticking out willy-nilly next to the surgeons' tents.

But this would be something else again, a nearly unfathomable defilement.

We are coming, Father Abraham. And how many shades, coming with him? All the years of slaughter. The whole brigade, killed many times over, cut down and reorganized, again and again with fresh boys, fresh recruits.

The dead so many they could easily be laid out from here to Washington City. Jackknifed along a thousand fences and trees, roads and woods and city streets—

"Easy now!"

They lowered his body down, out of the carriage. Pennybacker hovering about them, hopping from one foot to the other, unable to help himself. All of them breathing a sigh of relief when the casket was down, and remounted on the catafalque. Shuffling slowly on down the crowded platform then, out to the waiting funeral barge. Actually pretty good at this by now, learning how to carry the dead.

He is coming.

The City spread out for him across the broad, grey river. The way he had come to it then, during that bitter week nearly two years before. No smell of burning now, but the usual tang of coal and brine, fish and smelting metal. The town slowly emerging from the morning mists—blackened, piercing steeples. The brown, rectangular blocks of factories and warehouses—and the dense stockade of masts, all around them.

Where she is.

He stood near the prow of the barge, forgetting his discipline for just a moment. Rubbing one hand absently over the thick brown beard he had grown, now tinged with grey. Wondering at how old he must look now. Wondering what she would think to see him coming back here like this—*if* she saw him, he had not had time to write her before being plucked from the ranks for the funeral guard.

Sergeant Tom O'Kane, coming back on the President's funeral guard. Jesus, but that was a thing!

Standing proudly in the barge, scarcely able to believe it himself, but most of all just wanting to be home. *Remember yourself now.* Eyes front, staring straight ahead at the City as the tars rocked them slowly over through the swift, deceptive currents of the Hudson.

She is there, waiting, he thought. *And the rest of them. My family.*

When he had come back to the block, on that terrible day nearly two years before, he had held her and held her, out in the street, until the captain had finally made him push on with the rest of their makeshift detail. He had managed to finagle a few nights back with her, and the family, before they had to leave the City. Back again for only a few weeks' leave the next fall, after the terrible losses they had sustained, and all the men from the Irish Brigade had been given leave to go home, and make recruiting speeches for their regiments.

How he had hated that duty. Not wanting to convince any man they should take part in the slaughter he had endured. Some of the *b'hoys* had come 'round, cursing and hooting at them from the back of the crowd, but most of what he saw before him were young faces—black and white, milling around before the speaker's platform, staring curiously up at him and the other veterans in their dress uniforms. And he had stood there, not knowing what to say. Not wanting to talk about saving the Union, or freeing the slaves, or the glory of Ireland, or any of the things they had been instructed to talk about, as well and good as they might be.

"Come for us," he had told them finally. "Come for us, if ya want to come. To help us end it, once an' for all, and get us back home. That's the only reason I can tell you honestly why I want you to come."

It had been worth it, at least, to spend some time with Deirdre and his family. He had felt more fully than ever the weight of the burden he had put upon her, being away. Deirdre with that poor, touched thing, Maddy Boyle, to look after, and all of Ruth's children.

She had already written him by then about Billy Dove, lost out on the field at Cold Harbor, and he had been saddened but not surprised. The brigade had been pinned down in that mess, too, but the colored troops had gotten the worst of it—as they often did. The rebs would not let them surrender, they shot any Negroes they captured in uniform, and fought like the very devils whenever they were up against a colored regiment.

Yet, in the end, their sympathy for what happened to the colored troops—for what happened to anyone else—was limited. Just as Tom had felt a certain numbness even about Billy, with so many others already dead and gone. The war had gone on for too long, men were too hardened to the killing.

And yet, for whatever whim of God's, he had been one of those who had lived. Coming back to his home for good—

To Deirdre, and the girls, Eliza and Mary and Amanda. The boys, Henry and Andrew. One for the Virgin, and the rest with the high-toned Protestant names she loved. And then all the others—Ruth's poor bairns, to look after as well now. To have a family, in a place such as this—!

It was beyond words. He kept his eyes on the docks of the Desbrosses Street ferry, the crowds surging forward on the quay. The City swelling up around him in its vast cacophony. The church bells tolling now, and a band beginning to play, and the cannon and train whistles booming somewhere up the island.

82

HERBERT WILLIS ROBINSON

Everything in black.

The black mourning ribbons, wrapped around the arms of the men, and the shiny new hats of their officers. The black rosettes pinned to the curtains in a hundred thousand homes, great and humble. Black crepe everywhere, tacked up right over the red, white, and blue bunting just hung out for the great victory celebrations of the past two weeks.

Oh, false City! Is your heart black, too?

The barge moves across the river like a ghost. The men silent, the oars muffled, moving swiftly and implacably out of the morning gloom. We hold our breath to see it, the whole crowd along the wharf hushed now, waiting until the boat draws up into the ferry slip with a barely audible bump.

A choir from some German society steps forward, and begins to sing a lugubrious old Lutheran hymn, then a favorite camp song of the army.

> *Weeping, sad and lonely,*
> *Hopes and fears how vain!*
> *When this cruel war is over,*
> *Praying that we meet again—*

There is a drum roll, and the soldiers lift the coffin from its barge. They salute and pivot, whirl and lock arms, and load the casket into a huge, glass-sided hearse. It is pulled by eight splendid greys, each of them caparisoned in black blankets, and black plumes, and black bridles. The President's honor guard will march out in front, with the men from the City's Seventh Regiment, and after the hearse will come carriages for those of us in the press, various notables.

Behind even us—black men. Frederick Douglass at their front, looking as proud and fierce as a lion. Some ministers from the African Methodist Episcopal Church with him. The rest not quite so bold as Douglass but marching with their heads held high—no doubt keeping their eyes open for brickbats. The City fathers refused to so much as even let them march at first, were persuaded to it only by enough threats from the Union League, and Secretary Stanton growling down in Washington.

I see the minister from the Bethel Church, the man who told me during the riot that the only hope for his people was in the next world. He is still here, though, still in the City. He marches with his head held up, too—signifying hope, demonstrating hope, even if he has none left.

There are fewer of his race than ever among us now. Their old streets, their old houses burned out, or occupied by whites who look at you uncomprehendingly, or with absolute malice, if you ask them who used to live there.

Still, just over a year ago, they commissioned the first Negro regiment from New York—the 20th Colored Infantry. They formed in the park at Union Square before leaving for the war. Standing at attention while the wives of the Union League stepped forward to present them with their regimental flags, and press laurels on their brows— *"as an emblem of love and honor from the daughters of this great metropolis to her brave champions."*

There was much disgust and resistance to this idea from the usual quarters, of course. Governor Seymour refused to have anything to do with the black regiments, while Mr. Bennett raged in the *Herald:* *"This is a pretty fair start for miscegenation. Why, the phrase 'love and honor' needs only the little word 'obey' to become the equivalent of a marriage ceremony."*

I doubt that he even saw the ceremony. The troops parading crisply into the square, dark faces in dark blue uniforms. The lead standard-bearer for the regiment a tall, strikingly handsome sergeant—coal black, with just the faintest sheen of Indies red in his skin. He was an older man, at least in his late thirties, with a grave and almost fierce-looking face. He gripped the banner with beautiful, craftsman's hands, leaning down so the short white society woman in front of him could place the laurel on his head.

It might have seemed ludicrous, save for the solemn and powerful expression the man maintained throughout. He stood carefully back up, the evergreen bough balancing precariously over his infantryman's cap. Then he snapped a salute, and the rest of the black troops fell into line, behind their white officers. Marching down to the Battery quietly—the Seventh Regiment refused to lend their band for the occasion—but with a dignity and order all the more befitting the occasion. A small crowd along the sidewalks to see them off, most of them also men and women of color. Waving handkerchiefs and weeping just like all the others had as they passed, directly to the ships, and on to the war.

How we would have preserved the Union without them, I do not know. In the wake of the riot, The Forty Thieves voted with alacrity to pay the three hundred dollars to buy a substitute for any man who wanted out of the draft. *At last, the poor man and the rich man have finally been given equal standing!* Now both can feel free to shirk their civic duty.

After the riot most of our white troops were drawn from the worst dregs of the City. Felons or drunkards, most of them so depraved they had to be shipped South in chains so that they would not desert and sign up again, under another name, to get the enlistment bonus all over again.

So much for John Hughes's insistence that his parishioners urge the government to draft them. Two days after the army broke the back of the mob, it was announced that the Archbishop would speak to the draft. Greeley and the other Republican papers had been castigating him for not saying anything sooner, but who cared what they thought? Some five thousand of his flock came out to hear Dagger John. Traveling all the way up to Thirty-sixth Street and the Madison Avenue, where he was staying with friends.

They had to carry him out to the balcony. Too ill now to make it back to his pulpit, or even to stand, but still determined to show himself before his enemies. Glaring out like a wounded eagle at the journalists whom he knew were there to mock him.

The speech itself was a disappointment, a rambling address that went on for more than an hour. The man who once had held the best Protestant lawyers in the town at bay now had trouble reading his words off a piece of paper. Calling blandly for peace, and order. Lifting his head, his eyes murky behind his reading spectacles, as he cried out to the crowd—

"They tell me you are rioters. I cannot see a rioter's face among you!"

Greeley and the others roasted him for that—but of course he was right. Nearly the whole crowd was made up of peaceable, aspiring middle-class Irish and Bavarians, from the upper wards. Craftsmen and mechanics, the backbone of the aspiring, rising Union—most of them as alarmed by the riot as George Strong had been.

Who else would come out to hear such a speech? They listened dutifully, straining to catch their Archbishop's words. Yet even here, near the end of his address, some rude *b'hoys* at the edge of the crowd start to cry out, *"Stop the draft!"* Dagger John was thrown off his text again, left to peer, in confusion, out into the sea of his people.

He died soon after the new year, his great dream, his new cathedral, still moldering along the Fifth Avenue. At the funeral I met Father Knapp, still as modest as ever in his simple black cassock. I was almost too ashamed to talk to him by then, after the last time I had seen him—watching while the mob murdered poor Colonel O'Brien. To hide my embarrassment, I asked him if he had returned to his parish, now that the Archbishop had passed. He told me that he had— but that he had already received permission to go West, to the frontier, and minister to the Irish farmers and miners of Colorado, and the road gangs throwing the railroad across the continent, even in the midst of this war.

Stunned, I was bold enough to ask him if he had lost faith in his people here, in the City, after all we saw that day. But he only shook his head, impatient that I still did not understand.

"They're no better or worse than anyone else," he insisted. "It's me that's failed *them*. I should have taught them to be something more— something better than what they were. That is why I should go."

Yet many of his flock seem to be going as well. Soon after I spoke to him, I saw the boy again—the same one from that first day of the riot, wiping his bloody hand across his face—

Smiling up at me, while the blood in the gutter slowly folded up his little boat—

Now he was seated happily atop his parents' wagon, over in the Eighth Ward, as they stuffed it full of their possessions. On their way to points west, I imagined, to Colorado, or Kansas, or the Arizona Territory. Or just out to Brooklyn, or up to Yonkers. But away, at least—anywhere away from these close streets of the City, where boys daub their faces with blood like so many savages.

The funeral procession crawls east down Canal Street, then it cuts uptown, looping its way around Union Square and heading back to City Hall, where the President will lie in state. In Nineteenth Street, the procession stalls for a few moments, and I glimpse two young boys, up in a brownstone window, wearing beautiful little suits— gawking down at the grand parade, the caissons and bands and cavalry, that is halted so fortuitously by their home. One of them, evidently nearsighted, peers earnestly down through large round glasses, as if trying to commit the entire scene to memory.

The coachman whips up again, the procession jerking forward. Moving slowly past the reviewing stand now, the wooden benches sagging under the collective girth of our City fathers.

I spy Greeley sitting up there, looking distracted. His mind no doubt preoccupied with his own unending dreams of electoral glory. *How he can bend the Republicans to his will, now that Lincoln is gone—*

Like every other editor, he has been eulogizing the great man for days now, in print. (Lincoln has become one for our pages.) Yet just last summer, panicking again over Grant's losses, Horace tried to force some impossible peace settlement on the administration. Negotiating with his own mysterious rebel emissaries in Niagara Falls.

Lincoln had broken with him once and for all then, comparing him to an old shoe. Pinning him, as always, with the perfect phrase—*"He is not truthful. The stitches all tear out."*

Next to Greeley on the reviewing stand sit our elected leaders and financial magnates. Many of these, too, fled the City after the riot— for a little while. August Belmont and Fernando Wood took ship to

Europe for a season. Other Copperhead aldermen and street commissioners hightailing it up to Connecticut, or Saratoga.

They were all back in time for the next election, though, carrying the City for that popinjay, McClellan. Holding their usual monster rallies, trying to exploit all the renewed slaughter down in Virginia. Running under the banner *"Union as It Was, and Constitution as It Is,"* words more ignorant than even the usual political slogans.

Was it just sheer demagoguery? Or did they not understand—nothing could ever be just as it was, ever again. Not after three years of war. Not after the fighting in this very City, so many dead. The South would not surrender, and the slaves could not be unfreed. It could end in nothing else by now, save blood.

Yet perhaps theirs is the greater reality. The Republicans were able to save the national election, and carry the state, thank God. But in the wards it was still business as usual, under the same masters. Finn McCool got his brother elected to the assembly—winning at the same time an infinitely more powerful seat for himself, as a Tammany committeeman. When I saw him soon after, he actually had the audacity to speak to me, as if he had never tried to set a mob on me in the streets.

"You're a cool enough fellow!" I cried. "I should see you hanged!"

"That's as may be," he said with a shrug. "But then if they hanged every man who deserved it in this town, they would run out of lampposts."

"You scoundrel! Is that the best you can say for yourself? You nearly burned the City to the ground, you and your friends!"

"Ah, but that was the City then, an' now it's a very different thing," he replied, as insolent as ever. Running an adoring hand down his fancy new suit, his diamond stickpin.

"The City's always burnin' somewhere, little by little, or haven't ye noticed? It's never the same City one day to the next, any more than we're exactly the same person, now. Are we?"

While I was still sputtering with rage, he tapped me with his walking stick—a fine black cane he likely filched during the riots, one with the head of a golden dog, its ears long and pointed as a jackal's.

"You're smart enough, an' you're no fool," he told me confidentially. "Let me make it up to ya, I can tell you certain things about West Side lots. You mark my words—that's the comin' place."

He gives me a huge, insolent wink, and strolls away.

"Remember!" he calls back to me, still grinning. Referring, I think, to his real estate tip. "It's only a matter of time!"

Indeed. If anything, New York only seems to burn faster since the riot. The whole pace of the City is more frantic, more flashy, more vulgar than before. There are still more dance halls and more beautiful waiter girls. More naked tableaux vivants, and nightwalkers, and street girls selling whatever they can. More hoarders and stock jobbers and shoddy men, filling the hotel lobbies. More faro games, and shooting galleries, and block-and-fall joints; more piles of garbage and dead animals and excrement piling up in the street.

In Wall Street they are gambling now with petroleum stocks, as well as gold. There are more epidemics sweeping through the poor wards, smallpox in the Five Points, typhus in Mulberry Street, cholera on the waterfront—many of them maladies that might have been prevented by a simple vaccine. Instead, our health wardens are mostly liquor dealers with political connections, inclined to do nothing but burn camphor in the streets—as if we are all giant moths, drawn to the flame.

The ways in which men make money during a war! Such a society we shall have in the years ahead—the streets jammed even now with the sybarites of shoddy. They jostle each other in the funeral procession. Using the death of the Great Emancipator to show off their newest carriages, the latest in silken black veils and ribbons, black gloves and sashed top hats.

Even so this is not society's day. The hearse rides high on its great wheels so they can all get a glimpse—all the hod carriers and the fishmongers, the tinsmiths and the bricklayers and the sewing girls. The women from the brothels, waving sad little perfumed handerkchiefs at the coffin. Men still in uniform, their faces expressionless, hands thrust deep in their empty pockets. Others teetering on crutches and wood stumps, faces drawn and ragged, saluting the body of their chief. Come out to mourn him along the same streets where just two years earlier they clamored for his blood.

It is all different now. The crowds along Broadway are docile, even reverent. Paddies and Yankees and Negroes alike, simply straining for a glimpse. He is theirs, too, now. *Lincoln,* they already call him. *Lincoln* with that same reverence with which they utter *Washington* or

Jefferson or *Jackson,* all the secular saints of the Republic. All of us caught up now in the greater story, the epic of the nation, which leaves us breathless, swept along in spite of ourselves.

And as we pass, I search their faces. Wondering if Maddy is among them.

I look for her everywhere now. Thinking that I see her half a dozen times a day, in the crowds along the street. Searching for her along Park Row, where I first picked her up—and in the narrow alleys and the tenements of Paradise Alley.

I had thought she might return to me, but she never did. I tell myself that she was only a model, a diversion, but I look for her anyway. I tell myself I only want to make it right, what I have done to her, yet I know that my need is a more selfish one.

I even keep the rented house she lived in, still empty on Paradise Alley. Hoping that somehow it will lure her back—unable to fathom the hold she has on me, but needing her more than ever now. *Maddy.* Always trying, even when I am not thinking about it, to pick out her face from the crowd. Thinking that still, somehow, there must be a reconciliation, a way that we can live together.

In the meantime I keep observing, keep writing down all that I see—hack that I am. The line of people stretches nearly down to the Battery, all waiting patiently, just to see his coffin. I watch them making their way slowly past, the regular citizens of the City, and I scribble observations in my notebooks. Recording their reverence. Recording their awe, what they say and do—but all the time, looking for her face again. Thinking that surely she will come to see Lincoln.

The funeral procession pulls up by the city hall steps at last. The honor guard steps forward, carefully carrying his casket up to the Governor's Room.

He has come among us once again. The simple rustic, who hid everything behind a smile, a joke, a story. His secrets carried to the grave. I can still see him at the opera in Brooklyn, at his own masked ball. Giving away nothing. Sitting up there alone, high above the stage, as he listened to the divine music—that homely Western face still perfectly opaque and attentive.

Tomorrow, after he has lain in state, they will put him on the train up to Albany, and then back out to the West, where the fields and prairies run on and on, all the way out to the far mountains.

But that is for tomorrow. For now he must rest. We must have him on display, like everything else in this City, mounted for all of us to see, and to wonder over.

✅

83

TOM O'KANE

He trudged downtown in the slow parade, hoping to get a glimpse of them, somewhere, in the gawking crowds. *Nothing.* It didn't exactly surprise him. The mobs were enormous and he could see why she wouldn't want to risk it—a white woman taking a bunch of black children out into the streets. *Not after all they had been through.*

None of the men in the honor guard were allowed to leave the city hall while the body lay in state, and there was no way to send a message. He was hoping word would get through anyway, the way it always spread around the City somehow, faster than any telegraph.

Some word to reach her, to let her know he was here—

He stood his watch in the close, dark room, his eyes nearly closing in the heat. Nothing to see beyond the pregnant black window bunting that covered the windows—just a snatch of new green branches and grass. The rifle heavy on his shoulder—even the Springfield—after so long a tramp around the City. The smell of melting candle wax and the mounds of fresh-cut flowers filling his nostrils.

The endless, shuffling lines of people moved past, whispering and pointing. The gentlemen and merchants, the boilermakers and brass polishers, the parlor maids and cooks, and longshoremen, and the firemen in full uniform, with their canvas hats and bright, wide galluses. Winding their way slowly forward to see the closed, blind casket. To stand there and touch the flag draped over it, and wonder what they should think about it.

He saw men and women he knew, but he could not say anything—and they did not recognize him now anyway, his face thick with beard, the infantry cap pulled down over his brow. He almost felt as if he were dead himself, watching them walk up to him, unseeing, touch the coffin and walk away. Wanting to call out to them, wanted to say to them, *Tell her*. But of course it was forbidden.

He thought again of when he had seen her, on the last day of the riots. Her chestnut hair already beginning to turn grey at the edges—no longer quite the color of her eyes—but still so lovely. Standing out in the street, wondering what next—her face set in that way she had. Then she had caught sight of him. Clutching the ends of her skirts, her eyes welling up with surprise and relief—relief to be rescued, he knew, but more just to see him there, so unexpected and safe. He knew then, if he had ever doubted it, that she was the making of him.

He stood drenched in sweat by the coffin, itching in the wool uniform. Watching the line moving past, the faces blurring.

Wishing her to come. Willing her to come.

He tried to spy them from as far down the line as he could, hoping to spot her as she emerged from the gloom of the city hall corridors. Looking for some spot of recognition—the color of a dress, her hair, the way of her walk.

She will come.

He had lowered his own eyes for a moment, and then she was there. He thought it was an illusion at first. She wore a dark ribbon tied around her hair. The one black mourning dress she had, carefully sewn and resewn, the one she had worn at the burial of their first child, and the twins. Twisting a handkerchief in her hands. And her face, her face—a little older, still, a few more lines, more grey hairs, yet just as lovely as he remembered. The perfect brown eyes, looking about anxiously, but full of hope. Looking for something besides the great, obvious catafalque, he realized. Having heard somehow after all that he was here—

Then she saw him. The tears coming to her eyes when she did, but a small, secretive smile playing along her lips. So proud of him in his position, he knew. Not bothering to approach the coffin, just looking at *him*—and all he could do was to stare back helplessly from under his cap. Knowing she would like it that way, that she would want him to do his duty, but preferring it that way, too, for the time being. Wanting only to look at her just then, to see *her*.

His Deirdre. *His wife.*

A GLOSSARY OF WORDS
AND EXPRESSIONS

A DROP OF THE CREATURE: A drink, usually of whiskey.

BAWN: From the Gaelic, a fortification.

BEN: A fool, a rube; a gullible man.

B'HOY: From the Gaelic, usually meaning a young rowdy gang member.

BLACKBIRDERS: Slavecatchers, and illegal slave smugglers.

BLACK FEVER: A virulent form of typhus, common in Ireland during the famine. Also known as spotted fever, its symptoms included delirium, fever, twitching limbs, fits, and rashes and, in its final stages, vomiting, painful sores, gangrene, and the loss of toes, fingers, and feet. Its sufferers emitted an awful stench, often bad enough to make others vomit on approaching them. Its name stemmed from the impediment of the blood flow, which gave the faces of victims a dark hue.

BLACK LEG: The last stages of scurvy, characterized by a loss of teeth from spongy gums, the painful swelling of limbs, and the bursting of blood vessels to the point where they left dark marks beneath the skin.

BLIND PIG: An illegal, often hidden bar; a dive.

BLOCK-AND-FALL JOINTS: Low taverns, serving the sort of whiskey that leaves one to walk a block and fall down.

BLOOD-AND-THUNDER: A common type of play in Bowery theatres, usually featuring much dramatic and violent action.

BLOODSUCKER: A man who sucked the fighters' fists dry of blood during the bare-knuckle boxing matches of the day.

BLOODY FLUX: Dysentery.

BODHUN: Gaelic, for fortress.

BROKEN LEG: A woman who has an illegitimate child.

BUCKETSHOP: A low dive, often serving dregs of beer, gleaned from the old barrels of other bars. Also, a crooked stock brokerage.

CASA: In New York slang, as in Spanish, a house.

CAT: A prostitute, or a bad-tempered older woman.

CHAINS AND WIFE: New York slang, for ball and chain, manacles.

CODFISH ARISTOCRACY: A derisive term for the older, elite Yankee society of New York and other American cities.

COPPERHEADS: Northern opponents of the Civil War and Abraham Lincoln, and often Southern sympathizers.

COW: An aged, worn-down prostitute.

CROTON: A common New York term for water, following the completion of the first Croton Aqueduct in 1842. Its iron pipes stretched forty-one miles from the Croton Dam, and provided the city with the first steady supply of good water in its history. The early Croton hydrants were wooden, and painted green.

DEAD RABBIT RIOT: What came to be a generic name for large-scale, gang brawls—which New York was rife with—after the Irish Dead Rabbits, or "best sports" gang. Recently, historical research has suggested that the gang itself might have been an invention of the newspapers; however, the brawls were very real.

DOLLAR SIDE OF BROADWAY: The west side of lower Broadway, then filled with more fashionable and expensive shops than on the east, "shilling," side of the street.

ELEPHANT HUNTING: Slumming. "The elephant" was a general piece of slang, usually ironic, for any sensation—as in "going to see the elephant" or "the elephant has left town."

FAMINE DROPSY: The last stages of starvation, more correctly known as hunger edema. It was often characterized by the swelling of bodies and limbs until they actually burst.

FAWNEY: A ring.

FIRE TENORS: Popular singers who performed on the street while firemen battled large blazes.

FLINT CORN: Also known as Indian corn, or Peel's brimstone, after Robert Peel, the British prime minister during the famine. Dried corn and similar meal issued during the Irish famine, it was known for its indigestibility. When eaten unground, it even tended to pierce the intestines.

FORK: A pickpocket.

FORTY THIEVES: A nickname for the New York City Common Council.

FOURIERISM: A French socialist movement that enjoyed a brief vogue in the United States, particularly within the pages of Horace Greeley's New York *Tribune*.

FROG AND TOE: Slang for the city of New York, predating the Big Apple by many decades. I have yet to uncover its origin.

GOMBEEN MAN: Gaelic, for a loan shark, or pawnshop owner.

GOOHS: Prostitutes.

HACKUM: A gang tough, particularly one who is good with a knife.

HARDTACK: The main staple of the Union army diet throughout the Civil War. These were usually biscuits made from flour and water, and preferred by quartermasters for their durability. This same quality made them well loathed among soldiers; they were also known as teeth dullers and sheet-iron crackers, and were frequently served teeming with worms, maggots, or weevils. Soldiers would often try to deliver themselves from these uninvited messmates by soaking the crackers in coffee.

HEAD MONEY: The fee of two dollars per passenger that the states of Massachusetts, New York, and Pennsylvania required all shipping companies to produce, so as to assure that immigrants did not become indigent wards of the state.

HIGH PAD: A highway robber.

KIRK BUZZER: A thief who specializes in picking pockets and robbing the collection plate in church.

KITCHEN RACKET: A loud house party, usually held in the main room of an Irish cottage.

KNOW-NOTHINGS: A nickname for adherents of the anti-immigrant, racist Nativist Party, which flourished for a time in the 1840s and '50s. The party specialized in street brawling and secret meetings and ritual; when confronted about their organization, loyal members were supposed to reply, "I know nothing."

LACED MUTTON: A common woman.

LEATHERHEADS: Slang for police, owing to the leather helmets that they once wore, years before the start of this novel.

MABS: Prostitutes.

MOLL BUZZER: A thief who specializes in picking women's pockets or purses.

MOLLY: Street slang for a low woman.

MONSTER MEETINGS: Mass meetings, often of tens of thousands of people, common during Daniel O'Connell's campaign to repeal the many discriminatory acts against Catholics, then prevalent in the United Kingdom.

MORT: New York slang for a woman—usually derogatory.

MOSE, THE BOWERY B'HOY: New York's own version of Paul Bunyan, a legendary figure of gargantuan appetites. Modeled (loosely) after a real fireman named Moses Humphreys, he was a staple of the New York stage for many years, beginning in 1848. Accompanied by his loyal sidekick, Sykesy, and his best gal, Lize, Mose frequently engaged in such hijincks as standing in New York Harbor and blowing ships back to sea, or picking up entire streetcars, horses and all. It was Mose who was held responsible for the disappearance of all the cherry trees on Cherry Street and the mulberry trees on Mulberry Street; he had used them for toothpicks. For all of Mose's Rabelaisian aspects, he was also a new venture in realism on the New York stage. He appeared in the rather flamboyant outfit of the real Bowery gang *b'hoys*, and affected their speech and mannerisms. As such, he soon became a great crowd favorite.

NAB: Street slang for a policeman.

NEDDY: A type of blackjack; see "slung shot."

NIGHTWALKERS: Prostitutes who walked the streets at night. Later, as they became more brazen and all but ubiquitous in New York, the common term became "streetwalkers."

NORTH RIVER: The Hudson River; the two names were then used interchangeably.

NOTICE OF EJECTMENT: During the famine many Irish tenant farmers were ejected from their land by their largely English absentee landlords when they could no longer pay their meager rents.

PAINTING THE OLD GAL GREEN: Pumping very well at a fire, usually to the point where one's company flooded the engine of a rival company.

PLACE OF BLOOD: A large collection of slaughterhouses along East Houston Street.

POP: A pistol; also, "to pawn."

POPSHOP: A pawnbroker's shop.

POTATO MURRAIN: Another term for the virus that rotted the potatoes and caused the terrible Irish famine of 1845–48.

RABBIT: New York slang for a young sport.

RELAPSING FEVER: Another illness common in Ireland during the famine. Similar to yellow fever, it would often include symptoms of jaundice, as well as high fevers and compulsive vomiting. After extreme sweating the crisis of the fever would seem to break, leaving the victim exhausted. It would generally recur another three to four times, though, every six to seven days.

RIBBONMEN: Irish bandits, who tended to prey on landlords' cattle at night, sometimes in connection with patriotic causes.

ROUNDSMAN: A patrolman.

SABBATARIANISM: A movement that protested strongly against the pursuit of almost any activity on the Sabbath, and particularly the consumption of alcohol.

SCALPEEN: A makeshift shelter, usually crafted from the remnants of a tumbled-down house. A *scalp* was a lesser *scalpeen*, often just a roofed ditch by the side of the road.

SHANTY ON THE GLIMMER: A black eye.

SHEELAHS NIGHT OUT: A girls' night out.

SHINPLASTER MONEY: A common term used for the mistrusted new paper money issued by the federal government for the first time during the Civil War, in order to keep the economy afloat.

SHIP'S FEVER: Any of the debilitating, often fatal illnesses common in Ireland during the famine, but contracted or experienced onboard a ship to America.

SHODDY: A term used to describe second-rate, badly made goods, still used as a noun at the time of the Civil War. The many New York merchants who made money selling shoddy uniforms and even weapons to the Union army came to be known disparagingly as shoddyites, or the shoddy aristocracy.

SHOULDER-HITTERS: Strong-arm men or thugs, commonly used to intimidate opponents at political meetings. Every prominent machine politician would have his own entourage of such men.

SINGING THE MURPHY HYMN: Becoming a teetotaler. The abstemious were generally referred to as Murphys.

SKILLYGALEE: One of the many ingenious ways Civil War soldiers found to make hardtack more or less palatable, in this instance by soaking the crackers in cold water, then browning them in pork fat. Another recipe was to eat them as a sandwich, spread with sugar and a slice of fat pork.

SLUNG SHOT: A popular type of blackjack, a neddy.

SOW BELLY: Slag for another army staple, salt pork, which was described as "usually black, rusty, and strong and decidedly unpopular." Like army salt beef, it was usually encased in salt and often had gone bad anyway. Troops frequently had to soak it in water overnight before they could eat it.

SPARKS OR SPARKLERS: Diamonds.

STAR POLICE: A nickname for the New York City police, in one of their earlier incarnations, for the large, star-shaped badges they wore.

STIRABOUT: A sort of weak porridge.

STUSS DENS: Places to play stuss, or faro, then the most popular card game of the time.

TAMMANY HALL: A political clubhouse and the preeminent machine within the Democratic Party, as it would be for over a hundred years. It had not yet, however, achieved complete dominance over the party, as it frequently would in the city over the decades to come.

TAMH: A Gaelic word for "plague."

TEASCHA: A Gaelic word for "fevers." Like *tamh,* its roots go back to medieval times.

TOPER: A clever highwayman; also known as a Captain Toper.

VELVET: Tongue. "A free one with the velvet" would be a talkative person.

WALKING THE CAPSTAN: The main employment within the workhouses to which many of the poor were confined. The purpose was to grind corn, when any was actually available.

WALKING THE HALL: Being unemployed.

YEAR OF SLAUGHTER: *Bliadhain an air,* in Gaelic. This was the year of an earlier, shorter potato famine, in 1741. It was still much in the minds of the Irish people by the time of the great famine of 1845–48, and often referred to by them as they saw their own suffering increase.

A C K N O W L E D G M E N T S ,

A N D   A   N O T E   O N   S O U R C E S

It will come as no surprise to many readers that most of *Paradise Alley* is based very closely upon the actual events of the Irish famine and the emigration of the 1840s, life in the lower wards of New York City in the 1850s, the Civil War, and the infamous draft riots of 1863—to this date, probably the worst civic disturbance in the history of the United States.

Many of the specific incidents herein have also been drawn closely from real life. These include the murders of James Noe and Colonel O'Brien, the scenes from the Irish famine, the various battles and atrocities that took place during the draft riots, and Ruth's defense of her son against a street mob.

Billy Dove was, in fact, the name of one of the earliest African American residents of the area that became Central Park. Jupiter K. Zeuss was also a real denizen of the area. John Kennedy *was* New York's superintendent of police at the time of the draft riots—his name is not intended to carry any political connotations whatsoever. *The White Captive* was a very real sensation; it can be viewed to this day in the American wing of the Metropolitan Museum of Art, in New York.

.   .   .

I am greatly indebted, as always, to my historical sources. First and foremost among them, when it comes to descriptions of New York life, circa 1840 to 1865 in general, and the draft riot in particular, are three superb histories: Iver Bernstein's seminal work, *The New York City Draft Riots: Their Significance for American Society and Politics in the Age of the Civil War;* Ernest A. McKay's *The Civil War & New York City;* and Adrian Cook's *The Armies of the Streets: The New York City Draft Riots of 1863.*

On these subjects I also benefited greatly from Solon Robinson's contemporary best-seller, *Hot Corn: Life Scenes in New York Illustrated; The Diary of George Templeton Strong; Writing New York, A Literary Anthology,* edited by Phillip Lopate; Roy Rosenzweig and Elizabeth Blackmar's *The Park and the People, A History of Central Park;* Witold Rybczinski's *A Clearing in the Distance: Frederick Law Olmsted and America in the Nineteenth Century;* Francis R. Kowsky's *Country, Park & City: The Architecture and Life of Calvert Vaux;* Arthur Schlesinger Jr.'s *The Age of Jackson;* Jerome Mushkat's *Fernando Wood, A Political Biography;* Oliver E. Allen's *The Tiger: The Rise and Fall of Tammany Hall;* Alfred Connable and Edward Silberfarb's *Tigers of Tammany;* and Dennis T. Lynch's *"Boss" Tweed.*

My descriptions of New York's colorful volunteer fire companies have been gleaned primarily from Herbert Asbury's *Ye Olde Fire Laddies* and A. E. Costello's *Our Firemen.*

When it came to describing the New York literary life of the time, I relied upon Ronald Weber's *Hired Pens, Professional Writers in America's Golden Age of Print;* Jay Monaghan's *The Great Rascal: The Exploits of the Amazing Ned Buntline;* Hervey Allen's *Israfel: The Life and Times of Edgar Allan Poe;* Francis Brown's *Raymond of the Times;* Glyndon G. Van Deusen's *Horace Greeley: Nineteenth Century Crusader;* William Harlan Hale's *Horace Greeley: Voice of the People;* and Coy F. Cross II's *Go West Young Man: Horace Greeley's Vision for America.*

In a more general sense, I also found it helpful to refer to the works of Whitman and Poe, and to Melville's unforgettable poem on watching the draft riots from his home in Brooklyn, "The House-Top. A Night Piece. July, 1863."

My understanding of *all* aspects of New York City life was enhanced by what have become the three indispensable reference works on the city: Kenneth T. Jackson's *The Encyclopedia of New York City;* Edwin G. Burrows and Mike Wallace's *Gotham;* and Eric Homberger's *The Historical Atlas of New York City.*

In regard to the Irish potato famine, and nineteenth-century Irish life in general, I would have been lost without Cecil Woodham-Smith's *The Great Hunger;* Alexis de Tocqueville's *Journey in Ireland; The Irish Famine, A Documentary History* by Noel Kissane; Robert Kee's *The Green Flag* series; Thomas Keneally's *The Great Shame;* and *The Encyclopedia of Ireland.*

For the Irish immigrant experience, I used Carl Wittke's *The Irish in America;* Hasia R. Diner's *Erin's Daughters in America, Irish Immigrant Women in the Nineteenth Century;* William V. Shannon's *The American Irish;* Richard Shaw's *Dagger John: The Unquiet Life & Times of Archbishop John Hughes of New York;* Father Joseph P. Chinnici's *Living Stones, The History and Structure of Catholic Spiritual Life in the United States;* George Deshon's *Guide for Catholic Young Women, Especially for Those Who Earn Their Own Living;* Tyler Anbinder's *Five Points;* Noel Ignatiev's *How the Irish Became White;* Charles R. Morris's *American Catholic: The Saints and Sinners Who Built America's Most Powerful Church;* Jay P. Dolan's *The American Catholic Experience* and *The Immigrant Church: New York's Irish and German Catholics 1815–1865: A History from Colonial Times to the Present;* Robert E. Kennedy's *The Irish: Emigration, Marriage, and Fertility.*

The passages concerning the battles and camp life of the Civil War were drawn from a lifetime of reading on the subject, and most particularly the classic works by Bruce Catton and Shelby Foote. I also found Bell Irvin Wiley's *The Life of Billy Yank, The Common Soldier of the Union* to be invaluable in describing daily life in the Union army. In dealing specifically with Irish-American regiments, I was lucky enough to find William Burton's *Melting Pot, The Union's Ethnic Regiments; Irish Green and Union Blue, The Civil War Letters of Peter Welsh,* edited by Lawrence Frederick Kohl, with Margaret Cosse Richard; and especially *The History of the Irish Brigade: A Collection of Historical Essays,* edited by Pia Seija Seagrave.

My research into the history of cabinets of wonder was informed by Lorraine Daston and Katharine Park's *Wonders and the Order of Nature;* and Arthur K. Wheelock Jr.'s *A Collector's Cabinet.*

For my brief sojourn in Charleston, I turned to Robert N. Rosen's *A Short History of Charleston,* and Maury Klein's *Days of Defiance, Sumter, Secession, and the Coming of the Civil War.* The classic collection, *The Book of Boxing,* edited by W. C. Heinz and Nathan Ward, helped me with the fine art of bare-knuckle boxing.

Finally, no tour of the nineteenth-century demimonde in New York would be complete without the guidance of Luc Sante's *Low Life* and Herbert Asbury's *The Gangs of New York.*

In addition to all of the above sources and a number of others, I was able to utilize a wide variety of magazines and newspapers from the period, thanks to the facilities of the New York Public Library and Columbia University libraries.

Beyond these literary resources, my knowledge of the era and culture in question was expanded immeasurably by a number of recent shows at New York's many fine cultural institutions. These included a New-York Historical Society exhibit on Seneca Village and the construction of Central Park; a Brooklyn Museum exhibit on cabinets of wonder; and the Metropolitan Museum of Art's exhibit "Art and the Empire City." Ric Burns's wonderful documentary series on New York also provided me with some indelible images.

No resource, though, proved more helpful than the personal assistance afforded to me by Father Dominic Monti and Father John Knapp. Both were very generous with their time and patience in explaining the American Catholic Church in the nineteenth century to my poor old Presbyterian mind. I must also thank Father Jerome Massimino for setting up my interview with Father Monti.

I have been very fortunate in my friends, family, and colleagues. Their generosity has done more to enhance my career and my life than I can easily express.

My wife, Ellen Abrams, has been my helpmate, my confidante, and my great soul. I hope that she always will be.

Henry Dunow has filled the difficult dual roles of friend and agent with aplomb, and he has done wonderful things for my self-esteem, my sanity, and my bank account. I must also thank Jennifer Carlson and everyone else at the Henry Dunow Literary Agency.

Daniel Conaway, my editor at HarperCollins, has persevered through not only the (at times) unreasoning obstinacy of his writer, but also the birth of his son, Christopher. His suggestions were unfailingly candid, perceptive, and helpful, and he is entitled to a great share of the credit for whatever success *Paradise Alley* might have. Dan's assistant, Nikola Scott, has been a joy to work with, thanks to her unflagging enthusiasm and good nature. The same can readily be said for the rest of my colleagues at HarperCollins.

I was able to thank many of those who have given me their love, friendship, and support over the years in the acknowledgments of my last book. My sentiments are unchanged toward them—and I would like to extend the same to a number of those I overlooked, did not mention by name, or did not know yet. These would include my mother, Claire S. Baker; my stepfather, Lawrence Martin; my sister, Pamela Baker, and brother-in-law, Mark Kapsch; my aunt and uncle, Ann and Bruce Baker; Whitneys, one and all; and my dear friends Amanda Robb, Andrew Chesler, Pearl Solomon, Alix Spiegel, Deirdre Dolan, James Gray, Milton Allimadi, Mana Kasongo, Andy Staub, Delphine Taylor, John Kaehny, Ahmed White, John Sullivan, Mariana Johnson, Marc Aronson, Marina Budhos, Ingrid Krane-Mueschen, Michael Mueschen, Larry Davidson, Wendy Owen-Dunow, Agnes Rossi—and the next generation: Zoe, Julian, Griffin, Anik, Daisy, Gus, Teddy, Maddy, Max, Mary, Grace, Alina, Christopher, Julius, Sasha, Eloise, Cassius, and Selene.

📖 Perennial

Books by Kevin Baker:

PARADISE ALLEY
A Novel
ISBN 0-06-095521-X (paperback)

The bestselling story of three very different Irish immigrant women trapped together in the midst of events that would come to be known as the Draft Riots—perhaps the bloodiest, most destructive riots in American history. Baker captures the Irish immigrant experience—and the African-American experience—in the crucible of nineteenth-century New York.

"Kevin Baker is quickly altering the landscape of American historical fiction."
Christian Science Monitor

DREAMLAND
A Novel
ISBN 0-06-093480-8 (paperback)

A mesmerizing portrait of immigrant New York in the early part of the 20th century, in which its characters confront both the glowing promise and the harsh reality of the American dream. Baker delivers both a masterful, sweeping chronicle of an era of American history and an intimate, heart-wrenching portrait of the lives of its characters.

"An epic re-creation of an era. . . . A boisterous, rollicking carnival." —*People*

SOMETIMES YOU SEE IT COMING
A Novel
ISBN 0-06-053597-0 (paperback)

Based in part on the life of baseball legend Ty Cobb, *Sometimes You See It Coming*—Kevin Baker's first novel—tells the story of John Barr. An all-around superstar, Barr plays the game with a single-minded ferocity that makes his New York Mets team all but invincible. Barr himself is a mystery, with no past, no friends, no women, and no interests outside of hitting a baseball as hard and as far as he can.

"Put this one on the shelf with Bernard Malamud's *The Natural*." —*Time*

(((LISTEN TO)))

PARADISE ALLEY
A Novel

BY KEVIN BAKER

"Rich in color and drama. . . . Extraordinary."
—New York Times

*"An authoritative blend of
documentary realism and driving narrative
that's just about irresistible."*
—*Kirkus Reviews* (starred review)

"An engrossing epic." —*Entertainment Weekly*

ISBN 0-06-057514-X • $39.95 ($59.95 Can.)
12 Hours • 8 Cassettes • UNABRIDGED